CHILDREN'S CLASSICS

Little Women

LOUISA M. ALCOTT

Little Women

PARRAGON

Little Women
A Parragon Classic

This is a Siena Book
Siena is an imprint of Parragon

First published in 1868

This edition published in 1999 by
Parragon
13 Whiteladies Road
Clifton
Bristol BS8 1PB

Printed and bound in the UK

Preface

Go then, my little Book, and show to all
That entertain and bid thee welcome shall,
What thou dost keep close shut up in thy breast;
And wish what thou dost show them may be blest
To them for good, may make them choose to be
Pilgrims better by far, than thee or me.
Tell them of Mercy; she is one
Who early hath her pilgrimage begun.
Yea, let young damsels learn of her to prize
The world which is to come, and so be wise;
For little tripping maids may follow God
Along the ways which saintly feet have trod.

Adapted from JOHN BUNYAN

Chapter 1

PLAYING PILGRIMS

"Christmas won't be Christmas without any presents," grumbled Jo, lying on the rug.

"It's so dreadful to be poor!" sighed Meg, looking down at her old dress.

"I don't think it's fair for some girls to have plenty of pretty things, and other girls nothing at all," added little Amy, with an injured sniff.

"We've got Father and Mother and each other," said Beth, contentedly, from her corner.

The four young faces on which the firelight shone brightened at the cheerful words, but darkened again as Jo said sadly:

"We haven't got Father, and shall not have him for a long time." She didn't say "perhaps never", but each silently added it; thinking of father far away, where the fighting was.

Nobody spoke for a minute; then Meg said in an altered tone:

"You know the reason Mother proposed not having any presents this Christmas was because it is going to be a hard winter for everyone; and she thinks we ought not to spend money for pleasure when our men are suffering so in the army. We can't do much, but we can make our little sacrifices, and ought to do it gladly. But I am afraid I don't"; and Meg shook her head, and she thought regretfully of all the pretty things she wanted.

"But I don't think the little we should spend would do any good. We've each got a dollar, and the army wouldn't be much helped by our giving that. I agree not to expect anything from mother or you, but I do want to buy *Undine and Sintram* for myself; I've wanted it *so* long," said Jo, who was a bookworm.

"I planned to spend mine on new music," said Beth, with a little sigh, which no one heard but the hearth-brush and kettle-holder.

"I shall get a nice box of Faber's drawing pencils; I really need them," said Amy, decidedly.

"Mother didn't say anything about our money, and she won't wish us to give up everything. Let's each buy what we want, and have a little fun; I'm sure we work hard enough to earn it," cried Jo, examining the heels of her shoes in a gentlemanly manner.

"I know *I* do—teaching those tiresome children nearly all day when I am longing to enjoy myself at home," began Meg, in the complaining tone again.

"You don't have half such a hard time as I do," said Jo. "How would you like to be shut up for hours with a nervous, fussy old lady, who keeps you trotting, is never satisfied, and worries you till you're ready to fly out of the window or cry?"

"It's naughty to fret; but I do think washing dishes and keeping things tidy is the worst work in the world. It makes me cross; and my hands get so stiff, I can't practise well at all"; and Beth looked at her rough hands with a sigh that anyone could hear that time.

"I don't believe any of you suffer as I do," cried Amy; "for you don't have to go to school with impertinent girls, who plague you if you don't know your lessons, and laugh at your dresses, and label your father if he isn't rich, and insult you when your nose isn't nice."

"If you mean *libel,* I'd say so, and not talk about *labels,* as if papa was a pickle-bottle," advised Jo, laughing.

"I know what I mean, and you needn't be *statirical* about it. It's proper to use good words, and improve your *vocabulary,*" returned Amy, with dignity.

"Don't peck at one another, children. Don't you wish we had the money papa lost when we were little, Jo? Dear me! how happy and good we'd be, if we had no worries!" said Meg, who could remember better times.

"You said, the other day, you thought we were a deal happier than the King children, for they were fighting and fretting all the time, in spite of their money."

"So I did, Beth. Well, I think we are; for, though we do have to work, we make fun for ourselves, and are a pretty jolly set, as Jo would say."

"Jo does use such slang words!" observed Amy, with a reproving look at the long figure stretched on the rug. Jo immediately sat up, put her hands in her pockets, and began to whistle.

"Don't, Jo; it's so boyish!"

"That's why I do it."

"I detest rude, unladylike girls!"

"I hate affected, niminy-piminy chits!"

"'Birds in their little nests agree,' " sang Beth, the peacemaker, with such a funny face that both sharp voices softened to a laugh, and the "pecking" ended for that time.

"Really, girls, you are both to be blamed," said Meg, beginning to lecture in her elder-sisterly fashion. "You are old enough to leave off boyish tricks, and to behave better, Josephine. It didn't matter so much when you were a little girl; but now you are so tall, and turn up your hair, you should remember that you are a young lady."

"I'm not! and if turning up my hair makes me one, I'll wear it in two tails till I'm twenty!" cried Jo, pulling off her net, and shaking down her chestnut mane. "I hate to think I've got to grow up, and be Miss March, and wear long gowns, and look as prim as a China-aster! It's bad enough to be a girl, anyway, when I like boys' games and work and manners! I can't get over my disappointment in not being a boy; and it's worse than ever now, for I'm dying to go and fight with Papa, and I can only stay at home and knit, like a poky old woman!" And Jo shook the blue army sock till the needles rattled like castanets, and her ball bounded across the room.

"Poor Jo! It's too bad, but it can't be helped; so you must try to be contented with making your name boyish, and playing brother to us girls," said Beth, stroking the rough head at her knee with a hand that all the dish-washing and dusting in the world could not make ungentle in its touch.

"As for you, Amy," continued Meg, "you are altogether too particular and prim. Your airs are funny now; but you'll grow up an affected little goose, if you don't take care. I like your nice manners and refined ways of speaking when you don't try to be elegant; but your absurd words are as bad as Jo's slang."

"If Jo is a tomboy and Amy a goose, what am I, please?" asked Beth, ready to share the lecture.

"You're a dear, and nothing else," answered Meg, warmly; and no one contradicted her, for the "Mouse" was the pet of the family.

As young readers like to know "how people look", we will take this moment to give them a little sketch of the four sisters, who sat knitting away in the twilight, while the December snow fell quietly without, and the fire crackled cheerfully within. It was a comfortable old room, though the carpet was faded and the furniture very plain; for a good picture or two hung on the walls, books filled the recesses, chrysanthemums and Christmas roses bloomed in the windows, and a pleasant atmosphere of home-peace pervaded it.

Margaret, the eldest of the four, was sixteen, and very pretty, being plump and fair, with large eyes, plenty of soft, brown hair, a sweet mouth, and white hands, of which she was rather vain. Fifteen-year-old Jo was very tall, thin, and brown, and reminded one of a colt; for she never seemed to know what to do with her long limbs, which were very much in her way. She had a decided mouth, a comical nose, and sharp, grey eyes, which appeared to see everything, and were by turns fierce, funny, or thoughtful. Her long, thick hair was her one beauty; but it was usually bundled in a net, to be out of her way. Round shoulders had Jo, big hands and feet, a fly-away look to her clothes, and the uncomfortable appearance of a girl who was rapidly shooting up into a woman, and didn't like it. Elizabeth—or Beth, as everyone called her—was a rosy, smooth-haired, bright-eyed girl of thirteen, with a shy manner, a timid voice, and a peaceful expression, which was seldom disturbed. Her father called her "Little Tranquillity", and the name suited her excellently; for she seemed to live in a happy world of her own, only venturing out to meet the few whom she trusted and loved. Amy, though the youngest, was a most important person—in her own opinion at least. A regular snow-maiden, with blue eyes, and yellow hair, curling on her shoulders, pale and slender, and always carrying herself like a young lady mindful of her manners. What the characters of the four sisters were we will leave to be found out.

The clock struck six; and, having swept up the hearth, Beth put a pair of slippers down to warm. Somehow the sight of the old shoes had a good effect upon the girls; for Mother was coming, and everyone brightened to welcome her. Meg stopped lecturing, and lighted the lamp, Amy got out of the easy-chair without being asked, and Jo forgot how tired she was as she sat up to hold the slippers nearer to the blaze.

"They are quite worn out; Marmee must have a new pair."

"I thought I'd get her some with my dollar," said Beth.

"No, I shall!" cried Amy.

"I'm the oldest," began Meg, but Jo cut in with a decided:

"I'm the man of the family now Papa is away, and *I* shall provide the slippers, for he told me to take special care of Mother while he was gone."

"I'll tell you what we'll do," said Beth; "let's each get her something for Christmas, and not get anything for ourselves."

"That's like you, dear! What will we get?" exclaimed Jo.

Everyone thought soberly for a minute; then Meg announced as if the idea was suggested by the sight of her own pretty hands, "I shall give her a nice pair of gloves."

"Army shoes, best to be had," cried Jo.

"Some handkerchiefs, all hemmed," said Beth.

"I'll get a little bottle of cologne; she likes it, and it won't cost much, so I'll have some left to buy my pencils," added Amy.

"How will we give the things?" asked Meg.

"Put them on the table, and bring her in and see her open the bundles. Don't you remember how we used to do on our birthdays?" answered Jo.

"I used to be *so* frightened when it was my turn to sit in the big chair with the crown on, and see you all come marching round to give the presents, with a kiss. I liked the things and the kisses, but it was dreadful to have you sit looking at me while I opened the bundles," said Beth, who was toasting her face and the bread for tea, at the same time.

"Let Marmee think we are getting things for ourselves, and then surprise her. We must go shopping tomorrow afternoon, Meg; there is so much to do about the play for Christmas night," said Jo, marching up and down, with her hands behind her back and her nose in the air.

"I don't mean to act any more after this time; I'm getting too old for such things," observed Meg, who was as much a child as ever about "dressing-up" frolics.

"You won't stop, I know, as long as you can trail round in a white gown with your hair down, and wear gold-paper jewellery. You are the best actress we've got, and there'll be an end of everything if you quit the boards," said Jo. "We ought to rehearse tonight. Come here, Amy, and do the fainting scene, for you are as stiff as a poker in that."

"I can't help it; I never saw anyone faint, and I don't choose to make myself all black and blue, tumbling flat as you do. If I can go down easily, I'll drop; if I can't, I shall fall into a chair and be graceful; I don't care if Hugo does come at me with a pistol," returned Amy, who was not gifted with dramatic power, but was chosen because she was small enough to be borne out shrieking by the villain of the piece.

"Do it this way; clasp your hands so, and stagger across the room, crying frantically, 'Roderigo! save me! save me!' " and away went Jo, with a melodramatic scream which was truly thrilling. Amy followed, but she poked her hands out stiffly before her, and jerked herself along as if she went by machinery; and her "Ow!" was more suggestive of pins being run into her than of fear and anguish. Jo gave a despairing groan, and Meg laughed outright, while Beth let her bread burn as she watched the fun with interest.

"It's no use! Do the best you can when the time comes, and if the audience laugh, don't blame me. Come on, Meg."

Then things went smoothly, for Don Pedro defied the world in a speech of two pages without a single break; Hagar, the witch, chanted an awful incantation over her kettleful of simmering toads, with weird effect; Roderigo rent his chains asunder manfully, and Hugo died in agonies of remorse and arsenic, with a wild "Ha! ha!"

"It's the best we've had yet," said Meg, as the dead villain sat up and rubbed his elbows.

"I don't see how you can write and act such splendid things, Jo. You're a regular Shakespeare!" exclaimed Beth, who firmly believed that her sisters were gifted with wonderful genius in all things.

"Not quite," replied Jo modestly. "I do think '*The Witch's Curse, an Operatic Tragedy*', is rather a nice thing; but I'd like to try *Macbeth,* if we only had a trap-door for Banquo. I always wanted to do the killing part. 'Is that a dagger I see before me?' " muttered

Jo, rolling her eyes and clutching at the air, as she had seen a famous tragedian do.

"No, it's the toasting fork, with mother's shoe on it instead of the bread. Beth's stage-struck!" cried Meg, and the rehearsal ended in a general burst of laughter.

"Glad to find you so merry, my girls," said a cheery voice at the door, and actors and audience turned to welcome a tall, motherly lady, with a "can-I-help-you" look about her which was truly delightful. She was not elegantly dressed, but a noble-looking woman, and the girls thought the grey cloak and unfashionable bonnet covered the most splendid mother in the world.

"Well, dearies, how have you got on today? There was so much to do, getting the boxes ready to go tomorrow, that I didn't come home to dinner. Has anyone called, Beth? How is your cold, Meg? Jo, you look tired to death. Come and kiss me, baby."

While making these maternal inquiries, Mrs. March got her wet things off, her warm slippers on, and sitting down in the easy-chair, drew Amy to her lap, preparing to enjoy the happiest hour of her busy day. The girls flew about, trying to make things comfortable, each in her own way. Meg arranged the tea-table; Jo brought wood and set chairs, dropping, overturning, and clattering everything she touched; Beth trotted to and fro between parlour and kitchen, quiet and busy; while Amy gave directions to everyone, as she sat with her hands folded.

As they gathered about the table, Mrs. March said, with a particularly happy face, "I've got a treat for you after supper."

A quick, bright smile went round like a streak of sunshine. Beth clapped her hands, regardless of the biscuit she held, and Jo tossed up her napkin, crying, "A letter! a letter! Three cheers for Father!"

"Yes, a nice long letter. He is well, and thinks he shall get through the cold season better than we feared. He sends all sorts of loving wishes for Christmas, and an especial message to you girls," said Mrs. March, patting her pocket as if she had got a treasure there.

"Hurry and get done! Don't stop to quirk your little finger, and simper over your plate, Amy," cried Jo, choking in her tea, and dropping her bread, butter side down, on the carpet in her haste to get at the treat. Beth ate no more, but crept away, to sit in her shadowy corner and brood over the delight to come, till the others were ready.

"I think it was so splendid of Father to go as chaplain when he was too old to be drafted, and not strong enough for a soldier," said Meg, warmly.

"Don't I wish I could go as a drummer, a *vivan*—what's its name? or a nurse, so I could be near him and help him," exclaimed Jo, with a groan.

"It must be very disagreeable to sleep in a tent, and eat all sorts of bad-tasting things, and drink out of a tin mug," sighed Amy.

"When will he come home, Marmee?" asked Beth, with a little quiver in her voice.

"Not for many months, dear, unless he is sick. He will stay and do his work faithfully as long as he can, and we won't ask for him back a minute sooner than he can be spared. Now come and hear the letter."

They all drew to the fire, Mother in the big chair, with Beth at her feet, Meg and Amy perched on either arm of the chair, and Jo leaning on the back, where no one would see any sign of emotion if the letter should happen to be touching. Very few letters were written in those hard times that were not touching, especially those which fathers sent home. In this one little was said of the hardships endured, the dangers faced, or the home-sickness conquered; it was a cheerful, hopeful letter, full of lively descriptions of camp life, marches, and military news; and only at the end did the writer's heart overflow with fatherly love and longing for the little girls at home.

"Give them all my dear love and a kiss. Tell them I think of them by day, pray for them by night, and find my best comfort in their affection at all times. A year seems very long to wait before I see them, but remind them that while we wait we may all work, so that these hard days need not be wasted. I know they will remember all I said to them, that they will be loving children to you, will do their duty faithfully, fight their bosom enemies bravely, and conquer themselves so beautifully, that when I come back to them I may be fonder and prouder than ever of my little women."

Everybody sniffed when they came to that part; Jo wasn't ashamed of the great tear that dropped off the end of her nose, and Amy never minded the rumpling of her curls as she hid her face on her mother's shoulder and sobbed out, "I *am* a selfish girl! but I'll truly try to be better, so he mayn't be disappointed in me by and by."

"We all will!" cried Meg. "I think too much of my looks, and hate to work, but won't any more, if I can help it."

"I'll try and be what he loves to call me, 'a little woman', and not be rough and wild; but do my duty here instead of wanting to be somewhere else," said Jo, thinking that keeping her temper at home was a much harder task than facing a rebel or two down South.

Beth said nothing, but wiped away her tears with the blue army sock, and began to knit with all her might, losing no time in doing the duty that lay nearest her, while she resolved in her quiet little soul to be all that Father hoped to find her when the year brought round the happy coming home.

Mrs. March broke the silence that followed Jo's words, by saying in her cheery voice, "Do you remember how you used to play *Pilgrim's Progress* when you were little things? Nothing delighted you more than to have me tie my piece-bags on your backs for burdens, give you hats and sticks and rolls of paper, and let you travel through the house from the cellar, which was the City of Destruction, up, up, to the housetop, where you had all the lovely things you could collect to make a Celestial City."

"What fun it was, especially going by the lions, fighting Apollyon, and passing through the Valley where the hobgoblins were!" said Jo.

"I liked the place where the bundles fell off and tumbled downstairs," said Meg.

"My favourite part was when we came out on the flat roof where our flowers and arbours and pretty things were, and all stood and sang for joy up there in the sunshine," said Beth, smiling, as if that pleasant moment had come back to her.

"I don't remember much about it, except that I was afraid of the cellar and the dark entry, and always liked the cake and milk we had up at the top. If I wasn't too old for such things, I'd rather like to play it over again," said Amy, who began to talk of renouncing childish things at the mature age of twelve.

"We never are too old for this, my dear, because it is a play we are playing all the time in one way or another. Our burdens are here, our road is before us, and the longing for goodness and happiness is the guide that leads us through many troubles and mistakes to the peace which is a true Celestial City. Now, my little pilgrims, suppose you begin again, not in play, but in earnest, and see how far on you can get before Father comes home."

"Really, Mother? Where are our bundles?" asked Amy, who was a very literal young lady.

"Each of you told what your burden was just now, except Beth; I rather think she hasn't got any," said her mother.

"Yes, I have; mine is dishes and dusters, and envying girls with nice pianos, and being afraid of people."

Beth's bundle was such a funny one that everybody wanted to laugh; but nobody did, for it would have hurt her feelings very much.

"Let us do it," said Meg, thoughtfully. "It is only another name for trying to be good, and the story may help us; for though we do want to be good, it's hard work, and we forget, and don't do our best."

"We were in the Slough of Despond tonight, and Mother came and pulled us out as Help did in the book. We ought to have our roll of directions, like Christian. What shall we do about that?" asked Jo, delighted with the fancy which lent a little romance to the very dull task of doing her duty.

"Look under your pillows, Christmas morning, and you will find your guide-book," replied Mrs. March.

They talked over the new plan while old Hannah cleared the table; then out came the four little work-baskets, and the needles flew as the girls made sheets for Aunt March. It was uninteresting sewing, but tonight no one grumbled. They adopted Jo's plan of dividing the long seams into four parts, and calling the quarters Europe, Asia, Africa, and America, and in that way got on capitally, especially when they talked about the different countries, as they stitched their way through them.

At nine they stopped work, and sang, as usual, before they went to bed.

No one but Beth could get much music out of the old piano; but she had a way of softly touching the yellow keys, and making a pleasant accompaniment to the simple songs they sang. Meg had a voice like a flute, and she and her mother led the little choir, Amy chirped like a cricket, and Jo wandered through the airs at her own sweet will, always coming out at the wrong place with a croak or a quaver that spoilt the most pensive tune. They had always done this from the time they could lisp:

"Crinkle, crinkle, 'ittle 'tar."

and it had become a household custom, for the mother was a born singer. The first sound in the morning was her voice, as she went about the house singing like a lark; and the last sound at night was the same cheery sound, for the girls never grew too old for that familiar lullaby.

Chapter 2

A MERRY CHRISTMAS

Jo was the first to wake in the grey dawn of Christmas morning. No stockings hung at the fireplace, and for a moment she felt as much disappointed as she did long ago, when her little sock fell down because it was so crammed with goodies. Then she remembered her mother's promise, and, slipping her hand under her pillow, drew out a little crimson-covered book. She knew it very well, for it was that beautiful old story of the best life ever lived, and Jo felt that it was a true guide-book for any pilgrim going the long journey. She woke Meg with a "Merry Christmas", and bade her see what was under her pillow. A green-covered book appeared, with the same picture inside, and a few words written by their mother, which made their one present very precious in their eyes. Presently Beth and Amy woke, to rummage and find their little books also—one, dove-coloured, the other blue; and all sat looking at and talking about them, while the east grew rosy with the coming day.

In spite of her small vanities, Margaret had a sweet and pious nature, which unconsciously influenced her sisters, especially Jo, who loved her very tenderly, and obeyed her because her advice was so gently given.

"Girls," said Meg seriously, looking from the tumbled head beside her to the two little night-capped ones in the room beyond, "Mother wants us to read and love and mind these books, and we must begin at once. We used to be faithful about it; but since Father went away, and all this war trouble unsettled us, we have neglected many things. You can do as you please; but *I* shall keep my book on the table here, and read a little every morning as soon as I wake, for I know it will do me good, and help me through the day."

Then she opened her new book and began to read. Jo put her arm round her, and, leaning cheek to cheek, read also, with the quiet expression so seldom seen on her restless face.

"How good Meg is! Come, Amy, let's do as they do. I'll help you with the hard words, and they'll explain things if we don't understand," whispered Beth, very much impressed by the pretty books and her sisters' example. "I'm glad mine is blue," said Amy; and then the rooms were very still while the pages were softly turned, and the winter sunshine crept in to touch the bright heads and serious faces with a Christmas greeting.

"Where is Mother?" asked Meg, as she and Jo ran down to thank her for their gifts, half an hour later. "Goodness only knows. Some poor creeter come a-beggin', and your ma went straight off to see what was needed. There never *was* such a woman for givin' away vittles and drink, clothes, and firin'," replied Hannah, who had lived with the family since Meg was born, and was considered by them all more as a friend than a servant.

"She will be back soon, I think; so fry your cake, and have everything ready," said Meg, looking over the presents which were collected in a basket and kept under the sofa, ready to be produced at the proper time. "Why, where is Amy's bottle of cologne?" she added, as the little flask did not appear. "She took it out a minute ago, and went off with it to put a ribbon on it, or some such notion," replied Jo, dancing about the room to take the first stiffness off the new army-slippers.

"How nice my handkerchiefs look, don't they! Hannah washed and ironed them for me, and I marked them all myself," said Beth, looking proudly at the somewhat uneven letters which had cost her such labour.

"Bless the child! she's gone and put 'Mother' on them instead of 'M. March'. How funny!" cried Jo, taking up one.

"Isn't it right? I thought it was better to do it so, because Meg's initials are 'M. M.', and I don't want anyone to use these but Marmee," said Beth, looking troubled.

"It's all right, dear, and a very pretty idea—quite sensible, too, for no one can ever mistake them now. It will please her very much, I know," said Meg, with a frown for Jo and a smile for Beth.

"There's Mother. Hide the basket, quick!" cried Jo, as a door slammed, and steps sounded in the hall.

Amy came in hastily, and looked rather abashed when she saw her sisters all waiting for her.

"Where have you been, and what are you hiding behind you?"

asked Meg, surprised to see, by her hood and cloak, that lazy Amy had been out so early.

"Don't laugh at me, Jo! I didn't mean anyone should know till the time came. I only meant to change the little bottle for a big one, and I gave *all* my money to get it, and I'm truly trying not to be selfish any more."

As she spoke, Amy showed the handsome flask which replaced the cheap one; and looked so earnest and humble in her little effort to forget herself that Meg hugged her on the spot, and Jo pronounced her "a trump", while Beth ran to the window and picked her finest rose to ornament the stately bottle.

"You see, I felt ashamed of my present, after reading and talking about being good this morning, so I ran round the corner and changed it the minute I was up; and I'm *so* glad, for mine is the handsomest now."

Another bang of the street door sent the basket under the sofa, and the girls to the table, eager for breakfast.

"Merry Christmas, Marmee! Many of them! Thank you for our books; we read some, and mean to every day," they cried, in chorus.

"Merry Christmas, little daughters! I'm glad you began at once, and hope you will keep on. But I want to say one word before we sit down. Not far away from here lies a poor woman with a little new-born baby. Six children are huddled into one bed to keep from freezing, for they have no fire. There is nothing to eat over there; and the oldest boy came to tell tell me they were suffering hunger and cold. My girls, will you give them your breakfast as a Christmas present?"

They were all unusually hungry, having waited nearly an hour, and for a minute no one spoke; only a minute, for Jo exclaimed impetuously:

"I'm so glad you came before we began!"

"May I go and help carry the things to the poor little children?" said Beth, eagerly.

"*I* shall take the cream and the muffins," added Amy, heroically, giving up the articles she most liked.

Meg was already covering the buckwheats, and piling the bread onto one big plate.

"I thought you'd do it," said Mrs. March, smiling as if satisfied. "You shall all go and help me, and when we come back we will have bread and milk for breakfast, and make it up at dinner-time."

They were soon ready, and the procession set out. Fortunately it was early, and they went through back streets, so few people saw them, and no one laughed at the queer party.

A poor, bare, miserable room it was, with broken windows, no fire, ragged bed-clothes, a sick mother, wailing baby, and a group of pale, hungry children cuddled under one old quilt, trying to keep warm.

How the big eyes stared and blue lips smiled as the girls went in!

"*Ach, mein Gott*! it is good angels come to us!" said the poor woman, crying for joy.

"Funny angels in hoods and mittens," said Jo and set them laughing.

In a few minutes it really did seem as if kind spirits had been at work there. Hannah, who had carried wood, made a fire, and stopped up the broken panes with old hats and her own cloak. Mrs. March gave the mother tea and gruel, and comforted her with promises of help, while she dressed the little baby as tenderly as if it had been her own. The girls, meantime, spread the table, set the children round the fire, and fed them like so many hungry birds—laughing, talking, and trying to understand the funny broken English.

"*Das ist gut*!" "*Die Engelkinder*!" cried the poor things, as they ate, and warmed their purple hands at the comfortable blaze.

The girls had never been called angel children before, and thought it very agreeable, especially Jo, who had been considered a "Sancho" ever since she was born. That was a very happy breakfast, though they didn't get any of it; and when they went away, leaving comfort behind, I think there were not in all the city four merrier people than the hungry little girls who gave away their breakfasts and contented themselves with bread and milk on Christmas morning.

"That's loving our neighbour better than ourselves, and I like it," said Meg, as they set out their presents, while their mother was upstairs collecting clothes for the poor Hummels.

Not a very splendid show, but there was a great deal of love done up in the few little bundles; and the tall vase of red roses, white chrysanthemums, and trailing vines, which stood in the middle, gave quite an elegant air to the table.

"She's coming! Strike up, Beth! Open the door, Amy! Three cheers for Marmee!" cried Jo, prancing about, while Meg went to conduct Mother to the seat of honour.

Beth played her gayest march, Amy threw open the door, and

Meg enacted escort with great dignity. Mrs. March was both surprised and touched; and smiled with her eyes full as she examined her presents, and read the little notes which accompanied them. The slippers went on at once, a new handkerchief was slipped into her pocket, well scented with Amy's cologne, the rose was fastened in her bosom, and the nice gloves were pronounced a "perfect fit".

There was a good deal of laughing and kissing and explaining, in the simple, loving fashion which makes these home festivals so pleasant at the time, so sweet to remember long afterwards, and then all fell to work.

The morning charities and ceremonies took so much time that the rest of the day was devoted to preparations for the evening festivities.

Not rich enough to afford any great outlay for private performances, the girls put their wits to work, and—necessity being the mother of invention—made whatever they needed. Very clever were some of their productions—paste-board guitars, antique lamps made of old-fashioned butter-boats covered with silver paper, gorgeous robes of old cotton glittering with tin spangle from a pickle factory, and armour covered with the same useful diamond-shaped bits, left in the sheets when the lids of tin preserve-pots were cut out. The furniture was used to being turned topsy-turvy, and the big chamber was the scene of many innocent revels.

No gentlemen were admitted; so Jo played male parts to her heart's content, and took immense satisfaction in a pair of russet-leather boots given her by a friend. These boots, an old foil, and a slashed doublet once used by an artist for some picture, were Jo's chief treasures, and appeared on all occasions. The smallness of the company made it necessary for the two principal actors to take several parts apiece; and they certainly deserved some credit for the hard work they did in learning three or four different parts, whisking in and out of various costumes, and managing the stage besides. It was excellent drill for their memories, a harmless amusement, and employed many hours which otherwise would have been idle, lonely, or spent in less profitable society.

On Christmas night, a dozen girls piled on to the bed, which was the dress-circle, and sat before the blue and yellow chintz curtains in a most flattering state of expectancy. There was a good deal of rustling and whispering behind the curtain, a trifle of lamp-smoke, and an occasional giggle from Amy, who was apt to get hysterical in the excitement of the moment. Presently a bell sounded, the curtains flew apart, and the Operatic Tragedy began.

"A gloomy wood", according to the one playbill was represented by a few shrubs in pots, green baize on the floor, and a cave in the distance. This cave was made with a clothes-horse for a roof, bureaus for walls; and in it was a small furnace in full blast, with a black spot on it, and an old witch bending over it. The stage was dark, and the glow of the furnace had a fine effect, especially as real steam issued from the kettle when the witch took the cover. A moment was allowed for the first thrill to subside; then Hugo, the villain, stalked in with a clanking sword at his side, a slouched hat, black beard, mysterious cloak, and the boots. After pacing to and fro in much agitation, he struck his forehead, and burst out in a wild strain, singing of his hatred to Roderigo, his love for Zara, and his pleasing resolution to kill the one and win the other. The gruff tones of Hugo's voice, with an occasional shout when his feelings overcame him, were very impressive, and the audience applauded the moment he paused for breath. Bowing with the air of one accustomed to public praise, he stole to the cavern, and ordered Hagar to come forth with a commanding "What ho, minion! I need thee!"

Out came Meg, with grey horse-hair hanging about her face, a red and black robe, a staff, and cabbalistic signs upon her cloak. Hugo demanded a potion to make Zara adore him, and one to destroy Roderigo. Hagar, in a fine dramatic melody, promised both, and proceeded to call up the spirit who would bring the love philtre:

"Hither, hither, from my home,
Airy sprite, I bid thee come!
Born of roses, fed on dew,
Charms and potions canst thou brew?

"Bring me here, with elfin speed,
The fragrant philtre which I need;
Make it sweet and swift and strong,
Spirit, answer now my song!"

A soft strain of music sounded, and then at the back of the cave appeared a little figure in cloudy white, with glittering wings, golden hair, and a garland of roses on its head. Waving a wand, it sang:

"Hither I come,
From my airy home,
Afar in the silver moon.
Take this magic spell,
And use it well,
Or its power will vanish soon!"

And, dropping a small, gilded bottle at the witch's feet, the spirit vanished. Another chant from Hagar produced another apparition—not a lovely one; for, with a bang, an ugly black imp appeared, and, having croaked a reply, tossed a dark bottle at Hugo, and disappeared with a mocking laugh. Having warbled his thanks and put the potions in his boots, Hugo departed; and Hagar informed the audience that, as he had killed a few of her friends in times past, she has cursed him, and intends to thwart his plans, and be revenged on him. Then the curtain fell, and the audience reposed and ate candy while discussing the merits of the play.

A good deal of hammering went on before the curtain rose again; but when it became evident what a masterpiece of stage-carpentering had been got up, no one murmured at the delay. It was truly superb! A tower rose to the ceiling; half-way up appeared a window, with a lamp burning at it, and behind the white curtain appeared Zara in a lovely blue and silver dress, waiting for Roderigo. He came in gorgeous array, with plumed cap, red cloak, chestnut love-locks, a guitar, and the boots, of course. Kneeling at the foot of the tower, he sang a serenade in melting tones. Zara replied, and, after a musical dialogue, consented to fly. Then came the grand effect of the play. Roderigo produced a rope ladder, with five steps to it, threw up one end, and invited Zara to descend. Timidly she crept from her lattice, put her hand on Roderigo's shoulder, and was about to leap gracefully down, when, "Alas! alas for Zara!" she forgot her train—it caught in the window, the tower tottered, leant forward, fell with a crash, and buried the unhappy lovers in the ruins!

A universal shriek arose as the russet boots waved wildly from the wreck,and a golden head emerged, exclaiming, "I told you so! I told you so!" With wonderful presence of mind, Don Pedro, the cruel sire, rushed in, dragged out his daughter, with a hasty aside:

"Don't laugh! Act as if it was all right!"—and, ordering Roderigo up, banished him from the kingdom with wrath and scorn. Though decidedly shaken by the fall of the tower upon him,

Roderigo defied the old gentleman, and refused to stir. This dauntless example fired Zara: she also defied her sire, and he ordered them both to the deepest dungeons of the castle. A stout little retainer came in with chains, and led them away, looking very much frightened, and evidently forgetting the speech he ought to have made.

Act third was the castle hall; and here Hagar appeared, having come to free the lovers and finish Hugo. She hears him coming, and hides; sees him put the potions into two cups of wine, and bid the timid little servant, "Bear them to the captives in their cells, and tell them I shall come anon." The servant takes Hugo aside to tell him something, and Hagar changes the cups for two others which are harmless. Ferdinando, the "minion", carries them away, and Hagar puts back the cup which holds the poison meant for Roderigo. Hugo, getting thirsty after a long warble, drinks it, loses his wits and, after a good deal of clutching and stamping, falls flat and dies; while Hagar informs him what she has done in a song of exquisite power and melody.

This was a truly thrilling scene, though some persons might have thought that the sudden tumbling down of a quantity of long hair rather marred the effect of the villain's death. He was called before the curtain, and with great propriety appeared, leading Hagar, whose singing was considered more wonderful than all the rest of the performance put together.

Act fourth displayed the despairing Roderigo on the point of stabbing himself, because he has been told that Zara has deserted him. Just as the dagger is at his heart, a lovely song is sung under his window, informing him that Zara is true, but in danger, and he can save her, if he will. A key is thrown in, which unlocks the door, and in a spasm of rapture he tears off his chains, and rushes away to find and rescue his lady-love.

Act fifth opened with a stormy scene between Zara and Don Pedro. He wishes her to go into a convent, but she won't hear of it; and, after a touching appeal, is about to faint, when Roderigo dashes in and demands her hand. Don Pedro refuses, because he is not rich. They shout and gesticulate tremendously, but cannot agree, and Roderigo is about to bear away the exhausted Zara, when the timid servant enters with a letter and a bag from Hagar, who has mysteriously disappeared. The letter informs the party that she bequeaths untold wealth to the young pair, and an awful doom to Don Pedro, if he doesn't make them happy. The bag is opened, and several quarts of tin money shower down upon the stage, till it is quite glorified with the glitter. This entirely softens the "stern sire": he consents without a murmer, all join in a joyful chorus, and the curtain falls upon the lovers kneeling to receive Don Pedro's blessing in attitudes of the most romantic grace.

Tumultuous applause followed, but received an unexpected check; for the cot-bed, on which the "dress-circle" was built, suddenly shut up, and extinguished the enthusiastic audience. Roderigo and Don Pedro flew to the rescue, and all were taken out unhurt, though many were speechless with laughter. The excitement had hardly subsided, when Hannah appeared, with "Mrs. March's compliments, and would the ladies walk down to supper".

This was a surprise, even to the actors; and, when they saw the table, they looked at one another in rapturous amazement. It was like Marmee to get up a little treat for them; but anything so fine as this was unheard of since the departed days of plenty. There was ice-cream—actually two dishes of it, pink and white—and cake and fruit and distracting French bonbons, and, in the middle of the table, four great bouquets of hot-house flowers.

It quite took their breath away; and they stared first at the table and then at their mother, who looked as if she enjoyed it immensely.

"Is it fairies?" asked Amy.

"It's Santa Claus," said Beth.

"Mother did it"; and Meg smiled her sweetest, in spite of her grey beard and white eyebrows.

"Aunt March had a good fit, and sent the supper," cried Jo, with a sudden inspiration.

"All wrong. Old Mr. Laurence sent it," replied Mrs. March.

"The Laurence boy's grandfather! What in the world put such a thing into his head? We don't know him!" exclaimed Meg.

"Hannah told one of his servants about your breakfast party. He is an odd old gentleman, but that pleased him. He knew my father, years ago; and he sent me a polite note this afternoon, saying he hoped I would allow him to express his friendly feeling towards my children by sending them a few trifles in honour of the day. I could not refuse; and so you have a little feast at night to make up for the bread-and-milk breakfast."

"That boy put it into his head, I know he did! He's a capital fellow, and I wish we could get acquainted. He looks as if he'd like to know us; but he's bashful, and Meg is so prim she won't let me speak to him when we pass," said Jo, as the plates went round, and the ice began to melt out of sight, with "Ohs!" and "Ahs!" of satisfaction.

"You mean the people who live in the big house next door, don't you?" asked one of the girls. "My mother knows old Mr. Laurence; but says he's very proud, and doesn't like to mix with his neighbours. He keeps his grandson shut up, when he isn't riding or walking with his tutor, and makes him study very hard. We invited him to our party, but he didn't come. Mother says he's very nice, though he never speaks to us girls."

"Our cat ran away once, and he brought her back, and we talked over the fence, and were getting on capitally—all about cricket, and so on—when he saw Meg coming, and walked off. I mean to know him some day; for he needs fun, I'm sure he does," said Jo decidedly.

"I like his manners, and he looks like a little gentleman; so I've no objection to your knowing him, if a proper opportunity comes. He brought the flowers himself; and I should have asked him in, if I had been sure what was going on upstairs. He looked so wistful as he went away, hearing the frolic, and evidently having none of his own."

"It's a mercy you didn't, Mother," laughed Jo, looking at her boots. "But we'll have another play, some time, that he *can* see. Perhaps he'll help act, wouldn't that be jolly?"

"I never had such a fine bouquet before! How pretty it is!" And Meg examined her flowers with great interest.

"They *are* lovely. But Beth's roses are sweeter to me," said Mrs. March, smelling the half-dead posy in her belt.

Beth nestled up to her, and whispered softly, "I wish I could send my bunch to Father. I'm afraid he isn't having such a merry Christmas as we are."

Chapter 3

THE LAURENCE BOY

"Jo! Jo! where are you?" cried Meg, at the foot of the garret stairs.

"Here!" answered a husky voice from above; and, running up,

Meg found her sister eating apples and crying over the *Heir of Redclyffe*, wrapped up in a comforter on an old three-legged sofa by the sunny window. This was Jo's favourite refuge; and here she loved to retire with half a dozen russets and a nice book, to enjoy the quiet and the society of a pet rat who lived near by, and didn't mind her a particle. As Meg appeared, Scrabble whisked into his hole. Jo shook the tears off her cheeks, and waited to hear the news.

"Such fun! only see! a regular note of invitation from Mrs. Gardiner for tomorrow night!" cried Meg, waving the precious paper, and then proceeding to read it, with girlish delight.

"'Mrs. Gardiner would be happy to see Miss March and Miss Josephine at a little party on New Year's Eve.' Marmee is willing we should go; now what *shall* we wear?"

"What's the use of asking that, when you know we shall wear our poplins because we haven't got anything else?" answered Jo, with her mouth full.

"If I only had a silk!" sighed Meg. "Mother says I may when I'm eighteen, perhaps; but two years is an everlasting time to wait."

"I'm sure our pops look like silk, and they are nice enough for us. Yours is as good as new, but I forgot the burn and the tear in mine. Whatever shall I do? The burn shows badly and I can't take any out."

"You must sit still all you can, and keep your back out of sight; the front is all right. I shall have a new ribbon for my hair, and Marmee will lend me her little pearl pin, and my new slippers are lovely, and my gloves will do, though they aren't as nice as I'd like."

"Mine are spoilt with lemonade, and I can't get any new ones, so I shall have to go without," said Jo, who never troubled herself much about dress.

"You *must* have gloves, or I won't go," cried Meg decidedly, "gloves are more important than anything else. I should be so mortified if you didn't have them."

"Then I'll stay where I am."

"You can't ask Mother for new ones, they are so expensive, and you are so careless. She said, when you spoilt the others, that she shouldn't get you any more this winter. Can't you make them do?" asked Meg anxiously.

"I can hold them crumpled up in my hand, so no one will know how stained they are; that's all I can do. No, I'll tell you how we can manage—each wear one good one and carry a bad one; don't you see?"

"Your hands are bigger than mine, and you will stretch my glove dreadfully," began Meg, whose gloves were a tender point with her.

"Then I'll go without. I don't care what people say!" cried Jo, taking up her book.

"You may have it, you may! only don't stain it, and do behave nicely. Don't put your hands behind you, or stare, or say 'Christopher Columbus!' will you?"

"Don't worry about me; I'll be as prim as I can, and not get into any scrapes, if I can help it. Now go and answer your note; and let me finish this splendid story."

So Meg went away to "accept with thanks", look over her dress, and sing blithely as she did up her one real lace frill; while Jo finished her story, her four apples, and had a game of romps with Scrabble.

On New Year's Eve the parlour was deserted, for the two younger girls played dressing-maids, and the two older were absorbed in the all-important business of "getting ready for the party". Simple as the toilets were, there was a great deal of running up and down, laughing and talking, and at one time a strong smell of burnt hair pervaded the house. Meg wanted a few curls about her face, and Jo undertook to pinch the papered locks with a pair of hot tongs.

"Ought they to smoke like that?" asked Beth, from her perch on the bed.

"It's the dampness drying," replied Jo.

"What a queer smell! it's like burnt feathers," observed Amy, smoothing her own pretty curls with a superior air.

"There, now I'll take off the papers and you'll see a cloud of little ringlets," said Jo, putting down the tongs.

She did take off the papers, but no cloud of ringlets appeared, for the hair came with the papers, and the horrified hairdresser laid a row of little scorched bundles on the bureau before her victim.

"Oh, oh, oh! what *have* you done? I'm spoilt! I can't go! My hair, oh, my hair!" wailed Meg, looking with despair at the uneven frizzle on her forehead.

"Just my luck; you shouldn't have asked me to do it; I always spoil everything. I'm so sorry, but the tongs were too hot, and so I've made a mess," groaned poor Jo, regarding the black pancakes with tears of regret.

"It isn't spoilt: just frizzle it, and tie your ribbon so the ends come on your forehead a bit, and it will look like the last fashion. I've seen many girls do it so," said Amy, consolingly.

"Serves me right for trying to be fine. I wish I'd let my hair alone," cried Meg, petulantly.

"So do I, it was so smooth and pretty. But it will soon grow out again," said Beth, coming to kiss and comfort the shorn sheep.

After various lesser mishaps, Meg was finished at last, and by the united exertions of the family, Jo's hair was got up and her dress on. They looked very well in their simple suits. Meg in silvery drab, with a blue velvet snood, lace frills, and the pearl pin; Jo in maroon, with a stiff, gentlemanly linen collar and a white chrysanthemum or two for her only ornament. Each put on the one nice light glove, and carried one soiled one, and all pronounced the effect "quite easy and fine". Meg's high-heeled slippers were very tight, and hurt her, though she would not own it, and Jo's nineteen hair-pins all seemed stuck straight into her head, which was not exactly comfortable; but, dear me, let us be elegant or die!

"Have a good time, dearies!" said Mrs. March, as the sisters went daintily down the walk. "Don't eat much supper, and come away at eleven, when I send Hannah for you." As the gate clashed behind them, a voice cried from a window:

"Girls, girls! *have* you both got nice pocket-handkerchiefs?"

"Yes, yes, spandy nice, and Meg has cologne on hers," cried Jo, adding with a laugh, as they went on, "I do believe Marmee would ask that if we were all running away from an earthquake."

"It is one of her aristocratic tastes, and quite proper, for a real lady is always known by neat boots, gloves, and handkerchief," replied Meg, who had a good many little "aristocratic tastes" of her own.

"Now don't forget to keep the bad breadth out of sight, Jo. Is my sash right? and does my hair look *very* bad?" said Meg, as she turned from the glass in Mrs. Gardiner's dressing-room, after a prolonged prink.

"I know I shall forget. If you see me doing anything wrong just remind me by a wink, will you?" returned Jo, giving her collar a twitch and her hair a hasty brush.

"No, winking isn't ladylike; I'll lift my eyebrows if anything is wrong, and nod if you are all right. Now hold your shoulders straight and take short steps, and don't shake hands if you are introduced to anyone: it isn't the thing."

"How *do* you learn all the proper ways? I never can. Isn't that music gay?"

Down they went, feeling a trifle timid, for they seldom went to parties, and, informal as this little gathering was, it was an event to them. Mrs.Gardiner, a stately old lady, greeted them kindly, and handed them over to the eldest of her six daughters. Meg knew Sallie, and was at her ease very soon; but Jo, who didn't care much for girls or girlish gossip, stood about, with her back carefully against the wall and felt as much out of place as a colt in a flower garden. Half a dozen jovial lads were talking about skates in another part of the room, and she longed to go and join them, for skating was one of the joys of her life. She telegraphed her wish to Meg, but the eyebrows went up so alarmingly that she dared not stir. No one came to talk to her, and one by one the group near her dwindled away, till she was left alone. She could not roam about and amuse herself, for the burnt breadth would show, so she stared at people rather forlornly till the dancing began. Meg was asked at once, and the tight slippers tripped about so briskly that none would have guessed the pain their wearer suffered smilingly. Jo saw a big red-headed youth approaching her corner, and fearing he meant to engage her, she slipped into a curtained recess, intending to peep and enjoy herself in peace. Unfortunately, another bashful person had chosen the same refuge; for, as the curtain fell behind her, she found herself face to face with the "Laurence boy".

"Dear me, I didn't know anyone was here!" stammered Jo, preparing to back out as speedily as she had bounced in.

But the boy laughed, and said pleasantly, though he felt a little startled:

"Don't mind me; stay if you like."

"Shan't I disturb you?"

"Not a bit; I only came here because I don't know many people, and I felt rather strange at first, you know."

"So did I. Don't go away, please, unless you'd rather."

The boy sat down again and looked at his pumps, till Jo said, trying to be polite and easy:

"I think I've had the pleasure of seeing you before; you live near us, don't you?"

"Next door"; and he looked up and laughed outright, for Jo's prim manner was rather funny, when he remembered how they had chatted about cricket when he brought the cat home.

That put Jo at her ease; and she laughed too, as she said, in her heartiest way:

"We did have such a good time over your nice Christmas present."

"Grandpa sent it."

"But you put it into his head, didn't you, now?"

"How is your cat, Miss March?" asked the boy, trying to look sober, while his black eyes shone with fun.

"Nicely, thank you, Mr. Laurence; but I am not Miss March, I'm only Jo," returned the young lady.

"I'm not Mr. Laurence, I'm only Laurie."

"Laurie Laurence—what an odd name!"

"My first name is Theodore, but I don't like it, for the fellows called me Dora, so I made them say Laurie instead."

"I hate my name, too—so sentimental! I wish everyone would say Jo, instead of Josephine. How did you make the boys stop calling you Dora?"

"I thrashed 'em."

"I can't thrash Aunt March, so I suppose I shall have to bear it"; and Jo resigned herself with a sigh.

"Do you like parties?" she asked in a moment.

"Sometimes; you see I've been abroad a good many years, and haven't been in company enough yet to know how you do things here."

"Abroad!" cried Jo. "Oh, tell me about it! I love dearly to hear people describe their travels."

Laurie didn't seem to know where to begin; but Jo's eager questions soon set him going, and he told her how he had been at school in Vevey, where the boys never wore hats, and had a fleet of boats on the lake, and for holiday fun went on walking trips about Switzerland with their teachers.

"Don't I wish I'd been there!" cried Jo. "Did you go to Paris?"

"We spent last winter there."

"Can you talk French?"

"We were not allowed to speak anything else at Vevey."

"Do say some! I can read it, but can't pronounce."

"*Quel nom a cette jeune demoiselle en les pantoufles jolies?*" said Laurie, good-naturedly.

"How nicely you do it! Let me see—you said, 'Who is the young lady in the pretty slippers,' didn't you?"

"*Oui, mademoiselle.*"

"It's my sister Margaret, and you knew it was! Do you think she is pretty?"

"Yes; she makes me think of the German girls, she looks so fresh and quiet."

Jo quite glowed with pleasure at this boyish praise of her sister, and stored it up to repeat to Meg.

Both peeped and criticized and chatted, till they felt like old acquaintances. Laurie's bashfulness soon wore off; for Jo's gentlemanly demeanour amused and set him at his ease, and Jo was her merry self again, because her dress was forgotten, and nobody lifted their eyebrows at her.

She liked the "Laurence boy" better than ever, and took several good looks at him, so that she might describe him to the girls; for they had no brothers, very few male cousins, and boys were almost unknown creatures to them.

"Curly black hair; brown skin; big, black eyes; handsome nose; fine teeth; small hands and feet; taller than I am; very polite for a boy, and altogether jolly. Wonder how old he is?"

It was on the tip of Jo's tongue to ask; but she checked herself in time, and with unusual tact, tried to find out in a roundabout way.

"I suppose you are going to college soon? I see you pegging away at your books—no, I mean studying hard"; and Jo blushed at the dreadful "pegging" which had escaped her.

Laurie smiled, but didn't seem shocked, and answered, with a shrug:

"Not for a year or two; I won't go before seventeen, anyway."

"Aren't you but fifteen?" asked Jo, looking at the tall lad, whom she had imagined seventeen already.

"Sixteen, next month."

"How I wish I was going to college! You don't look as if you liked it."

"I hate it! Nothing but grinding or skylarking. And I don't like the way fellows do either in this country."

"What do you like?"

"To live in Italy, and to enjoy myself in my own way."

Jo wanted very much to ask what his own way was: but his black brows looked rather threatening as he knit them; so she changed the subject by saying, as her foot kept time, "That's a splendid piano in the next room. Why don't you go and try it?"

"If you will come too," he answered, with a gallant little bow.

"I can't; for I told Meg I wouldn't, because—" There Jo stopped, and looked undecided whether to tell or to laugh.

"Because what?" asked Laurie, curiously.

"You won't tell?"

"Never"

"Well, I have a bad trick of standing before the fire, and so I burn my frocks, and I scorched this one; and though it's nicely mended, it shows, and Meg told me to keep still, so no one would see it. You may laugh, if you want to; it is funny, I know." But Laurie didn't laugh; he only looked down a minute, and the expression of his face puzzled Jo, when he said very gently: "Never mind that. Please come."

Jo thanked him, and gladly went, wishing she had two neat gloves, when she saw the nice, pearl-coloured ones her partner wore.

When the music stopped, they sat down; and Laurie was in the midst of an account of a students' festival at Heidelberg, when Meg appeared in search of her sister. She beckoned, and Jo reluctantly followed her into a side room, where she found her on a sofa, holding her foot, and looking pale. "I've sprained my ankle. That stupid high heel turned, and gave me a sad wrench. It aches so I can hardly stand, and I don't know how I'm ever going to get home," she said, rocking to and fro in pain.

"I knew you'd hurt your feet with those silly shoes. I'm sorry, but I don't see what you can do, except get a carriage, or stay here all night," answered Jo, softly rubbing the poor ankle as she spoke.

"I can't have a carriage, without it costing ever so much. I daresay I can't get one at all; for most people come in their own, and it's a long way to the stable, and no one to lend."

"I'll go."

"No, indeed! It's past nine, and dark as Egypt. I can't stop here, for the house is full. Sallie has some girls staying with her. I'll rest till Hannah comes, and then do the best I can."

"I'll ask Laurie; he will go," said Jo, looking relieved as the idea occurred to her.

"Mercy, no! Don't ask or tell anyone. Get me my rubbers, and put these slippers with our things. As soon as supper is over, watch for Hannah, and tell me the minute she comes."

"They are going out to supper now. I'll stay with you; I'd rather."

"No, dear, run along, and bring me some coffee. I'm so tired, I can't stir!"

So Meg reclined, with rubbers well hidden, and Jo went blundering away to the dining-room, which she found after going into a china-closet, and opening the door of a room where old Mr. Gardiner was taking a little private refreshment. Making a dart at the table, she secured the coffee, which she immediately spilt, making the front of her dress as bad as the back.

"Oh, dear, what a blunderbuss I am!" exclaimed Jo, finishing Meg's glove by scrubbing her gown with it.

"Can I help you?" said a friendly voice; and there was Laurie, with a full cup in one hand, and a plate of ice in the other.

"I was trying to get something for Meg, who is very tired, and someone shook me; and here I am, in a nice state," answered Jo, glancing dismally from the stained skirt to the coffee-coloured glove.

"Too bad! I was looking for someone to give this to. May I take it to your sister?"

"Oh, thank you! I'll show you where she is. I don't offer to take it myself, for I should only get into another scrape if I did."

Jo led the way; and, as if used to waiting on ladies, Laurie drew up a little table, brought a second instalment of coffee and ice for Jo, and was so obliging that even particular Meg pronounced him a "nice boy". They had a merry time over the bonbons and mottoes, and were in the midst of a quiet game of "Buzz", with two or three other young people who had strayed in, when Hannah appeared. Meg forgot her foot, and rose so quickly that she was forced to catch hold of Jo, with an exclamation of pain.

"Hush! Don't say anything," she whispered, adding aloud, "It's nothing. I turned my foot a little, that's all"; and limped upstairs to put her things on.

Hannah scolded, Meg cried, and Jo was at her wit's end, till she decided to take things into her own hands. Slipping out, she ran down, and, finding a servant, asked if he could get her a carriage. It happened to be a hired waiter, who knew nothing about the neighbourhood; and Jo was looking round for help, when Laurie, who had heard what she said, came up, and offered his grandfather's carriage, which had just come for him, he said.

"It's so early! You can't mean to go yet?" began Jo, looking relieved, but hesitating to accept the offer.

"I always go early—I do, truly! Please let me take you home. It's all on my way, you know, and it rains, they say."

That settled it; and, telling him of Meg's mishap, Jo gratefully accepted, and rushed up to bring down the rest of the party. Hannah hated rain as much as a cat does; so she made no trouble, and they rolled away in the luxurious close carriage, feeling very festive and elegant. Laurie went on the box; so Meg could keep her foot up, and the girls talked over their party in freedom.

"I had a capital time. Did you?" asked Jo, rumpling up her hair, and making herself comfortable.

"Yes, till I hurt myself. Sallie's friend, Annie Moffat, took a fancy to me, and asked me to come and spend a week with her when Sallie does. She is going in the spring, when the opera comes; and it will be perfectly splendid, if Mother only lets me go," answered Meg, cheering up at the thought.

"I saw you with the red-headed man I ran away from. Was he nice?"

"Oh, very! His hair is auburn, not red; and he is very polite."

"He looked like a grasshopper in a fit. Laurie and I couldn't help laughing. Did you hear us?"

"No; but it was very rude. What *were* you about all that time, hidden away there?"

Jo told her adventures, and, by the time she had finished, they were at home. With many thanks, they said "Good-night", and crept in, hoping to disturb no one; but the instant their door creaked, two little night-caps bobbed up, and two sleepy but eager voices cried out:

"Tell about the party tell about the party!" With what Meg called "a great want of manners", Jo had saved some bonbons for the little girls; and they soon subsided, after hearing the most thrilling events of the evening. "I declare, it really seems like being a fine young lady to come home from the party in a carriage, and sit in my dressing-gown with a maid to wait on me," said Meg, as Jo bound up her foot with arnica, and brushed her hair.

"I don't believe fine young ladies enjoy themselves a bit more than we do, in spite of our burnt hair, old gowns, one glove apiece, and tight slippers that sprain our ankles when we are silly enough to wear them." And I think Jo was quite right.

CHAPTER 4

BURDENS

"Oh, dear, how hard it does seem to take up our packs and jog on," sighed Meg, the morning after the party; for, now the holidays were over, the week of merry-making did not fit her for going on easily with the task she never liked.

"I wish it was Christmas or New Year all the time; wouldn't it be fun?" answered Jo, yawning dismally.

"We shouldn't enjoy ourselves half so much as we do now. But it does seem so nice to have little suppers and bouquets, and go to parties, and drive home, and read and rest, and not work. It's like other people, you know, and I always envy girls who do such things; I'm so fond of luxury," said Meg, trying to decide which of two shabby gowns was the least shabby.

"Well, we can't have it, so don't let us grumble, but shoulder our bundles and trudge along as cheerfully as Marmee does.

"I'm sure Aunt March is a regular Old Man of the Sea to me, but I suppose when I've learnt to carry her without complaining, she will tumble off, or get so light that I shan't mind her."

This idea tickled Jo's fancy, and put her in good spirits; but Meg didn't brighten, for her burden, consisting of four spoilt children, seemed heavier than ever. She hadn't heart enough even to make herself pretty, as usual, by putting on a blue neck-ribbon, and dressing her hair in the most becoming way.

"Where's the use of looking nice, when no one sees me but those cross midgets, and no one cares whether I'm pretty or not?" she muttered, shutting her drawer with a jerk. "I shall have to toil and toil all my days, with only little bits of fun now and then, and get old and ugly and sour, because I'm poor, and can't enjoy my life as other girls do. It's a shame!"

So Meg went down, wearing an injured look, and wasn't at all agreeable at breakfast-time. Everyone seemed rather out of sorts, and inclined to croak. Beth had a headache, and lay on the sofa, trying to comfort herself with the cat and three kittens; Amy was fretting because her lessons were not learned, and she couldn't find her rubbers; Jo *would* whistle and make a great racket getting ready; Mrs. March was very busy trying to finish a letter which must go at once; and Hannah had the grumps, for being up late didn't suit her.

"There never *was* such a cross family!" cried Jo, losing her temper when she had upset an ink-stand, broken both boot-lacings, and sat down upon her hat.

"You're the crossest person in it!" returned Amy, washing out the sum, that was all wrong, with the tears that had fallen on her slate.

"Beth, if you don't keep these horrid cats down cellar, I'll have them drowned," exclaimed Meg, angrily, as she tried to get rid of the kitten, which had scrambled up her back, and stuck like a burr just out of reach.

Jo laughed, Meg scolded, Beth implored, and Amy wailed, because she couldn't remember how much nine times twelve was.

"Girls, girls, do be quiet one minute! I *must* get this off by the early mail, and you drive me distracted with your worry," cried Mrs. March, crossing out the third spoilt sentence in her letter.

There was a momentary lull, broken by Hannah, who stalked in, laid two hot turnovers on the table, and stalked out again. These turnovers were an institution; and the girls called them "muffs", for they had no others, and found the hot pies very comforting to their hands on cold mornings. Hannah never forgot to make them, no matter how busy or grumpy she might be, for the walk was long and bleak; the poor things got no other lunch, and were seldom home before two.

"Cuddle your cats, and get over your headache, Bethy. Good-bye, Marmee; we are a set of rascals this morning, but we'll come home regular angels. Now then, Meg!" and Jo tramped away, feeling that the pilgrims were not setting out as they ought to do.

They always looked back before turning the corner, for their mother was always at the window, to nod and smile, and wave her hand to them. Somehow it seemed as if they couldn't have got through the day without that; for, whatever their mood might be, the last glimpse of that motherly face was sure to affect them like sunshine.

"If Marmee shook her fist instead of kissing her hand to us, it would serve us right, for more ungrateful wretches than we are were never seen," cried Jo, taking a remorseful satisfaction in the snowy walk and bitter wind.

"Don't use such dreadful expressions," said Meg, from the depths of the veil in which she had shrouded herself like a nun sick of the world.

"I like good strong words that mean something," replied Jo, catching her hat as it took a leap off her head, preparatory to flying away altogether.

"Call yourself any names you like; but *I* am neither a rascal nor a wretch, and I don't choose to be called so."

"You're a blighted being, and decidedly cross today, because you can't sit in the lap of luxury all the time. Poor dear, just wait till I make my fortune, and you shall revel in carriages and ice-cream and high-heeled slippers and posies and red-headed boys to chat with."

"How ridiculous you are, Jo!" But Meg laughed at the nonsense, and felt better in spite of herself.

"Lucky for you I am; for if I put on crushed airs, and tried to be dismal, as you do, we should be in a nice state. Thank goodness, I can always find something funny to keep me up. Don't croak any more but come home jolly, there's a dear."

Jo gave her sister an encouraging pat on the shoulder as they parted for the day, each going a different way, each hugging her little warm turnover, and each trying to be cheerful in spite of wintry weather, hard work, and the unsatisfied desires of pleasure-loving youth.

When Mr. March lost his property in trying to help an unfortunate friend, the two oldest girls begged to be allowed to do something towards their own support, at least. Believing that they could not begin too early to cultivate energy, industry, and independence, their parents consented, and both fell to work with the hearty goodwill which, in spite of all obstacles, is sure to succeed at last. Margaret found a place as nursery governess, and felt rich with her small salary. As she said, she *was* "fond of luxury", and her chief trouble was poverty. She found it harder to bear than the others, because she could remember a time when home was beautiful, life full of ease and pleasure, and want of any kind unknown. She tried not to be envious or discontented but it was very natural that the young girl should long for pretty things, gay friends, accomplishments, and a happy life. At the Kings' she daily saw all she wanted, for the children's older sisters were just out, and Meg caught frequent glimpses of dainty party-dresses and bouquets, heard lively gossip about theatres, concerts, sleighing parties, and merry-makings of all kinds, and saw money lavished on trifles which would have been so precious to her. Poor Meg seldom complained, but a sense of injustice made her feel bitter towards everyone sometimes, for she had not yet learned to know how rich she was in the blessings which alone can make life happy.

Jo happened to suit Aunt March, who was lame, and needed an active person to wait upon her. The childless old lady had offered to adopt one of the girls when the troubles came, and was much offended because her offer was declined. Other friends told the Marches that they had lost all chance of being remembered in the rich old lady's will; but the unworldly Marches only said:

"We can't give up our girls for a dozen fortunes. Rich or poor, we will keep together and be happy in one another."

The old lady wouldn't speak to them for a time, but, happening to meet Jo at a friend's, something in her comical face and blunt manners struck the old lady's fancy, and she proposed to take her for a companion. This did not suit Jo at all; but she accepted the place since nothing better appeared, and, to everyone's surprise, got on remarkably well with her irascible relative. There was an occasional tempest, and once Jo had marched home, declaring she couldn't bear it any longer; but Aunt March always cleared up quickly, and sent for her back again with such urgency that she could not refuse, for in her heart she rather liked the peppery old lady.

I suspect that the real attraction was a large library of fine books, which was left to dust and spiders since Uncle March died. Jo remembered the kind old gentleman, who used to let her build railroads and bridges with his big dictionaries, tell her stories about the queer pictures in his Latin books, and buy her cards of gingerbread whenever he met her in the street. The dim, dusty room,with the busts staring down from the tall bookcases, the cosy chairs, the globes, and, best of all, the wilderness of books, in which she could wander where she liked, made the library a region of bliss to her. The moment Aunt March took her nap or was busy with company Jo hurried to this quiet place, and curling herself up in the easy-chair, devoured poetry, romance, history, travels, and pictures, like a regular book-worm. But, like all happiness, it did not last long; for as sure as she had just reached the heart of the story, the sweetest verse of the song, or the most perilous adventure of her traveller, a shrill voice called, "Josy-phine! Josy-phine!" and she had to leave her paradise to wind yarn, wash the poodle, or read Belsham's Essays by the hour together.

Jo's ambition was to do something very splendid; what it was she had no idea, as yet, but left it for time to tell her; and, meanwhile, found her greatest affliction in the fact that she couldn't read, run, and ride as much as she liked. A quick temper, sharp tongue, and restless spirit were always getting her into scrapes, and her life was a series of ups and downs, which were both comic and pathetic. But the training she received at Aunt March's was just what she needed; and the thought that she was doing something to support herself made her happy, in spite of the perpetual "Josy-phine!"

Beth was too bashful to go to school; it had been tried, but she suffered so much that it was given up, and she did her lessons at home with her father. Even when he went away, and her mother was called to devote her skill and energy to Soldiers' Aid Societies, Beth went faithfully on by herself, and did the best she could. She was a housewifely little creature, and helped Hannah keep home neat and comfortable for the workers, never thinking of any reward but to be loved. Long, quiet days she spent, not lonely nor idle, for her little world was peopled with imaginary friends, and she was by nature a busy bee. There were six dolls to be taken up and dressed every morning, for Beth was a child still, and loved her pets as well as ever. Not one whole or handsome one among them; all were outcasts till Beth took them in; for, when her sisters outgrew these idols, they passed to her, because Amy would have nothing old or ugly. Beth cherished them all the more tenderly for that very reason, and set up a hospital for infirm dolls. No pins were ever stuck into their cotton vitals; no harsh words or blows were ever given them; no neglect ever saddened the heart of the most repulsive: but all were fed and clothed, nursed and caressed, with an affection which never failed.

One forlorn fragment of *dollanity* had belonged to Jo; and, having led a tempestuous life, was left a wreck in the ragbag, from which dreary poor-house it was rescued by Beth, and taken to her refuge. Having no top to its head, she tied on a neat little cap, and, as both arms and legs were gone, she hid these deficiencies by folding it in a blanket, and devoting her best bed to this chronic invalid. If anyone had known the care lavished on that dolly, I think it would have touched their hearts, even while they laughed. She brought it bits of bouquets; she read to it, took it out to breathe the air, hidden under her coat; she sang it lullabies, and never went to bed without kissing its dirty face, and whispering tenderly, "I hope you'll have a good night, my poor dear."

Beth had her troubles as well as the others; and not being an angel, but a very human little girl, she often "wept a little weep", as Jo said, because she couldn't take music lessons and have a fine piano. She loved music so dearly, tried so hard to learn, and practised away so patiently at the jingling old instrument, that it did seem as if someone (not to hint Aunt March) ought to help her. Nobody did, however, and nobody saw Beth wipe the tears off the yellow keys that wouldn't keep in tune, when she was all alone. She sang like a little lark about her work, never was too tired to play for Marmee and the girls, and day after day said hopefully to herself, "I know I'll get my music some time, if I'm good."

There are many Beths in the world, shy and quiet, sitting in corners till needed, and living for others so cheerfully that no one sees the sacrifices till the little cricket on the hearth stops chirping, and the sweet, sunshiny presence vanishes, leaving silence and shadow behind.

If anybody had asked Amy what the greatest trial of her life was, she would have answered at once, "My nose". When she was a baby, Jo had accidentally dropped her into the coal-hod, and Amy insisted that the fall had ruined her nose for ever. It was not big, nor red, like poor "Petrea's"; it was only rather flat, and all the pinching in the world could not give it an aristocratic point. No one minded it but herself, and it was doing its best to grow, but Amy felt deeply the want of a Grecian nose, and drew whole sheets of handsome ones to console herself.

"Little Raphael", as her sisters called her, had a decided talent for drawing, and was never so happy as when copying flowers, designing fairies, or illustrating stories with queer specimens of art. Her teachers complained that, instead of doing her sums, she covered her slate with animals; the blank pages of her atlas were used to copy maps on; and caricatures of the most ludicrous description came fluttering out of all her books at unlucky moments. She got through her lessons as well as she could, and managed to escape reprimands by being a model of deportment. She was a great favourite with her mates, being good-tempered and possessing the happy art of pleasing without effort. Her little airs and graces were much admired, so were her accomplishments; for beside her drawing, she could play twelve tunes, crochet, and read French without mispronouncing more than two-thirds of the words. She had a plaintive way of saying "When Papa was rich we did so-and-so," which was very touching; and her long words were considered "perfectly elegant" by the girls.

Amy was in a fair way to be spoilt; for everyone petted her, and her small vanities and selfishness were growing nicely. One thing, however, rather quenched the vanities; she had to wear her cousin's clothes. Now Florence's mamma hadn't a particle of taste, and Amy suffered deeply at having to wear a red instead of a blue bonnet, unbecoming gowns, and fussy aprons that did not fit. Everything was good, well made, and little worn; but Amy's artistic eyes were much afflicted, especially this winter, when her school dress was a dull purple, with yellow dots, and no trimming.

"My only comfort," she said to Meg, with tears in her eyes, "is that Mother doesn't take tucks in my dresses whenever I'm naughty, as Maria Park's mother does. My dear, it's really dreadful; for sometimes she is so bad, her frock is up to her knees, and she can't come to school. When I think of this *deggerredation,* I feel that I can bear even my flat nose and purple gown, with yellow sky-rockets on it."

Meg was Amy's confidante and monitor, and, by some strange attraction of opposites, Jo was gentle Beth's. To Jo alone did the shy child tell her thoughts; and over her big harum-scarum sister Beth unconsciously exercised more influence than anyone in the family. The two elder girls were a great deal to one another, but each took one of the younger into her keeping, and watched over her in her own way; "playing mother" they called it, and put their sisters in the places of discarded dolls, with the maternal instincts of little women.

"Has anybody got anything to tell? It's been such a dismal day I'm really dying for some amusement," said Meg, as they sat sewing together that evening.

"I had a queer time with aunt today, and, as I got the best of it, I'll tell you about it," began Jo, who dearly loved to tell stories. "I was reading that everlasting Belsham, and droning away as I always do, for aunt soon drops off, and then I take out some nice book, and read like fury till she wakes up. I actually made myself sleepy; and, before she began to nod, I gave such a gape that she asked me what I meant by opening my mouth wide enough to take the whole book in at once.

"'I wish I could and be done with it,' said I, trying not to be saucy.

"Then she gave me a long lecture on my sins, and told me to sit and think them over while she just 'lost' herself for a moment. She never finds herself very soon; so the minute her cap began to bob, like a top-heavy dahlia, I whipped the *Vicar of Wakefield* out of my pocket, and read away, with one eye on him, and one on aunt. I'd just got to where they all tumbled into the water, when I forgot, and laughed out loud. Aunt woke up; and, being more good-natured after her nap, told me to read a bit, and show what frivolous work I preferred to the worthy and instructive Belsham. I did my very best, and she liked it, though she only said:

"'I don't understand what it's all about. Go back and begin it, child.'

"Back I went, and made the Primroses as interesting as ever I could. Once I was wicked enough to stop in a thrilling place, and say meekly, 'I'm afraid it tires you, ma'am; shan't I stop now?'

"She caught up her knitting, which had dropped out of her hands, gave me a sharp look through her specs, and said, in her short way:

"'Finish the chapter, and don't be impertinent, miss.'"

"Did she own she liked it?" asked Meg.

"Oh, bless you, no! but she let old Belsham rest; and, when I ran back after my gloves this afternoon, there she was, so hard at the Vicar that she didn't hear me laugh as I danced a jig in the hall, because of the good time coming. What a pleasant life she might have, if she only chose. I don't envy her much, in spite of her money, for after all, rich people have about as many worries as poor ones, I think," added Jo.

"That reminds me," said Meg, "that I've got something to tell. It isn't funny, like Jo's story, but I thought about it a good deal as I came home. At the Kings' today I found everybody in a flurry, and one of the children said that her oldest brother had done something deadful, and papa had sent him away. I heard Mrs. King crying and Mr. King talking very loud, and Grace and Ellen turned away their faces when they passed me, so I shouldn't see how red their eyes were. I didn't ask any questions, of course; but I felt so sorry for them, and was rather glad I hadn't any wild brothers to do wicked things and disgrace the family."

"I think being disgraced in school is a great deal try*inger* than anything bad boys can do," said Amy, shaking her head, as if her experience of life had been a deep one. "Susie Perkins came to school today with a lovely red carnelian ring; I wanted it dreadfully, and wished I was her with all my might.

"Well, she drew a picture of Mr. Davis, with a monstrous nose and a hump, and the words, 'Young ladies, my eye is upon you!' coming out of his mouth in a balloon thing. We were laughing over it, when all of a sudden his eye *was* on us, and he ordered Susie to bring up her slate. She was *parry*lized with fright, but she went, and oh, what *do* you think he did? He took her by the ear—the ear! just fancy how horrid!—and led her to the recitation platform, and made her stand there half an hour, holding that slate so everyone could see it."

"Didn't the girls laugh at the picture?" asked Jo, who relished the scrape.

"Laugh! Not one! They sat as still as mice and Susie cried

quarts, I know she did. I didn't envy her then; for I felt that millions of carnelian rings wouldn't have made me happy after that. I never, never should have got over such an agonizing mortification." And Amy went on with her work, in the proud consciousness of virtue, and the successful utterance of two long words in a breath.

"I saw something that I liked this morning, and I meant to tell it at dinner, but I forgot," said Beth, putting Jo's topsy-turvy basket in order as she talked.

"When I went to get some oysters for Hannah, Mr. Laurence was in the fish-shop; but he didn't see me, for I kept behind a barrel, and he was busy with Mr. Cutter, the fish-man. A poor woman came in, with a pail and a mop, and asked Mr. Cutter if he would let her do some scrubbing for a bit of fish, because she hadn't any dinner for her children, and had been disappointed of a day's work. Mr. Cutter was in a hurry, and said 'No,' rather crossly; so she was going away, looking hungry and sorry, when Mr. Laurence hooked up a big fish with.the crooked end of his cane, and held it out to her. She was so glad and surprised, she took it right in her arms, and thanked him over and over. He told her to 'go along and cook it', and she hurried off, so happy! Wasn't it good of him? Oh, she did look so funny, hugging the big, slippery fish, and hoping Mr.Laurence's bed in heaven would be 'aisy'."

When they had laughed at Beth's story, they asked their mother for one; and, after a moment's thought, she said soberly: "As I sat cutting out blue flannel jackets today, at the rooms, I felt very anxious about Father, and thought how lonely and helpless we should be if anything happened to him. It was not a wise thing to do; but I kept on worrying till an old man came in, with an order for some clothes. He sat down near me, and I began to talk to him; for he looked poor and tired and anxious."

"'Have you sons in the army?' I asked; for the note he brought was not to me.

"'Yes, ma'am. I had four, but two were killed, one is a prisoner, and I'm going to the other, who is very sick in a Washington hospital,' he answered, quietly.

"'You have done a great deal for your country, sir,' I said, feeling respect now instead of pity.

"'Not a mite more than I ought, ma'am. I'd go myself, if I was any use; as I ain't, I give my boys, and give 'em free.'

"He spoke so cheerfully, looked so sincere, and seemed so glad to give his all, that I was ashamed of myself. I'd given one man, and thought it too much, while he gave four without grudging them. I had all my girls to comfort me at home; and his last son was waiting, miles away, to say 'good-bye' to him, perhaps! I felt so rich, so happy, thinking of my blessings, that I made him a nice bundle, gave him some money, and thanked him heartily for the lesson he had taught me."

"Tell another story, Mother—one with a moral to it, like this. I like to think about them afterwards, if they are real, and not too preachy," said Jo, after a minute's silence.

Mrs. March smiled, and began at once; for she had told stories to this little audience for many years, and knew how to please them.

"Once upon a time, there were four girls, who had enough to eat and drink and wear, a good many comforts and pleasures, kind friends and parents, who loved them dearly, and yet they were not contented." (Here the listeners stole sly looks at one another, and began to sew diligently.) "These girls were anxious to be good, and made many excellent resolutions; but they did not keep them very well, and were constantly saying, 'If we only had this,' or 'If we could only do that,' quite forgetting how much they already had, and how many pleasant things they actually could do. So they asked an old woman what spell they could use to make them happy, and she said, 'When you feel discontented, think over your blessings and be grateful.'" (Here Jo looked up quickly, as if about to speak, but changed her mind, seeing that the story was not done yet.) "Being sensible girls, they decided to try her advice, and soon were surprised to see how well off they were. One discovered that money couldn't keep shame and sorrow out of rich people's houses; another that, though she was poor, she was a great deal happier, with her youth, health, and good spirits, than a certain fretful, feeble old lady, who couldn't enjoy her comforts; a third, that, disagreeable as it was to help get dinner, it was harder still to have to go begging for it; and the fourth, that even carnelian rings were not so valuable as good behaviour. So they agreed to stop complaining, to enjoy the blessings already possessed, and try to deserve them, lest they should be taken away entirely, instead of increased; and I believe they were never disappointed, or sorry that they took the old woman's advice."

"Now, Marmee, that is very cunning of you to turn our own stories against us, and give us a sermon instead of a romance!" cried Meg.

"I like that kind of sermon. It's the sort Father used to tell us," said Beth, thoughtfully, putting the needles straight on Jo's cushion.

"I don't complain near as much as the others do, and I shall be more careful than ever now; for I've had warning from Susie's downfall," said Amy, morally.

"We needed that lesson, and we won't forget it. If we do, you just say to us, as old Chloe did in *Uncle Tom*, 'Tink ob yer marcies, chillen! tink ob yer marcies!'" added Jo, who could not for the life of her help getting a morsel of fun out of the little sermon, though she took it to heart as much as any of them.

CHAPTER 5

BEING NEIGHBOURLY

"What in the world are you going to do now, Jo?" asked Meg, one snowy afternoon, as her sister came tramping through the hall, in rubber boots, old sack and hood, with a broom in one hand and a shovel in the other.

"Going out for exercise," answered Jo, with a mischievous twinkle in her eyes.

"I should think two long walks this morning would have been enough! It's cold and dull out; and I advise you to stay warm and dry, by the fire, as I do," said Meg, with a shiver.

"Never take advice! Can't keep still all day, and, not being a pussy-cat, I don't like to doze by the fire. I like adventures, and I'm going to find some."

Meg went back to toast her feet and read *Ivanhoe;* and Jo began to dig paths with great energy. The snow was light, and with her broom she soon swept a path all round the garden, for Beth to walk in when the sun came out; and the invalid dolls needed air. Now the garden separated the Marches' house from that of Mr. Laurence. Both stood in a suburb of the city, which was still country-like, with groves and lawns, large gardens, and quiet streets. A low hedge parted the two estates. On one side was an old, brown house, looking rather bare and shabby, robbed of the vines that in summer covered its walls, and the flowers which then surrounded it. On the other side was a stately stone mansion, plainly betokening every sort of comfort and luxury, from the big coach-house and well-kept grounds to the conservatory and the glimpses of lovely things one caught between the rich curtains. Yet it seemed a lonely, lifeless sort of house; for no children frolicked on the lawn, no motherly face ever smiled at the windows, and few people went in and out, except the old gentleman and his grandson.

To Jo's lively fancy, this fine house seemed a kind of enchanted palace, full of splendours and delights, which no one enjoyed. She had long wanted to behold these hidden glories, and to know the "Laurence boy", who looked as if he would like to be known, if he only knew how to begin. Since the party, she had been more eager than ever, and had planned many ways of making friends with him; but he had not been seen lately, and Jo began to think he had gone away, when she one day spied a brown face at an upper window, looking wistfully down into their garden, where Beth and Amy were snowballing one another.

"That boy is suffering for society and fun," she said to herself. "His grandpa does not know what's good for him, and keeps him shut up all alone. He needs a party of jolly boys to play with, or somebody young and lively. I've a great mind to go over and tell the old gentleman so!"

The idea amused Jo, who liked to do daring things, and was always scandalizing Meg by her queer performances. The plan of "going over" was not forgotten; and when the snowy afternoon came, Jo resolved to try what could be done. She saw Mr. Laurence drive off, and then sallied out to dig her way down to the hedge, where she paused and took a survey. All quiet—curtains down at the lower windows; servants out of sight, and nothing human visible but a curly black head leaning on a thin hand at the upper window.

"There he is," thought Jo, "poor boy! all alone and sick this dismal day. It's a shame! I'll toss up a snowball, and make him look out, and then say a kind word to him."

Up went a handful of soft snow, and the head turned at once, showing a face which lost its listless look in a minute, as the big eyes brightened and the mouth began to smile. Jo nodded and laughed, and flourished her broom as she called out:

"How do you do? Are you sick?"

Laurie opened the window, and croaked out as hoarsely as a raven:

"Better, thank you. I've had a bad cold, and been shut up a week."

"I'm sorry. What do you amuse yourself with?"

"Nothing; it's as dull as tombs up here."

"Don't you read?"

"Not much; they won't let me."

"Can't somebody read to you?"

"Grandpa does, sometimes; but my books don't interest him and I hate to ask Brooke all the time."

"Have someone come and see you, then."

"There isn't anyone I'd like to see. Boys make such a row, and my head is weak."

"Isn't there some nice girl who'd read and amuse you? Girls are quiet, and like to play nurse."

"Don't know any."

"You know us," began Jo, then laughed, and stopped.

"So I do! Will you come, please?" cried Laurie.

"I'm not quiet and nice; but I'll come, if Mother will let me. I'll go ask her. Shut that window, like a good boy, and wait till I come."

With that, Jo shouldered her broom and marched into the house, wondering what they would all say to her. Laurie was in a flutter of excitement at the idea of having company, and flew about to get ready; for, as Mrs. March said, he was "a little gentleman", and did honour to the coming guest by brushing his curly pate, putting on a fresh collar, and trying to tidy up the room, which, in spite of half a dozen servants, was anything but neat. Presently there came a loud ring, then a decided voice, asking for "Mr. Laurie", and a surprised-looking servant came running up to announce a young lady.

"All right, show her up, it's Miss Jo," said Laurie, going to the door of his little parlour to meet Jo, who appeared, looking rosy and kind and quite at her ease, with a covered dish in one hand and Beth's three kittens in the other.

"Here I am, bag and baggage," she said briskly. "Mother sent her love, and was glad if I could do anything for you. Meg wanted me to bring some of her blancmange; she makes it very nicely, and Beth thought her cats would be comforting. I knew you'd laugh at them, but couldn't refuse, she was so anxious to do something."

It so happened that Beth's funny loan was just the thing; for, in laughing over the kits, Laurie forgot his bashfulness, and grew sociable at once.

"That looks too pretty to eat," he said, smiling with pleasure, as Jo uncovered the dish, and showed the blancmange, surrounded by a garland of green leaves, and the scarlet flowers of Amy's pet geranium.

"It isn't anything, only they all felt kindly, and wanted to show it. Tell the girl to put it away for your tea; it's so simple, you can eat it; and, being soft it will slip down without hurting your sore throat. What a cosy room this is!"

"It might be if it was kept nice; but the maids are lazy, and I don't know how to make them mind. It worries me, though."

"I'll right it up in two minutes; for it only needs to have the hearth brushed, so—and the things made straight on the mantel-piece, so—and the books put here and the bottles there, and your sofa turned from the light, and the pillows plumped up a bit. Now, then, you're fixed."

And so he was; for, as she laughed and talked, Jo had whisked things into place, and given quite a different air to the room. Laurie watched her in respectful silence; and when she beckoned him to his sofa, he sat down with a sigh of satisfaction, saying gratefully:

"How kind you are! Yes, that's what it wanted. Now please take the big chair, and let me do something to amuse my company."

"No. I came to amuse you. Shall I read aloud?" and Jo looked affectionately towards some inviting books near by.

"Thank you; I've read all those, and if you don't mind I'd rather talk," answered Laurie.

"Not a bit; I'll talk all day if you'll only set me going. Beth says I never know when to stop."

"Is Beth the rosy one, who stays at home a good deal, and sometimes goes out with a little basket?" asked Laurie, with interest.

"Yes, that's Beth; she's my girl, and a regular good one she is, too."

"The pretty one is Meg, and the curly-haired one is Amy, I believe?"

"How did you find that out?"

Laurie coloured up, but answered frankly, "Why, you see, I often hear you calling to one another, and when I'm alone up here, I can't help looking over at your house, you always seem to be having such good times. I beg your pardon for being so rude, but sometimes you forget to put down the curtain at the window where the flowers are; and when the lamps are lighted, it's like looking at a picture to see the fire, and you all round the table with your mother; her face is right opposite, and it looks so sweet behind the flowers, I can't help watching it. I haven't got any mother, you know," and Laurie poked the fire to hide a little twitching of the lips that he could not control.

The solitary, hungry look in his eyes went straight to Jo's warm heart. She had been so simply taught that there was no nonsense in her head, and at fifteen she was as innocent and frank as any child. Laurie was sick and lonely; and, feeling how rich she was in home-love and happiness, she gladly tried to share it with him. Her face was very friendly and her sharp voice unusually gentle as she said:

"We'll never draw that curtain any more, and I give you leave to look as much as you like. I just wish, though, instead of peeping, you'd come over and see us. Mother is so splendid, she'd do you heaps of good, and Beth would sing to you if *I* begged her to, and Amy would dance; Meg and I would make you laugh over our funny stage properties, and we'd have jolly times. Wouldn't your grandpa let you?"

"I think he would, if your mother asked him. He's very kind, though he does not look so; and he lets me do what I like, pretty much, only he's afraid *I* might be a bother to strangers," began Laurie, brightening more and more.

"We are not strangers, we are neighbours, and you needn't think you'd be a bother. We want to know you, and I've been trying to do it this ever so long. We haven't been here a great while, you know, but we have got acquainted with all our neighbours but you."

"You see grandpa lives among his books, and doesn't mind much what happens outside. Mr. Brooke, my tutor, doesn't stay here, you know, and I have no one to go about with me, so I just stop at home and get on as I can."

"That's bad. You ought to make an effort, and go visiting everywhere you are asked; then you'll have plenty of friends, and pleasant places to go to. Never mind being bashful; it won't last long if you keep going."

Laurie turned red again, but wasn't offended at being accused of bashfulness; for there was so much goodwill in Jo, it was impossible not to take her blunt speeches as kindly as they were meant.

"Do you like your school?" asked the boy, changing the subject, after a little pause, during which he stared at the fire, and Jo looked about her, well pleased.

"Don't go to school; I'm a businessman—girl, I mean. I go to wait on my great-aunt, and a dear, cross old soul she is, too," answered Jo.

Laurie opened his mouth to ask another question; but remembering just in time that it wasn't manners to make too many inquiries into people's affairs; he shut it again, and looked uncomfortable. Jo liked his good breeding, and didn't mind having a laugh at Aunt March, so she gave him a lively description of the fidgety old lady, her fat poodle, the parrot that talked Spanish, and the library where she revelled. Laurie enjoyed that immensely; and when she told about the prim old gentleman who came once to woo Aunt March, and in the middle of a fine speech, how Polly had tweaked his wig off, to his great dismay, the boy lay back and laughed till the tears ran down his cheeks, and a maid popped her head in to see what was the matter.

"Oh! that does me no end of good. Tell on, please," he said, taking his face out of the sofa cushions, red and shining with merriment.

Much elated with her success, Jo did "tell on", all about their plays and plans, their hopes and fears for Father, and the most interesting events of the little world in which the sisters lived. Then they got to talking about books; and to Jo's delight, she found that Laurie loved them as well as she did, and had read even more than herself.

"If you like them so much, come down and see ours. Grandpa is out, so you needn't be afraid," said Laurie, getting up.

"I'm not afraid of anything," returned Jo, with a toss of the head.

"I don't believe you are!" exclaimed the boy, looking at her with much admiration, though he privately thought she would have good reason to be a trifle afraid of the old gentleman, if she met him in some of his moods.

The atmosphere of the whole house being summer-like, Laurie led the way from room to room, letting Jo stop to examine whatever struck her fancy; and so at last they came to the library, where she clapped her hands, and pranced, as she always did when especially delighted. It was lined with books, and there were pictures and statues and distracting little cabinets full of coins and curiosities, and sleepy-hollow chairs and queer tables, and bronzes; and, best of all, a great open fireplace, with quaint tiles all round it.

"What richness!" sighed Jo, sinking into the depth of a velvet chair, and gazing about her with an air of intense satisfaction. "Theodore Laurence, you ought to be the happiest boy in the world," she added impressively.

"A fellow can't live on books," said Laurie, shaking his head, as he perched on a table opposite.

Before he could say more, a bell rang, and Jo flew up, exclaiming with alarm, "Mercy me! it's your grandpa!"

"Well, what if it is? You are not afraid of anything, you know," returned the boy, looking wicked.

"I think I am a little bit afraid of him, but I don't know why I should be. Marmee said I might come, and I don't think you're any the worse for it," said Jo, composing herself, though she kept her eyes on the door.

"I'm a great deal better for it, and ever so much obliged. I'm only afraid you are very tired talking to me; it was *so* pleasant, I couldn't bear to stop," said Laurie, gratefully.

"The doctor to see you, sir," and the maid beckoned as she spoke.

"Would you mind if I left you for a minute? I suppose I must see him," said Laurie.

"Don't mind me. I'm as happy as a cricket here," answered Jo.

Laurie went away, and his guest amused herself in her own way. She was standing before a fine portrait of the old gentleman, when the door opened again, and without turning, she said decidedly, "I'm sure now that I shouldn't be afraid of him, for he's got kind eyes, though his mouth is grim, and he looks as if he had a tremendous will of his own. He isn't as handsome as *my* grandfather, but I like him."

"Thank you, ma'am," said a gruff voice behind her; and there, to her great dismay, stood old Mr. Laurence.

Poor Jo blushed till she couldn't blush any redder, and her heart began to beat uncomfortably fast as she thought what she had said. For a minute a wild desire to run away possessed her; but that was cowardly, and the girls would laugh at her; so she resolved to stay, and get out of the scrape if she could.

A second look showed her that the living eyes, under the bushy grey eyebrows, were kinder even than the painted ones; and there was a sly twinkle in them which lessened her fear a good deal. The gruff voice was gruffer than ever, as the old gentleman said abruptly, after that dreadful pause, "So you're not afraid of me, hey?"

"Not much, sir."

"And you don't think me as handsome as your grandfather?"

"Not quite, sir."

"And I've got a tremendous will, have I?"

"I only said I thought so."

"But you like me, in spite of it?"

"Yes, I do, sir."

That answer pleased the old gentleman; he gave a short laugh, shook hands with her, and, putting his fingers under her chin, turned up her face, examined it gravely, and let it go, saying, with a nod, "You've got your grandfather's spirit, if you haven't his face. He *was* a fine man, my dear; but, what is better, he was a brave and honest one, and I was proud to be his friend."

"Thank you, sir"; and Jo was quite comfortable after that, for it suited her exactly.

"What have you been doing to this boy of mine, hey?" was the next question, sharply put.

"Only trying to be neighbourly, sir"; and Jo told how her visit came about.

"You think he needs cheering up a bit, do you?"

"Yes, sir; he seems a little lonely, and young folks would do him good, perhaps. We are only girls, but we should be glad to help if we could, for we don't forget the splendid Christmas present you sent us," said Jo, eagerly.

"Tut, tut, tut! that was the boy's affair. How is the poor woman?"

"Doing nicely, sir"; and off went Jo, talking very fast, as she told all about the Hummels, in whom her mother had interested richer friends than they were.

"Just her father's way of doing good. I shall come and see your mother some fine day. Tell her so. There's the tea-bell; we have it early, on the boy's account. Come down, and go on being neighbourly."

"If you'd like to have me, sir."

"Shouldn't ask you if I didn't"; and Mr.Laurence offered her his arm with old-fashioned courtesy.

"What *would* Meg say to this?" thought Jo, as she was marched away, while her eyes danced with fun as she imagined herself telling the story at home.

"Hey! Why, what the dickens has come to the fellow?" said the old gentleman, as Laurie came running downstairs, and brought up with a start of surprise at the astonishing sight of Jo arm-in-arm with his redoubtable grandfather.

"I didn't know you'd come, sir," he began, as Jo gave him a triumphant little glance.

"That's evident, by the way you racket downstairs. Come to your tea, sir, and behave like a gentleman"; and having pulled the boy's hair by way of a caress, Mr.Laurence walked on, while Laurie went through a series of comic evolutions behind their backs, which nearly produced an explosion of laughter from Jo. The old gentleman did not say much as he drank his four cups of tea, but he watched the young people, who soon chatted away like old friends, and the change in his grandson did not escape him. There was colour, light, and life in the boy's face now, vivacity in his manner, and genuine merriment in his laugh.

"She's right; the lad *is* lonely. I'll see what these little girls can do for him," thought Mr. Laurence, as he looked and listened. He liked Jo, for her odd, blunt ways suited him; and she seemed to understand the boy almost as well as if she had been one herself.

If the Laurences had been what Jo called "prim and poky" she would not have got on at all, for such people always made her shy and awkward; but finding them free and easy, she was so herself, and made a good impression. When they rose, she proposed to go, but Laurie said he had something more to show her, and took her away to the conservatory, which had been lighted for her benefit. It seemed quite fairylike to Jo, as she went up and down the walks, enjoying the blooming walls on either side, the soft light, the damp, sweet air, and the wonderful vines and trees that hung above her—while her new friend cut the finest flowers till his hands were full; then he tied them up, saying, with the happy look Jo liked to see, "Please give these to your mother, and tell her I like the medicine she sent me very much."

They found Mr. Laurence standing before the fire in the great drawing-room, but Jo's attention was entirely absorbed by a grand piano, which stood open.

"Do you play?" she asked, turning to Laurie with a respectful expression.

"Sometimes," he answered, modestly.

"Please do now. I want to hear it so I can tell Beth."

"Won't you first?"

"Don't know how; too stupid to learn, but I love music dearly."

So Laurie played, and Jo listened, with her nose luxuriously buried in heliotrope and tea-roses. Her respect and regard for the "Laurence boy" increased very much, for he played remarkably well, and didn't put on any airs. She wished Beth could hear him, but she did not say so; only praised him till he was quite abashed and his grandfather came to the rescue. "That will do, that will do, young lady. Too many sugar-plums are not good for him. His music isn't bad, but I hope he will do as well in more important things. Going? Well, I'm much obliged to you, and I hope you'll come again. My respects to your mother. Good night, Doctor Jo."

He shook hands kindly, but looked as if something did not please him. When they got into the hall, Jo asked Laurie if she had said anything amiss. He shook his head.

"No, it was me; he doesn't like to hear me play."

"Why not?"

"I'll tell you some day. John is going home with you, as I can't."

"No need of that; I am not a young lady, and it's only a step. Take care of yourself, won't you?"

"Yes; but you will come again, I hope?"

"If you promise to come and see us after you are well."

"I will."

"Good-night, Laurie!"

"Good-night, Jo, good-night!"

When all the afternoon's adventures had been told, the family felt inclined to go visiting in a body, for each found something very attractive in the big house on the other side of the hedge: Mrs. March wanted to talk of her father with the old man who had not forgotten him; Meg longed to walk in the conservatory; Beth sighed for the grand piano; and Amy was eager to see the fine pictures and statues.

"Mother, why didn't Mr. Laurence like to have Laurie play?" asked Jo, who was of an inquiring disposition.

"I am not sure, but I think it was because his son, Laurie's father, married an Italian lady, a musician, which displeased the old man, who is very proud. The lady was good and lovely and accomplished, but he did not like her, and never saw his son after he married. They both died when Laurie was a little child, and then his grandfather took him home. I fancy the boy, who was born in Italy, is not very strong, and the old man is afraid of losing him, which makes him so careful. Laurie comes naturally by his love of music, for he is like his mother, and I dare say his grandfather fears that he may want to be a musician; at any rate, his skill reminds him of the woman he did not like, and so he 'glowered', as Jo said."

"Dear me, how romantic!" exclaimed Meg.

"How silly!" said Jo. "Let him be a musician, if he wants to, and not plague his life out sending him to college, when he hates to go."

"That's why he has such handsome black eyes and pretty manners, I suppose. Italians are always nice," said Meg, who was a little sentimental.

"What do you know about his eyes and his manners? You never spoke to him, hardly," cried Jo, who was *not* sentimental.

"I saw him at the party, and what you tell shows that he knows how to behave. That was a nice little speech about the medicine Mother sent him."

"He meant the blancmange, I suppose."

"How stupid you are, child! He meant you, of course."

"Did he?" and Jo opened her eyes as if it had never occurred to her before.

"I never saw such a girl! You don't know a compliment when you get it," said Meg, with the air of a young lady who knew all about the matter.

"I think they are great nonsense, and I'll thank you not to be silly, and spoil my fun. Laurie's a nice boy, and I like him, and I won't have any sentimental stuff about compliments and such rubbish. We'll all be good to him, because he hasn't got any mother, and he *may* come over and see us, mayn't he, Marmee?"

"Yes, Jo, your little friend is very welcome, and I hope Meg will remember that children should be children as long as they can."

"I don't call myself a child, and I'm not in my teens yet," observed Amy. "What do you say, Beth?"

"I was thinking about our *Pilgrim's Progress*," answered Beth, who had not heard a word. "How we got out of the Slough and through the Wicket Gate by resolving to be good, and up the steep hill by trying; and that maybe the house over there full of splendid things, is going to be our Palace Beautiful."

"We have got to get by the lions, first," said Jo, as if she rather liked the prospect.

CHAPTER 6

BETH FINDS THE PALACE BEAUTIFUL

The big house did prove a Palace Beautiful, though it took some time for all to get in, and Beth found it very hard to pass the lions. Old Mr. Laurence was the biggest one; but after he had called, said something funny or kind to each one of the girls, and talked over old times with their mother, nobody felt much afraid of him, except timid Beth. The other lion was the fact that they were poor and Laurie rich; for this made them shy of accepting favours which they could not return. But, after a while they found that he considered them the benefactors, and could not do enough to show how grateful he was for Mrs. March's motherly welcome, their cheerful society, and the comfort he took in that humble home of theirs. So they soon forgot their pride, and interchanged kindnesses without stopping to think which was the greater.

All sorts of pleasant things happened about that time; for the new friendship flourished like grass in spring. Everyone liked Laurie, and he privately informed his tutor that "the Marches were regular splendid girls". With the delightful enthusiasm of youth they took the solitary boy into their midst, and made much of him, and he found something very charming in the innocent companionship of these simple-hearted girls. Never having known mother or sisters, he was quick to feel the influences they brought about him; and their busy, lively ways made him ashamed of the indolent life he led. He was tired of books, and found people so interesting now that Mr. Brooke was obliged to make very unsatisfactory reports; for Laurie was always playing truant and running over to the Marches'.

"Never mind; let him take a holiday, and make it up afterwards," said the old gentleman. "The good lady next door says he is studying too hard, and needs young society, amusement, and exercise. I suspect she is right, and that I've been coddling the fellow as if I'd been his grandmother. Let him do what he likes, as long as he is happy. He can't get into mischief in that little nunnery over there; and Mrs. March is doing more for him than we can."

What good times they had, to be sure! Such plays and tableaux, such sleigh-rides and skating frolics, such pleasant evenings in the old parlour, and now and then such gay little parties at the great house. Meg could walk in the conservatory whenever she liked, and revel in bouquets; Jo browsed over the new library voraciously, and convulsed the old gentleman with her criticisms. Amy copied pictures and enjoyed beauty to her heart's content; and Laurie played "lord of the manor" in the most delightful style.

But Beth, though yearning for the grand piano, could not pluck up courage to go to the "Mansion of Bliss", as Meg called it. She went once with Jo; but the old gentleman, not being aware of her infirmity, stared at her so hard from under his heavy eyebrows, and said "Hey!" so loud, that he frightened her so much her "feet chattered on the floor", she told her mother; and she ran away, declaring she would never go there any more, not even for the dear piano. No persuasions or enticements could overcome her fears, till the fact coming to Mr. Laurence's ear in some mysterious way, he set about mending matters. During one of the brief calls he made, he artfully led the conversation to music, and talked away about great singers whom he had seen, fine organs he had heard, and told such charming anecdotes that Beth found it impossible to stay in her distant corner, but crept nearer and nearer, as if fascinated. At the back of his chair she stopped, and stood listening, with her great eyes wide open, and her cheeks red with the excitement of this unusual performance. Taking no more notice of her than if she had been a fly, Mr. Laurence talked on about Laurie's lessons and teachers; and presently, as if the idea had just occurred to him, he said to Mrs. March:

"The boy neglects his music now, and I'm glad of it, for he was getting too fond of it. But the piano suffers for want of use. Wouldn't some of your girls like to run over, and practise on it now and then, just to keep it in tune, you know, ma'am?"

Beth took a step forward, and pressed her hands tightly together to keep from clapping them, for this was an irresistible temptation; and the thought of practising on that splendid instrument quite took her breath away. Before Mrs. March could reply, Mr. Laurence went on with an odd little nod and smile:

"They needn't see or speak to anyone, but run in at any time; for I'm shut up in my study at the other end of the house, Laurie is out a great deal, and the servants are never near the drawing-room after nine o'clock."

Here he rose, as if going, and Beth made up her mind to speak, for that last arrangement left nothing to be desired. "Please tell the young ladies what I say; and if they don't care to come, why, never mind." Here a little hand slipped into his, and Beth looked up at him with a face full of gratitude, as she said, in her earnest, yet timid way:

"Oh, sir, they do care, very, very much!"

"Are you the musical girl?" he asked, without any startling "Hey!" as he looked down at her very kindly.

"I'm Beth. I love it dearly, and I'll come, if you are quite sure nobody will hear me—and be disturbed," she added, fearing to be rude, and trembling at her own boldness as she spoke.

"Not a soul, my dear. The house is empty half the day; so come and drum away as much as you like, and I shall be obliged to you."

"How kind you are, sir."

Beth blushed like a rose under the friendly look he wore; but she was not frightened now, and gave the big hand a grateful squeeze, because she had no words to thank him for the precious gift he had given her. The old gentleman softly stroked the hair of her forehead, and stooping down, he kissed her, saying, in a tone few people ever heard:

"I had a little girl once, with eyes like these. God bless you, my dear! Good-day, madam"; and away he went, in a great hurry.

Beth had a rapture with her mother, and then rushed up to impart the glorious news to her family of invalids, as the girls were not at home. How blithely she sang that evening, and how they all laughed at her, because she woke Amy in the night by playing the piano on her face in her sleep. Next day, having seen both the old and the young gentlemen out of the house, Beth, after two or three retreats, fairly got in at the side-door and made her way, as noiselessly as any mouse, to the drawing-room where her idol stood. Quite by accident of course, some pretty, easy music lay on the piano; and, with trembling fingers, and frequent stops to listen and look about, Beth at last touched the great instrument, and straightway forgot her fear, herself, and everything else but the unspeakable delight which the music gave her, for it was like the voice of a beloved friend.

She stayed till Hannah came to take her home to dinner; but she had no appetite, and could only sit and smile upon everyone in a general state of beatitude.

After that, the little brown hood slipped through the hedge nearly every day, and the great drawing-room was haunted by a tuneful spirit that came and went unseen. She never knew that Mr. Laurence often opened his study door to hear the old-fashioned airs he liked; she never saw Laurie mount guard in the hall to warn the servants away; she never suspected that the exercise-books and new songs which she found in the rack were put there for her especial benefit; and when he talked to her about music at home, she only thought how kind he was to tell things that helped her so much. So she enjoyed herself heartily, and found, what isn't always the case, that her granted wish was all she had hoped. Perhaps it was because she was so grateful for this blessing that a greater was given her; at any rate she deserved both.

"Mother, I'm going to work Mr. Laurence a pair of slippers. He is so kind to me, I must thank him, and I don't know any other way. Can I do it?" asked Beth, a few weeks after that eventful call of his.

"Yes, dear. It will please him very much, and be a nice way of thanking him. The girls will help you about them, and I will pay for the making up," replied Mrs. March, who took peculiar pleasure in granting Beth's requests, because she so seldom asked anything for herself.

After many serious discussions with Meg and Jo, the pattern was chosen, the materials bought, and the slippers begun. A cluster of grave yet cheerful pansies on a deeper purple ground was pronounced very appropriate and pretty; and Beth worked away early and late, with occasional lifts over hard parts. She was a nimble little needle-woman, and they were finished before anyone got tired of them. Then she wrote a very short, simple note, and, with Laurie's help, got them smuggled on to the study-table one morning before the old gentleman was up.

When this excitement was over, Beth waited to see what would happen. All that day passed, and a part of the next, before any acknowledgement arrived, and she was beginning to fear she had offended her crotchety friend. On the afternoon of the second day, she went out to do an errand, and give poor Joanna, the invalid doll, her daily exercise. As she came up the street, on her return, she saw three, yes, four, heads popping in and out of the parlour windows, and the moment they saw her, several hands were waved, and several joyful voices screamed:

"Here's a letter from the old gentleman! Come quick, and read it!"

"Oh, Beth, he's sent you—" began Amy, gesticulating with unseemly energy; but she got no further, for Jo quenched her by slamming down the window.

Beth hurried on in a flutter of suspense. At the door, her sisters seized and bore her to the parlour in a triumphal procession, all pointing, and all saying at once, "Look there! look there!" Beth did look, and turned pale with delight and surprise; for there stood a little cabinet piano, with a letter lying on the glossy lid, directed, like a signboard, to "Miss Elizabeth March".

"For me?" gasped Beth, holding on to Jo, and feeling as if she should tumble down, it was such an overwhelming thing altogether.

"Yes; all for you, my precious! Isn't it splendid of him? Don't you think he's the dearest old man in the world? Here's the key in the letter. We didn't open it, but we are dying to know what he says," cried Jo, hugging her sister, and offering the note.

"You read it! I can't! I feel so queer! Oh, it is too lovely! " and Beth hid her face in Jo's apron, quite upset by her present.

Jo opened the paper, and began to laugh, for the first words she saw were:

"'MISS MARCH:

"'Dear Madam'"—

"How nice it sounds! I wish someone would write to me so!" said Amy, who thought the old-fashioned address very elegant.

"'I have had many pairs of slippers in my life, but I never had any that suited me so well as yours,'" continued Jo. "'Heart's ease is my favourite flower, and these will always remind me of the gentle giver. I like to pay my debts; so I know you will allow "the old gentleman" to send you something which once belonged to the little granddaughter he lost. With hearty thanks and best wishes, I remain, your grateful friend and humble servant,

"'JAMES LAURENCE.'"

"There, Beth, that's an honour to be proud of, I'm sure. Laurie told me how fond Mr. Laurence used to be of the child who died, and how he kept all her little things carefully. Just think, he's given you her piano. That comes of having big blue eyes, and loving music," said Jo, trying to soothe Beth, who trembled, and looked more excited than she had ever been before.

"See the cunning brackets to hold candles, and the nice green silk, puckered up, with a gold rose in the middle, and the pretty rack and stool, all complete," added Meg, opening the instrument and displaying its beauties.

"'Your humble servant, James Laurence'; only think of his writing that to you. I'll tell the girls. They'll think it's splendid," said Amy, much impressed by the note.

"Try it, honey. Let's hear the sound of the baby pianny," said Hannah, who always took a share in the family joys and sorrows.

So Beth tried it; and everyone pronounced it the most remarkable piano ever heard. It had evidently been newly tuned and put in apple-pie order; but perfect as it was, I think the real charm of it lay in the happiest of all happy faces which leaned over it, as Beth lovingly touched the beautiful black and white keys and pressed the bright pedals.

"You'll have to go and thank him," said Jo, by way of a joke; for the idea of the child's really going never entered her head.

"Yes, I mean too. I guess I'll go now, before I get frightened thinking about it." And, to the utter amazement of the assembled family, Beth walked deliberately down the garden, through the hedge, and in at the Laurences' door.

"Well, I wish I may die if it ain't the queerest thing I ever see. The pianny has turned her head! She'd never have gone in her right mind," cried Hannah, staring after her, while the girls were rendered quite speechless by the miracle.

They would have been still more amazed if they had seen what Beth did afterwards. If you will believe me, she went and knocked at the study door before she gave herself time to think; and when a gruff voice called out, "Come in!" she did go in, right up to Mr. Laurence, who looked quite taken aback, and held out her hand, saying, with only a small quaver in her voice, "I came to thank you, sir, for— " But she didn't finish; for he looked so friendly, that she forgot her speech, and, only remembering that he had lost the little girl he loved, she put both arms round his neck, and kissed him.

If the roof of the house had suddenly flown off, the old gentleman wouldn't have been more astonished; but he liked it—oh, dear, yes, he liked it amazingly!—and was so touched and pleased by that confiding little kiss, that all his crustiness vanished; and he just set her on his knee, and laid his wrinkled cheek against her rosy one, feeling as if he had got his own little granddaughter back again. Beth ceased to fear him from that moment and sat there talking to him as cosily as if she had known him all her life; for love casts out fear, and gratitude can conquer pride. When she went home, he walked with her to her own gate, shook hands cordially, and touched his hat as he marched back again, looking very stately and erect, like a handsome, soldierly old gentleman, as he was. When the girls saw that performance, Jo began to dance a jig, by way of expressing her satisfaction; Amy nearly fell out of the window in her surprise; and Meg exclaimed, with uplifted hands, "Well, I do believe the world is coming to an end!"

CHAPTER 7

AMY'S VALLEY OF HUMILIATION

"That boy is a perfect Cyclops, isn't he?" said Amy, one day, as Laurie clattered by on horseback, with a flourish of his whip as he passed.

"How dare you say so, when he's got both his eyes? and very handsome ones they are, too," cried Jo, who resented any slighting remarks about her friend.

"I didn't say anything about his eyes, and I don't see why you need fire up when I admire his riding."

"Oh, my goodness! that little goose means a centaur, and she called him a Cyclops," exclaimed Jo, with a burst of laughter.

"You needn't be so rude; it's only a 'lapse of lingy', as Mr. Davis says," retorted Amy, finishing Jo with her Latin. "I just wish I had a little of the money Laurie spends on that horse," she added, as if to herself, yet hoping her sisters would hear.

"Why?" asked Meg, kindly, for Jo had gone off in another laugh at Amy's second blunder.

"I need it so much; I'm dreadfully in debt, and it won't be my turn to have the rag-money for a month."

"In debt, Amy? What do you mean?" and Meg looked sober.

"Why, I owe at least a dozen pickled limes, and I can't pay them, you know, till I have money, for Marmee forbade my having anything charged at the shop."

"Tell me all about it. Are limes the fashion now? It used to be pickling bits of rubber to make balls"; and Meg tried to keep her countenance, Amy looked so grave and important.

"Why, you see, the girls are always buying them, and unless you want to be thought mean, you must do it too. It's nothing but limes now, for everyone is sucking them in their desks in school-time, and trading them off for pencils, bead-rings, paper dolls, or something else at recess. If one girl likes another she gives her a lime; if she's mad with her she eats one before her face, and don't offer even a suck. They treat by turns; and I've had ever so many, but haven't returned them; and I ought, for they are debts of honour, you know."

"How much will pay them off, and restore your credit?" asked Meg, taking out her purse.

"A quarter would more than do it, and leave a few cents over for a treat for you. Don't you like limes?"

"Not much; you may have my share. Here's the money. Make it last as long as you can, for it isn't very plenty, you know."

"Oh, thank you! It must be so nice to have pocket-money! I'll have a grand feast, for I haven't tasted a lime this week. I felt delicate about taking any, as I couldn't return them, and I'm actually suffering for one."

Next day Amy was rather late at school; but could not resist the temptation of displaying, with pardonable pride, a moist, brown-paper parcel, before she consigned it to the inmost recesses of her desk. During the next few minutes the rumour that Amy March had got twenty-four delicious limes (she ate one on the way), and was going to treat, circulated through her "set", and the attentions of her friends became quite overwhelming. Katy Brown invited her to her next party on the spot; Mary Kingsley insisted on lending her her watch till recess; and Jenny Snow, a satirical young lady, who had basely twitted Amy upon her timeless state, promptly buried the hatchet, and offered to furnish answers to certain appalling sums. But Amy had not forgotten Miss Snow's cutting remarks about "some persons whose noses were not too flat to smell other people's limes, and stuck-up people who were not too proud to ask for them"; and she instantly crushed that "Snow girl's" hopes by the withering telegram, "You needn't be so polite all of a sudden, for you won't get any."

A distinguished personage happened to visit the school that morning, and Amy's beautifully drawn maps received praise, which honour to her foe rankled in the soul of Miss Snow, and caused Miss March to assume the airs of a studious young peacock. But, alas, alas! pride goes before a fall, and the revengeful Snow turned the tables with disastrous success. No sooner had the guest paid the usual stale compliments, and bowed himself out than Jenny, under pretence of asking an important question, informed Mr. Davis, the teacher, that Amy March had pickled limes in her desk.

Now Mr. Davis had declared limes a contraband article, and solemnly vowed to ferrule publicly the first person who was found breaking the law. This much-enduring man had succeeded in banishing chewing-gum after a long and stormy war, and had made a bonfire of the confiscated novels and newspapers, had suppressed a private post office, had forbidden distortions of the face, nicknames, and caricatures, and done all that one man could do to keep half-a-hundred rebellious girls in order. Boys are trying enough to human patience, goodness knows! but girls are infinitely more so, especially to nervous gentlemen, with tyrannical tempers, and no more talent for teaching than Dr. Blimber. Mr. Davis knew any quantity of Greek, Latin, Algebra, and ologies of all sorts, so he was called a fine teacher, and manners, morals, feelings, and examples were not considered of any particular importance. It was a most unfortunate moment for denouncing Amy, and Jenny knew it. Mr. Davis had evidently taken his coffee too strong that morning; there was an east wind, which always affected his neuralgia; and his pupils had not done him the credit which he felt he deserved: therefore, to use the expressive, if not elegant, language of a schoolgirl, "he was as nervous as a witch, and as cross as a bear". The word "limes" was like fire to powder; his yellow face flushed, and he rapped on his desk with an energy which made Jenny skip to her seat with unusual rapidity.

"Young ladies, attention, if you please!"

At the stern order the buzz ceased, and fifty pairs of blue, black, grey, and brown eyes were obediently fixed upon his awful countenance.

"Miss March, come to the desk."

Amy rose to comply with outward composure, but a secret fear oppressed her, for the limes weighed upon her conscience.

"Bring with you the limes you have in your desk," was the unexpected command which arrested her before she got out of her seat.

"Don't take all," whispered her neighbour, a young lady of great presence of mind.

Amy hastily shook out half a dozen, and laid the rest down before Mr. Davis, feeling that any man possessing a human heart would relent when that delicious perfume met his nose.

Unfortunately Mr. Davis particularly detested the odour of the fashionable pickle, and disgust added to his wrath.

"Is that all?"

"Not quite," stammered Amy.

"Bring the rest immediately."

With a despairing glance at her set, she obeyed.

"You are sure there are no more?"

"I never lie, sir."

"So I see. Now take these disgusting things two by two, and throw them out of the window."

There was a simultaneous sigh, which created quite a little gust, as the last hope fled, and the treat was ravished from their longing lips. Scarlet with shame and anger, Amy went to and fro six dreadful times; and as each doomed couple—looking oh! so plump and juicy—fell from her reluctant hands, a shout from the street completed the anguish of the girls, for it told them that their feast was being exulted over by the little Irish children, who were their sworn foes. This—this was too much; all flashed indignant or appealing glances at the inexorable Davis, and one passionate lime-lover burst into tears.

As Amy returned from her last trip, Mr. Davis gave a portentous "Hem!" and said, in his most impressive manner—"Young ladies, you remember what I said to you a week ago. I am sorry this has happened; but I never allow my rules to be infringed, and I *never* break my word. Miss March, hold out your hand."

Amy started and put both hands behind her, turning on him an imploring look which pleaded for her better than the words she could not utter. She was rather a favourite with "old Davis", as, of course, he was called, and it's my private belief that he *would* have broken his word if the indignation of one irrepressible young lady had not found vent in a hiss. That hiss, faint as it was, irritated the irascible gentleman, and sealed the culprit's fate.

"Your hand, Miss March!" was the only answer her mute appeal received; and, too proud to cry or beseech, Amy set her teeth, threw back her head defiantly, and bore without flinching several tingling blows on her little palm. They were neither many nor heavy, but that made no difference to her. For the first time in her life she had been struck; and the disgrace, in her eyes, was as deep as if he had knocked her down.

"You will now stand on the platform till recess," said Mr. Davis, resolved to do the thing thoroughly, since he had begun.

That was dreadful. It would have been bad enough to go to

her seat, and see the pitying faces of her friends, or the satisfied ones of her few enemies; but to face the whole school with that shame fresh upon her, seemed impossible, and for a second she felt as if she could only drop down where she stood, and break her heart with crying. A bitter sense of wrong, and the thought of Jenny Snow, helped her to bear it; and, taking the ignominious place, she fixed her eyes on the stove-funnel above what now seemed a sea of faces, and stood there, so motionless and white that the girls found it very hard to study, with that pathetic figure before them.

During the fifteen minutes that followed, the proud and sensitive little girl suffered a shame and pain which she never forgot. To others it might seem a ludicrous or trivial affair, but to her it was a hard experience; for during the twelve years of her life she had been governed by love alone, and a blow of that sort had never touched her before. The smart of her hand and the ache of her heart were forgotten in the sting of the thought—"I shall have to tell at home, and they will be so disappointed in me!"

The fifteen minutes seemed an hour; but they came to an end at last, and the word "Recess!" had never seemed so welcome to her before.

"You can go, Miss March," said Mr. Davis, looking, as he felt, uncomfortable.

He did not soon forget the reproachful glance Amy gave him, as she went, without a word to anyone, straight into the anteroom, snatched her things, and left the place "for ever", as she passionately declared to herself. She was in a sad state when she got home; and when the older girls arrived, some time later, an indignation meeting was held at once. Mrs. March did not say much, but looked disturbed, and comforted her afflicted little daughter in her tenderest manner. Meg bathed the insulted hand with glycerine and tears; Beth felt that even her beloved kittens would fail as a balm for griefs like this; Jo wrathfully proposed that Mr. Davis be arrested without delay; and Hannah shook her fist at the "villain", and pounded potatoes for dinner as if she had him under her pestle.

No notice was taken of Amy's flight, except by her mates; but the sharp-eyed demoiselles discovered that Mr. Davis was quite benignant in the afternoon, also unusually nervous. Just before school closed Jo appeared, wearing a grim expression, as she stalked up to the desk, and delivered a letter from her mother; then collected Amy's property and departed, carefully scraping the mud from her boots on the door-mat, as if she shook the dust of the place off her feet.

"Yes, you can have a vacation from school, but I want you to study a little every day with Beth," said Mrs. March that evening. "I don't approve of corporal punishment, especially for girls. I dislike Mr. Davis's manner of teaching, and don't think the girls you associate with are doing you any good, so I shall ask your father's advice before I send you anywhere else."

"That's good! I wish all the girls would leave, and spoil his old school. It's perfectly maddening to think of those lovely limes," sighed Amy, with the air of a martyr.

"I am not sorry you lost them, for you broke the rules, and deserved some punishment for disobedience," was the severe reply, which rather disappointed the young lady, who expected nothing but sympathy.

"Do you mean you are glad I was disgraced before the whole school?" cried Amy.

"I should not have chosen that way of mending a fault," replied her mother; "but I'm not sure that it won't do you more good than a milder method. You are getting to be rather conceited, my dear, and it is quite time you set about correcting it. You have a good many little gifts and virtues, but there is no need of parading them, for conceit spoils the finest genius. There is not much danger that real talent or goodness will be overlooked long; even if it is, the consciousness of possessing and using it well should satisfy one, and the great charm of all power is modesty."

"So it is!" cried Laurie, who was playing chess in a corner with Jo. "I knew a girl, once, who had a really remarkable talent for music, and she didn't know it, never guessed what sweet little things she composed when she was alone, and wouldn't have believed it if anyone had told her."

"I wish I'd known that nice girl; maybe she would have helped me, I'm so stupid," said Beth, who stood beside him, listening eagerly.

"You do know her, and she helps you better than anyone else could," answered Laurie, looking at her with such mischievous meaning in his merry black eyes, that Beth suddenly turned very red, and hid her face in the sofa-cushion, quite overcome by such an unexpected discovery.

Jo let Laurie win the game, to pay for that praise of her Beth, who could not be prevailed upon to play for them after her compliment.

So Laurie did his best, and sang delightfully, being in a particularly lively humour, for to the Marches he seldom showed the moody side of his character. When he was gone, Amy, who had been pensive all the evening, said suddenly, as if busy over some new idea: "Is Laurie an accomplished boy?"

"Yes; he has had an excellent education, and has much talent; he will make a fine man, if not spoilt by petting," replied her mother.

"And he isn't conceited, is he?" asked Amy

"Not in the least; that is why he is so charming, and we all like him so much."

"I see; it's nice to have accomplishments, and be elegant; but not to show off, or get perked up," said Amy, thoughtfully.

"These things are always seen and felt in a person's manner and conversation, if modestly used; but it is not necessary to display them," said Mrs. March. "Any more than it's proper to wear all your bonnets and gowns and ribbons at once, that folks may know you've got them," added Jo; and the lecture ended in a laugh.

Chapter 8

JO MEETS APOLLYON

"Girls, where are you going?" asked Amy, coming into their room one Saturday afternoon, and finding them getting ready to go out, with an air of secrecy, which excited her curiosity.

"Never mind; little girls shouldn't ask questions," returned Jo, sharply.

Now if there *is* anything mortifying to our feelings, when we are young, it is to be told that; and to be bidden to "run away, dear", is still more trying to us. Amy bridled up at this insult, and determined to find out the secret, if she teased for an hour. Turning to Meg, who never refused her anything very long, she said coaxingly, "Do tell me! I should think you might let me go too, for Beth is fussing over her piano, and I haven't got anything to do, and am *so* lonely."

"I can't, dear, because you aren't invited," began Meg; but Jo broke in impatiently, "Now, Meg, be quiet, or you will spoil it all. You can't go, Amy; so don't be a baby and whine about it."

"You are going somewhere with Laurie, I know you are; you were whispering and laughing together, on the sofa, last night, and you stopped when I came in. Aren't you going with him?"

"Yes, we are; now do be still and stop bothering."

Amy held her tongue, but used her eyes, and saw Meg slip a fan into her pocket.

"I know! I know! you're going to the hall to see 'The Seven Castles'!" she cried, adding resolutely, "and I *shall* go, for Mother said I might see it; and I've got my rag-money, and it was mean not to tell me in time."

"Just listen to me a minute, and be a good child," said Meg, soothingly. "Mother doesn't wish you to go this week, because your eyes are not well enough yet to bear the light of this fairy piece. Next week you can go with Beth and Hannah, and have a nice time."

"I don't like that half as well as going with you and Laurie. Please let me; I've been sick with this cold so long, and shut up, I'm dying for some fun. Do, Meg! I'll be ever so good," pleaded Amy, looking as pathetic as she could.

"Suppose we take her. I don't believe Mother would mind, if we bundle her up well?" began Meg.

"If *she* goes *I* shan't; and if I don't, Laurie won't like it; and it will be very rude, after he invited only us, to go and drag in Amy. I should think she'd hate to poke herself where she isn't wanted," said Jo, crossly, for she disliked the trouble of overseeing a fidgety child, when she wanted to enjoy herself.

Her tone and manner angered Amy, who began to put her boots on, saying, in her most aggravating way, "I *shall* go; Meg says I may; and if I pay for myself, Laurie hasn't anything to do with it."

"You can't sit with us, for our seats are reserved, and you mustn't sit alone; so Laurie will give you his place, and that will spoil our pleasure; or he'll get another seat for you, and that isn't proper, when you weren't asked. You shan't stir a step; so you may just stay where you are," scolded Jo, crosser than ever, having just pricked her finger in her hurry.

Sitting on the floor, with one boot on, Amy began to cry, and

Meg to reason with her, when Laurie called from below, and the two girls hurried down, leaving their sister wailing; for now and then she forgot her grown-up ways, and acted like a spoilt child. Just as the party were setting out, Amy called over the bannisters, in a threatening voice, "You'll be sorry for this, Jo March; see if you ain't."

"Fiddlesticks!" returned Jo, slamming the door.

They had a charming time, for "The Seven Castles of the Diamond Lake" was as brilliant and wonderful as heart could wish. But, in spite of the comical red imps, sparkling elves, and gorgeous princes and princesses, Jo's pleasure had a drop of bitterness in it; the fairy queen's yellow curls reminded her of Amy; and between the acts she amused herself with wondering what her sister would do to make her "sorry for it". She and Amy had had many lively skirmishes in the course of their lives, for both had quick tempers, and were apt to be violent when fairly roused. Amy teased Jo, Jo irritated Amy, and semi-occasional explosions occurred, of which both were much ashamed afterwards. Although the oldest, Jo had the least self-control, and had hard times trying to curb the fiery spirit which was continually getting her into trouble; her anger never lasted long, and having humbly confessed her fault she sincerely repented and tried to do better. Her sisters used to say that they rather liked to get Jo into a fury because she was such an angel afterwards. Poor Jo tried desperately to be good, but her bosom enemy was always ready to flame up and defeat her; and it took years of patient effort to subdue it.

When they got home they found Amy reading in the parlour. She assumed an injured air as they came in; never lifted her eyes from her book, or asked a single question. Perhaps curiosity might have conquered resentment, if Beth had not been there to inquire, and receive a glowing description of the play. On going up to put away her best hat, Jo's first look was towards the bureau; for, in their last quarrel, Amy had soothed her feelings by turning Jo's top drawer upside down on the floor. Everything was in its place, however, and after a hasty glance into her various closets, bags, and boxes, Jo decided that Amy had forgiven and forgotten her wrongs.

There Jo was mistaken; for next day she made a discovery which produced a tempest. Meg, Beth, and Amy were sitting together, late in the afternoon, when Jo burst into the room, looking excited, and demanding breathlessly, "Has anyone taken my book?"

Meg and Beth said "No," at once, and looked surprised; Amy poked the fire, and said nothing. Jo saw her colour rise, and was down upon her in a minute.

"Amy, you've got it."

"No, I haven't."

"You know where it is, then!"

"No, I don't."

"That's a fib!" cried Jo, taking her by the shoulders and looking fierce enough to frighten a much braver child than Amy.

"It isn't. I haven't got it, don't know where it is now, and don't care."

"You know something about it, and you'd better tell at once, or I'll make you," and Jo gave her a slight shake.

"Scold as much as you like, you'll never see your silly old book again," cried Amy, getting excited in her turn.

"Why not?"

"I burnt it up."

"What! my little book I was so fond of, and worked over? and meant to finish before Father got home! Have you really burnt it?" said Jo, turning very pale, while her eyes kindled and her hands clutched Amy nervously.

"Yes, I did! I told you I'd make you pay for being so cross yesterday, and I have, so—"

Amy got no further, for Jo's hot temper mastered her, and she shook Amy till her teeth chattered in her head; crying in a passion of grief and anger:

"You wicked, wicked girl! I never can write it again and I'll never forgive you as long as I live."

Meg flew to rescue Amy, and Beth to pacify Jo, but Jo was quite beside herself; and with a parting box on her sister's ear, she rushed out of the room up to the old sofa in the garret, and finished her fight alone.

The storm cleared up below, for Mrs. March came home, and, having heard the story, soon brought Amy to a sense of the wrong she had done her sister. Jo's book was the pride of her heart, and was regarded by her family as a literary sprout of great promise. It was only half a dozen little fairy tales, but Jo had worked over them patiently, putting her whole heart into her work, hoping to make something good enough to print. She had just copied them with great care, and had destroyed the old manuscript, so that Amy's bonfire had consumed the loving work of several years. It seemed a small loss to others, but to Jo it was a dreadful calamity, and she felt that it never could be made up to her. Beth mourned as for a departed kitten, and Meg refused to defend her pet; Mrs. March looked grave and grieved, and Amy felt that no one would love her till she had asked pardon for the act which she now regretted more than any of them.

When the tea-bell rang Jo appeared, looking so grim and unapproachable, that it took all Amy's courage to say meekly:

"Please forgive me, Jo; I'm very, very sorry."

"I never shall forgive you," was Jo's stern answer; and from that moment she ignored Amy entirely.

No one spoke of the great trouble—not even Mrs. March—for all had learned by experience that when Jo was in that mood words were wasted; and the wisest course was to wait till some little accident, or her own generous nature, softened Jo's resentment, and healed the breach. It was not a happy evening; for though they sewed as usual, while their mother read aloud from Bremer, Scott, or Edgeworth, something was wanting and the sweet home peace was disturbed. They felt this most when singing time came; for Beth could only play, Jo stood dumb as a stone, and Amy broke down, so Meg and Mother sang alone. But in spite of their efforts to be as cheery as larks, the flute-like voices did not seem to chord as well as usual, and all felt out of tune.

As Jo received her good-night kiss, Mrs. March whispered gently: "My dear, don't let the sun go down upon your anger; forgive each other, help each other, and begin again tomorrow."

Jo wanted to lay her head down on that motherly bosom, and cry her grief and anger all away, but tears were an unmanly weakness, and she felt so deeply injured that she really *couldn't* quite forgive yet. So she winked hard, shook her head, and said gruffly, because Amy was listening: "It was an abominable thing, and she don't deserve to be forgiven."

With that she marched off to bed, and there was no merry or confidential gossip that night.

Amy was much offended that her overtures of peace had been repulsed, and began to wish she had not humbled herself, to feel more injured than ever, and to plume herself on her superior virtue in a way which was particularly exasperating. Jo still looked like a thundercloud, and nothing went well all day.

It was bitter cold in the morning, she dropped her precious turnover in the gutter, Aunt March had an attack of fidgets, Meg was pensive, Beth *would* look grieved and wistful when she got home, and Amy kept making remarks about people who were always talking about being good, and yet wouldn't try, when other people set them a virtuous example.

"Everybody is so hateful, I'll ask Laurie to go skating. He is always kind and jolly, and will put me to rights, I know," said Jo to herself, and off she went.

Amy heard the clash of skates, and looked out with an impatient exclamation: "There! she promised I should go next time, for this is the last ice we shall have. But it's no use to ask such a cross-patch to take me."

"Don't say that; you *were* very naughty, and it *is* hard to forgive the loss of her precious little book; but I think she might do it now, and I guess she will, if you try her at the right minute," said Meg. "Go after them; don't say anything till Jo has got good-natured with Laurie, then take a quiet minute, and just kiss her, or do some kind thing, and I'm sure she'll be friends again with all her heart."

"I'll try," said Amy, for the advice suited her; and, after a flurry to get ready, she ran after the friends, who were just disappearing over the hill. It was not far to the river, but both were ready before Amy reached them. Jo saw her coming, and turned her back; Laurie did not see, for he was carefully skating along the shore, sounding the ice, for a warm spell had preceded the cold snap.

"I'll go on to the first bend, and see if it's all right, before we begin to race," Amy heard him say, as he shot away, looking like a young Russian, in his fur-trimmed coat and cap.

Jo heard Amy panting after her run, stamping her feet and blowing her fingers, as she tried to put her skates on; but Jo never turned, and went slowly zigzagging down the river, taking a bitter, unhappy sort of satisfaction in her sister's troubles. She had cherished her anger till it grew strong, and took possession of her, as evil thoughts and feelings always do, unless cast out at once. As Laurie turned the bend, he shouted back: "Keep near the shore, it isn't safe in the middle."

Jo heard, but Amy was just struggling to her feet, and did not catch a word. Jo glanced over her shoulder, and the little demon she was harbouring said in her ear: "No matter whether she heard or not, let her take care of herself."

Laurie had vanished round the bend; Jo was just at the turn, and Amy, far behind, striking out towards the smoother ice in the middle of the river. For a minute Jo stood still, with a strange feeling at her heart; then she resolved to go on, but something held and turned her round, just in time to see Amy throw up her hands and go down, with a sudden crash of rotten ice, the splash of water, and a cry that made Jo's heart stand still with fear. She tried to call Laurie, but her voice was gone; she tried to rush forward, but her feet seemed to have no strength in them; and, for a second, she could only stand motionless, staring, with a terror-stricken face, at the little blue hood above the black water. Something rushed swiftly by her, and Laurie's voice cried out: "Bring a rail; quick, quick!"

How she did it, she never knew; but for the next few minutes she worked as if possessed, blindly obeying Laurie, who was quite self-possessed, and, lying flat, held Amy up by his arm and hockey till Jo dragged a rail from the fence, and together they got the child out, more frightened than hurt.

"Now then, we must walk her home as fast as we can; pile our things on her, while I get off these confounded skates," cried Laurie, wrapping his coat round Amy, and tugging away at the straps, which never seemed so intricate before.

Shivering, dripping, and crying, they got Amy home; and, after an exciting time of it, she fell asleep, rolled in blankets, before a hot fire. During the bustle Jo had scarcely spoken, but flown about looking pale and wild, with her things half off, her dress torn, and her hands cut and bruised by ice and rails and refractory buckles. When Amy was comfortably asleep, the house quiet, and Mrs. March sitting by the bed, she called Jo to her, and began to bind up the hurt hands.

"Are you sure she is safe?" whispered Jo, looking remorsefully at the golden head, which might have been swept away from her sight for ever under the treacherous ice.

"Quite safe, dear; she is not hurt, and won't even take cold, I think, you were so sensible in covering her and getting her home quickly," replied her mother, cheerfully.

"Laurie did it all; I only let her go. Mother, if she *should* die, it would be my fault"; and Jo dropped down beside the bed, in a passion of penitent tears, telling all that had happened, bitterly condemning her hardness of heart, and sobbing out her gratitude for being spared the heavy punishment which might have come upon her.

"It's my dreadful temper! I try to cure it; I think I have, and then it breaks out worse than ever. Oh, Mother, what shall I do? what shall I do?" cried poor Jo, in despair.

"Watch and pray, dear; never get tired of trying; and never

think it is impossible to conquer your fault," said Mrs. March, drawing the blowzy head to her shoulder, and kissing the wet cheek so tenderly that Jo cried harder than ever.

"You don't know, and you can't guess how bad it is! It seems as if I could do anything when I'm in a passion; I get so savage, I could hurt anyone, and enjoy it. I'm afraid I *shall* do something dreadful some day, and spoil my life, and make everybody hate me. Oh, Mother, help me, do help me!"

"I will, my child, I will. Don't cry so bitterly, but remember this day, and resolve, with all your soul, that you will never know another like it. Jo, dear, we all have our temptations, some far greater than yours, and it often takes us all our lives to conquer them. You think your temper is the worst in the world; but mine used to be just like it."

"Yours, Mother? Why, you are never angry!" and, for the moment, Jo forgot remorse in surprise.

"I've been trying to cure it for forty years, and have only succeeded in controlling it. I am angry nearly every day of my life, Jo; but I have learned not to show it; and I still hope to learn not to feel it, though it may take me another forty years to do so."

The patience and the humility of the face she loved so well was a better lesson to Jo than the wisest lecture, the sharpest reproof. She felt comforted at once by the sympathy and confidence given her; the knowledge that her mother had a fault like hers, and tried to mend it, made her own easier to bear and strengthened her resolution to cure it; though forty years seemed rather a long time to watch and pray, to a girl of fifteen.

"Mother, are you angry when you fold your lips tight together, and go out of the room sometimes, when Aunt March scolds, or people worry you?" asked Jo, feeling nearer and dearer to her mother than ever before.

"Yes, I've learned to check the hasty words that rise to my lips; and when I feel that they mean to break out against my will, I just go away a minute, and give myself a little shake for being so weak and wicked," answered Mrs. March, with a sigh and a smile, as she smoothed and fastened up Jo's dishevelled hair.

"How did you learn to keep still? That is what troubles me—for the sharp words fly out before I know what I'm about; and the more I say the worse I get, till it's a pleasure to hurt people's feelings, and say dreadful things. Tell me how you do it, Marmee dear."

"My good mother used to help me—"

"As you do us—" interrupted Jo, with a grateful kiss.

"But I lost her when I was a little older than you are, and for years had to struggle on alone, for I was too proud to confess my weakness to anyone else. I had a hard time, Jo, and shed a good many bitter tears over my failures; for, in spite of my efforts, I never seemed to get on. Then your father came, and I was so happy that I found it easy to be good. But by and by, when I had four little daughters round me, and we were poor, then the old trouble began again; for I am not patient by nature, and it tried me very much to see my children wanting anything."

"Poor Mother! What helped you then?"

"Your father, Jo. He never loses patience—never doubts or complains—but always hopes and works and waits so cheerfully that one is ashamed to do otherwise before him. He helped and comforted me, and showed me that I must try to practise all the virtues I would have my little girls possess, for I was their example. It was easier to try for your sakes than for my own; a startled or surprised look from one of you, when I spoke sharply, rebuked me more than any words could have done; and the love, respect, and confidence of my children was the sweetest reward I could receive for my efforts to be the woman I would have them copy."

"Oh Mother, if I'm ever half as good as you, I shall be satisfied," cried Jo, much touched.

"I hope you will be a great deal better, dear; but you must keep watch over your 'bosom enemy' as Father calls it, or it may sadden, if not spoil your life. You have had a warning; remember it, and try with heart and soul to master this quick temper, before it brings you greater sorrow and regret than you have known today."

"I will try, Mother: I truly will. But you must help me, remind me, and keep me from flying out. I used to see Father sometimes put his finger on his lips, and look at you with a very kind but sober face, and you always folded your lips tight or went away: was he reminding you then?" asked Jo, softly.

"Yes; I asked him to help me so, and he never forgot it, but saved me from many a sharp word by that little gesture and kind look."

Jo saw that her mother's eyes filled and her lips trembled as she spoke; and, fearing that she had said too much, she whispered, anxiously, "Was it wrong to watch you, and to speak of it! I didn't mean to be rude, but it's so comfortable to say all I think of you, and feel so safe and happy here."

"My Jo, you may say anything to your mother, for it is my greatest happiness and pride to feel that my girls confide in me, and know how much I love them."

"I thought I'd grieved you."

"No, dear; but speaking of Father reminded me how much I miss him, how much I owe him, and how faithfully I should watch and work to keep his little daughters safe and good for him."

"Yet you told him to go, Mother, and didn't cry when he went, and never complain now, or seem as if you needed any help," said Jo, wondering.

"I gave my best to the country I love, and kept my tears till he was gone. Why should I complain, when we both have merely done our duty, and will surely be the happier for it in the end? If I don't seem to need help, it is because I have a better friend even than Father to comfort and sustain me. My child, the troubles and temptations of your life are beginning, and may be many; but you can overcome and outlive them all if you learn to feel the strength and tenderness of your Heavenly Father as you do that of your earthly one. The more you love and trust Him, the nearer you will feel to Him, and the less you will depend on human power and wisdom. His love and care never tire or change, can never be taken from you, but may become the source of lifelong peace, happiness, and strength. Believe this heartily, and go to God with all your little cares, and hopes, and sins, and sorrows, as freely and confidingly as you come to your mother."

Jo's only answer was to hold her mother close, and, in the silence which followed, the sincerest prayer she had ever prayed left her heart without words; for in that sad yet happy hour she had learned not only the bitterness of remorse and despair, but the sweetness of self-denial and self-control; and, led by her mother's hand, she had drawn nearer to the friend who welcomes every child with a love stronger than that of any father, tenderer than that of any mother.

Amy stirred, and sighed in her sleep; and, as if eager to begin at once to mend her fault, Jo looked up with an expression on her face which it had never worn before.

"I let the sun go down on my anger; I wouldn't forgive her, and today, if it hadn't been for Laurie, it might have been too late! How could I be so wicked?" said Jo, half aloud, as she leaned over her sister, softly stroking the wet hair scattered on the pillow.

As if she heard, Amy opened her eyes, and held out her arms, with a smile that went straight to Jo's heart. Neither said a word, but they hugged one another close, in spite of the blankets, and everything was forgiven and forgotten in one hearty kiss.

CHAPTER 9

MEG GOES TO VANITY FAIR

"I do think it was the most fortunate thing in the world that those children should have the measles just now," said Meg, one April day, as she stood packing the "go abroady" trunk in her room, surrounded by her sisters.

"And so nice of Annie Moffat not to forget her promise. A whole fortnight of fun will be regularly splendid," replied Jo, looking like a windmill, as she folded skirts, with her long arms.

"And such lovely weather; I'm so glad of that," added Beth, tidily sorting neck and hair ribbons in her best box, lent for the great occasion.

"I wish I was going to have a fine time, and wear all these nice things," said Amy, with her mouth full of pins, as she artistically replenished her sister's cushion.

"I wish you were all going; but as you can't, I shall keep my adventures to tell you when I come back. I'm sure it's the least I can do, when you have been so kind, lending me things, and helping me get ready," said Meg, glancing round the room at the very simple outfit, which seemed nearly perfect in their eyes.

"What did Mother give you out of the treasure-box?" asked Amy, who had not been present at the opening of a certain cedar chest, in which Mrs. March kept a few relics of past splendour as gifts for her girls when the proper time came.

"A pair of silk stockings, that pretty carved fan, and a lovely blue sash. I wanted the violet silk; but there isn't time to make it over, so I must be contented with my old tarlatan."

"It will look nicely over my new muslin skirt, and the sash will set it off beautifully. I wish I hadn't smashed my coral bracelet, for you might have had it," said Jo, who loved to give and lend, but whose possessions were usually too dilapidated to be of much use. "There is a lovely old-fashioned pearl set in the treasure-box; but Mother said real flowers were the prettiest ornament for a young girl, and Laurie promised to send me all I want," replied Meg. "Now, let me see; there's my new grey walking-suit—just curl up the feather in my hat, Beth—then my poplin, for Sunday, and the small party—it looks heavy for spring, doesn't it? The violet silk would be so nice; oh dear."

"Never mind; you've got the tarlatan for the big party, and you always look like an angel in white," said Amy, brooding over the little store of finery in which her soul delighted.

"It isn't low-necked, and it doesn't sweep enough, but it will have to do. My blue house-dress looks so well, turned and freshly trimmed, that I feel as if I'd got a new one. My silk sacque isn't a bit the fashion, and my bonnet doesn't look like Sallie's; I didn't like to say anything, but I was sadly disappointed in my umbrella. I told Mother black, with a white handle, but she forgot and bought a green one, with a yellowish handle. It's strong and neat, so I ought not to complain, but I know I shall feel ashamed of it beside Annie's silk one with a gold top," sighed Meg, surveying the little umbrella with great disfavour.

"Change it," advised Jo.

"I won't be so silly, or hurt Marmee's feelings, when she took so much pains to get my things. It's a nonsensical notion of mine, and I'm not going to give up to it. My silk stockings and two pairs of new gloves are my comfort. You are a dear, to lend me yours, Jo. I feel so rich, and sort of elegant, with two new pairs, and the old ones cleaned up for common"; and Meg took a refreshing peep at her glove box.

"Annie Moffat has blue and pink bows on her night-caps; would you put some on mine?" she asked, as Beth brought up a pile of snowy muslins, fresh from Hannah's hands.

"No, I wouldn't; for the smart caps won't match the plain gowns, without any trimming on them. Poor folks shouldn't rig," said Jo, decidedly.

"I wonder if I shall *ever* be happy enough to have real lace on my clothes, and bows on my caps?" said Meg, impatiently.

"You said the other day that you'd be perfectly happy if you could only go to Annie Moffat's," observed Beth, in her quiet way.

"So I did! Well, I *am* happy and I *won't* fret; but it does seem as if the more one gets the more one wants, doesn't it? There now, the trays are ready, and everything in but my party-dress, which I shall leave for Mother to pack," said Meg, cheering up, as she glanced from the half-filled trunk to the many-times pressed and mended white tarlatan, which she called her "party-dress", with an important air.

The next day was fine, and Meg departed in style, for a fortnight of novelty and pleasure. Mrs. March had consented to the visit rather reluctantly, fearing that Margaret would come back more discontented than she went. But she had begged so hard, and Sallie had promised to take good care of her, and a little pleasure seemed so delightful after a winter of irksome work, that the mother yielded, and the daughter went to take her first taste of fashionable life.

The Moffats *were* very fashionable, and simple Meg was rather daunted, at first, by the splendour of the house and the elegance of its occupants. But they were kindly people in spite of the frivolous life they led, and soon put their guest at her ease. Perhaps Meg felt, without understanding why, that they were not particularly cultivated or intelligent people and that all their gilding could not quite conceal the ordinary material of which they were made. It certainly was agreeable to fare sumptuously, drive in a fine carriage, wear her best frock every day, and do nothing but enjoy herself. It suited her exactly; and soon she began to imitate the manners and conversation of those about her; to put on little airs and graces, use French phrases, crimp her hair, take in her dresses, and talk about the fashions as well as she could. The more she saw of Annie Moffat's pretty things, the more she envied her, and sighed to be rich. Home now looked bare and dismal as she thought of it, work grew harder than ever, and she felt that she was a very destitute and much-injured girl, in spite of the new gloves and silk stockings.

She had not much time for repining, however, for the three young girls were busily employed in "having a good time". They shopped, walked, rode, and called all day; went to theatres and operas, or frolicked at home in the evening; for Annie had many friends and knew how to entertain them. Her older sisters were very fine young ladies, and one was engaged, which was extremely interesting and romantic, Meg thought. Mr. Moffat was a fat, jolly old gentleman, who knew her father; and Mrs. Moffat a fat, jolly old lady, who took as great a fancy to Meg as her daughter had done. Everyone petted her; and "Daisy", as they called her, was in a fair way to have her head turned.

When the evening for the "small party" came, she found that the poplin wouldn't do at all, for the other girls were putting on thin dresses, and making themselves very fine indeed; so out came the tarlatan, looking older, limper, and shabbier than ever, beside Sallie's crisp new one. Meg saw the girls glance at it and then at one another, and her cheeks began to burn, for, with all her gentleness, she was very proud. No one said a word about it, but Sallie offered to dress her hair, and Annie to tie her sash, and Belle, the engaged sister, praised her white arms; but in their kindness Meg saw only pity for her poverty, and her heart felt very heavy as she stood by herself, while the others laughed, chattered, and flew about like gauzy butterflies. The hard, bitter feeling was getting pretty bad, when the maid brought in a box of flowers. Before she could speak, Annie had the cover off, and all were exclaiming at the lovely roses, heath, and fern within.

"It's for Belle, of course; George always sends her some, but these are altogether ravishing," cried Annie, with a great sniff.

"They are for Miss March, the man said. And here's a note," put in the maid, holding it to Meg.

"What fun! Who are they from? Didn't know you had a lover," cried the girls, fluttering about Meg in a high state of curiosity and surprise.

"The note is from Mother, and the flowers from Laurie," said Meg, simply, yet much gratified that he had not forgotten her.

"Oh, indeed!" said Annie, with a funny look, as Meg slipped the note in her pocket, as a sort of talisman against envy, vanity, and false pride; for the few loving words had done her good, and the flowers cheered her up by their beauty.

Feeling almost happy again, she laid by a few ferns and roses for herself, and quickly made up the rest in dainty bouquets for the breasts, hair, or skirts of her friends, offering them so prettily that Clara, the elder sister, told her she was "the sweetest little thing she ever saw"; and they looked quite charmed with her small attention. Somehow the kind act finished her despondency, and when all the rest went to show themselves to Mrs. Moffat, she saw a happy, bright-eyed face in the mirror, as she laid her ferns against her rippling hair, and fastened the roses in the dress that didn't strike her as so *very* shabby now.

She enjoyed herself very much that evening; everyone was very kind, and she had three compliments. Annie made her sing, and someone said she had a remarkably fine voice; Major Lincoln asked who the "fresh little girl, with the beautiful eyes" was; and

Mr. Moffat insisted on paying special attention to her during the evening. So, altogether, she had a very nice time, till she overheard a bit of a conversation, which disturbed her extremely. She was sitting just inside the conservatory, waiting for someone to bring her an ice, when she heard a voice ask, on the other side of the flowery wall: "How old is he?"

"Sixteen or seventeen, I should say," replied another voice.

"It would be a grand thing for one of those girls, wouldn't it? Sallie says they are very intimate now, and the old man quite dotes on them."

"Mrs. M. has made her plans, I dare say, and will play her cards well, early as it is. The girl evidently doesn't think of it yet," said Mrs. Moffat.

"She told that fib about her mamma as if she did know, and coloured up when the flowers came quite prettily. Poor thing! she'd be so nice if she was only got up in style. Do you think she'd be offended if we offered to lend her a dress for Thursday?" asked another voice.

"She's proud, but I don't believe she'd mind, for that dowdy tarlatan is all she has got. She may tear it tonight, and that will be a good excuse for offering a decent one."

"We'll see. I shall ask young Laurence, as a compliment to her, and we'll have fun about it afterwards."

Here Meg's friend appeared, to find her looking much flushed and rather agitated. She *was* proud, and her pride was useful just then, for it helped her hide her mortification, anger, and disgust at what she had just heard; for innocent and unsuspicious as she was, she could not help understanding the gossip of her friends. She tried to forget it, but could not, and kept repeating to herself, "Mrs. M. has made her plans", "that fib about her mamma", and "dowdy tarlatan", till she was ready to cry, and rush home to tell her troubles and ask for advice. As that was impossible, she did her best to seem gay, and, being rather excited, she succeeded so well that no one dreamed what an effort she was making. She was very glad when it was all over, and she was quiet in her bed, where she could think and wonder and fume till her head ached, and her hot cheeks were cooled by a few natural tears. Those foolish, yet well-meant words had opened a new world to Meg, and much disturbed the peace of the old one, in which, till now, she had lived as happily as a child. Her innocent friendship with Laurie was spoilt by the silly speeches she had overheard; her faith in her mother was a little shaken by the worldly plans attributed to her by Mrs. Moffat, who judged others by herself; and the sensible resolution to be contented with the simple wardrobe which suited a poor man's daughter was weakened by the unnecessary pity of girls who thought a shabby dress one of the greatest calamities under heaven.

Poor Meg had a restless night, and got up heavy-eyed, unhappy, half resentful towards her friends, and half ashamed of herself for not speaking out frankly and setting everything right. Everybody dawdled that morning, and it was noon before the girls found energy enough even to take up their worsted work. Something in the manner of her friends struck Meg at once; they treated her with more respect, she thought, took quite a tender interest in what she said, and looked at her with eyes that plainly betrayed curiosity. All this surprised and flattered her, though she did not understand it till Miss Belle looked up from her writing and said, with a sentimental air:

"Daisy, dear, I've sent an invitation to your friend, Mr. Laurence, for Thursday. We should like to know him, and it's only a proper compliment to you."

Meg coloured, but a mischievous fancy to tease the girls made her reply, demurely:

"You are very kind, but I'm afraid he won't come."

"Why not, *chérie*?" asked Miss Belle.

"He's too old."

"My child, what do you mean? What is his age, I beg to know!" cried Miss Clara.

"Nearly seventy, I believe," answered Meg, counting stitches to hide the merriment in her eyes.

"You sly creature! Of course we meant the young man," exclaimed Miss Belle, laughing.

"There isn't any, Laurie is only a little boy," and Meg laughed also at the queer look which the sisters exchanged as she thus described her supposed lover.

"About your age," Nan said.

"Nearer my sister Jo's; *I* am seventeen in August," returned Meg, tossing her head.

"It's very nice of him to send you flowers, isn't it?" said Annie looking wise about nothing.

"Yes, he often does to all of us, for their house is full and we are so fond of them. My mother and old Mr. Laurence are friends, you know, so it is quite natural that we children should play together"; and Meg hoped they would say no more.

"It's evident Daisy isn't out yet," said Miss Clara to Belle, with a nod.

"Quite a pastoral state of innocence all round," returned Miss Belle, with a shrug.

"I'm going out to get some little matters for my girls; can I do anything for you, young ladies?" asked Mrs. Moffat, lumbering in, like an elephant, in silk and lace.

"No, thank you, ma'am," replied Sallie. "I've got my new pink silk for Thursday, and don't want a thing."

"Nor I—" began Meg, but stopped, because it occurred to her that she *did* want several things, and could not have them.

"What shall you wear?" asked Sallie.

"My old white one again, if I can mend it fit to be seen; it got sadly torn last night," said Meg, trying to speak quite easily, but feeling very uncomfortable.

"Why don't you send home for another?" said Sallie, who was not an observing young lady.

"I haven't got any other." It cost Meg an effort to say that, but Sallie did not see it, and exclaimed, in amiable surprise: "Only that? How funny—" She did not finish her speech, for Belle shook her head at her, and broke in, saying kindly:

"Not at all; where is the use of having a lot of dresses when she isn't out? There's no need of sending home, Daisy, even if you had a dozen, for I've got a sweet blue silk laid away, which I've outgrown, and you shall wear it to please me, won't you, dear?"

"You are very kind, but I don't mind my old dress, if you don't; it does well enough for a little girl like me," said Meg.

"Now do let me please myself by dressing you up in style. I admire to do it, and you'd be a regular little beauty with a touch here and there. I shan't let anyone see you till you are done, and then we'll burst upon them like Cinderella and her godmother going to the ball," said Belle, in her persuasive tone.

Meg couldn't refuse the offer so kindly made, for a desire to see if she would be "a little beauty" after touching up, caused her to accept, and forget all her former uncomfortable feelings towards the Moffats.

On the Thursday evening Belle shut herself up with her maid; and between them they turned Meg into a fine lady. They crimped and curled her hair, they polished her neck and arms with some fragrant powder, touched her lips with coralline salve, to make them redder, and Hortense would have added "a *soupçon* of rouge", if Meg had not rebelled. They laced her into a sky-blue dress which was so tight she could hardly breathe, and so low in the neck that modest Meg blushed at herself in the mirror. A set of silver filagree was added, bracelets, necklace, brooch, and even earrings, for Hortense tied them on with a bit of pink silk which did not show. A cluster of tea-rosebuds at the bosom and a *ruche* reconciled Meg to the display of her pretty white shoulders, and a pair of high-heeled blue silk boots satisfied the last wish of her heart. A laced handkerchief, a plummy fan, and a bouquet in a silver holder finished her off; and Miss Belle surveyed her with the satisfaction of a little girl with a newly-dressed doll.

"Mademoiselle is *charmante, très jolie,* is she not?" cried Hortense, clasping her hands in an affected rapture.

"Come and show yourself," said Miss Belle, leading the way to the room where the others were waiting.

As Meg went rustling after her, with her long skirts trailing, her earrings tinkling, her curls waving, and her heart beating, she felt as if her "fun" had really begun at last, for the mirror had plainly told her that she *was* "a little beauty". Her friends repeated the pleasing phrase enthusiastically; and for several minutes she stood, like the jackdaw in the fable, enjoying her borrowed plumes, while the rest chattered like a party of magpies.

"While I dress, do you drill her, Nan, in the management of her skirt, and those French heels, or she will trip herself up. Take your silver butterfly, and catch up that long curl on the left side of her head, Clara, and don't any of you disturb the charming work of my hands," said Belle, as she hurried away, looking well pleased with her success.

"I'm afraid to go down, I feel so queer and stiff and half-dressed," said Meg to Sallie, as the bell rang, and Mrs. Moffat sent to ask the young ladies to appear at once.

"You don't look a bit like yourself, but you are very nice. I'm nowhere beside you, for Belle has heaps of taste, and you're quite French, I assure you. Let your flowers hang; don't be so careful of them, and be sure you don't trip," returned Sallie; trying not to care that Meg was prettier than herself.

Keeping that warning carefully in mind, Margaret got safely downstairs, and sailed into the drawing-rooms, where the Moffats and a few early guests were assembled. She very soon discovered that there is a charm about fine clothes which attracts a certain class of people, and secures their respect. Several young ladies who had taken no notice of her before, were very affectionate all of a sudden; several young gentlemen, who had only stared at her at the other party, now not only stared, but asked to be introduced, and said all manner of foolish but agreeable things to her; and several old ladies, who sat on sofas and criticized the rest of the party, inquired who she was, with an air of interest. She heard Mrs. Moffat reply to one of them: "Daisy March—father a colonel in the army—one of our first families, but reverses of fortune, you know; intimate friends of the Laurences; sweet creature, I assure you; my Ned is quite wild about her."

"Dear me!" said the old lady, putting up her glass for another observation of Meg, who tried to look as if she had not heard, and been rather shocked at Mrs. Moffat's fibs.

The "queer feeling" did not pass away, but she imagined herself acting the new part of a fine lady, and so got on pretty well, though the tight dress gave her a side-ache, the train kept getting under her feet, and she was in constant fear lest her earrings should fly off, and get lost or broken. She was flirting her fan, and laughing at the feeble jokes of a young gentleman who tried to be witty, when she suddenly stopped laughing, and looked confused; for, just opposite, she saw Laurie. He was staring at her with undisguised surprise, and disapproval also, she thought, for, though he bowed and smiled, yet something in his honest eyes made her blush, and wish she had her old dress on. To complete her confusion, she saw Belle nudge Annie, and both glance from her to Laurie, who, she was happy to see, looked unusually boyish and shy.

"Silly creatures, to put such thoughts into my head! I won't care for it, or let it change me a bit," thought Meg, and rustled across the room to shake hands with her friend.

"I'm glad you've come, I was afraid you wouldn't," she said, with her most grown-up air.

"Jo wanted me to come, and tell her how you looked, so I did," answered Laurie, without turning his eyes upon her, though he half smiled at her maternal tone.

"What shall you tell her?" asked Meg, full of curiosity to know his opinion of her, yet feeling ill at ease with him, for the first time.

"I shall say I didn't know you; for you look so grown-up, and unlike yourself, I'm quite afraid of you," he said, fumbling at his glove-button.

"How absurd of you! The girls dressed me up for fun, and I rather like it. Wouldn't Jo stare if she saw me?" said Meg, bent on making him say whether he thought her improved or not.

"Yes, I think she would," returned Laurie, gravely.
"Don't you like me so?" asked Meg.
"No, I don't," was the blunt reply.
"Why not?" in an anxious tone.
He glanced at her frizzled head, bare shoulders, and fantastically trimmed dress, with an expression that abashed her more than his answer, which had not a particle of his usual politeness about it.
"I don't like fuss and feathers."
That was altogether too much from a lad younger than herself, and Meg walked away, saying petulantly: "You are the rudest boy I ever saw."
Feeling very much ruffled, she went and stood at a quiet window to cool her cheeks, for the tight dress gave her an uncomfortably brilliant colour. As she stood there, Major Lincoln passed by, and, a minute after, she heard him saying to his mother: "They are making a fool of that little girl; I wanted you to see her, but they have spoilt her entirely; she's nothing but a doll tonight."
"Oh dear!" sighed Meg; "I wish I'd been sensible, and worn my own things; then I should not have disgusted other people or felt so uncomfortable and ashamed of myself."
She leaned her forehead on the cool pane, and stood half hidden by the curtains, never minding that her favourite song had begun, till someone touched her; and, turning, she saw Laurie, looking penitent, as he said, with his very best bow, and his hand out: "Please forgive my rudeness, and come and have an ice with me."
"I'm afraid it will be too disagreeable to you," said Meg, trying to look offended, and failing entirely.
"Not a bit of it. Come, I'll be good; I don't like your gown, but I do think you are—just splendid"; and he waved his hands, as if words failed to express his admiration.
Meg smiled and relented, and whispered, as they stood waiting: "Take care my skirt don't trip you up; it's the plague of my life, and I was a goose to wear it."
"Pin it round your neck, and then it will be useful," said Laurie, looking down at the little blue boots, which he evidently approved of.
"Laurie, I want you to do me a favour; will you?" said Meg.
"Won't I!" said Laurie, with alacrity.
"Please don't tell them at home about my dress tonight. They won't understand the joke, and it will worry Mother."
"Then why did you do it?" said Laurie's eyes, so plainly that

Meg hastily added: "I shall tell them myself all about it and "fess' to Mother how silly I've been. But I'd rather do it myself; so you'll not tell, will you?"

"I give you my word I won't; only what shall I say when they ask me?"

"Just say I looked pretty well, and was having a good time."

"I'll say the first with all my heart; but how about the other? You don't look as if you were having a good time; are you?" and Laurie looked at her with an expression which made her answer, in a whisper: "No, not just now. Don't think I'm horrid; I only wanted a little fun, but this sort doesn't pay, I find, and I'm getting tired of it."

"Here comes Ned Moffat; what does he want?" said Laurie, knitting his black brows as if he did not regard his young host in the light of a pleasant addition to the party.

"What a bore!" said Meg, assuming a languid air, which amused Laurie immensely.

He did not speak to her again till supper-time, when he saw her drinking champagne with Ned and his friend Fisher, who were behaving "like a pair of fools," as Laurie said to himself, for he felt a brotherly sort of right to watch over the Marches, and fight their battles whenever a defender was needed.

"You'll have a splitting headache tomorrow, if you drink that stuff. I wouldn't, Meg; your mother doesn't like it, you know," he whispered, leaning over her chair, as Ned turned to refill her glass, and Fisher stooped to pick up her fan.

"I'm not Meg tonight; I'm a 'doll', who does all sorts of crazy things. Tomorrow I shall put away my 'fuss and feathers', and be desperately good again," she answered, with an affected little laugh.

"Wish tomorrow was here, then," muttered Laurie, walking off, ill-pleased at the change he saw in her.

Meg danced and flirted, chattered and giggled, as the other girls did; after supper she undertook the German polka, and blundered through it, nearly upsetting her partner with her long skirt, and romping in a way that scandalized Laurie, who looked on, and meditated a lecture. But he got no chance to deliver it, for Meg kept away from him till he came to say good-night.

"Remember!" she said, trying to smile, for the splitting headache had already begun.

"Silence *à la mort*," replied Laurie, with a melodramatic flourish, as he went away.

This little bit of byplay excited Annie's curiosity; but Meg was too tired for gossip, and went to bed feeling as if she had been to a masquerade, and hadn't enjoyed herself as much as she expected. She was sick all the next day, and on Saturday went home, quite used up with her fortnight's fun, and feeling that she had "sat in the lap of luxury" long enough.

"It does seem pleasant to be quiet, and not have company manners on all the time. Home *is* a nice place, though it isn't splendid," said Meg, looking about her with a restful expression as she sat with her mother and Jo on the Sunday evening.

"I'm glad to hear you say so, dear, for I was afraid home would seem dull and poor to you after your fine quarters," replied her mother, who had given her many anxious looks that day; for motherly eyes are quick to see any change in children's faces.

Meg had told her adventures gaily, and said over and over what a charming time she had had; but something still seemed to weigh upon her spirits, and, when the younger girls were gone to bed, she sat thoughtfully staring at the fire, saying little, and looking worried.

As the clock struck nine, and Jo proposed bed, Meg suddenly left her chair, and taking Beth's stool, leaned her elbows on her mother's knee, saying bravely:

"Marmee, I want to "fess'."

"I thought so; what is it, dear?"

"Shall I go away?" asked Jo, discreetly.

"Of course not; don't I always tell you everything? I was ashamed to speak of it before the children, but I want you to know all the dreadful things I did at the Moffats'."

"We are prepared," said Mrs. March, smiling, but looking a little anxious.

"I told you they dressed me up, but I didn't tell you that they powdered and squeezed and frizzled, and made me look like a fashion-plate. Laurie thought I wasn't proper; I know he did, though he didn't say so, and one man called me 'a doll'. I knew it was silly, but they flattered me, and said I was a beauty, and quantities of nonsense, so I let them make a fool of me."

"Is that all?" asked Jo, as Mrs. March looked silently at the downcast face of her pretty daughter, and could not find it in her heart to blame her little follies.

"No; I drank champagne, and romped, and tried to flirt and was altogether abominable," said Meg, self-reproachfully.

"There is something more, I think," and Mrs. March smoothed

the soft cheek, which suddenly grew rosy, as Meg answered slowly: "Yes; it's very silly, but I want to tell it, because I hate to have people say and think such things about us and Laurie."

Then she told the various bits of gossip she had heard at the Moffats'; and, as she spoke, Jo saw her mother fold her lips tightly, as if ill pleased that such ideas should be put into Meg's innocent mind.

"Well, if that isn't the greatest rubbish I ever heard," cried Jo, indignantly. "Why didn't you pop out and tell them so, on the spot?"

"I couldn't, it was so embarrassing for me. I couldn't help hearing at first, and then I was so angry and ashamed, I didn't remember that I ought to go away."

"Just wait till *I* see Annie Moffat, and I'll show you how to settle such ridiculous stuff. The idea of having 'plans', and being kind to Laurie because he's rich, and may marry us by and by! Won't he shout when I tell him what those silly things say about us poor children?" and Jo laughed, as if, on second thoughts, the thing struck her as a good joke.

"If you tell Laurie, I'll never forgive you! She mustn't, must she, Mother?" said Meg, looking distressed.

"No; never repeat that foolish gossip, and forget it as soon as you can," said Mrs. March, gravely. "I was very unwise to let you go among people of whom I know so little—kind, I dare say, but worldly, ill-bred, and full of these vulgar ideas about young people. I am more sorry than I can express for the mischief this visit may have done you, Meg."

"Don't be sorry, I won't let it hurt me; I'll forget all the bad, and remember only the good; for I did enjoy a great deal, and thank you very much for letting me go. I'll not be sentimental or dissatisfied, Mother; I know I'm a silly little girl, and I'll stay with you till I'm fit to take care of myself. But it is nice to be praised and admired, and I can't help saying I like it," said Meg, looking half ashamed of the confession.

"That is perfectly natural, and quite harmless, if the liking does not become a passion, and lead one to do foolish or unmaidenly things. Learn to know and value the praise which is worth having, and to excite the admiration of excellent people by being modest as well as pretty, Meg."

Margaret sat thinking a moment, while Jo stood with her hands behind her, looking both interested and a little perplexed; for it was a new thing to see Meg blushing and talking about admiration, lovers, and things of that sort; and Jo felt as if, during that fortnight, her sister had grown up amazingly, and was drifting away from her into a world where she could not follow.

"Mother, do you have 'plans', as Mrs. Moffat said?" asked Meg, bashfully.

"Yes, my dear, I have a great many; all mothers do, but mine differ somewhat from Mrs. Moffat's, I suspect. I will tell you some of them, for the time has come when a word may set this romantic little head and heart of yours right on a very serious subject. You are young, Meg, but not too young to understand me; and mother's lips are the fittest to speak of such things to girls like you. Jo, your turn will come in time, perhaps, so listen to my 'plans', and help me carry them out if they are good."

Jo went and sat on one arm of the chair, looking as if she thought they were about to join in some very solemn affair. Holding a hand of each, and watching the two young faces wistfully, Mrs. March said, in her serious yet cheery way:

"I want my daughters to be beautiful, accomplished, and good; to be admired, loved, and respected; to have a happy youth, to be well and wisely married, and to lead useful, pleasant lives, with as little care and sorrow to try them as God sees fit to send. To be loved and chosen by a good man is the best and sweetest thing which can happen to a woman; and I sincerely hope my girls may know this beautiful experience. It is natural to think of it, Meg; right to hope and wait for it, and wise to prepare for it; so that, when the happy time comes, you may feel ready for the duties and worthy of the joy. My dear girls, I *am* ambitious for you, but not to have you make a dash in the world—marry rich men merely because they are rich, or have splendid houses, which are not homes because love is wanting. Money is a needful and precious thing—and, when well used, a noble thing—but I never want you to think of it as the first or only prize to strive for. I'd rather see you poor men's wives, if you were happy, beloved, contented, than queens on thrones, without self-respect and peace."

"Poor girls don't stand any chance, Belle says, unless they put themselves forward," sighed Meg.

"Then we'll be old maids," said Jo, stoutly.

"Right, Jo; better be happy old maids than unhappy wives or unmaidenly girls, running about to find husbands," said Mrs. March, decidedly. "Don't be troubled, Meg; poverty seldom daunts a sincere lover. Some of the best and most honoured women I know were poor girls, but so love-worthy that they were not allowed to be old maids. Leave these things to time. Make this home happy, so that you may be fit for homes of your own if they are offered you, and contented here if they are not. One thing remember, my girls; Mother is always ready to be your confidante, Father to be your friend; and both of us trust and hope that our daughters, whether married or single, will be the pride and comfort of our lives."

"We will, Marmee, we will!" cried both, with all their hearts, as she bade them good-night.

Chapter 10

THE P.C. AND P.O.

As spring came on, a new set of amusements became the fashion, and the lengthening days gave long afternoons for work and play of all sorts. The garden had to be put in order, and each sister had a quarter of the little plot to do what she liked with. Hannah used to say, "I'd know which each of them gardings belonged to, ef I see 'em in Chiny"; and so she might, for the girls' tastes differed as much as their characters. Meg's had roses and heliotrope, myrtle, and a little orange tree in it. Jo's bed was never alike two seasons, for she was always trying experiments; this year it was to be a plantation of sunflowers, the seeds of which cheerful and aspiring plant were to feed "Aunt Cockle-top" and her family of chicks. Beth had old-fashioned, fragrant flowers in her garden—sweet peas and mignonette, larkspur, pinks, pansies, and southernwood, with chickweed for the bird, and catnip for the pussies. Amy had a bower in hers—rather small and earwiggy, but very pretty to look at—with honeysuckles and morning-glories hanging their coloured horns and bells in graceful wreaths all over it; tall white lilies, delicate ferns, and as many brilliant, picturesque plants as would consent to blossom there.

Gardening, walks, rows on the river, and flower-hunts

employed the fine days; and for rainy ones they had house diversions, some old, some new—all more or less original. One of these was the "P.C."; for, as secret societies were the fashion, it was thought proper to have one; and, as all of the girls admired Dickens, they called themselves the Pickwick Club. With a few interruptions, they had kept this up for a year, and met every Saturday evening in the big garret, on which occasions the ceremonies were as follows: Three chairs were arranged in a row before a table, on which was a lamp, also four white badges, with a big "P.C." in different colours on each, and the weekly newspaper, called *The Pickwick Portfolio,* to which all contributed something; while Jo, who revelled in pens and ink, was the editor. At seven o'clock the four members ascended to the club room, tied their badges round their heads, and took their seats with great solemnity. Meg, as the eldest, was Samuel Pickwick; Jo, being of a literary turn, Augustus Snodgrass; Beth, because she was round and rosy, Tracy Tupman; and Amy, who was always trying to do what she couldn't, was Nathaniel Winkle. Pickwick, the president, read the paper, which was filled with original tales, poetry, local news, filmy advertisements, and hints, in which they good-naturedly reminded each other of their faults and short-comings. On one occasion Mr. Pickwick put on a pair of spectacles without any glasses, rapped upon the table, hemmed, and, having stared hard at Mr. Snodgrass, who was tilting back in his chair till he arranged himself properly, began to read:

The Pickwick Portfolio.

MAY 20, 18—

Poet's Corner.

ANNIVERSARY ODE.

Again we meet to celebrate,
With badge and solemn rite,
Our fifty-second anniversary,
In Pickwick Hall, to-night.
We all are here in perfect health,
None gone from our small band;
Again we see each well-known face,
And press each friendly hand.

Our Pickwick, always at his post,
With reverence we greet,
As, spectacles on nose, he reads
Our well-filled weekly sheet.

Although he suffers from a cold,
We joy to hear him speak,
For words of wisdom from him fall,
In spite of croak or squeak.

Old six-foot Snodgrass looms on high
With elephantine grace,
And beams upon the company
With brown and jovial face.

Poetic fire lights up his eye,
He struggles 'gainst his lot
Behold ambition on his brow,
And on his nose a blot!

Next our peaceful Tupman comes,
So rosy, plump, and sweet,
Who chokes with laughter at the puns,
And tumbles off his seat.

Prim little Winkle too is here,
With every hair in place,
A mode' of propriety,
Though he hates to wash his face.

The year is gone, we still unite
To joke and laugh and read,
And tread the path of literature
That doth to glory lead.

Long may our paper prosper well,
Our club unbroken be,
And coming years their blessings pour
On the useful gay "P.C."

A. Snodgrass

★

THE MASKED MARRIAGE.

A TALE OF VENICE

Gondola after gondola swept up to the marble steps, and left its lovely load to swell the brilliant throng that filled the stately halls of Count de Adelon. Knights and ladies, elves and pages, monks and flower-girls, all mingled gaily in the dance. Sweet voices and rich melody filled the air; and so with mirth and music the masquerade went on.

"Has your Highness seen the Lady Viola tonight?" asked a gallant troubadour of the fairy queen who floated down the hall upon his arm.

"Yes; is she not lovely, though so sad? Her dress is well chosen, too, for in a week she weds Count Antonio, whom she passionately hates."

"By my faith, I envy him. Yonder he comes arrayed like a bridegroom, except the black mask. When that is off we shall see how he regards the fair maid whose heart he cannot win, though her stern father bestows her hand," returned the troubadour.

"'Tis whispered that she loves the young English artist who haunts her steps, and is spurned by the old count," said the lady, as they joined the dance.

The revel was at its height when a priest appeared, and, withdrawing the young pair to an alcove hung with purple velvet, he motioned them to kneel. Instant silence fell upon the gay throng; and not a sound, but the dash of fountains or the rustle of orange-groves sleeping in the moonlight, broke the hush, as Count de Adelon spoke thus—

"My lords and ladies, pardon the ruse by which I have gathered you here to witness the marriage of my daughter. Father we wait your services."

All eyes turned toward the bridal party, and a low murmur of amazement went through the throng, for neither bride nor groom removed their masks. Curiosity and wonder possessed all hearts, but respect restrained all tongues till the holy rite was over. Then the eager spectators gathered round the count, demanding an explanation.

"Gladly would I give it if I could; but I only know that it was the whim of my timid Viola, and I yielded to it. Now, my children, let the play end. Unmask, and receive my blessing."

But neither bent the knee; for the young bridegroom replied, in a tone that startled all listeners, as the mask fell, disclosing the noble face of Ferdinand Devereux, the artist lover; and, leaning on the breast where now flashed the star of an English earl, was the lovely Viola, radiant with joy and beauty.

"My lord, you scornfully bade me claim your daughter when I could boast as high a name and vast a fortune as the Count Antonio. I can do more; for even your ambitious soul cannot refuse the Earl of Devereux and De Vere, when he gives his ancient name and boundless wealth in return for the beloved hand of this fair lady now my wife."

The count stood like one changed to stone; and, turning to the bewildered crowd, Ferdinand added, with a gay smile of triumph, "To you, my gallant friends, I can only wish that your wooing may prosper as mine has done; and that you may all win as fair a bride as I have by this masked marriage."

S. Pickwick.

★

Why is the P.C. like the Tower of Babel? It is full of unruly members.

★

THE HISTORY OF A SQUASH.

Once upon a time a farmer planted a little seed in his garden, and after a while it sprouted and became a vine, and bore many squashes. One day in October, when they were ripe, he picked one and took it to market. A grocerman bought and put it in his shop. That same morning, a little girl, in a brown hat and blue dress, with a round face and a snub nose, went and bought it for her mother. She lugged it home, cut it up, and boiled it in the big pot; mashed some of it, with salt and butter, for dinner; and to the rest she added a pint of milk, two eggs, four spoons of sugar, nutmeg, and some crackers; put it in a deep dish, and baked it till it was brown and nice; and next day it was eaten by a family named March.

T. Tupman.

★

Mr. Pickwick, *Sir:* —

I address you upon the subject of sin the sinner I mean is a man named Winkle who makes trouble in his club by laughing and sometimes won't write his piece in this fine paper I hope you will pardon his badness and let him send a French fable because he can't write out of his head as he has so many lessons to do and no brains in future I will try to take time by the fetlock and prepare some work which will be all *commy la fo* that means all right I am in haste as it is nearly school time.

Yours respectably, N. Winkle.

[The above is a manly and handsome acknowledgement of past misdemeanours. If our young friend studied punctuation, it would be well.]

★

A SAD ACCIDENT

On Friday last we were startled by a violent shock in our basement, followed by cries of distress. On rushing, in a body, to the cellar, we discovered our beloved President prostrate on the floor, having tripped and fallen while getting wood for domestic purposes. A perfect scene of ruin met our eyes; for in his fall Mr. Pickwick had plunged his head and shoulders into a tub of water, uspet a keg of soft soap upon his manly form, and torn his garments badly. On being removed from his perilous situation, it was discovered that he had suffered no injury but several bruises; and, we are happy to add, is now doing well.

Ed.

The Public Bereavement.

It is our painful duty to record the sudden and mysterious disappearance of our cherished friend, Mrs. Snowball Pat Paw. This lovely and beloved cat was the pet of a large circle of warm and admiring friends; for her beauty attracted all eyes, her grace and virtues endeared her to all hearts, and her loss is deeply felt by the whole community.

When last seen, she was sitting at the gate, watching the butcher's cart; and it is feared that some villain, tempted by her charms, basely stole her. Weeks have passed but no trace of her has been discovered; and we relinquish all hope, tie a black ribbon to her basket, set aside her dish, and weep for her as one lost to us for ever.

A sympathising friend sends the following gem: –

A LAMENT.

FOR S. B. PAT PAW.

We mourn the loss of our little pet,
And sigh o'er her hapless fate,
For never more by the fire she'll sit,
Nor play by the old green gate.

The little grave where her infant sleeps
Is 'neath the chestnut tree;
But o'er her grave we may not weep,
We know not where it may be.

Her empty bed, her idle ball,
Will never see her more;
No gentle tap, no loving purr
Is heard at the parlour door.

Another cat comes after her mice,
A cat with a dirty face;
But she does not hunt as our darling did,
Nor play with her airy grace.

Her stealthy paws tread the very hall
Where Snowball used to play,
But she only spits at the dogs our pet
So gallantly drove away.

She is useful and mild, and does her best,
But she is not fair to see;
And we cannot give her your place, dear,
Nor worship her as we worship thee.

A. S.

ADVERTISEMENTS.

Miss ORANTHY BLUGGAGE, the accomplished Strong-Minded Lecturer, will deliver her famous Lecture on "WOMAN AND HER POSITION", at Pickwick Hall, next Saturday Evening, after the usual performances.

A WEEKLY MEETING will be held at Kitchen Place, to teach young ladies how to cook. Hannah Brown will preside; and all are invited to attend.

THE DUSTPAN SOCIETY will meet on Wednesday next, and parade in the upper story of the Club House. All members to appear in uniform and shoulder their brooms at nine precisely.

MRS. BETH BOUNCER will open her new assortment of Doll's Millinery next week. The latest Paris Fashions have arrived, and orders are respectfully solicited.

A NEW PLAY will appear at the Barnville Theatre, in the course of a few weeks, which will surpass anything ever seen on the American stage. "THE GREEK SLAVE, or Constantine the Avenger", is the name of this thrilling drama! ! !

HINTS.

If S. P. didn't use so much soap on his hands, he wouldn't always be late at breakfast. A. S. is requested not to whistle in the street. T. T. please don't forget Amy's napkin. A. W. must not fret because his dress has not nine tucks.

WEEKLY REPORT.

Meg—Good.
Jo—Bad.
Beth—Very good.
Amy—Middling.

As the President finished reading the paper (which I beg leave to assure my readers is a bona fide copy of one written by bona fide girls once upon a time), a round of applause followed and then Mr. Snodgrass rose to make a proposition.

"Mr. President and gentlemen," he began, assuming a parliamentary attitude and tone, "I wish to propose the admission of a new member—one who highly deserves the honour, would be deeply grateful for it, and would add immensely to the spirit of the club, the literary value of the paper, and be no end jolly and nice. I propose Mr. Theodore Laurence as an honorary member of the P.C. Come now, do have him."

Jo's sudden change of tone made the girls laugh; but all looked rather anxious, and no one said a word, as Snodgrass took his seat.

"We'll put it to the vote," said the President. "All in favour of this motion please to manifest it by saying 'Ay'."

A loud response from Snodgrass, followed, to everybody's surprise, by a timid one from Beth.

"Contrary minded say 'No'."

Meg and Amy were contrary minded; and Mr. Winkle rose to say, with great eloquence. "We don't wish any boys; they only joke and bounce about. This is a ladies' club, and we wish to be private and proper."

"I'm afraid he'll laugh at our paper, and make fun of us afterwards," observed Pickwick, pulling the little curl on her forehead, as she always did when doubtful.

Up rose Snodgrass, very much in earnest. "Sir, I give you my word as a gentleman, Laurie won't do anything of the sort. He likes to write, and he'll give a tone to our contributions, and keep us from being sentimental, don't you see? We can do so little for him, and he does so much for us, I think the least we can do is to offer him a place here, and make him welcome if he comes."

This artful allusion to benefits conferred brought Tupman to his feet, looking as if he had quite made up his mind.

"Yes, we ought to do it, even if we *are* afraid. I say he *may* come, and his grandpa too, if he likes."

This spirited outburst from Beth electrified the club, and Jo left her seat to shake hands approvingly. "Now then, vote again. Everybody remember it's our Laurie, and say 'Ay!'" cried Snodgrass, excitedly.

"Ay! ay! ay!" replied three voices at once.

"Good! Bless you! Now, as there's nothing like 'taking time by the *fetlock*', as Winkle characteristically observes, allow me to present the new member"; and, to the dismay of the rest of the club, Jo threw open the door of the closet, and displayed Laurie sitting on a rag-bag, flushed and twinkling with suppressed laughter.

"You rogue! you traitor! Jo, how could you?" cried the three girls, as Snodgrass led her friend triumphantly forth; and, producing both a chair and a badge, installed him in a jiffy.

"The coolness of you two rascals is amazing," began Mr. Pickwick, trying to get up an awful frown, and only succeeding in producing an amiable smile. But the new member was equal to the occasion; and, rising, with a graceful salutation to the Chair, said, in the most engaging manner, "Mr. President and ladies—I beg pardon, gentlemen—allow me to introduce myself as Sam Weller, the very humble servant of the club."

"Good! good!" cried Jo, pounding with the handle of the old warming-pan, on which she leaned.

"My faithful friend and noble patron," continued Laurie, with a wave of the hand, "who has so flatteringly presented me, is not to be blamed for the base stratagem of tonight. I planned it, and she only gave in after lots of teasing."

"Come now, don't lay it all on yourself; you know I proposed the cupboard," broke in Snodgrass, who was enjoying the joke amazingly.

"Never you mind what she says. I'm the wretch that did it, sir," said the new member, with a Welleresque nod to Mr. Pickwick. "But on my honour I never will do so again, and henceforth *devote* myself to the interest of this immortal club."

"Hear! hear!" cried Jo, clashing the lid of the warming-pan like a cymbal.

"Go on, go on!" added Winkle and Tupman, while the President bowed benignly.

"I merely wish to say, that as a slight token of my gratitude for the honour done me, and as a means of promoting friendly relations between adjoining nations, I have set up a post-office in the hedge in the lower corner of the garden; a fine, spacious building, with padlocks on the doors, and every convenience for the mails—also the females, if I may be allowed the expression. It's the old martin-house; but I've stopped up the door, and made the roof open, so it will hold all sorts of things, and save our valuable time. Letters, manuscripts, books, and bundles can be passed in there; and, as each nation has a key, it will be uncommonly nice,

I fancy. Allow me to present the club key; and, with many thanks for your favour, take my seat."

Great applause as Mr. Weller deposited a little key on the table, and subsided; the warming-pan clashed and waved wildly, and it was some time before order could be restored. A long discussion followed, and everyone came out surprisingly for everyone did her best; so it was an unusually lively meeting, and did not adjourn till a late hour, when it broke up with three shrill cheers for the new member. No one ever regretted the admittance of Sam Weller, for a more devoted, well-behaved, and jovial member no club could have. He certainly did add "spirit" to the meeting and "a tone" to the paper; for his orations convulsed his hearers, and his contributions were excellent, being patriotic, classical, comical, or dramatic, but never sentimental. Jo regarded them as worthy of Bacon, Milton, or Shakespeare; and remodelled her own works with good effect, she thought.

The P.O. was a capital little institution, and flourished wonderfully, for nearly as many queer things passed through it as through the real office. Tragedies and cravats, poetry and pickles, garden seeds and long letters, music and gingerbread, rubbers, invitations, scoldings and puppies. The old gentleman liked the fun, and amused himself by sending odd bundles, mysterious messages, and funny telegrams; and his gardener, who was smitten with Hannah's charms, actually sent a love-letter to Jo's care. How they laughed when the secret came out, never dreaming how many love-letters that little post-office would hold in the years to come!

CHAPTER 11

EXPERIMENTS

"The first of June! The Kings are off to the seashore tomorrow, and I'm free. Three months' vacation—how I shall enjoy it!" exclaimed Meg, coming home one warm day to find Jo laid upon the sofa in an unusual state of exhaustion, while Beth took off her dusty boots, and Amy made lemonade for the refreshment of the whole party.

"Aunt March went today, for which, oh, be joyful!" said Jo. "I was mortally afraid she'd ask me to go with her; if she had, I should have felt as if I ought to do it; but Plumfield is about as gay as a churchyard, you know, and I'd rather be excused.

"We had a flurry getting the old lady off, and I had a fright every time she spoke to me, for I was in such a hurry to be through that I was uncommonly helpful and sweet, and feared she'd find it impossible to part from me. I quaked till she was fairly in the carriage, and had a final fright, for, as it drove off, she popped out her head, saying, 'Josy-phine, won't you—?' I didn't hear any more, for I basely turned and fled; I did actually run, and whisked round the corner, where I felt safe."

"Poor old Jo! she came in looking as if bears were after her," said Beth, as she cuddled her sister's feet with a motherly air.

"Aunt March is a regular samphire, is she not?" observed Amy, tasting her mixture critically.

"She means *vampire,* not seaweed; but it doesn't matter; it's too warm to be particular about one's parts of speech," murmured Jo.

"What shall you do all your vacation?" asked Amy, changing the subject, with tact. "I shall lie abed late and do nothing," replied Meg, from the depths of the rocking-chair. "I've been routed up early all winter, and had to spend my days working for other people; so now I'm going to rest and revel to my heart's content."

"No," said Jo; "that dozy way wouldn't suit me. I've laid in a heap of books, and I'm going to improve my shining hours reading on my perch in the old apple-tree, when I'm not having l—"

"Don't say 'larks'!" implored Amy, as a return snub for the "samphire" correction.

"I'll say 'nightingales', then, with Laurie; that's proper and appropriate, since he's a warbler."

"Don't let us do any lessons, Beth, for a while, but play all the time, and rest, as the girls mean to," proposed Amy.

"Well, I will, if Mother doesn't mind. I want to learn some new songs, and my children need fitting up for the summer; they are dreadfully out of order, and really suffering for clothes."

"May we, Mother?" asked Meg, turning to Mrs. March, who sat sewing in what they called "Marmee's corner".

"You may try your experiment for a week, and see how you

like it. I think by Saturday night you will find that all play and no work is as bad as all work and no play."

"Oh, dear, no! it will be delicious, I'm sure," said Meg, complacently.

"I now propose a toast, as my 'friend and pardner, Sairy Gamp', says. Fun for ever, and no grubbing!" cried Jo, rising, glass in hand, as the lemonade went round.

They all drank it merrily, and began the experiment by lounging for the rest of the day. Next morning Meg did not appear till ten o'clock; her solitary breakfast did not taste nice and the room seemed lonely and untidy; for Jo had not filled the vases, Beth had not dusted, and Amy's books lay scattered about. Nothing was neat and pleasant but "Marmee's corner", which looked as usual; and there Meg sat, to "rest and read", which meant yawn, and imagine what pretty summer dresses she would get with her salary. Jo spent the morning on the river with Laurie, and the afternoon reading and crying over *The Wide, Wide World*, up in the apple-tree. Beth began by rummaging everything out of the big closet where her family resided; but, getting tired before half done, she left her establishment topsy-turvy, and went to her music, rejoicing that she had no dishes to wash. Amy arranged her bower, put on her best white frock, smoothed her curls, and sat down to draw, under the honeysuckles, hoping someone would see and inquire who the young artist was. As no one appeared but an inquisitive daddy-long-legs, who examined her work with interest, she went for a walk, got caught in a shower, and came home dripping.

At tea-time they compared notes, and all agreed that it had been a delightful, though unusually long day. Meg, who went shopping in the afternoon, and got a "sweet blue muslin", had discovered, after she had cut the breadths off, that it wouldn't wash, which mishap made her slightly cross. Jo had burnt the skin off her nose boating, and got a raging headache by reading too long. Beth was worried by the confusion of her closet, and the difficulty of learning three or four songs at once; and Amy deeply regretted the damage done her frock, for Katy Brown's party was to be the next day, and now, like Flora M'Flimsey, she had "nothing to wear". But these were mere trifles, and they assured their mother that the experiment was working finely. She smiled, said nothing, and, with Hannah's help, did their neglected work, keeping home pleasant, and the domestic machinery running smoothly. It was astonishing what a peculiar and uncomfortable state of things was produced by the "resting and revelling" process. The days kept getting longer and longer; the weather was unusually variable, and so were tempers; an unsettled feeling possessed everyone, and Satan found plenty of mischief for the idle hands to do. As the height of luxury, Meg put out some of her sewing, and then found time hang so heavily that she fell to snipping and spoiling her clothes, in her attempts to furbish them up *à la* Moffat. Jo read till her eyes gave out, and she was sick of books; got so fidgety that even good-natured Laurie had a quarrel with her, and so reduced in spirits that she desperately wished she had gone out with Aunt March. Beth got on pretty well, for she was constantly forgetting that it was to be *all play, and no work*, and fell back into her old ways now and then; but something in the air affected her, and more than once her tranquillity was much disturbed; so much so, that, on one occasion, she actually shook poor dear Joanna, and told her she was a "fright". Amy fared worst of all, for her resources were small; and when her sisters left her to amuse and care for herself, she soon found that accomplished and important little self a great burden. She didn't like dolls, fairy-tales were childish, and one couldn't draw all the time; tea parties didn't amount to much, neither did picnics, unless very well conducted. "If one could have a fine house, full of nice girls, or go travelling, the summer would be delightful; but to stay at home with three selfish sisters and a grown-up boy was enough to try the patience of a 'Boaz'," complained Miss Malaprop, after several days devoted to pleasure, fretting, and *ennui*. No one would own that they were tired of the experiment; but, by Friday night, each acknowledged to herself that she was glad the week was nearly done. Hoping to impress the lesson more deeply, Mrs. March, who had a good deal of humour, resolved to finish off the trial in an appropriate manner; so she gave Hannah a holiday, and let the girls enjoy the full effect of the play system. When they got up on Saturday morning, there was no fire in the kitchen, no breakfast in the dining-room, and no mother anywhere to be seen.

"Mercy on us! what *has* happened?" cried Jo, staring about her in dismay.

Meg ran upstairs, and soon came back again, looking relieved, but rather bewildered, and a little ashamed.

"Mother isn't sick, only very tired, and she says she is going to stay quietly in her room all day, and let us do the best we can. It's a very queer thing for her to do, she doesn't act a bit like herself; but she says it has been a hard week for her, so we mustn't grumble, but take care of ourselves."

"That's easy enough, and I like the idea; I'm aching for something to do—that is, some new amusement, you know," added Jo, quickly.

In fact it *was* an immense relief to them all to have a little work, and they took hold with a will, but soon realized the truth of Hannah's saying, "Housekeeping ain't no joke." There was plenty of food in the larder, and, while Beth and Amy set the table, Meg and Jo got breakfast, wondering, as they did so, why servants ever talked about hard work.

"I shall take some up to Mother, though she said we were not to think of her, for she'd take care of herself," said Meg, who presided, and felt quite matronly behind the teapot.

So a tray was fitted out before anyone began, and taken up with the cook's compliments. The boiled tea was very bitter, the omelette scorched, and the biscuits speckled with saleratus; but Mrs. March received her repast with thanks, and laughed heartily over it after Jo was gone.

"Poor little souls, they will have a hard time, I'm afraid; but they won't suffer, and it will do them good," she said, producing the more palatable viands with which she had provided herself, and disposing of the bad breakfast, so that their feelings might not be hurt—a motherly little deception for which they were grateful.

Many were the complaints below, and great the chagrin of the head cook at her failures. "Never mind, I'll get the dinner and be servant; you be mistress, keep your hands nice, see company, and give orders," said Jo, who knew still less than Meg about culinary affairs.

This obliging offer was gladly accepted; and Margaret retired to the parlour, which she hastily put in order by whisking the litter under the sofa, and shutting the blinds, to save the trouble of dusting. Jo, with perfect faith in her own powers, and a friendly desire to make up the quarrel, immediately put a note in the office, inviting Laurie to dinner.

"You'd better see what you have got before you think about having company," said Meg, when informed of the hospitable but rash act.

"Oh, there's corned beef and plenty of potatoes; and I shall get some asparagus, and a lobster, 'for a relish', as Hannah says. We'll have lettuce, and make a salad. I don't know how, but the book tells. I'll have blancmange and strawberries for dessert; and coffee, too, if you want to be elegant."

"Don't try too many messes, Jo, for you can't make anything but gingerbread and molasses candy fit to eat. I wash my hands of the dinner party; and since you have asked Laurie on your own responsibility, you may just take care of him."

"I don't want you to do anything but be civil to him, and help with the pudding. You'll give me your advice if I get in a muddle, won't you?" asked Jo, rather hurt.

"Yes; but I don't know much, except about bread, and a few trifles. You had better ask Mother's leave before you order anything," returned Meg, prudently.

"Of course I shall; I'm not a fool," and Jo went off in a huff at the doubts expressed of her powers.

"Get what you like, and don't disturb me; I'm going out to dinner, and can't worry about things at home," said Mrs. March, when Jo spoke to her. "I never enjoyed housekeeping, and I'm going to take a vacation today, and read, and write, go visiting, and amuse myself."

The unusual spectacle of her busy mother rocking comfortably and reading, early in the morning, made Jo feel as if some natural phenomenon had occurred; for an eclipse, an earthquake, or a volcanic eruption would hardly have seemed stranger.

"Everything is out of sorts somehow," she said to herself, going downstairs. "There's Beth crying; that's a sure sign that something is wrong with this family. If Amy is bothering, I'll shake her."

Feeling very much out of sorts herself, Jo hurried into the parlour to find Beth sobbing over Pip, the canary, who lay dead in the cage, with his little claws pathetically extended, as if imploring the food for want of which he had died.

"It's all my fault—I forgot him—there isn't a seed or a drop left. O Pip! O Pip! how could I be so cruel to you?" cried Beth, taking the poor thing in her hands, and trying to restore him.

Jo peeped into his half-open eye, felt his little heart, and finding him stiff and cold shook her head, and offered her domino box for a coffin.

"Put him in the oven, and maybe he will get warm and revive," said Amy, hopefully.

"He's been starved, and he shan't be baked, now he's dead. I'll make him a shroud, and he shall be buried in the garden; and I'll never have another bird, never, my Pip! for I'm too bad to own one," murmured Beth, sitting on the floor with her pet folded in her hands.

"The funeral shall be this afternoon, and we will all go. Now, don't cry, Betty; it's a pity, but nothing goes right this week, and Pip has had the worst of the experiment. Make the shroud, and lay him in my box; and, after the dinner party, we'll have a nice little funeral," said Jo, beginning to feel as if she had undertaken a good deal.

Leaving the others to console Beth, she departed to the kitchen, which was in a most discouraging state of confusion. Putting on a big apron she fell to work, and got the dishes piled up ready for washing, when she discovered that the fire was out. "Here's a sweet prospect!" muttered Jo, slamming the stove-door open, and poking vigorously among the cinders.

Having rekindled the fire, she thought she would go to market while the water heated. The walk revived her spirits; and flattering herself that she had made good bargains, she trudged home again, after buying a very young lobster, some very old asparagus, and two boxes of acid strawberries. By the time she got cleared up the dinner arrived, and the stove was red hot. Hannah had left a pan of bread to rise, Meg had worked it up early, set it on the hearth for a second rising, and forgotten it. Meg was entertaining Sallie Gardiner in the parlour, when the door flew open, and a floury, crocky, flushed, and dishevelled figure appeared, demanding tartly:

"I say, isn't bread 'riz' enough when it runs over the pans?"

Sallie began to laugh; but Meg nodded, and lifted her eyebrows as high as they would go, which caused the apparition to vanish, and put the sour bread into the oven without further delay. Mrs. March went out, after peeping here and there to see how matters went, also saying a word of comfort to Beth, who sat making a winding sheet, while the dear departed lay in state in the domino box. A strange sense of helplessness fell upon the girls as the grey bonnet vanished round the corner; and despair seized them when, a few minutes later, Miss Crocker appeared, and said she'd come to dinner. Now, this lady was a thin, yellow spinster, with a sharp nose and inquisitive eyes, who saw everything, and gossiped about all she saw. They disliked her, but had been taught to be kind to her, simply because she was old and poor, and had few friends. So Meg gave her the easy-chair, and tried to entertain her, while she asked questions, criticized everything, and told stories of the people who she knew.

Language cannot describe the anxieties, experiences, and exertions which Jo underwent that morning; and the dinner she served up became a standing joke. Fearing to ask any more advice, she did her best alone, and discovered that something more than energy and goodwill is necessary to make a cook. She boiled the asparagus for an hour, and was grieved to find the heads cooked off and the stalks harder than ever. The bread burnt black, for the salad-dressing so aggravated her that she let everything else go till she had convinced herself that she could not make it fit to eat. The lobster was a scarlet mystery to her, but she hammered and poked till it was unshelled, and its meagre proportions concealed in a grove of lettuce leaves. The potatoes had to be hurried, not to keep the asparagus waiting, and were not done at last. The blancmange was lumpy, and the strawberries not as ripe as they looked, having been skilfully "deaconed".

"Well, they can eat beef, and bread and butter, if they are hungry; only it's mortifying to have to spend your whole morning for nothing," thought Jo, as she rang the bell half an hour later than usual, and stood, hot, tired, and dispirited, surveying the feast spread for Laurie, accustomed to all sorts of elegance, and Miss Crocker, whose curious eyes would mark all failures, and whose tattling tongue would report them far and wide.

Poor Jo would gladly have gone under the table, as one thing after another was tasted and left; while Amy giggled, Meg looked distressed, Miss Crocker pursed up her lips, and Laurie talked and laughed with all his might, to give a cheerful tone to the festive scene. Jo's one strong point was the fruit, for she had sugared it well, and had a pitcher of rich cream to eat with it. Her hot cheeks cooled a trifle, and she drew a long breath, as the pretty glass plates went round, and everyone looked graciously at the little rosy islands floating in a sea of cream. Miss Crocker tasted first, made a wry face, and drank some water hastily. Jo, who had refused, thinking there might not be enough, for they dwindled sadly after the picking over, glanced at Laurie, but he was eating away manfully, though there was a slight pucker about his mouth, and he kept his eye fixed on his plate. Amy, who was fond of delicate fare, took a heaping spoonful, choked, hid her face in her napkin, and left the table precipitately.

"Oh, what is it?" exclaimed Jo, trembling.

"Salt instead of sugar, and the cream is sour," replied Meg, with a tragic gesture.

Jo uttered a groan, and fell back in her chair; remembering that she had given a last hasty powdering to the berries out of one of the two boxes on the kitchen table, and had neglected to put the milk in the refrigerator. She turned scarlet, and was on the verge of crying, when she met Laurie's eyes, which *would* look merry in spite of his heroic efforts; the comical side of the affair suddenly struck her, and she laughed till the tears ran down her cheeks. So did everyone else, even "Croaker", as the girls called the old lady; and the unfortunate dinner ended gaily, with bread and butter, olives, and fun.

"I haven't strength of mind enough to clear up now, so we will sober ourselves with a funeral," said Jo, as they rose; and Miss Crocker made ready to go, being eager to tell the new story at another friend's dinner-table. They did sober themselves for Beth's sake; Laurie dug a grave under the ferns in the grove, little Pip was laid in, with many tears, by his tender-hearted mistress, and covered with moss, while a wreath of violets and chickweed was hung on the stone which bore his epitaph, composed by Jo while she struggled with the dinner:

Here lies Pip March,
  Who died the 7th of June;
Loved and lamented sore,
  And not forgotten soon.

At the conclusion of the ceremonies, Beth retired to her room, overcome with emotion and lobster; but there was no place of repose, for the beds were not made, and she found her grief much assuaged by beating up pillows and putting things in order. Meg helped Jo clear away the remains of the feast, which took half the afternoon, and left them so tired that they agreed to be contented with tea and toast for supper. Laurie took Amy for a drive, which was a deed of charity, for the sour cream seemed to have had a bad effect upon her temper. Mrs. March came home to find the three older girls hard at work in the middle of the afternoon, and a glance at the closet gave her an idea of the success of one part of the experiment.

Before the housewives could rest several people called, and there was a scramble to get ready to see them; then tea must be got, errands done; and one or two necessary bits of sewing neglected till the last minute. As twilight fell, dewy and still, one by one they gathered in the porch where the June roses were budding beautifully, and each groaned or sighed as she sat down as if tired or troubled.

"What a dreadful day this has been!" began Jo, usually the first to speak.

"It has seemed shorter than usual, but so uncomfortable," said Meg.

"Not a bit like home," added Amy.

"It can't seem so without Marmee and little Pip," sighed Beth, glancing with full eyes at the empty cage above her head.

"Here's Mother, dear; and you shall have another bird tomorrow, if you want it."

As she spoke, Mrs. March came and took her place among them, looking as if her holiday had not been much pleasanter than theirs.

"Are you satisfied with your experiment, girls, or do you want another week of it?" she asked, as Beth nestled up to her, and the rest turned towards her with brightening faces, as flowers turn towards the sun.

"I don't," cried Jo, decidedly.

"Nor I," echoed the others.

"You think, then, that it is better to have a few duties, and live a little for others, do you?"

"Lounging and larking doesn't pay," observed Jo, shaking her head. "I'm tired of it, and mean to go to work at something right off."

"Suppose you learn plain cooking; that's a useful accomplishment which no woman should be without," said Mrs. March, laughing inaudibly at the recollection of Jo's dinner party; for she had met Miss Crocker, and heard her account of it.

"Mother, did you go away and let everything be, just to see how we'd get on?" cried Meg, who had had suspicions all day.

"Yes; I wanted you to see how the comfort of all depends on each doing her share faithfully. While Hannah and I did your work you got on pretty well, though I don't think you were very happy or amiable; so I thought, as a little lesson, I would show you what happens when everyone thinks only of herself. Don't you feel that it is pleasanter to help one another, to have daily duties which make leisure sweet when it comes, and to bear and forbear, that home may be comfortable and lovely to us all?"

"We do, Mother, we do!" cried the girls.

"Then let me advise you to take up your little burdens again; for though they seem heavy sometimes, they are good for us, and lighten as we learn to carry them. Work is wholesome, and there is plenty for everyone; it keeps us from *ennui* and mischief, is good for health and spirits, and gives us a sense of power and independence better than money or fashion."

"We'll work like bees, and love it too; see if we don't!" said Jo. "I'll learn plain cooking for my holiday task; and the next dinner party I have shall be a success."

"I'll make the set of shirts for father, instead of letting you do it, Marmee. I can and I will, though I'm not fond of sewing; that will be better than fussing over my own things, which are plenty nice enough as they are," said Meg.

"I'll do my lessons every day, and not spend so much time with my music and dolls. I am a stupid thing, and ought to be studying, not playing," was Beth's resolution; while Amy followed their example by heroically declaring, "I shall learn to make button-holes, and attend to my parts of speech."

"Very good! then I am quite satisfied with the experiment, and fancy that we shall not have to repeat it; only don't go to the other extreme, and delve like slaves. Have regular hours for work and play; make each day both useful and pleasant, and prove that you understand the worth of time by employing it well. Then youth will be delightful, old age will bring few regrets, and life become a beautiful success, in spite of poverty."

"We'll remember, Mother!" and they did.

Chapter 12

CAMP LAURENCE

Beth was postmistress, for, being most at home, she could attend to it regularly, and dearly liked the daily task of unlocking the little door and distributing the mail. One July day she came in with her hands full, and went about the house leaving letters and parcels like the penny post.

"Here's your posy, Mother! Laurie never forgets that," she said, putting the fresh nosegay in the vase which stood in "Marmee's corner", and was kept supplied by the affectionate boy.

"Miss Meg March, one letter and a glove," continued Beth, delivering the article to her sister, who sat near her mother, stitching wristbands.

"Why, I left a pair over there, and here is only one," said Meg, looking at the grey cotton glove. "Didn't you drop the other in the garden?"

"No, I'm sure I didn't; for there was only one in the office."

"I hate to have odd gloves! Never mind, the other may be found. My letter is only a translation of the German song I wanted; I think Mr. Brooke did it, for this isn't Laurie's writing."

Mrs. March glanced at Meg, who was looking very pretty in her gingham morning gown, with the little curls blowing about her forehead, and very womanly, as she sat sewing at her little work-table, full of tiny white rolls; so unconscious of the thought in her mother's mind as she sewed and sung, while her fingers flew, and her thoughts were busied with girlish fancies as innocent and fresh as the pansies in her belt, that Mrs. March smiled, and was satisfied.

"Two letters for Doctor Jo, a book, and a funny old hat, which covered the whole post-office, stuck outside," said Beth, laughing, as she went into the study, where Jo sat writing.

"What a sly fellow Laurie is! I said I wished bigger hats were the fashion, because I burn my face every hot day. He said, 'Why mind the fashion? Wear a big hat and be comfortable!' I said I would if I had one, and he has sent me this to try me. I'll wear it, for fun, and show him I don't care for the fashion"; and hanging the antique broad-brim on a bust of Plato, Jo read her letters.

One from her mother made her cheeks glow and her eyes fill, for it said to her:

MY DEAR—I write a little word to tell you with how much satisfaction I watch your efforts to control your temper. You say nothing about your trials, failures, or successes, and think, perhaps, that no one sees them but the friend whose help you daily ask, if I may trust the well-worn cover of your guide book. *I*, too, have seen them all, and heartily believe in the sincerity of your resolution, since it begins to bear fruit. Go on, dear, patiently and bravely, and always believe that no one sympathises more tenderly with you than your loving

MOTHER

"That does me good! that's worth millions of money and pecks of praise. Oh, Marmee, I do try! I will keep on trying, and not get tired, since I have you to help me."

Laying her head on her arm, Jo wet her little romance with a few happy tears, for she *had* thought no one saw and appreciated her efforts to do good; and this assurance was doubly precious, doubly encouraging, because unexpected, and from the person whose commendation she most valued. Feeling stronger than ever to meet and subdue her Apollyon, she pinned the note inside her frock, as a shield and a reminder, lest she be taken unawares, and proceeded to open her other letter, quite ready for either good or bad news. In a big, dashing hand, Laurie wrote:

Dear Jo,
What ho!
Some English girls and boys are coming to see me tomorrow, and I want to have a jolly time. If it's fine, I'm going to pitch my tent in Longmeadow, and row up the whole crew to lunch and croquet—have a fire, make messes, gipsy fashion, and all sorts of larks. They are nice people, and like such things. Brooke will go, to keep us boys steady, and Kate Vaughn will play propriety for the girls. I want you all to come; can't let Beth off at any price, and nobody shall worry her. Don't bother about rations—I'll see to that, and everything else—only do come, there's a good fellow!

In a tearing hurry,
Yours ever, LAURIE

"Here's richness!" cried Jo, flying in to tell the news to Meg. "Of course we can go, Mother? it will be such a help to Laurie, for I can row, and Meg see to the lunch, and the children be useful in some way."

"I hope the Vaughns are not fine, grown-up people. Do you know anything about them, Jo?" asked Meg.

"Only that there are four of them. Kate is older than you, Fred and Frank (twins) about my age, and a little girl (Grace), who is nine or ten. Laurie knew them abroad, and liked the boys; I fancied, from the way he primmed up his mouth in speaking of her, that he didn't admire Kate much."

"I'm so glad my French print is clean; it's just the thing, and so becoming!" observed Meg complacently. "Have you anything decent, Jo?"

"Scarlet and grey boating suit, good enough for me. I shall row and tramp about, so I don't want any starch to think of. You'll come, Betty?"

"If you won't let any of the boys talk to me."

"Not a boy!"

"I like to please Laurie; and I'm not afraid of Mr. Brooke, he is so kind; but I don't want to play, or sing, or say anything. I'll work hard and not trouble anyone; and you'll take care of me, Jo, so I'll go."

"That's my good girl; you do try to fight off your shyness, and I love you for it. Fighting faults isn't easy, as I know; and a cheery word kind of gives a lift. Thank you, Mother," and Jo gave the thin cheek a grateful kiss, more precious to Mrs. March than if it had given back the rosy roundness of her youth.

"I had a box of chocolate drops, and the picture I wanted to copy," said Amy, showing her mail.

"And I got a note from Mr. Laurence asking me to come over and play to him tonight before the lamps are lighted, and I shall go," added Beth, whose friendship with the old gentleman prospered finely.

"Now let's fly round and do double duty today, so that we can play tomorrow with free minds," said Jo, preparing to replace her pen with a broom.

When the sun peeped into the girls' room early the next morning, to promise them a fine day, he saw a comical sight. Each had made such preparation for the *fête* as seemed necessary and proper. Meg had an extra row of little curl papers across her forehead, Jo had copiously anointed her afflicted face with cold cream, Beth had taken Joanna to bed with her to atone for the approaching separation, and Amy had capped the climax by putting a clothes-pin on her nose, to uplift the offending feature. It was one of the kind artists used to hold the paper on their drawing-boards, therefore quite appropriate and effective for the purpose to which it was now put. This funny spectacle appeared to amuse the sun, for he burst out with such radiance that Jo woke up, and roused all her sisters by a hearty laugh at Amy's ornament.

Sunshine and laughter were good omens for a pleasure party, and soon a lively bustle began in both houses. Beth, who was ready first, kept reporting what went on next door, and enlivened her sisters' toilets by frequent telegrams from the window.

"There goes the man with the tent! I see Mrs. Barker doing up the lunch in a hamper and a great basket. Now Mr. Laurence is looking up at the sky and the weathercock; I wish he would go too. There's Laurie, looking like a sailor—nice boy! Oh, mercy me! here's a carriage full of people—a tall lady, a little girl, and two dreadful boys. One is lame; poor thing, he's got a crutch. Laurie didn't tell us that. Be quick, girls! it's getting late. Why, there is Ned Moffat, I do declare. Look, Meg, isn't that the man who bowed to you one day when we were shopping?"

"So it is. How queer that he should come. I thought he was at the Mountains. There is Sallie; I'm glad she's got back in time. Am I all right, Jo?" cried Meg, in a flutter.

"A regular daisy. Hold up your dress and put your hat straight, it looks sentimental tipped that way, and will fly off at the first puff. Now then, come on!"

"Oh, Jo, you are not going to wear that awful hat? It's too absurd! You shall *not* make a guy of yourself," remonstrated Meg, as Jo tied down, with a red ribbon, the broad-brimmed old-fashioned Leghorn Laurie had sent for a joke.

"I just will, though, for it's capital—so shady, light, and big. It will make fun; and I don't mind being a guy if I'm comfortable." With that Jo marched straight away, and the rest followed—a bright little band of sisters, all looking their best, in summer suits, with happy faces under the jaunty hat-brims.

Laurie ran to meet and present them to his friends in the most cordial manner. The lawn was the reception room, and for several minutes a lively scene was enacted there. Meg was grateful to see that Miss Kate, though twenty, was dressed with a simplicity that American girls would do well to imitate; and she was much flattered by Mr. Ned's assurances that he came especially to see her. Jo understood why Laurie "primmed up his mouth" when speaking of Kate, for that young lady had a stand-off-don't-touch-me air, which contrasted strongly with the free and easy demeanour of the other girls. Beth took an observation of the new boys, and decided that the lame one was not "dreadful", but gentle and feeble, and she would be kind to him on that account. Amy found Grace a well-mannered, merry little person; and after staring dumbly at one another for a few minutes, they suddenly became very good friends.

Tents, lunch, and croquet utensils had been sent on beforehand, the party was soon embarked, and the two boats pushed off together, leaving Mr. Laurence waving his hat on the shore. Laurie and Jo rowed one boat; Mr. Brooke and Ned the other; while Fred Vaughn, the riotous twin, did his best to upset both by paddling about in a wherry like a disturbed water-bug. Jo's funny hat deserved a word of thanks, for it was of general utility; it broke the ice in the beginning, by producing a laugh; it created quite a refreshing breeze, flapping to and fro as she rowed, and would make an excellent umbrella for the whole party if a shower came up, she said. Kate looked rather amazed at Jo's proceedings, especially as she exclaimed "Christopher Columbus!" when she lost her oar; and Laurie said, "My dear fellow, did I hurt you?" when he tripped over her feet in taking his place. But after putting up her glass to examine the queer girl several times, Miss Kate decided that she was "odd, but rather clever", and smiled upon her from afar.

Meg, in the other boat, was delightfully situated, face to face with the rowers, who both admired the prospect, and feathered their oars with uncommon "skill and dexterity". Mr. Brooke was a grave, silent young man, with handsome brown eyes and a pleasant voice. Meg liked his quiet manners, and considered him a walking encyclopedia of useful knowledge. He never talked to her much, but he looked at her a good deal, and she felt sure that he did not regard her with aversion. Ned, being in college, of course put on all the airs which freshmen think it their bounden duty to assume; he was not very wise, but very good-natured, and altogether an excellent person to carry on a picnic. Sallie Gardiner was absorbed in keeping her white piqué dress clean, and chattering with the ubiquitous Fred, who kept Beth in constant terror by his pranks.

It was not far to Longmeadow; but the tent was pitched and the wickets down by the time they arrived. A pleasant green field, with three wide-spreading oaks in the middle, and a smooth strip of turf for the croquet.

"Welcome to Camp Laurence!" said the young host, as they landed, with exclamations of delight.

"Brooke is commander-in-chief; I am commissary-general; the other fellows are staff-officers; and you, ladies, are company. The tent is for your especial benefit, and that oak is your drawing-room; this is the messroom, and the third is the camp-kitchen. Now, let's have a game before it gets hot, and then we'll see about dinner."

Frank, Beth, Amy, and Grace sat down to watch the game played by the other eight. Mr. Brooke chose Meg, Kate, and Fred; Laurie took Sallie, Jo, and Ned. The Englishers played well; but the Americans played better, and contested every inch of the ground as strongly as if the spirit of '76 inspired them. Jo and Fred had several skirmishes, and once narrowly escaped high words. Jo was through the last wicket, and had missed the stroke, which failure ruffled her a good deal. Fred was close behind her, and his turn came before hers; he gave a stroke, his ball hit the wicket, and stopped an inch on the wrong side. No one was very near; and running up to examine, he gave it a sly nudge with his toe, which put it just an inch on the right side.

"I'm through! Now, Miss Jo, I'll settle you, and get in first," cried the young gentleman, swinging his mallet for another blow.

"You pushed it! I saw you; it's my turn now," said Jo, sharply.

"Upon my word, I didn't move it; it rolled a bit, perhaps, but that is allowed; so stand off please, and let me have a go at the stake."

"We don't cheat in America, but you can, if you choose," said Jo, angrily.

"Yankees are a deal the most tricky, everybody knows. There you go!" returned Fred, croqueting her ball far away.

Jo opened her lips to say something rude, but checked herself in time, coloured up to her forehead, and stood a minute hammering down a wicket with all her might, while Fred hit the stake, and declared himself out with much exultation. She went off to get her ball, and was a long time finding it among the bushes; but she came back, looking cool and quiet, and waited her turn patiently. It took several strokes to regain the place she had lost; and, when she got there, the other side had nearly won, for Kate's ball was the last but one, and lay near the stake.

"By George, it's all up with us! Good-bye, Kate. Miss Jo owes me one, so you are finished," cried Fred, excitedly, as they all drew near to see the finish.

"Yankees have a trick of being generous to their enemies," said Jo, with a look that made the lad redden, "especially when they beat them," she added, as, leaving Kate's ball untouched, she won the game by a clever stroke.

Laurie threw up his hat; then remembering that it wouldn't do to exult over the defeat of his guests, he stopped in the middle of a cheer to whisper to his friend: "Good for you, Jo! He did cheat, I saw him; we can't tell him so, but he won't do it again, take my word for it."

Meg drew her aside, under pretence of pinning up a loose braid, and said approvingly: "It was dreadfully provoking; but you kept your temper, and I'm so glad, Jo."

"Don't praise me, Meg, for I could box his ears this minute. I should certainly have boiled over if I hadn't stayed among the nettles till I got my rage under enough to hold my tongue. It's simmering now, so I hope he'll keep out of my way," returned Jo, biting her lips, as she glowered at Fred from under her big hat.

"Time for lunch," said Mr. Brooke, looking at his watch. "Commissary-general, will you make the fire and get water while Miss March, Miss Sallie and I spread the table? Who can make good coffee?"

"Jo can!" said Meg, glad to recommend her sister. So Jo, feeling that her late lessons in cookery were to do her honour, went to preside over the coffee-pot, while the children collected dry sticks, and the boys made a fire, and got water from a spring near by. Miss Kate sketched, and Frank talked to Beth, who was making little mats of braided rushes to serve as plates. The commander-in-chief and his aides soon spread the tablecloth with an inviting array of eatables and drinkables, prettily decorated with green leaves. Jo announced that the coffee was ready, and everyone settled themselves to a hearty meal; for youth is seldom dyspeptic, and exercise develops wholesome appetites. A very merry lunch it was; for everything seemed fresh and funny, and frequent peals of laughter startled a venerable horse who fed near by. There was a pleasing inequality in the table, which produced many mishaps to cups and plates; acorns dropped into the milk, little black ants partook of the refreshments without being invited, and fuzzy caterpillars swung down from the tree to see what was going on. Three white-headed children peeped over the fence, and an objectionable dog barked at them from the other side of the river with all his might and main.

"There's salt here, if you prefer it," said Laurie, as he handed Jo a saucer of berries.

"Thank you, I prefer spiders," she replied, fishing up two unwary little ones who had gone to a creamy death. "How dare you remind me of that horrid dinner party, when yours is so nice in every way?" added Jo, as they both laughed, and ate out of one plate, the china having run short.

"I had an uncommonly good time that day, and haven't got over it yet. This is no credit to me, you know; I don't do anything; it's you and Meg and Brooke who make it go, and I'm no end obliged to you. What shall we do when we can't eat any more?" asked Laurie, feeling that his trump card had been played when lunch was over.

"Have games till it's cooler. I brought 'Authors', and I dare say Miss Kate knows something new and nice. Go and ask her; she's company, and you ought to stay with her more."

"Aren't you company, too? I thought she'd suit Brooke; but he keeps talking to Meg, and Kate just stares at them through that ridiculous glass of hers. I'm going, so you needn't try to preach propriety, for you can't do it, Jo."

Miss Kate did know several new games; and as the girls would not, and the boys could not, eat any more, they all adjourned to the drawing-room to play "Rigmarole".

"One person begins a story, any nonsense you like, and tells as long as he pleases, only taking care to stop short at some exciting point, when the next takes it up and does the same. It's very funny when well done, and makes a perfect jumble of tragical comical stuff to laugh over. Please start it, Mr. Brooke," said Kate with a commanding air, which surprised Meg, who treated the tutor with as much respect as any other gentleman.

Lying on the grass at the feet of the two young ladies, Mr. Brooke obediently began the story, with the handsome brown eyes steadily fixed upon the sunshiny river.

"Once upon a time a knight went out into the world to seek his fortune, for he had nothing but his sword and his shield. He travelled a long while, nearly eight-and-twenty years, and had a hard time of it, till he came to the palace of a good old king, who had offered a reward to any who would tame and train a fine but unbroken colt of which he was very fond. The knight agreed to try, and got on slowly but surely; for the colt was a gallant fellow, and soon learned to love his new master, though he was freakish and wild. Every day, when he gave his lessons to this pet of the king's, the knight rode him through the city; and, as he rode, he looked everywhere for a certain beautiful face, which he had seen many times in his dreams, but never found. One day, as he went prancing down a quiet street, he saw at the window of a ruinous castle the lovely face. He was delighted, inquired who lived in this old castle, and was told that several captive princesses were kept there by a spell, and spun all day to lay up money to buy their liberty. The knight wished intensely that he could free them; but he was poor, and could only go by each day, watching for the sweet face, and longing to see it out in the sunshine. At last he resolved to get into the castle and ask how he could help them. He went and knocked; the great door flew open, and he beheld—"

"A ravishingly lovely lady, who exclaimed, with a cry of rapture, 'At last! at last!'" continued Kate, who had read French novels, and admired the style. "'Tis she!' cried Count Gustave, and fell at her feet in an ecstasy of joy. 'Oh, rise!' she said, extending a hand of marble fairness. 'Never! till you tell me how I may rescue you,' swore the knight, still kneeling. 'Alas, my cruel fate condemns me to remain here till my tyrant is destroyed.' 'Where is the villain!' 'In the mauve salon. Go, brave heart, and save me from despair.' 'I obey, and return victorious or dead!' With these thrilling words he rushed away, and flinging open the door of the mauve salon, was about to enter, when he received—"

"A stunning blow from the big Greek lexicon, which an old fellow in a black gown fired at him," said Ned. "Instantly Sir What's his-name recovered himself, pitched the tyrant out of the window, and turned to join the lady victorious, but with a bump on his brow; found the door locked, tore up the curtains, made a rope ladder, got half-way down when the ladder broke, and he went head first into the moat, sixty feet below. Could swim like a duck, paddled round the castle till he came to a little door guarded by two stout fellows; knocked their heads together till they cracked like a couple of nuts, then, by a trifling exertion of his prodigious strength, he smashed in the door, went up a pair of stone steps covered with dust a foot thick, toads as big as your fist, and spiders that would frighten you into hysterics, Miss March. At the top of these steps he came plump upon a sight that took his breath away and chilled his blood—"

"A tall figure, all in white, with a veil over its face, and a lamp in its wasted hand," went on Meg. "It beckoned, gliding noiselessly before him down a corridor as dark and cold as any tomb. Shadowy effigies in armour stood on either side, a dead silence reigned, the lamp burned blue, and the ghostly figure ever and anon turned its face towards him showing the glitter of awful eyes through its white veil. They reached a curtained door, behind which sounded lovely music; he sprang forward to enter, but the spectre plucked him back, and waved threateningly before him a—"

"Snuff-box," said Jo, in a sepulchral tone, which convulsed the audience. "'Thankee,' said the knight, politely, as he took a pinch, and sneezed seven times so violently that his head fell off "Ha! ha!' laughed the ghost; and having peeped through the keyhole at the princesses spinning away for dear life, the evil spirit picked up her victim and put him in a large tin box, where there were eleven other knights packed together without their heads, like sardines, who all rose and began to—"

"Dance a hornpipe," cut in Fred, as Jo paused for breath; "and, as they danced, the rubbishy old castle turned to a man-of-war in full sail. 'Up with the jib, reef the tops'l halliards, helm hard a-lee, and man the guns!' roared the captain, as a Portuguese pirate hove in sight, with a flag black as ink flying from her foremast. 'Go in and win my hearties!' says the captain; and a tremendous fight began. Of course the British beat; they always do."

"No, they don't," cried Jo, aside.

"Having taken the pirate captain prisoner, sailed slap over the schooner, whose decks were piled with dead, and whose leescuppers ran blood, for the order had been 'Cutlasses, and die hard!' 'Bosun's mate, take a bright of the flying-jib sheet, and start this villain if he don't confess his sins double quick,' said the British captain. The Portuguese held his tongue like a brick, and walked the plank, while the jolly tars cheered like mad. But the sly dog dived, came up under the man-of-war, scuttled her, and down she went, with all sail set, 'To the bottom of the sea, sea, sea,' where—"

"Oh, gracious! what *shall* I say?" cried Sallie, as Fred ended his rigmarole, in which he had jumbled together, pell-mell, nautical phrases and facts out of one of his favourite books. "Well, they went to the bottom, and a nice mermaid welcomed them, but was much grieved on finding the box of headless knights, and kindly pickled them in brine, hoping to discover the mystery about them, for, being a woman, she was curious. By and by, a diver came down, and the mermaid said, 'I'll give you this box of pearls if you can take it up'; for she wanted to restore the poor things to life, and couldn't raise the heavy load herself. So the diver hoisted it up, and was much disappointed to find no pearls. He left it in a great lonely field, where it has found by a—"

"Little goosegirl, who kept a hundred fat geese in the field," said Amy, when Sallie's invention gave out. "The little girl was sorry for them, and asked an old woman what she should do to help them. 'Your geese will tell you, they know everything,' said the old woman. So she asked what she should use for new heads, since the old ones were lost, and all the geese opened their hundred mouths and screamed—"

"'Cabbages!'" continued Laurie, promptly. "'Just the thing,' said the girl, and ran to get twelve fine ones from her garden. She put them on, the knights revived at once, thanked her, and went on their way rejoicing, never knowing the difference, for there were so many other heads like them in the world that no one thought anything of it. The knight in whom I'm interested went back to find the pretty face, and learned that the princesses had spun themselves free, and all gone to be married but one. He was in a great state of mind at that; and mounting the colt, who stood by him through thick and thin, rushed to the castle to see which was left. Peeping over the hedge, he saw the queen of his affections picking flowers in her garden. 'Will you give me a rose?' said he. 'You must come and get it. I can't come to you; it isn't proper,' said she, as sweet as honey. He tried to climb over the hedge, but it seemed to grow higher and higher; then he tried to push through, but it grew thicker and thicker and he was in despair. So he patiently broke twig after twig till he had made a little hole, through which he peeped, saying imploringly, 'Let me in! let me in.' But the pretty princess did not seem to understand, for he picked her roses quietly, and left him to fight his way in. Whether he did or not, Frank will tell you."

"I can't; I'm not playing, I never do," said Frank, dismayed at the sentimental predicament out of which he was to rescue the absurd couple. Beth had disappeared behind Jo, and Grace was asleep.

"So the poor knight is to be left sticking in the hedge, is he?" asked Mr. Brooke, still watching the river and playing with the wild rose in his buttonhole.

"I guess the princess gave him a posy, and opened the gate after a while," said Laurie, smiling to himself, as he threw acorns at his tutor.

"What a piece of nonsense we have made! With practice we might do something quite clever. Do you know 'Truth'?" asked Sallie, after they had laughed over their story.

"I hope so," said Meg, soberly.

"The game, I mean?"

"What is it?" said Fred.

"Why, you pile up your hands, choose a number, and draw out in turn, and the person who draws at the number has to answer truly any questions put by the rest. It's great fun."

"Let's try it," said Jo, who liked new experiments.

Miss Kate and Mr. Brooke, Meg, and Ned declined, but Fred, Sallie, Jo, and Laurie piled and drew; and the lot fell to Laurie.

"Who are your heroes?" asked Jo.

"Grandfather and Napoleon."

"Which lady here do you think prettiest?" said Sallie.

"Margaret."

"Which do you like best?" from Fred.

"Jo, of course."

"What silly questions you ask!" and Jo gave a disdainful shrug, as the rest laughed at Laurie's matter-of-fact tone.

"Try again; Truth isn't a bad game," said Fred.

"It's a very good one for you," retorted Jo, in a low voice.

Her turn came next.

"What is your greatest fault?" asked Fred, by way of testing in her the virtue he lacked himself.

"A quick temper."

"What do you most wish for?" said Laurie.

"A pair of boot-lacings," returned Jo, guessing and defeating his purpose.

"Not a true answer; you must say what you really do want most."

"Genius; don't you wish you could give it to me, Laurie?" and she slyly smiled in his disappointed face.

"What virtues do you most admire in a man?" asked Sallie.

"Courage and honesty."

"Now my turn," said Fred, as his hand came last.

"Let's give it to him," whispered Laurie to Jo, who nodded, and asked at once: "Didn't you cheat at croquet?"

"Well, yes, a little bit."

"Good! Didn't you take your story out of *The Sea-Lion*?" said Laurie.

"Rather."

"Don't you think the English nation perfect in every respect?" asked Sallie.

"I should be ashamed of myself if I didn't."

"He's a true John Bull. Now, Miss Sallie, you shall have a chance without waiting to draw. I'll harrow up your feelings first by asking if you don't think you are something of a flirt," said Laurie, as Jo nodded to Fred, as a sign that peace was declared.

"You impertinent boy! of course I'm not," exclaimed Sallie, with an air that proved the contrary.

"What do you hate most?" asked Fred.

"Spiders and rice pudding."

"What do you like best?" asked Jo.

"Dancing and French gloves."

"Well, *I* think Truth is a very silly play; let's have a sensible game of Authors, to refresh our minds," proposed Jo.

Ned, Frank, and the little girls joined in this, and while it went on the three elder sat apart talking. Miss Kate took out her sketch again, and Margaret watched her, while Mr. Brooke lay on the grass, with a book which he did not read.

"How beautifully you do it! I wish I could draw," said Meg, with mingled admiration and regret in her voice.

"Why don't you learn? I should think you had taste and talent for it," replied Miss Kate, graciously.

"I haven't time."

"Your mamma prefers other accomplishments, I fancy. So did mine; but I proved to her that I had talent by taking a few lessons privately, and then she was quite willing I should go on. Can't you do the same with your governess?"

"I have none."

"I forgot; young ladies in America go to school more than with us. Very fine schools they are, too, Papa says. You go to a private one, I suppose?"

"I don't go at all; I am a governess myself."

"Oh, indeed!" said Miss Kate; but she might as well have said, "Dear me, how dreadful!" for her tone implied it, and something in her face made Meg colour, and wish she had not been so frank.

Mr. Brooke looked up, and said quickly, "Young ladies in America love independence as much as their ancestors did, and are admired and respected for supporting themselves."

"Oh, yes; of course it's very nice and proper in them to do so. We have many most respectable and worthy young women who do the same, and are employed by the nobility, because, being the daughters of gentlemen, they are both well-bred and accomplished, you know," said Miss Kate in a patronising tone, that hurt Meg's pride, and made her work seem not only more distasteful, but degrading.

"Did the German song suit, Miss March?" inquired Mr. Brooke, breaking an awkward pause.

"Oh yes; it was very sweet, and I'm much obliged to whoever translated it for me"; and Meg's downcast face brightened as she spoke.

"Don't you read German?" asked Miss Kate, with a look of surprise.

"Not very well. My father, who taught me, is away, and I don't get on very fast alone, for I've no one to correct my pronunciation."

"Try a little now; here is Schiller's *Mary Stuart*, and a tutor who loves to teach," and Mr. Brooke laid his book on her lap, with an inviting smile.

"It's so hard, I'm afraid to try," said Meg, grateful, but bashful in the presence of the accomplished young lady beside her.

"I'll read a bit to encourage you"; and Miss Kate read one of the most beautiful passages in a perfectly correct but perfectly expressionless manner.

Mr. Brooke made no comment as she returned the book to Meg, who said innocently:

"I thought it was poetry."

"Some of it is. Try this passage."

There was a queer smile about Mr. Brooke's mouth as he opened at poor Mary's lament.

Meg, obediently following the long grass blade which her new tutor used to point with, read slowly and timidly, unconsciously making poetry of the hard words by the soft intonation of her musical voice. Down the page went the green guide, and presently forgetting her listener in the beauty of the sad scene Meg read as if alone, giving a little touch of tragedy to the words of the unhappy queen. If she had seen the brown eyes then, she would have stopped short; but she never looked up, and the lesson was not spoiled for her.

"Very well indeed" said Mr. Brooke, as she paused, quite ignoring her many mistakes, and looking as if he did, indeed, "love to teach".

Miss Kate put up her glass, and having taken a survey of the little tableau before her, shut her sketch-book, saying, with condescension:

"You've a nice accent, and in time will be a clever reader. I advise you to learn, for German is a valuable accomplishment to teachers. I must look after Grace, she is romping"; and Miss Kate strolled away adding to herself, with a shrug, "I didn't come to chaperone a governess, though she *is* young and pretty. What odd people these Yankees are; I'm afraid Laurie will be quite spoilt among them."

"I forgot that English people rather turn up their noses at governesses, and don't treat them as we do," said Meg, looking after the retreating figure with an annoyed expression.

"Tutors, also, have rather a hard time of it there, as I know to my sorrow. There's no place like America for us workers, Miss Margaret"; and Mr. Brooke looked so contented and cheerful, that Meg was ashamed to lament her hard lot. "I'm glad I live in it, then. I don't like my work, but I get a good deal of satisfaction out of it after all, so I won't complain; I only wish I liked teaching as you do."

"I think you would if you had Laurie for a pupil. I shall be very sorry to lose him next year," said Mr. Brooke, busily punching holes in the turf.

"Going to college, I suppose?" Meg's lips asked that question, but her eyes added, "And what becomes of you?"

"Yes; it's high time he went, for he is ready; and as soon as he is off I shall turn soldier. I am needed."

"I am glad of that!" exclaimed Meg. "I should think every young man would want to go; though it is hard for the mothers and sisters who stay at home," she added, sorrowfully.

"I have neither, and very few friends, to care whether I live or die," said Mr. Brooke, rather bitterly, as he absently put the dead rose in the hole he had made and covered it up, like a little grave.

"Laurie and his grandfather would care a great deal, and we should all be very sorry to have any harm happen to you," said Meg, heartily.

"Thank you; that sounds pleasant," began Mr. Brooke, looking cheerful again; but before he could finish his speech Ned, mounted on the old horse, came lumbering up to display his equestrian skill before the young ladies, and there was no more quiet that day.

"Don't you love to ride?" asked Grace of Amy, as they stood resting, after a race round the field with the others, led by Ned.

"I dote upon it; my sister Meg used to ride when Papa was rich but we don't keep any horses now, except Ellen Tree," added Amy, laughing.

"Tell me about Ellen Tree; is it a donkey?" asked Grace, curiously.

"Why, you see, Jo is crazy about horses, and so am *I*, but we've only got an old side-saddle, and no horse. But in our garden is an apple-tree, that has a nice low branch; so Jo put the saddle on it, fixed some reins on the part that turns up, and we bounce away on Ellen Tree whenever we like."

"How funny!" laughed Grace. "I have a pony at home, and ride nearly every day in the park, with Fred and Kate; it's very nice, for my friends go too, and the Row is full of ladies and gentlemen."

"Dear, how charming! I hope I shall go abroad some day; but I'd rather go to Rome than the Row," said Amy, who had not the remotest idea what the Row was, and wouldn't have asked for the world.

Frank, sitting just behind the little girls, heard what they were saying, and pushed his crutch away from him with an impatient gesture, as he watched the active lads going through all sorts of comical gymnastics. Beth, who was collecting the scattered Author-cards, looked up, and said, in her shy yet friendly way:

"I'm afraid you are tired; can I do anything for you?"

"Talk to me, please; it's dull, sitting by myself," answered Frank, who had evidently been used to being made much of at home.

If he had asked her to deliver a Latin oration, it would not have seemed a more impossible task to bashful Beth; but there was no place to run to, no Jo to hide behind now, and the poor boy looked so wistfully at her, that she bravely resolved to try.

"What do you like to talk about?" she asked, fumbling over the cards, and dropping half as she tried to tie them up.

"Well, I like to hear about cricket and boating and hunting," said Frank, who had not yet learnt to suit his amusements to his strength.

"My heart! what shall I do? I don't know anything about them," thought Beth; and, forgetting the boy's misfortune in her flurry, she said, hoping to make him talk, "I never saw any hunting, but I suppose you know all about it."

"I did once; but I can never hunt again, for I got hurt leaping a confounded five-barred gate; so there are no more horses and hounds for me," said Frank, with a sigh that made Beth hate herself for her innocent blunder.

"Your deer are much prettier than our ugly buffaloes," she said, turning to the prairies for help, and feeling glad that she had read one of the boy's books in which Jo delighted.

Buffaloes proved soothing and satisfactory; and, in her eagerness to amuse another, Beth forgot herself, and was quite unconscious of her sisters' surprise and delight at the unusual spectacle of Beth talking away to one of the dreadful boys, against whom she had begged protection.

"Bless her heart! She pities him, so she is good to him," said Jo, beaming at her from the croquet ground.

"I always said she was a little saint," added Meg, as if there could be no further doubt about it.

"I haven't heard Frank laugh so much for ever so long," said Grace to Amy, as they sat discussing dolls, and making tea-sets out of the acorn-cups.

"My sister Beth is a very *fastidious* girl when she likes to be," said Amy, well pleased at Beth's success. She meant "fascinating", but as Grace didn't know the exact meaning of either word "fastidious" sounded well, and made a good impression. An impromptu circus, fox and geese, and an amicable game of croquet finished the afternoon. At sunset the tent was struck, hampers packed, wickets pulled up, boats loaded, and the whole party floated down the river, singing at the tops of their voices. Ned, getting sentimental, warbled a serenade with the pensive refrain:

"Alone, alone, ah! woe, alone,"

and at the lines:

"We each are young, we each have a heart,
Oh, why should we thus stand coldly apart,"

he looked at Meg with such a lackadaisical expression that she laughed outright and spoilt his song.

"How can you be so cruel to me?" he whispered, under cover of a lively chorus. "You've kept close to that starched-up English woman all day, and now you snub me."

"I didn't mean to; but you looked so funny I really couldn't help it," replied Meg, passing over the first part of his reproach; for it was quite true that she *had* shunned him, remembering the Moffat party and the talk after it.

Ned was offended, and turned to Sallie for consolation, saying to her, rather pettishly, "There isn't a bit of flirt in that girl, is there?"

"Not a particle; but she's a dear," returned Sallie, defending her friend, even while confessing her shortcomings.

"She's not a stricken deer, anyway," said Ned, trying to be witty, and succeeding as well as very young gentlemen usually do. On the lawn, where it had gathered, the little party separated, with cordial good-nights and good-byes, for the Vaughns were going to Canada. As the four sisters went home through the garden, Miss Kate looked after them, saying, without the patronising tone in her voice, "In spite of their demonstrative manners, American girls are very nice when one knows them."

"I quite agree with you," said Mr. Brooke.

CHAPTER 13

CASTLES IN THE AIR

Laurie lay luxuriously swinging to and fro in his hammock one warm September afternoon, wondering what his neighbours were about, but too lazy to go and find out. He was in one of his moods; for the day had been both unprofitable and unsatisfactory, and he was wishing he could live it over again. The hot weather made him indolent, and he had shirked his studies, tried Mr. Brooke's patience to the utmost, displeased his grandfather by practising half the afternoon, frightened the maid-servants half out of their wits by mischievously hinting that one of his dogs was going mad, and, after high words with the stableman about some fancied neglect of his horse, he had flung himself into his hammock, to fume over the stupidity of the world in general, till the peace of the lovely day quieted him in spite of himself. Staring up into the green gloom of the horse-chestnut trees above him, he dreamed dreams of all sorts, and was just imagining himself tossing on the ocean, in a voyage round the world, when the sound of voices brought him ashore in a flash. Peeping through the meshes of his hammock, he saw the Marches coming out, as if bound on some expedition.

"What in the world are those girls about now?" thought Laurie, opening his sleepy eyes to take a good look, for there was something rather peculiar in the appearance of his neighbours. Each wore a large, flapping hat, a brown linen pouch slung over one shoulder, and carried a long staff. Meg had a cushion, Jo a book, Beth a basket, and Amy a portfolio. All walked quietly through the garden, out at the little back gate, and began to climb the hill that lay between the house and the river.

"Well, that's cool!" said Laurie to himself, "to have a picnic and never ask me. They can't be going in the boat, for they haven't got the key. Perhaps they forgot it; I'll take it to them, and see what's going on."

Though possessed of half a dozen hats, it took him some time to find one; then there was a hunt for the key, which was at last discovered in his pocket; so that the girls were quite out of sight when he leaped the fence and ran after them. Taking the shortest way to the boathouse, he waited for them to appear: but no one came, and he went up the hill to take an observation. A group of pines covered one part of it, and from the heart of this green spot came a clearer sound than the soft sigh of the pines or the drowsy chirp of the crickets.

"Here's a landscape!" thought Laurie, peeping through the bushes, and looking wide awake and good-natured already.

It *was* rather a pretty little picture; for the sisters sat together in the shady nook, with sun and shadow flickering over them, the aromatic wind lifting their hair and cooling their hot cheeks, and all the little wood-people going on with their affairs, as if these were no strangers, but old friends. Meg sat upon her cushion, sewing daintily with her white hands, and looking as fresh and as sweet as a rose, in her pink dress among the green. Beth was sorting the cones that lay thick under the hemlock near by, for she made pretty things of them. Amy was sketching a group of ferns, and Jo was knitting as she read aloud. A shadow passed over the boy's face as he watched them, feeling that he ought to go away, because uninvited; yet lingering, because home seemed very lonely, and this quiet party in the woods most attractive to his restless spirit. He stood so still that a squirrel, busy with its harvesting, ran down a pine close beside him, saw him suddenly and skipped back, scolding so shrilly that Beth looked up, espied the wistful face behind the birches, and beckoned with a reassuring smile.

"May I come in, please? or shall I be a bother?" he asked, advancing slowly.

Meg lifted her eyebrows, but Jo scowled at her defiantly, and said at once, "Of course you may. We should have asked you before, only we thought you wouldn't care for such a girl's game as this."

"I always liked your games; but if Meg doesn't want me, I'll go away."

"I've no objection, if you do something; it's against the rules to be idle here," replied Meg, gravely but graciously.

"Much obliged; I'll do anything if you'll let me stop a bit, for it's as dull as the Desert of Sahara down there. Shall I sew, read, cone, draw, or do all at once? Bring on your bears; I'm ready," and Laurie sat down, with a submissive expression delightful to behold.

"Finish this story while I set my heel," said Jo, handing him the book.

"Yes'm," was the meek answer, as he began, doing his best to prove his gratitude for the favour of an admission into the "Busy Bee Society".

The story was not a long one, and, when it was finished, he ventured to ask a few questions, as a reward of merit.

"Please, ma'am, could I inquire if this highly instructive and charming institution is a new one?"

"Would you tell him?" asked Meg of her sisters.

"He'll laugh," said Amy, warningly.

"Who cares?" said Jo.

"I guess he'll like it," added Beth.

"Of course I shall! I give you my word I won't laugh. Tell away, Jo, and don't be afraid."

"The idea of being afraid of you! Well, you see we used to play *Pilgrim's Progress*, and we have been going on with it in earnest all winter and summer."

"Yes, I know," said Laurie, nodding wisely.

"Who told you?" demanded Jo.

"Spirits."

"No, I did; I wanted to amuse him one night when you were all away, and he was rather dismal. He did like it, so don't scold, Jo," said Beth, meekly.

"You can't keep a secret. Never mind; it saves trouble now."

"Go on! Go on, please," said Laurie, as Jo became absorbed in her work, looking a trifle displeased.

"Oh, didn't she tell you about this new plan of ours? Well, we have tried not to waste our holiday, but each has had a task, and worked at it with a will. The vacation is nearly over, the stints are all done, and we are ever so glad that we didn't dawdle."

"Yes, I should think so"; and Laurie thought regretfully of his own idle ways.

"Mother likes to have us out of doors as much as possible; so we bring our work here, and have nice times. For the fun of it we bring our things in these bags, wear the old hats, use poles to climb the hill, and play pilgrims, as we used to do years ago. We call this hill the 'Delectable Mountain', for we can look far away and see the country where we hope to live some time."

Jo pointed, and Laurie sat up to examine; for through an opening in the wood one could look across the wide blue river, the meadows on the other side, far over the outskirts of the great city, to the green hills that rose to meet the sky. The sun was low, and the heavens glowed with the splendour of an autumn sunset.

Gold and purple clouds lay on the hilltops; and rising high into the ruddy light were silvery white peaks, that shone like the airy spires of some Celestial City.

"How beautiful that is!" said Laurie, softly, for he was quick to see and feel beauty of any kind.

"It's often so; and we like to watch it, for it is never the same, but always splendid," replied Amy, wishing she could paint it.

"Jo talks about the country where we hope to live some time—the real country, she means, with pigs and chickens and haymaking. It would be nice, but I wish the beautiful country up there was real, and we could ever go to it," said Beth, musingly.

"There is a lovelier country even than that, where we *shall* go by and by, when we are good enough," answered Meg, with her sweet voice.

"It seems so long to wait, so hard to do; I want to fly away at once, as those swallows fly, and go in at that splendid gate."

"You'll get there, Beth, sooner or later; no fear of that," said Jo; "I'm the one that will have to fight and work, and climb and wait, and maybe never get in after all."

"You'll have me for company, if that's any comfort. I shall have to do a deal of travelling before I come in sight of your Celestial City. If I arrive late, you'll say a good word for me, won't you, Beth?"

Something in the boy's face troubled his little friend; but she said cheerfully, with her quiet eyes on the changing clouds, "If people really want to go, and really try all their lives, I think they will get in; for I don't believe there are any locks on that door, or any guards at the gate. I always imagine it is as it is in the picture, where the shining ones stretch out their hands to welcome poor Christian, as he comes up from the river."

"Wouldn't it be fun if all the castles in the air which we make could come true, and we could live in them?" said Jo, after a little pause.

"I've made such quantities it would be hard to choose which I'd have," said Laurie, lying flat, and throwing cones at the squirrel who had betrayed him.

"You'd have to take your favourite one. What is it?" asked Meg.

"If I tell mine, will you tell yours?"

"Yes, if the girls will too."

"We will. Now, Laurie."

"After I'd seen as much of the world as I want to, I'd like to settle in Germany, and have just as much music as I choose. I'm to be a famous musician myself, and all creation is to rush to hear me; and I'm never to be bothered about money or business, but just enjoy myself, and live for what I like. That's my favourite castle. What's yours, Meg?"

Margaret seemed to find it a little hard to tell hers, and waved a brake before her face, as if to disperse imaginary gnats, while she said slowly, "I should like a lovely house, full of all sorts of luxurious things—nice food, pretty clothes, handsome furniture, pleasant people, and heaps of money. I am to be mistress of it, and manage it as I like, with plenty of servants, so I never need work a bit. How I should enjoy it! for I wouldn't be idle, but do good and make everyone love me dearly."

"Wouldn't you have a master for your castle in the air?" asked Laurie, slyly.

"I said 'pleasant people', you know"; and Meg carefully tied up her shoe as she spoke, so that no one saw her face.

"Why don't you say you'd have a splendid, wise, good husband, and some angelic little children? You know your castle wouldn't be perfect without," said blunt Jo, who had no tender fancies yet, and rather scorned romance, except in books.

"You'd have nothing but horses, inkstands, and novels in yours," answered Meg, petulantly.

"Wouldn't I, though? I'd have a stable full of Arabian steeds, rooms piled with books, and I'd write out of a magic inkstand, so that my works should be as famous as Laurie's music. I want to do something splendid before I go into my castle—something heroic or wonderful, that won't be forgotten after I'm dead. I don't know what, but I'm on the watch for it, and mean to astonish you all some day. I think I shall write books, and get rich and famous: that would suit me, so that is *my* favourite dream."

"Mine is to stay at home safe with Father and Mother, and help take care of the family," said Beth, contentedly.

"Don't you wish for anything else?" asked Laurie.

"Since I had my little piano, I am perfectly satisfied. I only wish we may all keep well and be together; nothing else."

"I have ever so many wishes; but the pet one is to be an artist, and go to Rome, and do fine pictures, and be the best artist in the whole world," was Amy's modest desire.

"We're an ambitious set, aren't we? Every one of us, but Beth, wants to be rich and famous, and gorgeous in every respect. I do wonder if any of us will ever get our wishes," said Laurie, chewing grass, like a meditative calf.

"I've got the key to my castle in the air; but whether I can unlock the door remains to be seen," observed Jo, mysteriously.

"I've got the key to mine, but I'm not allowed to try it. Hang college!" muttered Laurie, with an impatient sigh.

"Here's mine!" and Amy waved her pencil.

"I haven't got any," said Meg, forlornly.

"Yes, you have," said Laurie at once.

"Where?"

"In your face."

"Nonsense; that's of no use."

"Wait and see if it doesn't bring you something worth having," replied the boy, laughing at the thought of a charming little secret which he fancied he knew.

Meg coloured behind the brake, but asked no questions, and looked across the river with the same expectant expression which Mr. Brooke had worn when he told the story of the knight.

"If we are all alive ten years hence, let's meet, and see how many of us have got our wishes, or how much nearer we are then than now," said Jo, always ready with a plan.

"Bless me! how old I shall be—twenty-seven!" exclaimed Meg, who felt grown up already, having just reached seventeen.

"You and I will be twenty-six, Teddy, Beth twenty-four, and Amy twenty-two. What a venerable party!" said Jo.

"I hope I shall have done something to be proud of by that time; but I'm such a lazy dog, I'm afraid I shall 'dawdle', Jo."

"You need a motive, Mother says; and when you get it she is sure you'll work splendidly."

"Is she? By Jupiter! I will, if I only get the chance!" cried Laurie, sitting up with sudden energy. "I ought to be satisfied to please Grandfather, and I do try, but it's working against the grain, you see, and comes hard. He wants me to be an India merchant, as he was, and I'd rather be shot. I hate tea and silk and spices, and every sort of rubbish his old ships bring, and I don't care how soon they go to the bottom when I own them. Going to college ought to satisfy him, for if I give him four years he ought to let me off from business; but he's set, and I've got to do just as he did, unless I break away and please myself, as my father did. If there was anyone left to stay with the old gentleman, I'd do it tomorrow."

Laurie spoke excitedly, and looked ready to carry his threat into execution on the slightest provocation; for he was growing up very fast, and, in spite of his indolent ways, had a young man's hatred of subjection, a young man's restless longing to try the world for himself.

"I advise you to sail away in one of your ships, and never come home again till you have tried your own way," said Jo, whose imagination was fired by the thought of such a daring exploit, and whose sympathy was excited by what she called "Teddy's wrongs".

"That's not right, Jo; you mustn't talk in that way, and Laurie mustn't take your bad advice."

"You should do just what your grandfather wishes, my dear boy," said Meg, in her most maternal tone. "Do your best at college, and when he sees that you try to please him, I'm sure he won't be hard or unjust to you. As you say, there is no one else to stay with and love him, and you'd never forgive yourself if you left him without his permission. Don't be dismal or fret, but do your duty; and you'll get your reward, as good Mr. Brooke has, by being respected and loved."

"What do you know about him?" asked Laurie, grateful for the good advice, but objecting to the lecture, and glad to turn the conversation from himself, after his unusual outbreak.

"Only what your grandpa told us about him—how he took good care of his own mother till she died, and wouldn't go abroad as tutor to some nice person, because he wouldn't leave her; and how he provides now for an old woman who nursed his mother; and never tells anyone, but is just as generous and patient and good as he can be."

"So he is, dear old fellow!" said Laurie, heartily, as Meg paused, looking flushed and earnest with her story. "It's like Grandpa to find out all about him without letting him know, and to tell all his goodness to others, so that they might like him. Brooke couldn't understand why your mother was so kind to him, asking him over with me, and treating him in her beautiful, friendly way. He thought she was just perfect, and talked about it for days and days, and went on about you all in flaming style. If ever I get my wish, you see what I'll do for Brooke."

"Begin to do something now, by not plaguing his life out," said Meg, sharply.

"How do you know I do, Miss?"

"I can always tell by his face when he goes away. If you have been good, he looks satisfied and walks briskly; if you have plagued him, he's sober and walks slowly, as if he wanted to go back and do his work better."

"Well, I like that! So you keep an account of my good and bad marks in Brooke's face, do you! I see him bow and smile as he passes your window, but I didn't know you'd got up a telegraph."

"We haven't; don't be angry, and oh, don't tell him I said anything! It was only to show that I cared how you get on, and what is said here is said in confidence, you know," cried Meg, much alarmed at the thought of what might follow from her careless speech.

"*I* don't tell tales," replied Laurie, with his "high and mighty" air, as Jo called a certain expression which he occasionally wore, "only, if Brooke is going to be a barometer, I must mind and have fair weather for him to report."

"Please don't be offended. I didn't mean to preach or tell tales or be silly; I only thought Jo was encouraging you in a feeling which you'd be sorry for by and by. You are so kind to us, we feel as if you were our brother, and say just what we think. Forgive me. I meant it kindly." And Meg offered her hand with a gesture both affectionate and timid.

Ashamed of his momentary pique, Laurie squeezed the kind little hand, and said frankly, "I'm the one to be forgiven; I'm cross, and have been out of sorts all day. I like to have you tell me my faults and be sisterly, so don't mind if I am grumpy sometimes; I thank you all the same."

Bent on showing that he was not offended, he made himself as agreeable as possible—wound cotton for Meg, recited poetry to please Jo, shook down cones for Beth, and helped Amy with her ferns, proving himself a fit person to belong to the "Busy Bee Society". In the midst of an animated discussion on the domestic habits of turtles (one of those amiable creatures having strolled up from the river), the faint sound of a bell warned them that Hannah had put the tea "to draw", and they would just have time to get home to supper.

"May I come again?" asked Laurie.

"Yes, if you are good, and love your book, as the boys in the primer are told to do," said Meg, smiling.

"I'll try."

"Then you may come, and I'll teach you to knit as the Scotchmen do; there's a demand for socks just now," added Jo, waving hers, like a big, blue worsted banner, as they parted at the gate.

That night, when Beth played to Mr. Laurence in the twilight, Laurie, standing in the shadow of the curtain, listened to the little

David, whose simple music always quieted his moody spirit, and watched the old man, who sat with his grey head on his hand, thinking tender thoughts of the dead child he had loved so much. Remembering the conversation of the afternoon, the boy said to himself, with the resolve to make the sacrifice cheerfully, "I'll let my castle go, and stay with the dear old gentleman while he needs me, for I am all he has."

CHAPTER 14

SECRETS

Jo was very busy in the garret, for the October days began to grow chilly, and the afternoons were short. For two or three hours the sun lay warmly in the high window, showing Jo seated on the old sofa, writing busily, with her papers spread out upon a trunk before her, while Scrabble, the pet rat, promenaded the beams overhead, accompanied by his young fellow, who was evidently very proud of his whiskers. Quite absorbed in her work, Jo scribbled away till the last page was filled, when she signed her name with a flourish, and threw down her pen, exclaiming:

"There, I've done my best! If this won't suit, I shall have to wait till I can do better."

Lying back on the sofa, she read the manuscript carefully through, making dashes here and there, and putting in many exclamation points, which looked like little balloons; then she tied it up with a smart, red ribbon, and sat a minute looking at it with a sober, wistful expression, which plainly showed how earnest her work had been. Jo's desk up here was an old tin kitchen, which hung against the wall. In it she kept her papers and a few books, safely shut away from Scrabble, who, being likewise of a literary turn, was fond of making a circulating library of such books as were left in his way, by eating the leaves. From this tin receptacle, Jo produced another manuscript; and, putting both in her pocket, crept quietly downstairs, leaving her friends to nibble her pens and taste her ink.

She put on her hat and jacket as noiselessly as possible, and, going to the back entry window, got out upon the roof of a low porch, swung herself down to the grassy bank, and took a roundabout way to the road. Once there, she composed herself, hailed a passing omnibus, and rolled away to town, looking very merry and mysterious.

If anyone had been watching her he would have thought her movements decidedly peculiar; for, on alighting, she went off at a great pace till she reached a certain number in a certain busy street; having found the place with some difficulty, she went into the doorway, looked up the dirty stairs, and, after standing stock still a minute, suddenly dived into the street, and walked away as rapidly as she came. This manoeuvre she repeated several times, to the great amusement of a black-eyed young gentleman lounging in the window of the building opposite. On returning for the third time, Jo gave herself a shake, pulled her hat over her eyes, and walked up the stairs, looking as if she were going to have all her teeth out.

There was a dentist's sign, among others which adorned the entrance, and, after staring a minute at the pair of artificial jaws which slowly opened and shut to draw attention to a fine set of teeth, the young gentleman put on his coat, took his hat, and went down to post himself in the opposite doorway, saying, with a smile and a shiver:

"It's like her to come alone, but if she has a bad time she'll need someone to help her home."

In ten minutes Jo came running downstairs with a very red face, and the general appearance of a person who had just passed through a trying ordeal of some sort.

When she saw the young gentleman she looked anything but pleased, and passed him with a nod; but he followed, asking with an air of sympathy:

"Did you have a bad time?"

"Not very."

'You got through quickly."

"Yes, thank goodness!"

"Why did you go alone?"

"Didn't want anyone to know."

"You're the oddest fellow I ever saw. How many did you have out?"

Jo looked at her friend as if she did not understand him; then began to laugh, as if mightily amused at something.

"There are two which I want to have come out, but I must wait a week."

"What are you laughing at? You are up to some mischief, Jo," said Laurie, looking mystified.

"So are you. What were you doing, sir, up in that billiard saloon?"

"Begging your pardon, ma'am, it wasn't a billiard saloon, but a gymnasium, and I was taking a lesson in fencing."

"I'm glad of that."

"Why?"

"You can teach me, and then when we play *Hamlet*, you can be Laertes, and we'll make a fine thing of the fencing scene."

Laurie burst out with a hearty boy's laugh, which made several passers-by smile in spite of themselves.

"I'll teach you, whether we play *Hamlet* or not; it's grand fun, and will straighten you up capitally. But I don't believe that was your reason for saying 'I'm glad', in that decided way; was it, now?"

"No, I was glad that you were not in the saloon, because I hope you never go to such places. Do you?"

"Not often."

"I wish you wouldn't."

"It's no harm, Jo. I have billiards at home, but it's no fun unless you have good players, so, as I'm fond of it, I come sometimes and have a game with Ned Moffat or some of the other fellows."

"Oh dear, I'm so sorry, for you'll get to liking it better and better, and will waste time and money, and grow like those dreadful boys. I did hope you'd stay respectable, and be a satisfaction to your friends," said Jo, shaking her head.

"Can't a fellow take a little innocent amusement now and then without losing his respectability?" asked Laurie, looking nettled.

"That depends upon how and where he takes it. I don't like Ned and his set, and wish you'd keep out of it. Mother won't let us have him at our house, though he wants to come; and if you grow like him she won't be willing to have us frolic together as we do now."

"Won't she?" asked Laurie, anxiously.

"No, she can't bear fashionable young men, and she'd shut us all up in bandboxes rather than have us associate with them."

"Well, she needn't get out her bandboxes yet; I'm not a fashionable party, and don't mean to be; but I do like harmless larks now and then, don't you?"

"Yes, nobody minds them, so lark away, but don't get wild, will you? or there will be an end of all our good times."

"I'll be a double-distilled saint."

"I can't bear saints; just be a simple, honest, respectable boy, and we'll never desert you. I don't know what I *should* do if you acted like Mr. King's son; he had plenty of money, but didn't know how to spend it, and got tipsy, and gambled, and ran away, and forged his father's name, I believe, and was altogether horrid."

"You think I'm likely to do the same? Much obliged."

"No, I don't—oh, *dear*, no!—but I hear people talking about money being such a temptation, and I sometimes wish you were poor; I shouldn't worry then."

"Do you worry about me, Jo?"

"A little, when you look moody or discontented, as you sometimes do; for you've got such a strong will, if you once get started wrong, I'm afraid it would be hard to stop you."

Laurie walked in silence for a few minutes, and Jo watched him, wishing she had held her tongue, for his eyes looked angry though his lips still smiled as if at her warnings.

"Are you going to deliver lectures all the way home?" he asked presently.

"Of course not; why?"

"Because, if you are, I'll take a bus; if you are not, I'd like to walk with you, and tell you something very interesting."

"I won't preach any more, and I'd like to hear the news immensely."

"Very well, then; come on. It's a secret, and if I tell you, you must tell me yours."

"I haven't got any," began Jo, but stopped suddenly, remembering that she had.

"You know you have—you can't hide anything; so up and 'fess, or I won't tell," cried Laurie.

"Is your secret a nice one?"

"Oh, isn't it! all about people you know, and such fun! You ought to hear it, and I've been aching to tell it this long time. Come, you begin."

"You'll not say anything about it at home, will you?"

"Not a word."

"And you won't tease me in private?"

"I never tease."

"Yes, you do; you get everything you want out of people. I don't know how you do it, but you are a born wheedler."

"Thank you; fire away."

"Well, I've left two stories with a newspaper man, and he's to give his answer next week," whispered Jo, in her confidant's ear.

"Hurrah for Miss March, the celebrated American authoress!" cried Laurie, throwing up his hat and catching it again, to the great delight of two ducks, four cats, five hens, and half a dozen Irish children; for they were out of the city now.

"Hush! It won't come to anything, I dare say; but I couldn't rest till I had tried, and I said nothing about it, because I didn't want anyone else to be disappointed."

"It won't fail. Why, Jo, your stories are works of Shakespeare, compared to half the rubbish that is published every day. Won't it be fun to see them in print; and shan't we feel proud of our authoress?"

Jo's eyes sparkled, for it is always pleasant to be believed in; and a friend's praise is always sweeter than a dozen newspaper puffs.

"Where's *your* secret? Play fair, Teddy, or I'll never believe you again," she said, trying to extinguish the brilliant hopes that blazed up at a word of encouragement.

"I may get into a scrape for telling; but I didn't promise not to, so I will, for I never feel easy in my mind till I've told you any plummy bit of news I get. I know where Meg's glove is."

"Is that all?" said Jo, looking disappointed, as Laurie nodded and twinkled, with a face full of mysterious intelligence. "It's quite enough for the present, as you'll agree when I tell you where it is."

"Tell then."

Laurie bent, and whispered three words in Jo's ear, which produced a comical change. She stood and stared at him for a minute, looking both surprised and displeased, then walked on, saying sharply, "How do you know?"

"Saw it."

"Where?"

"Pocket."

"All this time?"

"Yes; isn't that romantic?"

"No, it's horrid."

"Don't you like it?"

"Of course I don't. It's ridiculous; it won't be allowed. My patience! what would Meg say?"

"You are not to tell anyone; mind that."

"I didn't promise."

"That was understood, and I trusted you."

"Well, I won't for the present, anyway; but I'm disgusted, and wish you hadn't told me."

"I thought you'd be pleased."

"At the idea of anybody coming to take Meg away? No, thank you."

"You'll feel better about it when somebody comes to take you away."

"I'd like to see anyone try it," cried Jo, fiercely.

"So should I!" and Laurie chuckled at the idea.

"I don't think secrets agree with me; I feel rumpled up in my mind since you told me that," said Jo, rather ungratefully.

"Race down this hill with me, and you'll be all right," suggested Laurie.

No one was in sight; the smooth road sloped invitingly before her; and finding the temptation irresistible, Jo darted away, soon leaving hat and comb behind her, and scattering hairpins as she ran. Laurie reached the goal first, and was quite satisfied with the success of his treatment; for his Atalanta came panting up, with flying hair, bright eyes, ruddy cheeks, and no signs of dissatisfaction in her face.

"I wish I was a horse; then I could run for miles in this splendid air, and not lose my breath. It was capital; but see what a guy it's made me. Go, pick up my things, like a cherub as you are," said Jo, dropping down under a maple-tree which was carpeting the bank with crimson leaves.

Laurie leisurely departed to recover the lost property, and Jo bundled up her braids, hoping no one would pass by till she was tidy again. But someone did pass by, and who should it be but Meg, looking particularly ladylike in her state and festival suit, for she had been making calls.

"What in the world are you doing here?" she asked, regarding her dishevelled sister with well-bred surprise.

"Getting leaves," meekly answered Jo, sorting the rosy handful she had just swept up.

"And hairpins," added Laurie, throwing half a dozen into Jo's lap. "They grow on this road, Meg; so do combs and brown straw hats."

"You have been running, Jo; how could you? When *will* you be stopping such romping ways?" said Meg, reprovingly, as she settled her cuffs, and smoothed her hair, with which the wind had taken liberties.

"Never till I'm stiff and old, and have to use a crutch. Don't try to make me grow up before my time, Meg; it's hard enough to have you change all of a sudden; let me be a little girl as long as I can."

As she spoke, Jo bent over the leaves to hide the trembling of her lips; for lately she had felt that Margaret was fast getting to be a woman, and Laurie's secret made her dread the separation which must surely come some time, and now seemed very near. He saw the trouble in her face, and drew Meg's attention from it by asking quickly, "Where have you been calling all so fine?"

"At the Gardiners', and Sallie has been telling me all about Belle Moffat's wedding. It was very splendid, and they have gone to spend the winter in Paris. Just think how delightful that must be!"

"Do you envy her, Meg?" said Laurie.

"I'm afraid I do."

"I'm glad of it," muttered Jo, tying on her hat with a jerk.

"Why?" asked Meg, looking surprised.

"Because if you care much about riches, you will never go and marry a poor man," said Jo, frowning at Laurie, who was mutely warning her to mind what she said.

"I shall never '*go* and marry' anyone," observed Meg, walking on with great dignity, while the others followed, laughing, whispering, skipping stones, and "behaving like children", as Meg said to herself, though she might have been tempted to join them if she had not had her best dress on.

For a week or two, Jo behaved so queerly that her sisters were quite bewildered. She rushed to the door when the postman rang; was rude to Mr. Brooke whenever they met; would sit looking at Meg with a woebegone face, occasionally jumping up to shake, and then to kiss her, in a very mysterious manner; Laurie and she were always making signs to one another and talking about "Spread Eagles" till the girls declared they had both lost their wits. On the second Saturday after Jo got out of the window, Meg, as she sat sewing at her window, was scandalized by the sight of Laurie chasing Jo all over the garden, and finally capturing her in Amy's bower. What went on there, Meg could not see; but shrieks of laughter were heard, followed by the murmur of voices and a great flapping of newspapers.

"What shall we do with that girl? She never *will* behave like a young lady," sighed Meg, as she watched the race with a disapproving face.

"I hope she won't; she is so funny and dear as she is," said Beth, who had never betrayed that she was a little hurt at Jo's having secrets with anyone but her.

"It's very trying, but we can never make her *commy la fo*," added Amy, who sat making some new frills for herself, with her curls tied up in a very becoming way—two agreeable things, which made her feel unusually elegant and ladylike.

In a few minutes Jo bounced in, laid herself on the sofa, and affected to read.

"Have you anything interesting there?" asked Meg, with condescension.

"Nothing but a story; won't amount to much, I guess," returned Jo, carefully keeping the name of the paper out of sight.

"You'd better read it aloud; that will amuse us and keep you out of mischief," said Amy, in her most grown-up tone.

"What's the name?" asked Beth, wondering why Jo kept her face behind the sheet.

"The Rival Painters."

"That sounds well; read it," said Meg.

With a loud "Hem!" and a long breath, Jo began to read very fast. The girls listened with interest, for the tale was romantic, and somewhat pathetic, as most of the characters died in the end.

"I like that about the splendid picture," was Amy's approving remark, as Jo paused.

"I prefer the lovering part. Viola and Angelo are two of our favourite names; isn't that queer?" said Meg, wiping her eyes, for the "lovering part" was tragical.

"Who wrote it?" asked Beth, who had caught a glimpse of Jo's face.

The reader suddenly sat up, cast away the paper, displaying a flushed countenance, and, with a funny mixture of solemnity and excitement, replied in a loud voice, "Your sister."

"You?" cried Meg, dropping her work.

"It's very good," said Amy, critically.

"I knew it! I knew it! Oh, my Jo, I *am* so proud!" and Beth began to hug her sister, and exult over this splendid success.

Dear me, how delighted they all were, to be sure! how Meg wouldn't believe it till she saw the words "Miss Josephine March" actually printed in the paper; how graciously Amy criticised the artistic parts of the story, and offered hints for a sequel, which unfortunately couldn't be carried out, as the hero and heroine were dead; how Beth got excited, and skipped and sung with joy; how Hannah came in to exclaim "Sakes alive, well I never!" in great astonishment at "that Jo's doin's"; how proud Mrs. March was when she knew it; how Jo laughed, with tears in her eyes, as she declared she might as well be a peacock and done with it; and how the "Spread Eagle" might be said to flap his wings triumphantly over the House of March, as the paper passed from hand to hand.

"Tell us all about it." "When did it come?" "How much did you get for it?" "What *will* Father say?" "Won't Laurie laugh?" cried the family, all in one breath, as they clustered about Jo; for these foolish, affectionate people made a jubilee of every little household joy.

"Stop jabbering, girls, and I'll tell you everything," said Jo, wondering if Miss Burney felt any grander over her *Evelina*, than she did over her *Rival Painters*. Having told how she disposed of her tales, Jo added, "And when I went to get my answer, the man said he liked them both, but didn't pay beginners, only let them print in his paper, and noticed the stories. It was good practice, he said; and when the beginners improved, anyone would pay. So I let him have the two stories, and today this was sent to me, and Laurie caught me with it, and insisted on seeing it, so I let him; and he said it was good, and I shall write more, and he's going to get the next paid for, and I *am* so happy, for in time I may be able to support myself and help the girls."

Jo's breath gave out here; and, wrapping her head in the paper, she bedewed her little story with a few natural tears; for to be independent, and earn the praise of those she loved, were the dearest wishes of her heart, and this seemed to be the first step towards that happy end.

Chapter 15

A TELEGRAM

"November is the most disagreeable month in the whole year," said Margaret, standing at the window one dull afternoon, looking out at the frost-bitten garden.

"That's the reason I was born in it," observed Jo, pensively, quite unconscious of the blot on her nose.

"If something very pleasant should happen now, we should think it a delightful month," said Beth, who took a hopeful view of everything, even November.

"I dare say; but nothing pleasant ever *does* happen in this family," said Meg, who was out of sorts. "We go grubbing along day after day, without a bit of change, and very little fun. We might as well be in a treadmill."

"My patience, how blue we are!" cried Jo. "I don't much wonder, poor dear, for you see other girls having splendid times, while you grind, grind, year in and year out. Oh, don't I wish I could manage things for you as I do for my heroines! You're pretty enough and good enough already, so I'd have some rich relation leave you a fortune unexpectedly; then you'd dash out as an heiress, scorn everyone who has slighted you, go abroad and come home my Lady Something, in a blaze of splendour and elegance."

"People don't have fortunes left them in that style nowadays; men have to work, and women to marry for money. It's a dreadful, unjust world," said Meg, bitterly.

"Jo and I are going to make fortunes for you all; just wait ten years, and see if we don't," said Amy, who sat in a corner, making mud pies, as Hannah called her little clay models of birds, fruit, and faces.

"Can't wait, and I'm afraid I haven't much faith in ink and dirt, though I'm grateful for your good intentions."

Meg sighed, and turned to the frost-bitten garden again; Jo groaned, and leaned both elbows on the table, in a despondent attitude, but Amy patted away energetically; and Beth, who sat at the other window, said, smiling, "Two pleasant things are going to happen right away; Marmee is coming down the street, and Laurie is tramping through the garden as if he had something nice to tell."

In they both came, Mrs. March with her usual question, "Any letter from Father, girls?" and Laurie to say in his persuasive way, "Won't some of you come for a drive? I've been working away at mathematics till my head is in a muddle, and I'm going to freshen my wits by a brisk turn. It's a dull day, but the air isn't bad, and I'm going to take Brooke home, so it will be gay inside, if it isn't out. Come, Jo, you and Beth will go, won't you?"

"Of course we will."

"Much obliged, but I'm busy"; and Meg whisked out her work-basket, for she had agreed with her mother that it was best, for her at least, not to drive often with the young gentleman.

"We three will be ready in a minute," cried Amy, running away to wash her hands.

"Can I do anything for you, Madam Mother?" asked Laurie, leaning over Mrs. March's chair, with the affectionate look and tone he always gave her.

"No, thank you, except call at the office, if you'll be so kind, dear. It's our day for a letter, and the postman hasn't been. Father is as regular as the sun, but there's some delay on the way, perhaps."

A sharp ring interrupted her, and a minute after Hannah came in with a letter.

"It's one of them horrid telegraph things, mum," she said, handing it as if she was afraid it would explode and do some damage.

At the word "telegraph", Mrs. March snatched it, read the two lines it contained, and dropped back into her chair as white as if the little paper had sent a bullet to her heart. Laurie dashed downstairs for water, while Meg and Hannah supported her, and Jo read aloud, in a frightened voice:

"MRS. MARCH:
Your husband is very ill. Come at once.
S. HALE,
Blank Hospital, Washington."

How still the room was as they listened breathlessly, how strangely the day darkened outside, and how suddenly the whole world seemed to change, as the girls gathered about their mother, feeling as if all the happiness and support of their lives was about to be taken from them. Mrs. March was herself again directly; read the message over, and stretched out her arms to her daughters, saying, in a tone they never forgot, "I shall go at once, but it may be too late. Oh, children, children, help me to bear it!"

For several minutes there was nothing but the sound of sobbing in the room, mingled with broken words of comfort, tender assurances of help, and hopeful whispers that died away in tears. Poor Hannah was the first to recover, and with unconscious wisdom she set all the rest a good example; for, with her, work was the panacea for most afflictions.

"The Lord keep the dear man! I won't waste no time a cryin', but git your things ready right away, mum," she said, heartily, as she wiped her face on her apron, gave her mistress a warm shake of the hand with her own hard one, and went away, to work like three women in one.

"She's right; there's no time for tears now. Be calm, girls, and let me think."

They tried to be calm, poor things, as their mother sat up, looking pale, but steady, and put away her grief to think and plan for them.

"Where's Laurie?" she asked presently, when she had collected her thoughts, and decided on the first duties to be done.

"Here, ma'am. Oh, let me do something!" cried the boy, hurrying from the next room, whither he had withdrawn, feeling that their first sorrow was too sacred for even his friendly eyes to see.

"Send a telegram saying I will come at once. The next train goes early in the morning. I'll take that."

"What else? The horses are ready; I can go anywhere, do anything," he said, looking ready to fly to the ends of the earth.

"Leave a note at Aunt March's. Jo, give me that pen and paper."

Tearing off the blank side of one of her newly-copied pages, Jo drew the table before her mother, well knowing that money for the long, sad journey must be borrowed, and feeling as if she could do anything to add a little to the sum for her father.

"Now go, dear; but don't kill yourself driving at a desperate pace; there is no need of that."

Mrs. March's warning was evidently thrown away; for five minutes later Laurie tore by the window on his own fleet horse, riding as if for his life.

"Jo, run to the rooms and tell Mrs. King that I can't come. On the way get these things. I'll put them down; they'll be needed, and I must go prepared for nursing. Hospital stores are not always good. Beth, go and ask Mr. Laurence for a couple of bottles of old wine: I'm not too proud to beg for Father; he shall have the best of everything. Amy, tell Hannah to get down the black trunk; and Meg, come and help me find my things, for I'm half bewildered."

Writing, thinking, and directing, all at once, might well bewilder the poor lady, and Meg begged her to sit down quietly in her room for a little while, and let them work. Everyone scattered like leaves before a gust of wind; and the quiet, happy household was broken up as suddenly as if the paper had been an evil spell.

Mr. Laurence came hurrying back with Beth, bringing every comfort the kind old gentleman could think of for the invalid, and friendliest promises of protection for the girls during the mother's absence, which comforted her very much. There was nothing he didn't offer, from his own dressing-gown to himself as escort. But that last was impossible. Mrs. March would not hear of the old gentleman's undertaking the long journey; yet an expression of relief was visible when he spoke of it, for anxiety ill fits one for travelling. He saw the look, knit his heavy eyebrows, rubbed his hands, and marched abruptly away, saying he'd be back directly. No one had time to think of him again till, as Meg ran through the entry, with a pair of rubbers in one hand and a cup of tea in the other, she came suddenly upon Mr. Brooke.

"I'm very sorry to hear of this, Miss March," he said, in the kind, quiet tone which sounded pleasantly to her perturbed spirit. "I came to offer myself as escort to your mother. Mr. Laurence has commissions for me in Washington, and it will give me real satisfaction to be of service to her there."

Down dropped the rubbers, and the tea was very near following, as Meg put out her hand, with a face so full of gratitude, that Mr. Brooke would have felt repaid for a much greater sacrifice than the trifling one of time and comfort which he was about to make.

"How kind you all are! Mother will accept, I'm sure; and it will be such a relief to know that she has someone to take care of her. Thank you very, very much!"

Meg spoke earnestly, and forgot herself entirely, till something in the brown eyes looking down at her made her remember the cooling tea, and lead the way into the parlour, saying she would call her mother.

Everything was arranged by the time Laurie returned with a note from Aunt March enclosing the desired sum, and a few lines repeating what she had often said before—that she had always told them it was absurd for March to go into the army, always predicted that no good would come of it, and she hoped they would take her advice next time. Mrs. March put the note in the fire, the money in her purse, and went on with her preparations, with her lips folded tightly, in a way which Jo would have understood if she had been there.

The short afternoon wore away; all the other errands were done, and Meg and her mother busy at some necessary needlework, while Beth and Amy got tea, and Hannah finished her ironing with what she called a "slap and a bang", but still Jo did not come. They began to get anxious; and Laurie went off to find her, for no one ever knew what freak Jo might take into her head. He missed her, however, and she came walking in with a very queer expression of countenance, for there was a mixture of fun and fear, satisfaction and regret in it, which puzzled the family as much as did the roll of bills she laid before her mother, saying, with a little choke in her voice, "That's my contribution towards making Father comfortable, and bringing him home!"

"My dear, where did you get it? Twenty-five dollars? Jo, I hope you haven't done anything rash?"

"No, it's mine honestly; I didn't beg, borrow, or steal it. I earned it; and I don't think you'll blame me, for I only sold what was my own."

As she spoke, Jo took off her bonnet, and a general outcry arose, for all her abundant hair was cut short.

"Your hair! Your beautiful hair!" "Oh, Jo, how could you? Your one beauty." "My dear girl, there was no need of this." "She doesn't look like my Jo any more, but I love her dearly for it!"

As everyone exclaimed, and Beth hugged the cropped head tenderly, Jo assumed an indifferent air, which did not deceive anyone a particle, and said, rumpling up the brown bush, and trying to look as if she liked it, "It doesn't affect the fate of the nation, so don't wail, Beth. It will be good for my vanity; I was getting too proud of my wig. It will do my brains good to have that mop taken off; my head feels deliciously light and cool, and the barber said I could soon have a curly crop, which will be boyish, becoming, and easy to keep in order. I'm satisfied; so please take the money, and let's have supper."

"Tell me all about it, Jo. *I* am not quite satisfied, but I can't blame you, for I know how willingly you sacrificed your vanity, as you call it, to your love. But, my dear, it was not necessary, and I'm afraid you will regret it, one of these days," said Mrs. March.

"No, I won't!" returned Jo, stoutly, feeling much relieved that her prank was not entirely condemned.

"What made you do it?" asked Amy, who would as soon have thought of cutting off her head as her pretty hair.

"Well, I was wild to do something for Father," replied Jo, as they gathered about the table, for healthy young people can eat even in the midst of trouble. "I hate to borrow as much as Mother does, and I knew Aunt March would croak; she always does, if you ask for a ninepence. Meg gave all her quarterly salary toward the rent, and I only got some clothes with mine, so I felt wicked, and was bound to have some money, if I sold the nose off my face to get it."

"You needn't feel wicked, my child; you had no winter things, and got the simplest with your own hard earnings," said Mrs. March, with a look that warmed Jo's heart.

"I hadn't the least idea of selling my hair at first, but as I went along I kept thinking what I could do, and feeling as if I'd like to dive into some of the rich stores and help myself. In a barber's window I saw tails of hair with the prices marked; and one black tail, not so thick as mine, was forty dollars. It came over me all of a sudden that I had one thing to make money out of, and without stopping to think, I walked in, asked if they bought hair, and what they would give for mine."

"I don't see how you dared to do it," said Beth, in a tone of awe.

"Oh, he was a little man who looked as if he merely lived to oil his hair. He rather stared, at first, as if he wasn't used to having girls bounce into his shop and ask him to buy their hair. He said he didn't care about mine, it wasn't the fashionable colour, and he never paid much for it in the first place; the work put into it made it dear, and so on. It was getting late, and I was afraid, if it wasn't done right away, that I shouldn't have it done at all, and you know when I start to do a thing, I hate to give it up; so I begged him to take it, and told him why I was in such a hurry. It was silly, I dare say, but it changed his mind, for I got rather excited, and told the story in my topsy-turvy way, and his wife heard, and said so kindly: 'Take it, Thomas, and oblige the young lady; I'd do as much for our Jimmy any day if I had a spire of hair worth selling'."

"Who was Jimmy?" asked Amy, who liked to have things explained as they went along.

"Her son, she said, who was in the army. How friendly such things make strangers feel, don't they? She talked away all the time the man clipped, and diverted my mind nicely."

"Didn't you feel dreadfully when the first cut came?" asked Meg, with a shiver.

"I took a last look at my hair while the man got his things, and that was the end of it. I never snivel over trifles like that; I will confess, though, I felt queer when I saw the dear old hair laid out on the table, and felt only the short, rough ends on my head. It almost seemed as if I'd an arm or a leg off. The woman saw me look at it, and picked out a long lock for me to keep. I'll give it to you, Marmee, just to remember past glories by; for a crop is so comfortable I don't think I shall ever have a mane again."

Mrs. March folded the wavy chestnut lock, and laid it away with a short grey one in her desk. She only said, "Thank you, deary", but something in her face made the girls change the subject, and talk as cheerfully as they could about Mr. Brooke's kindness, the prospect of a fine day tomorrow, and the happy times they would have when Father came home to be nursed.

No one wanted to go to bed, when, at ten o'clock, Mrs. March put by the last finished job, and said, "Come, girls." Beth went to the piano and played the father's favourite hymn; all began bravely, but broke down one by one, till Beth was left alone, singing with all her heart, for to her music was always a sweet consoler.

"Go to bed and don't talk, for we must be up early, and shall need all the sleep we can get. Good-night, my darlings," said Mrs. March, as the hymn ended, for no one cared to try another.

They kissed her quietly, and went to bed as silently as if the dear invalid lay in the next room.

Beth and Amy soon fell asleep in spite of the great trouble, but Meg lay awake, thinking the most serious thoughts she had ever known in her short life. Jo lay motionless, and her sister fancied that she was asleep, till a stifled sob made her exclaim, as she touched a wet cheek: "Jo, dear, what is it? Are you crying about Father?"

"No, not now."
"What then?"
"My—my hair!" burst out poor Jo, trying vainly to smother her emotion in the pillow.
It did not sound at all comical to Meg, who kissed and caressed the afflicted heroine in the tenderest manner.
"I'm not sorry," protested Jo, with a choke. "I'd do it again tomorrow, if I could. It's only the vain, selfish part of me that goes and cries in this silly way. Don't tell anyone, it's all over now. I thought you were asleep, so I just made a little private moan for my one beauty. How came you to be awake?"
"I can't sleep, I'm so anxious," said Meg.
"Think about something pleasant, and you'll soon drop off."
"I tried it, but felt wider awake than ever."
"What did you think of?"
"Handsome faces—eyes particularly," answered Meg, smiling to herself, in the dark.
"What colour do you like best?"
"Brown—that is, sometimes; blue are lovely."
Jo laughed, and Meg sharply ordered her not to talk, then amiably promised to make her hair curl, and fell asleep to dream of living in her castle in the air.
The clocks were striking midnight, and the rooms were very still, as a figure glided quietly from bed to bed, smoothing a coverlid here, settling a pillow there, and pausing to look long and tenderly at each unconscious face, to kiss each with lips that mutely blessed, and to pray the fervent prayers which only mothers utter. As she lifted the curtain to look out into the dreary night, the moon broke suddenly from behind the clouds, and shone upon her like a bright, benignant face, which seemed to whisper in the silence, "Be comforted, dear soul! There is always light behind the clouds."

CHAPTER 16

LETTERS

In the cold grey dawn the sisters lit their lamp, and read their chapter with an earnestness never felt before; for now the shadow of a real trouble had come, the little books were full of help and comfort; and, as they dressed, they agreed to say good-bye cheerfully and hopefully, and send their mother on her anxious journey unsaddened by tears or complaints from them. Everything seemed very strange when they went down—so dim and still outside, so full of light and bustle within. Breakfast at that early hour seemed odd, and even Hannah's familiar face looked unnatural as she flew about her kitchen with her night-cap on. The big trunk stood ready in the hall, Mother's cloak and bonnet lay on the sofa, and Mother herself sat trying to eat, but looking so pale and worn, with sleeplessness and anxiety, that the girls found it very hard to keep their resolution. Meg's eyes kept filling in spite of herself; Jo was obliged to hide her face in the kitchen roller more than once; and the little girls wore a grave, troubled expression, as if sorrow was a new experience to them.

Nobody talked much, but as the time drew very near, and they sat waiting for the carriage, Mrs. March said to the girls, who were all busied about her, one folding her shawl, another smoothing out the strings of her bonnet, a third putting on her overshoes, and a fourth fastening up her travelling bag:

"Children, I leave you to Hannah's care and Mr. Laurence's protection. Hannah is faithfulness itself, and our good neighbour will guard you as if you were his own. I have no fears for you, yet I am anxious that you should take this trouble rightly. Don't grieve and fret when I am gone, or think that you can comfort yourselves by being idle and trying to forget. Go on with your work as usual, for work is a blessed solace. Hope and keep busy; and whatever happens, remember that you never can be fatherless."

"Yes, Mother."

"Meg, dear, be prudent, watch over your sisters, consult

Hannah, and, in any perplexity, go to Mr. Laurence. Be patient, Jo, don't get despondent or do rash things; write to me often, and be my brave girl, ready to help and cheer us all. Beth, comfort yourself with your music, and be faithful to the little home duties; and you, Amy, help all you can, be obedient, and keep happy, safe at home."

"We will, Mother! we will!"

The rattle of an approaching carriage made them all start and listen. That was the hard minute, but the girls stood it well; no one cried, no one ran away or uttered a lamentation, though their hearts were very heavy as they sent loving messages to Father, remembering, as they spoke, that it might be too late to deliver them. They kissed their mother quietly, clung about her tenderly, and tried to wave their hands cheerfully when she drove away.

Laurie and his grandfather came over to see her off, and Mr. Brooke looked so strong and sensible and kind that the girls christened him "Mr. Greatheart" on the spot.

"Good-bye, my darlings! God bless and keep us all!" whispered Mrs. March, as she kissed one dear little face after the other, and hurried into the carriage.

As she rolled away, the sun came out, and, looking back, she saw it shining on the group at the gate, like a good omen. They saw it also, and smiled and waved their hands; and the last thing she beheld, as she turned the corner, was the four bright faces, and behind them, like a bodyguard, old Mr. Laurence, faithful Hannah, and devoted Laurie.

"How kind everyone is to us!" she said, turning to find fresh proof of it in the respectful sympathy of the young man's face.

"I don't see how they can help it," returned Mr. Brooke, laughing so infectiously that Mrs. March could not help smiling; and so the long journey began with the good omens of sunshine, smiles, and cheerful words.

"I feel as if there had been an earthquake," said Jo, as their neighbours went home to breakfast, leaving them to rest and refresh themselves.

"It seems as if half the house was gone," added Meg, forlornly.

Beth opened her lips to say something, but could only point to the pile of nicely-minded hose which lay on Mother's table, showing that even in her last hurried moments she had thought and worked for them. It was a little thing, but it went straight to their hearts; and, in spite of their brave resolutions, they all broke down and cried bitterly.

Hannah wisely allowed them to relieve their feelings, and, when the shower showed signs of clearing up, she came to the rescue, armed with a coffee-pot.

"Now, my dear young ladies, remember what your ma said, and don't fret. Come and have a cup of coffee all round, and then let's fall to work and be a credit to the family."

Coffee was a treat, and Hannah showed great tact in making it that morning. No one could resist her persuasive nods, or the fragrant invitation issuing from the nose of the coffee-pot. They drew up to the table, exchanged their handkerchiefs for napkins, and in ten minutes were all right again.

"'Hope and keep busy', that's the motto for us, so let's see who will remember it best. I shall go to Aunt March, as usual. Oh, won't she lecture though!" said Jo, as she sipped with returning spirit.

"I shall go to my Kings, though I'd much rather stay at home and attend to things here," said Meg, wishing she hadn't made her eyes so red.

"No need of that, Beth and I can keep house perfectly well," put in Amy, with an important air.

"Hannah will tell us what to do, and we'll have everything nice when you come home," added Beth, getting out her mop and dish-tub without delay.

"I think anxiety is very interesting," observed Amy, eating sugar, pensively.

The girls couldn't help laughing, and felt better for it, though Meg shook her head at the young lady who could find consolation in a sugar-bowl.

The sight of the turnovers made Jo sober again; and when the two went out to their daily tasks, they looked sorrowfully back at the window where they were accustomed to see their mother's face. It was gone; but Beth had remembered the little household ceremony, and there she was, nodding away at them like a rosy-faced mandarin.

"That's so like my Beth!" said Jo, waving her hat, with a grateful face. "Good-bye, Meggy; I hope the Kings won't train today. Don't fret about Father, dear," she added, as they parted.

"And I hope Aunt March won't croak. Your hair *is* becoming, and it looks very boyish and nice," returned Meg, trying not to smile at the curly head, which looked comically small on her tall sister's shoulders.

"That's my only comfort"; and, touching her hat, *à la* Laurie, away went Jo, feeling like a shorn sheep on a wintry day.

News from their father comforted the girls very much; for, though dangerously ill, the presence of the best and tenderest of nurses had already done him good. Mr. Brooke sent a bulletin every day, and, as the head of the family, Meg insisted on reading the dispatches, which grew more and more cheering as the week passed. At first, everyone was eager to write, and plump envelopes were carefully poked into the letter-box by one or other of the sisters, who felt rather important with their Washington correspondence. As one of these packets contained characteristic notes from the party, we will rob an imaginary mail, and read them:

MY DEAREST MOTHER—It is impossible to tell you how happy your last letter made us, for the news was so good we couldn't help laughing and crying over it. How very kind Mr. Brooke is, and how fortunate that Mr. Laurence's business detains him near you so long, since he is so useful to you and Father. The girls are all as good as gold. Jo helps me with the sewing, and insists on doing all sorts of hard jobs. I should be afraid she might overdo, if I didn't know that her "moral fit" wouldn't last long. Beth is as regular about her tasks as a clock, and never forgets what you told her. She grieves about Father, and looks sober except when she is at her little piano. Amy minds me nicely, and I take great care of her. She does her own hair, and I am teaching her how to make buttonholes, and mend her stockings. She tries very hard, and I know you will be pleased with her improvement when you come. Mr. Laurence watches over us like a motherly old hen, as Jo says; and Laurie is very kind and neighbourly. He and Jo keep us merry, for we get pretty blue sometimes, and feel like orphans, with you so far away. Hannah is a perfect saint; she does not scold at all, and always calls me Miss "Margaret", which is quite proper, you know, and treats me with respect. We are all well and busy; but we long day and night to have you back. Give my dearest love to Father, and believe me, ever your own.

MEG.

This note, prettily written on scented paper, was a great contrast to the next, which was scribbled on a big sheet of thin foreign paper, ornamented with blots and all manner of flourishes and curly-tailed letters:

MY PRECIOUS MARMEE—Three cheers for dear Father. Brooke was a trump to telegraph right off, and let us know the minute he was better. I rushed up garret when the letter came and tried to thank God for being so good to us; but I could only cry, and say, "I'm glad! I'm glad!" Didn't that do as well as a regular prayer? for I felt a great many in my heart. We have such funny times; and now I can enjoy them, for everyone is so desperately good, it's like living in a nest of turtle doves. You'd laugh to see Meg head the table and try to be motherish. She gets prettier every day, and I'm in love with her sometimes. The children are regular archangels, and I—well, I'm Jo, and never shall be anything else. Oh, I must tell you that I came near having a quarrel with Laurie. I freed my mind about a silly little thing, and he was offended. I was right, but didn't speak as I ought, and he marched home, saying he wouldn't come again till I begged pardon. I declared I wouldn't and got mad. It lasted all day; I felt bad, and wanted you very much. Laurie and I are both so proud, it's hard to beg pardon; but I thought he'd come to it, for I *was* in the right. He didn't come; and just at night I remembered what you said when Amy fell into the river. I read my little book, felt better, resolved not to let the sun set on *my* anger, and ran over to tell Laurie I was sorry. I met him at the gate, coming for the same thing. We both laughed, begged each other's pardon, and felt all good and comfortable again.

I made a "pome" yesterday, when I was helping Hannah wash; and, as Father likes my silly little things, I put it in to amuse him. Give him the lovingest hug that ever was, and kiss yourself a dozen times for your

TOPSY-TURVY Jo.

A SONG FROM THE SUDS

Queen of my tub, I merrily sing,
  While the white foam rises high;
And sturdily wash and rinse and wring,
  And fasten the clothes to dry;
Then out in the free, fresh air they swing,
  Under the sunny sky.

I wish we could wash from our hearts and souls
  The stains of the week away,
And let water and air by their magic make
  Ourselves as pure as they;
Then on the earth there would be indeed
  A glorious washing day!

Along the path of a useful life,
  Will heart's-ease ever bloom;
The busy mind has no time to think
  Of sorrow or care or gloom;
And anxious thoughts may be swept away,
  As we bravely wield a broom.

I am glad a task to me is given,
  To labour at day by day;
For it brings me health and strength and hope,
  And I cheerfully learn to say,—
"Head, you may think, Heart, you may feel,
  But, Hand, you shall work alway!"

DEAR MOTHER—There is only room for me to send my love and some pressed pansies from the root I have been keeping safe in the house for Father to see. I read every morning, try to be good all day, and sing myself to sleep with Father's tune. I can't sing "Land of the Lea!" now; it makes me cry. Everyone is very kind, and we are as happy as we can be without you. Amy wants the rest of the page, so I must stop. I didn't forget to cover the holders, and I wind the clock and air the rooms every day.

Kiss dear Father on the cheek he calls mine. Oh, do come soon to your loving

LITTLE BETH.

MA CHERE MAMMA—We are all well. I do my lessons always and never corroborate the girls—Meg says I mean contradict so I put in both words and you can take the properest. Meg is a great comfort to me and lets me have jelly every night at tea; its so good for me, Jo says, because it keeps me sweet tempered. Laurie is not as respectful as he ought to be now I am almost in my teens, he calls me Chick and hurts my feelings by talking French to me very fast when I say Merci or Bon jour as Hattie King does. The sleeves of my blue dress were all worn out, and Meg put in new ones, but the full front came wrong and they are more blue than the dress. I felt bad but did not fret. I bear my troubles well but I do wish Hannah would put more starch in my aprons and have buckwheats every day. Can't she? Didn't I make that interrigation point nice? Meg says my punchtuation and spelling are disgraceful and I am mortyfied but dear me I have so many things to do, I can't stop. Adieu, I send heaps of love to Papa—Your affectionate daughter

AMY CURTIS MARCH.

DEAR MISS MARCH—I jes drop a line to say we git on fust rate. The girls is clever and fly round right smart. Miss Meg is going to make a proper good housekeeper; she hes the liking for it, and gits the hang of things surprisin quick. Jo doos beat all for going ahead, but she don't stop to cal'k'late fust, and you never know where she's like to bring up. She done out a tub of clothes on Monday, but she starched em afore they was wrenched, and blued a pink calico dress till I thought I should a died a laughin. Beth is the best of little creeters, and a sight of help to me, bein so forehanded and dependable. She tries to learn everything, and really goes to market beyond her years; likewise keeps accounts, with my help, quite wonderful. We have got on very economical so fur; I don't let the girls hev coffee only once a week, according to your wish, and keep em on plain wholesome vittles. Amy does well about frettin, wearin her best clothes and eatin sweet stuff. Mr. Laurie is as full of didoes as usual, and turns the house upside down frequent; but he heartens up the girls, and so I let em hev full swing. The old gentleman sends heaps of things, and is rather wearin, but means wal, and it aint my place to say nothin. My bread is riz, so no more at this time. I send my duty to Mr. March, and hope he's seen the last of his Pewmonia—Yours Respectful,

HANNAH MULLET.

HEAD NURSE OF WARD No. 2—All serene on the Rappahannock, troops in fine condition, commissary department well conducted, the Home Guard under Colonel Teddy always on duty, Commander-in-Chief General Laurence reviews the army daily, Quartermaster Mullet keeps order in camp, and Major Lion does picket duty at night. A salute of twenty-four guns was fired on receipt of good news from Washington, and a dress parade took place at headquarters. Commander-in-Chief sends best wishes, in which he is heartily joined by

COLONEL TEDDY.

DEAR MADAM—The little girls are all well; Beth and my boy report daily; Hannah is a model servant, and guards pretty Meg like a dragon. Glad the fine weather holds; pray make Brooke useful, and draw on me for funds if expenses exceed your estimate. Don't let your husband want anything. Thank God he is mending—Your sincere friend and servant,

JAMES LAURENCE.

CHAPTER 17

LITTLE FAITHFUL

For a week the amount of virtue in the old house would have supplied the neighbourhood. It was really amazing, for everyone seemed in a heavenly frame of mind, and self-denial was all the fashion. Relieved of their first anxiety about their father the girls insensibly relaxed their praiseworthy efforts a little, and began to fall back into the old ways. They did not forget their motto, but hoping and keeping busy seemed to grow easier; and after such tremendous exertions, they felt that Endeavour deserved a holiday, and gave it a good many.

Jo caught a bad cold through neglect to cover the shorn head enough, and was ordered to stay at home till she was better, for Aunt March didn't like to hear people read with colds in their heads. Jo liked this, and after an energetic rummage from garret to cellar, subsided on the sofa to nurse her cold with rosenicum and books. Amy found that housework and art did not go well together, and returned to her mud pies. Meg went daily to her pupils, and sewed, or thought she did, at home, but much time was spent in writing long letters to her mother, or reading the Washington dispatches over and over. Beth kept on, with only slight relapses into idleness or grieving.

All the little duties were faithfully done each day, and many of her sisters' also, for they were forgetful, and the house seemed like a clock whose pendulum was gone avisiting. When her heart got heavy with longings for Mother or fears for Father, she went away into a certain closet, hid her face in the folds of a certain dear old gown, and made her little moan and prayed her little prayer quietly by herself. Nobody knew what cheered her up after a sober fit, but everyone felt how sweet and helpful Beth was, and fell into a way of going to her for comfort or advice in their small affairs.

All were unconscious that this experience was a test of character; and when the first excitement was over, felt that they had done well, and deserved praise. So they did; but their mistake was in ceasing to do well, and they learned this lesson through much anxiety and regret.

"Meg, I wish you'd go and see the Hummels; you know Mother told us not to forget them," said Beth, ten days after Mrs. March's departure.

"I'm too tired to go this afternoon," replied Meg, rocking comfortably as she sewed.

"Can't you, Jo?" asked Beth.

"Too stormy for me with my cold."

"I thought it was almost well."

"It's well enough for me to go out with Laurie, but not well enough to go to the Hummels'," said Jo, laughing, but looking a little ashamed of her inconsistency.

"Why don't you go yourself?" asked Meg.

"I *have* been every day, but the baby is sick, and I don't know what to do for it. Mrs. Hummel goes away to work, and Lottchen takes care of it; but it gets sicker and sicker, and I think you or Hannah ought to go."

Beth spoke earnestly, and Meg promised she would go tomorrow.

"Ask Hannah for some nice little mess, and take it round, Beth; the air will do you good," said Jo, adding apologetically, "I'd go, but I want to finish my writing."

"My head aches and I'm tired, so I thought maybe some of you would go," said Beth.

"Amy will be in presently, and she will run down for us," suggested Meg.

"Well, I'll rest a little and wait for her."

So Beth lay down on the sofa, and others returned to their work, and the Hummels were forgotten. An hour passed: Amy did not come; Meg went to her room to try on a new dress; Jo was absorbed in her story, and Hannah was sound asleep before the kitchen fire, when Beth quietly put on her hood, filled her basket with odds and ends for the poor children, and went out into the chilly air, with a heavy head, and a grieved look in her patient eyes. It was late when she came back, and no one saw her creep upstairs and shut herself into her mother's room. Half an hour after, Jo went to "Mother's closet" for something, and there found Beth sitting on the medicine chest looking very grave, with red eyes, and a camphor-bottle in her hand.

"Christopher Columbus! What's the matter?" cried Jo, as Beth put out her hand as if to warn her off, and asked quickly:

"You've had the scarlet fever, haven't you?"

"Years ago, when Meg did. Why?"

"Then I'll tell you. Oh, Jo, the baby's dead!"

"What baby?"

"Mrs. Hummel's; it died in my lap before she got home," cried Beth, with a sob.

"My poor dear, how dreadful for you! I ought to have gone," said Jo, taking her sister in her arms as she sat down in her mother's big chair, with a remorseful face.

"It wasn't dreadful, Jo, only so sad! I saw in a minute that it was sicker, but Lottchen said her mother had gone for a doctor, so I took baby and let Lotty rest. It seemed asleep, but all of a sudden it gave a little cry, and trembled, and then lay very still. I tried to warm its feet, and Lotty gave it some milk, but it didn't stir, and I knew it was dead."

"Don't cry, dear! What did you do?"

"I just sat and held it softly till Mrs. Hummel came with the doctor. He said it was dead, and looked at Heinrich and Minna, who have got sore throats. 'Scarlet fever, ma'am. Ought to have called me before,' he said, crossly. Mrs. Hummel told him she was poor, and had tried to cure baby herself, but now it was too late, and she could only ask him to help the others, and trust to charity for his pay. He smiled then, and was kinder; but it was very sad, and I cried with them till he turned round, all of a sudden, and told me to go home and take belladonna right away, or I'd have the fever."

"No, you won't!" cried Jo, hugging her close, with a frightened look. "Oh, Beth, if you should be sick I never could forgive myself! What *shall* we do?"

"Don't be frightened, I guess I shan't have it badly. I looked in Mother's book, and saw that it begins with headache, sore throat, and queer feelings like mine, so I did take some belladonna, and I feel better," said Beth, laying her cold hands on her hot forehead, and trying to look well.

"If Mother was only at home!" exclaimed Jo, seizing the book, and feeling that Washington was an immense way off. She read a page, looked at Beth, felt her head, peeped into her throat, and then said gravely, "You've been over the baby for more than a week, and among the others who are going to have it; so I'm afraid *you* are going to have it, Beth. I'll call Hannah, she knows all about sickness."

"Don't let Amy come: she never had it, and I should hate to give it to her. Can't you and Meg have it over again?" asked Beth anxiously.

"I guess not; don't care if I do; serve me right, selfish pig, to let you go, and stay writing rubbish myself!" muttered Jo, as she went to consult Hannah.

The good soul was wide awake in a minute, and took the lead at once, assuring Jo that there was no need to worry, everyone had scarlet fever, and, if rightly treated, nobody died—all of which Jo believed, and felt much relieved as they went up to call Meg.

"Now I'll tell you what we'll do," said Hannah, when she had examined and questioned Beth; "we will have Dr. Bangs, just to take a look at you, dear, and see that we start right; then we'll send Amy off to Aunt March's for a spell, to keep her out of harm's way, and one of you girls can stay at home and amuse Beth for a day or two."

"I shall stay, of course; I'm oldest," began Meg, looking anxious and self-reproachful.

"*I* shall, because it's my fault she is sick; I told Mother I'd do the errands, and I haven't," said Jo, decidedly.

"Which will you have, Beth? there ain't no need of but one," said Hannah.

"Jo, please," and Beth leaned her head against her sister, with a contented look, which effectually settled that point.

"I'll go and tell Amy," said Meg, feeling a little hurt, yet rather relieved on the whole, for she did not like nursing, and Jo did.

Amy rebelled outright, and passionately declared that she had rather have the fever than go to Aunt March. Meg reasoned, pleaded, and commanded: all in vain. Amy protested that she would *not* go; and Meg left her in despair, to ask Hannah what should be done. Before she came back, Laurie walked into the parlour to find Amy sobbing, with her head in the sofa cushions. She told her story, expecting to be consoled; but Laurie only put his hands in his pockets, and walked about the room, whistling softly, as he knit his brows in deep thought. Presently he sat down beside her, and said, in his most wheedlesome tone, "Now, be a sensible little woman, and do as they say. No, don't cry, but hear what a jolly plan I've got. You go to Aunt March's, and I'll come and take you out every day driving or walking, and we'll have capital times. Won't that be better than moping here?"

"I don't wish to be sent off as if I was in the way," began Amy, in an injured voice.

"Bless your heart, child, it's to keep you well. You don't want to be sick, do you?"

"No, I'm sure I don't; but I dare say I shall be, for I've been with Beth all the time."

"That's the very reason you ought to go away at once, so that you may escape it. Change of air and care will keep you well, I dare say; or, if it does not entirely, you will have the fever more lightly. I advise you to be off as soon as you can, for scarlet fever is no joke, miss."

"But it's dull at Aunt March's, and she is so cross," said Amy, looking rather frightened.

"It won't be dull with me popping in every day to tell you how Beth is, and take you out gallivanting. The old lady likes me, and I'll be as sweet as possible to her, so she won't peck at us, whatever we do."

"Will you take me out in the trotting waggon with Puck?"

"On my honour as a gentleman."

"And come every single day?"

"See if I don't."

"And bring me back the minute Beth is well?"

"The identical minute."

"And go to the hall, truly?"

"A dozen halls, if we may."

"Well—I guess—I will," said Amy, slowly.

"Good girl! Call Meg, and tell her you'll give in," said Laurie, with an approving pat, which annoyed Amy more than the "giving in".

Meg and Jo came running down to behold the miracle which had been wrought and Amy, feeling very precious and self-sacrificing, promised to go, if the doctor said Beth was going to be ill.

"How is the little dear?" asked Laurie; for Beth was his especial pet, and he felt more anxious about her than he liked to show.

"She is lying down on Mother's bed, and feels better. The baby's death troubled her, but I dare say she has only got cold. Hannah *says* she thinks so; but she *looks* worried, and that makes me fidgety," answered Meg.

"What a trying world it is!" said Jo, rumpling up her hair in a fretful sort of way. "No sooner do we get out of one trouble than down comes another. There doesn't seem to be anything to hold on to when Mother's gone; so I'm all at sea."

"Well, don't make a porcupine of yourself, it isn't becoming. Settle your wig, Jo, and tell me if I shall telegraph to your mother or do anything?" asked Laurie, who never had been reconciled to the loss of his friend's one beauty.

"That is what troubles me," said Meg. "I think we ought to tell her if Beth is really ill, but Hannah says we mustn't, for Mother can't leave Father, and it will only make them anxious. Beth won't be sick long, and Hannah knows just what to do, and Mother said we were to mind her, so I suppose we must, but it doesn't seem quite right to me."

"Hum, well, I can't say; suppose you ask grandfather after the doctor has been."

"We will. Jo, go and get Dr. Bangs at once," commanded Meg; "we can't decide anything till he has been."

"Stay where you are, Jo; I'm errand-boy to this establishment," said Laurie, taking up his cap.

"I'm afraid you are busy," began Meg.

"No, I've done my lessons for today."

"Do you study in vacation time?" asked Jo.

"I follow the good example my neighbours set me," was Laurie's answer, as he swung himself out of the room.

"I have great hopes of my boy," observed Jo, watching him fly over the fence with an approving smile.

"He does very well—for a boy," was Meg's somewhat ungracious answer, for the subject did not interest her.

Dr. Bangs came, said Beth had symptoms of the fever, but thought she would have it lightly, though he looked sober over the Hummel story. Amy was ordered off at once, and, provided with something to ward off danger, she departed in great state, with Jo and Laurie as escort.

Aunt March received them with her usual hospitality.

"What do you want now?" she asked, looking sharply over her spectacles, while the parrot, sitting on the back of her chair, called out:

"Go away. No boys allowed here."

Laurie retired to the window, and Jo told her story.

"No more than I expected, if you are allowed to go poking about among poor folks. Amy can stay and make herself useful, if she isn't sick, which I've no doubt she will be—looks like it now. Don't cry, child, it worries me to hear people sniff."

Amy *was* on the point of crying, but Laurie slyly pulled the parrot's tail, which caused Polly to utter an astonished croak, and call out, "Bless my boots!" in such a funny way, that she laughed instead.

"What do you hear from your mother?" asked the old lady, gruffly.

"Father is much better," replied Jo, trying to keep sober.

"Oh, is he? Well, that won't last long, I fancy; March never had any stamina," was the cheerful reply.

"Hah, ha! never say die, take a pinch of snuff, good-bye, good-bye!" squalled Polly, dancing on her perch, and clawing at the old lady's cap as Laurie tweaked him in the rear.

"Hold your tongue, you disrespectful old bird! and, Jo, you'd better go at once; it isn't proper to be gadding about so late with a rattle-pated boy like—"

"Hold your tongue, you disrespectful old bird!" cried Polly, tumbling off the chair with a bounce, and running to peck the "rattle-pated boy", who was shaking with laughter at the last speech.

"I don't think I *can* bear it, but I'll try," thought Amy, as she was left alone with Aunt March.

"Get along, you fright!" screamed Polly; and at that rude speech Amy could not restrain a sniff.

Chapter 18

DARK DAYS

Beth did have the fever, and was much sicker than anyone but Hannah and the doctor suspected. The girls knew nothing about illness, and Mr. Laurence was not allowed to see her, so Hannah had everything all her own way, and busy Dr. Bangs did his best, but left a good deal to the excellent nurse. Meg stayed at home, lest she should infect the Kings, and kept house, feeling very anxious and a little guilty when she wrote letters in which no mention was made of Beth's illness. She could not think it right to deceive her mother, but she had been bidden to mind Hannah, and Hannah wouldn't hear of "Mrs. March bein' told, and worried just for sech a trifle". Jo devoted herself to Beth day and night; not a hard task, for Beth was very patient, and bore her pain uncomplainingly, as long as she could control herself. But there came a time when during the fever fits she began to talk in a hoarse, broken voice, to play on the coverlet, as if on her beloved little piano, and try to sing with a throat so swollen that there was no music left; a time when she did not know the familiar faces round her, but addressed them by wrong names, and called imploringly for her mother. Then Jo grew frightened, Meg begged to be allowed to write the truth, and even Hannah said she "would think of it, though there was no danger *yet*". A letter from Washington added to their trouble, for Mr. March had had a relapse, and could not think of coming home for a long while.

How dark the days seemed now, how sad and lonely the house, and how heavy were the hearts of the sisters as they worked and waited, while the shadow of death hovered over the once happy home! Then it was that Margaret, sitting alone with tears dropping often on her work, felt how rich she had been in things more precious than any luxuries money could buy—in love, protection, peace, and health, the real blessings of life. Then it was that Jo, living in the darkened room with that suffering little sister always before her eyes, and that pathetic voice sounding in her ears, learned to see the beauty and the sweetness of

Beth's nature, to feel how deep and tender a place she filled in all hearts, and to acknowledge the worth of Beth's unselfish ambition to live for others, and make home happy by the exercise of those simple virtues which all may possess, and which all should love and value more than talent, wealth, or beauty. And Amy, in her exile, longed eagerly to be at home, that she might work for Beth, feeling now that no service would be hard or irksome, and remembering, with regretful grief, how many neglected tasks those willing hands had done for her. Laurie haunted the house like a restless ghost, and Mr. Laurence locked the grand piano, because he could not bear to be reminded of the young neighbour who used to make the twilight pleasant for him. Everyone missed Beth. The milkman, baker, grocer, and butcher inquired how she did; poor Mrs. Hummel came to beg pardon for her thoughtlessness, and to get a shroud for Minna; the neighbours sent all sorts of comforts and good wishes, and even those who knew her best, were surprised to find how many friends shy little Beth had made.

Meanwhile she lay on her bed with old Joanna at her side, for even in her wanderings she did not forget her forlorn protégée. She longed for her cats, but would not have them brought, lest they should get sick; and, in her quiet hours, she was full of anxiety about Jo. She sent loving messages to Amy, bade them tell her mother that she would write soon; and often begged for pencil and paper to try and say a word, that Father might not think she had neglected him. But soon even these intervals of consciousness ended, and she lay hour after hour, tossing to and fro, with incoherent words on her lips, or sank into a heavy sleep which brought her no refreshment. Dr. Bangs came twice a day, Hannah sat up at night, Meg kept a telegram in her desk all ready to send off at any minute, and Jo never stirred from Beth's side.

The first of December was a wintry day indeed to them, for a bitter wind blew, snow fell fast, and the year seemed getting ready for its death. When Dr. Bangs came that morning, he looked long at Beth, held the hot hand in both his own a minute, and laid it gently down, saying, in a low tone, to Hannah: "If Mrs. March *can* leave her husband she'd better be sent for."

Hannah nodded without speaking, for her lips twitched nervously; Meg dropped down into a chair as the strength seemed to go out of her limbs at the sound of those words: and Jo, after standing with a pale face for a minute, ran to the parlour, snatched up the telegram, and, throwing on her things, rushed out into the storm. She was soon back, and, while noiselessly taking off her cloak, Laurie came in with a letter, saying that Mr. March was mending again. Jo read it thankfully, but the heavy weight did not seem lifted off her heart, and her face was so full of misery that Laurie asked quickly: "What is it? is Beth worse?"

"I've sent for Mother," said Jo, tugging at her rubber boots with a tragical expression.

"Good for you, Jo! Did you do it on your own responsibility?" asked Laurie, as he seated her in the hall chair, and took off the rebellious boots, seeing how her hands shook.

"No, the doctor told us to."

"Oh, Jo, it's not so bad as that?" cried Laurie, with a startled face.

"Yes, it is; she doesn't know us, she doesn't even talk about the flocks of green doves, as she calls the vine leaves on the wall; she doesn't look like my Beth, and there's nobody to help us bear it; Mother and Father both gone, and God seems so far away I can't find him."

As the tears streamed fast down poor Jo's cheeks, she stretched out her hand in a helpless sort of way, as if groping in the dark, and Laurie took it in his, whispering as well as he could, with a lump in his throat: "I'm here. Hold on to me, Jo, dear!"

She could not speak, but she did "Hold on", and the warm grasp of the friendly human hand comforted her sore heart, and seemed to lead her nearer to the Divine arm which alone could uphold her in her trouble. Laurie longed to say something tender and comfortable, but no fitting words came to him, so he stood silent, gently stroking her bent head as her mother used to do. It was the best thing he could have done; far more soothing than the most eloquent words, for Jo felt the unspoken sympathy, and in the silence, learned the sweet solace which affection administers to sorrow. Soon she dried the tears which had relieved her, and looked up with a grateful face.

"Thank you, Teddy, I'm better now; I don't feel so forlorn, and will try to bear it if it comes."

"Keep hoping for the best; that will help you, Jo. Soon your mother will be here, and then everything will be right."

"I'm so glad Father is better; now she won't feel so bad about leaving him. Oh, me ! it does seem as if all the troubles came in a heap, and I got the heaviest part on my shoulders," sighed Jo, spreading her wet handkerchief over her knees to dry.

"Doesn't Meg pull fair?" asked Laurie, looking indignant.

"Oh, yes; she tries to, but she can't love Bethy as I do; and she won't miss her as I shall. Beth is my conscience, and I *can't* give her up. I can't! I can't!" Down went Jo's face into the wet handkerchief, and she cried despairingly; for she had kept up bravely till now, and never shed a tear. Laurie drew his hand across his eyes, but could not speak till he had subdued the choking feeling in his throat and steadied his lips. It might be unmanly, but he couldn't help it, and I'm glad of it. Presently as Jo's sobs quieted, he said hopefully, "I don't think she will die; she's so good, and we all love her so much, I don't believe God will take her away yet."

"The good and dear people always do die," groaned Jo, but she stopped crying, for her friend's words cheered her up, in spite of her own doubts and fears.

"Poor girl, you're worn out. It isn't like you to be forlorn. Stop a bit; I'll hearten you up in a jiffy."

Laurie went off two stairs at a time, and Jo laid her wearied head down on Beth's little brown hood, which no one had thought of moving from the table where she left it. It must have possessed some magic, for the submissive spirit of its gentle owner seemed to enter into Jo; and, when Laurie came running down with a glass of wine, she took it with a smile and said bravely, "I drink health to my Beth! You are a good doctor, Teddy, and *such* a comfortable friend; how can I ever pay you?" she added; the kind words had refreshed her troubled mind.

"I'll send in my bill, by and by; and tonight I'll give you something that will warm the cockles of your heart better than quarts of wine," said Laurie, beaming at her with a face of suppressed satisfaction at something.

"What is it?" cried Jo, forgetting her woes for a minute, in her wonder.

"I telegraphed to your mother yesterday, and Brooke answered she'd come at once, and she'll be here tonight, and everything will be all right. Aren't you glad I did it?"

Laurie spoke very fast, and turned red and excited all in a minute, for he had kept his plot a secret, for fear of disappointing the girls or harming Beth.

Jo grew quite white, flew out of her chair, and the moment he stopped speaking she electrified him by throwing her arms round his neck, and crying out, with a joyful cry, "Oh, Laurie! Oh, Mother! I *am* so glad!" She did not weep again, but laughed hysterically, and trembled and clung to her friend as if she was a little bewildered by the sudden news.

Laurie, though decidedly amazed, behaved with great presence of mind; he patted her back soothingly and, finding that she was recovering, followed it up by a bashful kiss or two, which brought Jo round at once. Holding on to the banisters, she put him gently away, saying breathlessly, "Oh, don't! I didn't mean to; it was dreadful of me; but you were such a dear to go and do it in spite of Hannah that I couldn't help flying at you. Tell me all about it, and don't give me wine again; it makes me act so stupidly."

"I don't mind," laughed Laurie, as he settled his tie. "Why, you see I got fidgety, and so did Grandpa. We thought Hannah was overdoing the authority business, and your mother ought to know. She'd never forgive us if Beth— well, if anything happened, you know. So I got Grandpa to say it was high time we did something, and off I pelted to the office yesterday, for the doctor looked sober, and Hannah most took my head off when I proposed a telegram. I *never* can bear to be 'lorded' over, so that settled my mind, and I did it. Your mother will come, I know, and the late train is in at 2 a.m. I shall go for her, and you've only got to bottle up your rapture, and keep Beth quiet, till that blessed lady gets here."

"Laurie, you're an angel! How shall I ever thank you?"

"Fly at me again; I rather like it," said Laurie, looking mischievous—a thing he had not done for a fortnight.

"No, thank you. I'll do it by proxy, when your grandpa comes. Don't tease, but go home and rest, for you'll be up half the night. Bless you, Teddy, bless you!"

Jo had backed into a corner; and, as she finished her speech, she vanished precipitately into the kitchen, where she sat down upon a dresser, and told the assembled cats, that she was "happy, oh, *so* happy!" while Laurie departed, feeling that he had made rather a neat thing of it.

"That's the interferingest chap I ever see; but I forgive him, and do hope Mrs. March is coming on right away," said Hannah, with an air of relief, when Jo told the good news.

Meg had a quiet rapture, and then brooded over the letter, while Jo set the sick-room in order, and Hannah "knocked up a couple of pies in case of company unexpected". A breath of fresh air seemed to blow through the house, and something better than sunshine brightened the quiet rooms. Everything appeared to feel the hopeful change; Beth's bird began to chirp again, and a half-blown rose was discovered on Amy's bush in the window, and fires seemed to burn with unusual cheeriness; and every time the girls met, their pale faces broke into smiles as they hugged one another, whispering encouragingly, "Mother's coming, dear! Mother's coming!" Everyone rejoiced but Beth; she lay in that heavy stupor, alike unconscious of hope and joy, doubt and anger. It was a piteous sight—the once rosy face so changed and vacant, the once busy hands so weak and wasted, the once smiling lips quite dumb, and the once pretty, well-kept hair scattered rough and tangled on the pillow.

All day she lay so, only rousing now and then to mutter, "Water!" with lips so parched they could hardly shape the word; all day Jo and Meg hovered over her, watching, waiting, hoping, and trusting in God and Mother; and all day the snow fell, the bitter wind raged, and the hours dragged slowly by. But night came at last; and every time the clock struck, the sisters, still sitting on either side of the bed, looked at each other with brightening eyes, for each hour brought help nearer. The doctor had been in to say that some change, for better or worse, would probably take place about midnight, at which time he would return.

Hannah, quite worn out, lay down on the sofa at the bed's foot, and fell fast asleep; Mr. Laurence marched to and fro in the parlour, feeling that he would rather face a rebel battery than Mrs. March's anxious countenance as she entered; Laurie lay on the rug, pretending to rest, but staring into the fire with the thoughtful look which made his black eyes beautifully soft and clear.

The girls never forgot that night, for no sleep came to them, as they kept their watch with that dreadful sense of powerlessness which comes to us in hours like those.

"If God spares Beth I never will complain again," whispered Meg, earnestly.

"If God spares Beth I'll try to love and serve him all my life," answered Jo, with equal fervour.

"I wish I had no heart, it aches so," sighed Meg, after a pause.

"If life is often as hard as this, I don't see how we ever shall get through it," added her sister, despondently.

Here the clock struck twelve, and both forgot themselves in watching Beth, for they fancied a change passed over her wan face. The house was still as death, and nothing but the wailing of the wind broke the deep hush. Weary Hannah slept on, and no one but the sisters saw the pale shadow which seemed to fall upon the little bed. An hour went by, and nothing happened except Laurie's quiet departure for the station. Another hour—still no one came; and anxious fears of delay in the storm or accidents by the way, or, worst of all, a great grief at Washington, haunted the poor girls.

It was past two, when Jo, who stood at the window thinking how dreary the world looked in its winding sheet of snow, heard a movement by the bed, and, turning quickly, saw Meg kneeling before her mother's easy-chair, with her face hidden. A dreadful fear passed coldly over Jo, as she thought, "Beth is dead, and Meg is afraid to tell me."

She was back in her post in an instant, and to her excited eyes a great change seemed to have taken place. The fever flush and the look of pain were gone, and the beloved little face looked so pale and peaceful in its utter repose, that Jo felt no desire to weep or to lament. Leaning low over this dearest of her sisters, she kissed the damp forehead with her heart on her lips, and softly whispered, "Good-bye, my Beth; good-bye!"

As if waked by the stir, Hannah started out of her sleep, hurried to the bed, looked at Beth, felt her hands, listened at her lips, and then, throwing her apron over her head, sat down to rock to and fro, exclaiming, under her breath, "The fever's turned; she's sleeping nat'ral; her skin's damp, and she breathes easy. Praise be given! Oh, my goodness me!"

Before the girls could believe the happy truth, the doctor came to confirm it. He was a homely man, but they thought his face quite heavenly when he smiled, and said, with a fatherly look at them, "Yes, my dears, I think the little girl will pull through this time. Keep the house quiet; let her sleep, and when she wakes, give her—" What they were to give, neither heard; for both crept into the dark hall, and sitting on the stairs, held each other close, rejoicing with hearts too full for words. When they went back to be kissed and cuddled by faithful Hannah, they found Beth lying, as she used to do, with her cheek pillowed on her hand, the dreadful pallor gone, and breathing quietly, as if just fallen asleep.

"If Mother would only come now!" said Jo, as the winter night began to wane.

"See," said Meg, coming up with a white, half-opened rose, "I thought this would hardly be ready to lay in Beth's hand tomorrow if she—went away from us. But it has blossomed in the night, and now I mean to put it in my vase here, so that when the darling wakes, the first things she sees will be the little rose, and Mother's face."

Never had the sun risen so beautifully, and never had the world seemed so lovely, as it did to the heavy eyes of Meg and Jo, as they looked out in the early morning, when their long, sad vigil was done.

"It looks like a fairy world," said Meg, smiling to herself, as she stood behind the curtain, watching the dazzling sight.

"Hark!" cried Jo, starting to her feet.

Yes, there was a sound of bells at the door below, a cry from Hannah, and then Laurie's voice saying, in a joyful whisper, "Girls, she's come! she's come!"

CHAPTER 19

AMY'S WILL

While these things were happening at home, Amy was having hard times at Aunt March's. She felt her exile deeply, and, for the first time in her life, realized how much she was beloved and petted at home. Aunt March never petted anyone; she did not approve of it; but she meant to be kind, for the well-behaved little girl pleased her very much, and Aunt March had a soft place in her old heart for her nephew's children, though she didn't think proper to confess it. She really did her best to make Amy happy, but, dear me, what mistakes she made! Some old people keep young at heart in spite of wrinkles and grey hair, can sympathize with children's little cares and joys, make them feel at home, and can hide wise lessons under pleasant plays, giving and receiving friendship in the sweetest way. But Aunt March had not this gift, and she worried Amy very much with her rules and orders, her prim ways, and long, prosy talks. Finding the child more docile and amiable than her sister, the old lady felt it her duty to try and counteract, as far as possible, the bad effects of home freedom and indulgence. So she took Amy in hand, and taught her as she herself had been taught sixty years ago—a process which carried dismay to Amy's soul, and made her feel like a fly in the web of a very strict spider.

She had to wash the cups every morning, and polish up the old-fashioned spoons, the fat silver tea-pot, and the glasses, till they shone. Then she must dust the room, and what a trying job that was! Not a speck escaped Aunt March's eye, and all the furniture had claw legs, and much carving, which was never dusted to suit. Then Polly must be fed, the lap-dog combed, and a dozen trips upstairs and down, to get things, to deliver orders, for the old lady was very lame, and seldom left her big chair. After these tiresome labours, she must do her lessons, which was a daily trial of every virtue she possessed. Then she was allowed one hour for exercise or play, and didn't she enjoy it? Laurie came every day, and wheedled Aunt March, till Amy was allowed to go out with him, when they walked and rode, and had capital times. After dinner, she had to read aloud, and sit still while the old lady slept, which she usually did for an hour, as she dropped off over the first page. Then patchwork or towels appeared, and Amy sewed with outward meekness and inward rebellion till dusk, when she was allowed to amuse herself as she liked till tea-time. The evenings were the worst of all, for Aunt March fell to telling long stories about her youth, which were so unutterably dull that Amy was always ready to go to bed, intending to cry over her hard fate, but usually going to sleep before she had squeezed out more than a tear or two.

If it had not been for Laurie, and old Esther, the maid, she felt that she never could have got through that dreadful time. The parrot alone was enough to drive her distracted, for he soon felt that she did not admire him, and revenged himself by being as mischievous as possible. He pulled her hair whenever she came near him, upset his bread and milk to plague her when she had newly cleaned his cage, made Mop bark by pecking at him while Madam dozed; called her names before company, and behaved in all respects like a reprehensible old bird. Then she could not endure the dog —a fat, cross beast, who snarled and yelped at her when she made his toilet, and who lay on his back, with all his legs in the air and a most idiotic expression of countenance when he wanted something to eat, which was about a dozen times a day. The cook was bad-tempered, the old coachman deaf, and Esther the only one who ever took any notice of the young lady.

Esther was a French woman, who had lived with "Madame", as she called her mistress, for many years, and who rather tyrannized over the old lady, who could not get along without her. Her real name was Estelle, but Aunt March ordered her to change it, and she obeyed, on condition that she was never asked to change her religion. She took a fancy to Mademoiselle, and amused her very much, with odd stories of her life in France, when Amy sat with her while she got up Madame's laces. She also allowed her to roam about the great house, and examine the curious and pretty things stored away in the big wardrobes and the ancient chests; for Aunt March hoarded like a magpie. Amy's chief delight was an Indian cabinet, full of queer drawers, little pigeonholes, and secret places, in which were kept all sorts of ornaments, some precious, some merely curious, all more or less antique. To examine and arrange these things gave Amy great satisfaction, especially the jewel-cases, in which, on velvet cushions, reposed the ornaments which had adorned a belle forty years ago. There was the garnet set which Aunt March wore when she came out, the pearls her father gave her on her wedding day, her lover's diamonds, the jet mourning rings and pins, and queer lockets, with portraits of dead friends, and weeping willows made of hair inside; the baby bracelets her one little daughter had worn; Uncle March's big watch, with the red seal so many childish hands had played with, and in a box, all by itself, lay Aunt March's wedding-ring, too small now for her fat finger, but put carefully away, like the most precious jewel of them all.

"Which would Mademoiselle choose if she had her will?" asked Esther, who always sat near to watch over and lock up the valuables.

"I liked the diamonds best, but there is no necklace among them, and I'm fond of necklaces, they are so becoming. I should choose this if I might," replied Amy, looking with great admiration at a string of gold and ebony beads, from which hung a heavy cross of the same.

"I, too, covet that, but not as a necklace; ah, no! to me it is a rosary, and as such I should use it like a good Catholic," said Esther, eyeing the handsome thing wistfully.

"Is it meant to use as you use the string of good-smelling wooden beads hanging over your glass?" asked Amy.

"Truly, yes, to pray with. It would be pleasing to the saints if one used so fine a rosary as this, instead of wearing it as a vain bijou. If Mademoiselle went apart each day to meditate and pray, as did the good mistress whom I served before Madame, it would be well. She had a little chapel, and in it found solacement for much trouble."

"Would it be right for me to do so too?" asked Amy, who, in her loneliness, felt the need of help of some sort, and found that she was apt to forget her little book, now that Beth was not there to remind her of it.

"It would be excellent and charming; and I shall gladly arrange the little dressing-room for you if you like it. Say nothing to Madame, but when she sleeps go you and sit alone a while to think good thoughts, and pray the dear God to preserve your sister."

Esther was truly pious, and quite sincere in her advice; for she had an affectionate heart, and felt much for the sisters in their anxiety. Amy liked the idea and gave her leave to arrange the light closet next her room, hoping it would do her good.

"I wish I knew where all these pretty things would go when Aunt March dies," she said, as she slowly replaced the shining rosary, and shut the jewel-cases one by one.

"To you and your sisters. I know it; Madame confides in me; I witnessed her will, and it is to be so," whispered Esther, smiling.

"How nice! but I wish she'd let us have them now. Pro-cras-ti-nation is not agreeable," observed Amy, taking a last look at the diamonds.

"It is too soon yet for the young ladies to wear these things. The first one who is affianced will have the pearls—Madame has said it; and I have a fancy that the little turquoise ring will be given to you when you go, for Madame approves your good behaviour and charming manners."

"Do you think so? Oh, I'll be a lamb, if I can only have that lovely ring! It's ever so much prettier than Kitty Bryant's. I do like Aunt March after all"; and Amy tried on the blue ring with a delightful face, and a firm resolve to earn it.

From that day she was a model of obedience, and the old lady complacently admired the success of her training. Esther fitted up the closet with a little table, placed a foot-stool before it, and over it a picture taken from one of the shut-up rooms. She thought it was of no great value, but, being appropriate, she borrowed it, well knowing that Madame would never know it, nor care if she did. It was, however, a very valuable copy of one of the famous pictures of the world, and Amy's beauty-loving eyes were never tired of looking up at the sweet face of the divine mother, while tender thoughts of her own were busy at her heart. On the table she laid her little testament and hymn-book, kept a vase always full of the best flowers Laurie brought her, and came every day to sit alone, "thinking good thoughts, and praying the dear God to preserve her sister". Esther had given her a rosary of black beads, with a silver cross, but Amy hung it up and did not use it, feeling more than doubtful as to its fitness for Protestant prayers.

The little girl was very sincere in all this, for, being left alone outside the safe home-nest, she felt the need of some kind hand to hold by so sorely, that she instinctively turned to the strong and tender friend, Whose fatherly love most closely surrounds His little children. She missed her mother's help to understand and rule herself, but having been taught where to look, she did her best to find the way, and walk in it confidingly. But Amy was a young pilgrim, and just now her burden seemed very heavy. She tried to forget herself, to keep cheerful, and be satisfied with doing right, though no one saw or praised her for it. In her first effort at being very, very good, she decided to make her will, as Aunt March had done; so that if she *did* fall ill and die, her possessions might be justly and generously divided. It cost her a pang even to think of giving up the little treasures which in her eyes were as precious as the old lady's jewels.

During one of her play-hours she wrote out the important document as well as she could, with some help from Esther as to certain legal terms, and, when the good-natured French woman had signed her name, Amy felt relieved, and laid it by to show Laurie, whom she wanted as a second witness. As it was a rainy day, she went upstairs to amuse herself in one of the large chambers, and took Polly with her for company. In this room there was a wardrobe full of old-fashioned costumes, with which Esther allowed her to play, and it was her favourite amusement to array herself in the faded brocades, and parade up and down before the long mirror, making stately courtesies, and sweeping her train about, with a rustle which delighted her ears. So busy was she on this day that she did not hear Laurie's ring, nor see his face peeping in at her, as she gravely promenaded to and fro, flirting her fan and tossing her head, on which she wore a great pink turban, contrasting oddly with her blue brocade dress and yellow quilted petticoat. She was obliged to walk carefully, for she had on high-heeled shoes, and, as Laurie told Jo afterwards, it was a comical sight to see her mince along in her gay suit, with Polly sidling and bridling just behind her, imitating her as well as he could, and occasionally stopping to laugh or exclaim, "Ain't we fine? Get along, you fright! Hold your tongue! Kiss me, dear! Ha! ha!"

Having with difficulty restrained an explosion of merriment lest it should offend her majesty, Laurie tapped, and was graciously received.

"Sit down and rest while I put these things away; then I want to consult you about a very serious matter," said Amy, when she had shown her splendour, and driven Polly into a corner. "That bird is the trial of my life," she continued, removing the pink mountain from her head, while Laurie seated himself astride of a chair. "Yesterday, when Aunt was asleep, and I was trying to be as still as a mouse, Polly began to squall and flap about in his cage; so I went to let him out, and found a big spider there. I poked it out, and it ran under the bookcase; Polly marched straight after it, stooped down and peeped under the bookcase, saying, in his funny way, with a cock of his eye, 'Come out and take a walk, my dear.' I *couldn't* help laughing, which made Poll swear, and Aunt woke up and scolded us both."

"Did the spider accept the old fellow's invitation?" asked Laurie, yawning.

"Yes; out it came, and away ran Polly, frightened to death, and scrambled up on Aunt's chair, calling out, 'Catch her! catch her! catch her!' as I chased the spider."

"That's a lie! Oh, lor!" cried the parrot, pecking at Laurie's toes.

"I'd wring your neck if you were mine, you old torment," cried Laurie, shaking his fist at the bird, who put his head on one side, and gravely croaked, "Allyluyer! bless your buttons, dear!"

"Now I'm ready," said Amy, shutting the wardrobe, and taking a paper out of her pocket. "I want you to read that, please, and tell me if it is legal and right. I felt that I ought to do it, for life is uncertain and I don't want any ill-feeling over my tomb."

Laurie bit his lips, and turning a little from the pensive speaker read the following document, with praiseworthy gravity, considering the spelling:

"MY LAST WILL AND TESTAMENT

"I, Amy Curtis March, being in my sane mind, do give and bequeath all my earthly property—viz., to wit:— namely

"To my Father, my best pictures, sketches, maps, and works of art, including frames. Also my $100, to do what he likes with.

"To my Mother, all my clothes, except the blue apron with pockets—also my likeness, and my medal, with much love.

"To my dear sister Margaret, I give my turkquoise ring (if I get it), also my green box with the doves on it, also my piece of real lace for her neck, and my sketch of her as a memorial of her 'little girl'.

"To Jo I leave my breast-pin, the one mended with sealing wax, also my bronze inkstand—she lost the cover—and my most precious plaster rabbit, because I am sorry I burnt up her story.

"To Beth (if she lives after me) I give my dolls and the little bureau, my fan, my linen collars, and my new slippers if she can wear them being thin when she gets well. And I herewith also leave her my regret that I ever made fun of old Joanna.

"To my friend and neighbour Theodore Laurence I bequeath my paper marshay portfolio, my clay model of a horse though he did say it hadn't any neck. Also in return for his great kindness in the hour of affliction any one of my artistic works he likes, Noter Dame is the best.

"To our venerable benefactor Mr. Laurence I leave my purple box with a looking glass in the cover which will be nice for his pens and remind him of the departed girl who thanks him for his favours to her family, specially Beth.

"I wish my favourite playmate Kitty Bryant to have the blue silk apron and my gold bead ring with a kiss.

"To Hannah I give the bandbox she wanted and all the patch work I leave hoping she will 'remember me, when it you see'.

"And now having disposed of my most valuable property I hope all will be satisfied and not blame the dead. I forgive everyone, and trust we may all meet when the trump shall sound. Amen.

"To this will and testament I set my hand and seal on this 20th day of Nov. Anni Domino 1861.

"AMY CURTIS MARCH.

"Witnesses { ESTELLE VALNOR,
THEODORE LAURENCE."

The last name was written in pencil, and Amy explained that he was to rewrite it in ink, and seal it up for her properly.

'What put it into your head? Did anyone tell you about Beth's giving away her things?" asked Laurie, soberly, as Amy laid a bit of red tape, with sealing-wax, a taper, and a standish before him.

She explained; and then asked anxiously, "What about Beth?"

"I'm sorry I spoke: but as I did I'll tell you. She felt so ill one day that she wanted to give her piano to Meg, her cats to you, and the poor old doll to Jo, who would love it for her sake. She was sorry she had so little to give, and left locks of hair to the rest of us, and her best love to Grandpa. *She* never thought of a will."

Laurie was signing and sealing as he spoke, and did not look up till a great tear dropped on the paper. Amy's face was full of trouble; but she only said, "Don't people put sort of postscripts to their wills, sometimes?"

"Yes; 'codicils', they call them."

"Put one in mine, then—that I wish *all* my curls cut off, and given round to my friends. I forgot it; but I want it done, though it will spoil my looks."

Laurie added it, smiling at Amy's last and greatest sacrifice. Then he amused her for an hour, and was much interested in all her trials. But when he came to go, Amy held him back to whisper, with trembling lips, "Is there really any danger about Beth?"

"I'm afraid there is; but we must hope for the best, so don't cry, dear"; and Laurie put his arm about her with a brotherly gesture which was very comforting.

When he had gone, she went to her little room, and sitting in the twilight, prayed for Beth, with streaming tears and an aching heart, feeling that a million turquoise rings would not console her for the loss of her gentle little sister.

Chapter 20

CONFIDENTIAL

I don't think I have any words in which to tell the meeting of the mother and daughters; such hours are beautiful to live, but very hard to describe, so I will leave it to the imagination of my readers, merely saying that the house was full of genuine happiness, and that Meg's tender hope was realized; for when Beth woke from that long, healing sleep, the first objects on which her eyes fell *were* the little rose and Mother's face. Too weak to wonder at anything, she only smiled, and nestled close into the loving arms about her, feeling that the hungry longing was satisfied at last. Then she slept again, and the girls waited upon their mother; for she would not unclasp the thin hand which clung to hers even in sleep.

Hannah had "dished up" an astonishing breakfast for the traveller, finding it impossible to vent her excitement in any other way; and Meg and Jo fed their mother like dutiful young storks, while they listened to her whispered account of Father's state, Mr. Brooke's promise to stay and nurse him, the delays which the storm occasioned on the homeward journey, and the unspeakable comfort Laurie's hopeful face had given her when she arrived, worn out with fatigue, anxiety, and cold.

What a strange, yet pleasant day that was! so brilliant and gay without, for all the world seemed abroad to welcome the first snow; so quiet and reposeful within, for everyone slept, spent with watching, and a sabbath stillness reigned through the house, while nodding Hannah mounted guard at the door. With a blissful sense of burdens lifted off, Meg and Jo closed their weary eyes, and lay at rest, like storm-beaten boats, safe at anchor in a quiet harbour. Mrs. March would not leave Beth's side, but rested in the big chair, waking often to look at, touch, and brood over her child, like a miser over some recovered treasure.

Laurie, meanwhile, posted off to comfort Amy, and told his story so well that Aunt March actually "sniffed" herself, and never once said, "I told you so". Amy came out so strong on this occasion that I think the good thoughts in the little chapel really began to bear fruit. She dried her tears quickly, restrained her impatience to see her mother, and never even thought of the turquoise ring, when the old lady heartily agreed in Laurie's opinion, that she behaved "like a capital little woman". Even Polly seemed impressed, for he called her "good girl", blessed her buttons, and begged her to "come and take a walk, dear!" in his most affable tone. She would very gladly have gone out to enjoy the bright wintry weather; but, discovering that Laurie was dropping with sleep in spite of manful efforts to conceal the fact, she persuaded him to rest on the sofa, while she wrote a note to her mother. She was a long time about it, and, when she returned, he was stretched out, with both arms under his head, sound asleep, while Aunt March had pulled down the curtains, and sat doing nothing in an unusual fit of benignity.

After a while, they began to think he was not going to wake till night, and I'm not sure that he would, had he not been effectually roused by Amy's cry of joy at sight of her mother. There probably were a good many happy little girls in and about the city that day, but it is my private opinion that Amy was the happiest of all, when she sat in her mother's lap and told her trials, receiving consolation and compensation in the shape of approving smiles and fond caresses. They were alone together in the little room, to which her mother did not object when its purpose was explained to her.

"On the contrary, I like it very much, dear," looking from the footstool to the well-worn little book, and the lovely picture with its garland of evergreen. "It is an excellent plan to have some place where we can go to be quiet, when things vex or grieve us. There are a good many hard times in this life of ours, but we can always bear them if we ask help in the right way. I think my little girl is learning this?"

"Yes, Mother; and when I go home I mean to have a corner in the big closet to put my books, and the copy of that picture which I've tried to make. The woman's face is not good—it's too beautiful for me to draw—but the baby is done better, and I love it very much. I like to think he was a little child once, for then I don't seem so far away, and that helps me."

As Amy pointed to the smiling Christ-child on His mother's knee, Mrs. March saw something on the lifted hand that made her smile. She said nothing, but Amy understood the look, and, after a minute's pause, she added, gravely:

"I wanted to speak to you about this, but I forgot it. Aunt gave me the ring today; she called me to her and kissed me, and put it on my finger, and said I was a credit to her, and she'd like to keep me always. She gave me that funny guard to keep the turquoise on, as it's too big. I'd like to wear them, Mother; can I?"

"They are very pretty, but I think you're rather too young for such ornaments, Amy," said Mrs. March, looking at the plump little hand, with the band of sky-blue stones on the forefinger, and the quaint guard, formed of two tiny golden hands clasped together.

"I'll try not to be vain," said Amy. "I don't think I like it only because it's so pretty; but I want to wear it as the girl in the story wore her bracelets, to remind me of something."

"Do you mean Aunt March?" asked her mother, laughing.

"No, to remind me not to be selfish." Amy looked so earnest and sincere about it, that her mother stopped laughing, and listened respectfully to the little plan.

"I've thought a great deal lately about my 'bundle of naughties', and being selfish is the largest one on it; so I'm going to try hard to cure it, if I can. Beth isn't selfish, and that's the reason everyone loves her and feels so bad at the thought of losing her. People wouldn't feel half so bad about me if I was sick, and I don't deserve to have them; but I'd like to be loved and missed by a great many friends, so I'm going to try and be like Beth all I can. I'm apt to forget my resolutions; but if I had something always about me to remind me, I guess I should do better. May I try this way?"

"Yes; but I have more faith in the corner of the big closet. Wear your ring, dear, and do your best; I think you will prosper, for the sincere wish to be good is half the battle. Now I must go back to Beth. Keep up your heart, little daughter, and we will soon have you home again."

That evening, while Meg was writing to her father, to report the traveller's safe arrival, Jo slipped upstairs into Beth's room, and, finding her mother in her usual place, stood a minute twisting her fingers in her hair, with a worried gesture and an undecided look.

"What is it, deary?" asked Mrs. March, holding out her hand, with a face which invited confidence.

"I want to tell you something, Mother."

"About Meg?"

"How quickly you guessed! Yes, it's about her, and though it's a little thing, it fidgets me."

"Beth is asleep; speak low, and tell me all about it. That Moffat hasn't been here, I hope?" asked Mrs. March, rather sharply.

"No, I should have shut the door in his face if he had," said Jo, settling herself on the floor at her mother's feet. "Last summer Meg left a pair of gloves over at the Laurences', and only one was returned. We forgot all about it, till Teddy told me that Mr. Brooke had it. He kept it in his waistcoat pocket, and once it fell out, and Teddy joked him about it, and Mr. Brooke owned that he liked Meg, but didn't dare say so, she was so young and he so poor. Now, isn't it a *dreadful* state of things?"

"Do you think Meg cares for him?" asked Mrs. March, with an anxious look.

"Mercy me! I don't know anything about love and such nonsense!" cried Jo, with a funny mixture of interest and contempt. "In novels, the girls show it by starting and blushing, fainting away, growing thin, and acting like fools. Now Meg does not do anything of the sort; she eats and drinks and sleeps, like a sensible creature; she looks straight in my face when I talk about that man, and only blushes a little bit when Teddy jokes about lovers. I forbid him to do it, but he doesn't mind me as he ought."

"Then you fancy that Meg is *not* interested in John?"

"Who?" cried Jo, staring.

"Mr. Brooke. I call him 'John' now; we fell into the way of doing so at the hospital, and he likes it."

"Oh, dear! I know you'll take his part: he's been good to Father, and you won't send him away, but let Meg marry him, if she wants to. Mean thing! to go petting Papa and helping you, just to wheedle you into liking him"; and Jo pulled her hair again with a wrathful tweak.

"My dear, don't get angry about it, and I will tell you how it happened. John went with me at Mr. Laurence's request, and was so devoted to poor Father that we couldn't help getting fond of him. He was perfectly open and honourable about Meg, for he told us he loved her, but would earn a comfortable home before he asked her to marry him. He only wanted our leave to love her and work for her, and the right to make her love him if he could. He is a truly excellent young man, and we could not refuse to listen to him; but I will not consent to Meg engaging herself so young."

"Of course not; it would be idiotic! I knew there was mischief brewing; I felt it; and now it's worse than I imagined. I just wish I could marry Meg myself, and keep her safe in the family."

This odd arrangement made Mrs. March smile; but she said gravely, "Jo I confide in you, and don't wish you to say anything to Meg yet. When John comes back, and I see them together, I can judge better of her feelings towards him."

"She'll see his in those handsome eyes that she talks about, and then it will be all up with her. She's got such a soft heart, it will melt like butter in the sun if anyone looks sentimentally at her. She read the short reports he sent more than she did your letters, and pinched me when I spoke of it, and likes brown eyes, and doesn't think John an ugly name, and she'll go and fall in love, and there's an end of peace and fun, and cosy times together. I see it all! they'll go lovering around the house, and we shall have to dodge; Meg will be absorbed, and no good to me any more; Brooke will scratch up a fortune somehow, carry her off, and make a hole in the family; and I shall break my heart, and everything will be abominably uncomfortable. Oh, dear me! why weren't we all boys, then there wouldn't be any bother."

Jo leaned her chin on her knees, in a disconsolate attitude, and shook her fist at the represhensible John. Mrs. March sighed, and Jo looked up with an air of relief.

"You don't like it, Mother? I'm glad of it. Let's send him about his business, and not tell Meg a word of it, but all be happy together as we always have been."

"I did wrong to sigh, Jo. It is natural and right you should all go to homes of your own, in time; but I do want to keep my girls as long as I can; and I am sorry that this happened so soon, for Meg is only seventeen, and it will be some years before John can make a home for her. Your father and I have agreed that she shall not bind herself in any way, nor be married, before twenty. If she and John love one another, they can wait, and test the love by doing so. She is conscientious, and I have no fear of her treating him unkindly. My pretty, tender-hearted girl! I hope things will go happily with her."

"Hadn't you rather have her marry a rich man?" asked Jo, as her mother's voice faltered a little over the last words.

"Money is a good and useful thing, Jo; and I hope my girls will never feel the need of it too bitterly, nor be tempted by too much. I should like to know that John was firmly established in some good business, which gave him an income large enough to keep free from debt and make Meg comfortable. I'm not ambitious for a splendid fortune, a fashionable position, or a great name for my girls. If rank and money come with love and virtue, also, I should accept them gratefully, and enjoy your good fortune; but I know, by experience, how much genuine happiness can be had in a plain little house, where the daily bread is earned, and some privations give sweetness to the few pleasures. I am content to see Meg begin humbly, for, if I am not mistaken, she will be rich in the possession of a good man's heart, and that is better than a fortune."

"I understand, Mother, and quite agree; but I'm disappointed about Meg, for I'd planned to have her marry Teddy by and by, and sit in the lap of luxury all her days. Wouldn't it be nice?" asked Jo, looking up, with a brighter face.

"He is younger than she, you know," began Mrs.March; but Jo broke in: "Only a little; he's old for his age, and tall; and can be quite grown-up in his manners if he likes. Then he's rich and generous and good, and loves us all; and *I* say it's a pity my plan is spoilt."

"I'm afraid Laurie is hardly grown up enough to Meg, and altogether too much of a weathercock, just now, for anyone to depend on. Don't make plans, Jo; but let time and their own hearts mate your friends. We can't meddle safely in such matters, and had better not get 'romantic rubbish', as you call it, into our heads, lest it spoil our friendship."

"Well, I won't; but I hate to see things going all criss-cross and getting snarled up, when a pull here and a snip there would straighten it out. I wish wearing flat-irons on our heads would keep us from growing up. But buds will be roses, and kittens, cats—more's the pity!"

"What's that about flat-irons and cats?" asked Meg, as she crept into the room, with the finished letter in her hand.

"Only one of my stupid speeches. I'm going to bed; come, Meggy," said Jo, unfolding herself, like an animated puzzle.

"Quite right, and beautifully written. Please add that I send my love to John," said Mrs. March, as she glanced over the letter, and gave it back.

'Do you call him 'John'?" asked Meg, smiling, with her innocent eyes looking down into her mother's.

"Yes; he has been like a son to us, and we are very fond of him," replied Mrs. March, returning the look with a keen one.

"I'm glad of that, he is so lonely. Good-night, Mother dear. It is so inexpressibly comfortable to have you here," was Meg's quiet answer.

The kiss her mother gave her was a very tender one; and, as she went away, Mrs. March said, with a mixture of satisfaction and regret, "She does not love John yet, but will soon learn to."

CHAPTER 21

LAURIE MAKES MISCHIEF, AND JO MAKES PEACE

Jo's face was a study next day, for the secret rather weighed upon her, and she found it hard not to look mysterious and important. Meg observed it, but did not trouble herself to make inquiries, for she had learned that the best way to manage Jo was by the law of contraries, so she felt sure of being told everything if she did not ask. She was rather surprised, therefore, when the silence remained unbroken, and Jo assumed a patronizing air, which decidedly aggravated Meg, who in her turn assumed an air of dignified reserve, and devoted herself to her mother. This left Jo to her own devices; for Mrs. March had taken her place as nurse, and bade her rest, exercise, and amuse herself after her long confinement. Amy being gone, Laurie was her only refuge; and, much as she enjoyed his society, she rather dreaded him just then, for he was an incorrigible tease, and she feared he would coax her secret from her.

She was quite right; for the mischief-loving lad no sooner suspected a mystery than he set himself to find it out, and led Jo a trying life of it. He wheedled, bribed, ridiculed, threatened, and scolded; affected indifference, that he might surprise the truth from her; declared he knew, then that he didn't care; and, at last, by dint of perseverance, he satisfied himself that it concerned Meg and Mr. Brooke. Feeling indignant that he was not taken into his tutor's confidence, he set his wits to work to devise some proper retaliation for the slight.

Meg meanwhile had apparently forgotten the matter, and was absorbed in preparations for her father's return; but all of a sudden a change seemed to come over her, and, for a day or two, she was quite unlike herself. She started when spoken to, blushed when looked at, was very quiet, and sat over her sewing, with a timid, troubled look on her face. To her mother's inquiries she answered that she was quite well, and Jo's she silenced by begging to be let alone.

"She feels it in the air—love, I mean—and she's going very fast. She's got most of the symptoms—is twittery and cross, doesn't eat, lies awake, and mopes in corners. I caught her singing that song he gave her, and once she said 'John', as you do, and then turned as red as a poppy. Whatever shall we do?" said Jo, looking ready for any measures, however violent.

"Nothing but wait. Let her alone, be kind and patient, and Father's coming will settle everything," replied her mother.

"Here's a note to you, Meg, all sealed up! How odd! Teddy never seals mine," said Jo, next day, as she distributed the contents of the little post-office.

Mrs. March and Jo were deep in their own affairs, when a sound from Meg made them look up to see her staring at her note with a frightened face.

"My child, what is it?" cried her mother, running to her, while Jo tried to take the paper which had done the mischief.

"It's all a mistake—he didn't send it. Oh, Jo, how could you do it?" and Meg hid her face in her hands, crying as if her heart was quite broken.

"Me! I've done nothing! What's she talking about?" cried Jo, bewildered.

Meg's mild eyes kindled with anger as she pulled a crumpled note from her pocket, and threw it at Jo, saying reproachfully: "You wrote it, and that bad boy helped you. How could you be so rude, so mean, and cruel to us both?"

Jo hardly heard her, for she and her mother were reading the note, which was written in a peculiar hand.

MY DEAREST MARGARET—I can no longer restrain my passion and must know my fate before I return. I dare not tell your parents yet, but I think they would consent if they knew that we adore one another. Mr. Laurence will help me to some good place, and then, my sweet girl, you will make me happy. I implore you to say nothing to your family yet, but to send one word of hope through Laurie to

Your devoted JOHN.

"Oh, the little villain! that's the way he meant to pay me for keeping my word to Mother. I'll give him a hearty scolding, and bring him over to beg pardon," cried Jo, burning to execute immediate justice. But her mother held her back, saying, with a look she seldom wore: "Stop, Jo, you must clear yourself first. You have played so many pranks, that I am afraid you have had a hand in this."

"On my word, Mother, I haven't! I never saw that note before, and I don't know anything about it, as true as I live!" said Jo, so earnestly that they believed her. "If I *had* taken a part in it I'd have done it better than this, and have written a sensible note. I should think you'd have known Mr. Brooke wouldn't write such stuff as that," she added, scornfully tossing down the paper.

"It's like his writing," faltered Meg, comparing it with the note in her hand.

"Oh, Meg, you didn't answer it?" cried Mrs. March, quickly.

"Yes, I did!" and Meg hid her face again, overcome with shame.

"Here's a scrape! *Do* let me bring that wicked boy over to explain, and be lectured. I can't rest till I get hold of him"; and Jo made for the door again.

"Hush! let me manage this, for it is worse than I thought. Margaret, tell me the whole story," commanded Mrs. March, sitting down by Meg, yet keeping hold of Jo, lest she should fly off.

"I received the first letter from Laurie, who didn't look as if he knew anything about it," began Meg, without looking up. "I was worried at first, and meant to tell you; then I remembered how you liked Mr. Brooke, so I thought you wouldn't mind if I kept my little secret for a few days. I'm so silly that I liked to think no one knew; and, while I was deciding what to say I felt like the girls in books, who have such things to do.

"Forgive me, Mother, I'm paid for my silliness now; I never can look him in the face again."

"What did you say to him?" asked Mrs. March.

"I only said I was too young to do anything about it yet; that I didn't wish to have secrets from you, and he must speak to Father. I was very grateful for his kindness, and would be his friend, but nothing more, for a long while."

Mrs. March smiled, as if pleased, and Jo clapped her hands, exclaiming, with a laugh:

"You are almost equal to Caroline Percy, who was a pattern of prudence! Tell on, Meg. What did he say to that?"

"He writes in a different way entirely, telling me that he never sent any love letter at all, and is very sorry that my roguish sister, Jo, should take such liberties with our names. It's very kind and respectful, but think how dreadful for me!"

Meg leaned against her mother, looking the image of despair, and Jo tramped about the room, calling Laurie names. All of a sudden, she stopped, caught up the two notes, and, after looking at them closely, said decidedly, "I don't believe Brooke ever saw either of these letters. Teddy wrote both, and keeps yours to crow over me with, because I wouldn't tell him my secret."

"Don't have any secrets Jo; tell it to Mother, and keep out of trouble, as I should have done," said Meg, warningly.

"Bless you, child! Mother told me."

"That will do, I'll comfort Meg while you go and get Laurie. I shall sift the matter to the bottom, and put a stop to such pranks at once."

Away ran Jo, and Mrs. March gently told Meg Mr. Brooke's real feelings. "Now, dear, what are your own? Do you love him enough to wait till he can make a home for you, or will you keep yourself quite free for the present?"

"I've been so scared and worried, I don't want to have anything to do with lovers for a long while—perhaps never," answered Meg, petulantly. "If John *doesn't* know anything about this nonsense, don't tell him, and make Jo and Laurie hold their tongues. I won't be deceived and plagued and made a fool of—it's a shame!"

Seeing that Meg's usually gentle temper was roused, and her pride hurt by this mischievous joke, Mrs. March soothed her by promises of entire silence, and great discretion for the future.

The instant Laurie's step was heard in the hall, Meg fled into the study, and Mrs. March received the culprit alone. Jo had not told him why he was wanted, fearing he wouldn't come; but he knew the minute he saw Mrs. March's face, and stood twirling his hat, with a guilty air which convicted him at once. Jo was dismissed, but chose to march up and down the hall like a sentinel, having some fear that the prisoner might bolt. The sound of voices in the parlour rose and fell for half an hour; but what happened during that interview the girls never knew.

When they were called in, Laurie was standing by their mother, with such a penitent face that Jo forgave him on the spot, but did not think it wise to betray the fact. Meg received his humble apology, and was much comforted by the assurance that Brooke knew nothing of the joke.

"I'll never tell him to my dying day—wild horses shan't drag it out of me; so you'll forgive me, Meg, and I'll do anything to show how out-and-out sorry I am," he added, looking very much ashamed of himself.

"I'll try; but it was a very ungentlemanly thing to do. I didn't think you could be so sly and malicious, Laurie," replied Meg, trying to hide her maidenly confusion under a gravely reproachful air.

"It was altogether abominable, and I don't deserve to be spoken to for a month; but you will, though, won't you?" and Laurie folded his hands together with such an imploring gesture, as he spoke in his irresistibly persuasive tone, that it was impossible to frown upon him, in spite of his scandalous behaviour. Meg pardoned him, and Mrs. March's grave face relaxed, in spite of her efforts to keep sober, when she heard him declare that he would atone for his sins by all sorts of penances and abase himself like a worm before the injured damsel. Jo stood aloof, meanwhile, trying to harden her heart against him, and succeeding only in primming up her face into an expression of entire disapprobation. Laurie looked at her once or twice, but, as she showed no sign of relenting, he felt injured, and turned his back on her till the others were done with him, when he made her a low bow, and walked off without a word.

As soon as he had gone, she wished she had been more forgiving; and when Meg and her mother went upstairs she felt lonely and longed for Teddy. After resisting for some time, she yielded to the impulse and, armed with a book to return, went over to the big house.

"Is Mr. Laurence in?" asked Jo, of a housemaid, who was coming downstairs.

"Yes, miss; but I don't believe he's seeable just yet."
"Why not? is he ill?"
"La, no, miss, but he's had a scene with Mr. Laurie, who is in one of his tantrums about something, which vexes the old gentleman, so I dursn't go nigh him."
"Where is Laurie?"
"Shut up in his room, and he won't answer, though I've been a-tapping. I don't know what's to become of the dinner, for it's ready, and there's no one to eat it."
"I'll go and see what the matter is. I'm not afraid of either of them."
Up went Jo, and knocked smartly at the door of Laurie's little study.
"Stop that, or I'll open the door and make you!" called out the young gentleman, in a threatening tone.
Jo immediately knocked again; the door flew open, and in she bounced, before Laurie could recover from his surprise. Seeing that he really *was* out of temper, Jo, who knew how to manage him, assumed a contrite expression, and going artistically down upon her knees, said meekly, "Please forgive me for being so cross. I came to make it up, and can't go away till I have."
"It's all right. Get up, and don't be a goose, Jo," was the cavalier reply to her petition.
"Thank you; I will. Could I ask what's the matter? You don't look exactly easy in your mind."
"I've been shaken, and I won't bear it!" growled Laurie, indignantly.
"Who did it?" demanded Jo.
"Grandfather; if it had been anyone else I'd have—" And the injured youth finished his sentence by an energetic gesture of the right arm.
"That's nothing; I often shake you, and you don't mind," said Jo, soothingly.
"Pooh! you're a girl, and it's fun; but I'll allow no man to shake *me*."
"I don't think anyone would care to try it, if you looked as much like a thundercloud as you do now. Why were you treated so?"
"Just because I wouldn't say what your mother wanted me for. I'd promised not to tell, and of course I wasn't going to break my word."

"Couldn't you satisfy your grandpa in any other way?"

"No; he *would* have the truth, the whole truth, and nothing but the truth. I'd have told my part of the scrape, if I could without bringing Meg in. As I couldn't, I held my tongue, and bore the scolding till the old gentleman collared me. Then I got angry, and bolted, for fear I should forget myself."

"It wasn't nice, but he's sorry, I know; so go down and make up. I'll help you."

"Hanged if I do! I'm not going to be lectured and pummelled by everyone, just for a bit of a frolic. I *was* sorry about Meg, and begged pardon like a man; but I won't do it again, when I wasn't in the wrong."

"He didn't know that."

"He ought to trust me, and not act as if I was a baby. It's no use, Jo; he's got to learn that I'm able to take care of myself, and don't need anyone's apron strings to hold on by."

"What pepper-pots you are!" sighed Jo. "How do you mean to settle this affair?"

"Well, he ought to beg pardon, and believe me when I say I can't tell him what the fuss is about."

"Bless you! he won't do that."

"I won't go down till he does."

"Now, Teddy, be sensible; let it pass, and I'll explain what I can. You can't stay here, so what's the use of being melodramatic?"

"I don't intend to stay here long, anyway. I'll slip off and take a journey somewhere, and when grandpa misses me he'll come round fast enough."

"I dare say; but you ought not to go and worry him."

"Don't preach. I'll go to Washington and see Brooke; it's gay there, and I'll enjoy myself after the troubles."

"What fun you'd have! I wish I could run off too," said Jo, forgetting her part of Mentor in lively visions of material life at the capital.

"Come on, then! Why not? You go and surprise your father, and I'll stir up old Brooke.

"It would be a glorious joke; let's do it, Jo. We'll leave a letter saying we are all right, and trot off at once. I've got money enough; it will do you good, and be no harm, as you go to your father."

For a moment Jo looked as if she would agree; for, wild as the plan was, it just suited her. She was tired of care and confinement, Longed for change, and thoughts of her father blended temptingly with the novel charms of camps and hospitals, liberty and fun. Her eyes kindled as they turned wistfully toward the window, but they fell on the old house opposite. And she shook her head with sorrowful decision.

"If I was a boy, we'd run away together, and have a capital time; but as I'm a miserable girl, I must be proper, and stop at home. Don't tempt me, Teddy, it's a crazy plan."

"That's the fun of it," began Laurie, who had got a wilful fit on him, and was possessed to break out of bounds in some way.

"Hold your tongue! " cried Jo, covering her ears. "'Prunes and prisms' are my doom, and I may as well make up my mind to it. I came here to moralise, not to hear about things that make me skip to think of."

"I know Meg would wet-blanket such a proposal, but I thought you had more spirit," began Laurie, insinuatingly.

"Bad boy, be quiet! Sit down and think of your own sins, don't go making me add to mine. If I get Grandpa to apologize for the shaking, will you give up running away?" asked Jo, seriously.

"Yes, but you won't do it," answered Laurie, who wished to "make up", but felt that his outraged dignity must be appeased first.

"If I can manage the young one I can the old one," muttered Jo, as she walked away, leaving Laurie bent over a railroad map, with his head propped up on both hands.

"Come in! " and Mr. Laurence's gruff voice sounded gruffer than ever, as Jo tapped at his door.

"It's only me, sir, come to return a book," she said, blandly, as she entered.

"Want any more?" asked the old gentleman, looking grim and vexed, but trying not to show it.

"Yes, please. I like old Sam so well, I think I'll try the second volume," returned Jo, hoping to propitiate him by accepting a second dose of Boswell's *Johnson* as he had recommended that lively work.

The shaggy eyebrows unbent a little, as he rolled the steps towards the shelf where the Johnsonian literature was placed. Jo skipped up, and sitting on the top step, affected to be searching for her book, but was really wondering how best to introduce the dangerous object of her visit. Mr. Laurence seemed to suspect that something was brewing in her mind; for, after taking several brisk turns about the room, he faced round on her, speaking so abruptly that *Rasselas* tumbled face downward on the floor.

"What has that boy been about? Don't try to shield him. I know he has been in mischief by the way he acted when he came home. I can't get a word from him; and when I threatened to shake the truth out of him he bolted upstairs, and locked himself into his room."

"He did do wrong, but we forgave him, and all promised not to say a word to anyone," began Jo, reluctantly.

"That won't do; he shall not shelter himself behind a promise from you soft-hearted girls. If he's done anything amiss, he shall confess, beg pardon, and be punished. Out with it, Jo! I won't be kept in the dark."

Mr. Laurence looked so alarming, and spoke so sharply, that Jo would gladly have run away, if she could, but she was perched aloft on the steps, and he stood at the foot, a lion in the path, so she had to stay and brave it out.

"Indeed, sir, I cannot tell; Mother forbade it. Laurie has confessed, asked pardon, and been punished quite enough. We don't keep silence to shield him, but someone else, and it will make more trouble if you interfere. Please don't; it was partly my fault, but it's all right now; so let's forget it, and talk about the *Rambler*, or something pleasant."

"Hang the *Rambler!* come down and give me your word that this harum-scarum boy of mine hasn't done anything ungrateful or impertinent. If he has, after all your kindness to him, I'll thrash him with my own hands."

The threat sounded awful, but did not alarm Jo, for she knew the irascible old gentleman would never lift a finger against his grandson, whatever he might say to the contrary. She obediently descended, and made as light of the prank as she could without betraying Meg or forgetting the truth.

"Hum—ha—well, if the boy held his tongue because he promised, and not from obstinacy, I'll forgive him. He's a stubborn fellow, and hard to manage," said Mr. Laurence, rubbing up his hair till it looked as if he had been out in a gale, and smoothing the frown from his brow with an air of relief.

"So am I; but a kind word will govern me when all the king's horses and all the king's men couldn't," said Jo, trying to say a kind word for her friend, who seemed to get out of one scrape only to fall into another.

'You think I'm not kind to him, hey?" was the sharp answer.

"Oh, dear, no, sir; you are rather too kind sometimes, and then just a trifle hasty when he tries your patience. Don't you think you are?"

Jo was determined to have it out now, and tried to look quite placid, though she quaked a little after her bold speech. To her great relief and surprise, the old gentleman only threw his spectacles on to the table, with a rattle, and exclaimed frankly: "You're right, girl, I am! I love the boy, but he tries my patience past bearing, and I don't know how it will end, if we go on so."

"I'll tell you, he'll run away." Jo was sorry for that speech the minute it was made; she meant to warn him that Laurie would not bear much restraint, and hoped he would be more forbearing with the lad.

Mr. Laurence's ruddy face changed suddenly, and he sat down, with a troubled glance at the picture of a handsome man, which hung over his table. It was Laurie's father, who *had* run away in his youth, and married against the imperious old man's will. Jo fancied he remembered and regretted the past, and she wished she had held her tongue.

"He won't do it unless he is very much worried, and only threatens it sometimes, when he gets tired of studying. I often think I should like to, especially since my hair was cut; so, if you ever miss us, you may advertise for two boys, and look among the ships bound for India."

She laughed as she spoke, and Mr. Laurence looked relieved, evidently taking the whole thing as a joke.

'You hussy, how dare you talk in that way? Where's your respect for me, and your proper bringing up? Bless the boys and girls! What torments they are; yet we can't do without them," he said, pinching her cheeks good-humouredly. "Go and bring that boy down to his dinner, tell him it's all right, and advise him not to put on tragedy airs with his grandfather. I won't bear it."

"He won't come, sir; he feels badly because you didn't believe him when he said he couldn't tell. I think the shaking hurt his feelings very much."

Jo tried to look pathetic, but must have failed, for Mr. Laurence began to laugh, and she knew the day was won.

"I'm sorry for that, and ought to thank him for not shaking *me*, I suppose. What the dickens does the fellow expect?" and the old gentleman looked a trifle ashamed of his own testiness.

"If I were you, I'd write him an apology, sir. He says he won't come down till he has one, and talks about Washington, and goes on in an absurd way. A formal apology will make him see how foolish he is, and bring him down quite amiable. Try it; he likes fun, and this way is better than talking. I'll carry it up, and teach him his duty."

Mr. Laurence gave her a sharp look, and put on his spectacles, saying slowly, "You're a sly puss, but I don't mind being managed by you and Beth. Here, give me a bit of paper, and let us have done with this nonsense."

The note was written in the terms which one gentleman would use to another after offering some deep insult. Jo dropped a kiss on the top of Mr. Laurence's bald head, and ran up to slip the apology under Laurie's door, advising him, through the keyhole, to be submissive, decorous, and a few other agreeable impossibilities. Finding the door locked again, she left the note to do its work, and was going quietly away, when the young gentleman slid down the banisters, and waited for her at the bottom, saying, with his most virtuous expression of countenance, "What a good fellow you are, Jo! Did you get blown up?" he added, laughing.

"No; he was pretty mild, on the whole."

"Ah! I got it all round; even you cast me off over there, and I felt just ready to go to the deuce," he began, apologetically.

"Don't talk in that way; turn over a new leaf and begin again, Teddy, my son."

"I keep turning over new leaves, and spoiling them, as I used to spoil my copy-books; and I make so many beginnings there never will be an end," he said, dolefully.

"Go and eat your dinner; you'll feel better after it. Men always croak when they are hungry," and Jo whisked out at the front door after that.

"That's a 'label' on my 'sect'", answered Laurie, quoting Amy, as he went to partake of humble-pie dutifully with his grandfather, who was quite saintly in temper, and overwhelmingly respectful in manner, all the rest of the day.

Everyone thought the matter ended and the little cloud blown over; but the mischief was done, for, though others forgot it, Meg remembered. She never alluded to a certain person, but she thought of him a good deal, dreamed dreams more than ever; and once Jo, rummaging her sister's desk for stamps, found a bit of paper scribbled over with the words, "Mrs. John Brooke"; whereat she groaned tragically, and cast it into the fire, feeling that Laurie's prank had hastened the evil day for her.

CHAPTER 22

PLEASANT MEADOWS

Like sunshine after storm were the peaceful weeks which followed. The invalids improved rapidly, and Mr. March began to talk of returning early in the new year. Beth was soon able to lie on the study sofa all day, amusing herself with the well-beloved cats at first, and, in time, with dolls' sewing, which had fallen sadly behind hand. Her once active limbs were so stiff and feeble that Jo took her a daily airing about the house in her strong arms. Meg cheerfully blackened and burnt her white hands cooking delicate messes for the "dear"; while Amy, a loyal slave of the ring, celebrated her return by giving away as many of her treasures as she could prevail on her sisters to accept.

As Christmas approached, the usual mysteries began to haunt the house, and Jo frequently convulsed the family by proposing utterly impossible or magnificently absurd ceremonies, in honour of this unusually merry Christmas. Laurie was equally impractical, and would have had bonfires, sky-rockets, and triumphal arches, if he had his own way. After many skirmishes and snubbings, the ambitious pair were considered effectually quenched, and went about with forlorn faces, which were rather belied by explosions of laughter when the two got together.

Several days of unusually mild weather fitly ushered in a splendid Christmas Day. Hannah "felt in her bones" that it was going to be an unusually fine day, and she proved herself a true prophetess, for everybody and everything seemed bound to produce a grand success. To begin with, Mr. March wrote that he should soon be with them; then Beth felt uncommonly well that morning, and, being dressed in her mother's gift—a soft crimson merino wrapper—was borne in triumph to the window to behold the offering of Jo and Laurie. The Unquenchables had done their best to be worthy of the name, for, like elves, they had worked by night, and conjured up a comical surprise. Out in the garden stood a stately snow-maiden, crowned with holly, bearing a basket of fruit and flowers in one hand, a great roll of new music in the other, a perfect rainbow of an Afghan round her chilly shoulders, and a Christmas carol issuing from her lips, on a pink paper streamer:

THE JUNGFRAU TO BETH
God bless you, dear Queen Bess!
  May nothing you dismay,
But health and peace and happiness
  Be yours, this Christmas Day.
Here's fruit to feed our busy bee,
  And flowers for her nose;
Here's music for her pianee,
  An Afghan for her toes.
A portrait of Joanna, see,
  By Raphael No. 2,
Who laboured with great industry
  To make it fair and true.
Accept a ribbon red, I beg,
  For Madam Purrer's tail;
And ice-cream made by lovely Peg—
  A Mont Blanc in a pail.
Their dearest love, my makers laid
  Within my breast of snow:
Accept it, and the Alpine maid,
  From Laurie and from Jo.

How Beth laughed when she saw it, how Laurie ran up and down to bring in the gifts, and what ridiculous speeches Jo made as she presented them!

"I'm so full of happiness, that, if Father was only here, I couldn't hold one drop more," said Beth, quite sighing with contentment, as Jo carried her off to the study to rest after the excitement and to refresh herself with some of the delicious grapes the "Jungfraun" had sent her.

"So am I," added Jo, slapping the pocket wherein reposed the long-desired *Undine and Sintram*.

"I'm sure I am," echoed Amy, poring over the engraved copy

of the Madonna and Child, which her mother had given her, in a pretty frame.

"Of course I am!" cried Meg, smoothing the silver folds of her first silk dress; for Mr. Laurence had insisted on giving it.

"How can *I* be otherwise?" said Mrs. March, gratefully, as her eyes went from her husband's letter to Beth's smiling face, and her hand caressed the brooch made of grey and golden, chestnut and dark brown hair, which the girls had just fastened on her breast. Now and then, in this workaday world, things do happen in the delightful story-book fashion, and what a comfort that is. Half an hour after everyone had said they were so happy they could only hold one drop more, the drop came. Laurie opened the parlour door, and popped his head in very quietly. He might just as well have turned a somersault and uttered an Indian war-whoop; for his face was so full of suppressed excitement and his voice so treacherously joyful, that everyone jumped up, though he only said, in a queer breathless voice, "Here's another Christmas present for the March family."

Before the words were well out of his mouth, he was whisked away somehow, and in his place appeared a tall man, muffled up to the eyes, leaning on the arm of another tall man, who tried to say something and couldn't. Of course there was a general stampede; and for several minutes everybody seemed to lose their wits, for the strangest things were done, and no one said a word. Mrs. March became invisible in the embrace of four pairs of loving arms; Jo disgraced herself by nearly fainting away, and had to be doctored by Laurie in the china-closet; Mr. Brooke kissed Meg entirely by mistake, as he somewhat incoherently explained; and Amy, the dignified, tumbled over a stool, and, never stopping to get up, hugged and cried over her father's boots in the most touching manner. Mrs. March was the first to recover herself, and held up her hand with a warning, "Hush! remember Beth!"

But it was too late; the study door flew open, the little red wrapper appeared on the threshold—joy put strength into the feeble limbs—and Beth ran straight into her father's arms. Never mind what happened just after that; for the full hearts overflowed, washing away the bitterness of the past, and leaving only the sweetness of the present.

It was not at all romantic, but a hearty laugh set everybody straight again, for Hannah was discovered behind the door, sobbing over the fat turkey, which she had forgotten to put down when she rushed up from the kitchen. As the laugh subsided, Mrs.

March began to thank Mr. Brooke for his faithful care of her husband, at which Mr. Brooke suddenly remembered that Mr. March needed rest, and, seizing Laurie, he precipitately retired. Then the two invalids were ordered to repose, which they did, by both sitting in one big armchair, and talking hard.

Mr. March told how he had longed to surprise them, and how when the fine weather came, he had been allowed by his doctor to take advantage of it; how devoted Brooke had been, and how he was altogether a most estimable and upright young man. Why Mr. March paused a minute just there, and, after a glance at Meg, who was violently poking the fire, looked at his wife with an inquiring lift of the eyebrows, I leave you to imagine; also why Mrs. March gently nodded her head, and asked, rather abruptly, if he wouldn't have something to eat. Jo saw and understood the look; and she stalked grimly away to get beef-tea, muttering to herself, as she slammed the door, "I hate estimable young men with brown eyes!"

There never *was* such a Christmas dinner as they had that day. The fat turkey was a sight to behold, when Hannah sent him up, stuffed, browned, and decorated; so was the plum-pudding, which quite melted in one's mouth; likewise the jellies, in which Amy revelled like a fly in a honey-pot. Everything turned out well; which was a mercy, Hannah said, "For my mind was that flustered, mum, that it's a merrycle I didn't roast the pudding, and stuff the turkey with raisins, let alone bilin' of it in a cloth."

Mr. Laurence and his grandson dined with them, also Mr. Brooke—at whom Jo glowered darkly, to Laurie's infinite amusement. Two easy-chairs stood side by side at the head of the table, in which sat Beth and her father, feasting modestly on chicken and a little fruit. They drank healths, told stories, sang songs, "reminisced", as the old folk say, and had a thoroughly good time. A sleigh-ride had been planned, but the girls would not leave their father; so the guests departed early, and, as twilight gathered, the happy family sat together round the fire.

"Just a year ago we were groaning over the dismal Christmas we expected to have. Do you remember?" asked Jo, breaking a short pause which had followed a long conversation about many things.

"Rather a pleasant year on the whole!" said Meg, smiling at the fire, and congratulating herself on having treated Mr. Brooke with dignity.

"I think it's been a pretty hard one," observed Amy, watching the light shine on her ring, with thoughtful eyes.

"I'm glad it's over, because we've got you back," whispered Beth, who sat on her father's knee.

"Rather a rough road for you to travel, my little pilgrims, especially the latter part of it. But you have got on bravely; and I think the burdens are in a fair way to tumble off very soon," said Mr. March, looking with fatherly satisfaction at the four young faces gathered round him.

"How do you know? Did Mother tell you?" asked Jo.

"Not much; straws show which way the wind blows, and I've made several discoveries today."

"Oh, tell us what they are!" cried Meg, who sat beside him.

"Here is one!" and taking up the hand which lay on the arm of his chair, he pointed to the roughened forefinger, a burn on the back, and two or three little hard spots on the palm.

"I remember a time when this hand was white and smooth, and your first care was to keep it so. It was very pretty then, but to me it is much prettier now—for in these seeming blemishes I read a little history. A burnt-offering has been made of vanity; this hardened palm has earned something better than blisters; and I'm sure the sewing done by these pricked fingers will last a long time, so much goodwill went into the stitches. Meg, my dear, I value the womanly skill which keeps home happy more than white hands or fashionable accomplishments. I'm proud to shake this good, industrious little hand, and hope I shall not soon be asked to give it away."

If Meg had wanted a reward for hours of patient labour, she received it in the hearty pressure of her father's hand, and the approving smile he gave her.

"What about Jo? Please say something nice; for she has tried so hard, and been so very, very good to me," said Beth, in her father's ear. He laughed, and looked across at the tall girl who sat opposite, with an unusually mild expression in her brown face.

"In spite of the curly crop, I don't see the 'son Jo' whom I left a year ago," said Mr. March. "I see a young lady who pins her collar straight, laces her boots neatly, and neither whistles, talks slang, nor lies on the rug as she used to do. Her face is rather thin and pale, just now, with watching and anxiety; but I like to look at it, for it has grown gentler, and her voice is lower; she doesn't bounce, but moves quietly, and takes care of a certain little person in a motherly way which delights me. I rather miss my wild girl;

but if I get a strong, helpful, tender-hearted woman in her place, I shall feel quite satisfied. I don't know whether the shearing sobered our black sheep, but I do know that in all Washington I couldn't find anything beautiful enough to be bought with the five-and-twenty dollars which my good girl sent me."

Jo's keen eyes were rather dim for a minute, and her thin face grew rosy in the firelight, as she received her father's praise, feeling that she did deserve a portion of it.

"Now, Beth," said Amy, longing for her turn, but ready to wait.

"There's so little of her, I'm afraid to say much, for fear of she will slip away altogether, though she is not so shy as she used to be," began their father cheerfully; but recollecting how nearly he *had* lost her, he held her close, saying tenderly, with her cheek against his own, "I've got you safe, my Beth, and I'll keep you so, please God."

After a minute's silence, he looked down at Amy, who sat on the cricket at his feet, and said, with a caress of the shining hair:

"I observed that Amy took drumsticks at dinner, ran errands for her mother all the afternoon, gave Meg her place tonight, and has waited on everyone with patience and good-humour. I also observe that she does not fret much nor look in the glass, and has not even mentioned a very pretty ring which she wears; so I conclude that she has learned to think of other people more and of herself less, and has decided to try and mould her character as carefully as she moulds her little clay figures. I am glad of this; for though I should be very proud of a graceful statue made by her, I shall be infinitely prouder of a lovable daughter, with a talent for making life beautiful to herself and others."

"What are you thinking of, Beth?" asked Jo, when Amy had thanked her father and told about her ring.

"I read in *Pilgrim's Progress* today, how, after many troubles, Christian and Hopeful came to a pleasant green meadow, where lilies bloomed all the year round, and there they rested happily, as we do now, before they went on to their journey's end," answered Beth; adding, as she slipped out of her father's arms, and went slowly to the instrument, "It's singing time now, and I want to be in my old place. I'll try to sing the song of the shepherd-boy which the pilgrims heard. I made the music for Father, because he likes the verses."

So, sitting at the dear little piano, Beth softly touched the keys, and, in the sweet voice they had never thought to hear again, sung to her own accompaniment the quaint hymn, which was a singularly fitting song for her:

> "He that is down need fear no fall,
>   He that is low no pride;
> He that is humble ever shall
>   Have God to be his guide.
> "I am content with what I have,
>   Little be it or much;
> And, Lord! contentment still I crave,
>   Because thou savest such.
> "Fullness to them a burden is,
>   That go on pilgrimage;
> Here little, and hereafter bliss,
>   Is best from age to age!"

CHAPTER 23

AUNT MARCH SETTLES THE QUESTION

Like bees swarming after their queen, mother and daughters hovered about Mr. March the next day, neglecting everything to look at, wait upon, and listen to the new invalid, who was in a fair way to be killed by kindness. As he sat propped up in a big chair by Beth's sofa, with the other three close by, and Hannah popping in her head now and then to "peek at the dear man", nothing seemed needed to complete their happiness. But something was needed, and the elder ones felt it, though none confessed the fact. Mr. and Mrs. March looked at one another with an anxious expression, as their eyes followed Meg. Jo had sudden fits of sobriety, and was seen to shake her fist at Mr. Brooke's umbrella, which had been left in the hall; Meg was absent-minded, shy, and silent, started when the bell rang, and coloured when John's name was mentioned; Amy said, "Everyone seemed waiting for something, and couldn't settle down, which was queer, since Father was safe at home," and Beth innocently wondered why their neighbours didn't run over as usual.

Laurie went by in the afternoon, and, seeing Meg at the window, seemed suddenly possessed with a melodramatic fit, for he fell down upon one knee in the snow, beat his breast, tore his hair, and clasped his hands imploringly, as if begging some boon; and when Meg told him to behave himself and go away, he wrung imaginary tears out of his handkerchief, and staggered round the corner as if in utter despair.

"What does the goose mean?" said Meg, laughing, and trying to look unconscious.

"He's showing you how your John will go on by and by. Touching, isn't it?" answered Jo, scornfully.

"Don't say *my John*, it isn't proper or true"; but Meg's voice lingered over the words as if they sounded pleasant to her. "Please don't plague me, Jo; I've told you I don't care *much* about him, and there isn't to be anything said, but we are all to be friendly, and go on as before."

"We can't, for something *has* been said, and Laurie's mischief has spoilt you for me. I see it, and so does Mother; you are not like your old self a bit, and seem ever so far away from me. I don't mean to plague you, and will bear it like a man, but I do wish it was all settled. I hate to wait; so if you mean ever to do it, make haste and have it over quickly," said Jo, pettishly.

"*I* can't say or do anything till he speaks, and he won't, because Father said I was too young," began Meg, bending over her work, with a queer little smile, which suggested that she did not quite agree with her father on that point.

"If he did speak, you wouldn't know what to say, but would cry or blush, or let him have his own way, instead of giving a good, decided No."

"I'm not so silly and weak as you think. I know just what I should say, for I've planned it all, so I needn't be taken unawares; there's no knowing what may happen, and I wish to be prepared."

Jo couldn't help smiling at the important air which Meg had unconsciously assumed, and which was as becoming as the pretty colour varying in her cheeks.

"Would you mind telling me what you'd say?" asked Jo, more respectfully.

"Not at all; you are sixteen now, quite old enough to be my

confidante, and my experience will be useful to you by-and-by, perhaps, in your own affairs of this sort."

"Don't mean to have any; it's fun to watch other people philander, but I should feel like a fool doing it myself," said Jo, looking alarmed at the thought.

"I think not, if you liked anyone very much, and he liked you." Meg spoke as if to herself, and glanced out at the lane, where she had often seen lovers walking together in the summer twilight.

"I thought you were going to tell your speech to that man," said Jo, rudely shortening her sister's little reverie.

"Oh, I should merely say, quite calmly and decidedly, 'Thank you, Mr. Brooke, you are very kind, but I agree with Father that I am too young to enter into any engagement at present; so please say no more, but let us be friends as we were.'"

"Hum! that's stiff and cool enough. I don't believe you'll ever say it, and I know he won't be satisfied if you do. If he goes on like the rejected lovers in books, you'll give in, rather than hurt his feelings."

"No, I won't. I shall tell him I've made up my mind, and shall walk out of the room with dignity."

Meg rose as she spoke, and was just going to rehearse the dignified exit, when a step in the hall made her fly into her seat and begin to sew as if her life depended on finishing that particular seam in a given time. Jo smothered a laugh at the sudden change, and, when someone gave a modest tap, opened the door with a grim aspect, which was anything but hospitable.

"Good-afternoon. I came to get my umbrella—that is, to see how your father finds himself today," said Mr. Brooke, getting a trifle confused as his eye went from one tell-tale face to the other.

"It's very well, he's in the rack, I'll get him, and tell it you are here," and having jumbled her father and the umbrella well together in her reply, Jo slipped out of the room to give Meg a chance to make her speech and air her dignity. But the instant she vanished, Meg began to sidle towards the door, murmuring, "Mother will like to see you. Pray sit down, I'll call her."

"Don't go; are you afraid of me, Margaret?" and Mr. Brooke looked so hurt that Meg thought she must have done something very rude. She blushed up to the little curls on her forehead, for he had never called her Margaret before, and she was surprised to find how natural and sweet it seemed to hear him say it. Anxious to appear friendly and at her ease, she put out her hand with a confiding gesture, and said gratefully: "How can I be afraid when you have been so kind to Father? I only wish I could thank you for it."

"Shall I tell you how?" asked Mr. Brooke, holding the small hand fast in both his own, and looking down at Meg with so much love in the brown eyes, that her heart began to flutter, and she both longed to run away and to stop and listen.

"Oh no, please don't—I'd rather not," she said, trying to withdraw her hand, and looking frightened in spite of her denial.

"I won't trouble you, I only want to know if you care for me a little, Meg. I love you so much, dear," added Mr. Brooke tenderly.

This was the moment for the calm, proper speech, but Meg didn't make it; she forgot every word of it, hung her head, and answered, "I don't know," so softly, that John had to stoop down to catch the foolish little reply.

He seemed to think it was worth the trouble, for he smiled to himself as if quite satisfied, pressed the plump hand gratefully, and said, in his most persuasive tone, "Will you try and find out? I want to know *so* much; for I can't go to work with any heart until I learn whether I am to have my reward in the end or not."

"I'm too young," faltered Meg, wondering why she was so fluttered, yet rather enjoying it.

"I'll wait; and in the meantime, you could be learning to like me. Would it be a very hard lesson, dear?"

"Not if I chose to learn it, but—"

"Please choose to learn, Meg. I love to teach, and this is easier than German," broke in John, getting possession of the other hand, so that she had no way of hiding her face, as he bent to look into it.

His tone was properly beseeching; but, stealing a shy look at him, Meg saw that his eyes were merry as well as tender, and that he wore the satisfied smile of one who had no doubt of his success. This nettled her; Annie Moffat's foolish lessons in coquetry came into her mind, and the love of power, which sleeps in the bosoms of the best of little women, woke up all of a sudden and took possession of her. She felt excited and strange, and, not knowing what to do, followed a capricious impulse, and, withdrawing her hands, said petulantly, "I *don't* choose. Please go away and let me be!"

Poor Mr. Brooke looked as if his lovely castle in the air was tumbling about his ears, for he had never seen Meg in such a mood before, and it rather bewildered him.

"Do you really mean that?" he asked, anxiously, following her as she walked away.

"Yes, I do; I don't want to be worried about such things. Father says I needn't; it's too soon and I'd rather not."

"Mayn't I hope you'll change your mind by-and-by? I'll wait, and say nothing till you have had more time. Don't play with me, Meg. I didn't think that of you."

"Don't think of me at all. I'd rather you wouldn't," said Meg, taking a naughty satisfaction in trying her lover's patience and her own power. He was grave and silent now; and looked decidedly more like the novel heroes whom she admired; but he neither slapped his forehead nor tramped about the room, as they did; he just stood looking at her so wistfully, so tenderly, that she found her heart relenting in spite of her. What would have happened next I cannot say, if Aunt March had not come hobbling in at this interesting minute.

The old lady couldn't resist her longing to see her nephew; for she had met Laurie as she took her airing, and, hearing of Mr. March's arrival, drove straight out to see him. The family were all busy in the back part of the house, and she had made her way quietly in, hoping to surprise them. She did surprise two of them so much that Meg started as if she had seen a ghost, and Mr. Brooke vanished into the study.

"Bless me, what's all this?" cried the old lady, with a rap of her cane, as she glanced from the pale young gentleman to the scarlet young lady.

"It's Father's friend. I'm *so* surprised to see you!" stammered Meg, feeling that she was in for a lecture now.

"That's evident," returned Aunt March, sitting down. "But what is Father's friend saying to make you look like a peony? There's mischief going on, and I insist upon knowing what it is," with another rap.

"We were merely talking. Mr. Brooke came for his umbrella," began Meg, wishing that Mr. Brooke and the umbrella were safely out of the house.

"Brooke? That boy's tutor? Ah! I understand now. I know all about it. Jo blundered into a wrong message in one of your father's letters, and I made her tell me. You haven't gone and accepted him, child?" cried Aunt March, looking scandalized.

"Hush! he'll hear. Shan't I call Mother?" said Meg, much troubled.

"Not yet. I've something to say to you, and I must free my mind at once. Tell me, do you mean to marry this Cook? If you do, not one penny of my money ever goes to you. Remember that, and be a sensible girl," said the old lady, impressively.

Now Aunt March possessed in perfection the art of rousing the spirit of opposition in the gentlest people, and enjoyed doing it. The best of us have a spice of perversity in us, especially when we are young and in love. If Aunt March had begged Meg to accept John Brooke, she would probably have declared she couldn't think of it; but as she was peremptorily ordered *not* to like him, she immediately made up her mind that she would. Inclination as well as perversity made the decision easy, and, being already much excited, Meg opposed the old lady with unusual spirit.

"I shall marry whom I please, Aunt March, and you can leave your money to anyone you like," she said, nodding her head with a resolute air.

"Highty tighty! Is that the way you take my advice, miss? You'll be sorry for it, by and by, when you've tried love in a cottage, and found it a failure."

"It can't be a worse one than some people find in big houses," retorted Meg.

Aunt March put on her glasses and took a look at the girl, for she did not know her in this new mood. Meg hardly knew herself, she felt so brave and independent—so glad to defend John, and assert her right to love him, if she liked. Aunt March saw that she had begun wrong, and, after a little pause, made a fresh start, saying, as mildly as she could, "Now, Meg, my dear, be reasonable, and take my advice. I mean it kindly, and don't want you to spoil your whole life by making a mistake at the beginning. You ought to marry well, and help your family; it's your duty to make a rich match, and it ought to be impressed upon you."

"Father and Mother don't think so; they like John, though he *is* poor."

"Your parents, my dear, have no more worldly wisdom than two babies."

"I'm glad of it," cried Meg, stoutly.

Aunt March took no notice, but went on with her lecture, "This Rook is poor, and hasn't got any rich relations, has he?"

"No, but he has many warm friends."

"You can't live on friends; try it, and see how cool they'll grow. He hasn't any business, has he?"

"Not yet; Mr. Laurence is going to help him."

"That won't last long. James Laurence is a crotchety old fellow, and not to be depended upon. So you intend to marry a man without money, position, or business, and go on working harder than you do now, when you might be comfortable all your days by minding me and doing better? I thought you had more sense, Meg."

"I couldn't do better if I waited half my life! John is good and wise; he's got heaps of talent; he's willing to work, and sure to get on, he's so energetic and brave. Everyone likes and respects him, and I'm proud to think he cares for me, though I'm so poor and young and silly," said Meg, looking prettier than ever in her earnestness.

"He knows *you* have got rich relations, child; that's the secret of his liking, I suspect."

"Aunt March, how dare you say such a thing? John is above such meanness, and I won't listen to you a minute if you talk so," cried Meg, indignantly, forgetting everything but the injustice of the old lady's suspicions. "My John wouldn't marry for money, any more than I would. We are willing to work, and we mean to wait. I'm not afraid of being poor, for I've been happy so far and I know I shall be with him, because he loves me, and I—"

Meg stopped there, remembering all of a sudden that she hadn't made up her mind; that she had told "her John" to go away, and that he might be overhearing her inconsistent remarks.

Aunt March was very angry, for she had set her heart on having her pretty niece make a fine match, and something in the girl's happy young face made the lonely old woman feel both sad and sour.

"Well, I wash my hands of the whole affair. You are a wilful child, and you've lost more than you know by this piece of folly. No, I won't stop; I'm disappointed in you, and haven't spirits to see your father now. Don't expect anything from me when you are married; your Mr. Book's friends must take care of you. I've done with you for ever."

And, slamming the door in Meg's face, Aunt March drove off in high dudgeon. She seemed to take all the girl's courage with her; for, when left alone, Meg stood a moment, undecided whether to laugh or cry. Before she could make up her mind, she was taken possession of by Mr. Brooke, who said, all in one breath, "I couldn't help hearing, Meg. Thank you for defending me and Aunt March for proving that you *do* care for me a little bit."

"I didn't know how much till she abused you," began Meg.

"And I needn't go away, but may stay and be happy, may I, dear?"

Here was another fine chance to make the crushing speech and the stately exit, but Meg never thought of doing either, and disgraced herself for ever in Jo's eyes by meekly whispering, "Yes, John," and hiding her face on Mr. Brooke's waistcoat.

Fifteen minutes after Aunt March's departure, Jo came softly downstairs, paused an instant at the parlour door, and, hearing no sound within, nodded and smiled, with a satisfied expression, saying to herself, "She has sent him away as we planned, and that affair is settled. I'll go and hear the fun, and have a good laugh over it."

But poor Jo never got her laugh, for she was transfixed upon the threshold by a spectacle which held her there, staring with her mouth nearly as wide open as her eyes. Going to exult over a fallen enemy, and to praise a strong-minded sister for the banishment of an objectionable lover, it certainly *was* a shock to behold the aforesaid enemy serenely sitting on the sofa, with the strong-minded sister enthroned upon his knee, and wearing an expression of the most abject submission. Jo gave a sort of gasp as if a cold shower-bath had suddenly fallen upon her—for such an unexpected turning of the tables actually took her breath away. At the odd sound the lovers turned and saw her. Meg jumped up, looking both proud and shy; but "that man", as Jo called him, actually laughed, and said coolly, as he kissed the astonished newcomer, "Sister Jo, congratulate us!"

That was adding insult to injury—it was altogether too much—and making some wild demonstration with her hands, Jo vanished without a word. Rushing upstairs, she startled the invalids by exclaiming tragically, as she burst into the room:

"Oh, *do* somebody go down quick; John Brooke is acting dreadfully, and Meg likes it!"

Mr. and Mrs. March left the room with speed; and, casting herself upon the bed, Jo cried and scolded tempestuously, as she told the awful news to Beth and Amy. The little girls, however, considered it a most agreeable and interesting event, and Jo got little comfort from them; so she went up to her refuge in the garret, and confided her troubles to the rats.

Nobody ever knew what went on in the parlour that afternoon, but a great deal of talking was done, and quiet Mr. Brooke astonished his friends by the eloquence and spirit with which he pleaded his suit, told his plans, and persuaded them to arrange everything just as he wanted it.

The tea-bell rang before he had finished describing the paradise which he meant to earn for Meg, and he proudly took her in to supper, both looking so happy that Jo hadn't the heart to be jealous or dismal. Amy was very much impressed by John's devotion and Meg's dignity, Beth beamed at them from a distance, while Mr. and Mrs. March surveyed the young couple with such tender satisfaction that it was perfectly evident Aunt March was right in calling them as "unworldly as a pair of babies". No one ate much, but everyone looked very happy, and the old room seemed to brighten up amazingly when the first romance of the family began there.

"You can't say nothing pleasant ever happens now, can you, Meg?" said Amy, trying to decide how she would group the lovers in the sketch she was planning to make.

"No, I'm sure I can't. How much has happened since I said that! It seems a year ago," answered Meg, who was in a blissful dream, lifted far above such common things as bread and butter.

"The joys come close upon the sorrows this time, and I rather think the changes have begun," said Mrs. March. "In most families there comes, now and then, a year full of events; this has been such a one, but it ends well after all."

"Hope the next will end better," muttered Jo, who found it very hard to see Meg absorbed in a stranger before her face; for Jo loved a few persons very dearly, and dreaded to have their affection lost or lessened in any way.

"I hope the third year from this *will* end better; I mean it shall, if I live to work out my plans," said Mr. Brooke, smiling at Meg, as if everything had become possible to him now.

"Doesn't it seem very long to wait?" asked Amy, who was in a hurry for the wedding.

"I've got so much to learn before I shall be ready, it seems a short time to me," answered Meg, with a sweet gravity in her face, never seen there before.

"You have only to wait; *I* have to do the work," said John, beginning his labours by picking up Meg's napkin, with an expression which caused Jo to shake her head, and then say to herself, with an air of relief, as the front door banged, "Here comes Laurie. Now we shall have a little sensible conversation." But Jo was mistaken; for Laurie came prancing in, overflowing with spirits, bearing a great bridal-looking bouquet for "Mrs. John

Brooke", and evidently labouring under the delusion that the whole affair had been brought about by his excellent management.

"I knew Brooke would have it all his own way, he always does; for when he makes up his mind to accomplish anything, it's done, though the sky falls," said Laurie, when he had presented his offering and his congratulations.

"Much obliged for that recommendation. I take it as a good omen for the future, and invite you to my wedding on the spot," answered Mr. Brooke, who felt at peace with all mankind, even his mischievous pupil.

"I'll come if I'm at the ends of the earth; for the sight of Jo's face alone on that occasion would be worth a long journey. You don't look festive, ma'am; what's the matter?" asked Laurie, following her into a corner of the parlour, whither all had adjourned to greet Mr. Laurence.

"I don't approve of the match, but I've made up my mind to bear it, and shall not say a word against it," said Jo, solemnly. "You can't know how hard it is for me to give up Meg," she continued, with a little quiver in her voice.

"You don't give her up. You only go halves," said Laurie, consolingly.

"It never can be the same again. I've lost my dearest friend," sighed Jo.

"You've got me, anyhow. I'm not good for much, I know; but I'll stand by you, Jo, all the days of my life; upon my word I will!" and Laurie meant what he said.

"I know you will, and I'm ever so much obliged; you are always a great comfort to me, Teddy," returned Jo, gratefully shaking hands.

"Well, now, don't be dismal, there's a good fellow. It's all right, you see. Meg is happy; Brooke will fly round and get settled immediately; Grandpa will attend to him, and it will be very jolly to see Meg in her own little house. We'll have capital times after she is gone, for I shall be through college before long, and then we'll go abroad, or some nice trip or other. Wouldn't that console you?"

"I rather think it would; but there's no knowing what may happen in three years," said Jo, thoughtfully.

"That's true. Don't you wish you could take a look forward and see where we shall all be then? I do," returned Laurie.

"I think not, for I might see something sad; and everyone looks so happy now, I don't believe they could be much improved"; and Jo's eyes went slowly round the room, brightening as they looked, for the prospect was a pleasant one.

Father and Mother sat together, quietly re-living the first chapter of the romance which for them began some twenty years ago. Amy was drawing the lovers, who sat apart in a beautiful world of their own, the light of which touched their faces with a grace the little artist could not copy. Beth lay on her sofa, talking cheerily with her old friend, who held her little hand as if he felt that it possessed the power to lead him along the peaceful way she walked. Jo lounged in her favourite low seat, with the grave, quiet look which best became her; and Laurie, leaning on the back of her chair, his chin on a level with her curly head, smiled with his friendliest aspect, and nodded at her in the long glass which reflected them both.

So grouped, the curtain falls upon Meg, Jo, Beth, and Amy. Whether it ever rises again, depends upon the reception given to the first act of the domestic drama called

LITTLE WOMEN

CHILDREN'S CLASSICS

Heidi

JOHANNA SPYRI

Heidi

PARRAGON

Heidi
A Parragon Classic

This is a Siena Book
Siena is an imprint of Parragon

This edition published in 1999 by
Parragon
13 Whiteladies Road
Clifton
Bristol BS8 1PB

Printed and bound in the UK

CHAPTER 1

UP TO THE ALM-UNCLE

From the old and pleasantly situated town of Mayenfeld a path leads through green, shady meadows to the foot of the mountains which look down from their majestic heights upon the valley below. As the footpath begins to slope gently upwards, the fragrance of the nearby heath, with its short grass and vigorous mountain plants, fills the air; then the way becomes more rugged and the path rises steeply towards the Alps.

One bright, sunny morning in June, a tall, sturdy-looking girl of this mountainous country climbed the narrow mountain path, leading a child by the hand. The little girl's cheeks were aglow and the bright crimson shone even through her brown, sunburnt skin. This was not surprising, for in spite of the scorching sun the child was wrapped up as though for protection against bitter frost. She wore two, if not three frocks, one on top of the other, and, in addition, a big red shawl was tied all round her body so that her little five-year-old figure was scarcely discernible. In her heavy, nailed mountain shoes, she toiled laboriously up the slope. The two figures had been climbing from the valley for about an hour when they reached the hamlet called Dörfli which is situated half-way up the Alm. Here they were greeted with friendly calls from every doorway, for this was the girl's birthplace. But she hurried on until she had reached the last of the scattered little houses, and as she passed, a voice called from the doorway, "Wait for me, Dete, if you are going up and I will come too!"

She stood still, and the child let go of her and sat down on the ground. "Are you tired, Heidi?" asked the older girl.

"No, I am hot, though," answered Heidi.

"We shall soon reach the top now. If you can be brave and walk strongly for a little longer we shall get there in an hour," said Dete encouragingly.

The stout pleasant-looking woman who had hailed them, came out of her house and joined them, chattering and laughing with Dete, who was an old acquaintance.

"Where are you taking the child, Dete?" she asked. "I suppose it is your sister's child—the orphan?"

"Yes," answered Dete. "I am taking her to stay with the Alm-Uncle."

"Surely you aren't going to leave the child with *him*. You must be out of your mind, Dete! The old man is sure to turn you away, in any case!"

"He can't do that! He is her grandfather. I have looked after the child up till now, and I can tell you, Barbel, I am not going to turn down the offer of a good job on her account. From now on the grand-father will have to do his bit."

"Oh, well, if he were like other people—" replied Barbel, "but you know him as well as I do. How can he look after a child, and especially such a little one? Oh, she will never stay with him! But where are *you* going, Dete?"

"To a very good job in Frankfurt," explained Dete. "I looked after the people I am going to at the Baths last summer. They wanted me to go away with them then, but of course I could not go. Now they have asked me again you can be sure that I am not going to let the opportunity pass!"

"Well, I wouldn't like to be the child," said Barbel disapprovingly. "Nobody knows anything about the old man up there. He never speaks to anybody, and he never goes to church. If he is seen, occasionally, everyone keeps away from him and his stick. With his bushy eyebrows and terrible beard he looks a positive savage. The whole village is afraid of him and not many people would want to be alone with him."

"Still," Dete persisted, "he is the grandfather and it's up to him to look after the child."

"They say all sorts of terrible things about the old man," said Barbel, glancing keenly at her companion. "There must be something on his conscience, that he should live such an isolated life up there. You must surely have heard his history from your sister, eh, Dete?"

"Perhaps I have, but I shan't say. It would be a fine thing for me if he found out I had been talking!"

Barbel had been eager for a long time to learn something about the old man whom everybody referred to as the Alm-Uncle. She wanted to know why he seemed to hate everybody and why he lived all by himself up on the mountain. Besides, she wondered why the villagers in Dörfli called him Alm-Uncle. He was obviously not everyone's uncle. Barbel was much the same as all the others though, and referred to him by the same name.

Barbel had married and come to Dörfli quite recently, so she was not familiar with local history. Dete, on the other hand, had spent her childhood and youth in Dörfli, until she had gone into service in the large hotel at Ragatz Baths the previous year.

This morning Dete had come all the way from Ragatz on this special journey with little Heidi. Barbel was quite determined not to miss this golden opportunity to find out as much as she could about the strange old man. Confidentially she took Dete's arm. "Do tell me more about him, now! You have nothing to fear," she coaxed.

"I can't be expected to tell you much about an old fellow who is nearly fifty years older than me. He must be at least seventy! However, if I could be absolutely certain that whatever I told you would be kept completely confidential, then I dare say I could tell you a few things I have found out about him, as he came from Domleschg, where my mother was born."

"Whatever do you mean, Dete?" retorted Barbel, red in the face. "I am not one of those village gossips and you can take my word that I know how to keep a secret."

"All right then, I'll tell you," said Dete, lowering her voice, "but I don't want the child to hear." She looked round to see whether Heidi were nearby and might hear what she had to say, but the little one was not in sight. Dete stopped in some consternation, and looked back. There was no sign of the child.

"Now I see her!" cried Barbel at last. "Over there!" She pointed far away from the path. "She is climbing the slopes with Peter, the goat-herd, and his goats. He can look after the child, and you will be able to go on with your story."

"She's good enough at looking after herself," said Dete, "and perhaps it's a good thing, for the old man will not be able to provide for her very well. He has nothing now but his two goats and the Alm cottage."

"Did he have more in his younger days?" asked Barbel.

"Yes, I should think he did!" replied Dete with conviction. "He was brought up on one of the finest farms in Domleschg. He was the eldest son. But he lost the farm with his gambling and drinking, and, when the whole story of his wild extravagance came out, his parents died of grief. He disappeared after that and at first nobody knew where he had gone. Some said he joined the army in Naples. No more news came for about twelve to fifteen years. Then, suddenly, he appeared again in Domleschg with an almost grown-up boy and tried to find a home for him with relations. But every door was closed against him."

"That so embittered him that he vowed he would never again set foot in Domleschg and came with the boy to Dörfli to live. His wife must have been a native of the Grisons. He probably met and married her there and she died shortly afterwards. It seems he still had a little money left—enough for the boy, Tobias, to be apprenticed to a carpenter. He was a good boy and well liked by everyone in Dörfli. But nobody trusted the old man. There was a rumour that he had to get out of Naples to avoid serious trouble, because it was said that he had killed a man—of course, not in the war, you understand, but in some brawl. But we did not break our connection with him since we were closely related. My great-grand-mother on my mother's side was his grandmother's sister, you know. We called him 'Uncle', and as we are related on my father's side to almost everybody in Dörfli, the whole village called him 'Uncle', too. And because he lived on the Alm he was called the 'Alm-Uncle'."

"But what happened to Tobias?" asked Barbel eagerly.

"Wait a moment, I am coming to that," replied Dete. "Tobias served his apprenticeship in Mels, and as soon as he had finished he came home to Dörfli and married my sister, Adelheid. They were very happy together, but their happiness was short-lived. Two years later, while Tobias was working at the building of a house, a beam fell on him and killed him, and when his mutilated body was brought home, Adelheid fell into a violent fever as a result of the shock, and never recovered. In any case, she was not very strong and sometimes took strange fits when we couldn't tell whether she was asleep or awake."

"Only a few weeks after Tobias died, Adelheid too was buried. Some said it was the uncle's punishment for the wicked life he had led, and they even told him so to his face. The pastor, too, begged him to repent of his past sins, but the uncle only grew more fierce and embittered. He would not speak to anyone, and everyone, in turn, kept clear of him. Then we heard he had come to live on the Alm and he has remained up there in solitude ever since, at war with God and the world."

"Mother and I took in Adelheid's little child. She was only a year old then. When Mother died last summer and I had to go and work at the health resort, I took the child with me and left her in charge of old Ursel up in Pfaferserdorf. I was kept on at the health resort during the winter, for I could knit and sew and plenty of people gave me work to do, and early in the spring some Frankfurt people I had served during the summer came back. They offered me a job, and I am going away with them to Frankfurt. We leave the day after tomorrow."

"And you are going to leave the poor child with that terrible old man!" said Barbel reproachfully.

"Well, what else can I do?" replied Dete defensively. "I have done what I can for the child, and can't take her with me. But, goodness! Where are you going, Barbel? We are already halfway up the Alm."

"I have almost come as far as I need," answered Barbel. "I want to speak to Peter's grandmother. She spins for me in winter. Goodbye, then, Dete! And good luck!"

Dete shook her friend's hand and stopped while Barbel

walked towards the little brown Alm hut which was situated in a sheltered spot some yards off the path. The hut was more than half-way up the Alm from the village. It was fortunate it stood in such a sheltered place, for it looked dilapidated beyond repair. Even situated as it was, it was hardly safe to live in when gales swept the mountains. Then everything in the hut, doors and windows and all the old beams, would shake and crack.

The goat-herd lived here with his mother and his old blind grand-mother. Peter was eleven years old. Every morning he collected goats from the village and drove them up to the Alm where they grazed till evening. At sunset, Peter would go running nimbly down the mountainside with his goats, until, on reaching Dörfli he would whistle through his fingers. The piercing sound summoned the owners of the goats, who then took them home. Usually the little boys and girls came to collect the animals, for they were not in the least frightened of the gentle goats, and this hour of the day, during the long summer, was the time when Peter could see his little friends. For the rest of the day he was alone on the mountain with only the goat for company. He often got home very late from Dörfli, for he stayed as long as possible to play with his friends. So he was left with just enough time to eat his bread and milk, sleep and get up again early the next morning. His father had been killed in a wood-cutting accident several years before. His mother, Brigitta, was always called the goat-herd's wife, and his blind grandmother was just "grandmother" to all and sundry.

Dete stood looking impatiently in all directions to catch a glimpse of the children and the goats; but they had taken a very roundabout way. At first the little girl had toiled hard to climb with the goat-herd, panting in the heat and making a great effort under her heavy encumbrance of clothes. She did not say a word but looked steadily, now at Peter who jumped about on his bare feet, now at the goats who climbed still more easily on their slender little legs. Suddenly the child sat down on the ground and quickly removed her shoes and stockings. Then, standing up, she began to take off her hot red shawl, then her Sunday frock and her everyday frock, which Dete had also made her wear, until, clad only in her light little petticoat, she stood with her bare arms stretched happily into the air. Then she put everything neatly into a little pile and jumped and climbed behind the goats. As she came skipping along in her new garb, Peter grinned broadly. He looked back, and when he saw the little pile of clothes lying on the path he grinned even more, but he said nothing. The child, feeling free at last, began to chatter to the boy, asking him how many goats he had, where he was going with them and what he would do there. So at last the children arrived at the cottage and caught sight of Aunt Dete. She no sooner spotted the group than she cried, "Heidi! What a sight you are! Where are your clothes? And the new shoes I bought you, and the stockings I knitted? Where have you put them?"

The child quietly pointed down the hill.

The aunt followed the direction of her finger. There was, indeed, something lying on the ground. "You dreadful child!" she cried in great annoyance. "What's the meaning of this? Why have you taken everything off?"

"I didn't need them," said the child, not looking at all penitent.

"Oh, have you no sense?" lamented the aunt. "Who is to go back down for them? It's all of half an hour's walk." Then turning to Peter, she ordered, "Peter! Run back and fetch the clothes!"

"I am late already," said Peter slowly, and remained motionless, both hands in his pockets.

"Don't just stand there staring!" Aunt Dete cried. "This will never do! Come here! I will give you something good. Look!" And she held up a bright new coin. The boy's eyes shone at the sight of it. Suddenly he jumped up and made off down the Alm by the shortest way. Soon he reached the little pile of clothes, gathered them up and sped back so quickly that the aunt could not but be pleased, and at once gave him the coin. Peter put it in his pocket, his face wreathed in smiles for he didn't often come by such a prize.

"You can take the clothes up to the uncle's since you are

going that way," Aunt Dete said as she started to climb the steep slope which rose just behind Goat Peter's cottage. Readily Peter carried out the order and followed as she walked ahead; his left arm round the bundle, the goats' stick swinging in his right hand. Heidi and the goats leaped joyously at his side. Thus, in three quarters of an hour, the little group reached the top of the Alm where the old uncle's cottage stood on a ledge of the mountain. Behind the hut were three ancient fir trees, and beyond these, the mountain rose in an almost sheer wall, the lower parts still overgrown with grasses and flowers, with stonier slopes above leading to the black, bare, jagged peaks. Along the side of the cottage facing the valley, the uncle had made himself a bench, and here he now sat puffing his pipe, both hands on his knees, calmly watching the children, the goats and Aunt Dete as they climbed. Heidi arrived first. She went straight up to the old man, stretched out her hand towards him and said, "Good evening, Grandfather!"

"Well, well! What is the meaning of this?" asked the old man gruffly. He took the child's hand abruptly and as he did so a long, piercing glance shot from beneath his bushy eyebrows. Heidi returned his look without blinking. The grandfather presented a fearsome aspect. His face seemed covered in beard and eyebrows, and Heidi could not take her fascinated gaze away from him.

In the meantime, the aunt and Peter had arrived.

"I wish you good day!" said Dete shortly. "This is Tobias' and Adelheid's child. You will hardly recognise her because you have not seen her since she was a year old."

"What have I to do with the child?" asked the old man brusquely. "And you, there!" he called to Peter. "Take yourself off with your goats! You are late as it is."

Peter obeyed at once, for the uncle had given him an angry look which did not make him wish to linger.

"The child just has to stay with you, Uncle," said Dete. "I have done my bit for four years. Now it is your turn."

"Indeed!" mumbled the old man, his glance flashing at Dete. "And if the child starts fretting for you as children do, being such difficult things, what shall I do with her then?"

"That's up to you," replied Dete. "No one told me what to do with the little one when she was left in my care, and only one year old, too. Now I have to make my own living and you are the child's nearest relative. If you can't look after her it's your responsibility and you must answer for any harm that comes to her. And I shouldn't think you can afford to add another to your list of wicked deeds."

At that point Dete realised she had said more than she should have.

At her words, the old man got up. He looked so threatening that she took a step backwards. Flinging out his arm, he shouted at her, "Be off! And don't be in a hurry to show your face here again!"

Dete did not need a second telling. "Good-bye, then!" she said hurriedly. "And you, too, Heidi!" And with that she turned and ran down the mountain, and didn't stop until she reached Dörfli.

This time, people were even more eager to stop and question her, wondering what had become of the child. They all knew Dete well, and also the history of the child. When voices called from every door and window, "Where is the child, Dete? What have you done with her?" she replied angrily, "With the Alm-Uncle, of course! I left her with the Alm-Uncle, just as I said." The women of the village began to cry out at her: "Shame on you for leaving a little girl up there! What a terrible thing to do."

Dete ran through the village as fast as she could go. Her one thought was to get away from Dörfli and to avoid speaking to any one, for she was far from easy in her conscience about what she had done. The child's dying mother had asked Dete to take care of Heidi, and here she was, abandoning the girl to an unknown fate. However, she consoled herself with the thought of being better able to provide for the child with her newly earned money, and with the wonderful prospect of soon being free to enjoy her new position far away from all the village talk.

CHAPTER 2

THE GRANDFATHER'S HUT

Long after Dete had gone, the grandfather went back to his seat outside the hut, and sat silently blowing clouds of smoke from his pipe while Heidi began to inspect her new surroundings. She found a shed, attached to one side of the hut, which housed the goats. She peeped in and then walked round to the other side of the cottage where there stood three old fir trees. A strong wind shook their thick branches and the child stood still, listening to the moaning of the wind in the ancient trees. Then she completed the circuit of the cottage and returned to where the grandfather sat. He hadn't moved an inch since she'd left him, so she went across and stood in front of him, her hands clasped behind her back, her steady eyes looking at him.

The old man raised his head. Heidi stayed where she was and continued to gaze at him. "Well, what are we going to do now" he said.

"I would like to see inside the cottage."

"Come, then!" The grandfather got up. "And bring your bundle of clothes!"

"I don't need them any more," declared Heidi.

The old man turned and looked searchingly at the child. Heidi's dark eyes were shining with delight at the prospect of seeing inside the cottage. "She doesn't lack sense, anyway," he said quietly to himself. Then, "Why don't you need them any more?" he asked aloud.

"I would rather be dressed like the goats with their bare legs."

"All right, then, but bring the things!" commanded the grandfather. "We will put them in the cupboard."

Heidi obediently picked up her bundle and followed the old man inside. The door opened directly on to a big room which was the full breadth of the cottage. The only furniture in the room was a table and a chair. In one corner stood the grandfather's bed and in the opposite wall the fireplace above which hung a big kettle. On the same side as the bed, in the middle of the wall, there was a door which the grandfather now opened. This was the cupboard where he kept his belongings. On a shelf lay a couple of shirts, socks and some rough sack-cloth sheets. On another stood plates, cups and glasses, and on the top shelf there was a round loaf, a sausage, ham and cheese. Everything that Alm-Uncle possessed in the way of food and clothing was kept in this cupboard. As soon as the door was opened Heidi came forward and pushed her own clothes as far behind the grandfather's as possible so that they would be well out of the way. Then she turned her attention to the room and asked, "Where shall I sleep, Grandfather?"

"Wherever you want to."

This seemed to please the child and she began to inspect every corner. By the grandfather's bed, wooden steps went up, and when the child climbed the little ladder she found herself in the hayloft. A bale of hay, fresh and sweet-smelling, lay on the floor, and from a little window in the roof she could see far down into the valley.

"Oh, this is where I want to sleep!" she cried joyfully. "It is lovely! Come and see how lovely it is, Grandfather!"

"I have seen it before!" came from below.

"I am going to make my bed," the child called again and ran busily to and fro. "You must bring me a sheet to lie upon, Grandfather!"

"Indeed!" remarked the grandfather, and after a while he went to the cupboard and raked about amongst the clothes. Presently he pulled out a long, coarse piece of sack-cloth which might serve as a sheet. He carried it up to the loft and there he saw that a very nice little bed had been made amongst the hay, with extra hay piled up into a pillow at one end, and arranged in such a way that whoever lay on the improvised bed would be able to look up at the little window.

"Well done!" exclaimed the grandfather. "Now the sheet goes on. But wait——I" and here he took a big bunch of hay and made the bed twice as thick so that the hardness of the floor would not come through.

"Now bring it here!"

Heidi quickly grasped the sheet but it was so thick and heavy, she staggered under the weight, It was just as well though, as the thickness of the cloth would prevent the sharp stalks of hay from sticking into her. Together they spread the sheet and now the bed looked very trim and tidy; but Heidi stood back and regarded it critically.

"There is still something we have forgotten, Grandfather."

"Now what?" he asked.

"A top sheet. When you get into bed you need something to pull over you."

"Oh, indeed! But what if I haven't got any?"

"Don't worry, Grandfather," Heidi consoled him. "We can use more hay for a cover," and she began to gather another bundle.

"Wait a moment!" The old man went down the steps to his own bed. Back he came presently with a big, heavy, linen sack which he laid on the floor.

"Isn't that better than hay?" he asked, helping her to spread it on the bed, for Heidi's little frame couldn't manage to lift and spread the heavy cover out smoothly.

Heidi stood admiringly before her new sleeping-place. "The cover is beautiful!" she declared ecstatically, "and the bed is just perfect! I wish it were night-time already so that I could go to sleep on it!"

"I think we should eat first," the grandfather advised.

In her eagerness, Heidi had forgotten everything except the new bed, but now, when she thought of it, she did indeed feel very hungry, for she had had nothing to eat since that morning before the journey, when she had breakfasted meagerly on a piece of bread and a small cup of watery coffee. "Yes, I think so, too!" she agreed.

"Well, then, since we are in such complete agreement, let's go down," said the old man, guiding the child towards the stairs.

In the room below he went over to the fireplace, pushed

back the big kettle and brought a little one forward on the chain. Then he sat down on a three-legged stool and blew up the fire. It was soon blazing merrily and the little kettle began to boil. Next the old man cut a big piece of cheese, and piercing it with a long, iron fork, he held it over the fire, turning it constantly to and fro until it was golden brown all over. Heidi had watched all these operations with the closest attention and apparently some new ideas had entered her head for suddenly she jumped up and went to the cupboard. When the grandfather had decided that the cheese was nicely toasted and took it to the table, there was the round loaf, two plates and two knives neatly laid, for Heidi had been quick to see what was wanted and had brought everything from the cupboard.

"So you can think for yourself! That's good!" said the grandfather and spread the toasted cheese on the bread. "But there is still something missing."

Heidi's eyes alighted on the steaming pot by the fire and she knew at once what it was. Quickly she ran back to the cupboard but could find only one little bowl. She hesitated only a moment for right at the back were two glasses. Presently she came back and put the little bowl and glasses on the table.

"Very good! Very good!" said the old man. "You have found a way out of the difficulty. But now, where are *you* going to sit?" and he drew his own chair up to the table.

Heidi ran to the hearth and brought back the little three-legged stool.

"You have got a seat, at any rate," said the grandfather, "though it is rather low! Even on my chair you would be too small to reach the table. But now you must eat. Come along!"

He filled the little bowl with milk and placing it on his own chair pushed it near the stool so that Heidi had a little table of her own. Then he filled a plate with a big piece of bread and some of the yellow, toasted cheese and laid it also on the chair. He himself sat on the corner of the table and began his meal. Heidi lifted her little bowl and drank without stopping. Then she drew a deep breath—for she had been so thirsty that she hadn't even stopped to breathe—and put down the empty bowl.

"Do you like the milk?" the grandfather asked.

"It is the best milk I have ever tasted!" replied Heidi.

"You can have more," said the grandfather, filling the little bowl again and putting it before her. She spread the bread with her slice of golden cheese and began eating hungrily.

The cheese was soft as butter and tasted good. From time to time Heidi took a drink from the bowl and looked blissfully happy.

When the meal was finished, the grandfather went out to the goat-house where there was work to be done. Heidi watched him attentively, observing how he first swept everything clean with the broom then spread fresh straw for the little animals to sleep on. At last the goat-house was finished and he went into the shed which was close by. Here he chopped several round sticks to equal lengths; then he carefully shaped a flat piece of wood and drilled four holes into one side. He put the round sticks into the holes—and there was a chair like the grandfather's, only much higher! Speechless with admiration, Heidi gazed at it.

"What do you think it is, Heidi?" asked the grandfather.

"It is *my* chair, because it is so high. But you made it so quickly, Grandfather!" said the little girl in amazement.

"She has eyes in her head all right," thought the grandfather as he walked round the cottage, fixing a loose board at the door and repairing anything that needed attention. Heidi followed close behind. Nothing escaped her notice, and everything she saw gave her new pleasure.

Evening came, and the old fir trees behind the cottage began to rustle more loudly as a strong wind swept along, roaring amongst the branches. Heidi's heart beat faster. She thought she had never heard anything so beautiful and went skipping and running for sheer joy under the trees. All the while the grandfather watched the child from the doorway.

There was the sound of a shrill whistle. Heidi stood still and the grandfather stepped out of the cottage. From above, the goats came jumping like wild creatures and in the midst of them was Peter. With a joyful cry, Heidi rushed to welcome her old friends of the morning. At the cottage, children and animals came to a halt and two pretty, slender goats, one brown, one white, ran from the herd towards the grandfather. Eagerly they licked his hands for in the palms he held a little salt which the goats liked very much. Peter disappeared with the rest of the flock and Heidi fell to caressing first one and then the other of the goats and jumped gaily round them.

"Do they belong to us, Grandfather? Do they really belong to us?" she asked. "Will they stay in the little shed? Do they always stay with us?" Heidi scarcely gave the grandfather a chance to put in his steady, "Yes! Yes!" between one question and the next.

When the goats had finished licking the salt from his hands, the old man commanded, "Go and fetch your little bowl and the bread!"

Heidi obeyed at once. Then the grandfather milked the white goat into the little bowl which was soon full to the brim. He cut a piece of bread and handing it to the child said, "Eat now, and then go upstairs to sleep. I suppose your night things are in the bundle Aunt Dete made up, which I put in the cupboard. Get it out if you need it. I have to tie up the goats for the night. Sleep well!"

"Good night, Grandfather! But what are the goats' names? Tell me, Grandfather!" cried the child, running behind the old man's receding figure.

"The white one is called 'Little Swan' and the brown one is 'Little Bear'," the grandfather called over his shoulder.

"Good night, Little Swan! Good night, Little Bear!" cried Heidi happily as all three disappeared into the goat-house.

Heidi went back to the bench outside the cottage where she sat and took her bread and milk. The wind was so strong she was almost blown from her seat, so she finished hurriedly and went into the house and upstairs to bed where she was soon fast asleep, as soundly and happily as though on the best feather-bed. Not long after, and before the darkness had come completely, the grandfather, too, had gone to bed, for he always rose at sunrise, which was at a very early hour during the long summer months. All night long the wind blew strongly so that the whole cottage seemed to shake and every beam cracked and groaned.

In the middle of the night the grandfather rose, saying half aloud to himself, "Perhaps she is afraid." He climbed the steps and stood by Heidi's bed. At intervals the moon shone brightly, then as clouds were chased across it everything became dark again. At that moment a shaft of moonlight came through the little window, falling directly on Heidi's bed. Her cheeks were flushed from sleep and her head rested quietly and peacefully on her little round arm. Her dreams appeared to be happy ones for a smile played about her mouth. The grandfather gazed at the sleeping child until the moon was again overshadowed. Then he went back to his bed.

CHAPTER 3

ON THE ALM

Early in the morning, Heidi was awakened by a loud whistle. As she opened her eyes, a gleam of sunshine came through the little window on to her bed and shone on the hay nearby so that everything was bathed in golden light. Then, from outside, she heard the grandfather's deep, quiet voice and she remembered that she was up on the Alm. She no longer lived with old Ursel who was almost stone deaf and always wanted to have Heidi by her side, so that sometimes the child had felt like a prisoner and would have liked to run away from the stuffy room where she had to sit all day. For Ursel was always too cold and insisted on keeping the room unbearably hot. So Heidi was very glad when she awoke and found herself in her new home. She remembered all the exciting things she had seen the previous day and wondered what this new day had in store for her. Above all she looked forward to seeing Little Swan and Little Bear again. Quickly she jumped out of bed and in a few minutes had dressed herself. Then she climbed down the steps and ran out to the front of the cottage. Peter, the goat-herd, was already there with his flock and the grandfather was leading out Little Swan and Little Bear to join them. Heidi ran forward to say good-morning to him and the goats.

"How would you like to go with them to the pasture?" asked the grandfather.

Heidi was overjoyed. That was the thing she would like best of all.

"But first you must wash yourself or the sun, shining brightly up there, will laugh at you when he looks down and sees how dirty you are! See! This is where you wash." The grandfather pointed towards a big flat tub filled with water which stood in the sun before the cottage door. Heidi jumped towards it and splashed and scrubbed until she was perfectly clean. In the meantime the grandfather went into the cottage, calling to Peter, "Come here, goat-general, and bring your rucksack!"

Amazed, Peter answered the call and laid down the rucksack in which he carried his meagre lunch.

"Open it!" ordered the old man, and then put in a big piece of bread and an equally big piece of cheese. Peter opened his round eyes very wide for this food was twice as much as he had for his own lunch.

"And now the little bowl has to go in, too," the old man continued. "At lunch-time you will milk for her two little bowlfuls, for she is going, too, and can stay with you until you come back in the evening. Take care she doesn't fall over the precipice!"

Now Heidi came running towards them. "Grandfather, the sun can't laugh at me now!" For fear of the sun's mockery she had rubbed her face, neck and arms so vigorously with the rough cloth which the grandfather had hung up beside the water-tub, that she was almost as red as a lobster.

The old man smiled. "No, he has no reason to laugh now," he agreed. "But do you know what happens when you come home in the evening? You go right into the tub like a fish because if you run like the goats your feet will get dirty. Now, off you go!"

Happily the children climbed up the Alm. The high winds during the night had blown away the last little cloud and now the sky was a vast expanse of deep blue out of which the sun shone and glittered on the green slopes. The little blue and yellow mountain flowers opened their cups and seemed to nod merrily at Heidi who romped everywhere. Here and there were big patches of pretty red primroses, and china-blue gentians, and enchanted by this sparkling, waving sea of flowers, she forgot all about Peter, even about the goats. All along the way she picked flowers until she had a big bunch which she wrapped in her pinafore, for she wanted to take them home and put them in her bedroom, so that it would look as pretty as the fields themselves.

Peter was quite dazed trying to look in every direction at once, for the goats, like Heidi, were jumping from one place to another. He had to whistle and shout and brandish his stick to bring the goats together again.

"Where are you now, Heidi?" came the boy's exasperated and rather angry cry.

"Here!" came the reply, but Peter could see no one. Heidi was sitting, hidden from view, behind a little hillock which was covered with sweet-smelling prunella. The air was filled with the perfume of these beautiful flowers, and Heidi was sitting taking in deep breaths of the scented air and thinking how wonderful it all was.

"Come here!" Peter called again. "You are not to go near the precipice—the uncle said so!"

"Where is that?" asked Heidi, still not moving from her hiding-place.

"Up there! Right on the top the old eagle sits on the look-out for his prey."

That did the trick.

At once Heidi jumped up and ran to Peter with her apron-ful of flowers.

"That is enough flower-picking for now," he said as they climbed up together, "if you are going to keep pace with me. And if you pick all the flowers to-day there will be none left for to-morrow."

Heidi was convinced. Moreover, her pinafore was so full that it could hardly hold another one. So she now walked quietly beside Peter. The goats were also quieter, as they were anxious to reach their delicious pasture, and climbed unhesitatingly towards their grazing ground. The pasture which Peter usually chose and where he spent the day was situated at the foot of the high rocks. Bushes and fir trees covered the lower parts but nearer the summit the rocks rose bare and rugged towards the sky. On one side of the mountain, jagged clefts stretched far down and the grandfather had been right to warn Peter of the danger. When they had reached the pasture, Peter carefully put his rucksack into a little hollow in the ground, for the wind often blew with great violence across this part of the country and Peter did not want to see his precious possessions rolling down the mountainside. Then the boy, tired after the strenuous climb, stretched himself out at full length on the sunny pasture.

Heidi, by this time, had undone her pinafore and rolled it neatly round the flowers which she laid beside Peter's rucksack in the hollow. Then she sat down beside him and looked around. The valley lay far below, bathed in the sparkling morning sunshine. In front of Heidi a big, broad snowfield rose up to the dark blue sky and on the left stood a huge pile of rocks above which a bare rocky peak reached towards the sky, towering majestically above the child. Heidi sat motionless. A great silence was all around and only the delicate blue harebells and yellow cistus swayed softly in the gentle breeze, nodding joyfully on their slender little stems. Peter had fallen asleep and the goats were climbing high up amongst the bushes. Heidi had never been so happy. The golden sunlight, the fresh breezes and the delicate perfume of the flowers filled her with delight and she only wished that she might stay there for ever. She gazed so long at the mountains that it seemed to her that each had a face and that these mountain faces were as familiar to her as old friends.

Suddenly Heidi heard a loud, harsh cry and when she looked up she saw, circling overhead, a huge bird, larger than she had ever seen before. His large wings were outspread and he flew in a wide circle, coming back again and again and uttering loud, piercing shrieks above Heidi's head.

"Peter! Peter! Wake up!" cried Heidi. "Look! There is a big bird just above us!"

Peter got up and watched the bird, too, as it rose higher and higher and at last disappeared behind the grey rocks.

"Where has he gone to?" asked Heidi who had been watching the bird with keen interest.

"Home to his nest," replied Peter.

"Is his home up there? Oh, how nice to live so high up! How terrible he cries! Let's climb up there and see where his nest is!"

"Oh, no!" replied Peter emphatically. "Even the goats can't climb so high and the uncle said you were not to climb the rocks."

Suddenly Peter started to whistle and call loudly. Heidi could not think what this meant, but the goats apparently understood, for, one after another, they came springing down until they were all gathered together on the green slope. Some continued to nibble and others ran about, playfully pushing each other with their horns. Heidi jumped up and ran amongst them. She delighted in their individual antics and quickly made friends with each of them in turn, for to her they were like separate people with their own personalities. While she played with the goats Peter fetched the rucksack and laid out the four pieces of bread on the ground, the big ones on Heidi's side and the small ones on his own. Then he took the little bowl, drew some milk into it from Little Swan and placed it in the centre. "Stop skipping now! It is time to eat," he said. But he had to shout again, for Heidi was so absorbed in her games with the goats that she was oblivious to everything else. So Peter called until the rocks themselves echoed his voice, and then Heidi appeared and ran to join Peter and the feast spread out on the ground before him.

She sat down. "Is the milk for me?" she asked.

"Yes," replied Peter, "and the two big pieces of bread and cheese are yours too, and when you have finished you get another bowlful from Little Swan." "And where do you get your milk?" asked Heidi. "From my own goat. Go on and eat," urged Peter.

Heidi began to drink her milk and as soon as she put down her empty bowl Peter filled it again. Then Heidi gave a big piece of her bread to Peter and all the cheese as well, saying, "You can have it all. I have had enough."

Peter gazed at her, speechless with surprise. Never in his life could he have given away as much as that. He hesitated a little, for he could not believe that Heidi meant it seriously. She held out the pieces, but as Peter still did not take them she laid the food on his knees. Peter had never before had such a satisfying lunch.

The animals had begun to climb up again towards the bushes; some skipping gaily over everything, others stopping to taste the tender herbs. Heidi watched the goats, and after a while she said, "Tell me their names, Peter."

Peter knew them all, of course, and told Heidi the name of each, pointing them out as he did so. Heidi listened carefully and very soon she had learnt their names of by heart and could call to each one, for they all had distinguishing characteristics.

Turk was the big one, with enormous horns with which he was always trying to butt the others. So he was mostly left on his own as the rest of them were frightened of his bullying.

Only one, little Goldfinch, would face him without fear, and would rush at him nimbly, several times, so that Turk simply stood still in bewilderment, not knowing which way to turn, for her little horns were sharp.

There was also a sad little goat called White Snowflake, who bleated plaintively, and Heidi had frequently to go and comfort it and stroke its little soft head. Just then, it cried again, and Heidi ran over, and clasping her arms around it, beseeched it to tell her what was wrong. The goat snuggled to Heidi and stopped bleating.

Peter called out, between mouthfuls of bread and cheese, "She is missing her mother, an old goat who was sold at Mayenfeld the other day."

"Hasn't she a grandfather or a grandmother?" called back Heidi.

"She has neither," replied Peter.

"Oh, poor Snowflake," cried Heidi. "Please don't cry any more; I will come with you every day, and I will never leave you alone again, I promise."

The young goat nuzzled Heidi's shoulder and seemed more content.

Peter now joined Heidi, who had come to the conclusion that the best and most distinctive goats by far were the two which were owned by her grandfather. They even treated the arrogant Turk with total indifference.

"Peter," Heidi said presently, "the prettiest of all are Little Swan and Little Bear." These two were light on their feet, and always seemed to find the best leaves to nibble. Heidi watched them with pleasure.

"I know," Peter replied. "The uncle brushes and washes them, and gives them salt, and has the nicest shed."

Suddenly Peter jumped up and bounded after the goats. Heidi followed. Something must have happened and she simply could not stay behind. Peter forced his way through the middle of the herd to that side of the Alm where the bare and jagged rocks fell away steeply. Here, a heedless little goat might easily tumble down and break his legs. Peter had noticed inquisitive little Goldfinch jumping in that direction. The boy arrived just in time, for the little goat was just about to jump towards the edge of the precipice. Peter, lunging towards the goat, fell down and only managed to seize one of its legs as he fell. Goldfinch gave an angry cry at finding herself caught and tried desperately to free herself. Peter could not get up and shouted for Heidi to help because he was afraid Goldfinch might wrench her leg. Heidi was already there and at once saw the danger. She quickly gathered some sweet-smelling plants from the ground and held them out towards Goldfinch, saying coaxingly, "Come along, Goldfinch, and be good! Look! You might fall down and hurt yourself."

The little goat turned quickly and ate the herbs from Heidi's outstretched hand. In the meantime Peter got to his feet again and held Goldfinch by the cord with which her little bell was fastened to her neck. Heidi grasped the goat in the same way at the other side of its head and together they led the truant back to the peacefully grazing flock. As soon as Peter got her back to safety, he raised his stick and started to give her a good beating. Goldfinch, however, knowing what was in store, timidly shrank back, and Heidi cried, "No, Peter! No! You mustn't beat her! Look how frightened she is!"

"She deserves it," Peter muttered, about to strike; but Heidi threw herself against his arm, crying indignantly, "Don't touch her! You will hurt her! Leave her alone!"

Peter turned surprised eyes on the fierce little girl and his stick dropped to his side. "All right, then, I'll let her off—if you give me some of your cheese to-morrow again," he bargained.

"You can have it all, to-morrow and every day. I don't want it," Heidi consented. "And I'll give you the bread, too, the same as today, but you must promise never to beat Goldfinch or Snowflake, or any of the goats."

"Suits me," said Peter, and that was as good as a promise. He let Goldfinch go and the little goat leapt joyously towards the herd.

So the day passed quickly and the sun began to sink behind the mountains. Heidi was sitting quietly on the ground, gazing at the cistus and the harebells which glistened in the evening sunshine; rocks and grass shimmered in a golden glow. Suddenly she jumped up and cried, "Peter! Peter! They are on fire! They are all on fire! All the mountains are burning! And the great snow mountain also, and the sky! Oh, look at the lovely fiery snow! Peter, get up and look! The fire is at the great bird's nest, too. Look at the rocks and the grass and the fir trees! Everything is on fire!"

"It is always like that," replied Peter with great unconcern, continuing to peel his stick, "but it is not real fire."

"What is it, then?" asked Heidi, gazing eagerly around. She ran back and forth looking from side to side, as if she could not take in enough of the majestic sight. "What is it, Peter?"

"It just gets like that," Peter tried to explain.

"Oh, look, look, Peter!" cried Heidi again in great excitement. "Everything is turning a rosy pink colour. Look at the snow and the high rocks! What are their names Peter"

"Mountains don't have names," replied Peter.

"Oh, how beautiful. Crimson snow! Oh, now all the rocks are turning grey—now the colour is all gone. Now it is all over, Peter."

Heidi sat down, looking as distressed as if everything really had come to an end.

"To-morrow it will be the same," said Peter. "Get up now. We must go home."

"Will it be like this every day we are on the pasture?" asked Heidi insistently, as she walked down the Alm at Peter's side. She waited breathlessly for his answer, hoping that he would be able to set her mind at rest.

"Mostly," he replied. "But will it definitely be like that again tomorrow" Heidi persisted. "Yes, yes; it will certainly come tomorrow," Peter replied.

Heidi was very happy. She had absorbed so many new impressions . . . had so many new things to think about that she was quite silent until they reached the hut and saw the grandfather sitting on the bench under the fir trees. Here he sat in the evenings, waiting for his goats.

Heidi ran up to him, followed by Little Swan and Little Bear, for the goats knew their master.

"Good night!" Peter called after Heidi, and then added, "come again, tomorrow!" because he was very anxious for her to go with him. Heidi ran back and gave her hand to Peter, promising him that she would go with him, and then ran over to little Snowflake, whom she clasped gently round the neck, saying, "Sleep well, and don't forget that I will be back tomorrow, so you needn't be sad." Snowflake looked at her happily and then leapt off after the other goats.

Heidi raced towards her grandfather.

"Oh, Grandfather, it was wonderful" she cried long before she reached him. "The fire on the snow and the rocks and the blue and yellow flowers, and look what I have brought for you!" Heidi unfolded her pinafore and all the flowers fell at the grandfather's feet. But what a sight the poor flowers were! Heidi did not recognise them. They were like withered grass and not a single little cup was open. "Grandfather, what is the matter with the flowers?" cried Heidi, quite alarmed. "They weren't like that before. What is wrong with them?"

"They would rather be out in the sun than tied up in a pinafore," explained the grandfather.

"Then I will never gather any more. But Grandfather, why did the eagle screech so?" Heidi asked.

"You had better have your bath now," said the grandfather, "and I shall fetch some milk from the shed. Afterwards, when we are having our supper, I will tell you about everything."

Later, when Heidi sat in her high chair, the little bowl of milk in front of her and the grandfather at her side, she again asked her question.

"Why did the great bird scream at us, Grandfather?"

"He screams in mockery of the people in the villages down in the valley where they sit gossiping together. He wants to say, 'If you would all mind your own business or climb up into the heights like me you would be much happier!'"

The grandfather spoke these words with such vehemence that Heidi seemed to hear again the croaking of the great bird.

"Why don't the mountains have names, Grandfather?" asked Heidi again.

"They have names," he answered, "and if you can describe one to me so that I can recognise it, then I will tell you its name."

Heidi tried to describe the rocky mountain with the two high peaks exactly as she had seen it. Presently the grandfather interrupted, "Yes, I know that one. Its name is Falknis. Did you notice any others?"

Then Heidi recalled the mountain with the large snowfield which looked at first as if it were on fire and then turned rose-coloured, then pale pink, and at last faded back to its own grey colour.

"I know that one, too," said the grandfather. "That is the Scesaplana. Did you like being on the pasture?"

Now Heidi told him everything: how wonderful it had been and particularly about the fire in the evening. Heidi wanted the grandfather to explain why this had happened, since Peter had been unable to do so.

"You see," the grandfather instructed her, "that's what the sun does when he says good night to the mountains. He throws his most beautiful rays over them so that they won't forget him before morning."

Heidi was delighted. She could hardly wait for the next day when she would again be allowed to go to the pasture, to watch how the sun said good night to the mountains. But first she had to go to bed, and how soundly she slept all night on her hay bed and dreamt of nothing but glistening mountains tinged with red, and Little Snowflake running happily about!

CHAPTER 4

PETER'S GRANDMOTHER

Next morning, the sun shone brightly as Peter appeared with the goats and they all went up together to the pasture. And so it continued every day. Heidi grew stronger and sturdier with living so much in the open and her little sunburnt face shone with health. When autumn came and the wind blew with greater force over the mountains, the grandfather would sometimes say, "To-day you had better stay at home, Heidi. A little one like you might easily be swept down the mountain-side by the wind."

But when Peter heard this in the morning he would look very miserable. He found it dull now without Heidi; and, of course, he got less to eat. On such days the goats would become so stubborn that he had twice as much trouble with them. They, too, had grown so accustomed to Heidi that they would hardly move off without her.

Heidi herself was never bored because she always saw something new and exciting to take up her attention. Best of all she liked to go up the Alm with the goats to where the great bird was, where there was such a lot to see, and so much to experience with the little goats and their different personalities. But she also liked to watch the grandfather at work, helping him all she could at the carpenter's bench.

Then a very special treat for Heidi was to watch the grandfather prepare the lovely round goat's milk cheese. But even in the midst of such exciting activities she would sometimes steal away when the wind blew strongest to stand and listen beneath the old fir trees, catching her breath as the wind roared amongst the branches. Nothing sounded so strange and mysterious to her as the stirring of the tree-tops. She would stand directly beneath them and look up at the bending, swaying, roaring branches, bowing to the mighty wind sweeping through them.

As the season changed, the sun lost the fierce heat of summer and Heidi looked out her warm stockings and shoes and her wool dress. Gradually the weather grew colder and as Heidi stood beneath the trees, she would feel as if the wind were blowing straight through her, but she could never tear herself away and go indoors while the stirring branches beckoned her. As it grew ever colder, Peter would appear early in the morning blowing on his hands to warm them. Then one morning they awoke to find the whole Alm covered in snow. Not one blade of grass was visible. Peter and the goats did not appear and Heidi watched from the window of the hut as the big snowflakes fell. The snow fell thickly until it reached above the window so that it was impossible to open it and Heidi and the Alm-Uncle were imprisoned in the hut. This amused Heidi and she ran from one window to another expecting the hut to be covered right over at any moment. The next day it had stopped snowing and the grandfather forced his way out and shovelled the snow away from around the hut. Soon the snow was heaped up around the cottage and they were able to open the window again. In the afternoon, as Heidi and the grandfather sat together by the fire there came a great thumping outside the door. At last the door opened and there stood Peter, knocking the snow from his boots. He had struggled through deep snowdrifts and he still had great lumps of frozen snow clinging to his clothes.

"Good evening!" he said coming in and at once getting as near as possible to the fire. After this salutation the boy lapsed into complete silence but nevertheless his whole face beamed with joy.

Heidi looked at him in amazement for the snow which had covered him from head to foot was beginning to melt and ran from him in rivulets.

"Well, General, and how are things going?" called the grandfather. "Now that the goat army has been disbanded you will have to turn to nibbling at the slate pencil."

"Why must he nibble the slate pencil?" asked Heidi at once.

"In winter the boy has to go to school," explained the grandfather. "There he learns to read and write and that is sometimes difficult; and then it helps a little if one can nibble the slate pencil, isn't that so, General?"

"Yes, that's true," acknowledged Peter.

Now Heidi's interest was thoroughly aroused. She asked Peter many questions about school and everything to be seen and heard there. Since conversation with Peter was inclined to be a slow business he had ample opportunity to get thoroughly dry. He always had great difficulty in putting his thoughts into words and on the subject of school this was particularly hard. By the time he had managed to think of the answer to one question Heidi had already thought of two or three more to ask and they were all of a kind which required much answering. The grandfather kept silent during this dialogue but an occasional twitch of amusement at the corners of his mouth showed that he was listening.

"Well, General, now you have been under fire and must be in need of some refreshment!" As he spoke, the old man rose and got the supper from the cupboard and Heidi brought the chairs up to the table. The grandfather had also made a bench for two people, hinged into the wall, and several different seats here and there, so that he and Heidi could sit together, as she had a way of staying close beside him whatever he was doing. So there was plenty of room for all of them to sit in comfort.

Peter's round eyes opened wider when he saw what a large piece of delicious meat the grandfather put on his plate. He had not enjoyed himself so much for a long time. As they finished the meal it began to grow dark and Peter prepared to go home. He had already bade them good night, but turned again at the door and said: "I'll come back again on Sunday, a week to-day, but the grandmother said she would like you to come to see her some time."

This new idea of going to visit somebody appealed to Heidi at once and on the following morning her first words were, "Grandfather, I must go down and see the grandmother today. She will be expecting me."

"The snow is too deep," replied the grandfather to put her off. But Heidi was determined to go since she had got the grandmother's message. Not a day passed without her pleading, "Grandfather, I must go now! The grandmother is waiting for me!"

On the fourth day a hard frost had set in and the ground cracked at every step. But the bright sun peeped in at the window and fell on Heidi where she sat on her high chair at the table. Soon she had begun her customary little speech, "Today I must go to the grandmother or she will be tired of waiting for me."

The grandfather rose and going up to the hayloft brought down the thick sack which was Heidi's bedcover. "Come, then!" he said. Joyously the child skipped out into the glittering snow world. The old fir trees were silent now and on every branch the snow lay thickly.

The grandfather went into the shed and brought out a large sleigh. There was a pole fixed at the side and from the low seat the sleigh could be guided by the feet pressing against the ground and with the help of the pole.

The grandfather took his seat on the sleigh and placed the child on his knee, wrapping her carefully in the sack to keep her warm. His left arm held her secure and this was necessary for the long drive ahead. Then he grasped the pole with his right hand and gave a push with his feet. The sleigh shot down the Alm with such rapidity that Heidi felt she was flying through the air like a bird. She shouted aloud with joy.

By and by the sleigh stopped with a jerk just outside Goat Peter's cottage. The grandfather lifted the child and unwrapped her, saying, "Now in you go and when it starts to get dark come straight home!" Then he turned and pulled the sleigh back up the mountain.

Heidi opened the cottage door and found herself in a small, rather dark room. She could see a fireplace and a shelf with some dishes so she concluded that this was the kitchen. Then she saw a door and she found that it led into another, narrower room. This cottage was quite different from her grandfather's and everything looked very poor and shabby. When Heidi entered the room she saw a table, and at the table a woman was sitting patching a jacket which Heidi recognised at once as Peter's. In the corner, an old bent woman sat spinning. Heidi went straight to her. "Good day, Grandmother!" she said. "Here I am to see you. Did you think I was long in coming?"

The old woman lifted her head and groped for the hand which Heidi held out to her. When she had found it she held it for a while, thoughtfully. Then she said, "Are you the child who stays with the Alm-Uncle? Are you Heidi?"

"Yes," said Heidi. "I have just come down in the sleigh with Grandfather."

"How can it be? Your hands are quite warm. Brigitta, did the Alm-Uncle himself come with the child?"

Peter's mother, Brigitta, who had been mending at the table got up and looked curiously at the little girl. "I don't know, Mother," she said. "I suppose the child knows if the Alm-Uncle came himself."

Heidi looked at the woman and said firmly, "I know very well who wrapped me in the cover and brought me down in the sleigh. It was Grandfather."

"Then there must be something in what Peter said about the Alm-Uncle although we didn't believe him at the time," said the grandmother. "Who could believe it possible! I didn't think the child would stay up there more than three weeks. How does she look, Brigitta?"

By this time Brigitta had carefully inspected Heidi from every angle so she was able to report: "She is as finely built as Adelheid was, but she has the dark eyes and curly hair of Tobias and the old man. I think she resembles both her parents."

During this time, Heidi's attention had not been idle. She had looked round carefully at everything in the room. Suddenly she said, "Look Grandmother! One of your shutters is loose. The grandfather would put a nail in and then the shutter would be all right. It will break the window-pane soon. See how it shakes!"

"Ah, my child," said the grandmother, "I can't see but I can hear, and much more than the shutter banging. Everything in this house cracks and rattles as soon as the wind blows. It comes in from all sides. Everything seems to be loose. During the night, when the others are asleep, I often fear that the house is going to fall to pieces and kill us all. Alas, there is no one here to repair things. Peter doesn't know how to."

"But can't you see the shutter banging, Grandmother? Look! There it is, just over there!" said Heidi, pointing towards the shutter.

"Alas, child, I can see nothing, nothing!" lamented the grand-mother.

"But if I go outside and open the shutter properly so that it is lighter, won't you see then, Grandmother?"

"No, not even then. Nobody can ever make it light for me."

"But if you go outside into the white snow then surely it will be light. Come with me, Grandmother, and I will show you." Heidi, beginning to feel very distressed, took the old woman's hand and tried to lead her.

"Just let me sit, child. It will always be dark for me."

"But surely in summer it will be different, Grandmother," comforted Heidi, becoming more and more anxious to help. "Surely then it will be light for you! When the sun shines on the mountains and on the flowers and turns them all to crimson and gold, then everything will be bright and wonderful for you."

"Ah, child, I shall never again see the flaming mountains nor the little golden flowers up there. It will never again be light for me on this earth, never!"

Suddenly, Heidi began to cry. Full of compassion she sobbed, "Who then can help you? Is there no one?"

The grandmother tried to comfort the child. The old woman was touched to hear her sob so bitterly. Heidi rarely cried, but when she did her grief was not easily overcome. At last the grandmother said, "Come, my dear Heidi, come and I will explain something to you. You see, when one can't see one likes to hear a kind word and I like to hear you talking. Come, sit here close to me and tell me what you have been doing up there and all about the grandfather. I knew him very well years ago. But for many years now I have only heard of him from Peter, and Peter doesn't talk much."

Suddenly, Heidi had a new idea. Quickly she wiped away her tears and said comfortingly, "You wait, Grandmother, and I shall tell Grandfather everything. He will make it light for you again and will repair the cottage for you. He can do everything."

The grandmother was silent now and Heidi began to give a lively account of her life, of summer days on the pasture and her present life in winter with the grandfather. She described the things he could make from wood—benches and chairs and beautiful mangers where the hay was put for Little Swan and Little Bear, and a big new tub for bathing in summer, a new milk bowl and a spoon. Heidi was quite carried away describing all the beautiful things which could be made from pieces of wood. The grandmother listened intently and every now and then she would say, "Do you hear, Brigitta? Do you hear what she says about the Alm-Uncle?"

Suddenly the story was interrupted by a loud clatter at the door and in tramped Peter. He stopped abruptly and gaped when he saw Heidi, but managed a friendly grin as she greeted him, "Good evening, Peter!"

"Is the boy back from school already?" asked the grandmother in surprise. "An afternoon has not passed so quickly for me for a long time! Good evening, Peter. How did you get on with your reading to-day?"

"Just as usual," answered Peter.

"Well, well," sighed the grandmother gently. "I thought

there might perhaps be a change by this time, especially as you are going to be twelve years old in February."

"What do you mean by change, Grandmother?" Heidi asked with interest.

"I hoped he would be able to learn to read," explained the grand-mother. "Up there on the shelf is an old hymn book with beautiful hymns in it. I have not heard them for a very long time and I can't remember them now. So I had hoped if Peter could learn to read he would be able to read the hymns to me. But he can't learn the letters. It is too difficult for him."

"I think I had better light the lamp. It is getting quite dark," said Peter's mother, who was still busy patching his jacket. "This afternoon has flown by without my noticing."

Heidi jumped up from her chair, stretched out her hand quickly to the grandmother and said, "Good-bye, Grandmother. I have to go home when it gets dark." She said good night to Peter and his mother and went towards the door. But the grandmother called anxiously, "Wait, wait, Heidi! You mustn't go alone. Peter will go with you. Do you hear? Take care of the child, Peter, and see that she doesn't fall down. And don't loiter on the way in case she catches cold, do you hear? Has she got a warm scarf?"

"I haven't got a scarf," replied Heidi, "but I shall not be cold."

With these words she was outside the house and away so quickly that Peter could hardly keep pace. "Run after her, Brigitta!" the grandmother called. The child will be frozen to death on such a night. Take my scarf! Hurry up now and run quickly!"

Brigitta obeyed. The children had only gone a little way up the mountain when they saw the grandfather coming down and soon he stood beside them.

"Good, Heidi! You have kept your word," he praised her. Then wrapping her snugly in the cover he picked her up and turned back up the mountain.

Brigitta saw the old man lift the child, well wrapped up, into his arms. She returned with Peter to the cottage and told the grandmother with amusement what she had seen.

The grandmother was both astonished and glad. "God be thanked that he is good to the child! If only he would allow her to come again! She is a great comfort and what a kind heart she has!" Until the grandmother went to bed she kept repeating, "If only she could come again! Then I might have something to look forward to in this world! She has done me so much good. She has such a loving little heart and how good she is at telling her story."

Brigitta agreed with her mother, and Peter was well pleased, saying, "I told you so," with great satisfaction.

All the way, Heidi chatted to the grandfather although he could not make out a word of the muffled voice coming from inside the sack. So he said, "Wait until we get home, then you can tell me all about it."

As soon as they entered the hut and Heidi was released from her wrapping she said, "Grandfather, to-morrow we must take the hammer and plenty of long nails to fix the grandmother's shutters and all the loose boards because her house rattles and shakes all over!"

"Must we, indeed! And who told you so?" inquired the grandfather.

"Nobody told me but I know myself," replied Heidi, "for everything is loose and the grandmother cannot sleep if she is afraid that any minute the house will fall down on their heads. And for her everything is dark and she thinks that nobody can ever make it light for her again; but you can do it, Grandfather, I am sure. Think how sad it is for her always having to sit in the dark, and being frightened; and only you can help her. To-morrow we will go and help her, won't we, Grandfather?"

Heidi clung tightly to the grandfather and looked up at him with eagerness and confidence. For a little while the old man looked down at the child, then he said, "Yes, Heidi, we will go and see about the repairs. We can do that to-morrow."

The child started to skip round the room, chanting joyfully, "Tomorrow we'll go! To-morrow we'll go!"

The grandfather kept his promise and on the following afternoon they took the same sleigh drive as they had done the previous day. Once again the old man set the child down before the door of Goat Peter's cottage and said, "Go in now and come away again whenever it gets dark!"

Scarcely had Heidi opened the door and skipped into the room when the grandmother called from the corner, "It is Heidi! Here comes the child!" In her eagerness, she let the thread drop from her fingers and the wheel stood still as both her arms stretched out towards the child. Heidi ran to her at once, and drawing the little chair close to her she sat down at her side. Once again there was so much she had to tell the grandmother and so many questions she had to ask. But suddenly such heavy blows sounded against the wall that the grandmother started violently and nearly upset the spinning wheel. "Mercy on us!" she exclaimed, trembling. "What is that? The house must be falling about us!" Heidi grasped her arm firmly and comforted her, "No, no, Grandmother! Don't be afraid! It is only Grandfather hammering. He will fix everything so that you don't need to be afraid any more."

"Is it possible? Then the Lord has not forgotten us!" the grandmother exclaimed. "Did you hear that, Brigitta? If it is the Alm-Uncle, go and tell him to come in so that I can thank him!"

Brigitta went outside. The Alm-Uncle was busy nailing some strong planks to the wall, knocking in the nails with great vigour. Brigitta approached and said, "Good evening, Uncle! Mother and I want to thank you for your kindness and she would like to tell you herself how grateful she is."

"That will do," interrupted the old man. "I know what you think of the Alm-Uncle. Go back inside. I can find out for myself what is needed here."

Brigitta obeyed at once for the Uncle expressed himself in a way which brooked no opposition.

He knocked and hammered his way all round the house and then climbed the narrow little stair up to the roof, and hammered away there until he had used his last nail. By the time he had finished, darkness had fallen and he had no sooner come down and got out the sleigh from behind the shed than Heidi appeared. As on the previous day, the grandfather wrapped her up and took her in his arms, and, dragging the sleigh behind, made his way back up the mountain. For although he had to drag the heavy sleigh, he was afraid that if Heidi sat in it alone, her wrappings would come loose and then she would get very cold; so he carried her snug and warm in his arms.

And so the winter passed. After many lonely years a great happiness had entered the joyless life of the old blind grandmother, and her days were no longer dreary and dark for now she had something to look forward to. From early morning she listened for Heidi's familiar tripping steps. The child became very attached to the old grandmother. And Heidi, sitting beside her, would chat so merrily that the grandmother hardly noticed the passing of time, and never bothered to ask Brigitta whether the day was over, as she used to do. Indeed, as Heidi left, the old lady would remark on how short the afternoon had been. She continually asked Brigitta to say if the child looked well and Brigitta always replied, "She looks the picture of health!" As soon as she understood that nobody, not even the grandfather, could help the old woman, Heidi was very sad; but the grandmother told her again and again that she felt the darkness much less when Heidi was with her. So every fine winter's day Heidi came down on the sleigh. Without any fuss, the grandfather always packed in his tools and he spent many afternoons repairing the cottage. All his good work soon had its effect and the cottage no longer rattled and groaned when the wind blew around it. The grandmother said she had not slept so well for many a year and that she would never forget what the Alm-Uncle had done for her.

Chapter 5

TWO VISITORS TO THE ALM-HUT

Quickly the winter passed, and more quickly still the happy days of summer; and now another winter was drawing to its close. Heidi was happy as a bird and each day she looked forward eagerly to the coming of spring when the warm south wind would sweep through the fir trees and across the valley, melting the last patch of snow on the lower slopes. Long days on the pasture would return and this seemed to Heidi the greatest joy of all. She was eight years old now and had learnt a great deal during the time she had lived with the Alm-Uncle. She knew how to manage the goats, and Little Swan and Little Bear would follow her about, bleating at the very sound of her voice.

Twice during this winter Peter had come from the school in Dorfli with a message from the teacher telling the Alm-Uncle that the child he had staying with him should go to school since she was over the age and should, indeed, have attended the previous winter. On both occasions, the Alm-Uncle had replied that he had no intention of sending the child to school.

When the sun had melted all the snow on the mountain, and the snowdrops were appearing and the fir trees had shaken off the weight of snow and were once again waving their green branches in the wind, Heidi ran back and forth with pleasure between the goat shed, the trees and the hut, to show her grandfather how big the area of green grass under the trees had grown. One sunny morning in March, as she ran out of the house, she was startled to come face to face with an old gentlemen dressed in black. He stood regarding her gravely for a time and then, thinking that his unexpected appearance had frightened her, he said kindly, "It is all right. You need not be afraid of me. You are Heidi, are you not? Where is your grandfather?"

"He is sitting at the table, making wooden spoons," replied Heidi and at once led him inside.

It was the old pastor from Dörfli who had known the uncle well in the old days. He walked towards the old man who was bent over his work, and addressed him.

"Good morning, neighbour!"

Astonished, the grandfather looked up, then rose, saying, "Good morning, pastor!" Offering his seat to the visitor, he added, "Pray sit down, if you do not mind a wooden seat."

The pastor seated himself. "I have not seen you for a long time, neighbour," he said.

"Nor I you!"

"I have come to-day to discuss something with you," continued the pastor. "I think perhaps you know what it is I want to talk to you about, and that I am anxious to hear what you intend to do about a certain matter."

There was a silence. The pastor glanced quickly towards the child, who stood by the door and watched the newcomer with interest.

"Heidi, go and see how the goats are getting along!" said the grandfather. "You may take them a little salt, and stay with them until I come!"

Heidi disappeared at once.

"The child should have gone to school a year ago," said the pastor now. "The school master reminded you often but you ignored him. What is it you intend should become of the child, neighbour?"

"I intend that she should not go to school!"

The pastor looked with surprise at the old man who sat on his bench with his arms folded determinedly.

"But how is the child going to grow up?" asked the pastor reasonably.

"She will grow up with the goats and birds. That way she will learn nothing evil."

"But the child is neither a goat nor a bird but a human being," pleaded the pastor. "Though she learns nothing evil from her companions, they cannot teach her her A B Cs! Learn she must, and the time has come to begin. I came to speak a word to you in time, neighbour, so that you may think it over at your leisure and make arrangements during the summer. The child must not be allowed to run about another winter without taking lessons. Next winter she must attend school regularly!"

"No, she will not go, pastor!" muttered the old man with unwavering determination.

"Do you really think there is no way of making you see reason if you insist so stubbornly on this decision?" asked the pastor, beginning to lose patience. "You have lived in the world and have seen and learnt a lot. I should have thought you would have had more sense, neighbour."

"You think so? asked the old man, and the tremor in his voice betrayed that he was no longer calm. "And do you really think that next winter I shall send a delicate child on a two hours' walk down the mountain on ice-cold mornings in storm and snow, and allow her to return at night when there may be a wind raging fit to blow a man over, let alone a child? Perhaps the pastor still remembers the child's mother, Adelheid. She was a sleep-walker and had a delicate constitution. Might not the health of this child, who is also finely built, be endangered by so much exertion? I wonder who can force me to send her? I shall take it to the highest law court in the country and then we shall see who can force me!"

"You are quite right, neighbour," agreed the pastor, amicably. "It would not be possible to send the child from here. But I see the child is dear to you. For her sake, do what you ought to have done long ago. Come down into Dörfli and live amongst us! What a life you live here, alone and embittered towards God and men. If anything should happen to you up here in the mountains who would come to your assistance? I cannot understand how you are not frozen to death in this hut of yours in the winter-time. How does this delicate child stand up to it?"

"I see to it that she is not cold, and that she has a good warm bed, I should like the pastor to know. And another thing: I get all the wood I need. If the pastor cares to look into my wood-shed he will soon see! There is plenty there! The fire is never out in my hut all through the winter. As for living down in the valley, it is out of the question. The people down there despise me and I them. For all our sakes, it is better we stay apart."

"No, no, you are quite wrong!" the pastor said warmly. "The people down below don't dislike you half as much as you think. Take my advice, neighbour! Make your peace with God, ask His forgiveness and then come and see how people will change towards you and how happy you will be!"

The pastor rose. He held out his hand to the old man and repeated with kindly emphasis, "I am counting on it, neighbour! Next winter you'll come back to live with us in the valley and we'll be good neighbours again, as we used to be. I would be disappointed to think that you were coming back only because of the school business. Promise me that you will live amongst us again, reconciled to God and man!"

The Alm-Uncle shook hands with the pastor but insisted firmly, "I know you mean well, but as to what you expect me to do—no! Once and for all I tell you I will not send the child, nor will I come down to live in the valley."

"Then God help you!" sighed the pastor and sadly made his way back down the mountain to the village.

As a result of the interview, the Alm-Uncle was in a very black mood, and when Heidi asked in the afternoon, "Shall we go down to the grandmother's now?" he replied harshly, "Not to-day!" He was silent the whole day and the following morning, when Heidi asked again, "Shall we go to-day to see the grandmother?" he turned away abruptly, mumbling, "Perhaps."

But before the dinner dishes had been cleared away another visitor had arrived. It was cousin Dete, dressed in a beautiful gown which swept the floor and wearing on her head a very fine hat with feathers. The Alm-Uncle examined her from head to foot in amazement. But Dete was all prepared to make friendly conversation and at once adopted a flattering tone.

"How well the child looks! I hardly recognised her! I can see that she has not had a bad time with the Alm-Uncle, far from it! I have often thought of taking the child back for I can imagine that she is in your way. Day and night I have thought about what to do with her and that's why I am here to-day. I have just heard of something that would be a piece of luck for Heidi. I have fixed everything. It is really a wonderful chance. The people I am in service with have some very wealthy relations. They live in the most beautiful house in Frankfurt and they have an only daughter who is an invalid and has to be wheeled in a chair. She is very much alone and has her lessons with a private teacher, which, of course, is very boring for her. Now she would like a playmate so her people have asked my mistress to help them find a companion. The lady house-keeper thinks that a simple, unspoilt child, one different from the children now-a-days, would be most suitable. Naturally I thought of Heidi and went at once to the lady and told her all about our child's character. She agreed immediately to take her. No one can foresee what good fortune will be in store for Heidi. If the people become fond of her and if something should happen to their own little daughter—and who knows when she is so weak—then in all likelihood they would not want to be without a child—then it would be the most unheard-of luck—"

"Do you think you have just about finished?" interrupted the Alm-Uncle who had held his peace up till now.

"Ugh!" exclaimed Dete, tossing her head. "You behave as though I were telling you something of no consequence. Anybody in Prattigau would thank God if I were to bring such news!"

"You may take your news where you like. I want to hear no more of it," replied the Uncle dryly.

This threw Dete immediately into a passion. "Well!" she stormed, "if that is all you have to say, Uncle, I will speak my mind, too. The child is eight years old now, but she knows nothing. You neither want her to attend school nor to go to church. Oh, I have heard all about it in Dörfli. She is my sister's child and I am responsible for what happens to her. When such a good chance comes her way only one who cared nothing for her welfare would oppose it. But I tell you, I won't give in and people are on my side. There is not a single person who would not take my part—and they are all against you. And if you are thinking of taking it to law, think well, Uncle! There are things that could be brought up against you which you wouldn't like to hear."

"Hold your tongue!" thundered the uncle, his eyes ablaze with anger. "Very well, then. Take the child away and ruin her! And never let me set eyes on you again, with that ridiculous hat on your head and such words on your tongue!" Then the uncle turned from her abruptly and strode from the hut.

"You have made Grandfather angry," said Heidi, fixing dark, smouldering eyes on her aunt.

"Oh, he'll soon get over it," replied Dete impatiently. "Come along now! Where are your clothes?"

"I won't go!" said Heidi defiantly.

"What did you say?" asked the aunt, about to fly into a temper. Then she softened her tone a little and continued more persuasively, "Come, come! You don't know any better. You have no idea how well off you will be." Then, going to the wardrobe, she took out Heidi's things and parcelled them together. "Come now! Here is your hat! What a sight it is! But never mind! It will do for to-day. Put it on, quickly."

"I am going to stay here," repeated Heidi.

"Don't be so silly. You are as obstinate as a goat. I suppose that is what you have learnt from them. But you've got to understand, the grandfather is cross and doesn't want to see us again, you heard him say so. He wants you to go with me, so now you mustn't make him more angry. You have no idea how nice it is in Frankfurt. But, of course, if you don't like it you can always come back here. By that time the grandfather will have recovered himself."

"Can I come straight home again tonight if I want to?" asked Heidi.

"Come along now and don't be silly! I said you can go home when you like. To-day we are only going as far as Mayenfeld but tomorrow we will travel by train, and the train can carry you home again as fast as the wind."

Aunt Dete took the bundle of clothes under one arm, grasped Heidi firmly by the other hand, and together they started to climb down the hill. It was still too early in the spring to take the goats up to the pasture, so Peter was still going to school in Dörfli, but once in a while he took a day's holiday, for learning to read seemed not nearly as attractive a proposition as wandering about looking for thick sticks which might come in useful.

As Dete and Heidi approached the grandmother's hut, Peter appeared from round a corner of the cottage. He was carrying a huge bundle of thick hazel twigs, when the two figures approached. He stopped to stare at them as they passed by; then he called out after them, "Where are you going?"

"I have to go at once to Frankfurt with Aunt," answered Heidi, "but I am going to say good-bye to the grandmother first. She will be waiting for me and I must see her before I go."

"No, no," interrupted the aunt quickly. "It is much too late. You can see her next time you come back. Come along, now!" And she pulled the child along, afraid that she might again take it into her head to stay and that the grandmother would support her wishes.

Peter dashed into the cottage and dropped his bundle of sticks so noisily that the grandmother started up from her spinning, exclaiming fretfully, "What is it now? What is it?" And Peter's mother, who had been sitting by the table, said in her patient way, "What is it, Peter? What is the matter?"

"She is taking Heidi away!" gasped Peter.

"Who?" asked the grandmother in distress. "Taking her where, Peter?" But she soon guessed what had taken place, for her daughter had told her not long ago that she had seen Dete going up to the Alm-Uncle's. The old woman unfastened the window with trembling fingers and called out imploringly, "Dete, Dete, don't take the child away from us! Don't take Heidi away!"

Dete and Heidi heard the voice. Dete had evidently made out the grandmother's words for she grasped the child's hand still more firmly and ran as fast as she could.

Heidi, struggling to get her hand free, cried, "The grandmother is calling! I want to go to her!"

But that was exactly what the aunt did not want. She tried to soothe the child.

"Come quickly now or it will be too late and we will not be able to continue our journey to-morrow. You will soon see how much you will like Frankfurt. Perhaps you will never want to come back again. But if you do it will be quite simple. You could even take something home for the grandmother—something she would like."

This appealed to Heidi and she stopped trying to resist and started to run, too.

After a little while she asked, "What could I get for Grandmother?"

"Something nice," said the aunt. "Perhaps some nice soft rolls. She would enjoy that. It would be such a change from the dark bread."

"Oh, yes! She always gives it to Peter and says 'It is too hard for me.' I have heard her myself", admitted Heidi. "Let us hurry, then, Aunt Dete! We may reach Frankfurt to-day and I shall soon be back with the rolls." And Heidi started to run so fast that the aunt with her bundle could hardly keep pace with her. But she was glad to be having no more difficulty with the child for now they had almost reached the first houses in Dörfli and a lot of talk and questions might have made Heidi change her mind again. So Dete strode straight ahead holding Heidi's hand tightly so that every one would see that she had to hurry along because of the child. To every question she merely answered, "I can't stop now. We have a long way to go."

"Are you going away?" Is she fleeing from the Alm-Uncle?" "It's amazing that she has survived!" "But how healthy she looks!" Questions and exclamations came from all sides and Dete was glad that she didn't have to stop and that Heidi didn't say a word but hurried on eagerly.

From that day on the Alm-Uncle looked even more fierce and terrifying when he came down to Dörfli. He spoke to no one and looked more threatening with his cheese-basket on his back and his mountain stick in his hand. The old man ignored everyone as he strode through the village to the valley where he sold cheese and bought bread and meat. After he had gone, the villagers stood around watching his retreating back and everyone commented on his wild appearance and his total lack of response to anyone's greeting.

They all agreed that it was a good thing that the child had been taken from him—they had noticed how Heidi hurried along as though afraid that her grandfather might catch them up. Everybody was of the same opinion; that it was a great blessing that the child had been taken away. Only the blind grandmother took the old man's part. When people came to the house to give her some spinning to do, she would tell them again and again how kind and good he had been to the child and what he had done for herself and her daughter; how he had spent many afternoons repairing the cottage which, without his help, would undoubtedly have collapsed upon them.This story soon got about in Dörfli, but most people thought the grandmother was too old to understand and too blind and hard of hearing to know exactly what went on around her.

It was as well it had been repaired, for the Alm-Uncle never came to Goat Peter's cottage now and the grandmother's days were once more passed in sighing and fretting. "Alas, all the joy and happiness has gone with the child!" she would say, "and the days are long and dreary! If only I might see Heidi again before I die!"

CHAPTER 6

A NEW START FOR HEIDI

In the house in Frankfurt, the little daughter of Herr Sesemann sat in the comfortable invalid chair in which all her life was spent and in which she had to be wheeled from room to room. Now she was in the room which they called the study, and where she had her lessons.

Clara's little face was pale and thin and her soft, gentle blue eyes were fixed at this moment on the door. To-day, time seemed to pass very slowly for her, for she was saying rather impatiently, "But isn't it time yet, Fräulein Rottenmeier?"

The lady thus addressed sat very upright at a small work-table and nodded. Principally because of her rather odd and very severe style of dress, Fräulein Rottenmeier presented an awe-inspiring appearance. Over her shoulders she wore a cape with a stiff collar and on her head a very elaborate cap. Since the death of Frau Sesemann, several years ago, Fräulein Rottenmeier had acted as house-keeper and manager of the domestic staff. Herr Sesemann very often went off on business trips, leaving Fräulein Rottenmeier in sole charge of the house, stipulating only that no decisions should be taken without first consulting his little daughter and that nothing should be done against her wish.

Just as Clara was asking the same question a second time, Dete and Heidi arrived at the door. Dete asked the coachman, who had descended from is box, whether it was too late to see Fräulein Rottenmeier.

"That's nothing to do with me," he muttered. "Ring the bell you'll find in the hall and Sebastian will come."

Dete rang the bell and the butler came down the stairs, the big round buttons of his livery in keeping with his round eyes which stared blankly at the two strangers.

"I wonder if it is too late to see Fräulein Rottenmeier?" Dete asked.

Sebastian stared frostily for a moment, then pressed a bell and disappeared without a word. Next a maid appeared. A spotless white cap was perched on top of her head. Regarding the visitors haughtily from the top of the stairs, "What is it?" she asked.

Dete repeated her request. Tinette disappeared, but very soon came back and called from above, "Come this way! You are expected."

Dete and Heidi went upstairs and followed Tinette into the study. At the door Dete stopped politely, still holding Heidi's hand firmly for there was no knowing what the child might do in strange surroundings.

Fräulein Rottenmeier rose slowly and came forward to examine the new playmate for the daughter of the house. She did not appear to be very pleased with what she saw. Heidi wore her simple little cotton dress and on her head, her old, crushed, straw hat. She gazed innocently from underneath it, staring with unconcealed surprise at the lady's towering headgear.

"What is your name?" asked Fräulein Rottenmeier, after a

lengthy inspection of the child, who had returned her gaze steadily and inquiringly throughout.

"Heidi," the child answered distinctly.

"What? That is not a Christian name! You were surely not baptised so! What name were you given when you were christened?"

"I can't remember now," replied Heidi.

"What a foolish answer!" exclaimed the lady, shaking her head disapprovingly. "Dete, is the child stupid or impertinent?"

"I am so sorry! Would you kindly allow me to speak for the child? She is not accustomed to strangers," said Dete hastily, secretly nudging Heidi for having given such an unsuitable answer. "She certainly is not stupid, nor impertinent. It is just that she always says exactly what she is thinking. This is the first time she has ever been in an upper-class house and she knows nothing about good manners. She is docile and willing to learn if madam will have the patience. She was christened Adelheid for her mother, my late sister."

"Well, at least that's a name one can pronounce," remarked Fräulein Rottenmeier. "But Dete, I must say that for her age the child looks to me a little strange. I told you that a companion for Fräulein Clara had to be of her age to be able to share her lessons and everything. Fräulein Clara is twelve now. What is the age of the child?"

"With your permission," began Dete elaborately, "I am not quite sure myself but I think she is a little younger, but not much. She will be ten, or perhaps a little more."

"I am eight now, the grandfather said," declared Heidi. The aunt gave her another push but Heidi was not in the least embarrassed.

"What! Only eight years old!" cried Fräulein Rottenmeier indignantly. "Four years younger! What use is that? And what have you learnt? Which books did you use for your lessons?"

"None," replied Heidi.

"What? How did you learn to read?"

"I never learnt. Neither did Peter," said Heidi.

"Mercy! You cannot read! Is that true that you cannot read?"

demanded Fräulein Rottenmeier, deeply shocked. What did you learn, then?"

"Nothing," said Heidi.

"Dete!" cried Fräulein Rottenmeier when she had recovered from this shock. "This is not the agreement at all! How dare you bring this child to me!"

But Dete was not easily frightened and replied boldly, "With madam's permission, the child is just what I understood madam wanted. Madam told me she wanted a companion unlike ordinary children. Therefore I chose this one because the older ones are not so unspoilt. But now I am afraid I must go. My mistress will be expecting me. If I may, I shall come again soon to see how the child is getting on."

With a curtsy, Dete left the room and quickly ran downstairs. For a moment Fräulein Rottenmeier was too surprised to speak, then she ran after Dete. There were many things which must be discussed if the child were to stay and the aunt seemed determined that she should.

Heidi still stood by the door where she had remained since she entered the room. So far Clara had watched silently; now she beckoned to Heidi to come nearer.

Heidi went up to her.

"Would you rather be called Heidi or Adelheid?" asked Clara.

"I am always called Heidi," Heidi replied.

"Then I shall always call you that, too," said Clara "I like the name although never before have I heard it or seen a little girl like you. Has your hair always been short and curly like that?"

"Yes, I think so," replied Heidi.

"Did you come to Frankfurt yesterday, and are you pleased to be here?" Clara continued to ask.

"No, we came to-day. But to-morrow I am going home again with some white rolls for the grandmother."

"How strange you are!" Clara burst out. "You have been brought here to stay with me and share my lessons with me. What fun it will be now because you can't read at all. At least it will be a change. It is usually very dull and the mornings are so long! You see, every morning at ten my tutor comes and the lessons go on till two. That is far too long! Sometimes the tutor holds his book close to his face as if he had suddenly become short-sighted but I know quite well it is only because he is yawning; and Fräulein Rottenmeier takes out her handkerchief and holds it to her face as if she were affected by what we are reading, but she too only wants to yawn. But I don't dare, because if I only did it once Fräulein Rottenmeier would fetch the cod liver oil and say I was getting weak again, and the worst thing of all is to take cod liver oil. But it will be much more fun now. I can listen to you learning to read."

Heidi shook her head doubtfully at the mention of her learning to read.

"Of course, Heidi, you have to learn to read. Everybody has to learn to read and my tutor is very kind. He is never cross and he will explain everything to you. But nevertheless, you won't be able to understand what he explains. Don't ask any questions, as you will only encourage him to continue explaining and you'll understand even less. The best thing to do is to wait until you've learnt more and know about everything on your own, then what he says will have some sort of meaning."

Just then Fräulein Rottenmeier came back into the room. She had not succeeded in calling Dete back and was apparently very annoyed about it. She had wanted at least to persuade Dete that Heidi was totally unsuitable to be Clara's companion and to complain at Dete's misleading behaviour. She felt even more annoyed at the thought that she herself had brought the problem on to her own head by agreeing to Heidi being fetched.

What was she going to do about it? She ran to and fro in a bother from the dining room to the study, and then began scolding Sebastian, who was studying the table he had just laid, to make sure nothing had been missed out.

"You can carry on day-dreaming tomorrow morning," she said crossly, "hurry up or we'll get no dinner today."

Then she bustled out, calling Tinette, but in such an irritable voice that the maid came up with even more of a swagger than usual. She looked so pert that Fräulein Rottenmeier did not dare scold her.

"See that a room is made ready for the child who has just

arrived," she said, tight-lipped. "It's all ready; it just needs a duster over it." Sebastian had opened the folding doors of the study and quietly wheeled Clara into the other room. While he adjusted the chair Heidi placed herself before him and stared steadily up at him.

"Well, what is it you are looking at?" he grumbled.

When Fräulein Rottenmeier returned she was just in time to hear Heidi say, "You look like Peter."

She raised her hands in horror. "Really!" she murmured. "She treats the butler as an equal! The child knows absolutely nothing!"

Sebastian helped Clara to her seat at the table and Fräulein Rottenmeier seated herself beside her, motioning Heidi to sit opposite. Beside Heidi's plate lay a lovely white roll. She glanced at it happily. The resemblance Heidi had discovered in Sebastian seemed to have given her confidence in him for she sat as quiet as a mouse until he came to her side to serve the fish, then she pointed to the roll and asked, "May I have it?"

Sebastian nodded, glancing sideways at Fräulein Rottenmeier to see what effect the question had had on her.

Immediately Heidi took the roll and put it into her pocket. Sebastian hid a smile. Motionless and silent, he stood at her side, waiting for her to take her helping of fish for it was not his place to speak or move away until Heidi had helped herself. For a few seconds Heidi looked at him wonderingly, then she asked, "May I have a little of that, too?" Sebastian nodded again. "Then give me some, please," she said, looking calmly at her plate. At this breach of etiquette Sebastian was almost in danger of losing control of his features and the arm which held the dish was beginning to shake.

"You can leave the dish on the table and come back afterwards," ordered Fräulein Rottenmeier, looking very severe, and Sebastian disappeared at once.

"Adelheid, I see I shall have to teach you the first simple rules of good behaviour," said the lady with a deep sigh. "First of all I will show you how to behave at the table and improve your manners."

She instructed Heidi thoroughly and clearly on what she had

to do. "Then," she went on to explain, "I must impress upon you particularly that you are not to speak to Sebastian at table unless the question or remark is absolutely necessary, and even then you must not address him as a friend. Do you understand? And so with Tinette. You will address *me* as you hear others do. Clara will decide for herself what you are to call her."

"Clara, of course!" Clara interrupted.

Then followed a long list of rules about getting up and going to bed, about entering and leaving a room, about being tidy and shutting doors. All of a sudden Heidi's eyes closed, for she had been up since five o'clock that morning and had had a long journey. She leaned back in her chair, fast asleep. When Fräulein Rottenmeier had finished her lecture at last, she said, "Now, remember everything I have said, Adelheid! Have you understood it all?"

"Heidi has been asleep for ever so long," Clara said with amusement. She had not had such an entertaining dinner for a long time!

"It is really shocking how much trouble this child is causing," exclaimed Fräulein Rottenmeier angrily and rang the bell so violently that both Sebastian and Tinette came rushing in. But in spite of all the noise Heidi slept on and it was only with great difficulty that they succeeded in awakening her so that she could be shown to her bedroom which was at the end of a long passage, beyond those of Clara and Fräulein Rottenmeier.

CHAPTER 7

AN EVENTFUL DAY

Heidi awoke in the morning and looked around in bewilderment. She blinked and rubbed her eyes but it did not help her to remember where she was. She was lying in a high white bed in a big room and daylight streamed in between long white curtains. There were two arm-chairs covered in a floral material. A sofa stood against the wall with a round table in front of it and in the corner there was a wash-stand with all sorts of objects on it which were entirely new to Heidi.

Suddenly she remembered that she was in Frankfurt and the events of the previous day came back to her quite clearly. She remembered the long list of instructions given to her by Fräulein Rottenmeier, up to the point at which she must have fallen asleep. Heidi jumped out of bed and dressed; then went from one window to the other to try to get a glimpse of the sky and the countryside outside. Behind the big curtains she felt like a bird in a cage. As she could not manage to pull them aside she crept underneath to get to the window. It was so high that she could only just see over the sill. However, the view was not one of pleasant green fields but only of walls and windows. She ran backwards and forwards from one window to another, but the view was just the same. It frightened her to think that she could not see the sky, for she was used to rising early and running outside straight away to inspect the meadows, the blue sky, the sun and the trees and flowers. Heidi couldn't believe that there might be no green grass or snow on the mountain slopes. She was like a captive bird, trying to fly out into the free air through the bars of its cage. But the windows would not open, and her little fingers were not strong enough to prise them open from the bottom. At last she realised that her efforts were in vain, and she started to consider going outside and round the house until she found the grass. Then she remembered that the previous night when she arrived, she had seen only hard pavements in front of the house. Presently there came a knock at the door and Tinette popped her head round, saying in a bored voice, "Breakfast is ready!"

Heidi failed to understand that this was an invitation, for the sour expression on Tinette's face had suggested rather a warning to stay away. So it seemed to Heidi, at any rate, and she acted accordingly. She took the little stool from under the table, put it in a corner, sat down and waited quietly to see what would happen next. After some time Fräulein Rottenmeier bustled along with a great deal of noise. Once again she seemed to be thoroughly annoyed and shouted at Heidi, "What is the matter with you, Adelheid? Don't you know what breakfast is? Come along!"

This Heidi understood and followed at once. Clara had been seated in the dining-room for some time and she greeted Heidi in a friendly way. Her face wore a much happier expression than usual for she was looking forward to all kinds of unexpected events that day. Breakfast passed without incident. Heidi ate her rolls very nicely and when they had finished Clara was wheeled back to the study. Fräulein Rottenmeier told Heidi to follow and remain with Clara until the tutor arrived to begin lessons. As soon as the children were alone together Heidi asked, "How can I see right down to the ground?"

"You just open the window and look out!" replied Clara, amused.

"But the windows won't open," replied Heidi sadly.

"Oh yes," Clara assured her, "but you can't do it alone. Neither can I. But if you see Sebastian he will open them for you."

Heidi sighed with relief, for the house had begun to make her feel as though she were a prisoner. Then Clara began to ask Heidi about her home and Heidi was delighted to tell her all about the Alm and the goats and the pasture and everything that was dear to her.

In the meantime the tutor had arrived, but Fräulein Rottenmeier did not show him into the study as usual. She wanted to talk to him first and led him to the dining-room. There, in great agitation, she began to describe to him the awkward situation which had arisen and told him how, some time ago, she had persuaded Herr Sesemann to get a companion for Clara as it would help Clara at her lessons and give her some amusement during her leisure hours. In actual fact, Fräulein Rottenmeier had wanted this for her own benefit, as it would no longer necessitate her own continual attendance on the sick child. The father had replied that he was delighted for his daughter to have a companion, as long as she was given exactly the same kindness and care as Clara, for he would not tolerate any tormenting of the child—"a quite unnecessary and tactless remark," added Fräulein Rottenmeier. She recounted how dreadfully she had been deceived and she went on to enlighten the tutor on all the dreadful things of which Heidi had so far been found guilty, and how, in view of Heidi's complete ignorance, the tutor would have to begin at the very beginning with the A B C, and how she herself had had to give the child instruction on the simplest rules of behaviour. There was only one way out of the situation, in Fräulein Rottenmeier's opinion, and that was for the tutor to insist that it was impossible to teach two children so far apart in age without retarding-Clara's progress. That would be a very good reason for Herr Sesemann's sending the child back home. Herr Sesemann knew the child had arrived and without his consent Fräulein Rottenmeier could not send her away again.

However, the tutor was cautious and unwilling to commit himself. With many words of comfort he assured Fräulein Rottenmeier that though the child were backward in some things she might be quite advanced in other respects and that regular lessons might very well restore the balance. When Fräulein Rottenmeier at last realised that she would get very little support from the tutor she opened the door to the study and allowed him him to go through to the children. She paced up and down the dining room, silently pondering how the servants should be instructed to address Adelheid. The father had expressly stated that she was to be treated exactly like his own daughter, and this would probably refer particularly to her dealings with the servants. However, her musing was suddenly interrupted, for before many minutes had passed, a dreadful noise came from the study. Then there was a loud cry from Sebastian. Fräulein Rottenmeier rushed in to find the whole room in complete disorder; books, copy-books, ink-stand; and across the table, on to the floor and across the carpet there flowed a stream of ink. Heidi was nowhere to be seen.

"What is all this?" cried Fräulein Rottenmeier. "Carpet,

books, work basket, everything covered with ink! I never saw such a mess! I have no doubt that wretched child is to blame!"

The tutor looked very distressed but Clara was following events with obvious amusement.

"Yes, Heidi did it, but not on purpose. She mustn't be punished. It was just that she was in such a hurry to get away that she tugged the tablecloth and then everything fell on the floor. She wanted to see the carriages passing; that's why she rushed out. Perhaps she has never seen one before!"

"What did I tell you? The creature doesn't know the first thing! She has no idea what a lesson is—that she must sit still and listen. But where is the little trouble-maker? Surely she hasn't run away! Whatever will Herr Sesemann say?"

Fräulein Rottenmeier ran downstairs. There stood Heidi in the open doorway looking out into the street in complete bewilderment.

"What is the matter? What are you thinking of to run away like that?" Fräulein Rottenmeier shouted at the child.

"I thought I heard the fir trees rustling but I can't find them and I don't hear them any more," said Heidi disconsolately, turning her head in the direction of the disappearing carriages. The rumbling of their wheels had seemed to her like the howling of the wind in the fir trees at home and she had tried to follow the sound.

"Fir trees! What nonsense! Do you think we live in a wood! Come and see the mess you have made!"

Heidi followed Fräulein Rottenmeier upstairs. She gazed in astonishment at the havoc she had created, for in her haste to get downstairs she had noticed nothing.

"You won't do this a second time," warned Fräulein Rottenmeier. "During lessons you will sit still and pay attention! And if you can't do that I will have to tie you to your chair. Do you understand?"

"Yes," said Heidi. "I shall be good now."

Sebastian and Tinette were called in to restore order and the tutor went away because there could be no more lessons that day— there had not even been time for yawning!

Clara always rested in the afternoons, so Heidi was told she might do as she pleased. This suited her perfectly because there was something she very much wanted to do. But she needed assistance, and for this reason she posted herself in front of the dining-room door, right in the centre of the hall so that she would not miss the person to whom she wished to speak. It was not very long before Sebastian came upstairs carrying a large tray. Heidi addressed him formally, as Fräulein Rottenmeier had instructed her.

"Is there something the little fräulein wants?" inquired Sebastian, carrying the silver into the dining-room. "I only wanted to ask you something—but nothing nasty like this morning," said Heidi, hastily, eager to placate him, for Sebastian appeared to be in a bad mood, and Heidi was sure that it was because she had spilt ink on the floor.

"Oh yes, and why are you talking to me in that manner?" replied Sebastian, in an offended tone, obviously still cross.

"Fräulein Rottenmeier ordered me always to speak to you like that," said Heidi.

Sebastian laughed, to Heidi's astonishment, and added in a friendly way, "What is it that the little fräulein wants?"

"My name is Heidi, not fräulein," replied Heidi, now put out herself.

"Exactly, but the lady in question has ordered me to call you fräulein," he explained.

"Oh, well, I had better accept it," said Heidi quietly, for she had realised that whatever Fräulein Rottenmeier said was to be obeyed absolutely. "So now I have three names," she sighed.

"What was it the little fräulein wanted to ask?" said Sebastian kindly as he went through to the dining room to put away the cutlery.

"How do you open a window, Sebastian?"

"Like this!" And he opened one of the large windows in the dining-room.

Heidi crossed over to the window but she was not tall enough to be able to see out.

"Here you are!" said Sebastian, bringing a high stool. "Now the little fräulein can see everything that is going on in the street down below."

Cheerfully Heidi climbed up and at last managed to see out of the window. Greatly disappointed, she withdrew her head almost at once. "But I can only see the stony street! Nothing else!" she said sadly. "If you go round the house what do you see on the other side, Sebastian?"

"Just the same!" he replied.

"But where have you to go to see over the whole valley?" she asked.

"Then you must climb a high tower or a church steeple, like that one with the golden ball. From there you can see ever so far."

At that, Heidi quickly jumped down from her stool and raced downstairs into the street. But it was not so easy as she had imagined. When she saw the steeple from the window it looked as though she only had to cross the street to reach it. But although she had walked right down the street she had not come to the steeple and she could not even see it any longer. She walked on and on. Many people passed but they all seemed to be in such a hurry that Heidi did not like to stop any of them to ask the way. Then Heidi saw a boy standing on the street corner with a barrel organ and, perched on his arm, a very strange-looking little animal. Heidi went forward and asked, "Where is the tower with the golden ball on the top?"

"Don't know!" answered the boy.

"Who can tell me, then?" asked Heidi again.

"Don't know."

"Don't you know of any church with a high steeple?"

"Yes, I know one!"

"Well, then, come and show it to me!"

"You show me first what you will give me for it!" said the boy, holding his hand out. Heidi searched in her pocket and found a pretty little card on which was printed a wreath of red roses. It was not easy to part with it for it had been given to her by Clara only that morning. But she longed to be able to look down over the green slopes into the valley. "There," said Heidi, "would you like this?"

The boy withdrew his hand and shook his head.

"What do you want, then?" asked Heidi, cheerfully putting away her little picture.

"Money," said the boy.

"I haven't got any now, but Clara will give me some later. How much do you want?"

"Twopence."

"Well, come along, then!"

They walked down a long street and on the way Heidi asked her companion what he was carrying on his back. He told her it was a barrel organ which played beautiful music when you turned the handle. All at once they found themselves in front of an old church with a high steeple. The boy stood still and pointed at it.

"But how can I get in?" asked Heidi when she saw that the doors were closed.

"Don't know," came the reply.

"Perhaps I could ring the bell as we do for Sebastian." Heidi had discovered a bell in the wall which she now pulled as hard as she could.

"When I go up you must wait here for me for I don't know my way back and you must show it to me."

"What will I get for it?"

"What do you want?"

"Another twopence."

They heard steps inside and the door creaked open. An old man appeared, looking first surprised and then angry when he saw the children. "How dare you ring-the bell like that!" he shouted at them. "Can't you read the notice? 'Visitors wishing to go to the top of the tower, please ring!' "

The boy said nothing but pointed to Heidi.

"But that's just what I want!" said Heidi.

"Why do you want to go up there?" asked the caretaker. "Did somebody send you?"

"No," said Heidi. "I would just like to go up to the top and look down."

"Be off with you! And don't dare to try this trick on me again!" said the old man and was about to close the door; but Heidi grasped his coat and cried beseechingly, "Let me go up just once!"

The imploring look in Heidi's eyes made the old man change his mind. He took her hand and said kindly, "If you really want it so much I will take you up."

The boy sat down on the stone steps and prepared to wait.

Together Heidi and the old man climbed many, many steps which became smaller and smaller as they went up, until at last, a very narrow little stair led up to the top of the tower. The caretaker lifted Heidi up to let her see out of the window. "Now you can look down," he said.

Heidi saw nothing but roofs, steeples and chimneys. She withdrew her head presently and said, very dispiritedly, "It is not at all as I expected."

"There! You see how a little one like you knows nothing about views. Now come down and never ring my bell again!"

The old man put Heidi back down on the floor and went ahead of her down the narrow stair. When the steps got broader they came to the caretaker's little room and beside it, underneath the sloping roof, stood a big basket. In front of it sat a big grey cat which snarled and spat because inside the basket lived her family and she wanted to warn everybody not to meddle with them. Heidi looked at her in amazement. She had never seen such a big cat. There were scores of mice in the old tower and the cat had no difficulty in catching half a dozen every day, for her kittens. The caretaker saw the look of delight on Heidi's face and said, "Come! She won't hurt you when I am here. You can still look at the kittens."

Heidi went over to the basket and exclaimed joyfully, "Oh, what sweet little kittens!"

'Would you like one?" asked the old man as he watched Heidi with amusement.

"For myself? To keep?" whispered Heidi, who could hardly believe her luck.

"Yes, you can have them all if you like," he said, thinking this would be a better way of getting rid of them than drowning.

Heidi was overjoyed. There was certainly plenty of room in the big house and how happy the kittens would make Clara!

"But how can I carry them away?" asked Heidi, picking

some of them up, but the big cat sprang at her arm and hissed at her so fiercely that she shrank back.

"I will bring them if you tell me the address," said the old man.

"Herr Sesemann's. On the door there is a dog's head with a gold ring in its mouth."

The caretaker did not need such a detailed description. He had been in the church for many years and knew every house in the district.

"I know the house."

"If only I could take one or two with me—one for me and one for Clara! May I?"

"Yes! Take them."

Heidi's eyes shone with delight. She chose a white one and a tabby and put one into her right and one into her left pocket. Then they went downstairs.

The boy was still sitting on the steps outside. He jumped up when he saw Heidi but it took Heidi several minutes of detailed description of the house and its surroundings before the boy realised where she had to go and they then quickly reached the house. Heidi rang the bell and Sebastian opened the door. When he saw Heidi he hustled her inside.

"Quickly! Into the dining-room! They are all at table and Fräulein Rottenmeier looks like a loaded cannon. But why did you run away like that?"

Heidi went into the room. Fräulein Rottenmeier did not look up, Clara said nothing and it was an altogether uneasy atmosphere. When Heidi was seated Fräulein Rottenmeier began in a very severe and solemn voice:

"Adelheid! I shall talk to you afterwards. I will only say now that you have behaved exceedingly badly, leaving the house without permission and wandering about the streets until such a late hour without telling anyone. Your conduct is unparalleled!"

"Miaow!" It sounded like an answer.

Now the lady's temper rose, "What Adelheid! You are rude as well as naughty! I warn you!"

"I didn't—," began Heidi. "Miaow! Miaow!"

Sebastian could conceal his amusement no longer and had to leave the room.

"That will do!" Fräulein Rottenmeier tried to say, but her voice cracked with excitement. "Get up and leave the room!"

Heidi, frightened, got up and tried to explain, "I really didn't— Miaow! Miaow!"

"But Heidi," Clara said reproachfully, "when you see it makes Fräulein Rottenmeier angry why do you go on saying 'Miaow'?

"I didn't. It is the kittens!"

"What! Cats!" screamed Fräulein Rottenmeier. "Sebastian! Tinette! Find the horrid animals! Remove them at once!"

The lady rushed into the study and locked the door for she disliked cats more than anything.

Sebastian had to wait outside the door until his face was straight again. When he had served Heidi he had noticed the little kitten's head peeping out of her pocket and had guessed what would happen. When at last he entered the room everything seemed quiet and peaceful again. Clara had the kittens on her lap and Heidi knelt beside her. Both played happily with the two tiny animals.

"Sebastian," said Clara. "You must help us to find a place for the kittens where Fräulein Rottenmeier will not find them, because she is afraid of them and wants to get rid of them. Where can we put them?"

"I shall see to that, Fräulein Clara," replied Sebastian willingly. "I shall prepare a nice bed in a basket and put it in a place where madam is not likely to go; rely on me!" He made ready at once, chuckling to himself, for he realised that there would be a further to-do about this at some time in the future, and Sebastian was by no means unhappy at the thought of Fräulein Rottenmeier being unsettled.

Much later Fräulein Rottenmeier opened the door an inch or two and called through the slit, "Are the horrid animals away?"

"Yes! Yes!" answered Sebastian, quietly collecting the kittens from Clara's lap and disappearing with them.

The lecture for Heidi was put off until the following day as

Fräulein Rottenmeier felt too exhausted, after her ordeal of irritation, anger and fear, through which the innocent Heidi had put her, so she retired quietly. Clara and Heidi went cheerfully to bed, knowing that the kittens were all right.

CHAPTER 8

A COMMOTION IN THE HOUSE

The following morning, shortly after Sebastian had admitted the tutor, the door bell rang again, so loudly this time that the butler thought the master himself had arrived home unexpectedly. He rushed downstairs and threw open the door, and there stood a little ragged boy with a barrel organ on his shoulder.

"What do you want?" asked Sebastian irritably. "I'll teach you to ring the bell like that! Be off with you!"

"I want to see Clara," the urchin replied.

"You cheeky little brat. Don't you know to say *Fräulein* Clara? What could you possibly have to see Fräulein Clara about?" stormed Sebastian.

"She owes me fourpence," said the boy.

"You must be insane! What makes you think Fräulein Clara lives here, anyway?"

"Yesterday I showed her the way for twopence; and back again; that was fourpence."

"You are telling a pack of lies! Fräulein Clara never goes out—she can't walk. Be off with you now before I take my boot to you!"

But the boy was not to be turned away so easily. He stood firm and repeated determinedly, "But I have seen her in the street and can tell you what she looks like. She has short, curly hair and she wears a brown dress. She talks different from us."

"Ho!" thought Sebastian. "So this is more mischief the little fräulein has been up to!" He chuckled to himself as an idea occurred to him, then he said aloud, "Very well. Come with me, but wait outside the door until I call you, and when I let you into the room begin right away to play a tune on your barrel organ for the young lady. That will please her."

Sebastian knocked on the study door and went in. "There is a boy outside who says he has a message for Fräulein Clara," he announced.

This unexpected interruption to the lesson delighted Clara. "Let him come in at once!" she begged, turning to her tutor. "You see, he wants to speak to me particularly."

The boy entered, and at once started to play his organ according to Sebastian's instructions. Fräulein Rottenmeier was busy in the dining-room when the sound came to her ears. Was it in the street? Yet it seemed so much nearer! But who could be playing an organ in the study? And yet . . . She rushed into the study, and there, incredible as it seemed, there stood the ragged organ player. The tutor looked as though he were making an effort to speak, but failed. Clara and Heidi were listening happily.

"Stop! Stop at once!" commanded Fräulein Rottenmeier, but her voice was drowned by the music. She was walking towards the boy when suddenly on the floor between her feet she caught sight of a horrible, dark, crawling animal. It was a tortoise! At the sight of it, Fräulein Rottenmeier leaped into the air, shrieking at the top of her voice,"Sebastian! Sebastian!"

The organ player stopped abruptly. Sebastian stood behind the door, convulsed with laughter. At last he came in.

"Take them away! All of them! Boy, animal and all! At once, Sebastian!"

Sebastian dragged off the boy with the tortoise, at the same time putting something into his hand and whispering, "Fourpence for Fräulein Clara and fourpence for the music. You have done well!"

The door closed behind the little organ player, peace returned to the study and the lesson continued. This time Fräulein Rottenmeier remained in the room, grimly determined to prevent further incident.

Again a knock came to the study door and Sebastian appeared with the news that someone had brought a large basket to be delivered to Fräulein Clara. He carried in a covered basket and then disappeared.

"I think we will finish the lesson first," said Fräulein Rottenmeier, "and then we will see what is inside the basket."

Clara could not imagine what it could be and looked longingly at the basket. She broke off in the midst of her declensions to ask the tutor if she might have just one peep inside. The tutor frowned and was just about to refuse his permission when the lid of the basket lifted of its own accord and out jumped one, two, three, and then another two, and then several more kittens, and they all raced about the room in every direction. They climbed up on to Fräulein Rottenmeier's dress and scampered about her feet. They climbed up on Clara's chair, and, in fact, went into every corner of the room, scratching and maiowing. Clara cried delightedly, "Oh, look at them, Heidi! Aren't they sweet!"

Heidi raced about after them and the tutor, in a dilemma, moved uncomfortably from one foot to the other, at a complete loss to know what to do. At first, Fräulein Rottenmeier was too horror-stricken to utter a word, then she began to scream, "Tinette! Sebastian! Sebastian! Tinette!" She was terrified to move from her chair until Sebastian and Tinette appeared at last and removed the kittens only to put them in the basket with the others.

There had been no yawning during lessons that day.

In the evening, Fräulein Rottenmeier held an inquiry into the affair. She summoned Sebastian and Tinette and it soon became evident that Heidi, on her excursion of the previous day, had been responsible for all these alarming occurrences. Fräulein Rottenmeier was pale with anger. She gave a sign for Sebastian and Tinette to withdraw, then she turned to Heidi who stood beside Clara's chair, not very sure of what crime she had been guilty.

"Adelheid," Fräulein Rottenmeier began in a stern voice, "I know of only one punishment which will make you aware of your frightful misconduct for you are nothing but a little barbarian. We shall see if a spell down in the dark cellar with the rats and black beetles will tame you a little so that you will know not to do such things in future."

Heidi listened in silence and was rather surprised at the threatened punishment for she had never been in such a cellar. The room which the grandfather called the cellar at home was a very pleasant place where the fresh cheese and milk was kept.

But Clara started to cry, sobbing, "No! No! Fräulein Rottenmeier! You must wait till Papa comes home. He said in his letter that he would come back soon and when he does I will tell him everything and he shall decide what is to be done with Heidi."

Fräulein Rottenmeier was obliged to agree and she got up and left the room, grumbling, "Well, Clara, I too will have something to say to Herr Sesemann."

Although a few days passed quietly after this, Fräulein Rottenmeier failed to regain her peace of mind. She was constantly aware of the disappointment that Heidi had been and of the fact that since her arrival the whole household had been upset. But Clara was very happy indeed. She was never bored now, for during lessons something amusing was always happening. Instead of trying to learn the letters, Heidi would cry out, "Oh, it is shaped like a goat's horn!" or "It is like an eagle!" until the poor tutor would completely lose patience. Then, after lessons were over, in the late afternoon, Heidi would sit by Clara and tell her about the Alm and how much she wanted to go back. Indeed, she would talk about her old home until the longing to go back became so great that she would say, "I must go home again! To-morrow I must really go!" But Clara would persuade her to stay, saying, "Just wait until Papa comes home!" And Heidi would remember that each day she stayed meant that she could add another roll to her collection. Every night at supper she found a soft white roll on her plate and she would quietly slip it into her pocket. So she now had quite an amazing quantity of rolls to take back to the grandmother!

Every afternoon, while Clara rested, Heidi found herself

alone and then she would sit by herself and think about the Alm. One day, the memory of the snowcapped peaks, the yellow flowers glittering in the sun, and the green valley made heı feel so homesick that she could hardly control her longing to be home again. Dete, after all, had said that she could go home whenever she wanted. She hastily put the rolls into her red scarf, put on her little straw hat and started of for home. But she got no farther than the front door, for there stood Fräulein Rottenmeier, just returned from her walk. Her sharp eyes looked Heidi up and down. "What is the meaning of this? Didn't I forbid you to run about in the streets? And you are surely not going out dressed like a beggar child!"

"I wasn't going to run about, I just wanted to go home," explained Heidi, frightened.

"Wanted to go home, indeed! I wonder what Herr Sesemann would have to say to this? Running away from his beautiful house! What do you find wrong with it, I should like to know? Are you not treated better than you deserve? Have you ever in your life had such a splendid place to live in or had so many servants to wait upon you? Have you?"

"No," said Heidi.

"I should think not," continued the lady. "You are an exceedingly ungrateful child who thinks of nothing but getting into mischief."

This rebuke was too much for Heidi and she began to pour out all the things that she had kept hidden for so long. "I only want to go home because Snowflake will be crying and the grandmother is waiting for me; and Goldfinch gets beaten when Goat Peter doesn't get part of my lunch. Here I can never watch the sun saying good night to the mountains, and if the great bird were to fly over Frankfurt he would croak even louder about so many people huddling together, gossiping, and not living in the mountains where it is so much nicer."

"Mercy! The child has gone out of her mind!" cried Fräulein Rottenmeier, rushing upstairs and colliding with Sebastian. "Take the unfortunate creature upstairs at once!" she called to him.

"What mischief have we been up to now, eh?" said Sebastian good-humouredly. Heidi stood trembling and frightened, and when Sebastian saw the distress on her little face he said kindly, "Now, now! Don't take it so much to heart! Cheer up and everything will be all right! Come! We'd better do as we were told and go upstairs."

Heidi looked such a picture of dejection as she slowly climbed the stairs that Sebastian felt really sorry for her. "Don't you give in!" he said encouragingly. "There's a brave little girl! Never a tear all the time she is with us, and others at her age cry twelve times a day. And the kittens are so happy! You should just see them jumping about in the loft! Afterwards we shall go up and look at them, together, shall we?—when madam is not here."

Heidi nodded, but not very cheerfully, and disappeared into her room.

At supper Fräulein Rottenmeier did not speak but kept casting very odd glances in Heidi's direction as though she expected the child to do something extraordinary at any moment. But Heidi sat silently at the table, neither eating nor drinking although the roll had, as usual, disappeared quickly into her pocket.

Next morning, when the tutor arrived, Fräulein Rottenmeier took him into the dining-room and told him her worries about Heidi and of her attempt to go home the previous day. "I really think the child has gone mad," she concluded. The tutor managed to quieten her fears, explaining that Adelheid was perhaps a little strange but with careful handling and education the balance would soon be restored. He was quite sure of this having now heard Fräulein Rottenmeier's revelation, and having so far failed to teach Heidi the alphabet. He felt that she was perhaps just a little eccentric, but it was nothing that perseverance would not cure.

Fräulein Rottenmeier felt quite relieved after this conversation and during the afternoon she began to recall Heidi's outlandish appearance when she had prepared to set out on her journey. She decided that the child had better have one or two things from Clara's wardrobe before Herr Sesemann arrived. Clara was completely in favour of the plan and the lady went into Heidi's room to inspect her wardrobe. Very soon she returned, wearing an expression of complete disgust. "Adelheid!" she said. "I have never seen anything like it! In a wardrobe of all places, what do I find? Heaps of little rolls! Who ever heard of keeping bread in a wardrobe? Tinette! Go and remove all that stale bread from Heidi's wardrobe—and you can take away the old straw hat, too! "

"No! No!" screamed Heidi. "Not the hat! And the rolls are for Grandmother!" And she began to run after Tinette until Fräulein Rottenmeier stopped her.

"Stay just where you are!" she said. "All that rubbish must be thrown out."

Then Heidi threw herself into Clara's chair, crying in despair. "Now Grandmother won't get her rolls. She has taken them away!" and she sobbed as though her heart would break.

Clara was very much alarmed at this outburst and pleaded, "Heidi! Heidi! Don't cry! Listen to me! I will give you as many rolls as you want when you go home and they will be soft and fresh. Yours were quite stale. Don't cry any more, Heidi!"

It was a long time before Heidi could stop sobbing but Clara's promise had comforted her and when she had assured herself that Clara would indeed give her as many or more rolls than she had collected, she quietened down.

At supper, Heidi's eyes were still swollen with crying and when she looked at her roll she started to sob again; but with a great effort she managed to control herself for she knew that she had to be quiet at table. Whenever Sebastian came near he smiled at her encouragingly as if to say, "I will put everything right for you." He made signs at her all evening, pointing to his head and hers, nodding and smiling.

When it came time for Heidi to go to bed, what did she find under the bed-cover but her old hat! She hugged it with delight, knocking it more out of shape than ever; then she wrapped it in a handkerchief and put it right at the back of the wardrobe. Sebastian had seen Tinette with the hat and had taken it from her quickly, saying, "It's all right. I shall dispose of this." This had been the reason for all the nods and smiles which Sebastian had given Heidi at supper.

Chapter 9

NEWS FROM THE MASTER

A few days later there was great excitement in the house because Herr Sesemann had returned. Sebastian and Tinette were kept busy carrying up parcels and suitcases from the carriage. They were packed with all sorts of exciting presents which Clara's father was in the habit of bringing back from his travels.

It was late afternoon when Herr Sesemann arrived and he came straight into the study where Clara and Heidi were sitting together. Father and daughter greeted each other affectionately for they loved each other very much, then Herr Sesemann held out his hand to Heidi and said kindly, "And this is our little Swiss girl? Come and shake hands with me? That's right! Now, you and Clara are great friends, are you not? Or are you always quarrelling with each other?"

"No, Clara is very good to me," answered Heidi.

"And Heidi," interjected Clara, "has never quarrelled with me."

"That's good! I'm delighted to hear it," said Herr Sesemann, rising from his chair. "Now, Clara, you must allow me to go and have something to eat. I have had nothing since breakfast. Later I shall see you again and show you all the things I have brought home."

In the dining-room he found Fräulein Rottenmeier inspecting the table which had been laid for dinner. Herr Sesemann sat down and Fräulein Rottenmeier, looking the picture of gloom, took her place opposite.

"What is the matter, Fräulein Rottenmeier?" asked Herr Sesemann. "You look very dismal. Have you had a stroke of bad luck? Clara seems to be cheerful enough. What is wrong?"

With a very long face, the lady began, "Herr Sesemann, we have been completely deceived—and it concerns Clara."

"In what way?" Herr Sesemann asked calmly.

"You know we decided that Clara should have a companion, and as I knew you were anxious to have a nicely brought up girl, I thought of a little Swiss girl of whom I had heard a great deal. You know what I wanted—the sort of child of whom I often read, who is so at ease living the natural life high in the mountains, that she would be like a pure being from another world!"

"And what do you think Clara would have in common with such a person as you describe, Fräulein?"

"I do not jest, Herr Sesemann. I have been terribly cheated. Completely taken in! Really shockingly!"

"But what is so shocking? I see nothing shocking in the child," remarked Herr Sesemann, still completely unperturbed.

"Oh, if you only knew the type of people—and the animals!— this creature has brought into your house! The tutor can tell you all about it."

"Animals? What am I to understand from that, Fräulein Rottenmeier"

"Herr Sesemann, it is beyond *my* understanding! Her whole behaviour would be beyond comprehension were it not for one thing. She has spells of mental disturbance!" concluded Fräulein Rottenmeier with conviction.

Up till now, Herr Sesemann had not thought the affair of any great importance; but mental disturbance! That could easily have a harmful effect on his little daughter.

He looked quickly at Fräulein Rottenmeier as though to assure himself that it was not she who was the victim of a troubled mind. Just then, the door opened and the tutor entered.

"Ah, here is our tutor! Perhaps he can clear this matter up for us," Herr Sesemann exclaimed. "Come, sit down and have a cup of coffee with us," he said, addressing the tutor. "No need for ceremony. Now tell me what is wrong with this child who has come to be a companion to my daughter. What's this about her bringing animals into the house, and about her mental faculties?"

The tutor began in his usual roundabout way, "Since you

ask me for my opinion about this young girl, Herr Sesemann, I should like to direct your attention to the fact that, although there may be a lack of development, caused by more or less neglected education, or rather by somewhat delayed tuition, on the one hand, there is, on the other hand, I think we must admit, a certain benefit to be gained from such a solitary life in the mountains, and we must consider—"

"My dear friend," interrupted Herr Sesemann, "you take too much trouble. Tell me, did her bringing animals to the house alarm you too, and what is your opinion of her as a companion for my little daughter?"

"I have no wish to say anything against the young girl," the tutor began again. "If on the one hand there is a certain inexperience of social custom, owing to the somewhat uncivilised life she led up to the time she came to Frankfurt, on the other hand she has gifts not to be overlooked, and if carefully led—"

"My dear sir, you must please excuse me now. I must speak to my daughter." And with these words Herr Sesemann quickly left the room.

In the study, he sat down beside his little girl and turning to Heidi said, "Listen, little one, will you go and fetch me—ah—fetch me—" Herr Sesemann wanted the child out of the room but was having difficulty in thinking up an excuse. "Fetch me a glass of water?"

Heidi disappeared at once.

"And now, my dear Clara," said Herr Sesemann, pulling his chair closer and taking his daughter's hand, "tell me quite frankly, what kind of animals did your little friend bring into the house? And what makes Fräulein Rottenmeier think that she is sometimes not quite right in her mind?"

Clara had no difficulty in explaining. She told her father the story of the tortoise and the kittens and explained all the remarks which Fräulein Rottenmeier had thought so odd, and which seemed to upset her so much.

Herr Sesemann laughed heartily. "Well, then, you don't want me to send the child home, Clara? You are not tired of her?" asked her father.

"No! No! Papa, Please don't!" exclaimed Clara in alarm.

"The time has passed so quickly since Heidi came. Something happens every day, and it used to be so dull. And she always has so much to tell me."

"Very well, then. Ah! Here is our little friend! Have you brought me nice fresh water?" Herr Sesemann asked as Heidi handed him the glass.

"Yes. It is fresh from the pump," answered Heidi.

"Did you go yourself to the pump, Heidi?" asked Clara.

"Yes, but I had to go a long way because at the first pump there were ever so many people and at the second there were just as many. Then I went into another street and got the water there. The gentleman with the white hair sends his kind regards to Herr Sesemann."

"Well, that was a long expedition," laughed Herr Sesemann. "And who is this gentleman?"

"As he was passing the pump he stopped and said, 'Since you have got a glass would you mind giving me a drink? To whom are you taking the glass of water?' And I said, 'To Herr Sesemann.' And he laughed and gave me the message for you and said 'he hoped Herr Sesemann would enjoy the water."

"And what did this gentleman look like who sends me so many good wishes?" asked Herr Sesemann with a smile.

"He wore a thick gold chain with a big red stone hanging from it; and the top of his stick was a horse's head."

"That is our old friend, the doctor," cried Clara and her father at the same instant. Herr Sesemann smiled to himself as he wondered what their friend would think of the new way in which the Sesemanns went about quenching their thirst.

That very evening, he told Fräulein Rottenmeier that Heidi would remain; that he found the child perfectly normal and that his daughter preferred her company to any other. "I am anxious, therefore," said Herr Sesemann emphatically, "that this child should always be treated in a friendly way and that her little peculiarities should not be treated as crimes. And, by the way, if you find difficulty in managing the child there is a prospect that you will be relieved of this duty. I am expecting my mother very soon for a long visit, and, as you know, she gets along with everybody, Fräulein Rottenmeier," he concluded pointedly.

"Yes, I know," Herr Sesemann," said Fräulein Rottenmeier rather sourly.

Herr Sesemann remained only a short time at home and after a fortnight he set off for Paris, comforting his little daughter with the prospect of the arrival of her grandmother in a day or two.

On the day after Herr Sesemann's departure, a letter came announcing Frau Sesemann's arrival on the following day. Clara was overjoyed and talked so much about her grandmother that Heidi, too, called her Grandmamma.

Later, when Heidi was going to her bedroom, Fräulein Rottenmeier took her into her own room and instructed her that she should never address Frau Sesemann as Grandmamma but always as 'madam'. "Do you understand?" she asked.

Heidi really did not understand at all why she should call the lady by this title but Fräulein Rottenmeier's face wore such a severe expression that Heidi did not dare ask for an explanation.

Chapter 10

ANOTHER GRANDMOTHER

The following evening great preparations were afoot in the Sesemann house. It was clear that the lady who was to arrive was held in great esteem by all and presently there was the sound of a carriage stopping at the front door. Sebastian and Tinette rushed downstairs and put footstools everywhere, that the lady might find one wherever she wanted to put her feet. Fräulein Rottenmeier followed, but slowly and with dignity.

She knew that she would have to be there to welcome Frau Sesemann, but was not going to let her authority be undermined by the presence of another woman. Suddenly the carriage rolled up to the door, and the servants ran down the step to assist their important visitor. Heidi, who had been ordered to wait in her room until she was called, sat in a corner and repeated over and over again to herself the little speech which she had been instructed to address to Frau Sesemann.

Before very long Tinette came to call her. Putting her head round the door, she announced in her usual saucy manner "You're to go into the study."

Heidi made her way to the study, still turning the words over in her mind and still hardly able to believe that she should address any one in the peculiar way Fräulein Rottenmeier had told her. As she opened the door, the grandmother said in a kind voice, "Ah, here is the child! Come here and let me look at you!"

Heidi approached, and said very distinctly in her clear voice, "Good evening, Mrs madam!"

"Well," said the grandmother, laughing. "Is that how you address people on the Alm?"

"No. At home nobody has a name like that," said Heidi gravely.

"Neither do they here!" said the grandmother, still smiling, and patted Heidi's cheek. "When I am with children I am always Grandmamma. Can you remember that?"

"Yes, very well," Heidi assured her, "because that's what I used to say."

"I understand," said the grandmother, shaking her head a little. She looked more closely at Heidi and Heidi's steady, serious eyes looked back at her eagerly, for there was a warmth about the old woman which attracted the child. Heidi gazed entranced at the beautiful white hair which was adorned with a lacy frill, ending in two broad ribbons which floated gently about the grandmother's head as though blown by a soft breeze.

"And what is your name, child?"

"It is really Heidi, but if you call me Adelheid I shall try to remember—" Heidi stopped guiltily, remembering that sometimes she failed to answer when Fräulein Rottenmeier called her by this name. Just at that moment, Fräulein Rottenmeier entered.

"Frau Sesemann will agree that I had to choose a name which one could pronounce, and, of course, on account of the servants—"

"Very correct, I have no doubt, Rottenmeier," replied Frau Sesemann, "but if the child is called Heidi and is accustomed to that name, I shall call her by it; so that's settled."

Fräulein Rottenmeier found it very embarrassing to be called by her surname but since the grandmother would have her own way there was nothing she could do about it. She was a very alert old lady and had her wits about her, and she very soon knew exactly what was going on in the house.

The following afternoon, after sitting by Clara's bed until she fell asleep, Frau Sesemann went upstairs and knocked at Fräulein Rottenmeier's door. Fräulein Rottenmeier looked startled at this unexpected visit.

"Where is the Heidi child and what is she doing, I should like to know," said Frau Sesemann, coming straight to the point.

"She is in her room where she could find something useful to do if she had the slightest inclination," replied Fräulein Rottenmeier. "But if Frau Sesemann only knew the queer things she imagines and does—I can hardly bring myself to talk of them."

"And so would I, if I were in her place, I don't doubt. Tell the little one to come to my room. I have some nice books to give her."

"But that's just it!" replied Fräulein Rottenmeier, throwing up her hands in despair. "Of what use are books to her? She does not even know the alphabet yet! It is quite impossible to teach her anything. The tutor will tell you so himself. If he didn't have the patience of a saint he would have given up trying to teach her long ago."

"Well, that is strange. The child does not strike me as being stupid," said Frau Sesemann shortly. "Now go and fetch her. She can look at the pictures for the time being."

Fräulein Rottenmeier was about to say more but Frau Sesemann turned and went quickly into her room. She was very surprised at Fräulein Rottenmeier's remarks and was determined to find out more about the whole matter. Perhaps the tutor would help, although his conversation was so round-about and lengthy that she felt it might be difficult to get to the root of the problem.

Heidi was greatly delighted with the beautiful coloured pictures in the books which the grandmother had brought. Suddenly she cried aloud as the grandmother turned a page, and when the old lady looked at the child she saw that tears were streaming down her cheeks. She looked at once at the picture. It depicted a beautiful green pasture with all sorts of animals grazing. In the midst, the shepherd leant upon his stick and looked happily at his flock. Everything was bathed in a golden light for the sun was just setting on the far horizon.

The grandmother took Heidi's hand gently. "Come, come! child! Don't cry! It has reminded you of something, perhaps. But look, there is a beautiful story about it and I am going to tell it to you tonight. There are many beautiful stories in this book which can be read over and over again. Come now, we must have a chat, so dry your tears and stand in front of me so that I can look at you. That's right. Now we are happy again."

Heidi tried very hard to stop sobbing and when at last she succeeded the grandmother said, "Now I want you to tell me something, child. How are you getting on with your lessons? Do you like them? Are you doing well?"

"Oh, no!" answered Heidi with a sigh. "But I knew it would be impossible."

"What is impossible, Heidi? What do you mean?"

"To learn to read. It is too difficult."

"Well I never! And who told you this?"

"Peter did, and he knows for he has tried and tried but he can't learn. It is too difficult."

"What a boy Peter must be! But listen to me, Heidi. We must never believe what the 'Peters' say but try for ourselves. I am sure you have never paid enough attention to the tutor or looked properly at the letters."

"It is no use," said Heidi with a great sigh of resignation.

"Now, Heidi. Listen to what I say! You have not been able to learn to read because you believed what Peter said. Now you must believe what I say when I tell you that you can learn to read like many other children who are like you and not like Peter, and in a very short time. First you must know what happens when you are able to read. Do you see the shepherd on the beautiful green pasture? Well, as soon as you can read you shall have the book for your own and then you will know the whole story just as if someone were to tell it to you—what the shepherd did with his sheep and goats and the wonderful things that happened to him. Wouldn't you like to know all that, Heidi?"

Heidi had been listening with keen attention and now exclaimed with sparkling eyes "Oh, if only I could read already!"

"You will learn in no time—I can see that, Heidi. But now we must go to Clara. Come, we will take the books with us!"

The grandmother took Heidi's hand and they went together into the study.

From the day Heidi had tried to go home and Fräulein Rottenmeier had scolded her for being so wicked and ungrateful, a change had come over the child. She knew now that she could not go home whenever she liked, as Aunt Dete had told her, but that she had to stay in Frankfurt for a long time, maybe for ever. She also understood that Herr Sesemann would think her very ungrateful, and Clara and the grandmother, too, if she again showed signs of wanting to leave. So there was nobody to whom she could reveal how homesick she was, for she could not face giving the grandmother, who was so kind to her, cause to be angry, as Fräulein Rottenmeier had been.

But the strain of keeping all this to herself became almost more than she could bear. She lost her appetite and every day grew paler and paler. At night she would lie awake for a long time, for as soon as she was alone with everything quiet around her, she would see again in her thoughts the Alm and the sunshine and the flowers; and when at last she fell asleep she would see in her dreams the red summits of the crags and the crimson snowfield in the evening sun. Awakening in the morning she wanted to run out happily into the sun—but she soon realised that she was in the big bed at Frankfurt, far, far away from home. Then Heidi would weep long and quietly, her head pressed into the pillow so that no one could hear.

Heidi's unhappiness did not escape the grandmother. She waited a few days to see if there might be a change. But as Heidi remained subdued and when she noticed that often in the early morning the child looked as though she had been crying, the grandmother took her, one day, into her room and said lovingly, "Now tell me, Heidi, what is the matter? Are you worrying about something?"

But not for the world would Heidi show ingratitude to the grandmother who had been so kind, so she replied:

"Please, I cannot tell you."

"Could you tell Clara, then?"

"Oh, no! Nobody," said Heidi, looking so pitiful that the grandmother was filled with compassion.

"Come here, little one, and I will tell you something. If one is in trouble and can't speak about it to any one, then one tells it to God who is in Heaven and prays to Him for help because he is able to take away all our troubles. Do you know that? Do you pray every night to your Heavenly Father and thank Him for all he has done for you and ask Him to keep you from harm?"

"Oh, no! I never do that," answered Heidi.

"Have you never prayed, Heidi? Don't you know what it is?"

"Sometimes I used to pray with the first grandmother but it is a long time ago and I have forgotten it."

"You see, Heidi, because you have nobody to help you, you are unhappy. Think how wonderful it is when our hearts are heavy with sadness, to be able to go any moment to God and tell Him everything and ask Him for help when no one else can give it. He is always able to help and can give us what makes us happy again."

A gleam of joy came into Heidi's eyes, "May I tell Him everything?"

"Everything, Heidi. Everything."

Heidi drew away the hand which the grandmother held affectionately and asked hastily, "May I go?"

"Certainly, certainly!" answered the grandmother and Heidi

ran off to her room. She sat down on her little stool, folded her hands and told God about everything that made her so unhappy and begged Him with all her heart to let her go home to the grandfather.

A little more than a week after this the tutor asked to see Frau Sesemann as he had something very remarkable to tell her. When he was shown into her room Frau Sesemann held out her hand, saying, "I am pleased to see you. Sit down, won't you? Now tell me why you wish to see me. I hope it is not a complaint."

"On the contrary, madam," the tutor began. "Something has occurred—something which I did not expect. In the light of all my previous experience it was an impossibility and yet it really has happened. It is like a miracle. Contrary to all I had expected—"

"Am I to understand that the child, Heidi, has learned to read after all?" Frau Sesemann guessed.

Speechless with surprise the tutor looked at her.

"It is indeed nothing short of a miracle. In spite of my painstaking explanations, she never seemed to be able to learn the alphabet, and now she has learnt it with such rapidity—overnight, so to say—and so correctly! It is most unusual with a beginner."

"Life is full of miracles," Frau Sesemann smiled. "Of course, there might be such a happy coincidence as a fresh zeal for learning and a new method of teaching. Now we must be glad the child has made such a good beginning and hope for her future progress."

After she had seen the tutor to the door, she went straight to the study to make sure of the good news. Sure enough, Heidi was seated beside Clara and was reading a story to her with great eagerness, evidently surprised herself to find the black letters turning into real people and exciting adventures.

That same evening, at the dinner table, Heidi found by her plate the big book with the lovely pictures and when she looked questioningly at the grandmother the old lady nodded her confirmation, "Yes, it is yours, now."

"Always? Even when I go home?" asked Heidi, flushed with happiness.

"Of course, for ever!" assured the grandmother. "To-morrow we shall start to read it."

"But you are not going home yet, Heidi," Clara put in. "Not for many years. I want you to stay with me, especially when grandmother goes away."

Before she went to bed, Heidi looked at her book, and from that day on, her greatest pleasure was to read over and over again the stories which belonged to the beautiful pictures.

When, in the evening, the grandmother said, "Now Heidi will read to us," the child was delighted and when she read aloud, the stories seemed to be still more beautiful and interesting. The picture she liked best was the one with the green pasture and the shepherd leaning happily on his crook. He was tending his father's fine flock. But the next picture showed how the shepherd had run away from home and had to look after a herd of swine. He had grown quite thin for all he had to eat was husks. In this picture, the sun did not shine so golden and the land was grey and misty. But then there was still another picture to this story. In it the old father was running with outstretched arms to meet his returning and repentant son, welcoming him as he approached timidly, tired and dirty and dressed in rags. This was Heidi's favourite story which she read again and again without ever tiring of hearing the grandmother's explanations of the meaning of the story. There were many other beautiful tales in the book, and with reading and studying the pictures the days passed quickly and the time came for the grandmother's departure.

CHAPTER 11

HEIDI LEARNS A GREAT DEAL

Every afternoon during her visit, the grandmother sat beside Clara for a time while she was resting, and afterwards she would call Heidi into her room and would talk to her and keep her occupied in all sorts of ways. The grandmother had pretty little dolls and showed Heidi how to make little dresses and coats for them so that without knowing it Heidi had learnt to sew. Since Heidi could now read she was allowed to read aloud to the grandmother and this she enjoyed very much, growing more fond of the stories the more she read them. But still, Heidi never looked really happy and her sparkling eyes were never as bright as before.

One afternoon during the last week of the grandmother's visit, when Heidi was paying her customary afternoon call, the grandmother asked, "Tell me, child, why is it you are not happy? Is there still the same grief in your heart?"

"Yes," Heidi nodded.

"Have you told God about it?"

"Yes."

"And do you say your prayers every day so that all will be well and you will be happy again?"

"Oh, no. I don't pray at all now."

"What is this, Heidi? Why don't you pray any more?"

"It is no use. God does not listen, and I can understand it; when there are so many people in Frankfurt all praying to Him, He cannot possibly listen to them all. He certainly has not heard me."

"What makes you so sure, Heidi?"

"I have prayed for the same thing every day for weeks and weeks and God has never done it."

"Oh, Heidi! That is not the way in which to think of Him. You see, God is our Heavenly Father and always knows what is best for us, even when we ourselves do not. If we ask for something which is not good for us, He does not grant it but instead gives us the thing that is best for us. If we go on praying earnestly and never run away or lose faith our prayers will be answered. You see, Heidi, what you asked for was not good for you just at the moment. God has certainly heard you. He can hear every one at the same time because He is God and not a human being like you or me. And because He knows what is good for you He says, 'Yes, Heidi shall have what she wants but only when it is good for her; because if I give her what she wants right away and then, by and by, she sees that it would have been better for her not to have had her own way, she will say, "If only God had not given me what I asked for! It is not so good as I thought."' Since God watched over you, you should have trusted in Him, come with everything to Him and prayed every day; but you ran away, stopped praying and forgot all about Him!

"But you see, when someone behaves like you so that God never hears his voice among those who pray, He lets him go his own way. And when he gets into trouble and then complains, 'There is no one to help me!' God says, 'Why did you run away from Me? I cannot help you when you run away.' Do you want that, Heidi? Or would you rather go and ask Him to forgive you for running away, and pray to Him every day and trust that He will make everything right for you and that you will be happy again?"

Every word the grandmother said had touched the child's heart and she said repentantly, "At once I will ask God to forgive me and I will never forget Him again. I will go and pray now."

"That is a good child. He will help you at the right moment, never fear!" And Heidi ran to her room and prayed to God to forgive her and asked Him not to forget her.

It was a sad time for Clara and Heidi when the day of the grandmother's departure arrived, but the old lady insisted on making it quite a party so that they would not think too much about her going. After the grandmother had driven off in her carriage the house seemed very empty and silent and Clara and Heidi felt quite lost.

The next day, when the children sat together in the afternoon, Heidi suggested to Clara that she should read aloud to her every afternoon. Clara was very pleased with this idea and Heidi began with great enthusiasm. But the first story turned out to be about a dying grandmother and Heidi, who took all the stories very seriously and believed every word was true, at once thought that it was the grandmother on the Alm who was dead and burst into tears. Clara tried to explain that the story was about a quite different grandmother, but the idea that such a thing could happen had entered Heidi's mind and she realised with a great shock that the grandmother and the grandfather also might die while she was so far away and if she did not go home for a very long time everything on the Alm might be silent and dead and she would be all alone and would never see her dear ones again. And these sad thoughts made her sob the louder.

In the midst of Clara's explanation Fräulein Rottenmeier had entered the room and as Heidi still continued to sob she burst out impatiently, "Adelheid! That will do! I warn you, if you continue to give way to these outbursts whenever you read I will take the book away from you for good."

Heidi turned pale at such a thought. The book was her most treasured possession. Hurriedly she dried her tears. The stratagem had worked all right. No matter what the story, Heidi never cried again. But sometimes it was so difficult to keep back the tears that Clara would say, "Heidi, what terrible faces you are making!" But grimaces made no noise and did not attract Fräulein Rottenmeier's attention.

Heidi began to lose her appetite again and grew so pale and thin that Sebastian was extremely perturbed when she refused to take any of the delicious food which he served. Often he would whisper encouragingly as he held out a dish, "Take a little of this, Fräulein Heidi! It is so good! No, not like that! A heaped spoonful, and another one!" and other pieces of fatherly advice. But it was no use. Heidi hardly ate anything and as she lay in bed at night she would begin to think about home and what might be happening there, and she would turn her face into her pillow so that no one would hear, and cry as though her heart would break.

The days went by and Heidi could hardly tell whether it were winter or summer, for all she ever saw of the outside world was the same grey walls and roofs. She was only allowed out when Clara was well enough to go for a short drive (which never took them farther than the neighbouring streets) and never had a glimpse of grass or flowers, let alone fir trees and mountains. Heidi's longing for the beautiful, remembered things grew every day so that she could not speak or think of them without her eyes filling with tears.

Autumn and winter passed and the spring sun shone on the white walls of the house opposite, and Heidi knew it would soon be the time when Peter climbed up to the Alm with his goats, the flowers glittered in the sunshine and in the evening the mountains turned to crimson in the setting sun. Heidi would sit in her lonely little room and press her palms into her eyes so that she would not be able to see the sunshine striking the wall, and so she sat, silently struggling against her homesickness until she heard Clara's voice calling her.

CHAPTER 12

THE HOUSE IS HAUNTED

For some time, very strange things had been happening in the house. Every morning when the servants came down they found the front door wide open. During the first few days when this had happened all the rooms in the house were carefully searched for signs of burglary, but nothing was missing. At night every care was taken. The door was carefully locked and bolted, and to make it even more secure the wooden bar was put across. But all these precautions were of no avail; in the morning, the servants would again find the door wide open. Fräulein Rottenmeier would never go alone to some parts of the house, and would invent some excuse for one of the servants to accompany her. She was especially nervous if she had to visit the upper guest rooms, or go down to the strange, vast council chambers, where every footfall sounded and the ancient senators in their austere robes looked down sternly at her.

The cook meanwhile, would stand by her stove, shaking her head and muttering to herself, "To think that I should live to see such strange goings-on." At last John and Sebastian plucked up courage and promised to sit up all night in the room off the hall and watch to see what took place. Fräulein Rottenmeier, thinking they should be armed against any intruders, got out two of Herr Sesemann's pistols, and brought up a bottle of wine from the cellar with which the watchers might fortify their courage.

On the appointed night, the two installed themselves in the downstairs room and at once felt in need of a little stimulant. At first the wine made them very talkative, and by and by very sleepy, so they both leaned back in their arm-chairs and fell fast asleep. Sebastian awoke as the old church clock struck midnight. He called to his companion but John remained fast asleep. Sebastian did not go to sleep again but sat uneasily in the quietness of the night, only now and then giving John a quiet poke to see if he were awake. The clock struck the hour and John awoke with a start. He jumped to his feet and with a great show of courage said, "Now, Sebastian, we had better go outside and see what is going on. You aren't feeling scared, are you? Come on! I'll go first."

John opened the door wide and stepped into the hall. A sudden draught put out the light which he carried and he turned quickly, pushing against Sebastian, and stumbled back into the room, slamming the door and turning the key in the lock with feverish haste. Then he relit the candle. Sebastian did not know what to make of this odd behaviour and turned a puzzled look on John. In the light of the candle he saw that John was as white as a sheet and trembled all over. "What is it?" Sebastian asked hurriedly. "What did you see?"

"The door wide open," gasped John, "and on the stairs, a white figure—then, poof! and it was gone."

Sebastian shuddered with horror and felt as though his knees were going to give way. For the rest of the night the two sat close together and did not move again until the morning light came streaming through the window and the sound of passers-by came from the street. Then they went out and closed the front door and made their way upstairs to tell their story to Fräulein Rottenmeier. Straight away, she wrote a long letter to Herr Sesemann, telling him all about the open door and the ghostly figure, and insisting upon his immediate return as every one in the house now went in fear of his life and there was no knowing what the dreadful consequences of these incidents might be. But Herr Sesemann replied that it was impossible for him to return home just then, and altogether treated the affair very lightly. He suggested that should the ghost not have already disappeared, the grandmother should be summoned by letter to come and dispense with the nuisance.

Fräulein Rottenmeier was not at all satisfied. She wrote immediately to Frau Sesemann, but received a similarly indifferent reaction, and the tone of the letter, was to her mind, quite uncivil. Frau Sesemann implied that she did not care to undertake the journey from Holstein to Frankfurt, simply because Rottenmeier imagined she saw ghosts. She had never known a ghost in the house, and if there was now one in residence, it must be alive, in which case Rottenmeier should be able to deal with it.

Fräulein Rottenmeier was beginning to feel that she had had quite enough of this particular worry. She had never told the children of the apparition for fear of upsetting them, but now she had an idea. In a hushed voice and with much colourful detail, she told them of the nightly visitations. The story so frightened Clara that she began to scream for her father to come home. She was in such a state of fright that she would not be left alone for a minute. She insisted that everyone should sleep in the same room, and leave the light burning all the time; and Tinette should be next door, and Sebastian and John upstairs in the hall in order to frighten the ghost as soon as it appeared. Fräulein Rottenmeier wrote another letter to Herr Sesemann saying she would not answer for the serious consequences the mysterious occurrences might have on his daughters's delicate constitution. This had the desired effect.

Two days later Herr Sesemann came home. He stood and rang the front door-bell in such a way that everyone rushed down and stood trembling as if they thought the ghost was up to his tricks in broad daylight.

Sebastian peered through a window, and at once there was

another, very human and impatient ring on the bell. Clara was over-joyed to see him, and when he saw in what good spirits she was, a look of great relief spread over his features. Indeed, she was so pleased to see him that she was almost grateful to the ghost, for being responsible for his homecoming.

"And how is the ghost behaving?" he asked Fräulein Rottenmeier with a twinkle in his eye.

"It is no joke," she replied tartly. "I am sure by to-morrow Herr Sesemann will no longer consider it a laughing matter."

"Well, we shall see," replied Herr Sesemann, "but I must request you not to suspect my honourable forefathers. Now send Sebastian to me."

Herr Sesemann knew that Sebastian and Fräulein Rottenmeier were not always on the best of terms and he had his own ideas as to the cause of the disturbances.

"Now, Sebastian," he said, "tell me frankly. Have you been playing ghosts to tease Fräulein Rottenmeier?"

"On my honour, sir, no" replied Sebastian with unmistakable sincerity; "Please don't think that! I have been feeling very uncomfortable myself about this thing."

"Well, if that is so, I will have to show you and the brave John how ghosts look in the daylight. You should be ashamed of yourself, Sebastian, a big strong fellow like you running away from a ghost! But now go at once to my old friend Dr. Classen. Give him my kind regards and ask him to come here to-night at nine o'clock. Tell him I have come specially from Paris to consult him and will he make arrangements to spend the night here. Do you understand?" Sebastian indicated that he understood perfectly, and Herr Sesemann went to reassure Clara, telling her that the ghost would soon be found out and done away with.

Promptly at nine o'clock the doctor arrived after both Fräulein Rottenmeier and the children had gone to bed. He was a grey-haired man with bright, kindly eyes. At first he looked a little worried but presently he burst out laughing. "Well, well! For a patient with whom I am to sit up all night you don't look too bad."

"Not so hasty, my friend. Wait until I tell you this. There's a ghost in the house! This place is haunted."

The doctor laughed uproariously.

"That's a fine way of showing your sympathy I must say," Herr Sesemann continued. "It's a pity my friend Rottenmeier can't enjoy it. She is convinced that some ancient member of the family is prowling about the house."

"And how did she make his acquaintance?" asked the doctor, still chuckling. Herr Sesemann told him how the front door was found open every morning, as everyone in the house was willing to swear, and he had prepared two loaded revolvers in readiness for any untoward event. It could be that an elaborate practical joke was being played by a friend of one of the servants—in which case a pistol shot would frighten him sufficiently, or it was a thief, thinking to create safe access for himself at a future time, by pretending to be a ghost with whom everyone would become familiar and used to seeing in the house.

When the doctor had heard the whole story the two gentlemen went downstairs to the room where Sebastian and John had kept watch. There, a bottle of wine was put at their disposal, and the two revolvers together with two large lamps. They settled themselves comfortably in arm-chairs and smoked and chatted together with such enjoyment that in what seemed no time at all they heard the clock strike twelve.

"The ghost seems to have got wind of us and does not choose to come to-night," said the doctor.

"Hold on! It usually comes before one o'clock," replied his friend.

They resumed their conversation and until one o'clock struck there was not a sound to be heard. Then suddenly the doctor lifted a-finger.

"Hush, Sesemann. Don't you hear something?"

They both listened and heard distinctly the bar on the door being softly pushed aside, the key turning in the lock and the door opening. Herr Sesemann seized one of the pistols which lay ready on the table.

"You are not afraid are you?" whispered the doctor.

"As well to be careful," Herr Sesemann replied, picking up the lamp. The doctor took the other pistol and together they stepped out into the hall.

Moonlight streamed through the open door and fell on a white figure which stood motionless on the threshold.

"Who is there?" the doctor demanded loudly, his voice echoing through the hall. As both gentlemen advanced towards the figure it turned and gave a little cry. In her little white nightgown and with her bare feet, Heidi stood there trembling and blinking at the light and the weapons pointed in her direction.

The gentlemen exchanged surprised glances.

"Well if it isn't the little water-carrier!" said the doctor.

"Child, what does this mean?" asked Herr Sesemann. "Why have you come downstairs?"

Pale and trembling with fright, Heidi stood before him. "I don't know," she whispered.

Then the doctor intervened. "Sesemann, this is something I shall have to deal with. Go and sit by the fire while I take the child up to bed."

The doctor put down his revolver and taking the child in his arms he carried her upstairs, reassuring her gently all the while, and laying her on her bed he covered her carefully with the quilt. Then he sat on the edge of the bed, and taking her hand, he said kindly, "Everything is all right now. Tell me where you wanted to go."

"I didn't want to go at all," said Heidi. "I didn't know I was going downstairs but suddenly I was there."

"Were you dreaming about something which you could see and hear everything as if you were there?"

"Yes, I dream every night and it is always the same. I think I am with Grandfather and outside I hear the fir trees rustling and I think how beautifully the stars will be shining and I run quickly and open the door of the cottage. But when I awake I am still in Frankfurt." Heidi struggled to swallow the lump which rose in her throat.

"And have you a pain anywhere? In your head or in your back?"

"No. Only a feeling as if there were a big stone here."

"As though you had eaten something and it would not go down?"

"No, not like that. But so heavy that it makes me want to cry and cry."

"I see, and then you have a good cry?"

"Oh, no, I mustn't. Fräulein Rottenmeier doesn't allow it."

"Then you just swallow hard, is that it? But you like being in Frankfurt, don't you?"

"Yes," said Heidi in a flat voice which made it sound more like 'no'.

"And where did you live when you were with your grandfather?"

"Always on the Alm."

"And wasn't that rather dull?"

"Oh, no, it was beautiful. It was so beautiful—" Heidi could not go on. Remembrance of the past, the recent excitement and the long-suppressed weeping overwhelmed the child. Tears gushed from her eyes and her little body was shaken with sobs. The doctor rose. Gently he laid Heidi's head on the pillow. "Cry a little. It will do no harm, and then sleep. To-morrow everything will be all right."

The doctor went downstairs and joined his friend. He lowered himself into the opposite arm-chair and looked across at him gravely. "Sesemann, your little protégé is a sleep-walker. Every night, without knowing it, she has been opening the front door and alarming your staff. The child is pining away with homesickness. Didn't you see how pathetically thin she is? Now there is only one remedy for her overstretched nerves, and that is to send her back home at once. My advice is that the child should travel home to-morrow."

Herr Sesemann got up in a great state of agitation and strode up and down the room. "Ill, Homesick! Wasting away! In my house! And nobody seems to have noticed it! And you, doctor, suggest that I should send her back home in that pathetic state. No, doctor, I cannot do it. You take the child in hand and restore her to health; then I shall send her home if she wants to go."

"Sesemann," said the doctor, "consider! This is not an illness that can be cured with pills and powders. The child does not have a strong constitution but if she gets back home to the mountain air she will very quickly recover; if not—wouldn't you rather send the child back ill than not at all?"

Such blunt words alarmed Herr Sesemann and he agreed at once. "Well, if you think that is the only way then we must act at once." They discussed the matter further and after a while the doctor took his leave. When the master of the house opened the door the bright morning light shone in.

CHAPTER 13

BACK TO THE ALM

In great agitation, Herr Sesemann went upstairs to Fräulein Rottenmeier's room. His loud rap on the door awakened the lady and she was startled to hear him say, "Come down to the dining-room quickly, please! We must make preparations for a journey."

Fräulein Rottenmeier had never before been obliged to get up so early. It was only half-past four in the morning. What could possibly have happened? She was so flustered that she could hardly manage to dress. Herr Sesemann proceeded to rouse the whole staff and his urgent cries convinced them that the ghost had attacked the master and he needed their help. But, to their surprise, they found him walking up and down in the dining-room and not looking at all terrified. John was ordered to get the horses and carriage ready; Tinette had to wake Heidi and help her to dress and Sebastian was sent off to the house where Dete was in service, to bring her along.

At last Fräulein Rottenmeier was ready and came downstairs although she had put her cap on back to front in her hurry of preparation. Herr Sesemann instructed her to pack a trunk with the Swiss child's belongings and to add one or two things of Clara's so that the child would have some decent clothes to go home with. All this had to be done at once, Herr Sesemann insisted.

Poor Fräulein Rottenmeier stared in bewilderment at Herr Sesemann. She had expected to hear a hair-raising account of an encounter with a ghost in which she would have revelled in broad daylight and instead she was being given these practical instructions. Unable to believe her ears, she waited silently for Herr Sesemann to say something further; but he had no time for lengthy explanations and bustled off to Clara's room, leaving her standing there. He found Clara lying awake, wondering what could be the cause of such an upheaval in the house. Sitting beside her bed, her father told her all that had happened; about the doctor's verdict and how he thought that as Heidi was in a very overwrought state her sleep walking might take her somewhere dangerous. So they had decided to send Heidi home again at once.

Clara was distressed and made all sorts of suggestions for keeping Heidi with her, but her father remained firm, promising that if she were a good girl and did not make a fuss he would take her to Switzerland the following year. Eventually Clara gave in to him, on condition that Heidi's box would be packed in her room so that it would be possible for Clara to add things to it if she wanted.

In the meantime, Dete had arrived and was waiting downstairs wondering what on earth had happened that she should be summoned at such an early hour. Herr Sesemann told her about Heidi and that she was to go home that very day, accompanied by Dete herself.

Dete was very disappointed for this was the last thing she had expected to hear. She recalled the Uncle saying that he never wished to see her again, and it occurred to her that it would not be a safe undertaking to once again take the child to him, having once already delivered her and taken her away. Quickly she made as many excuses as she could muster, speaking low and fluently, so that Herr Sesemann, sensing her reluctance, told her to go away.

Herr Sesemann told Sebastian that he would have to accompany the child on her journey, the first day as far as Basle and the next day to her destination. He would be furnished with an explanatory letter to the grandfather, after presenting which he could return at once.

"But the main thing is this, Sebastian," concluded Herr Sesemann, "and I want you to see it is carried out. On this card I have written the name of the hotel in Basle. Show it to the manager and you will be given accommodation for the child and yourself. Go into the child's room and see that the windows are securely fastened, and when he has gone to bed, lock the door from the outside, for the child is a sleep-walker."

"Ah, so that was the ghost! I understand!" exclaimed Sebastian in great surprise.

"Yes, you foolish fellow. What cowards you all were," said Herr Sesemann and went off to his room to write a letter to the Alm-Uncle. Sebastian stayed where he was, feeling sheepish, and wishing that he had not let John drag him back into the room, instead of going after the small white figure. "I should certainly follow it if I saw it now," he said to himself. But of course everything was clearly illuminated by daylight.

All this time, Heidi was completely ignorant of what was afoot and was standing dressed in her Sunday best without the faintest notion why. Tinette had helped her to dress without uttering a word, for she considered her a common child and not fit to be spoken to.

The letter written, Herr Sesemann returned to the dining-room where breakfast was ready, and demanded, "Where is the child?"

Heidi was fetched and as she said good morning, Herr Sesemann looked into her sad little face. "Now what do you say to this, little one?" he asked kindly.

Heidi looked at him in surprise.

"Don't you know about it yet?" Herr Sesemann laughed. "You are going home to-day."

"Home?" repeated Heidi faintly, turning pale. For a moment she could hardly breathe, she was so overcome by the news.

"Perhaps you don't want to go," suggested Herr Sesemann.

"Oh, yes, I do want to go home," she replied, her face aglow with pleasure.

"Very well, then, you must take a good breakfast and then off you go in the carriage."

But hard as she tried, Heidi could scarcely swallow a mouthful for excitement. It all seemed like a dream and she thought that at any moment she might wake and find herself at the front door, shivering in her nightgown.

"Tell Sebastian to take plenty of provisions, for naturally the child can't eat just at present," Herr Sesemann told Fräulein Rottenmeier, who just at that moment entered the room. And turning to Heidi, he said kindly, "Go and join Clara until the carriage arrives."

Heidi rose eagerly and ran upstairs to Clara's room. In the middle of the floor was a big trunk which Clara had packed with dresses, pinafores, handkerchiefs and all sorts of clothes. "Look what I have packed for you," said Clara "Aren't you pleased, Heidi? And look, Heidi!" Triumphantly she held up a basket. Heidi peeped in and jumped for joy, for inside were twelve beautiful white rolls for the grandmother.

The children were so happily absorbed in their preparations that they had forgotten completely that the time for parting had come, and when the carriage was ready there was no time left for sadness.

Remembering her favourite book, Heidi ran back quickly to her own room and took it from under the pillow, the place where she always kept it, and racing back she put it into the basket with the rolls. Then she went and had a last look in the wardrobe and, sure enough, there was her old red shawl, which Fräulein Rottenmeier had not thought worth including with the rest of her luggage. Heidi wrapped it up and carefully hid it amongst the other luggage so that it would not be seen.

The children had to say good-bye quickly for Herr Sesemann was waiting to see Heidi to the carriage. Fräulein Rottenmeier was waiting at the top of the stairs and somehow a peep of red amongst Heidi's luggage caught her eye. She at once pulled out the red shawl and threw it aside.

"No, Adelheid," she scolded, "you cannot possibly take that old thing with you. Good-bye, then!"

Heidi did not dare lift up the little bundle but looked

imploringly at the master of the house with an expression which suggested that her greatest treasure had been taken from her.

"No, no," objected Herr Sesemann very firmly. "The child can take home whatever she pleases, whether it be kittens or tortoises and we won't be upset about it either, Fräulein Rottenmeier."

Heidi quickly lifted up her bundle and her eyes beamed with gratitude. Herr Sesemann shook hands with her, wished her a happy journey and said that he and Clara would always remember her. Heidi thanked him for all his kindness and said finally, "And please say good-bye to the doctor for me and thank him very, very much." She had not forgotten his words of the night before when he had said, "And to-morrow everything will be all right." And now these words had really come true and Heidi was convinced that it was all of his doing.

She was lifted into the carriage, and trunk, basket and provisions followed. Finally Sebastian climbed up beside her. Once more Herr Sesemann wished her a good journey and the carriage rolled away.

Very soon Heidi was sitting beside Sebastian in the train, her basket on her lap. She would not let go of it for a second, for inside were the rolls for the Grandmother. For many hours she sat silent. Only now did she fully realise that she was on her way home to the grandfather, the grandmother and Goat Peter; and the familiar scene rose before her eyes. She thought of how beautiful everything would look at home, but then a sudden thought came to her and suddenly she turned anxiously to Sebastian. "Sebastian, are you sure the grandmother on the Alm is not dead?"

"No, no," he replied comfortingly, "I am sure she will still be alive."

Once more Heidi became preoccupied with her own thoughts, occasionally peeping into the basket. After some time she asked again, "Sebastian, if I only knew for certain that grandmother is still alive!"

"Yes, yes," said Sebastian, half asleep. "She will be alive. Why should she be dead?"

After a while Heidi fell asleep, too, and slept so soundly that she did not wake up until Sebastian shook her by the arm and said, "Wake up! Wake up! We are in Basle. This is where we get out!"

The next morning they had to start again on a long train journey, and as they reached their destinations Heidi was too excited to talk and again sat with her basket held tightly. When she least expected it, a voice shouted, "Mayenfeld!" Up she jumped from her seat and Sebastian followed. As they stood on the platform beside Heidi's luggage, Sebastian looked regretfully after the disappearing train, for he much preferred that comfortable mode of transport to the tiring and dangerous climb up into the mountains in this, as he considered it, barbarous country. Cautiously he looked round to see of whom he might inquire the safest road to Dörfli. He spotted a broad-shouldered man loading a cart with big heavy sacks which had just arrived by train. Sebastian addressed his inquiry to him.

"All the roads here are safe," answered the man.

So Sebastian asked which was the best way one could take without being in danger of falling over a precipice, and also how to get a trunk up to Dörfli. The man regarded the trunk and then declared that if it was not too heavy, he would take it on his cart, as he was on his way there. After further conversation, the man agreed to take both the child and the trunk as far as Dörfli and from there somebody would take her up to the Alm.

"I can go by myself. I know the way from Dörfli to the Alm," said Heidi, who had been listening attentively to the conversation.

Sebastian was greatly relieved not to have to do any climbing. He took Heidi aside and gave her a heavy little leather bag and the letter to the grandfather, explaining; "This little bag is a present from Herr Sesemann. It must go to the bottom of the basket, under the rolls, and the little fräulein must be very careful with it for Herr Sesemann would be very angry if she were to lose it."

"I won't lose it," said Heidi confidently and at once put both the bag and the letter at the bottom of her basket.

The trunk was hoisted on to the cart and then Sebastian helped Heidi with her basket on to the driver's seat. He shook hands with her and reminded her once more about the contents of the basket. (Sebastian was rather worried as he knew he was supposed to see the child right to her destination.) The driver swung himself up beside Heidi and the cart moved off. Sebastian, glad to have rid himself of a wearisome duty, sat down in the station to wait for the return train.

The man with the cart was the miller from Dörfli who was taking home his sacks of flour. He had never seen Heidi before but felt sure this must be the much-discussed child whose parents he had known. He began to wonder what had happened that she should be returning here. "Aren't you the little girl who lived with the uncle on the Alm?" he shouted to Heidi above the noise of the cart.

"Yes," replied Heidi.

"You are soon back, aren't you? Didn't they treat you well there?"

"No, it wasn't that. Nobody could have been treated better than I was in Frankfurt."

"What brings you back then?"

"Because Herr Sesemann allowed me."

"But wouldn't you rather have stayed?"

"Oh, I'd rather be with the grandfather on the Alm than anywhere else in the world!"

"Maybe you'll think differently once you're there," muttered the baker, and then said to himself, "It's very odd, she must surely know what it's like up there." Then he started to whistle and said no more.

Heidi looked round and trembled with excitement as she began to recognise the trees on the road and above, the great towering peaks which seemed to welcome her back like old friends. Heidi nodded to them in turn, and at every bend of the road grew more and more happy until she felt she would burst with joy. More than anything she wanted to leap from the plodding cart and run as fast as she could until she reached the Alm. But instead, she sat still and patient, despite her inward excitement. As they drove into Dörfli the clock was striking five. A group of women and children clustered round the cart and wanted to know where they had come from and where they were going. As the baker lifted Heidi down she said quickly, "Thank you. Grandfather will fetch the trunk later," and tried to run off. She was at once stopped by questions from all sides but she pushed her way through the crowd with such a worried expression that the people were compelled to stand aside and let her through. It was certain, in their minds, that she would not go back to the grandfather if she had anywhere else to go, but the baker quickly enlightened them, declaring that although she had had the chance to live in a house where she had everything, it was her own wish to return to the grandfather. "There you are," they said to each other, "you can see she's frightened, and no wonder." They whispered about the Alm-Uncle and how he had deteriorated during the year, never saying one word, and looking like thunder at those he met. This news amazed everybody and it was soon spread around Dörfli that Heidi had given up a luxurious home to return to the hut on the Alm.

As fast as she could, Heidi climbed up from Dörfli. As she reached the top the path got steeper and the basket seemed to get heavier and heavier, so that she was obliged to pause now and then to get her breath. There was only one thought in her mind. Would she find the grandmother still in her usual corner by the spinning wheel? Suddenly she caught sight of the cottage and her heart began to pound. She ran as fast as she could until she reached the door ant trembled so much with excitement that she could hardly open it. But then she was inside and standing in the middle of the little room with no breath left to say a word.

"Dear Lord!" a voice cried from the corner, "that sounded like Heidi. If only I could have her with me again. Who is there?"

"But it *is* Heidi, Grandmother! I am back!" called Heidi and rushed towards the old woman. She put her arms round her and hugged her, unable to speak for joy. At first the grandmother was too overwhelmed to utter a word; then she caressed Heidi's curly head and said, "It is her hair, and her voice. Thank God that He has granted this to me!" Tears of joy spilled from her blind eyes. "Is it really you, Heidi? Have you come back to me?"

"Yes, Grandmother, it is true," assured Heidi. "Don't cry. I am really back and will come to you every day and never go away again. And you won't have to eat hard bread for a while. Look, Grandmother, look!"

Heidi unpacked her basket and piled the twelve rolls in the grandmother's lap.

"Ah, child, what a blessing you bring with you," she said, feeling the rolls, of which there seemed to be a countless number, but the greatest blessing is you yourself," and again she touched Heidi's hair and her hot cheek. "Speak to me, child," she murmured, "so that I can hear your voice again."

Heidi was in the midst of telling the grandmother how she had feared she might never see her again when the door opened and Peter's mother walked in. For a moment she stood perplexed, then she cried, "Can it possibly be you, Heidi?"

Brigitta's quick glance soon took in Heidi's appearance, and with little gasps of admiration she exclaimed to the grandmother, "Mother, if you could only see what a pretty frock she is wearing and how grand she looks! I hardly recognise her. And this hat with the feather, is it yours, too, Heidi? Put it on and let me see how you look in it."

"No, I don't care about it," replied Heidi. "If you like it, please have it. I still have my old one." Heidi opened the little red bundle and took out her own hat which looked more crushed than ever after the long journey. But that did not trouble Heidi. She still remembered all the grandfather had had to say about hats with feathers, on Dete's last visit. This was why she had looked after her old hat so lovingly, for she had always the thought of going home again in the back of her mind. And taking off her pretty frock, she wrapped the red shawl round her shoulders. "But now," she said, taking the grandmother's hand, "I must go home to Grandfather. To-morrow I shall come back. Good night, Grandmother!"

"Yes, come again, Heidi, come again to-morrow," begged the grandmother and pressed the child's hands.

"But why have you taken off your pretty dress?" Brigitta wanted to know.

"Because I would rather go to Grandfather like this in case he shouldn't recognise me. You hardly knew me at first."

Brigitta thought she was silly, and told her not to give it away. Perhaps Heidi should sell it to the schoolmaster's daughter in Dörfli. But Heidi did not change her mind, and later hid the hat behind the grandmother's chair. Brigitta accompanied her to the door and there said to her, "You could have kept the dress, he would have recognised you; but approach him carefully, for Peter says that Alm-Uncle never talks to anyone these days and is very moody."

Heidi said good night and went off up to the Alm. The big snow-field at the Scesaplana sparkled in the evening sun. A red shimmer fell on the grass at Heidi's feet and she turned round. She had not remembered, even in her dreams, how beautiful this picture was. The two peaks of the Falkins rose like twin flames, the snowfield was aglow and above it floated rose-tinted clouds. Far below stretched the valley, and above and around everything glittered and sparkled. Tears crept down Heidi's cheeks at the sight of all this splendour. Earnestly she pressed her hands together and thanked God for bringing her home again. She stood still, her heart full of thankfulness, until the light began to fade, and then all at once she ran up the mountain as fast as she could. Presently the tops of the fir trees waving in the wind and then the hut came into view, and there was the grandfather sitting on his bench and smoking his pipe. Heidi ran faster and before the Alm-Uncle was aware of anything Heidi had thrown her basket to the ground and put her two arms round his neck, unable to say more than, "Grandfather! Grandfather! Grandfather!"

The old man could say nothing. For the first time for many years his eyes were wet with tears and he brushed them roughly away with the back of his hand. Then he lifted Heidi on to his knee and looked at her. "So you have come home again to me, Heidi," he began. "You don't look very much of a lady. Did they send you away?"

"Oh, no, Grandfather. You mustn't think that. They were all

very good to me, Clara and Grandmamma and Herr Sesemann. It was just that I couldn't bear being away from you any longer. Sometimes I felt I would choke, but I never said anything because it would have been ungrateful. Then suddenly one morning Herr Sesemann called for me very early—I think maybe it was the doctor who told him—but perhaps it is all in the letter—" and Heidi jumped down and fetched the letter and the little bag from her basket and handed them both to the grandfather.

"I think that belongs to you," he declared, laying the little leather bag beside him on the bench. Then he read the letter and without a word put it into his pocket.

"Do you think you could still drink milk with me?" he asked Heidi and took her hand to go into the hut. "But take your money! You can buy a proper bed with it and enough clothes to last several years."

"I don't need it, Grandfather," assured Heidi. "I have got a bed already and Clara packed such a lot of clothes in my trunk that I shall never have to buy any ever again. It's wonderful."

"Take the money and put it into the cupboard, then. Some day you will want it."

Heidi obeyed and followed the grandfather into the hut. Joyfully she ran about and looked into every corner. Then she went up the ladder, but she stopped short when she put her head into the loft. "Oh, Grandfather, where is my bed?" she cried reproachfully.

"It will soon be there again," came from below. "How was I to know you were coming back? Come down and drink your milk."

Heidi came down and took her old seat in the high chair. Eagerly she drank her milk as though nothing had ever tasted so delicious. Then she took a deep breath and declared, "There is nothing in the whole world so good as our milk, Grandfather!"

Suddenly a shrill whistle sounded. Quick as lightning Heidi rushed outside, and there were the goats, skipping and jumping down the steep heights with Peter in their midst. Speechlessly he stared at Heidi.

"Good evening, Peter!" she said. "Do you still know me?"

The little goats had evidently recognised her voice, for they rubbed their heads against her eagerly. Heidi was wild with joy to see her old companions once more and called each one by name as they came scampering and leaping down to her. Even shy little Snowflake pushed the Great Turk out of her way in such a sure manner that he was left standing looking very put out by her bravado.

Heidi was thrilled to be back with all her old friends. She threw her arms around Snowflake's neck, stroked Goldfinch, and was pushed and nuzzled on all sides.

Slowly Peter came towards her. "So you are back again!" he managed to say at last. Then, just as in the old days, he asked, "Will you come up to the pasture, to-morrow?"

"No, not to-morrow, but the next day. To-morrow I must go and see the grandmother as I have been worried about her."

"I am glad you are back!" Peter said, beaming with happiness, and began to urge the goats down the mountain.

When Heidi got back into the cottage her bed was already made up for her. With a sigh of contentment she lay down and slept as she had not done for a whole year. During the night the grandfather got up again and again and listened anxiously to hear if Heidi slept quietly. But Heidi never stirred. Now there was nothing to make her wander about in the night-time for her longing was satisfied. She had seen the mountains again and had heard the wind in the fir trees. She was home on the Alm.

Chapter 14

THE BELLS RING OUT

Heidi stood under the fir trees and waited for the Alm-Uncle who was going to take her as far as the grandmother's and then go on to Dörfli to fetch her trunk. She was impatient to hear how the grandmother had enjoyed the white rolls and thought the grandfather would never be finished with his tasks, but at the same time she could not listen enough to the whispering of the trees, or breathe in the beautiful flower-filled air of the pastures. At last the old man appeared and announced, "Well, I have finished."

It was a Saturday, which was Alm-Uncle's day for cleaning and tidying the house. He had spent the morning doing this so that he could go with Heidi in the afternoon, and the hut was now shining bright and clean.

At Goat Peter's cottage they parted and Heidi ran inside. The grandmother heard her step and called lovingly, "Are you there, child? Have you come back again?" She took Heidi's hand and told her how much she had enjoyed the rolls and how much stronger she felt already. Brigitta explained how the grandmother would only take one roll each day for fear they would be finished too soon. At that Heidi exclaimed, "I know what I shall do, Grandmother. I shall write to Clara and I am sure she will send as many rolls as you want."

"That is very good of you," said Brigitta, "but I am afraid they would get very hard and stale. If only I had money! The baker in Dörfli makes them too, but I can't afford to buy them. I have hardly enough money for the ordinary black bread."

"Oh, but I have lots of money!" the child cried delightedly. "Now I know how I shall spend it. Every day Grandmother will have a white roll and two on Sundays and Peter will get them in Dörfli."

"No, no, my child," remonstrated the grandmother. "The money you have got is not for that; you must give it to the grandfather and he will tell you what to do with it."

But Heidi took no notice and continued to chatter happily, "Now Grandmother can eat a roll every day and will get quite strong. Perhaps it's only dark for you because you are so weak, Grandmother."

The grandmother said nothing. She did not want to spoil the child's joy.

Suddenly Heidi caught sight of the grandmother's hymn book and a new thought struck her:

"Grandmother, I can read now. Shall I read to you one of the hymns from your old book?"

"Yes, indeed," replied the grandmother, both surprised and delighted. "But do you really know how to read, child?"

Heidi had climbed on a chair and lifted down the dusty book which had lain untouched on the shelf for a very long time.

She blew the dust off and then sat down on the stool beside the old woman, asking which hymn she wanted to hear.

"Whichever you like, child! Whichever you like!" And she waited in eager expectation while Heidi turned over the pages and read softly a line here and there.

"Here is one about the sun. I shall read that one, Grandmother."

And Heidi read the hymn aloud, very touchingly.

The grandmother sat with folded hands while Heidi read and the face of the aged woman shone with an indescribable joy such as Heidi had never seen before, and her eyes glistened with tears. When the child stopped reading, "Once more, Heidi, please. Read it once more," she begged, and Heidi read the hymn again.

The morning breaks,
And warm and bright
The earth lies still
In golden light—
For Dawn has scattered the clouds of night.

God's handiwork
Is seen around
Things great and small
To his praise abound—
Where are the signs of his love not found.

All things must pass
But God shall still
His will fulfill—
Sure and unshaken is His will.

His saving grace
Will never fail
Though grief and fear
The heart assail—
O'er life's wild seas he will prevail.

Joy shall be ours
In that garden blest,
Where after storm
We find our rest—
I wait in peace—God's time is best.

"Oh, Heidi, that is enough to fill my heart with light. How comforting the words are!"

As the grandmother spoke, there was a knock at the window and the grandfather stood outside, beckoning Heidi to come home. She went at once, but not without promising the grandmother that she would come again to-morrow. She was completely happy because she could make the grandmother's life cheerful again. It was an even greater source of happiness to her than the goats and the pasture.

Heidi had so much to tell the grandfather, particularly about the rolls. "Surely, Grandfather," she said, "if Grandmother won't take the money you will give me money from the bag so that I can give it to Peter to buy the rolls every day!"

"What about a bed, Heidi?" asked the grandfather. "A proper bed for you would be nice and there would still be plenty left over for the rolls?"

But Heidi gave him no peace and at last the old man said, "The money is yours to do with as you please. You will be able to buy rolls for the Grandmother with it for many, many years."

Heidi was jubilant. "Oh, Grandfather, isn't everything wonderful!" Then she became serious. "If God had answered when I prayed to come here at once, everything would have been different. I would only have come for a short time and Grandmother would only have got a few rolls and I wouldn't have been able to read to her. But God has thought it out much better than I ever could, just as Grandmamma told me in Frankfurt. Everything has turned out as she said. Oh, how glad I am that God did not let me have my way! Now I shall always pray as Grandmamma taught me and if God does not do what I ask I shall think at once, 'I am sure it is just the same as at Frankfurt and God knows a much better way.' So we will pray every day, please, Grandfather, and we will never forget Him so that He does not forget us."

"And if somebody does forget Him?" murmured the grandfather.

"Oh, it will be the worse for him! Because then God will forget *him*, and nobody will pity him because he ran away from God who could have helped him."

"That is true, Heidi. But how do you know?"

"From Grandmamma She explained it all to me."

The grandfather walked on silently, then, lost in his own thoughts. He said, "But nobody can go back once he has forgotten God and God has forgotten him for ever."

"Oh, no, Grandfather! It's possible to go back. I know that, too, from Grandmamma, and it even says so in the lovely story in my book, but you have not read it yet. As soon as we are home you shall hear what a beautiful story it is."

As soon as they reached the top of the hill Heidi ran into the cottage to get her book and returned presently with it under her arm. The grandfather, busy with his own thoughts, was seated on the bench. Heidi climbed up beside him and opened her book at her favourite story.

Now Heidi began to read the story of the Prodigal Son who, although he had all he could wish for at home tending his father's flock, longed for wealth and riches, and asked for his share of his father's wealth so that he could go out into the world and be his own master. After he had foolishly spent all he had, he was obliged to work as a swine-herd with nothing to wear but rags and nothing to eat but the husks which the pigs left. Then he remembered his father and thought what an ungrateful son he had been, and he wept bitterly. So he decided, 'I shall go to my father and ask forgiveness and say to him, "I am not worthy to be called thy son; make me one of thy day labourers."' But when he was still a great distance from his father's house, his father recognised him and hastened forward—

"And what do you think happens now, Grandfather?" Heidi could not help stopping to ask. "Do you think the father in still angry and will say to him, 'Go away!' Listen now to what happens next!"

"And when the father saw him coming he had compassion on him and embraced him, and the son said, 'Father, I have sinned against Heaven and in thy sight and am not worthy to be called thy son.' But his father said to his servants, 'Bring the best robe for him. Put a ring on his finger and bring shoes for his feet. And bring forth the fatted calf and kill it and let us eat and be merry, for this, my son, was dead and is alive again; he was lost and is found.'

"Isn't that a beautiful story, Grandfather?" asked Heidi when she saw that he was still absorbed in his thoughts.

"Yes, Heidi, the story is beautiful," answered the grandfather, his face still grave. So Heidi was silent for a while and looked at the pictures in her book. After a while she laid the book on his lap and said, "Look, Grandfather, he is so happy standing there," pointing to the figure of the prodigal son, who was standing by his father in new clothes, as one of the family.

A few hours later when Heidi had been asleep for a long time, the grandfather climbed up the ladder and put his lamp beside her bed so that its light fell on the sleeping child. She was lying with folded hands, as if she had fallen asleep saying her prayers. On her little face was an expression of peace and trust. For a long time the old man stood gazing at the child, then he folded his hands and half aloud he prayed with bent head, "Father, I have sinned against Heaven and in Thy sight and am not worthy to be called Thy son." As he spoke tears rolled down the old man's cheeks.

Early next morning the Alm-Uncle stood in front of his hut, smiling gently as he looked around him. It was a beautiful Sunday morning and he could hear the church bells ringing down in the valley. He went back into the hut and called up to the loft, "Get up, Heidi! Put on your nice frock for we are going to church together."

Heidi was soon dressed in her pretty Frankfurt clothes and came downstairs quickly, her curiosity aroused by this unusual summons from the Alm-Uncle; but great was her surprise when she caught a glimpse of him. "Oh, Grandfather, I have never seen you in this coat with the silver buttons. How nice you look in your Sunday coat!"

The old man smiled and said, "You too, in your pretty dress. Come along now!" He took Heidi's hand in his and they walked down the mountain together. The bells were ringing on every side and the sound of them filled the whole valley and rose up echoing among the mountains. As they descended, the peals sounded louder and richer and Heidi listened rapturously. "Listen, Grandfather! It is like a great festival."

When the grandfather and Heidi entered the church the singing had already begun so they sat down together at the back. But before the hymn was finished there was subdued whispering on all sides, "The Alm-Uncle, did you see the Alm-Uncle?"

Soon everybody knew that the Alm-Uncle was in church and the women, hardly able to believe, kept turning their heads to look. When the sermon began, everybody became more attentive and forgot, for the time being, about the uncle.

As soon as the service was finished the old uncle walked with the child in the direction of the pastor's house. Some of the people followed him curiously and when they saw him and the child go inside, they gathered in excited groups to discuss the extraordinary event, for they could not imagine what had brought the old man down from his mountain-top. It soon became evident that many of them were beginning to change their opinion of the old man. They had noticed what great care he took of the little one and surely, they thought, he cannot be so very wicked or he would be afraid to face the pastor. Then the baker reminded them, "Didn't I tell you? What child would give up a wonderful home with the best life can offer to go back to a grandfather who had been unkind and of whom she is afraid?" And so a friendly feeling for the grandfather began to spread amongst the people and they waited patiently at the pastor's door as though to welcome back an old friend who had been gone a long time.

The uncle knocked at the door of the pastor's study and the pastor greeted him as though he had expected the old man. His appearance in church had not escaped the pastor's notice and he shook hands warmly. At first the Alm-Uncle could not find words, then, pulling himself together, he began, "Pastor, I have come to ask you to forget the words I spoke to you on the Alm and not to hold it against me that I was too obstinate to take your well-meant advice. I see now that you were right and I was wrong, so I am following your advice and I would like to take the house in Dörfli for the winter, for the cold season up there is not good for the child. She is too delicate. Of course, the people here do not trust me and I deserve no better."

The kind eyes of the pastor brightened with joy. Once more he grasped the old man's hand and said with deep emotion, "Neighbour, I am sincerely glad; and you will never have cause to regret coming back to live amongst us. You will always be welcome in my house and I hope to spend many a pleasant winter evening with you for I value your friendship. And we shall also find playmates for the little one."

The pastor laid his hand affectionately on Heidi's curly head, and taking her by the hand, accompanied them both to the door. When they stood outside on the doorstep he bade them good-bye and everybody noticed that the pastor shook hands with the Alm-Uncle as if they were the best of friends.

As soon as the door closed the old man was assailed by friendly greetings from every one, "How nice to see you again, Uncle!" "It's good to see you back, Uncle. I have been wanting to have a talk with you for a long time." And when the Uncle told them that he was going to live again in his old house in Dörfli for the winter months, there was such a chorus of joyful shouts that it seemed as though the Alm-Uncle was the most popular person in Dörfli. The farming people accompanied the old man and the child far up the mountain path and when they said farewell every one invited him to call next time he was down. When they parted, the old man followed them with his eyes and his face reflected an inner light so that Heidi could not take her eyes off him. "Grandfather," she said, "today you look nicer every minute. I have never seen you like this before."

"Do you think so?" asked the old man, smiling. "You see, Heidi, I am so happy to-day. To be at peace with God and man is good! God was good to me when He sent you to the Alm."

When they arrived at Goat Peter's hut, the grandfather opened the door and they walked inside.

"Good morning, Grandmother!" he said. "I think we will have to do some more patching before the autumn winds come."

"Mercy!" exclaimed the grandmother. "That is the uncle!" and her voice was both surprised and pleased. "Now I can thank you for all you have done for us, Uncle. God bless you! God bless you!" And when he held her trembling hand she said, "If I have ever hurt you, don't punish me by taking Heidi away from me. Oh, you do not know what the child means to me." And she held Heidi close to her.

"Have no fear, Grandmother. I shall not punish either you or myself. We shall all stay together now and, if God wills it, for a long time."

Brigitta beckoned the Uncle into a corner, and showed him the hat with the feathers, explaining how it came to be there and insisting that she could not take such a thing from a child. But the grandfather, glancing towards Heidi, replied that Brigitta should indeed take the hat, as Heidi was free to decide if she didn't want it.

Brigitta was thrilled. "It is worth more than ten shillings," she said, displaying it for all to admire. "And what changes for the good Heidi has brought with her from Frankfurt. I've a good mind to send Peter there for a while—I am sure it would benefit him tremendously."

The grandfather's eyes twinkled. He thought it would probably do Peter good, but he meant to wait for the right moment to broach the subject to him.

At that moment, Peter himself rushed in noisily and evidently in a great hurry. He held a letter in his hand which was a rare enough occurrence to account for his excitement. It was a letter for Heidi which had been given to Peter at the post office in Dörfli. Heidi opened her letter and read it aloud. It was from Clara.

She told Heidi how dull it had been since she had gone and how, for this reason, she had persuaded her father to take her to Ragatz next autumn so that she might have a chance of seeing her again. Grandmamma wished to come too, for she also wished to visit Heidi and the grandfather on the Alm; and Grandmamma was sending some coffee so that the grandmother would not have to eat the rolls dry. And she was looking forward to visiting the grandmother herself if Heidi would take her.

There were so many questions to ask and so much to discuss after this news that even the grandfather did not notice how quickly time was passing. Everybody was happy about the news but, as the grandmother said, the greatest delight of all was to see an old friend return like old times. "Come again, soon, Uncle, and you, child, tomorrow!"

They both promised. But now it was time to leave. As in the morning the bells had greeted them, so now the peaceful evening chimes accompanied them on their way up to the sunny Alm cottage which shone with an air of Sunday calm in the red glow of the evening sky. But when Grandmamma arrives next autumn there will be even more surprises for Heidi and for the grandmother; for a proper bed will certainly be put up in the hay loft. If Grandmamma has anything to do with it, everything turns out very well.

Chapter 15

PREPARATIONS FOR A JOURNEY

It was a sunny morning in September and the good doctor, who had been the cause of Heidi's going home, was on his way to the Sesemann's house. There was a look of great sadness on his face and he seemed to have aged considerably since the spring. The doctor had had an only daughter in whom, since the death of his wife, he had found his only happiness. A few months before, she had died and, ever since, all the doctor's brightness and cheerfulness had gone.

Sebastian opened the door with marked civility, for the doctor was not only the best friend of the master but also of his little daughter, and because of his warmth and kindness was beloved by everyone in the house.

"Everything all right?" he asked Sebastian in his pleasant voice as he preceded the servant upstairs.

"Ah, I am glad you are here!" exclaimed Herr Sesemann as he stepped forward to welcome his friend. "We must definitely discuss again this Swiss journey. Do you still stick by your decision in spite of the fact that Clara's health shows signs of improvement?"

"My dear Sesemann, what am I to think of you!" replied the doctor. "This is the third time to-day you have called me in to ask the same question."

"Yes, you are perfectly right and I cannot blame you for becoming impatient; but you must understand, my dear friend, how difficult it is for me to deny the child now, at the last minute, something which I promised her so faithfully and to which she has been looking forward for months. It is only the prospect of this journey and the thought of seeing her friend again which has enabled Clara to suffer so patiently these last bad weeks and now, suddenly, I am to deprive the poor child of this joy. I simply cannot do it."

"Sesemann, it has to be done," replied the doctor firmly, and when he saw his friend silent and depressed he continued, "now think it out for yourself. For years Clara hasn't had such a bad summer as this last one. There can be no question of travelling without risk of the worst consequences. And after all, it is September, and although there is a chance that it is still fine up there, it may very easily be cold. The days are getting shorter and the journey from Ragatz to the Alm would take several hours as Clara would have to be carried up the mountain. In short, Sesemann, it is quite impossible. But I shall speak to her myself. She is a sensible child. If she is taken to Ragatz next May for very special care and if she is stronger she will enjoy the excursion up the mountain far more than now. Only with the greatest care and attention can she have a chance of recovery."

Herr Sesemann suddenly turned to the doctor and said bluntly: "Tell me honestly, Doctor: do you really think she may one day recover?"

The doctor shrugged. "I don't hold out much hope," he said quietly. "But think what I have to go through. You still have a loving child to watch for you and to be there when you arrive home. You do not return to a lonely house, and Clara is comfortable there too. Despite all the things she has to miss she has many things for which to be grateful. No, my friend, you have not a great deal to be sorry about."

Herr Sesemann rose and walked up and down the room as was his habit when something occupied his mind.

Suddenly he tapped his friend on the shoulder.

"Doctor, I have a suggestion to make. You don't look well and are not the same as you used to be. You need a change and do you know what has occurred to me? You should go and visit Heidi on the Alm in our name."

This suggestion surprised the doctor very much and he started to make objections, but Herr Sesemann gave him no opportunity. He was so enthusiastic about his new plan that he took his friend by the arm and drew him into Clara's room. Clara was always pleased to see the doctor, for he nearly always had some funny story to tell her. Recently he had been more serious, but Clara knew why, and would have given anything to see him lively and cheerful once more.

Herr Sesemann took Clara's hand in his and began to talk about the Swiss journey and how he himself had looked forward to it. He passed quickly over the main point—that it was impossible now for Clara to go—for he could not bear the thought of the tears which would be bound to fall, and then told her of his latest plan to persuade their good friend, the doctor, to take this holiday.

Tears came into Clara's eyes although she tried to hide them for her father's sake, but it was a great disappointment to her to have to give up this journey which had been her only joy and comfort during many lonely hours. She knew, however, that her father would only deny her something which would do her harm; so she swallowed her tears and tuned her thoughts to the only remaining hope. She took the doctor's hand and said imploringly:

"Please, doctor, go and see Heidi and then come back and tell me what it is like there and how Heidi is getting on; and the grandfather, and Peter and the goats. I feel I know them all so well! And then you can take to Heidi all the things I have for her, and something for the grandmother. Please go, doctor, and I'll take as much cod liver oil as you like."

It may not have been this promise which altogether decided the doctor but he certainly replied smilingly: "Then I suppose I must go, Clara, if we are to see you grow plump and strong! And when have you decided I am to start?"

"As soon as possible, doctor. To-morrow morning," replied Clara.

"She is quite right," interrupted her father. "The weather is fine and it would be a pity to miss a single day which you could enjoy on the Alm."

The doctor could not help laughing a little. "Soon you'll reproach me for not being there already, Sesemann. I see I shall have to make haste."

But Clara still detained him. She had to give him lots of messages for Heidi. She would send round the presents later on. The doctor promised to deliver them all faithfully and to bring back a full account of everything that happened.

The servants of a household have a strange capacity for knowing what is going on long before they are informed about it by the master. Tinette, having been rung for, went into Clara's room. Clara asked her to fill a box with the cakes normally served with coffee. Tinette picked it up, and swinging it carelessly, carried it out. "I wouldn't have bothered if I'd been you," she said cheekily as she went out. Sebastian, as he opened the front door for the doctor, said with his usual deference: "May I ask the doctor to give my regards to the little fräulein?"

"Ah, Sebastian," the doctor smiled, "you know already about my going?"

Sebastian looked embarrassed, "Well, I—not exactly—as a matter of fact—well, you see, I just happened to go into the dining-room when I heard the little fräulein's name mentioned, and then I thought—"

"I see! I see!" smiled the doctor. "Good-bye, Sebastian! I'll be sure to remember your message."

The doctor stepped across the threshold, and then jumped back again quickly. The doorway was blocked by Fräulein Rottenmeier returning from her walk which she had been prevented from concluding by the rough wind. It was a very gusty day and the wind blew out her skirts so that she looked like a ship in full sail. The doctor drew aside to let her pass, but the wind was so strong she was blown right into the doorway and, gasping for breath, crashed into the doctor. The poor lady was very much upset by this loss of dignity for she had a great admiration for the doctor, but he very quickly smoothed her down and told her of his plans, asking her in a most amiable voice to pack the parcel for Heidi in the way in which only she could do it. Then off he went.

Clara had expected that Fräulein Rottenmeier would make all sorts of objections to sending the many presents to Heidi, but she was mistaken. Fräulein Rottenmeier was in an exceptionally good temper and everything was laid out on a large table where Clara could watch it all being packed. This was not an easy task, for the presents were all of different shapes and size. There was the little warm coat with the hood which Clara had herself designed for Heidi, so that during the long, cold winter she could be warm enough to visit the grandmother whenever he wanted. Then came a thick warm shawl for the grandmother in which she could wrap herself up and not feel the draught from the cold wind and also a large cake as a change from the rolls. There was the large box full of cakes, also for the grandmother, as a change from bread when she had her coffee. Then there was a delicious sausage which

Clara had at first meant for Peter as he never had anything to eat except bread and cheese, but had later decided to send to Brigitta, since there might be a danger of Peter eating it all himself, and Brigitta could be depended upon to divide it up between all of them for supper. There was a packet of tobacco for the grandfather who was so fond of his pipe, and last of all, there were a lot of mysterious little packages which Clara had especially enjoyed putting together, as they had been made up specially to be put in as individual surprises for Heidi.

At last the job was done and an imposing-looking parcel lay on the floor ready for transport. Fräulein Rottenmeier looked at it with a satisfied smile, pleased with her efforts at the art of packing. Clara gazed at it blissfully, imagining Heidi's squeals of delight when it arrived.

Fräulein Rottenmeier rang for Sebastian and with an energetic swing he lifted the parcel on to his shoulder and carried it off to be despatched at once to the doctor's house.

CHAPTER 16

A VISITOR TO THE ALM

The morning sky was all aglow, shedding its light upon the mountains, and a fresh breeze stirred in the fir trees, swaying their ancient branches. Heidi opened her eyes, awakened by the sound of the wind in the trees, and jumping out of bed, dressed herself very quickly. When she came down the ladder, the grandfather was already standing outside and was looking at the sky to see what sort of weather it was going to be. Little pink clouds floated across the sky and gradually more and more blue patches appeared. The sun was just rising and touched the mountain tops with gold.

"Oh, how lovely!" cried Heidi. "Good morning, Grandfather!"

"Are you awake already?" he said, patting the child's head. She ran off to listen to the fir trees, and with every new gust of wind which blew through their old branches, she thrilled with pleasure.

The grandfather went off to milk the goats and brought them out ready for their climb up to the pastures. There came the sound of Peter's whistle and presently Heidi was surrounded by the whole flock who were all bleating, nuzzling and rubbing against her so that she could hardly move. Little Bear pushed rather harder than he should, and was gently reproached by Heidi; whereupon Little Swan lifted her head daintily, as if to imply that she would not stoop to such behaviour. Heidi, meanwhile, had pushed her way through to where Snowflake was standing, for the little goat had tried to reach her and had been pushed aside by the others. Peter at last gave one more piercing blast on his whistle, and the goats moved off.

"Are you coming with us to-day?" he asked and it was clear from the tone of his voice that he was anxious for Heidi to accompany him.

"No, Peter, I can't come to-day," replied Heidi. "The friends from Frankfurt may arrive at any moment and I must be here when they come."

"That's what you always say," grumbled Peter. "And I shall go on saying it until they arrive," returned Heidi. "How could you think that I would not stay here to greet them?" "The uncle is always here. So I can't see that it matters," he muttered.

Just at that point the uncle himself called out, "What's wrong with the army to-day, it isn't on the move? Is it the General's fault or is it the troops'?"

Peter turned at once and cracked his whip in the air, and the goats, who knew the sound well, started off up the mountain with Peter trotting after them.

Since Heidi had come back she thought of all sorts of things to do about the house which had not occurred to her before.

Every morning she made her bed carefully, then she went downstairs and tidied the kitchen. She put the chairs straight and anything which was lying about she put into the cupboard. Next she would get out a duster, and climbing on to a chair, would rub the table until it shone. All this pleased the grandfather and he would look round, saying, "The house is so well kept nowadays it always looks as though it were Sunday! Heidi's trip certainly hasn't been in vain!"

To-day Heidi had begun her chores as usual but the beautiful weather seemed to draw her outside and she was not making much progress with her work. A sunbeam slanting through the open window seemed to be calling: "Come, Heidi! Come out!" She simply could not stay indoors any longer and ran outside. The sunlight sparkled on the mountains and shone down on the valley. Heidi had to sit down for a minute and look about her. However, she soon jumped up and ran back to the hut when she remembered that her stool was still standing in the middle of the floor and that the table had still not been rubbed properly.

Hardly had she set about her tasks again when she heard the fir trees calling her and off she ran again to listen to their song. The grandfather was working in the shed and came out from time to time to look smilingly at the child. He had just gone back to his work when Heidi called out loudly, "Grandfather! Grandfather! Come quickly!" The old man came out at once, afraid that something had happened to the child. He saw Heidi running towards the path, calling as she went, "They are coming! They are coming! The doctor is first!"

Heidi rushed forward to welcome her old friend who stretched out his hand in greeting. As soon as she reached him she clasped his out-stretched arm affectionately. "Good morning, doctor, and thank you, ever so much, I am so grateful to you."

"God bless you, Heidi! And what is it you are grateful to me for?"

"For arranging it so that I could come home to be with Grandfather," explained the child.

The doctor's face brightened with joy. He had not expected

such a welcome. He had climbed the steep mountain path feeling lonely and depressed and with never a thought for the beautiful scenery around him. Convinced that Heidi would hardly even recognise him again he had pictured the disappointment his arrival without the expected friends would cause. But instead, here was Heidi beaming with joy and full of love and gratitude, and still clinging to his arm.

With fatherly tenderness the doctor took the child by the hand. "Take me to your grandfather, Heidi, and show me where you live."

But Heidi did not go on. Her gaze was fixed on the path down the mountain and her little face showed disappointment. "Where are Clara and Grandmamma?" she asked.

"I have something to tell you, Heidi, and I know you will be as sorry about it as I am," replied the doctor. "You see, Heidi, I have come alone. Clara has been very ill and could not travel, so the grandmamma did not come either. But in the spring, when the days begin to get warmer and longer, they will certainly come."

Heidi looked perplexed. It was difficult for her to realise that everything she had looked forward to was not to be. She stood frozen for a moment, overwhelmed by the sudden disappointment. The doctor stood silently before her and there was no sound save the sighing of the wind in the fir trees. Then it occurred to Heidi that after all the doctor had come and she looked up at him. The eyes that looked down into hers were sad. Heidi had never seen him look like this in Frankfurt and her heart was at once full of sorrow for him. No doubt, she decided, it was because Clara and the grandmamma could not come and she tried to think quickly of a way to comfort him.

"Oh, it won't be long until the spring and then they'll be sure to come, won't they?" she asked. "The winter is never very long here, and when they do come, they will be able to stay much longer. Clara will certainly like that! Now let's go up to the grandfather."

Hand in hand with the doctor, she climbed up to the cottage and called out cheerfully to the grandfather. "They haven't come yet, but it won't be long."

The doctor was no stranger to the grandfather, for Heidi had talked about him a great deal. The old man welcomed his guest heartily and then the two men sat down on the bench before the cottage and there was still a little place for Heidi beside the doctor. The doctor started to explain:

"Herr Sesemann wanted me to come and I allowed myself to be persuaded because I have not been well for quite a time and I thought the fresh mountain air would do me good. Heidi," said the doctor, stooping towards her, "there will be something coming up here which has travelled with me all the way from Frankfurt—something which will give you more pleasure than the old doctor."

Heidi was intensely interested to know what it could be but the doctor would not give a hint.

The grandfather encouraged the doctor to spend the beautiful autumn days on the Alm, or at least, to come up every fine day. "I cannot invite you to stay here, as I have no accommodation, but if you would take a room down in Dörfli in the pleasant little inn instead of going back to Ragatz you could come up here in the mornings. There are many places round about which I would take pleasure in showing you."

This proposal delighted the doctor and so it was settled.

Time had passed quickly and it was now noon. The wind had dropped and the fir trees were quiet in the sun. The air was beautifully clean up there, but was nevertheless warm and gentle with its fill of sunlight. The Alm-Uncle rose and went into the cottage and brought back a little table which he placed in front of the bench. "Now, Heidi. Fetch everything we need for the meal," he ordered. "The doctor has to be content with our simple fare but he must admit that the dining-room is very pleasant."

"It is, indeed," agreed the doctor, looking down into the sunlit valley, "I gladly accept your kind invitation. Everything is bound to taste good in such surroundings."

Heidi ran to and fro like a busy little squirrel and brought whatever she could find in the cupboard for she wanted to show her pleasure in being able to entertain the doctor. The grandfather prepared the meal and appeared presently with the steaming milk jug and golden-brown toasted cheese. From the meat which he had cured himself he cut nice thin slices and the doctor ate more heartily than he had done for a whole year.

"Yes, Clara must certainly come here," he said. "It will give her new strength, and if her appetite is as good as mine has been to-day she'll grow plump and strong in no time."

As the doctor spoke, a man appeared coming up the path with a big bundle on his back. Panting, he arrived at the hut and put it down with a sigh of relief. "This is what I have brought with me all the way from Frankfurt," said the doctor, rising. The bundle was opened and when the first wrapping had been taken off he said: "Now, child, you go on and get out the treasure for yourself."

Heidi looked with big, astonished eyes at each item as it was unwrapped, speechless with pleasure. The doctor lifted the lid of one of the boxes. "Look, Heidi. Something the grandmother can have with her coffee!"

Heidi picked up the cake and skipped around with it joyfully: "Oh, a cake for the grandmother!" Heidi wanted to go down at once to the grandmother with the presents, but the grandfather persuaded her to wait until the evening when she could accompany the doctor on his way down and take the presents at the same time.

Now Heidi found the packet of tobacco and handed it to the grandfather who started at once to fill his pipe. The two men went back and sat down on the bench, leaving Heidi to continue her inspection of Clara's parcel alone. After she had admired them all sufficiently, Heidi put away the many presents and came back to where the men were sitting. As soon as there was a gap in the conversation she addressed their guest very solemnly:

"No, the parcel did not give me as much pleasure as your visit, doctor."

The two men could not help laughing at her childish gravity.

As the sun set behind the mountains, the guest rose to take his leave and begin his walk down to Dörfli. The grandfather took the presents under his arm, the box with the cake, the big sausage and the shawl; the doctor took Heidi's hand and so all three walked down to Goat Peter's cottage where Heidi was to wait for her grandfather, who would first accompany their guest into Dörfli. Here Heidi said good night to the doctor and asked: "Would you like to come with the goats to-morrow?"

"Very well, Heidi. We'll go together," he replied. Now the two men walked on down the valley and Heidi ran into the cottage; taking first the cake box, then bringing in the big sausage, and last of all the shawl. She put everything very close to the grandmother so that the old woman would be able to touch the presents; and she laid the shawl on her knees.

"It has all come from Clara and the grandmamma in Frankfurt," she told the astonished Brigitta and the grandmother, Brigitta watching in amazement as one heavy package after another was dragged through the door.

"Aren't you delighted with the cake, Grandmother?" Heidi wanted to know again and again.

"Yes, Heidi. What kind people they must be!" Then she felt the warm, soft shawl and said, "How cosy it will be in the winter-time! I never dreamt I would possess anything so luxurious."

Heidi was surprised that the grandmother was more pleased about the shawl than the cake.

Brigitta was gazing at the sausage with a look in her eyes little short of worship. Never in her life had she seen such an enormous sausage, and she had certainly never owned one. She shook her head and looking puzzled, said, "I still have to ask Uncle what we should do with it."

But Heidi replied straight away, "You must eat it! That's what it's for."

Then Peter came rushing in. "The Alm-Uncle is just behind me, Heidi—" Peter stopped and gasped with astonishment as he caught sight of the sausage. Heidi understood immediately that she must leave, for it was getting late and although the grandfather always stopped by nowadays to greet the old lady, they would have a dark climb to the hut tonight. The grandfather never let Heidi go to bed too late, for she was always up at sunrise, so on this occasion he wished everyone goodnight through the open door, and started back with Heidi straight away, climbing to their peaceful home under a star-filled sky.

CHAPTER 17

A COMPENSATION

Early next morning the doctor climbed up to the Alm with Peter and the goats. The man and the boy walked in silence. In vain the kindly doctor had tried to start up a conversation with the boy but Peter remained obstinately silent and would not be coaxed into chatting about himself. Up at the Alm cottage Heidi waited with her two goats looking as sunny and sparkling as the morning.

"Are you coming?" asked Peter as he did every morning.

"Of course, if the doctor is coming, too," replied Heidi.

Peter cast a suspicious glance at the gentleman.

The Alm-Uncle came out of the hut carrying the lunch bag which he flung across Peter's shoulder. It was heavier than usual, for the uncle had put in something extra for the doctor in case he decided to stay long enough on the pasture to have his lunch with the children. When Peter felt the extra weight a grin spread across his face and the sulky look vanished. His thoughts were busy with the special tit-bits which the uncle might have put in the bag.

Now the trip started. The goats came crowding round Heidi as usual, so that she could hardly move forward, and eventually she stopped and told them to go on ahead properly and behave themselves. Gradually she was able to push them on in front of her, leaving her space to walk with the doctor, who took her by the hand. He had no difficulty this time in making conversation, for Heidi had so much to say about the goats, the mountains, the flowers and the birds, that time passed quickly and they soon found themselves at the pasture. All the way up Peter had cast hostile glances at the doctor, which had fortunately gone unnoticed by Heidi and her companion. Heidi led the doctor to her favourite spot where she liked to sit, and the doctor sat down on the grass beside her, casting a contented glance around him at the wide, green, sunlit valley. The snowfield glittered in the clear autumn sunlight, and the two rocky peaks were sharply silhouetted against the deep blue sky. A gentle breeze blew across the valley, gently ruffling the late summer flowers which still waved amongst the grasses. The eagle flew silently above them. Heidi looked around her with delight. Everything was so perfect. Her eyes sparkled with happiness and she glanced round at her friend to see if he too was enchanted with the beautiful scenery. The doctor had been sitting, silent and thoughtful, but when he met Heidi's eager, inquiring eyes, he said, "Yes, Heidi, it is beautiful, but if one's heart is sad how is it possible to enjoy all this beauty? Can you tell me?"

"Oh!" Heidi exclaimed confidently. "No one is ever sad here. That only happens in Frankfurt."

The doctor smiled quietly, then he asked again, "But if somebody brings all the sadness from Frankfurt up here, Heidi, do you know what to do then?"

"When we don't know what to do we have only to tell God about our troubles," said Heidi seriously.

"Well, my dear, that seems to be a good idea," remarked the doctor, "but what if God Himself has sent the sorrow? What can one say to Him, then?"

Heidi had to think about this. "Then, we must wait," she said, "and just keep thinking, 'soon God will make things right.' We have only to have a little patience and not run away; then something will turn up and we will see quite clearly that all the time it was all for the bet. At the time we only think of the sadness."

"You have a wonderful faith, Heidi, and you must never lose it." The doctor was silent, gazing at the towering mountains above them. Then he said again, "You see, Heidi, when someone has a great grief he cannot enjoy anything lovely, and beauty, like this around us, only makes him more sad. Can you understand that?"

Heidi thought sadly of the old grandmother who would never see again the splendour of the sun and the mountains. Every time she thought about darkness Heidi sorrowed anew for the grandmother, and for a while she said nothing. Then, "Yes, I can understand that." Then she said softly, "That's how it was with the grandmother until I read the hymns for her from the old book. She says they made everything light for her again and made her happy."

"Can you remember any of the hymns, Heidi?" asked the doctor.

"Yes, shall I say one to you?" replied Heidi eagerly.

The doctor nodded, and Heidi folded her hands and started to recite the grandmother's favourite hymn.

Let not your heart be troubled
Nor fear your soul dismay,
There is a wise Defender
And he will be your stay.
Where you have failed, he conquers,
See, how the foeman flies
And all your tribulation
Is turned to glad surprise.

If for awhile it seemeth
His mercy is withdrawn,
That he no longer careth
For his wandering child forlorn,
Doubt not His great compassion,
His love can never tire,
To those who wait in patience
He gives their heart's desire.

She stopped. The doctor did not look as though he were listening. He was sitting quite still, with his hand over his eyes. Heidi thought he had perhaps fallen asleep. But he was wide awake, and thinking about a very long time ago, when he had been a little boy, and his mother had read him the very same hymn. He could see his mother's loving gaze and hear her dear voice, and she seemed to be saying many things to him. It was some while before he stirred, to see Heidi looking at him in a puzzled way.

"That was a beautiful hymn, Heidi," he said. "I would like you to read it to me again net time we come here together."

All this time Peter had been standing apart and growing more and more angry because the old gentleman sat beside Heidi all the time so that Peter had not once had a chance to speak to her. He felt so cross, he stood behind the doctor and shook his fist at him. Peter knew by the sun that it was midday and time for lunch, so he called out at the top of his voice, "Dinnertime!"

Heidi got up to bring the rucksack to where they sat, but the doctor said he was not hungry and only wanted a glass of milk and wanted to climb higher. Heidi did not feel very hungry either and she wanted to take the doctor to the spot where Greenfinch had nearly jumped to her death, so she ran to Peter and asked him to fetch two bowls of milk, one for the doctor and one for herself. Peter looked at her in surprise and asked, "What about all the food in the rucksack?"

"You can have it, Peter," replied Heidi, "but bring the milk first."

Peter had never been so quick in all his life and when he opened the rucksack and saw all the good food he was ashamed of making such faces at the doctor's back. So he ran to where he had stood shaking his fist at the doctor. There he held up his unclenched hands to show that he no longer bore any ill-will, then raced back down to his enormous meal, knowing his conscience was clear.

Heidi and the doctor wandered about together and talked for a long time until the doctor decided it was time for him to go home. Heidi accompanied him down the mountain as far as the Alm-hut. She held his hand all the way and chattered to him about the joys of life on the mountain, where the most beautiful flowers grew and so on. Heidi could name every

Alpine flower growing, for her grandfather had taught her well.

At last the doctor insisted on Heidi's returning to the hut, and then he went on alone, turning now and again to see Heidi still standing on the same spot and waving to him just as his own little daughter might have done.

The month remained beautiful throughout. The doctor came up to the Alm every morning and sometimes went out with the Alm-Uncle whose conversation he enjoyed very much, for the old man knew the ways of all the wild animals and had many interesting stories to tell. He knew all kinds of uses for the plants on the mountainside, from the scented pines, to the curling moss which was found everywhere.

He also had marvellous tales to relate of the animals living in holes, caves and trees all over the mountain.

And so the lovely month of September passed. On the finest days, the doctor would climb the Alm with Heidi, and they would sit together whilst Heidi read hymns and talked of things which she had learnt from her life there.

Peter sat some way away from them, but was more or less resigned to the situation, and no longer flew into tantrums. One morning the doctor did not look quite so happy as usual and told them that this would be his last day and that he would have to return to Frankfurt. "I am very sad to go," he admitted, "for I feel now as if the Alm were my home."

The Alm-Uncle was sorry to hear this news of the doctor's departure for he too had enjoyed his companionship. Heidi could hardly believe that her dear friend had to go and she looked at him beseechingly; but the doctor's smile told her that his visit was at an end. She accompanied him a little of the way until the doctor stopped and said lovingly, stroking her curly hair, "Heidi, I have to go away now. How I would love to take you with me to Frankfurt!"

Heidi recalled Frankfurt, with its many houses and long streets. She remembered Fräulein Rottenmeier and Tinette and replied despondently, "I would rather you came back to us."

"You are right. That will be better," said the doctor. "Good-bye, then, Heidi." His kind eyes looked down on her for an instant and then he turned away quickly and continued his walk down the valley.

Heidi did not move. The sight of tears in the doctor's eyes had upset her and suddenly she started to cry. Then she ran after the doctor as fast as she could, and as soon as she was beside him she sobbed, "I want to come with you! Just let me go back and tell Grandfather!"

The doctor tried to soothe the excited child. "Oh, my dear Heidi," he comforted her, "you must stay here among the fir trees or you may become ill again. But you can promise me this: if I should ever become ill and lonely would you come then and stay with me? If I could know that there would be someone to care for me then."

"Oh, yes, I would come at once. I love you nearly as much as the grandfather."

Once again the doctor said farewell and Heidi stood and waved as long as he remained in sight. As he turned for the last time he whispered to himself, "It is good to live up there. One is restored, body and soul, and knows again what it is to be happy."

Chapter 18

WINTER IN DÖRFLI

Snow lay high around the Alm cottage until the windows appeared to be level with the ground. If the Alm-Uncle had still been living there he would have to have done the same as Peter did every day. When snow had fallen during the night Peter had to jump out of the window, and if there was no frost he sank so deeply into the snow that he had to struggle with both hands and feet to get out again. Then his mother would hand him a shovel and he would scrape a path to the door.

He had to dig the snow well clear of the house, otherwise the pile of snow would fall inside as soon as the door was opened. But if there was severe frost the house was shut in altogether except for the little window through which only Peter was able to creep. But the great advantage of the frost was that once Peter got through the little window he would be on hard, frozen snow. His mother would hand him his little sleigh through the window and Peter would go where he pleased, for the whole Alm was one huge sledging track.

The Alm-Uncle had kept his word. As soon as the first snows began to fall he had shut up the cottage and the shed and had taken Heidi and the goats down to Dörfli to live. Near the church stood a building which had, once upon a time, been a mansion house. A famous soldier had once lived there; he had been cited for bravery whilst fighting in Spain and had returned home much the richer. On his return he used some of his money to build a beautiful house where he intended to live.

But rural life was too quiet for him, and it was not long before he left again, this time never to return. After many years a relative took over the house, being certain that the soldier must have died. It was in such a poor state of repair that he did not wish to incur the expense of rebuilding it, so it was let for a nominal rent to the poor people of the district. Thus, if part of it fell down, it was not replaced. Although it was now half in ruins it still retained something of its former dignity. When the uncle had come to Dörfli with his son, Tobias, he had lived in this neglected house, and since that time it had been empty, for no one could live in it who did not know how to close up all the gaps and holes to keep out the wind which blew out the candle and made draughts all through the dilapidated old house.

But all this the uncle could fix, and when he had decided to spend the winter in Dörfli he had come down many times in the autumn to repair the house. Then, in October, he and Heidi had taken up their abode.

Entering from the back, one came first into a tumbledown building where, on one side, the wall had collapsed completely. Although the other wall was half in ruins the arch of an old window was still visible but thickly overgrown with ivy. The roof was vaulted and this had apparently been the chapel.

Next one entered a large hall where the walls and the ceiling had partly collapsed, and to prevent further ruin, strong pillars had been put in for support. Here the Alm-Uncle had built a partition and had covered the ground with straw, for this was to be the goat-house.

After going through many passages where in places the broken roof revealed patches of sky, one at last entered, through a heavy oak door, a spacious room which was still in good condition. The four strong walls with dark panelling were unbroken, and in one corner a stove reached to the ceiling. On white tiles big blue pictures were painted, representing old castles buried amidst high trees, huntsmen with their dogs or quiet lakes bordered by shady trees with a fisherman in the foreground. A bench was built all round the stove and here one could sit and study the pictures.

This attracted Heidi at once, and as soon as they entered the room she ran to the stove, sat down on the bench and began to look at the pictures. But as she slid along and round towards the back of the stove she found something else to attract her attention. Between stove and wall four boards had been put up. It might have been a place for storing apples but there were no apples there now and it was, quite obviously, going to be Heidi's bed just like the one on the Alm; a high straw bed with a sheet on it and the sack as a cover. Heidi was overjoyed. "Oh, Grandfather! This is going to be my room. How nice! But where are you going to sleep?"

"Your room has to be near the stove to keep you warm," declared the grandfather. "But you shall see mine, too."

Heidi ran through the huge room behind the grandfather who opened a door on the other side. This led into a small room where the old man had made up his bed. Then there was another door, and Heidi stood amazed when she looked into the spacious kitchen. In this room there were many signs of the grandfather's activity but there still remained a great deal of work to be done to fill up all the holes and crannies through which the wind still whistled. He had already made the old door strong, with the judicious use of screws and nails, and it served well as protection against the elements and the numerous insects which lived in the weeds surrounding the building.

Heidi was delighted with their new home, and the next day when Peter came she showed him all over the house, for she had already explored every corner. She insisted that he inspect each and every thing to be found in it, before he went.

Heidi slept comfortably and well in her warm corner, but every time she woke she thought immediately of the mountain and had to restrain herself from the impulse to rush outside and see why the trees were so quiet. She had to remind herself of her surroundings, and occasionally felt uneasy when she realised that she was not in her real home. But then the comforting sound of her grandfather's voice, and the bleating of the goats would reassure her, and once again Heidi was happy, and would leap out of bed and run to join the animals as quickly as she could.

Four days after they had settled down Heidi announced to the grandfather one morning that she must go and visit the grandmother. "I can't leave her alone any longer," she said. But the grandfather would not agree.

"Not to-day or to-morrow," he said. "The Alm is covered fathom-deep in snow, and it is still falling; Peter can hardly get through. A little one like you would soon be buried and no one would be able to find you. Wait a little until it freezes and then you can walk up quite comfortably."

At first Heidi was impatient at the thought of having to wait, but the days were busy and passed quickly. Every morning and afternoon she went to school and learned eagerly. She hardly ever saw Peter there for he seldom turned up. The teacher was a kind man and would remark tolerantly, "Peter absent to-day again! Ah, well, the snow is lying high, he won't be able to get through."

But in the evening, when school was finished, Peter always seemed able to come down to see Heidi no matter how deep the snow! After a few days the sun came out again and shone strongly on the wintry landscape, but the days were short and at night the moon would take up the vigil, clear and huge and sparkling, so that the whole mountain glittered.

One morning, when Peter, as usual sprang from the window into the snow he found that it had hardened with the strong frost of the previous night. The hard ice came as a surprise to him and he could not stop himself sliding off down the Alm which was frozen over as hard as iron. This delighted Peter because he knew that Heidi would be able to come up now to the cottage. Quickly he rushed back to the house and hurriedly swallowing his breakfast he announced, "I must be off to school!"

"Yes, go and learn as much as you can," said his mother.

Peter climbed through the little window, got on to his sledge and went shooting rapidly down the mountain. He went so fast that when he reached Dörfli he was quite unable to stop and the sledge skimmed along until it reached level ground when it stopped of its own accord. Peter got up and looked about. The headlong drive had taken him some way beyond Mayenfeld. It would take him an hour to climb up again and that would be much too late for school, thought Peter, so he might as well take his time. He arrived back in Dörfli just as Heidi and the grandfather were sitting down to dinner. Peter entered and as he had something special to tell them to-day he began right away.

"It's done it!" he fairly shouted.

"Eh! What has?" asked the old man. "You sound quite warlike to-day, General."

"The snow—frozen!" announced Peter.

"Oh, now I can go to the grandmother!" rejoiced Heidi, who was quick to understand Peter's odd way of expressing himself. "But why didn't you come to school? You could easily have come on the sledge," she added reproachfully, for she felt that it was not the thing to do to stay away if it were possible to attend.

"Took me too far down," said Peter. "So it was too late."

"Now that's what I'd call desertion," said the uncle, "and people who do that get their ears pulled; do you hear?"

Peter fidgeted uncomfortably, for there was no one whom he feared and respected more than the Alm-Uncle.

"And a leader like you should be doubly ashamed of himself," continued the uncle. "What would you do if your goats ran anywhere they liked?"

"Beat them," Peter replied smartly.

"And if a boy behaved like that and got a good beating, what would you say then?"

"Serves him right," was the answer.

"Very well, then, if it should happen again that your sledge passes the school when you should be inside, come to me and get what you deserve!"

At last the meaning of the uncle's little speech was beginning to dawn on Peter. He looked quite thunderstruck and retreated into a corner looking round in a frightened way in case there should be a stick in sight similar to the one he sometimes used on the goats. But the uncle said cheerfully, "Come now and eat with us and then Heidi can go up with you. In the evening you can bring her home again and have your supper here."

This unexpected turn to the conversation cheered Peter immensely. He obeyed at once and sat beside Heidi, who could hardly eat for excitement about going to the grandmother's. She pushed aside her plate of potatoes and toasted cheese, and offered it to Peter, together with the helping which the Uncle was already giving him. He was not put off, however, by the enormous amount of food on his P!ate, and started eating heartily straight away.

Heidi ran to the cupboard and brought out the little warm coat with the hood which Clara had given her. Putting it on she stood waiting beside Peter and as soon as he had swallowed his last bite she said, "Come along now!" On the way, Heidi told Peter how unhappy the two goats had been at first in their new surroundings, and how they would not eat nor make any sound. She had asked her grandfather why this was so, and he told her that they were feeling as she had.

When they arrived at the cottage, Peter's mother was alone in the room. She told them that the grandmother was not very well and had had to stay in bed because it was so cold. Heidi had always been accustomed to seeing the grandmother in her place in the corner. She ran to the other room and there lay the old woman in her narrow bed with only a thin coverlet over her, but wrapped in the warm grey shawl . . . .

"Thank God!" exclaimed the old woman when she heard Heidi running in, for she had had a secret fear that the gentleman from Frankfurt, with whom Heidi had been seen out walking on the Alm, would take the child away.

"Are you very ill, Grandmother?" asked Heidi with concern.

"No, no, child!" said the old woman and patted Heidi lovingly. "It is only the frost getting into my bones a little."

"Will you be better as soon as it is warm again?' Heidi persisted.

"Yes, yes, and with God's help before that so that I can get back to my spinning," said the grandmother, noticing how worried the child was.

This cheered Heidi a little, for she had never seen the grandmother ill in bed before, and was greatly upset. "Grandmother, in Frankfurt people put on a shawl when they go for a walk. Did you think it was for going to bed?" she said thoughtfully.

"I have put the shawl on in bed to keep warm, Heidi. You see the cover is rather thin."

"But, Grandmother," Heidi started again, "your pillow goes downhill instead of uphill!"

"Yes, I know, child." The grandmother tried to find a more comfortable place on the thin pillow which looked as hard as a board. "You see, the pillow has never been particularly soft and now I have slept on it for so many years that it has become quite flat."

"If only I had asked Clara if I could take my bed home! I had three big, thick pillows and they were so high I could hardly sleep for my head slipping off them. Could you have slept on them, Grandmother?"

"I am sure I could. One keeps warmer that way and breathes more easily when the head is high. However, don't let's speak about it. I have so much for which to thank God. The nice rolls

I get, and the lovely warm shawl, and you coming to see me, Heidi. Would you care to read some of my favourite hymns to me to-day?"

Heidi got down the old hymn book and chose the most beautiful verses for they were all familiar to her now and she was as pleased as the old lady to hear them again. As the grandmother listened, a joyous smile lightened her face which had looked so worn and tired before.

Heidi stopped. "Grandmother, are you feeling better already? she asked.

"Yes, child, I am much better already. Please read to the end." Heidi read the last lines:—

"As the eyes grow dim, and darkness
Closes round, the soul grows clearer,
Sees the goal to which it travels,
Gladly feels its home is nearer."

As she read them, the grandmother repeated the words softly to herself, with a serene expression on her face. Heidi remembered the beautiful day of her return home and her face lit up with joy.

"Grandmother, I know just what it means to be going home."

The grandmother made no reply but the happy expression stayed on her face.

After a while the child said: "I must go home now, Grandmother. It is getting late. I am so glad you are feeling better." The grandmother held Heidi's hand.

"I feel at peace again, even if I have to stay here. It is dreadful to have to lie alone for days on end, without light or sound. It makes me sad and I sometimes feel that it is too much for me to stand. But to hear you read the hymns to me gives me comfort and peace in my heart once more."

Heidi said good-bye to the grandmother and she and Peter set off quickly, for the darkness was already coming down. As Peter got out his sledge the moon came through and shone brightly on the white snow so that it seemed as if the day were about to break. Peter sat in front, and off they shot down the Alm like two birds.

That night, as Heidi lay in her warm bed behind the stove, she thought about the grandmother and how she would like to visit her every day, for if she could read to her more often, perhaps the peace and light which came to her would help make her better. But Heidi knew one or two weeks might pass before she was allowed to go up again. She thought and thought about how things could be arranged. Suddenly she had an idea and she could hardly wait for daylight to carry out her plan. She suddenly sat upright in bed, for she had been so busy thinking about her plan that in her excitement she had forgotten to say her prayers.

When she had prayed from the bottom of her heart for the grandfather and the grandmother and all the people she knew, she lay down on the soft hay and slept soundly and peacefully until the morning.

Chapter 19

WINTER CONTINUES

Next morning, Peter turned up at school in good time. He had brought his lunch with him, as did all the children who lived any distance from the school. They all sat at tables at mid-day and with their lunches on their knees and their feet upon the benches, ate heartily, whilst the other children went home to Dörfli.

They were free to do whatever they liked until one o'clock, when school recommenced. As was his usual habit when he happened to be at school, Peter paid a visit afterwards to the uncle. To-day, immediately he entered the house, Heidi rushed to him."Peter, I have thought of something!" she exclaimed.

"What is it?" he asked.

"You must learn to read now," was her reply.

"I know how to read—a little."

"Yes, yes, Peter, but I mean so well that you can read easily and quickly."

"I'll never be able to do that," remarked Peter gloomily.

"I don't believe that, and neither would anybody else," said Heidi with determination. "Grandmamma told me some time ago that I was not to believe you. I shall teach you. I know quite well how to do it. You must learn now, and then you will be able to read one or two hymns to Grandmother every day."

"Oh, I don't care about *that*!" Peter grumbled.

This obstinacy towards something which she considered was kind and right annoyed Heidi. With flashing eyes she stood before the boy and said threateningly, "Then I will tell you what will happen if you refuse to learn. Your mother has said already that she will send you to Frankfurt to be taught, and I have seen the building where the boys go to school. Clara showed it to me. But they don't go there just when they are boys, but always, even when they are grown up. And don't think there is only one teacher as in our school."

A cold shudder ran down Peter's back.

"And you will have to go there among all the teachers and pupils," Heidi continued, "and if you cannot even read, and make mistakes with your spelling, you'll see how much they will laugh at you; much worse than Tinette, and if you only knew what she was like!"

"All right, then. I will," said Peter reluctantly.

Heidi was mollified at once. "That's right. We can start today," she decided joyfully. She dragged Peter to the table and brought out the necessary books. In Clara's big parcel there had been a book which Heidi thought was just right for teaching Peter, for it was an A B C book with verses.

They both bent over the book and the lesson began. Peter had to spell out the first verse again and again for Heidi wanted him to be able to read it correctly and fluently. At last she said, "You still don't know the verse so I shall read it to you. If you know the meaning it will be easier for you to spell it." And Heidi read:

"Learn A B C without a grudge
Or you'll be brought before the judge."

"I won't," said Peter obstinately.

"What?" asked Heidi.

"Go before the judge," was the answer.

"Hurry up then and learn these three letters and you won't need to."

Peter started again and repeated the three letters until Heidi said, "Now you can read these three! And read them carefully!"

As she noticed the effect this verse had had upon Peter she thought it would be a good idea to prepare him a little for the following lessons.

"Wait! I'll read the other verses to you now," she continued, "and you'll see what else can happen."

And she began to read very slowly and clearly:

"D E F G must smoothly flow
Or you will get a nasty blow.

If you forget H I J K
The fatal blow will fall to-day.

To learn L M is not a strain
And will prevent a lot of pain.

Remember well N O P Q
Or you'll get what's in store for you.

R S T may save a smack
If you will make a quick attack."

Here Heidi stopped because Peter was so quiet. All these secret hints and threats had petrified him with fright and he stared anxiously at Heidi. Her kind heart was touched at once and she said reassuringly, "You don't need to be afraid, Peter. If you come every evening and learn as well as you have done to-day you will soon know the letters and nothing will happen to you. But you must come *every* day and not just sometimes as you did with school—even if it snows. The snow doesn't trouble you anyway."

Peter promised. Fear of punishment had made him quite docile. Then he set off home.

He followed Heidi's advice and arrived promptly every evening. The letters were studied with zeal and the verses taken to heart. Often the grandfather listened to the lessons while he contentedly smoked his pipe. Every now and then his face would twitch with amusement. Peter was usually asked to stay to supper with them which was a great compensation to him for the anxiety which the verses caused.

So the winter passed. Peter appeared regularly and made good progress. He had now got as far as U and Heidi read:

"Who still mistakes the U for V
May go where he won't like to be."

This gave Peter an uncomfortable feeling but made him learn all the quicker lest the threat were carried out. The following evening the verse was:

"If W is still unknown
The stick may come into its own."

Peter remarked sneeringly, "There isn't one."

But Heidi reminded him that the grandfather had a very big stick in his cupboard, at least as thick as Peter's arm and this made him bend over his W in a feverish effort to memorise it. Next was:

"X is a cross you may recall
And this is easiest of them all."

And Heidi quickly prompted him to learn another letter as well so that only the last one remained for the following day. Although Peter tried to object, Heidi read out:

"To stop at Y will never do
And all the world will laugh at you."

Peter at once attacked the Y with energy, imagining the gentlemen of Frankfurt in their tall black hats, jeering at him and scorning his inadequacy. He did not give up until he could close his eyes and still remember what it looked like.

Peter arrived the next day feeling very jaunty because there was only one more letter to be learnt and when Heidi read the verse:

"Who still forgets the Z you know
Straight to the Hottentots will go,"

he said sarcastically, "Who knows where they live?"

"Grandfather does. Wait! I shall ask him at once. He is only across the road with the pastor."

Heidi was about to run to the door when Peter exclaimed in alarm, "Wait a moment!" In his imagination he saw both the pastor and the uncle carrying him off and sending him away to the Hottentots—because he really had forgotten completely what Z was like.

"What is the matter?" Heidi asked in surprise.

"Nothing! Come back! I shall learn now," muttered Peter.

Heidi, though, wanted to know just where the Hottentots were to be found, and persisted in her suggestion that she should ask the grandfather, but Peter seemed so desperately anxious that she should not, that she eventually changed her mind. Instead, she made him repeat the letter until it was engraved on his brain, and in addition she began to teach him spelling, at which Peter made a very good start indeed. And from day to day Peter made progress with his reading.

The ice had thawed and new snow had fallen every day so that about three weeks had passed since Heidi's visit to the grandmother. This made her work all the harder with Peter so that he would be able to take her place and read to the old woman.

One evening Peter went home and announced, "I can do it now!"

"What can you do, Peter?" asked his mother.

"Read," he answered.

"Did you hear that, Grandmother?" Brigitta exclaimed.

Grandmother did hear and was wondering how this had come about.

"I have to read a hymn now. Heidi said so."

Brigitta quickly fetched the book and the grandmother smiled in anticipation of hearing the comforting words once more. Peter sat down ant began to read and his mother sat beside him, listening, and saying after each verse, in a voice full of astonishment and admiration, "Who would have thought it!"

The grandmother, too, followed the verses with the greatest attention but she did not say anything.

The following day at school when it was Peter's turn to read, the teacher said, "Well, Peter, must we pass you again or would you like to try?"

Without hesitation, Peter read three lines. The teacher laid down his book and stared at Peter as if he had never see him before. Then he said, "Peter, this is a miracle! With all the patience in the world I did not succeed in teaching you even your letters and here you are reading beautifully. How did this come about?"

"It was Heidi," Peter answered.

In surprise the teacher turned towards Heidi who sat on her bench looking as though nothing out of the ordinary had happened.

The teacher continued, "I have noticed a change in you altogether. You have been attending school very regularly lately. What can have brought about this change for the better?"

"The uncle," came the reply.

With ever-growing astonishment the teacher looked at Heidi, then back again at Peter.

As soon as school was over, the teacher hastened to tell the pastor what had happened and what a good influence the uncle and Heidi had been.

Every night now Peter read a hymn in obedience to Heidi's instructions, but he refused to read a second one and indeed the grandmother never encouraged him to do so.

Brigitta was always delighted that her Peter had achieved so much but the grandmother said, "Yes, it is good that he has learnt so well but still I shall be glad when it is spring and Heidi can come up again. When Peter reads there always seem to be some words missing in the hymn so that I don't understand them so well as when Heidi reads them."

The reason was, of course, that Peter was rather lazy about reading for the grandmother and if a word was too difficult or too long, he just skipped over it thinking it would not matter very much to the grandmother, seeing there were so many words! Thus it was that most of the important words in the hymns were missing altogether when Peter read them.

Chapter 20

NEWS FROM CLARA

May had come again and from the heights the streamlets rippled eagerly down into the valley. The last snow had melted and the golden sun had dried up the last traces of winter. The spring breeze was rustling the tops of the old fir trees and last year's dark green pine needles were being replaced by bright, shiny light green ones. The great eagle flew high above, lazily circling in the blue air, and the warmth of the sunshine seeped into the ground beneath, and warmed the ancient timbers of the grandfather's hut. Heidi was happy to be on the Alm again and jumped about for joy, and it seemed to her that the little wild creatures which started about were as happy as she and all were humming and singing, "On the Alm! On the Alm!" At one moment she would stand listening to the strange sounds of the wind blowing down from the mountain tops and bending the fir trees until they strained with its force. Then she would rush round to the front of the hut, and sitting on the ground in the sunshine she would watch the tiny flowers gradually opening in the warmth of the sun. Joyfully, she followed the antics of all the thousands of little insects going about their lives in the glorious spring weather, All the, while, she could not stop thinking how beautiful the mountain looked.

Familiar sounds came from the carpenter's shed. Heidi knew what the sounds meant, for they had been familiar to her ever since her first arrival on the Alm. The grandfather was busy finishing a beautiful new chair and another one, already finished, stood outside.

"Oh, I know what these are for!" cried Heidi. "We will need them when they come from Frankfurt. This one is for Grandmamma and the one you are making now is for Clara. Will there be another one, Grandfather?" she asked hesitantly. "Perhaps Fräulein Rottenmeier is coming too."

"Well, I am not sure at the moment," replied the grandfather, "but it is best to make an extra one just in case she does come."

Heidi gazed at the simple wooden chair, and couldn't imagine Fräulein Rottenmeier actually sitting down on it. After a few moments' contemplation she said doubtfully, "Grandfather, I really don't think that Fräulein Rottenmeier would be suitable for that chair."

"In that case she can enjoy the comfortable bed with the mattress of green grass," was the grandfather's reply.

Suddenly there was a great whistling and shouting and Heidi knew immediately it was Peter. She rushed outside and immediately found herself crowded on all sides by her animal friends. They too were delighted to be on the mountain once more, for they were frolicking and bleating with joy, nudging and pushing Heidi in their anxiety to show her how pleased they were to see her. A harsh command from Peter sent them scattering, however, for he had something to deliver to Heidi. There he stood brandishing a letter. It was addressed to Heidi.

"How did you get this?" she asked in surprise.

"I found it inside my dinner bag," replied Peter. This was only partly true. The letter had been handed to him the previous evening by the postman at Dörfli, and Peter had put it at the bottom of his bag. This fine morning he had filled the bag with his bread and cheese and had completely forgotten about the letter when he collected the grandfather's two goats. He only remembered it when he had finished his lunch and was checking for any additional food which might have been missed. Carefully Heidi read the address, then ran towards the grandfather, holding out her letter. "From Frankfurt! From Clara! Do you want to hear it?"

Of course, both he and Peter wanted to hear it, so Heidi began to read:

"DEAR HEIDI,

Everything is packed and ready and in two or three days we shall be on our way. Papa will not be coming with us as he has to go to Paris first. The doctor comes to see me every day and as he comes into the room he always calls, 'Off you go now! Off to the Alm as quickly as you can!' He says everybody must become healthy and happy there. He, too, is his own self again after being with you. He has come almost every day during the winter, and has spent long hours telling me everything about life up there. He tells me of all he did with you two, and talks of the flowers and the light and the peacefulness of the mountains, high above the noise of the towns and villages. And he takes a deep breath, as though he were breathing your pure mountain air, and says that no-one can fail to get better up there. He is altogether changed since he saw you, and looks much younger and happier. Oh, how I am looking forward to seeing everything, to being with you and also to getting to know Peter and the goats! I have to go to Ragatz first, for six weeks, as the doctor has ordered. Then we will go to Dörfli, and every day, if the weather is good, I shall be carried up to see you. Grandmamma is coming with me and is looking forward greatly to seeing you. But what about this: Fräulein Rottenmeier has adamantly refused to join us. Grandmamma often asks her if she would not like to accompany us, but she always refuses, very politely of course. Apparently Sebastian gave her a fright by emphasising the dangers of the mountains and the precipices, and she quite lost interest in the idea of a journey. Tinette is just as frightened, so Sebastian will come with us as far as Ragatz, and we will finish the journey alone. I can hardly bear to wait. Good-bye, Heidi! Grandmamma sends her love,

Your affectionate friend,

CLARA."

Peter was not at all thrilled with the news of the arrival of the guests from Frankfurt. It made him very cross indeed and he ran outside, waving his stick in the air so wildly that he frightened the goats, and they scrambled down the mountain ahead of him. Peter tore after them, brandishing his stick as though he would strike someone.

He was furious at the thought of the prospective visitors, who would again take Heidi's company away from him. Heidi was overflowing with happiness. As soon as possible she called at the grandmother's to tell her the good news. She knew the grandmother would be interested in all she had to tell, for Heidi had talked to her of all the people who were to arrive, and she had sympathised with the troubles which had beset her life at Frankfurt. Heidi called on her in the afternoon, while the sun was high in the sky, and she raced down the mountain, with the breeze blowing her along. The grandmother was sitting spinning once more in her usual corner. She was no longer confined to bed, but although she was so much better her face wore an expression of sadness. Peter had told her the news about the people who were coming from Frankfurt and the grandmother had her own ideas of what might come to pass. She could not help dreading that they might take Heidi away again. Heidi rushed in, and sitting on her little stool began a stream of excited chatter about the events which were about to happen.

As she was in the midst of telling the grandmother the great news, she had to stop suddenly and ask with concern, "What is the matter, Grandmother? Aren't you happy about all this?"

"Yes, yes, I am glad for you, Heidi," said the old woman, trying to put on a more cheerful expression. "Is it that you think Fräulein Rottenmeier may come after all?" asked Heidi nervously.

"No, Heidi, don't worry," said the old lady. "Hold my hand, and I'll know that you're here with me. Perhaps it would be a good thing if you went, although I doubt if I could bear the parting."

"Grandmother, nothing would give me pleasure if you could not bear it," said Heidi, and her voice was so positive that the grandmother thought that perhaps even if the Frankfurt people did want to take Heidi, she might refuse to go. But, oh dear, that too would be all wrong. She was anxious to hide her fears and suggested, "I know something, Heidi, that would calm my thoughts. Read the hymn for me which begins: 'All things will work for good.'"

Heidi quickly found the hymn and read:—

> All things will work for good
> To those who trust in Me;
> I come with healing in my wings
> To save and set thee free.

When she had finished reading the grandmother said, "Yes, that is right! If one trusts in God one knows that whatever happens is for our good. Read it once more so that we won't forget." Heidi repeated the verse, reassuring herself as well as her grandmother.

Heidi returned home as evening descended, and rejoiced to see the stars glittering overhead. Eventually, entranced by the vast sparkling sky she said to herself, "I understand now why we should be happy and go bravely on our way; it is because God knows what is best for us, and what will bring us most happiness." The stars twinkled back at her all the way home, where she found her grandfather also star-gazing, overwhelmed by the beauty of the night sky.

The month of May had seldom before been so beautiful and sunny.

The sky was clear blue day after day and the grandfather exclaimed repeatedly, "This is indeed a good year. The sun will make the plants grow strong and nourishing. Take care, Peter, that your flock doesn't get out of hand from overfeeding!"

Peter's answer could be clearly read in his face.

"I can manage them!"

May had passed and June arrived, bringing hot, long days filled with the scent of the flowers carpeting the mountainside. The month was drawing to its close when one morning Heidi ran out of the hut. She had intended to visit the fir trees and then climb up to see if the rock roses were in bloom. Just as she turned the corner she gave a loud cry which brought the uncle hurrying to see what had happened.

"Grandfather! Grandfather!" the child called excitedly, "Come over here! Come and look!"

He came, and his eyes followed the direction of her outstretched arm. A strange procession could be seen coming up the mountain path. In front came two men carrying a sedan chair in which a young girl sat, wrapped in many shawls. A horse followed, mounted by a stately lady who looked about her with keen interest. Another man pushed an empty wheelchair, for it was easier and safer to carry the invalid up the mountain in the sedan.

"Here they are! Here they are!" cried Heidi joyfully.

When the eagerly expected guests reached the Alm, Heidi sprang forward and the two children embraced each other lovingly. Grandmamma, too, was welcomed with the greatest affection. Then Grandmamma turned to the Alm-Uncle who came forward to bid them welcome. They all felt like old friends, as they had heard so much about each other.

Grandmamma was delighted with the beautiful situation. "What a marvellous place to live, Uncle. I would never have believed it could be so very beautiful. You would be envied by the richest of men. And how well my little Heidi is looking!" she remarked, patting the child's rosy cheeks. "What do *you* think, Clara? Isn't it delightful here?"

Clara was entranced. Never in her life before had she seen or imagined anything so beautiful. "Oh, how lovely it is! How I wish I could always live here with Heidi, Grandmamma!"

Meantime the uncle had pushed the invalid chair nearer and now he suggested, "Wouldn't it be better to put the little daughter into her accustomed seat?" And without waiting for assistance he lifted Clara in his strong arms and very gently placed her in her own comfortable chair, putting some of the wraps over her knees and doing it all as expertly as if he had looked after invalids all his life. Grandmamma was greatly impressed by his care and attention.

"If I knew where you had come by your skill, I would pack every nurse I know off to learn to handle their patients as gently as you. How on earth do you know what should be done?"

Alm-Uncle smiled sadly and said, "I know from my own experience." He saw again a painful scene of many years before, of a crippled man lying helpless and unable to move. It was his captain, who had been mortally wounded during some fierce fighting in Sicily. The Uncle had carried him from the battlefield and nursed him until his death.

Thus it had seemed easy and natural to him to adopt the role of nurse once again. Clara could not find words to express her delight in everything around her. "Oh, Heidi," she said, "if only I could go about and see all the things you have described to me!"

With a great effort Heidi succeeded in wheeling the chair on to the grass so that Clara could see the magnificent old fir trees which had gazed down undisturbed for so many years on the valley below. The sky extended a clear blue for as far as the eye could see, and Clara was fascinated. She had never seen such trees before. The grandmamma had followed them and was equally amazed at the appearance of strength of the magnificent great firs, which had seen so much change beneath their spreading branches. Heidi wheeled Clara to the goat-house next, and opened the door so that Clara could see inside.

"If only I could wait till Peter comes with the goats!" Clara said regretfully. "How I should love to see Little Swan and Little Bear! If we must always leave as early as you say, Grandmamma, we shall never see them!"

"My dear child, let us enjoy the things we can and not think of those we may miss."

"Oh, how pretty the flowers are! If only I could get up and pick some!"

Heidi ran and gathered a big bunch. "But that is nothing, Clara," she said. "If you come with us up to the pasture you will see ever so many. There are flowers of every colour you can think of, and they smell so lovely. There are so many there is hardly room to move amongst them. They are as thick as a carpet and if you sit down amongst them you never want to get up again."

Heidi's eyes sparkled with longing to be able to show it all to her friend, and Clara's soft blue eyes reflected Heidi's enthusiasm.

"Oh, Grandmamma! Do you think I shall ever be allowed to go up as high as that?" she asked. "If only I could go with you, Heidi! I should like to climb all over the Alm."

"I shall push your chair," said Heidi stoutly, and to show how easy it was she made a rush at the chair which nearly sent it rolling down the slope. But the grandfather was near at hand and stopped it in time.

Grandfather had been busy preparing the meal and he had brought the table and the chairs outside beside the bench. Soon the meal was ready and the whole company sat down merrily. Grandmamma was delighted with this dining-room under the blue sky where she could sit and enjoy the magnificent view far down into the valley. "Can I believe my eyes?" she exclaimed when she saw Clara taking a second helping of toasted cheese which she was eating with a great appetite.

"Yes, Grandmamma. It tastes so good. Better than the whole menu at Ragatz," Clara assured her.

"That's right. Eat all you can," encouraged the uncle. "Our mountain air makes up for the deficiency of the kitchen."

Grandmamma and the uncle chatted together as though they had known each other for years. They had much in common, and the time passed quickly in lively conversation. But suddenly Grandmamma remembered, "We will have to go presently, Clara. The sun will be going down soon and the men with the chair will be here."

"Just let's stay another hour, Grandmamma," pleaded Clara.

"We haven't seen inside the cottage yet and we must see Heidi's bed."

Grandmamma wanted to see inside the cottage, too, and the uncle invited them to go in. Clara's chair, however, was too broad to pass through the door, but without hesitation, the uncle lifted Clara out of the chair and carried her inside.

Grandmamma looked around with interest and was very much impressed by the tidiness and cosy atmosphere of the house. "Is your bed up there, Heidi" she asked and started to climb up to the loft. "Oh, what a lovely scent! This should be a healthy bedroom," she exclaimed.

Grandfather followed, carrying Clara, and Heidi came after. They all stood around Heidi's bed. "Heidi, how jolly!" exclaimed Clara. "From your bed you can look straight up into the sky! And you will always have the lovely smell of the hay and will be able to listen to the fir trees rustling! It is quite the loveliest bedroom I have ever seen."

The uncle looked at Grandmamma. "I have an idea," he said. "I think if we could agree to have your little grand-daughter staying here with us for a while, she would be bound to get strong and well. With all the rugs you have brought we could make a fine soft bed and I myself would look after her."

Clara and Heidi were as happy as two birds let out of their cage at this suggestion and the Grandmamma's face beamed. "My dear Uncle, you are kindness itself," she said. "I have just been thinking how good a holiday so high up in the mountains would be for the child. But the nursing, the trouble and the inconvenience for you! And you make the offer as if it were nothing at all. I thank you from the bottom of my heart." The old lady took his hand and the uncle nodded happily. He carried Clara back to her chair outside, with Heidi skipping along after them. Then he picked up a huge pile of shawls and furs which had been carried up the mountain for Clara and said, "What a good thing Grandmamma brought all these with her; they will be most useful."

He at once started to get Clara's bed ready and he and the Grandmamma spread the rugs over it. When they had finished, the bed was so smooth and thick, not a single bit of hay could penetrate. Satisfied, Grandmamma climbed down the ladder and joined the children who were already discussing how they would spend their time. But, how long would Clara be allowed to stay, was the great question. Grandmamma replied, "Grandfather knows best. You must ask him."

The grandfather thought four weeks would be just right to decide if the mountain air was agreeing with the child. The prospect of being together for so long surpassed the children's expectations and they both shouted for joy.

The chair-bearers appeared at the cottage but they were immediately sent down the mountain again.

"It is not farewell, Grandmamma," said Clara as they parted. "You will come and visit us here on the Alm and see what we are doing and how we are getting on, won't you?"

Heidi could only express her happiness with a high jump.

Grandmamma mounted her horse and the Alm-Uncle set off to lead her down the mountain path. She tried to persuade him to go back, but he insisted on seeing her safely to Dörfli for it was a rocky and dangerous path for those who did not know it well.

She decided to return to Ragatz rather than stay alone in Dörfli. From there she could equally well pay occasional visits to the Alm.

Peter and the goats arrived while the Uncle was escorting Grandmamma, and as soon as they saw Heidi the animals rushed towards her. She and Clara were soon in the midst of a pushing, nudging, bleating crowd. Clara made acquaintance with each and every one as Heidi introduced them, including little Snowflake, and Goldfinch, about whom she had heard so much.

Peter, meanwhile, stood sullenly to one side, not looking at all pleased at the attention being given Clara.

The two girls greeted him in a friendly way, but he turned on his heel, and waving his stick in the air, rushed off, with the goats following him.

The day closed for Clara with the most overwhelming experience of all. She lay in the big soft bed in the loft with

Heidi near, and looked through the round open window right into the middle of the starlit sky. "Oh, Heidi!" she exclaimed. "It seems as if we were riding through the sky!"

"Do you know why the stars twinkle so happily?" asked Heidi.

"No, why do you think?"

"Because they see how well God has arranged everything for men so that nobody needs to be afraid and can be quite sure that everything will turn out for the best. But we must not forget to pray, Clara, and to ask God to remember us."

The children sat up and said their prayers together; then Heidi put her head on her arm and fell asleep at once. But Clara lay awake a long time. She had never been able to see the stars at home because she had never been outside the house at night, and inside, the heavy curtains were always drawn long before the stars came out. So she could not gaze long enough at the sparkling heavens and lay looking out of the little round window until at last her eyes closed of their own accord and she saw the stars in her dreams.

CHAPTER 21

LIFE ON THE ALM

The Alm-Uncle had been standing outside the hut as was his habit, watching the early mists rising and the new day awakening. The morning clouds grew brighter and brighter until the sun appeared in its full glory and flooded the rocks, woods and mountains with golden light.

The uncle went back into the hut and quietly climbed up the little ladder. Clara had just opened her eyes and did not know at first where she was. Then she saw the sleeping Heidi beside her and heard the kindly voice of the grandfather whispering, "Did you sleep well?"

Clara assured him that she had slept soundly all night. The grandfather was pleased and straight away began to attend to her so gently and sympathetically that one would think that he had been looking after sick children all his life. Now Heidi was awake and watched the grandfather carry Clara downstairs. Quickly she got up and dressed and ran down the ladder after them and out into the open air.

There a surprise awaited her, for the grandfather had not been idle after the children had retired for the night. He had noticed that it was impossible for Clara's chair to be carried through the hut door. So he loosened two boards at one side, which would allow for the chair to go through whenever required. Clara was just being wheeled into the sunshine. There he left her while he went to attend to the goats, and Heidi joined her friend.

The soft morning breeze touched their faces, and Clara could smell the fresh scent of the fir trees. She took a deep breath of pleasure and noticed how well and comfortable she felt.

She had never before been out in the country so early in the day, and it was sheer delight for her to breathe the clear mountain air and feel the warm sun caressing her face and hands. It was better than Clara had ever imagined it could be.

"Oh, Heidi, if only I could stay in the mountains with you always!" she exclaimed.

"Do you understand now why I said that the best place in the world is on the Alm with Grandfather?"

Just at that moment the grandfather appeared with two bowls of foaming milk. "This will give you strength," he said to Clara. "It is from Little Swan, and will help you regain your health."

Clara had never tasted goats' milk before and she smelt it first. But when she saw Heidi drinking hers to the last drop, she did the same. It tasted sweet and strong, as though it contained sugar and cinnamon. Soon her bowl was empty, too.

"To-morrow we may be able to take two," the grandfather suggested, observing with satisfaction how Clara had followed Heidi's example.

Soon Peter arrived with his flock and the uncle took him

aside to tell him to be sure to take Little Swan high up where she would get the best grass. "She knows where the best food is, and if it should mean going a little higher, never mind. Follow her; a bit of extra climbing won't do you any harm. I want the best possible milk from her and you can ensure that she eats well. Why are you staring over there as though you wanted to eat somebody?" the grandfather exclaimed in the midst of his instructions. "Now be off! And remember what I have said!"

Peter marched off at once, but it was obvious that there was something going on in his mind. When Heidi appeared amongst the goats he said to her threateningly, "You had better come with me because Little Swan has to get special attention and someone will have to stay with the others."

"No, I can't," replied Heidi. "I can't come so long as Clara is with me. But Grandfather has promised that some time we shall come together."

As she said this she ran back to Clara and Peter made threatening gestures towards the invalid chair. Then he quickly climbed up until he was out of sight for he was afraid the uncle might have seen him.

Clara and Heidi had so many plans that they hardly knew what to do first. Heidi suggested that they should first write to Grandmamma for they had promised to write every day and tell her all their experiences.

"Must we write the letter inside the cottage?" asked Clara who preferred to stay outside and enjoy the lovely scenery.

Heidi went into the cottage to get all the things they needed and then they both settled down to write the letter. After almost every sentence Clara had to stop and look around. It was far too beautiful for writing. The wind was no longer cool, and gently caressed her face. Insects danced and hummed in the air and a deep silence lay on the sunny fields. The whole, broad valley lay peacefully below and only now and then was the silence broken by the yodelling of a shepherd boy, and the sound echoed softly amongst the rocks.

The morning passed so quickly, the children were surprised to see the uncle bringing the lunch which they took out of doors just as they had done the day before. He had decided that as long as there was a ray of light from the sun, the little daughter should have the benefit of the fresh air. In the afternoon they sat in the shadow of the fir trees and Clara related all the things that had happened at Frankfurt since Heidi left. The greater their animation as they talked, the louder chorused the birds above, as if they, too, wished to join in the conversation. Time flew past, and they hardly realised that the afternoon was nearly over.

Evening was approaching and the goats came rushing down the mountain, their keeper following them with a not very pleasant expression on his face. He did not even answer the children's friendly call but went on chasing the goats.

When Clara saw that the grandfather had taken Little Swan away for milking she suddenly felt very impatient to taste the milk. "Isn't it strange!" she said. "I never used to like to eat. Everything tasted like cod liver oil, and now I can hardly wait until supper-time when Grandfather brings the milk." Heidi understood—she remembered the dreadful times in Frankfurt, when she had felt unable to eat. Clara though, was puzzled. She did not realise that it was simply that she had never ever spent a complete day out-of-doors, let alone in the pure, healthy mountain air.

This time, when the milk arrived, Clara even finished hers before Heidi and asked the grandfather for a second helping. He nodded cheerfully, and taking both bowls, went back into the cottage. When he returned with the milk he brought two large slices of bread, spread with plenty of butter which he had got fresh from a herdsman's cottage that afternoon. It tasted delicious and the grandfather smiled with satisfaction to see the two children eat so heartily.

That night, when they went to bed, Clara wanted to look up again at the stars but her eyes would not stay open and she was soon fast asleep like Heidi and slept as she had never done before in her life.

So the days passed happily. One day the children were surprised to see two porters climbing up the mountain. Each of them carried a bed on his back, complete with sheets and mattress. The men also brought a letter from Grandmamma in which she said that the beds were for Clara and Heidi. She instructed Heidi to sleep in the proper bed, and to take it with her to Dörfli in winter, leaving the other behind, so that there would always be a bed for Clara if she visited. She also thanked the children for their letters and encouraged them to continue to write and tell her about everything that happened. The grandfather moved all the hay out of Heidi's room, and then enlisted help in moving the two beds up to the loft. There they were set close enough for both the children to be able to watch the stars.

Grandmamma was very pleased that Clara was enjoying the Alm so much and she was quite content to wait a little before she repeated her visit to the Alm because the ride up the steep mountain was rather trying for her.

Clara had now spent three weeks on the Alm and was enjoying life more every day. She could not praise sufficiently the love and care with which the grandfather nursed her. As for Heidi, her cheerful chatter and amusing companionship made her presence even more enjoyable than in Frankfurt. Every morning Clara expressed her delight in the good fortune which had brought her there.

Grandmamma decided, on the basis of the optimistic reports coming daily from the mountain, that she would postpone her visit for a while, for it was by no means an easy journey for her. During the last few days, when Grandfather carried Clara downstairs to put her into her chair he asked her, "Wouldn't the little daughter like to try to stand on the ground?" Clara had always tried to please him but had soon been forced to cry out, "Oh, it hurts!" and had clung to him; but each day he allowed her to stand just a little longer without her noticing.

For years they had not had such a splendid summer on the Alm. Every day the sun shone brilliantly out of a cloudless sky.

Heidi never tired of describing the high pasture to her friend. She talked of the golden light from the setting sun, and the myriads of beautiful flowers carpeting the ground. As she told Clara about the lovely rock roses and the vivid blue harebells she longed suddenly to be up there once again, and she sprang up and asked the grandfather, "Will you come to the pasture with us to-morrow?"

He consented. "But the little daughter must do me a favour too. To-night she must try her very best to stand."

Cheerfully Heidi ran with this news to Clara who promised to try to stand on her feet as much as ever Grandfather wanted, for she was looking forward immensely to this excursion.

As soon as Heidi caught sight of Peter in the evening she exclaimed, "Peter! Peter! To-morrow we shall come up too and stay all day on the pasture."

But Peter just grumbled like a bear in a temper and was about to give Goldfinch a hefty whack out of sheer bad feeling, but nimble Goldfinch saw what was coming and leaped out of the way in time.

That night Clara and Heidi went to their new beds full of anticipation of the next day. They agreed to stay awake all night to talk about their plans, but hardly had their heads touched the pillows when the conversation suddenly ceased. Clara saw in her dreams a big pasture thickly covered with flowers and Heidi heard the eagle crying, "Come! Come! Come!"

Chapter 22

AN UNEXPECTED EVENT

Early next morning the old man looked out to see what sort of day it would be. The dark shadows in the valley lifted and gradually a rosy light spread across the mountains until above and below were bathed in colour. The sun had risen. A gentle breeze was moving the branches of the fir trees back and forth as the sun caught the tips of the trees in its warm glow.

The uncle brought the invalid chair from the shed and

placed it in front of the house, and then went inside to tell the children what a beautiful morning it was.

Peter came lumbering up the hill. All the jealousy and temper in him had reached a climax. For weeks he had not had Heidi to himself. Even the goats avoided him as much as they could, for he would brandish his stick and hit them hard without any justification, and they no longer trusted him as they had in former days. When he came in the morning the strange child was carried out to her chair and Heidi's attention was completely taken up with her. In the evening, the invalid was still there and again Heidi had no time for him. Not once, all during the summer, had Heidi come up to the pasture, and though she came to-day she would still be accompanied by her friend and would still have no time for him. Peter anticipated this and it made him quite wild with rage.

When he caught sight of the chair, standing so proudly on its wheels, it seemed to him that here was the enemy who had done all this harm to him and would, to-day, hurt him still more. There was no one about and everything was quiet. Wildly he rushed forward, and, seizing the chair, he pushed it with all his might down the slope. He pushed with such violence that it disappeared almost at once. Peter then rushed up the Alm and took cover behind a big black-berry bush. Here he was hidden from the uncle's sight but could watch the chair's progress down the mountain. Far below, he saw it gather speed, bouncing off the rocks until it turned over and over and flew into a hundred pieces. The sight filled Peter with such an indescribable joy that he laughed aloud and stamped his feet. The boy raced round in circles, completely beside himself at the destruction of his enemy.

And now he thought of all the pleasant things for him which would result from the disaster. The stranger would have to leave because she could not get about without her chair; then Heidi would be free again to come with him up to the pasture. Everything would be as it had been in days gone by. It did not occur to Peter that if we do something wrong, trouble is sure to follow.

Presently Heidi came out and ran to the shed. The door was

wide open. She looked everywhere, puzzled to know what had become of the chair.

"Did you move the chair, Heidi?" asked the grandfather.

"I have looked everywhere for it. You said it was by the door," replied Heidi.

The wind suddenly grew stronger and rattled the door of the shed, blowing it back against the wall with a bang.

"Grandfather, it must have been the wind," called Heidi. "Oh, if it has blown the chair down the valley we will never get it back in time."

"If it has rolled a far as that we will never get it back at all," said the grandfather. "By now it will be in a thousand pieces," and he went round the corner of the hut to look down the path. "It is very odd," he said to himself. "The chair would have had to have turned the corner outside the shed."

"Oh, what a pity! Now we can't go," lamented Clara "If I have no chair I am sure I shall have to go home. Oh, what a pity!" Heidi, however, looked confidently at her grandfather, and said, "You will help, won't you, Grandfather, so that Clara doesn't have to go home?"

"We will go to-day as we intended," replied the uncle. "Then we shall see what else can be done."

The children were delighted.

The uncle then went back into the hut and bringing out some of the rugs, spread them out on the sunniest spot for Clara to sit on. Then he brought the milk for the children and led Little Swan and Little Bear out of the shed.

"I wonder why the boy is not here yet?" thought the uncle, for Peter had not greeted them with his usual whistle that morning.

He picked up Clara and, carrying her on one arm and the rugs on the other he said, "Now, let's be off! The goats will come with us."

With one arm round Little Swan's neck and the other round Little Bear's, Heidi walked behind the grandfather. The little goats were so pleased to be with her again that they almost pushed her over with their loving nudges and squeezes.

When they arrived on the pasture they saw here and there

on the slopes, goats peacefully grazing, and in the midst of them, on the ground, Peter was lying.

"I'll teach you to pass my house another time, you lazy fellow!" called the uncle "What does this mean?"

Peter shot up at the sound of the familiar voice. "There was nobody up," he answered.

"Did you see anything of the chair?" the uncle continued.

"Of what?" Peter answered back obstinately.

The uncle said no more but spread the rugs on the sunny slope and set Clara down upon them, asking if she was comfortable.

"As comfortable as in the chair," she said gratefully, "and I think this most be the most beautiful spot on earth. Oh, Heidi, how lovely it is!"

The grandfather got ready to leave them. "Enjoy yourselves!" he said. "When dinner-time comes, Heidi will get the food from the rucksack which I have put in the shade. Peter will provide the milk but Heidi must see that it is milk from Little Swan, and in the evening I will come back to fetch you. Now I must go and look for the chair and see what has happened to it." It was a truly beautiful day. The sky was a deep, clear, azure blue, and the high snowfields glittered as though covered in a thousand jewels. The great mountain summits rose majestically to the sky, and the great eagle hovered above. The wind blew down from the mountains and swept cool draughts of air around the children sitting in the sun.

The children had never been so happy together. The goats would gather round them in a friendly way and they had even got to know Clara well enough to rub their heads affectionately against her shoulder. Little Snowflake came to see Heidi most often, laying her head in Heidi's lap, and only going away when another goat pushed her out of the way.

So the hours went by, and Heidi thought she would like to go to her favourite spot where the flowers grew so profusely, and see if the cups were open now and as beautiful as last year. Clara could only be taken there in the evening when the grandfather came back, but by that time the flower bells would have closed again. Heidi could not resist the temptation to go and look. Hesitatingly she asked Clara, "Do you mind, Clara, if I leave you for a few minutes? I would so much like to go and see the flowers. But wait!" Heidi had an idea She led Snowflake up to Clara. "There, now! You won't be lonely."

Clara encouraged Heidi to go. She was quite content to be with the little goat. Heidi had thrown some leaves into Clara's lap and Clara held them out to Snowflake one by one. The little goat ate the leaves slowly from her hands and seemed contented and trusting in her new-found friend. As she sat alone on the mountain and looked at the little animal which seemed to look up to her for protection, she thought how wonderful it would be to be able, one day, to help others instead of always being dependent as she was now. A great many thoughts came into her mind and she longed to be able to go on living in the sun and to lead a useful life.

She suddenly felt extraordinarily happy, as if she saw everything in a new and beautiful light, and in a fit of gaiety she threw her arms round Snowflake's neck and cried, "Oh, Snowflake—it is so wonderful here; I would so like to stay here for ever with you."

Heidi reached the lovely flower patch and the ground seemed to be completely covered with sparkling gold. It was more beautiful than ever and she breathed in the sweet fragrance. Suddenly she turned and ran back to Clara, out of breath with excitement. "You must come and see it!" she called from a distance. "The flowers are so beautiful now and in the evening they may have changed. I can carry you, don't you think, Clara?"

Clara shook her head. "No, no, Heidi! You are much smaller than I. Oh, if only I could walk!"

Heidi looked about as if searching for something. Up above, Peter sat staring at the children, as if he couldn't believe his eyes. Didn't he destroy the hated chair so that the stranger would not be able to move about and here she sat beside Heidi? Heidi spotted Peter and called, "Come down, Peter!"

"No, I don't want to," was the reply.

"But you must! Come! I can't carry Clara by myself. You have to help me. Come quickly!" Heidi urged him.

"I don't want to," he shouted again.

Heidi came up the hill towards him. With flaming eyes she stood before him and said, "Peter, if you don't come at once I shall do something which you won't like at all, I can tell you!"

Fear seized Peter. He knew he had done something wicked which he did not want anybody to know about and here was Heidi speaking as though she knew all about it. What if she told the uncle! Peter feared nobody so much as him. Tortured with anxiety, he got up and went down to Heidi.

"I am coming, but you mustn't do what you said," he pleaded timidly so that Heidi felt quite sorry for him.

"There's nothing to be afraid of. Come with me now."

Heidi told him to take Clara's arm and she would support her from the other side. But the difficulty was how to make her walk when she could not even stand. So Heidi ordered Peter to give her his arm to lean on and asked her to put her other arm firmly round Heidi's neck. "Then we can carry you."

But Peter had never in his life before given his arm to anybody and kept it stiffly by his body.

"That's not the way," said Heidi and showed him how to do it.

But in spite of it all they did not get on very well. Clara was not light and the team was too unequal—down on the one side and up on the other. Clara tried to help by putting forward first one foot and then the other but she always drew them back quickly again.

"Put your foot down firmly," Heidi suggested.

"Do you think—" Clara hesitated.

But she obeyed, and ventured first one step on the ground and then another. The pain made her moan a little. Then she put a foot out again and cried joyfully that it was less painful already.

"Try again!" urged Heidi eagerly.

Clara went on trying, again and again, and suddenly she exclaimed, "I can do it, Heidi! Oh, I can! Look! I can make steps—one after the other!"

"Can you really walk now? Can you really walk all by yourself? Oh if only Grandfather were here!" cried Heidi. "You can walk, you can walk!"

Clara had still to hold on to both Peter and Heidi, but with every step she felt safer, and it was less and less uncomfortable.

Heidi was quite beside herself with joy. "Now we will b able to come here every day and you will be able to walk like me and you will be healthy! Oh, this is the most marvellous thing that could have happened."

Clara joyfully agreed. She could think of nothing in the world more wonderful than being able to walk around like normal people and never again to have to lie all day in her invalid chair.

It was not far to the slope where the beautiful flowers grew. The children could already see the yellow and blue patches. Soon they reached it.

"Let's sit down here," said Clara. They sat down in the midst of the flowers. Heidi thought she had never seen it so beautiful before. Clara was silent, overcome with happiness at the beauty around her and at the wonderful prospect which had opened up before her . . . the joy of being able to walk about like other people. Surrounding her were the many colours of the flowers waving in the grass, and their mixed perfumes enveloped her in an aura of fragrance, so that she could hardly believe the beauty of it all.

Heidi thought of Clara's cure, and the thought made everything so perfect that she wanted to shout aloud with pleasure. Clara could not speak, she was so totally overwhelmed by the prospect of new life which had opened before her, and the perfection of her situation. Peter was quiet, too, and lay quite still on the ground. He was fast asleep. Occasionally, Heidi ran to and fro to look more closely at the groups of flowers, and whichever way she turned they seemed to smell sweeter and to grow in greater abundance.

The children remained there for a long time. It was long past noon when some of the goats approached the slope and started to bleat loudly. They did not care to eat flowers, and they looked like a small deputation with Goldfinch as their spokesman, who had come to protest at the absence of their companions. The chorus awoke Peter and he remembered with a pang of misgiving his wicked deed of the morning. He willingly obeyed Heidi's every command in the hope that she would not report him to the uncle. The three of them went back to the pasture and had their meal, Heidi running to get the bag, for unknown to Peter, her threat to him had been related to Peter's dinner. She had noticed the lovely things which her grandfather had packed for them, and had been pleased at the thought of Peter sharing them, and she had originally intended that he should pay for his moodiness by going without dinner. Since he had, after all, complied with her wish to help Clara, she now divided the food equally into large helpings. They all three ate well, but although Peter ate up every bit as usual he did not enjoy it very much, tortured as he was by the fear of punishment.

Soon after they had finished, the grandfather appeared, climbing up the slope, and Heidi rushed towards him to tell him the good news. The grandfather's face brightened and he smiled happily at Clara. "You have made the effort and you have won," he said.

He lifted Clara up and with his left arm behind her she walked, with his strong support, much more confidently than before. Heidi skipped happily beside them. Then the grandfather lifted Clara into his arms. "We mustn't overdo it," he said. "In any case it is time to go home."

Later in the evening, when Peter arrived in Dörfli with his goats, a crowd of people had gathered. They were looking at something which lay on the ground. Peter wanted to see too, and eventually elbowed his way through. There lay the pitiful remains of Clara's chair. There was a part of the back and some red padding and a few shiny nails; it was clearly the same chair and although it was broken beyond repair it was easy to see that it had once been a beautiful piece of workmanship.

"I saw them carry it up," said the baker. "I bet it's worth a lot of money. I wonder if somebody did this deliberately? When the gentleman from Frankfurt hears of this he is sure to investigate. Suspicion is going to fall on all those who have been up on the Alm lately. I'm glad I haven't been up there for two years at least." "Alm-Uncle said that it may have been the wind," said one of the women, admiring the shiny red upholstery.

"Just as well," returned the baker, "for whoever else might have been responsible for such a deed would surely be in trouble if he were found."

Peter had heard enough. Stealthily he crept away from the crowd and ran up the mountain path as though the devil were after him.

He was in a terrible state by the time he reached home. He would not answer when he was spoken to, refused to eat, and went up to bed as soon as he could, only to put his head under the sheets and torture himself with fears about what was to happen to him.

As the children lay in bed that night, looking out at the stars, Heidi said, "I have been thinking all day how good it is that God does not give us just what we ask. He always knows of something better for us."

"Why do you think that, Heidi?" asked Clara.

"Because when I was in Frankfurt I prayed to be allowed to go home at once and when it did not happen I thought God did not hear. But, you see, if I had run away at once you would never have come here and would never have got well."

Clara thought hard. "But, Heidi," she said, "that would mean that we must never pray for anything because God knows better than we do."

"Yes, Clara, but we must do it like this," Heidi replied eagerly. "Every day we must thank God for everything to let Him know that we haven't forgotten that it all comes from Him. But, you know, if we don't get what we have asked for we must not think that God has not heard, and stop praying. We must say then, 'Now I know, dear Father, that you have something better in mind and I am glad that you will make it right in the end, no matter what happens now.'"

"How well you can explain it, Heidi," remarked Clara.

"Grandmamma explained it all to me and it turned out to be true. But I think we have to thank God particularly to-day because He has given us this great happiness—that you can walk now." They each silently prayed and thanked God from the bottom of their hearts for His goodness to Clara.

The following morning, the grandfather suggested that they should invite the grandmamma to the Alm because they had something new to show her. But the children wanted to give Grandmamma a great surprise and wanted to wait until Clara could go for a little walk supported only by Heidi. They thought it would be about a week before this could happen and in their next letter Grandmamma was eagerly invited to come for a visit; but they did not give away the secret.

Every day walking became easier and less painful for Clara and longer walks were undertaken. The exercise gave her such an appetite that the grandfather had to cut the bread a little bit thicker every day, and he was very pleased when he saw it disappearing.

So another week went by, and the day of the grandmamma's visit approached.

Chapter 23

PROMISES TO MEET AGAIN

The Grandmamma wrote to announce the day of her arrival and Peter brought the letter up from Dörfli that morning. Everyone was already up and about and the goats were waiting for him in their customary high spirits. The grandfather stood looking with pleasure at his happy healthy brood. As Peter approached he slowed his pace, and handing the letter apprehensively to the Alm-Uncle he then turned quickly and fled back down the mountain.

"Grandfather," asked Heidi. "Why does Peter always behave now as if he expected to be punished for something? He is like the goats running away for fear of the stick."

"Maybe he, too, is afraid of the stick which he sometimes thoroughly deserves," replied the grandfather. Peter ran without stopping until he was out of sight. Then he stopped. He was nervous and jumpy, as if he expected someone to leap on him and arrest him at any moment.

Heidi tidied the hut in preparation for the grandmamma's arrival, and when everything was in order the children sat down on the bench outside the cottage, ready to welcome her. The grandfather came and sat down beside them. He held in his hands a lovely bunch of gentians which he had picked that morning. Heidi ran forward every now and then to see if there was any sign of their guest's arrival. Soon she saw a group of people toiling up the mountain path. First there came a guide, and then a white horse on which rode the grandmamma, and last of all a porter with grandmamma's luggage. At last the procession arrived and the old lady caught sight of the children.

"Why, what is this?" she cried out. "Clara, you aren't in your chair! I can't believe my eyes!" And before even shaking hands with any one she still exclaimed, "Clara, is this really you? Your cheeks have become quite round and rosy. I hardly recognise you, child."

She came forward to embrace Clara, but Heidi quickly slipped from the bench, and, with Clara leaning on her shoulder, they walked slowly towards the grandmamma.

The old lady stood transfixed. Then she embraced her little grandchild, then Heidi, then Clara again. She gazed at them both speechlessly. At last she saw the Alm-Uncle who had been watching the proceedings with a broad smile. With Clara on her arm she walked with her to the bench, and, letting Clara sit down, she grasped the old man's hand.

"My dear Uncle! How can I thank you? This is your doing! Your care and nursing—"

"And God's sunshine and mountain air," interrupted the grandfather, smiling.

"And also Little Swan's good milk," put in Clara. "Grandmamma, you should have seen how much milk I have been drinking!"

"I can see it, Clara, by your cheeks! What a change! You have become plump and strong and taller, too. I simply can't take my eyes off You! But now we must send a telegram to my son in Paris. He must come at once—but I shan't tell him why. This will be the most wonderful surprise he has ever had. Uncle, have the men gone? How can we send a telegram?"

"They have gone, but, if you are in a hurry, I will call Peter. He will do it."

A piercing whistle summoned Peter and he came running down from the high rocks. His face was pale and drawn, for he was convinced that the moment of truth had arrived and that Uncle was about to hand him over to the police. He was given a piece of paper on which the message was written and the uncle told him to take it to the post office at Dörfli. Peter hurried away, quite relieved to see that no policeman had arrived so far.

So now, everyone sat down to a delicious meal outside the hut, and grandmamma was regaled with elated accounts from all sides of the progress made with Clara, and the way in which her cure had come about. They told her how grandfather had persuaded Clara to do a little every day, first standing, then taking a few steps, and how, finally, after the chair had blown down the mountain, they had managed to take Clara up to the pasture. Grandmamma could hardly believe all that had taken place, and exclaimed with delight at every turn of events.

Clara and Heidi were of course beside themselves at Grandmamma's reaction.

In Paris, Herr Sesemann had finished his business and he also had a surprise in store. Without giving any warning, he took the train to Basle, for he had a great longing to see his little daughter from whom he had been separated all summer. He arrived at Ragatz a few hours after his mother's departure, and this fitted in nicely with his plans. He took a coach to Mayenfeld, where he learned that he could drive as far as Dörfli. The climb from there seemed to him very long and fatiguing, and when the cottage failed to come into view he began to wonder uneasily if he had chosen the right path or if the hut was on the other side of the mountain. He looked around, but no human being was to be seen of whom he could ask the way. He was beginning to wonder uneasily if he was on the right track. Just then, a boy came running from above; it was Peter with the telegram. He did not keep to the footpath but ran straight down the mountainside. Herr Sesemann beckoned to him and reluctantly Peter came forward.

"Come here, boy!" Herr Sesemann encouraged him. "Tell me, is this the way to the hut where the old man lives with the child, Heidi, and where the people from Frankfurt are staying now?"

A gasp was the only answer that came from Peter, and in his haste to get away, the boy fell head over heels and catapulted down the mountainside, just as the chair had done—except that Peter did not break up into pieces! The telegram, however, was torn to scraps.

"What a timid boy!" exclaimed Herr Sesemann, thinking that the appearance of a stranger had had this extraordinary effect on the simple boy of the mountains. And he continued on his way.

Peter had been convinced that this was the policeman from Frankfurt. He was overcome with terror at the sight of the visitor and was utterly certain that he had been sent to collect him and take him away to Frankfurt. He tumbled on down the mountainside until at last he managed to catch hold of a bush. He had to lie still for a moment or two to recover, and then he picked himself up.

"Well, well, and what is this that comes hurtling down the mountain?" said a voice behind him. Peter jumped, and saw the baker standing there chuckling. He had been most amused to see Peter tumbling down the mountain just like the chair had done.

Peter did not answer but began to scramble back up the slope. He wanted to go home and hide, but the goats were still up there waiting for him, and he dared not delay for fear of fresh recriminations from the Uncle. He was in a sorry state: bruised and shaken from his fall, and in an agony of fear and apprehension about the fate that was to befall him.

Shortly after meeting Peter, Herr Sesemann reached the first hut and knew that he was on the right road. So he climbed higher and higher and at last, after a long, strenuous walk, his goal came in sight. There stood the Alm hut.

Herr Sesemann joyfully climbed the last steep path. Before he had reached the top he was recognised by the party outside the cottage and quickly a surprise was prepared for him. As he left the path to approach the hut, two figures came towards him. A tall girl with fair hair and rosy cheeks leaned on her smaller companion. Herr Sesemann stood still and stared at them.

"Papa don't you know me?" called Clara "Have I changed so much?"

At once Herr Sesemann rushed to embrace his little daughter.

"Yes, you have changed indeed! Is it possible? Can this be my little Clara?" he exclaimed repeatedly.

Grandmamma had come forward. "My dear son, what do you think of this?" she cried. "You had prepared a pleasant surprise for us but I think we have an even pleasanter one for you! But now you must meet the Alm-Uncle who is our greatest benefactor."

"Gladly, and also our dear little Heidi," replied Herr Sesemann, shaking hands with Heidi. "I don't need to ask if you are well and happy. No alpine rose could look more blooming."

Heidi looked up with sparkling eyes at the kind Herr Sesemann who had always been so good to her. How glad she was that he could find such happiness on the Alm.

Then the grandmamma led her son to the Alm-Uncle. As the two men shook hands, Herr Sesemann expressed his heartfelt thanks and his great astonishment at the miracle.

Her eyes filled with tears, and the grandmamma turned away and looked towards the ancient fir trees. A patch of blue caught her eye. It was a beautiful bouquet of blue gentians. "How exquisite!" she exclaimed. "Heidi, did you pick them for me?"

"No," replied Heidi, "but I think I know who did."

Suddenly, a slight rustling sound came from behind the trees. It was Peter. At the sight of the strange gentleman with the Alm-Uncle, he had tried to slip away unobserved. But the grandmamma recognised him. She thought that perhaps it was he who had brought her the flowers, and that he was sidling along in the background from shyness at the possibility of her discovering them. She felt that she should reward him for his kindness. "Come here, my boy," she said loudly. "Don't be afraid."

Paralysed with fright, Peter looked out from behind the trees. "It is all up now!" he thought. His face distorted with terror, he began to creep forward.

"Come along now," encouraged the grandmamma. "Now tell me, boy, did you do this?"

Peter never lifted his eyes and, of course, did not see where the grandmamma's finger pointed. All he had noticed was the uncle standing at the corner of the hut, looking piercingly at him, and, what was most terrifying of all, beside him stood the policeman from Frankfurt. Trembling all over, Peter could only mutter something which sounded like "Yes."

"Well, what is so dreadful about that?" asked the grandmamma.

"That it is broken to pieces and can't be put together again." With great difficulty Peter managed to stammer the words and his legs shook so much he could hardly stand.

Grandmamma went over to the Alm-Uncle. "My dear Uncle, is there something seriously wrong with the poor boy?" she asked sympathetically.

"Nothing," replied the uncle, "but I think the lad may have been the 'wind' which chased the invalid chair down the mountain and now he is expecting his well-deserved punishment."

Grandmamma could hardly believe this for she did not think he looked such a bad boy; and there seemed no reason for him to destroy the chair. But to the uncle, Peter's confession only confirmed the suspicion which he had had from the beginning. The angry looks Peter had cast on Clara and the signs of resentment towards the newcomers to the Alm had not escaped the uncle. He had put two and two together and explained it all now to grandmamma. When he had finished, the lady said, "No, no, my dear Uncle, we don't want to punish the poor boy any more. One must be fair. We strangers have, for weeks, taken Heidi away from him, so he sits, day after day, and broods all by himself. No, no, we must be fair. Anger and resentment drove the boy to his revenge which was, perhaps, a little foolish; but we are all foolish when we are angry."

Grandmamma went over to Peter and sat down on the bench under the fir trees. In a kind voice she said, "Come, my boy, stand in front of me. I want to speak to you. Stop trembling and listen. You pushed the chair down the slope to destroy it; that was wicked and you knew that you deserved to be punished. So to avoid that you took a lot of trouble to hide the truth; but you see, he who does something wrong and thinks nobody will find out is always mistaken. God sees and hears everything and when He notices that somebody wants to hide a wrong deed He wakes up the little watchman whom He has placed inside us from our birth and who sleeps inside us until we do something wrong. This little watchman has a little prong in his hand and he prods us with it all the time so that we do not have a minute's peace. His voice torments us, too, for it keeps calling. 'Soon you will be found out! Now they'll come and drag you away!' So we live in terror and anxiety and never have a moment's happiness. Did you feel something like that, Peter?"

Peter nodded penitently, for that was exactly how he had felt.

"In still another way you miscalculated, for you wanted to do something wrong and something good came out of it. Because Clara had no chair and she wanted to see the beautiful flowers she tried hard to walk; and she succeeded, and in the end, was able to go every day to the pasture—much more frequently than she would have done in the chair. You see, Peter, God can turn evil into good for the one who was meant to be harmed; harm comes to the evil-doer instead. Do you understand, Peter? If so, don't forget; and if you ever again want to do something wrong, remember the little watch-man inside with his prong and unpleasant voice, will you?"

"Yes, I will," answered Peter, very depressed for he still did not know how the affair would end.

"Then everything is all right and the whole matter is settled," finished the grandmamma. "But now you shall have a souvenir from the Frankfurt visitors. Tell me, my boy, what would you like?"

Slowly Peter lifted his head and gazed at the grandmamma in astonishment.

He had expected some awful punishment and now he was being asked what he would like. He was completely confused.

"Yes, I am quite serious," continued the grandmamma "You shall have something as a remembrance and as a token that the people from Frankfurt think no more than that you did something wrong. Do you understand, my boy?"

Now it began to dawn on Peter that he need not fear any punishment and that the kind lady had saved him from arrest by the police. It was a great weight off his mind. Now he saw, too, that it was better to confess at once if one had done something wrong and suddenly he stammered, "And I also lost the paper."

The grandmamma had to think for a moment what this meant but soon she recalled the telegram and said kindly:

"That is right. Always confess at once what you have done and everything will be all right. And now have you any special wish?"

Peter felt quite giddy at the thought of being able to have anything he wanted. The annual fair at Maienfeld flashed before his eyes with all the beautiful things he had admired so often and never hoped to possess. There were the red whistles, which he could use for his goats; and the fascinating knives. Peter was deeply absorbed in his thoughts and he could not decide which of the two he would like the better. Suddenly he had a brainwave. "A penny," he said.

The grandmamma laughed. "That is not an extravagant wish," she said. "Come here!" She pulled out her purse and took from it four bright round shillings and on top of them she put four pennies. "Well, we want to settle our accounts," she said. "I will explain it to you. Here are just as many pennies as there are weeks in the year and so you will be able to spend a penny every week for a whole year."

"All my life?" asked Peter innocently.

Now the grandmamma could not help laughing heartily so that the gentlemen interrupted their talk to hear what was going on.

"Yes, my boy, that's a passage for my will," said the old lady. "I will put down, 'A penny a week to Peter as long as he lives.'" Herr Sesemann nodded his agreement and laughed too.

Peter looked once more at the present in his hand. He still could hardly believe his eyes. Then he said, "God bless you!" and off he went, running and leaping, all fear and anxiety gone. His joy sent him flying over the rocks and boulders with twice his usual agility. He was forgiven, and he was to have a penny every week for the rest of his life.

After dinner, Clara took her father aside and said to him, "If you only knew, Papa, what the grandfather has done for me! I shall never forget it all my life. And I keep wondering, what could I give him or do for him, that would give him half the pleasure he has given me!"

"That is my dearest wish, too, my child," replied her father.

Herr Sesemann now went to the Alm-Uncle and seizing his hand, said, "My dear friend, let us have a word together. Believe me when I say that for years I have not known such happiness. Money and possessions have meant nothing to me since they have not helped to make my poor child well and happy. You have restored her health and given new life to her and me. Now, tell me, how can I show my gratitude? I can never repay what you have done, but whatever is in my power is at your disposal. Tell me, my friend, what can I do?"

The Alm-Uncle had listened in silence. Now he looked at Herr Sesemann and smiled. "Believe me, Herr Sesemann, I too am over-joyed at the girl's recovery on our Alm and my trouble has been well repaid by that. For your kind offer I thank you, but there is nothing I need; as long as I live I have enough for Heidi and myself. But if one wish only could be fulfilled I should have no more worries in this life."

"Speak, my dear friend," urged Herr Sesemann.

"I am old," continued the uncle, "and cannot expect to be here much longer. When I have passed away there will be nothing for the child and she has no relatives of any account. If you will promise that Heidi will never have to go out and earn her living among strangers then you will have amply repaid what I have done for your child."

"But there could never be any question about it!" exclaimed Herr Sesemann. "The child is one of us. Ask my mother and my daughter. They will never allow Heidi to go to strangers. This I promise you, both during my life and after, the child will never have to go among strangers. But she has made good friends, one of whom is our friend, the doctor. He is winding up his affairs and intends to come and settle here this autumn, in the Swiss mountains, for he has never felt so well and happy as in the company of you and the child. You see, Heidi will now have two protectors. May they both live long!"

"God grant that will be so!" added the grandmamma and shook hands warmly with the Alm-Uncle. Then she embraced Heidi, who stood beside her.

"And you, my dear Heidi, come, tell me, don't you have a particular wish?"

"Yes, certainly," replied Heidi, looking cheerfully up at the grandmamma.

"What is it child?" she encouraged.

"I would like my bed from Frankfurt with the three high pillows and the thick cover, so that Grandmother needn't lie with her head downhill and won't need to put her shawl on in bed any more because she is cold."

"My dear child, it is good you remind me to think of others in our happiness, those who are not so well off as we are. I will wire at once to Frankfurt. The bed will be here in two days and, with God's help, the grandmother will soon be sleeping comfortably in it."

Heidi skipped delightedly round the grandmamma. She wanted to go down at once and give the grandmother this happy message for she felt she had been away from her far too long, especially since the grandmother was in such discomfort the last time Heidi had seen her, but the grandfather said reprovingly, "No, no, Heidi! When you have guests you can't run away like that!"

But the grandmamma supported Heidi. "My dear Uncle, we shall go together. We can then go on to Dörfli and send the wire off to Frankfurt. What do you think, my son?"

Until now Herr Sesemann had not given much thought to his holiday plans. Originally, he had thought of taking a trip through Switzerland with his mother and had wondered if Clara would be fit to accompany them for part of the journey. But now he would be able to enjoy the company of his daughter more fully. He did not want to miss any of these beautiful days of late summer and decided to stay the night at Dörfli and the next morning to fetch Clara when all three would go to Ragatz and start their journey from there.

Clara was a little upset at the thought of leaving the Alm but there was so much to look forward to and so little time to think that she was soon quite cheerful again. Heidi bounced for joy as they all went down the mountain. She told grandmamma all about the grandmother, and how cold she was, and what she lacked in the way of food.

Brigitta was standing outside the cottage when the little company approached and she rushed inside quickly crying, "They are coming, Mother."

"Alas, it is true, then," sighed the grandmother. "Do you think they are taking the child with them? Did you see her?"

Presently the door flew open and Heidi rushed into the room, going at once to the Grandmother's corner and embracing her affectionately.

"Grandmother, Grandmother! My bed is coming from Frankfurt, and the three pillows and also the thick cover. It will be here in two days. Grandmamma has promised."

The grandmother smiled a little sadly, "What a kind lady! I wish I could be happy that she is taking you with her, Heidi."

"What is all this? Who has been telling my good, old grandmother such tales?" said a kind voice. Grandmamma had overheard the conversation.

"No, no, that is out of the question! Heidi will stay with the grandmother, but we will come back to the Alm every year for we have good reason to thank God for this spot, and especially for the miracle He has wrought on our girl."

The grandmother's face lit up. Unable to speak, she pressed Frau Sesemann's hand again and again, and two large tears ran down her wrinkled cheeks.

Heidi clung affectionately to her and said, "Hasn't it all happened as in the hymn I read to you? When the bed comes from Frankfurt you will be much better too, Grandmother."

"Ah, yes, Heidi. God has sent me so many good things. Is it possible that there are such kind people who trouble themselves about a poor old woman?"

"My good Grandmother," interrupted Frau Sesemann, "in the eyes of God we are all equally poor and need His help; and He does not forget us. We must say good-bye now, but only until we meet again next year, and we certainly never will forget the dear grandmother."

Frau Sesemann took the grandmother's hand again, and with the old woman's blessing, Herr Sesemann and his mother continued their journey down into the valley.

Next morning, Clara was very sad about leaving the Alm where she had been so happy; but Heidi did her best to comfort her. "Summer will soon come again, and then it will be better still, for you are well now and we can go every day with the goats up to the pastures."

Clara dried her tears, "Don't forget to remember me to Peter and the goats," she said. Heidi suggested that Clara send Little Swan some salt, for she loved to lick some from out of the grandfather's hand in the evening. Clara promised to send a hundred pounds of salt so that Little Swan would never forget her.

Herr Sesemann had arrived and was beckoning to the children for it was time to go. Heidi stood at the very edge of the slope and waved to Clara until she disappeared from sight.

Frau Sesemann did not forget how cold it could be in winter

on the mountain. She sent a big parcel to Goat Peter's hut; it contained warm clothing of every description so that the grandmother would never again have to sit trembling with cold.

The doctor arrived in Dörfli, and, on the Alm-Uncle's advice, he bought the house where the old man and Heidi stayed during the winter. The doctor decided to have it rebuilt, part of it for himself and the other part for the uncle and Heidi for their winter lodgings.

As the days went by, the doctor and the Alm-Uncle became very good friends and often their conversation would turn to Heidi because, for both of them, it was the greatest joy to have the child with them in their new house.

One day, when the doctor and the uncle were standing together, seeing how the new building was getting on, the doctor said to the old man; "I share your happiness in the child and I feel I am the nearest to her after you; I want to share also the responsibilities and to provide for her as best I can, so that I may hope that in my old age she will stay with me. That is my greatest wish, that Heidi should have the same claims on me as though she were my own child. Then we will be able to leave her free of worries when you and I have departed."

The grandfather pressed the doctor's hand and the doctor could read in the eyes of his friend how greatly touched he was by these words.

At this moment Heidi and Peter were sitting with the grandmother. Heidi had such a story to tell them that she hardly took time to breathe. They had seen very little of each other during the summer, and how much had happened!

It was difficult to tell which of the three radiant faces shone most happily.

Brigitta, with Heidi's help, at last understood the story of Peter's miraculous weekly penny and her face beamed, perhaps most radiantly of all.

At last, the grandmother said to Heidi, "Read one of the hymns to me, child! I want to thank our Heavenly Father for all the mercy He has bestowed on us!"

The Railway Children

E. Nesbit

The Railway Children

PARRAGON

The Railway Children
A Parragon Classic

This is a Siena Book
Siena is an imprint of Parragon

First published in 1908

This edition published in 1999 by
Parragon
13 Whiteladies Road
Clifton
Bristol BS8 1PB

Printed and bound in the UK

Chapter 1

THE BEGINNING OF THINGS

They were not railway children to begin with. I don't suppose they had ever thought about railways except as a means of getting to Maskelyne and Cook's, the Pantomime, Zoological Gardens, and Madame Tussaud's. They were just ordinary suburban children, and they lived with their Father and Mother in an ordinary red-brick-fronted villa, with coloured glass in the front door, a tiled passage that was called a hall, a bath-room with hot and cold water, electric bells, french windows, and a good deal of white paint, and "every modern convenience", as the house-agents say.

There were three of them. Roberta was the eldest. Of course, Mothers never have favourites, but if their Mother *had* had a favourite, it might have been Roberta. Next came Peter, who wished to be an Engineer when he grew up; and the youngest was Phyllis, who meant extremely well.

Mother did not spend all her time in paying dull calls to dull ladies, and sitting dully at home waiting for dull ladies to pay calls to her. She was almost always there, ready to play with the children, and read to them, and help them to do their home-lessons. Besides this she used to write stories for them while they were at school, and read them aloud after tea, and she always made up funny pieces of poetry for their birthdays and for other great occasions, such as the christening of the new kittens, or the refurnishing of the dolls' house, or the time when they were getting over the mumps.

These three lucky children always had everything they needed: pretty clothes, good fires, a lovely nursery with heaps of toys, and a Mother Goose wall-paper. They had a kind and merry nursemaid, and a dog who was called James, and who was their very own. They also had a Father who was just perfect—never cross, never unjust, and always ready for a game—at least, if at any time he was *not* ready, he always had an excellent reason for it, and explained the reason to the children so interestingly and funnily that they felt sure he couldn't help himself.

You will think that they ought to have been very happy. And so they were, but they did not know *how* happy till the pretty life in Edgecombe Villa was over and done with, and they had to live a very different life indeed.

The dreadful change came quite suddenly.

Peter had a birthday—his tenth. Among his other presents was a model engine more perfect than you could ever have dreamed of. The other presents were full of charm, but the Engine was fuller of charm than any of the others were.

Its charm lasted in its full perfection for exactly three days. Then, owing either to Peter's inexperience or Phyllis's good intentions, which had been rather pressing, or to some other cause, the Engine suddenly went off with a bang. James was so frightened that he went out and did not come back all day. All the Noah's Ark people who were in the tender were broken to bits, but nothing else was hurt except the poor little engine and the feelings of Peter. The others said he cried over it—but of course boys of ten do not cry, however terrible the tragedies may be which darken their lot. He said that his eyes were red because he had a cold. This turned out to be true, though Peter did not know it was when he said it; the next day he had to go to bed and stay there. Mother began to be afraid that he might be sickening for measles, when suddenly he sat up in bed and said:

"I hate gruel—I hate barley water—I hate bread and milk. I want to get up and have something *real* to eat."

"What would you like?" Mother asked.

"A pigeon-pie," said Peter, eagerly, "a large pigeon-pie. A very large one."

So Mother asked the Cook to make a large pigeon-pie. The pie was made. And when the pie was made, it was cooked. And when it was cooked, Peter ate some of it. After that his cold was better. Mother made a piece of poetry to amuse him while the pie was being made. It began by saying what an unfortunate but worthy boy Peter was, then it went on:

He had an engine that he loved
With all his heart and soul,
And if he had a wish on earth
It was to keep it whole.
One day—my friends, prepare your minds;
I'm coming to the worst—
Quite suddenly a screw went mad,
And then the boiler burst!
With gloomy face he picked it up
And took it to his Mother,
Though even he could not suppose
That she could make another;
For those who perished on the line
He did not seem to care,
His engine being more to him
Than all the people there.
And now you see the reason why
Our Peter has been ill:
He soothes his soul with pigeon-pie
His gnawing grief to kill.
He wraps himself in blankets warm
And sleeps in bed till late,
Determined thus to overcome
His miserable fate.
And if his eyes are rather red,
His cold must just excuse it:
Offer him pie; you may be sure
He never will refuse it.

Father had been away in the country for three or four days. All Peter's hopes for the curing of his afflicted Engine were now fixed on his Father, for Father was most wonderfully clever with his fingers. He could mend all sorts of things. He had often acted as veterinary surgeon to the wooden rocking-horse; once he had saved its life when all human aid was despaired of, and the poor creature was given up for lost, and even the carpenter said he didn't see his way to do anything. And it was Father who mended the doll's cradle when no one else could; and with a little glue and some bits of wood and a pen-knife made all the Noah's Ark beasts as strong on their pins as ever they were, if not stronger.

Peter, with heroic unselfishness, did not say anything about his Engine till after Father had had his dinner and his after-dinner cigar. The unselfishness was Mother's idea—but it was Peter who carried it out. And needed a good deal of patience, too.

At last Mother said to Father, "Now, dear, if you're quite rested, and quite comfy, we want to tell you about the great railway accident, and ask your advice."

"All right," said Father, "fire away!"

So then Peter told the sad tale, and fetched what was left of the Engine.

"Hum," said Father, when he had looked the Engine over very carefully.

The children held their breaths.

"Is there *no* hope?" said Peter, in a low, unsteady voice.

"Hope? Rather! Tons of it," said Father, cheerfully; "but it'll want something besides hope—a bit of brazing say, or some solder, and a new valve. I think we'd better keep it for a rainy day. In other words, I'll give up Saturday afternoon to it, and you shall all help me."

"*Can* girls help to mend engines?" Peter asked doubtfully.

"Of course they can. Girls are just as clever as boys, and don't you forget it! How would you like to be an engine-driver, Phil?"

"My face would be always dirty, wouldn't it?" said Phyllis, in unemotional tones, "and I expect I should break something."

"I should just love it," said Roberta—"do you think I could when I'm grown up, Daddy? Or even a stoker?"

"You mean a fireman," said Daddy, pulling and twisting

at the engine. "Well, if you still wish it, when you're grown up, we'll see about making you a fire-woman. I remember when I was a boy—"

Just then there was a knock at the front door.

"Who on earth!" said Father. "An Englishman's house is his castle, of course, but I do wish they built semi-detached villas with moats and drawbridges."

Ruth—she was the parlour-maid and had red hair—came in and said that two gentlemen wanted to see the master.

"I've shown them into the Library, Sir," said she.

"I expect it's the subscription to the Vicar's testimonial," said Mother, "or else it's the choir holiday fund. Get rid of them quickly, dear. It does break up an evening so, and it's nearly the children's bedtime."

But Father did not seem to be able to get rid of the gentlemen at all quickly.

"I wish we *had* got a moat and drawbridge," said Roberta; "then, when we didn't want people, we could just pull up the drawbridge and no one else could get in. I expect Father will have forgotten about when he was a boy if they stay much longer."

Mother tried to make the time pass by telling them a new fairy story about a Princess with green eyes, but it was difficult because they could hear the voices of Father and the gentlemen in the Library, and Father's voice sounded louder and different from the voice he generally used to people who came about testimonials and holiday funds.

Then the Library bell rang, and everyone heaved a breath of relief.

"They're going now," said Phyllis; "he's rung to have them shown out."

But instead of showing anybody out, Ruth showed herself in, and she looked queer, the children thought.

"Please'm," she said, "the Master wants you to just step into the study. He looks like the dead, mum; I think he's had bad news. You'd best prepare yourself for the worst, 'm—p'raps it's a death in the family or a bank busted or—"

"That'll do, Ruth," said Mother gently; "you can go."

Then Mother went into the Library. There was more

talking. Then the bell rang again, and Ruth fetched a cab. The children heard boots go out and down the steps. The cab drove away, and the front door shut. Then Mother came in. Her dear face was as white as her lace collar, and her eyes looked very big and shining. Her mouth looked like just a line of pale red—her lips were thin and not their proper shape at all.

"It's bedtime," she said. "Ruth will put you to bed."

"But you promised we should sit up late tonight because Father's come home," said Phyllis.

"Father's been called away—on business," said Mother. "Come, darlings, go at once."

They kissed her and went. Roberta lingered to give Mother an extra hug and to whisper:

"It wasn't bad news, Mammy, was it? Is anyone dead—or—"

"Nobody's dead—no," said Mother, and she almost seemed to push Roberta away. "I can't tell you anything tonight, my pet. Go, dear, go *now*."

So Roberta went.

Ruth brushed the girls' hair and helped them to undress. (Mother almost always did this herself.) When she had turned down the gas and left them she found Peter, still dressed, waiting on the stairs.

"I say, Ruth, what's up?" he asked.

"Don't ask me no questions and I won't tell you no lies," the red-headed Ruth replied. "You'll know soon enough."

Late that night Mother came up and kissed all three children as they lay asleep. But Roberta was the only one whom the kiss woke, and she lay mousey-still, and said nothing.

"If Mother doesn't want us to know she's been crying," she said to herself as she heard through the dark the catching of her Mother's breath, "we *won't* know it. That's all."

When they came down to breakfast the next morning, Mother had already gone out.

"To London," Ruth said, and left them to their breakfast.

"There's something awful the matter," said Peter, breaking his egg. "Ruth told me last night we should know soon enough."

"Did you *ask* her?" said Roberta, with scorn.

"Yes, I did!" said Peter, angrily. "If you could go to bed without caring whether Mother was worried or not, I couldn't. So there."

"I don't think we ought to ask the servants things Mother doesn't tell us," said Roberta.

"That's right, Miss Goody-Goody," said Peter, "preach away."

"*I'm* not goody," said Phyllis, "but I think Bobbie's right this time."

"Of course. She always is. In her own opinion," said Peter.

"Oh, *don't!*" cried Roberta, putting down her egg-spoon; "don't let's be horrid to each other. I'm sure some dire calamity is happening. Don't let's make it worse!"

"Who began, I should like to know?" said Peter.

Roberta made an effort, and answered:

"I did, I suppose, but—"

"Well, then," said Peter, triumphantly. But before he went to school he thumped his sister between the shoulders and told her to cheer up.

The children came home to one o'clock dinner, but Mother was not there. And she was not there at tea-time.

It was nearly seven before she came in, looking so ill and tired that the children felt they could not ask her any questions. She sank into an arm-chair. Phyllis took the long pins out of her hat, while Roberta took off her gloves, and Peter unfastened her walking-shoes and fetched her soft velvety slippers for her.

When she had had a cup of tea, and Roberta had put eau-de-Cologne on her poor head that ached, Mother said:

"Now, my darlings, I want to tell you something. Those men last night did bring very bad news, and Father will be away for some time. I am very worried about it, and I want you all to help me, and not to make things harder for me."

"As if we would!" said Roberta, holding Mother's hand against her face.

"You can help me very much," said Mother, "by being good and happy and not quarrelling when I'm away"—

Roberta and Peter exchanged guilty glances—"for I shall have to be away a good deal."

"We won't quarrel. Indeed we won't," said everybody. And meant it, too.

"Then," Mother went on, "I want you not to ask me any questions about this trouble; and not to ask anybody else any questions."

Peter cringed and shuffled his boots on the carpet.

"You'll promise this, too, won't you?" said Mother.

"I did ask Ruth," said Peter, suddenly. "I'm very sorry, but I did."

"And what did she say?"

"She said I should know soon enough."

"It isn't necessary for you to know anything about it," said Mother; "it's about business, and you never do understand business, do you?"

"No," said Roberta; "is it something to do with Government?" For Father was in a Government Office.

"Yes," said Mother. "Now it's bed-time, my darlings. And don't *you* worry. It'll all come right in the end."

"Then don't *you* worry either, Mother," said Phyllis, "and we'll all be as good as gold."

Mother sighed and kissed them.

"We'll begin being good the first thing tomorrow morning," said Peter, as they went upstairs.

"Why not *now*?' said Roberta.

"There's nothing to be good *about* now, silly," said Peter.

"We might begin to try to *feel* good," said Phyllis, "and not call names."

"Who's calling names?" said Peter. "Bobbie knows right enough that when I say 'silly', it's just the same as if I said Bobbie."

" *Well*," said Roberta.

"No, I don't mean what you mean. I mean it's just a—what is it Father calls it?—a term of endearment! Good night."

The girls folded up their clothes with more than usual neatness—which was the only way of being good that they could think of.

"I say," said Phyllis, smoothing out her pinafore, "you used to say it was so dull—nothing happening, like in books. Now something *has* happened."

"I never wanted things to happen to make Mother unhappy," said Roberta. "Everything's perfectly horrid."

Everything continued to be perfectly horrid for some weeks.

Mother was nearly always out. Meals were dull and dirty. The between-maid was sent away, and Aunt Emma came on a visit. Aunt Emma was much older than Mother. She was going abroad to be a governess. She was very busy getting her clothes ready, and they were very ugly, dingy clothes, and she had them always littering about, and the sewing-machine seemed to whir—on and on all day and most of the night. Aunt Emma believed in keeping children in their proper places. And they more than returned the compliment. Their idea of Aunt Emma's proper place was anywhere where they were not. So they saw very little of her. They preferred the company of the servants, who were more amusing. Cook, if in a good temper, could sing comic songs, and the housemaid, if she happened not to be offended with you, could imitate a hen that has laid an egg, a bottle of champagne being opened, and could mew like two cats fighting. The servants never told the children what the bad news was that the gentlemen had brought to Father. But they kept hinting that they could tell a great deal if they chose—and this was not comfortable.

One day when Peter had made a booby trap over the bath-room door, and it had acted beautifully as Ruth passed through, that red-haired parlour-maid caught him and boxed his ears.

"You'll come to a bad end," she said furiously, "you nasty little limb, you! If you don't mend your ways, you'll go where your precious Father's gone, so I tell you straight!"

Roberta repeated this to her Mother, and next day Ruth was sent away.

Then came the time when Mother came home and went to bed and stayed there two days and the Doctor came, and the children crept wretchedly about the house and wondered if the world was coming to an end.

Mother came down one morning to breakfast, very pale and with lines on her face that used not to be there. And she smiled, as well as she could, and said:

"Now, my pets, everything is settled. We're going to leave this house, and go and live in the country. Such a ducky dear little white house. I know you'll love it."

A whirling week of packing followed—not just packing clothes, like when you go to the seaside, but packing chairs and tables, covering their tops with sacking and their legs with straw.

All sorts of things were packed that you don't pack when you go to the seaside. Crockery, blankets, candlesticks, carpets, bedsteads, saucepans, and even fenders and fire-irons.

The house was like a furniture warehouse. I think the children enjoyed it very much. Mother was very busy, but not too busy now to talk to them, and read to them, and even to make a bit of poetry for Phyllis to cheer her up when she fell down with a screwdriver and ran it into her hand.

"Aren't you going to pack this, Mother?" Roberta asked, pointing to the beautiful cabinet inlaid with red turtleshell and brass.

"We can't take everything," said Mother.

"But we seem to be taking all the ugly things," said Roberta.

"We're taking the useful ones," said Mother; "we've got to play at being Poor for a bit, my chickabiddy."

When all the ugly useful things had been packed up and taken away in a van by men in green-baize aprons, the two girls and Mother and Aunt Emma slept in the two spare rooms where the furniture was all pretty. All their beds had gone. A bed was made up for Peter on the drawing-room sofa.

"I say, this is larks," he said, wriggling joyously, as Mother tucked him up, "I do like moving! I wish we moved once a month."

Mother laughed.

"I don't!" she said. "Good night, Peterkin."

As she turned away Roberta saw her face. She never forgot it.

"Oh, Mother," she whispered all to herself as she got into bed, "how brave you are! How I love you! Fancy being brave enough to laugh when you're feeling like *that*!"

Next day boxes were filled, and boxes and more boxes; and then late in the afternoon a cab came to take them to the station.

Aunt Emma saw them off. They felt that *they* were seeing *her* off, and they were glad of it.

"But, oh, those poor little foreign children that she's going to governess!" whispered Phyllis. "I wouldn't be them for anything!"

At first they enjoyed looking out of the window, but when it grew dusk they grew sleepier and sleepier, and no one knew how long they had been in the train when they were roused by Mother's shaking them gently and saying:

"Wake up, dears. We're there."

They woke up, cold and melancholy, and stood shivering on the draughty platform while the baggage was taken out of the train. Then the engine, puffing and blowing, set to work again, and dragged the train away. The children watched the tail-lights of the guard's van disappear into the darkness.

This was the first train the children saw on that railway which was in time to become so very dear to them. They did not guess then how they would grow to love the railway, and how soon it would become the centre of their new life nor what wonders and changes it would bring to them. They only shivered and sneezed and hoped the walk to the new house would not be long. Peter's nose was colder than he ever remembered it to have been before. Roberta's hat was crooked, and the elastic seemed tighter than usual. Phyllis's shoe-laces had come undone.

"Come," said Mother, "we've got to walk. There aren't any cabs here."

The walk was dark and muddy. The children stumbled

a little on the rough road, and once Phyllis absently fell into a puddle, and was picked up damp and unhappy. There were no gas-lamps on the road, and the road was uphill. The cart went at a slow pace, and they followed the gritty crunch of its wheels. As their eyes got used to the darkness, they could see the mound of boxes swaying dimly in front of them.

A long gate had to be opened for the cart to pass through, and after that the road seemed to go across fields—and now it went downhill. Presently a great dark lumpish thing showed over to the right.

"There's the house," said Mother. "I wonder why she's shut the shutters."

"Who's *she*?" asked Roberta.

"The woman I engaged to clean the place, and put the furniture straight and get supper."

There was a low wall, and trees inside.

"That's the garden," said Mother.

"It looks more like a dripping-pan full of black cabbages," said Peter.

The cart went on along by the garden wall, and round to the back of the house, and here it clattered into a cobble-stoned yard and stopped at the back door.

There was no light in any of the windows.

Everyone hammered at the door, but no one came.

The man who drove the cart said he expected Mrs Viney had gone home.

"You see your train was that late," said he.

"But she's got the key," said Mother: "What are we to do?"

"Oh, she'll have left that under the doorstep," said the cart man; "folks do hereabouts." He took the lantern off his cart and stooped.

"Ay, here it is, right enough," he said.

He unlocked the door and went in and set his lantern on the table.

"Got e'er a candle?" said he.

"I don't know where anything is." Mother spoke rather less cheerfully than usual.

He struck a match. There was a candle on the table, and he lighted it. By its thin little glimmer the children saw a large bare kitchen with a stone floor. There were no curtains, no hearth-rug. The kitchen table from home stood in the middle of the room. The chairs were in one corner, and the pots, pans, brooms, and crockery in another. There was no fire, and the black grate showed cold, dead ashes.

As the cart man turned to go out after he had brought in the boxes, there was a rustling, scampering sound that seemed to come from inside the walls of the house.

"Oh, what's that?" cried the girls.

"It's only the rats," said the cart man. And he went away and shut the door, and the sudden draught of it blew out the candle.

"Oh, dear," said Phyllis, "I wish we hadn't come!" and she knocked a chair over.

"*Only* the rats!" said Peter, in the dark.

Chapter 2

PETER'S COAL-MINE

"What fun!" said Mother, in the dark, feeling for the matches on the table. "How frightened the poor mice were—I don't believe they were rats at all."

She struck a match and relighted the candle and everyone looked at each other by its winky, blinky light.

"Well," she said, "you've often wanted something to happen and now it has. This is quite an adventure, isn't it? I told Mrs Viney to get us some bread and butter and meat and things, and to have supper ready. I suppose she's laid it in the dining-room. So let's go and see."

The dining-room opened out of the kitchen. It looked

much darker than the kitchen when they went in with the one candle, because the kitchen was whitewashed, but the dining-room was dark wood from floor to ceiling, and across the ceiling there were heavy black beams. There was a muddled maze of dusty furniture—the breakfast-room furniture from the old home where they had lived all their lives. It seemed a very long time ago, and a very long way off.

There was a table certainly, and there were chairs, but there was no supper.

"Let's look in the other rooms," said Mother; and they looked. And in each room was the same kind of blundering half-arrangement of furniture, and fire-irons and crockery, and all sorts of odd things on the floor, but there was nothing to eat; even in the pantry there were only a rusty cake-tin and a broken plate with whitening mixed in it.

"What a horrid old woman!" said Mother; "she's just walked off with the money and not got us anything to eat at all."

"Then shan't we have any supper at all?" asked Phyllis, dismayed, stepping back on to a soap-dish that cracked responsively.

"Oh, yes," said Mother, "only it'll mean unpacking one of those big cases that we put in the cellar. Phil, do mind where you're walking to, there's a dear. Peter, hold the light."

The cellar door opened out of the kitchen. There were five wooden steps leading down. It wasn't a proper cellar at all, the children thought, because its ceiling went up as high as the kitchen's. A bacon-rack hung under its ceiling. There was wood in it, and coal. Also the big cases.

Peter held the candle, all on one side, while Mother tried to open the great packing-case. It was very securely nailed down.

"Where's the hammer?" asked Peter.

"That's just it," said Mother. "I'm afraid it's inside the box. But there's a coal-shovel—and there's the kitchen poker."

And with these she tried to get the case open.

"Let me do it," said Peter, thinking he could do it better himself. Everyone thinks this when he sees another person stirring a fire, or opening a box, or untying a knot in a bit of string.

"You'll hurt your hands, Mammy," said Roberta; "let me."

"I wish Father was here," said Phyllis; "he'd get it open in two shakes. What are you kicking me for, Bobbie?"

"I wasn't," said Roberta.

Just then the first of the long nails in the packing-case began to come out with a scrunch. Then a lath was raised and then another, till all four stood up with long nails in them shining fiercely like iron teeth in the candle-light.

"Hooray!" said Mother; "here are some candles—the very first thing! You girls go and light them. You'll find some saucers and things. Just drop a little candle-grease in the saucer and stick the candle upright in it."

"How many shall we light?"

"As many as ever you like," said Mother, gaily. "The great thing is to be cheerful. Nobody can be cheerful in the dark except owls and dormice."

So the girls lighted candles. The head of the first match flew off and stuck to Phyllis's finger; but, as Roberta said, it was only a little burn, and she might have had to be a Roman martyr and be burned whole if she had happened to live in the days when those things were fashionable.

Then, when the dining-room was lighted by fourteen candles, Roberta fetched coal and wood and lighted a fire.

"It's very cold for May," she said, feeling what a grown-up thing it was to say.

The fire-light and the candle-light made the dining-room look very different, for now you could see that the dark walls were of wood, carved here and there into little wreaths and loops.

The girls hastily "tidied" the room, which meant putting the chairs against the wall, and piling all the odds and ends into a corner and partly hiding them with the big leather-chair that Father used to sit in after dinner.

"Bravo!" cried Mother, coming in with a tray full of

things. "This is something like! I'll just get a tablecloth and then—"

The tablecloth was in a box with a proper lock that was opened with a key and not with a shovel, and when the cloth was spread on the table, a real feast was laid out on it.

Everyone was very, very tired, but everyone cheered up at the sight of the funny and delightful supper. There were biscuits, the Marie and the plain kind, sardines, preserved ginger, cooking raisins, and candied peel and marmalade.

"What a good thing Aunt Emma packed up all the odds and ends out of the store cupboard," said Mother. "Now, Phil, *don't* put the marmalade spoon in among the sardines."

"No, I won't, Mother," said Phyllis, and put it down among the Marie biscuits.

"Let's drink Aunt Emma's health," said Roberta, suddenly; "what would we have done if she hadn't packed up these things? Here's to Aunt Emma!"

And the toast was drunk in ginger wine and water, out of willow-patterned tea-cups, because the glasses couldn't be found.

They all felt that they had been a little hard on Aunt Emma. She wasn't a nice cuddly person like Mother, but after all it was she who had thought of packing up the odds and ends of things to eat.

It was Aunt Emma, too, who had aired all the sheets ready; and the men who had moved the furniture had put the bedsteads together, so the beds were soon made.

"Good night, chickies," said Mother. "I'm sure there aren't any rats. But I'll leave my door open, and then if a mouse comes, you need only scream, and I'll come and tell it exactly what I think of it."

Then she went to her own room. Roberta woke to hear the little travelling clock chime two. It sounded like a church clock ever so far away, she always thought. And she heard, too, Mother, still moving about in her room.

Next morning Roberta woke Phyllis by pulling her hair gently, but quite enough for her purpose.

"Wassermarrer?" asked Phyllis, still almost wholly asleep.

"Wake up! wake up!" said Roberta "We're in the new house—don't you remember? No servants or anything. Let's get up and begin to be useful. We'll just creep down mouse-quietly, and have everything beautiful before Mother gets up. I've woken Peter. He'll be dressed as soon as we are."

So they dressed quietly and quickly. Of course, there was no water in their room, so when they got down they washed as much as they thought was necessary under the spout of the pump in the yard. One pumped and the other washed. It was splashy but interesting.

"It's much more fun than basin washing," said Roberta. "How sparkly the weeds are between the stones, and the moss on the roof—oh, and the flowers!"

The roof of the back kitchen sloped down quite low. It was made of thatch and it had moss on it, and house-leeks and stone-crop and wallflowers, and even a clump of purple flag-flowers, at the far corner.

"This is far, far and away prettier than Edgecombe Villa," said Phyllis. "I wonder what the garden's like."

"We mustn't think of the garden yet," said Roberta, with earnest energy. "Let's go in and begin to work."

They lighted the fire and put the kettle on, and they arranged the crockery for breakfast; they could not find all the right things, but a glass ash-tray made an excellent salt-cellar, and a newish baking-tin seemed as if it would do to put bread on if they had any.

When there seemed to be nothing more that they could do, they went out again into the fresh bright morning.

"We'll go into the garden now," said Peter. But somehow they couldn't find the garden. They went round the house and round the house. The yard occupied the back, and across it were stables and outbuildings. On the other three sides the house stood simply in a field, without a yard of garden to divide it from the short smooth turf. And yet they had certainly seen the garden wall the night before.

It was a hilly country. Down below they could see the

line of the railway, and the black yawning mouth of a tunnel. The station was out of sight. There was a great bridge with tall arches running across one end of the valley.

"Never mind the garden," said Peter; "let's go down and look at the railway. There might be trains passing."

"We can see them from here," said Roberta, slowly; "let's sit down a bit."

So they all sat down on a great flat grey stone that had pushed itself up out of the grass; it was one of many that lay about on the hillside, and when Mother came out to look for them at eight o'clock, she found them deeply asleep in a contented, sun-warmed bunch.

They had made an excellent fire, and had set the kettle on it at about half past five. So that by eight the fire had been out for some time, the water had all boiled away, and the bottom was burned out of the kettle. Also they had not thought of washing the crockery before they set the table.

"But it doesn't matter—the cups and saucers, I mean," said Mother. "Because I've found another room—I'd quite forgotten there was one. And it's magic! And I've boiled the water for tea in a saucepan."

The forgotten room opened out of the kitchen. In the agitation and half darkness the night before its door had been mistaken for a cupboard's. It was a little square room, and on its table, all nicely set out, was a joint of cold roast beef, with bread and butter, cheese, and a pie.

"Pie for breakfast!" cried Peter; "how perfectly ripping!"

"It isn't pigeon-pie," said Mother; "it's only apple. Well, this is the supper we ought to have had last night. And there was a note from Mrs Viney. Her son-in-law has broken his arm, and she had to get home early. She's coming this morning at ten."

That was a wonderful breakfast. It is unusual to begin the day with cold apple pie, but the children all said they would rather have it than meat.

"You see it's more like dinner than breakfast to us," said Peter, passing his plate for more, "because we were up so early."

The day passed in helping Mother to unpack and arrange

things. Six small legs quite ached with running about while their owners carried clothes and crockery and all sorts of things to their proper places. It was not till quite late in the afternoon that Mother said:

"There! That'll do for today. I'll lie down for an hour, so as to be as fresh as a lark by supper-time."

Then they all looked at each other. Each of the three expressive countenances expressed the same thought. That thought was double, and consisted, like the bits of information in the *Child's Guide to Knowledge*, of a question and an answer.

Q. Where shall we go?

A. To the railway.

So to the railway they went, and as soon as they started for the railway they saw where the garden had hidden itself. It was right behind the stables, and it had a high wall all round.

"Oh, never mind about the garden now!" cried Peter. "Mother told me this morning where it was. It'll keep till tomorrow. Let's get to the railway."

The way to the railway was all downhill over smooth, short turf with here and there furze bushes and grey and yellow rocks sticking out like candied peel from the top of a cake.

The way ended in a steep run and a wooden fence—and there was the railway with the shining metals and the telegraph wires and posts and signals.

They all climbed on to the top of the fence, and then suddenly there was a rumbling sound that made them look along the line to the right, where the dark mouth of a tunnel opened itself in the face of a rocky cliff; next moment a train had rushed out of the tunnel with a shriek and a snort, and had slid noisily past them. They felt the rush of its passing, and the pebbles on the line jumped and rattled under it as it went by.

"Oh!" said Roberta, drawing a long breath; "it was like a great dragon tearing by. Did you feel it fan us with its hot wings?"

"I suppose a dragon's lair might look very like that tunnel from the outside," said Phyllis.

But Peter said:

"I never thought we should ever get so near to a train as this. It's the most ripping sport!"

"Better than toy-engines, isn't it?" said Roberta.

(I am tired of calling Roberta by her name. I don't see why I should. No one else did. Everyone else called her Bobbie, and I don't see why I shouldn't.)

"I don't know; it's different," said Peter. "It seems so odd to see *all* of a train. It's awfully tall, isn't it?"

"We've always seen them cut in half by platforms," said Phyllis.

"I wonder if that train was going to London," Bobbie said. "London's where Father is."

"Let's go down to the station and find out," said Peter.

So they went.

They walked along the edge of the line, and heard the telegraph wires humming over their heads. When you are in the train, it seems such a little way between post and post, and one after another the posts seem to catch up the wires almost more quickly than you can count them. But when you have to walk, the posts seem few and far between.

But the children got to the station at last.

Never before had any one of them been at a station, except for the purpose of catching trains—or perhaps waiting for them—and always with grown-ups in attendance, grown-ups who were not themselves interested in stations, except as places from which they wished to get away.

Never before had they passed close enough to a signal-box to be able to notice the wires, and to hear the mysterious "ping, ping", followed by the strong, firm clicking of machinery.

The very sleepers on which the rails lay were a delightful path to travel by—just far enough apart to serve as the stepping-stones in a game of foaming torrents hastily organized by Bobbie.

Then to arrive at the station, not through the booking office, but in a freebooting sort of way by the sloping end of the platform. This in itself was joy.

Joy, too, it was to peep into the porters' room, where the lamps are, and the Railway almanac on the wall, and one porter half asleep behind a paper.

There were a great many crossing lines at the station; some of them just ran into a yard and stopped short, as though they were tired of business and meant to retire for good. Trucks stood on the rails here, and on one side was a great heap of coal—not a loose heap, such as you see in your coal cellar, but a sort of solid building of coals with large square blocks of coal outside used just as though they were bricks, and built up till the heap looked like the picture of the Cities of the Plain in *Bible Stories for Infants*. There was a line of whitewash near the top of the coaly wall.

When presently the Porter lounged out of his room at the twice-repeated tingling thrill of a gong over the station door, Peter said, "How do you do?" in his best manner, and hastened to ask what the white mark was on the coal for.

"To mark how much coal there be," said the Porter, "so we'll know if anyone nicks it. So don't you go off with none in your pockets, young gentleman!"

This seemed, at the time, but a merry jest, and Peter felt at once that the Porter was a friendly sort with no nonsense about him. But later the words came back to Peter with a new meaning.

Have you ever gone into a farmhouse kitchen on a baking day, and seen the great crock of dough set by the fire to rise? If you have, and if you were at that time still young enough to be interested in everything you saw, you will remember that you found yourself quite unable to resist the temptation to poke your finger into the soft round dough that curved inside the pan like a giant mushroom. And you will remember that your finger made a dent in the dough, and that slowly, but quite surely, the dent disappeared, and the dough looked quite the same as it did before you touched it. Unless, of course, your hand was extra dirty in which case, naturally, there would be a little black mark.

Well, it was just like that with the sorrow the children

had felt at Father's going away, and at Mother's being so unhappy. It made a deep impression, but the impression did not last long.

They soon got used to being without Father, though they did not forget him; and they got used to not going to school, and to seeing very little of Mother, who was now almost all day shut up in her upstairs room writing, writing, writing. She used to come down at tea-time and read aloud the stories she had written. They were lovely stories.

The rocks and hills and valleys and trees, the canal, and above all, the railway, were so new and so perfectly pleasing that the remembrance of the old life in the villa grew to seem almost like a dream.

Mother had told them more than once that they were "quite poor now," but this did not seem to be anything but a way of speaking. Grown-up people, even Mothers, often make remarks that don't seem to mean anything in particular, just for the sake of saying something, seemingly. There was always enough to eat, and they wore the same kind of nice clothes they had always worn.

But in June came three wet days; the rain came down, straight as lances, and it was very, very cold. Nobody could go out, and everybody shivered. They all went up to the door of Mother's room and knocked.

"Well, what is it?" asked Mother from inside.

"Mother," said Bobbie, "mayn't I light a fire? I do know how."

And Mother said: "No, my ducky-love. We mustn't have fires in June—coal is so dear. If you're cold, go and have a good romp in the attic. That'll warm you."

"But, Mother, it only takes such a very little coal to make a fire."

"It's more than we can afford, chickeny-love," said Mother, cheerfully. "Now run away, there's darlings—I'm madly busy!"

"Mother's always busy now," said Phyllis, in a whisper to Peter. Peter did not answer. He shrugged his shoulders. He was thinking.

Thought, however, could not long keep itself from the suitable furnishing of a bandit's lair in the attic. Peter was the bandit, of course. Bobbie was his lieutenant, his band of trusty robbers, and, in due course, the parent of Phyllis, who was the captured maiden for whom a magnificent ransom—in horse-beans—was unhesitatingly paid.

They all went down to tea flushed and joyous as any mountain brigands.

But when Phyllis was going to add jam to her bread and butter, Mother said:

"Jam or butter, dear—not jam *and* butter. We can't afford that sort of reckless luxury nowadays."

Phyllis finished the slice of bread and butter in silence, and followed it up by bread and jam. Peter mingled thought and weak tea.

After tea they went back to the attic and he said to his sisters:

"I have an idea."

"What's that?" they asked politely.

"I shan't tell you," was Peter's unexpected rejoinder.

"Oh, very well," said Bobbie; and Phil said, "Don't then."

"Girls," said Peter, "are always so hasty tempered."

"I should like to know what boys are !" said Bobbie, with fine disdain. "I don't want to know about your silly ideas."

"You'll know some day," said Peter, keeping his own temper by what looked exactly like a miracle; "if you hadn't been so keen on a row, I might have told you about it being only noble-heartedness that made me not tell you my idea. But now I shan't tell you anything at all about it—so there!"

And it was, indeed, some time before he could be induced to say anything, and when he did it wasn't much. He said:

"The only reason why I won't tell you my idea that I'm going to do is because it may be wrong, and I don't want to drag you into it."

"Don't you do it if it's wrong, Peter," said Bobbie; "let me do it." But Phyllis said:

"*I* should like to do wrong if *you're* going to!"

"No," said Peter, rather touched by this devotion; "it's a

forlorn hope, and I'm going to lead it. All I ask is that if Mother asks where I am, you won't blab."

"We haven't got anything *to* blab," said Bobbie, indignantly.

"Oh, yes, you have!" said Peter, dropping horse-beans through his fingers. "I've trusted you to the death. You know I'm going to do a lone adventure—and some people might think it wrong—I don't. And if Mother asks where I am, say I'm playing at mines."

"What sort of mines?"

"You just say mines."

"You might tell *us*, Pete."

"Well, then, *coal*-mines. But don't you let the word pass your lips on pain of torture."

"You needn't threaten," said Bobbie, "and I do think you might let us help."

"If I find a coal-mine, you shall help cart the coal," Peter condescended to promise.

"Keep your secret if you like," said Phyllis.

"Keep it if you *can*," said Bobbie.

"I'll keep it right enough," said Peter.

Between tea and supper there is an interval even in the most greedily regulated families. At this time Mother was usually writing, and Mrs Viney had gone home.

Two nights after the dawning of Peter's idea he beckoned the girls mysteriously at the twilight hour.

"Come hither with me," he said, "and bring the Roman Chariot."

The Roman Chariot was a very old perambulator that had spent years of retirement in the loft over the coach-house. The children had oiled its works till it glided noiseless as a pneumatic bicycle, and answered to the helm as it had probably done long ago in its best days.

"Follow your dauntless leader," said Peter, and led the way down the hill towards the station.

Just above the station many rocks had pushed their heads out through the turf as though they, like the children, were interested in the railway.

In a little hollow between three rocks lay a heap of dried brambles and heather.

Peter halted, turned over the brushwood with a well-scarred boot and said:

"Here's the first coal from the St Peter's Mine. We'll take it home in the chariot. Punctuality and despatch. All orders carefully attended to. Any shaped lump cut to suit regular customers."

The chariot was packed full of coal. And when it was packed it had to be unpacked again because it was so heavy that it couldn't be got up the hill by the three children, not even when Peter harnessed himself to the handle with his braces, and firmly grasping his waistband in one hand pulled while the girls pushed behind.

Three journeys had to be made before the coal from Peter's mine was added to the heap of Mother's coal in the cellar.

Afterwards Peter went out alone, and came back very black and mysterious.

"I've been to my coal-mine," he said; "tomorrow evening we'll bring home the black diamonds in the chariot."

It was a week later that Mrs Viney remarked to Mother how well this last lot of coal was holding out.

The children hugged themselves and each other in complicated wriggles of silent laughter as they listened on the stairs. They had all forgotten by now that there had ever been any doubt in Peter's mind as to whether coal-mining was wrong.

But there came a dreadful night when the Station Master put on a pair of old sand shoes that he had worn at the seaside on his summer holiday, and crept out very quietly to the yard where the Sodom and Gomorrah heap of coal was, with the whitewashed line round it. He crept out there, and he waited like a cat by a mousehole. On the top of the heap something small and dark was scrabbling and rattling furtively among the coal.

The Station Master concealed himself in the shadow of a brake-van that had a little tin chimney and was labelled:

G. N. & S. R.
34576

Return at once to
White Heather Sidings,

and in this concealment he lurked till the small thing on the top of the heap ceased to scrabble and rattle, came to the edge of the heap, cautiously let itself down, and lifted something after it. Then the arm of the Station Master was raised, the hand of the Station Master fell on a collar, and there was Peter firmly held by the jacket, with an old carpenter's bag full of coal in his trembling clutch.

"So I've caught you at last, have I, you young thief?" said the Station Master.

"I'm not a thief," said Peter, as firmly as he could. "I'm a coal-miner."

"Tell that to the Marines," said the Station Master.

"It would be just as true whoever I told it to," said Peter.

"You're right there," said the man who held him. "Stow your jaw, you young rip, and come along to the station."

"Oh, no," cried in the darkness an agonized voice that was not Peter's.

"Not the *police* station!" said another voice from the darkness.

"Not yet," said the Station Master. "The Railway Station first. Why, it's a regular gang. Any more of you?"

"Only us," said Bobbie and Phyllis, coming out of the shadow of another truck labelled Stavely Colliery, and bearing on it the legend in white chalk: "Wanted in No.1 Road."

"What do you mean by spying on a fellow like this?" said Peter, angrily.

"Time someone did spy on you, *I* think," said the Station Master. "Come along to the station."

"Oh, *don't*!" said Bobbie. "Can't you decide *now* what you'll do to us? It's our fault just as much as Peter's. We helped to carry the coal away—and we knew where he got it."

"No, you didn't," said Peter.

"Yes, we did," said Bobbie. "We knew all the time. We only pretended we didn't just to humour you."

Peter's cup was full. He had mined for coal, he had struck coal, he had been caught, and now he learned that his sisters had "humoured" him.

"Don't hold me!" he said. "I won't run away."

The Station Master loosed Peter's collar, struck a match and looked at them by its flickering light.

"Why," said he, "you're the children from the Three Chimneys up yonder. So nicely dressed, too. Tell me now, what made you do such a thing? Haven't you ever been to church or learned your catechism or anything, not to know it's wicked to steal?" He spoke much more gently now, and Peter said:

"I didn't think it was stealing. I was almost sure it wasn't. I thought if I took it from the outside part of the heap, perhaps it would be. But in the middle I thought I could fairly count it only mining. It'll take thousands of years for you to burn up all that coal and get to the middle parts."

"Not quite. But did you do it for a lark or what?"

"Not much lark carrying that beastly heavy stuff up the hill," said Peter, indignantly.

"Then why did you?" The Station Master's voice was so much kinder now that Peter replied:

"You know that wet day? Well, Mother said we were too poor to have a fire. We always had fires when it was cold at our other house, and—"

"*Don't*" interrupted Bobbie, in a whisper.

"Well," said the Station Master, rubbing his chin thoughtfully, "I'll tell you what I'll do. I'll look over it this once. But you remember, young gentleman, stealing is stealing, and what's mine isn't yours, whether you call it mining or whether you don't. Run along home."

"Do you mean you aren't going to do anything to us? Well, you are a brick," said Peter, with enthusiasm.

"You're a dear," said Bobbie.

"You're a darling," said Phyllis.

"That's all right," said the Station Master.

And on this they parted.

"Don't speak to me," said Peter, as the three went up the hill. "You're spies and traitors—that's what you are."

But the girls were too glad to have Peter between them, safe and free, and on the way to Three Chimneys and not to the Police Station, to mind much what he said.

"We *did* say it was us as much as you," said Bobbie, gently.

"Well—and it wasn't."

"It would have come to the same thing in Courts with judges," said Phyllis. "Don't be snarky, Peter. It isn't our fault your secrets are so jolly easy to find out." She took his arm, and he let her.

"There's an awful lot of coal in the cellar, anyhow," he went on.

"Oh, don't!" said Bobbie. "I don't think we ought to be glad about *that*."

"I don't know," said Peter, plucking up spirit. "I'm not at all sure, even now, that mining is a crime."

But the girls were quite sure. And they were also quite sure that he was quite sure, however little he cared to own it.

CHAPTER 3

THE OLD GENTLEMAN

After the adventure of Peter's coal-mine, it seemed well to the children to keep away from the station—but they did not, they could not, keep away from the railway. They had lived all their lives in a street where cabs and omnibuses rumbled by at all hours, and the carts of butchers and bakers and candlestick makers (I never saw a candlestick maker's cart; did you?) might occur at any moment. Here in the deep silence of the sleeping country the only things that went by were the trains. They seemed to be all that was left to link the children to the old life that had once been theirs. Straight down the hill in front of Three Chimneys the daily passage of their six feet began to mark a path across the crisp, short turf. They began to know the hours when certain trains passed, and they gave names to them. The 9.15 up was called the Green Dragon. The 10.7 down was the Worm of Wantley. The midnight town express, whose shrieking rush they sometimes woke from their dreams to hear, was the Fearsome Fly-by-night. Peter got up once, in chill starshine, and, peeping at it through his curtains, named it on the spot.

It was by the Green Dragon that the old gentleman travelled. He was a very nice-looking old gentleman, and he looked as if he were nice, too, which is not at all the same thing. He had a fresh-coloured, clean-shaven face and white hair, and he wore rather odd-shaped collars and a top-hat that wasn't exactly the same kind as other people's. Of course the children didn't see all this at first. In fact the first thing they noticed about the old gentleman was his hand.

It was one morning as they sat on the fence waiting for the Green Dragon, which was three and a quarter minutes late by Peter's Waterbury watch that he had had given him on his last birthday.

"The Green Dragon's going where Father is," said Phyllis; "if it were a really real dragon, we could stop it and ask it to take our love to Father."

"Dragons don't carry people's love," said Peter; "they'd be above it."

"Yes, they do, if you tame them thoroughly first. They fetch and carry like pet spaniels," said Phyllis, "and feed out of your hand. I wonder why Father never writes to us."

"Mother says he's been too busy," said Bobbie; "but he'll write soon, she says."

"I say," Phyllis suggested, "let's all wave to the Green Dragon as it goes by. If it's a magic dragon, it'll understand

and take our love to Father. And if it isn't, three waves aren't much. We shall never miss them."

So when the Green Dragon tore shrieking out of the mouth of its dark lair, which was the tunnel, all three children stood on the railing and waved their pocket-handkerchiefs without stopping to think whether they were clean handkerchiefs or the reverse. They were, as a matter of fact, very much the reverse.

And out of a first-class carriage a hand waved back. A quite clean hand. It held a newspaper. It was the old gentleman's hand.

After this it became the custom for waves to be exchanged between the children and the 9.15.

And the children, especially the girls, liked to think that perhaps the old gentleman knew Father, and would meet him "in business", wherever that shady retreat might be, and tell him how his three children stood on a rail far away in the green country and waved their love to him every morning, wet or fine.

For they were now able to go out in all sorts of weather such as they would never have been allowed to go out in when they lived in their villa house. This was Aunt Emma's doing, and the children felt more and more that they had not been quite fair to this unattractive aunt, when they found how useful were the long gaiters and waterproof coats that they had laughed at her for buying for them.

Mother, all this time, was very busy with her writing. She used to send off a good many long blue envelopes with stories in them—and large envelopes of different sizes and colours used to come to her. Sometimes she would sigh when she opened them and say:

"Another story come home to roost. Oh, dear! Oh, dear!" and then the children would be very sorry.

But sometimes she would wave the envelope in the air and say:

"Hooray, hooray. Here's a sensible Editor. He's taken my story and this is the proof of it."

At first the children thought "the proof" meant the letter the sensible Editor had written, but they presently got to know that the proof was long slips of paper with the story printed on them.

Whenever an Editor was sensible there were buns for tea.

One day Peter was going down to the village to get buns to celebrate the sensibleness of the Editor of the *Children's Globe*, when he met the Station Master.

Peter felt very uncomfortable, for he had now had time to think over the affair of the coal-mine. He did not like to say "Good morning" to the Station Master, as you usually do to anyone you meet on a lonely road, because he had a hot feeling, which spread even to his ears, that the Station Master might not care to speak to a person who had stolen coals. "Stolen" is a nasty word, but Peter felt it was the right one. So he looked down; and said nothing.

It was the Station Master who said "Good morning" as he passed by. And Peter answered, "Good morning." Then he thought:

"Perhaps he doesn't know who I am by daylight, or he wouldn't be so polite."

And he did not like the feeling which thinking this gave him. And then before he knew what he was going to do he ran after the Station Master, who stopped when he heard Peter's hasty boots crunching the road, and coming up with him very breathless and with his ears now quite magenta-coloured, he said:

"I don't want you to be polite to me if you don't know me when you see me."

"Eh?" said the Station Master.

"I thought perhaps you didn't know it was me that took the coals," Peter went on, "when you said 'Good morning'. But it was, and I'm sorry. There."

"Why," said the Station Master, "I wasn't thinking anything at all about the precious coals. Let bygones be bygones. And where were you off to in such a hurry?"

"I'm going to buy buns for tea," said Peter.

"I thought you were all so poor," said the Station Master.

"So we are," said Peter, confidentially, "but we always have three-pennyworth of halfpennies for tea whenever Mother sells a story or a poem or anything."

"Oh," said the Station Master, "so your Mother writes stories, does she?"

"The beautifulest you ever read," said Peter.

"You ought to be very proud to have such a clever Mother."

"Yes", said Peter, "but she used to play with us more before she had to be so clever."

"Well," said the Station Master, "I must be getting along. You give us a look in at the Station whenever you feel so inclined. And as to coals, it's a word that—well—oh, no, we never mention it, eh?"

"Thank you," said Peter. "I'm very glad it's all straightened out between us." And he went on across the canal bridge to the village to get the buns, feeling more comfortable in his mind than he had felt since the hand of the Station Master had fastened on his collar that night among the coals.

Next day when they had sent the threefold wave of greeting to Father by the Green Dragon, and the old gentleman had waved back as usual, Peter proudly led the way to the station.

"But ought we?" said Bobbie.

"After the coals, she means," Phyllis explained.

"I met the Station Master yesterday," said Peter, in an offhand way, and he pretended not to hear what Phyllis had said; "he expressly invited us to go down any time we liked."

"After the coals?" repeated Phyllis. "Stop a minute—my bootlace is undone again."

"It always *is* undone again," said Peter, "and the Station Master was more of a gentleman than you'll ever be, Phil—throwing coal at a chap's head like that."

Phyllis did up her bootlace and went on in silence, but her shoulders shook, and presently a fat tear fell off her nose and splashed on the metal of the railway line. Bobbie saw it.

"Why, what's the matter, darling?" she said, stopping short and putting her arm round the heaving shoulders.

"He called me un—un—ungentlemanly," sobbed Phyllis.

"I didn't never call him unladylike, not even when he tied my Clorinda to the firewood bundle and burned her at the stake for a martyr."

Peter had indeed perpetrated this outrage a year or two before.

"Well, you began, you know," said Bobbie, honestly, "about coals and all that. Don't you think you'd better both unsay everything since the wave, and let honour be satisfied?"

"I will if Peter will," said Phyllis, sniffing.

"All right," said Peter; "honour is satisfied. Here, use my hankie, Phil, for goodness' sake, if you've lost yours as usual. I wonder what you do with them."

"You had my last one," said Phyllis, indignantly, "to tie up the rabbit-hutch door with. But you're very ungrateful. It's quite right what it says in the poetry-book about sharper than a serpent it is to have a toothless child—but it means ungrateful when it says toothless. Miss Lowe told me so."

"All right," said Peter, impatiently, "I'm sorry, *There*! Now will you come on?"

They reached the station and spent a joyous two hours with the Porter. He was a worthy man and seemed never tired of answering the questions that began with "Why—" which many people in higher ranks of life often seem weary of.

He told them many things that they had not known before—as, for instance, that the things that hook carriages together are called couplings, and that the pipes like great serpents that hang over the couplings are meant to stop the train with.

"If you could get a hold of one o' them when the train is going and pull 'em apart," said he, "she'd stop dead off with a jerk."

"Who's she?" said Phyllis.

"The train, of course," said the Porter. After that the train was never again "It" to the children.

"And you know the thing in the carriages where it says on it, 'Five pounds' fine for improper use.' If you was to improperly use that, the train 'ud stop."

"And if you used it properly?" said Roberta.

"It 'ud stop just the same, I suppose," said he, "but it isn't proper use unless you're being murdered. There was an old lady once—someone kidded her on it was a refreshment-room bell, and she used it improper, not being in danger of her life, though hungry, and when the train stopped and the guard came along expecting to find someone weltering in their last moments, she says, 'Oh, please, Mister, I'll take a glass of stout and a bath bun,' she says. And the train was seven minutes behind her time as it was."

"What did the guard say to the old lady?"

"*I* dunno," replied the Porter, "but I lay she didn't forget it in a hurry, whatever it was."

In such delightful conversation the time went by all too quickly.

The Station Master came out once or twice from that sacred inner temple behind the place where the hole is that they sell you tickets through, and was most jolly with them all.

"Just as if coal had never been discovered," Phyllis whispered to her sister.

He gave them each an orange, and promised to take them up into the signal-box one of these days, when he wasn't so busy.

Several trains went through the station, and Peter noticed for the first time that engines have numbers on them, like cabs.

"Yes," said the Porter, "I knowed a young gent as used to take down the numbers of every single one he seed; in a green note-book with silver corners it was, owing to his father being very well-to-do in the wholesale stationery."

Peter felt that he could take down numbers, too, even if he was not the son of a wholesale stationer. As he did not happen to have a green leather note-book with silver corners, the Porter gave him a yellow envelope and on it he noted:

379
663

and felt that this was the beginning of what would be a most interesting collection.

That night at tea he asked Mother if she had a green leather note-book with silver corners. She had not; but when she heard what he wanted it for she gave him a little black one.

"It has a few pages torn out," said she; "but it will hold quite a lot of numbers, and when it's full I'll give you another. I'm so glad you like the railway. Only, please, you mustn't walk on the line."

"Not if we face the way the train's coming?" asked Peter, after a gloomy pause, in which glances of despair were exchanged.

"No—really not," said Mother.

Then Phyllis said, "Mother, didn't *you* ever walk on the railway lines when you were little?"

Mother was an honest and honourable Mother, so she had to say, "Yes."

"Well, then," said Phyllis.

"But, darlings, you don't know how fond I am of you. What should I do if you got hurt?"

"Are you fonder of us than Granny was of you when you were little?" Phyllis asked. Bobbie made signs to her to stop, but Phyllis never did see signs, no matter how plain they might be.

Mother did not answer for a minute. She got up to put more water in the teapot.

"No one," she said at last, "ever loved anyone more than my mother loved me."

Then she was quiet again, and Bobbie kicked Phyllis hard under the table, because Bobbie understood a little bit the thoughts that were making Mother so quiet—the thoughts of the time when Mother was a little girl and was all the world to *her* mother. It seems so easy and natural to run to Mother when one is in trouble. Bobbie understood a little how people do not leave off running to their mothers when they are in trouble even when they are grown up, and she thought she knew a little what it must be to be sad, and have no mother to run to any more.

So she kicked Phyllis, who said:

"What are you kicking me like that for, Bob?"

And then Mother laughed a little and sighed and said:

"Very well, then. Only let me be sure you do know which way the trains come—and don't walk on the line near the tunnel or near corners."

"Trains keep to the left like carriages," said Peter, "so if we keep to the right, we're bound to see them coming."

"Very well," said Mother, and I dare say you think that she ought not to have said it. But she remembered about when she was a little girl herself, and she did say it—and neither her own children nor you nor any other children in the world could ever understand exactly what it cost her to do it. Only some few of you, like Bobbie, may understand a very little bit.

It was the very next day that Mother had to stay in bed because her head ached so. Her hands were burning hot, and she would not eat anything, and her throat was very sore.

"If I was you, Mum," said Mrs Viney, "I should take and send for the doctor. There's a lot of catchy complaints a-going about just now. My sister's eldest—she took a-chill and it went to her inside, two year ago come Christmas, and she's never been the same gell since."

Mother wouldn't at first, but in the evening she felt so much worse that Peter was sent to the house in the village that had three laburnum trees by the gate, and on the gate a brass plate with W. W. Forrest, M.D., on it.

W. W. Forrest, M.D., came at once. He talked to Peter on the way back. He seemed a most charming and sensible man, interested in railways, and rabbits, and really important things.

When he had seen Mother, he said it was influenza

"Now, Lady Grave-airs," he said in the hall to Bobbie, "I suppose you'll want to be head-nurse."

"Of course," said she.

"Well, then, I'll send down some medicine. Keep up a good fire. Have some strong beef tea made ready to give her as soon as the fever goes down. She can have grapes now, and beef essence—and soda-water and milk, and you'd better get in a bottle of brandy. The best brandy. Cheap brandy is worse than poison."

She asked him to write it all down, and he did.

When Bobbie showed Mother the list he had written, Mother laughed. It was a laugh, Bobbie decided though it was rather cold and feeble.

"Nonsense," said Mother, lying in bed with eyes as bright as beads. "I can't afford all that rubbish. Tell Mrs Viney to boil two pounds of scrag-end of the neck for your dinners tomorrow, and I can have some of the broth. Yes, I should like some more water now, love. And will you get a basin and sponge my hands?"

Roberta obeyed. When she had done everything she could to make Mother less uncomfortable, she went down to the others. Her cheeks were very red, her lips set tight, and her eyes shone as bright as Mother's.

She told them what the Doctor had said, and what Mother had said.

"And now," said she, when she had told all, "there's no one but us to do anything, and we've got to do it. I've got the shilling for the mutton."

"We can do without the beastly mutton," said Peter; "bread and butter will support life. People have lived on less on desert islands many a time."

"Of course," said his sister. And Mrs Viney was sent to the village to get as much brandy and soda-water and beef tea as she could buy for a shilling.

"But even if we never have anything to eat at all," said Phyllis, "you can't get all those other things with our dinner money."

"No," said Bobbie, frowning, "we must find out some other way. Now *think* everybody, just as hard as ever you can."

They did think. And presently they talked. And later, when Bobbie had gone up to sit with Mother in case she wanted anything, the other two were very busy with scissors and a white sheet, and a paint brush, and the pot of Brunswick black that Mrs Viney used for grates and fenders. They did not manage to do what they wished, exactly, with the first sheet, so they took another out of the linen cupboard. It did not occur to them that they were spoiling good sheets which cost good money. They only knew that they were making a good—but what they were making comes later.

Bobbie's bed had been moved into Mother's room, and several times in the night she got up to mend the fire, and to give her mother milk and soda-water. Mother talked to herself a good deal, but it did not seem to mean anything. And once she woke up suddenly and called out: "Mamma, mamma!" and Bobbie knew she was calling for Granny, and that she had forgotten that it was no use calling, because Granny was dead.

In the early morning Bobbie heard her name and jumped out of bed and ran to Mother's bedside.

"Oh—ah—yes—I think I was asleep," said Mother. "My poor little duck, how tired you'll be—I do hate to give you all this trouble."

"Trouble!" said Bobbie.

"Ah, don't cry, sweet," Mother said; "I shall be all right in a day or two."

And Bobbie said, "Yes," and tried to smile.

When you are used to ten hours of solid sleep, to get up three or four times in your sleep-time makes you feel as though you had been up all night. Bobbie felt quite stupid and her eyes were sore and stiff, but she tidied the room, and arranged everything neatly before the Doctor came.

This was at half past eight.

"Everything going on all right, little Nurse?" he said at the front door. "Did you get the brandy?"

"I've got the brandy," said Bobbie, "in a little flat bottle."

"I didn't see the grapes or the beef tea, though," said he.

"No," said Bobbie, firmly, "but you will tomorrow. And there's some beef stewing in the oven for beef tea."

"Who told you to do that" he asked.

"I noticed what Mother did when Phil had mumps."

"Right," said the Doctor. "Now you get your old woman to sit with your mother, and then you eat a good breakfast, and go straight to bed and sleep till dinnertime. We can't afford to have the head-nurse ill."

He was really quite a nice doctor.

When the 9.15 came out of the tunnel that morning the old gentleman in the first-class carriage put down his newspaper, and got ready to wave his hand to the three children on the fence. But this morning there were not three. There was only one. And that was Peter.

Peter was not on the railings either, as usual. He was standing in front of them in an attitude like that of a showman showing off the animals in a menagerie, or of the kind clergyman when he points with a wand at the "Scenes from Palestine," when there is a magic-lantern and he is explaining it.

Peter was pointing, too. And what he was pointing at was a large white sheet nailed against the fence. On the sheet there were thick black letters more than a foot long.

Some of them had run a little, because of Phyllis having put the Brunswick black on too eagerly, but the words were quite easy to read.

And this was what the old gentleman and several other people in the train read in the large black letters on the white sheet:

LOOK OUT AT THE STATION

A good many people did look out at the station and were disappointed, for they saw nothing unusual. The old gentleman looked out, too, and at first he too saw nothing more unusual than the gravelled platform and the sunshine and the wall-flowers and forget-me-nots in the station borders. It was only just as the train was beginning to puff and pull itself together to start again that he saw Phyllis. She was quite out of breath with running.

"Oh," she said, "I thought I'd missed you. My bootlaces would keep coming down, and I fell over them twice. Here, take it."

She threw a warm, dampish letter into his hand as the train moved.

He leaned back in his corner. and opened the letter. This is what he read:

DEAR MR We do not know your name.

Mother is ill and the doctor says to give her the things at the end of the letter, but she says she can't afford it and to get mutton for us and she will have the broth. We do not know anybody here but you, because Father is away and we do not know the address. Father will pay you, or if he has lost all his money, or anything, Peter will pay you when he is a man. We promise it on our honer. I. O. U. for all the things Mother wants

sined PETER

Will you give the parsel to the Station Master, because of us not knowing what train you come down by? Say it is for Peter that was sorry about the coals and he will know all right.

ROBERTA
PHYLLIS
PETER

Then came the list of things the Doctor had ordered.

The old gentleman read it through once, and his eyebrows went up. He read it twice and smiled a little. When he had read it twice, he put it in his pocket and went on reading *The Times*.

At about six that evening there was a knock at the back door. The three children rushed to open it, and there stood the friendly Porter, who had told them so many interesting things about railways. He dumped down a big hamper on the kitchen flags.

"Old gent," he said; "he asked me to fetch it up straight away."

"Thank you very much," said Peter, and then, as the Porter lingered, he added:

"I'm most awfully sorry I haven't got twopence to give you like Father does, but—"

"You drop it if you please," said the Porter, indignantly. "I wasn't thinking about no tuppences. I only wanted to say I was sorry your Mamma wasn't so well, and to ask how she finds herself this evening—and I've fetched her along a bit of sweetbriar, very sweet to smell it is. Twopence indeed," said he, and produced a bunch of sweetbriar from his hat, "just like a conjurer," as Phyllis remarked afterwards.

"Thank you very much," said Peter, "and I beg your pardon about the twopence."

"No offence," said the Porter, untruly but politely, and went.

Then the children undid the hamper. First there was straw, and then there were fine shavings, and then came all the things they had asked for, and plenty of them, and then a good many things they had not asked for; among others peaches and port wine and two chickens, a cardboard box of big red roses with long stalks, and a tall thin green bottle of lavender water, and three smaller fatter bottles of eau-de-Cologne. There was a letter, too.

"Dear Roberta and Phyllis and Peter," it said; "here are the things you want. Your mother will want to know where they came from. Tell her they were sent by a friend who heard she was ill. When she is well again you must tell her all about it, of course. And if she says you ought not to have asked for the things, tell her that I say you were quite right, and that I hope she will forgive me for taking the liberty of allowing myself a great pleasure."

The letter was signed G. P. something that the children couldn't read.

"I think we *were* right," said Phyllis.

"Right? Of course we were right," said Bobbie.

"All the same," said Peter, with his hands in his pockets, "I don't exactly look forward to telling Mother the whole truth about it."

"We're not to do it till she's well," said Bobbie, "and when she's well we shall be so happy we shan't mind a little fuss like that. Oh, just look at the roses! I must take them up to her."

"And the sweetbriar," said Phyllis, sniffing it loudly: "don't forget the sweetbriar."

"As if I should!" said Roberta "Mother told me the other day there was a thick hedge of it at her mother's house when she was a little girl."

Chapter 4

THE ENGINE-BURGLAR

What was left of the second sheet and the Brunswick black came in very nicely to make a banner bearing the legend

SHE IS NEARLY WELL, THANK YOU

and this was displayed to the Green Dragon about a fortnight after the arrival of the wonderful hamper. The old gentleman saw it, and waved a cheerful response from the train. And when this had been done the children saw that now was the time when they must tell Mother what they had done when she was ill. And it did not seem nearly so easy as they had thought it would be. But it had to be done. And it was done. Mother was extremely angry. She was seldom angry, and now she was angrier than they had ever known her. This was horrible. But it was much worse when she suddenly began to cry. Crying is catching, I believe, like measles and whooping-cough. At any rate, everyone at once found itself taking part in a crying-party.

Mother stopped first. She dried her eyes and then she said:

"I'm sorry I was so angry, darlings, because I know you didn't understand."

"We didn't mean to be naughty, Mammy," sobbed Bobbie, and Peter and Phyllis sniffed.

"Now, listen," said Mother; "it's quite true that we're poor, but we have enough to live on. You mustn't go telling everyone about our affairs—it's not right. And you must never, never, never ask strangers to give you things. Now always remember that—won't you?"

They all hugged her and rubbed their damp cheeks against hers and promised that they would.

"And I'll write a letter to your old gentleman, and I shall tell him that I didn't approve—oh, of course I shall thank him, too, for his kindness. It's *you* I don't approve of, my darlings, not the old gentleman. He was as kind as ever he could be. And you can give the letter to the Station Master to give him—and we won't say any more about it."

Afterwards, when the children were alone, Bobbie said:

"Isn't Mother splendid? You catch any other grown-up saying they were sorry they had been angry."

"Yes," said Peter, "she *is* splendid; but it's rather awful when she's angry."

"She's like Avenging and Bright in the song," said Phyllis. "I should like to look at her if it wasn't so awful. She looks so beautiful when she's really downright furious."

They took the letter down to the Station Master.

"I thought you said you hadn't got any friends except in London," said he.

"We've made him since," said Peter.

"But he doesn't live hereabouts?"

"No—we just know him on the railway."

Then the Station Master retired to that sacred inner temple behind the little window where the tickets are sold, and the children went down to the Porter's room and talked to the Porter. They learned several interesting things from him—among others that his name was Perks, that he was married and had three children, that the lamps in front of engines are called head-lights and the ones at the back tail-lights.

"And that just shows," whispered Phyllis, "that trains really *are* dragons in disguise, with proper heads and tails."

It was on this day that the children first noticed that all engines are not alike.

"Alike?" said the Porter whose name was Perks, "lor, love you, no, Miss. No more alike nor what you an' me are. That little 'un without a tender as went by just now all on her own, that was a tank, that was—she's off to do some shunting t'other side o' Maidbridge. That's as it might be you, Miss. Then there's goods engines, great, strong things with three wheels each side joined with rods to strengthen 'em as it might be me. Then there's main-line engines as it might be this 'ere young gentleman when he grows up and wins all the races at 'is school—so he will. The main-line engine she's built for speed as well as power. That's one to the 9.15 up."

"The Green Dragon," said Phyllis.

"We call her the Snail, Miss, among ourselves," said the Porter. "She's oftener be'ind and nor any train on the line."

"But the engine's green," said Phyllis.

"Yes, Miss," said Perks, "so's a snail some seasons o' the year."

The children agreed as they went home to dinner that the Porter was most delightful company.

Next day was Roberta's birthday. In the afternoon she was politely but firmly requested to get out of the way and keep there till tea-time.

"You aren't to see what we're going to do till it's done; it's a glorious surprise," said Phyllis.

And Roberta went out into the garden all alone. She tried to be grateful, but she felt she would much rather have helped in whatever it was than have to spend her birthday afternoon by herself, no matter how glorious the surprise might be.

Now that she was alone, she had time to think, and one of the things she thought of most was what Mother had said in one of those feverish nights when her hands were so hot and her eyes so bright.

The words were: "Oh, what a doctor's bill there'll be for this!"

She walked round and round the garden among the rose-bushes that hadn't any roses yet, only buds, and the lilac bushes and syringas and American currants, and the more she thought of the doctor's bill, the less she liked the thought of it.

And presently she made up her mind. She went out through the side door of the garden and climbed up the steep field to where the road runs along by the canal. She walked along until she came to the bridge that crosses the canal and leads to the village, and here she waited. It was very pleasant in the sunshine to lean one's elbow on the warm stone of the bridge and look down at the blue water of the canal. Bobbie had never seen any other canal, except the Regent's Canal, and the water of that is not at all a pretty colour. And she had never seen any river at all except the Thames, which also would be all the better if its face was washed.

Perhaps the children would have loved the canal as much as the railway, but for two things. One was that they had found the railway *first*—on that first, wonderful morning when the house and the country and the moors and rocks and great hills were all new to them. They had not found the canal till some days later. The other reason was that everyone on the railway had been kind to them—the Station Master, the Porter, and the old gentleman who waved. And the people on the canal were anything but kind.

The people on the canal were, of course, the bargees, who steered the slow barges up and down, or walked beside the old horses that trampled up the mud of the towing-path, and strained at the long tow-ropes.

Peter had once asked one of the bargees the time, and had been told to "get out of that," in a tone so fierce that he did not stop to say anything about his having just as much right on the towing-path as the man himself. Indeed, he did not even think of saying it till some time later.

Then another day when the children thought they would like to fish in the canal, a boy in a barge threw lumps of coal at them, and one of these hit Phyllis on the back of the neck. She was just stooping down to tie up her bootlace—and though the coal hardly hurt at all it made her not care very much about going on fishing.

On the bridge, however, Roberta felt quite safe, because she could look down on the canal, and if any boy showed signs of meaning to throw coal, she could duck behind the parapet.

Presently there was a sound of wheels, which was just what she expected.

The wheels were the wheels of the Doctor's dogcart, and in the cart, of course, was the Doctor.

He pulled up and called out:

"Hullo, head-nurse! Want a lift?"

"I wanted to see you," said Bobbie.

"Your mother's not worse, I hope?" said the Doctor.

"No—but—"

'Well, step in, then, and we'll go for a drive."

Roberta climbed in and the brown horse was made to turn round—which it did not like at all, for it was looking forward to its tea—I mean its oats.

"This is jolly," said Bobbie, as the dogcart flew along the road by the canal.

"We could throw a stone down any one of your three chimneys," said the Doctor, as they passed the house.

"Yes," said Bobbie, "but you'd have to be a jolly good shot."

"How do you know I'm not?" said the Doctor. "Now, then, what's the trouble?"

Bobbie fidgeted with the hook of the driving apron.

"Come, out with it," said the Doctor.

"It's rather hard, you see," said Bobbie, "to out with it; because of what Mother said."

"What *did* Mother say?"

"She said I wasn't to go telling everyone that we're poor. But you aren't everyone, are you?"

"Not at all," said the Doctor cheerfully. "Well?"

"Well, I know doctors are very extravagant—I mean expensive, and Mrs Viney told me that her doctoring only cost her twopence a week because she belonged to a Club."

"Yes?"

"You see she told me what a good doctor you were, and I asked her how she could afford you, because she's much poorer than we are. I've been in her house and I know. And then she told me about the Club, and I thought I'd ask you—and—oh, I don't want Mother to be worried! Can't we be in the Club, too, the same as Mrs Viney?"

The Doctor was silent. He was rather poor himself, and he had been pleased at getting a new family to attend. So I think his feelings at that minute were rather mixed.

"You aren't cross with me, are you?" said Bobbie, in a very small voice.

The Doctor roused himself.

"Cross? How could I be? You're a very sensible little woman. Now look here, don't you worry. I'll make it all right with your Mother, even if I have to make a special brand-new Club all for her. Look here, this is where the Aqueduct begins."

"What's an Aque—what's its name?" asked Bobbie.

"A water bridge," said the Doctor. "Look."

The road rose to a bridge over the canal. To the left was a steep rocky cliff with trees and shrubs growing in the cracks of the rock. And the canal here left off running along the top of the hill and started to run on a bridge of its own—a great bridge with tall arches that went right across the valley.

Bobbie drew a long breath.

"It *is* grand, isn't it?" she said. "It's like pictures in the *History of Rome*."

"Right!" said the Doctor, "that's just exactly what it *is* like. The Romans were dead nuts on aqueducts. It's a splendid piece of engineering."

"I thought engineering was making engines."

"Ah, there are different sorts of engineering—making roads and bridges and tunnels is one kind. And making fortifications is another. Well, we must be turning back. And, remember, you aren't to worry about doctor's bills or you'll be ill yourself, and then I'll send you a bill as long as the aqueduct."

When Bobbie had parted from the doctor at the top of the field that ran down from the road to Three Chimneys, she could not feel that she had done wrong. She knew that Mother would perhaps think differently. But Bobbie felt that for once she was the one who was right, and she scrambled down the rocky slope with a really happy feeling.

Phyllis and Peter met her at the back door. They were unnaturally clean and neat, and Phyllis had a red bow in her hair. There was only just time for Bobbie to make herself tidy and tie up her hair with a blue bow before a little bell rang.

"There!" said Phyllis, "that's to show the surprise is ready. Now you wait till the bell rings again and then you may come into the dining-room."

So Bobbie waited.

"Tinkle, tinkle," said the little bell, and Bobbie went into the dining-room, feeling rather shy. Directly she opened the door she found herself, as it seemed, in a new world of light and flowers and singing. Mother and Peter and Phyllis were standing in a row at the end of the table. The shutters were shut and there were twelve candles on the table, one for each of Roberta's years. The table was covered with a sort of pattern of flowers, and at Roberta's place was a thick wreath of forget-me-nots and several most interesting little packages. And Mother and Phyllis and Peter were singing—to the first part of the tune of St Patrick's Day. Roberta knew that Mother had written the words on purpose for her birthday. It was a little way of Mother's on birthdays. It had begun on Bobbie's fourth birthday when Phyllis was a baby. Bobbie remembered learning the verses to say to Father "for a surprise". She wondered if Mother had remembered, too. The four-year-old verse had been:

Daddy dear, I'm only four
And I'd rather not be more.
Four's the nicest age to be,
Two and two and one and three.
What I love is two and two,

Mother, Peter, Phil, and you
What you love is one and three,
Mother, Peter, Phil and me.
Give your little girl a kiss
Because she learned and told you this.

The song the others were singing now went like this:

Our darling Roberta,
No sorrow shall hurt her
If we can prevent it
Her whole life long.
Her birthday's our fête day,
We'll make it our great day,
And give her our presents
And sing her our song.
May pleasures attend her
And may the Fates send her
The happiest journey
Along her life's way.
With skies bright above her
And dear ones to love her!
Dear Bob! Many happy
Returns of the day!

When they had finished singing they cried, "Three cheers for our Bobbie!" and gave them very loudly. Bobbie felt exactly as though she were going to cry—you know that odd feeling in the bridge of your nose and the pricking in your eyelids? But before she had time to begin they were all kissing and hugging her.

"Now," said Mother, "look at your presents."

They were very nice presents. There was a green and red needle-book that Phyllis had made herself in secret moments. There was a darling little silver brooch of Mother's shaped like a butter-cup, which Bobbie had known and loved for years, but which she had never, never thought would come to be her very own. There was also a pair of blue glass vases from Mrs Viney. Roberta had seen and admired them in the village shop. And there were three birthday cards with pretty pictures and wishes.

Mother fitted the forget-me-not crown on Bobbie's brown head.

"And now look at the table," she said.

There was a cake on the table covered with white sugar, with "Dear Bobbie" on it in pink sweets, and there were buns and jam; but the nicest thing was that the big table was almost covered with flowers—wallflowers were laid all round the tea-tray—there was a ring of forget-me-nots round each plate. The cake had a wreath of white lilac round it, and in the middle was something that looked like a pattern all done with single blooms of lilac or wallflower or laburnum.

"What is it?" asked Roberta.

"It's a map—a map of the railway!" cried Peter. "Look—those lilac lines are the metals—and there's the station done in brown wallflowers. The laburnum is the train, and there are the signal-boxes, and the road up to here—and those fat red daisies are us three waving to the old gentleman—that's him, the pansy in the laburnum train."

"And there's 'Three Chimneys' done in the purple primroses," said Phyllis. "And that little tiny rose-bud is Mother looking for us when we're late for tea. Peter invented it all, and we got all the flowers from the station. We thought you'd like it better."

"That's my present," said Peter, suddenly dumping down his adored steam-engine on the table in front of her. Its tender had been lined with fresh white paper, and was full of sweets.

"Oh, Peter!" cried Bobbie, quite overcome by this munificence, "not your own dear little engine that you're so fond of?"

"Oh, no," said Peter, very promptly, "not the engine. Only the sweets."

Bobbie couldn't help her face changing a little—not so much because she was disappointed at not getting the engine, as because she had thought it so very noble of Peter, and now she felt she had been silly to think it. Also she felt she must have seemed greedy to expect the engine as well as the sweets. So her face changed. Peter saw it. He hesitated a minute; then his face changed, too, and he said: "I mean not *all* the engine. I'll let you go halves if you like."

"You're a brick," cried Bobbie; "it's a splendid present." She said no more aloud, but to herself she said:

"That was awfully decent of Peter because I know he didn't mean to. Well, the broken half shall be my half of the engine, and I'll get it mended and give it back to Peter for his birthday."—"Yes, Mother dear, I should like to cut the cake," she added, and tea began.

It was a delightful birthday. After tea Mother played games with them—any game they liked—and of course their first choice was blindman's-buff, in the course of which Bobbie's forget-me-not wreath twisted itself crookedly over one of her ears and stayed there. Then, when it was near bed-time and time to calm down, Mother had a lovely new story to read to them.

"You won't sit up late working, will you, Mother?" Bobbie asked as they said good-night.

And Mother said no, she wouldn't—she would only just write to Father and then go to bed.

But when Bobbie crept down later to bring up her presents—for she felt she really could not be separated from them all night— Mother was not writing, but leaning her head on her arms and her arms on the table. I think it was rather good of Bobbie to slip quietly away, saying over and over, "She doesn't want me to know she's unhappy, and I won't know; I won't know." But it made a sad end to the birthday.

*

The very next morning Bobbie began to watch her opportunity to get Peter's engine mended secretly. And the opportunity came the very next afternoon.

Mother went by train to the nearest town to do shopping. When she went there, she always went to the Post-office. Perhaps to post her letters to Father, for she never gave them to the children or Mrs Viney to post, and she never went to the village herself. Peter and Phyllis went with her. Bobbie wanted an excuse not to go, but try as she would she couldn't think of a good one. And just when she felt that all was lost, her frock caught on a big nail by the kitchen door and there was a great criss-cross tear all along the front of the skirt. I assure you this was really an accident. So the others pitied her and went without her, for there was no time for her to change, because they were rather late already and had to hurry to the station to catch the train.

When they had gone, Bobbie put on her everyday frock, and went down to the railway. She did not go into the station, but she went along the line to the end of the platform where the engine is when the down train is along-side the platform—the place where there are a water tank and a long, limp, leather hose, like an elephant's trunk. She hid behind a bush on the other side of the railway. She had the toy engine done up in brown paper, and she waited patiently with it under her arm.

Then when the next train came in and stopped, Bobbie went across the metals of the up-line and stood beside the engine. She had never been so close to an engine before. It looked much larger and harder than she had expected, and it made her feel very small indeed, and, somehow, very soft—as if she could very, very easily be hurt rather badly.

"I know what silk-worms feel like now," said Bobbie to herself.

The engine-driver and fireman did not see her. They were leaning out of the other side, telling the Porter a tale about a dog and a leg of mutton.

"If you please," said Roberta—but the engine was blowing off steam and no one heard her.

"If you please, Mr Engineer," she spoke a little louder, but the Engine happened to speak at the same moment, and of course Roberta's soft little voice hadn't a chance.

It seemed to her that the only way would be to climb on to the engine and pull at their coats. The step was high, but she got her knee on it, and clambered into the cab; she stumbled and fell on hands and knees on the base of the great heap of coals that led up to the square opening in the tender. The engine was not above the weaknesses of its fellows; it was making a great deal more noise than there was the slightest need for. And just as Roberta fell on the coals, the engine-driver, who had turned without seeing her, started the engine, and when Bobbie had picked herself up, the train was moving—not fast, but much too fast for her to get off.

All sorts of dreadful thoughts came to her all together in one horrible flash. There were such things as express trains which went on, she supposed, for hundreds of miles without stopping. Suppose this should be one of them? How would she get home again? She had no money to pay for the return journey.

"And I've no business here. I'm an engine-burglar—that's what I am," she thought. "I shouldn't wonder if they could lock me up for this." And the train was going faster and faster.

There was something in her throat that made it impossible for her to speak. She tried twice. The men had their backs to her. They were doing something to things that looked like taps.

Suddenly she put out her hand and caught hold of the nearest sleeve. The man turned with a start, and he and Roberta stood for a minute looking at each other in silence. Then the silence was broken by them both.

The man said, "Here's a bloomin' go!" and Roberta burst into tears.

The other man said he was blooming well blest—or something like it—but though naturally surprised they were not exactly unkind.

"You're a naughty little girl, that's what you are," said the fireman, but the engine-driver said:

"Darling little piece, I call her," but they made her sit down on an iron seat in the cab and told her to stop crying and tell them what she meant by it.

She did stop, as soon as she could. One thing that helped her was the thought that Peter would give almost his ears to be in her place—on a real engine—really going. The children had often wondered whether any engine-driver could be found noble enough to take them for a ride on an engine—and now here she was. She dried her eyes and sniffed earnestly.

"Now, then," said the fireman, "out with it. What do you mean by it, eh?"

"Oh, please," sniffed Bobbie, and stopped.

"Try again," said the engine-driver, encouragingly.

Bobbie tried again.

"Please, Mr Engineer," she said, "I did call out to you from the line, but you didn't hear me—and I just climbed up to touch you on the arm—quite gently I meant to do it—and then I fell into the coals—and I am so sorry if I frightened you. Oh, don't be cross—oh, please don't!" She sniffed again.

"We ain't so much *cross*," said the fireman, "as interested like. It ain't every day a little gell tumbles into our coal bunker outer the sky, is it, Bill? What did you *do* it for—eh?"

"That's the point," agreed the engine-driver; "what did you do it *for*?"

Bobbie found that she had not quite stopped crying. The engine-driver patted her on the back and said: "Here, cheer up, Mate. It ain't so bad as all that 'ere, I'll be bound."

"I wanted," said Bobbie, much cheered to find herself addressed as "Mate"—"I only wanted to ask you if you'd be so kind as to mend this." She picked up the brown-paper parcel from among the coals and undid the string with hot, red fingers that trembled.

Her feet and legs felt the scorch of the engine fire, but her shoulders felt the wild chill rush of the air. The engine lurched and shook and rattled, and as they shot under a bridge the engine seemed to shout in her ears.

The fireman shovelled on coals.

Bobbie unrolled the brown paper and disclosed the toy engine.

"I thought," she said wistfully, "that perhaps you'd mend this for me—because you're an engineer, you know."

The engine-driver said he was blowed if he wasn't blest.

"I'm blest if I ain't blowed," remarked the fireman.

But the engine-driver took the little engine and looked at it—and the fireman ceased for an instant to shovel coal, and looked, too.

"It's like your precious cheek," said the engine-driver—"whatever made you think we'd be bothered tinkering with penny toys?"

"I didn't mean it for precious cheek," said Bobbie; "only everybody that has anything to do with railways is so kind and good. I didn't think you'd mind. You don't really—do you?" she added, for she had seen a not unkindly wink pass between the two.

"My trade's driving of a engine, not mending her—especially such a hout-size in engines as this 'ere," said Bill. "An' 'ow are we a-goin' to get you back to your sorrowing friends and relations, and all be forgiven and forgotten?"

"If you'll put me down next time you stop," said Bobbie, firmly, though her heart beat fiercely against her arm as she clasped her hands, "and lend me the money for a third-class ticket, I'll pay you back—honour bright. I'm not a confidence trick like in the newspapers—really, I'm not."

"You're a little lady, every inch," said Bill, relenting suddenly and completely. "We'll see you get home safe. An' about this engine—Jim—ain't you got ne'er a pal as can use a soldering iron? Seems to me that's about all the little bounder wants doing to it."

"That's what Father said," Bobbie explained eagerly. "What's that for?"

She pointed to a little brass wheel that he had turned as he spoke.

"That's the injector."

"In—what?"

"Injector to fill up the boiler."

"Oh," said Bobbie, mentally registering the fact to tell the others; "that is interesting."

"This 'ere's the automatic brake," Bill went on, flattered by her enthusiasm. "You just move this 'ere little handle—do it with one finger, you can—and the train jolly soon stops. That's what they call the Power of Science in the newspapers."

He showed her two little dials, like clock faces, and told her how one showed how much steam was going, and the other showed if the brake was working properly.

By the time she had seen him shut off steam with a big shining steel handle, Bobbie knew more about the inside working of an engine than she had ever thought there was to know, and Jim had promised that his second cousin's wife's brother should solder the toy engine, or Jim would know the reason why. Besides all the knowledge she had gained Bobbie felt that she and Bill and Jim were now friends for life, and that they had wholly and forever forgiven her for stumbling uninvited among the sacred coals of their tender.

At Stacklepoole Junction she parted from them with warm expressions of mutual regard. They handed her over to the guard of a returning train—a friend of theirs—and she had the joy of knowing what guards do in their secret fastnesses, and understood how when you pull the communication cord in railway carriages, a wheel goes round under the guard's nose and a loud bell rings in his ears. She asked the guard why his van smelt so fishy, and learned that he had to carry a lot of fish every day, and that the wetness in the hollows of the corrugated floor had all drained out of boxes full of plaice and cod and mackerel and soles and smelts.

Bobbie got home in time for tea, and she felt as though her mind would burst with all that had been put into it since she parted from the others. How she blessed the nail that had torn her frock!

"Where have you been?" asked the others.

"To the station, of course," said Roberta. But she would not tell a word of her adventures till the day appointed, when she mysteriously led them to the station at the hour of 3.19's transit, and proudly introduced them to her friends, Bill and Jim. Jim's second cousin's wife's brother had not been unworthy of the sacred trust imposed in him. The toy engine was, literally, as good as new.

"Good-bye—oh, good-bye," said Bobbie, just before the engine screamed *its* good-bye. "I shall always, always love you—and Jim's second cousin's wife's brother as well!"

And as the three children went home up the hill, Peter hugging the engine, now quite its old self again, Bobbie told, with joyous leaps of the heart, the story of how she had been an Engine-burglar.

Chapter 5

PRISONERS AND CAPTIVES

It was one day when Mother had gone to Maidbridge. She had gone alone, but the children were to go to the station to meet her. And, loving the station as they did, it was only natural that they should be there a good hour before there was any chance of Mother's train arriving, even if the train were punctual, which was most unlikely. No doubt they would have been just as early, even if it had been a fine day, and the delights of woods and fields and rocks and rivers had been open to them. But it happened to be a very wet day and, for July, very cold. There was a wild wind that drove flocks of dark purple clouds across the sky "like herds of dream elephants," as Phyllis said. And the rain stung sharply, so that the way to the station was finished at a run. Then the rain fell faster and harder, and beat slantwise against the windows of the booking office and of the chill place that had General Waiting Room on its door.

"It's like being in a besieged castle," Phyllis said; "look at the arrows of the foe striking against the battlements!"

"It's much more like a great garden-squirt," said Peter.

They decided to wait on the up side, for the down platform looked very wet indeed, and the rain was driving right into the little black shelter where down-passengers have to wait for their trains.

The hour would be full of incident and of interest, for there would be two up trains and one down to look at before the one that should bring Mother back.

"Perhaps it'll have stopped raining by then," said Bobbie; "anyhow, I'm glad I brought Mother's waterproof and umbrella."

They went into the desert spot labelled General Waiting Room, and the time passed pleasantly enough in a game of advertisements. You know the game, of course. It is something like dumb Crambo. The players take it in turns to go out, and then come back and look as like some advertisement as they can, and the others have to guess what advertisement it is meant to be. Bobbie came in and sat down under Mother's umbrella and made a sharp face, and everyone knew she was the fox who sits under the umbrella in the advertisement. Phyllis tried to make a Magic Carpet of Mother's waterproof, but it would not stand out stiff and raft-like as a Magic Carpet should, and nobody could guess it. Everyone thought Peter was carrying things a little too far when he blacked his face all over with coal-dust and struck a spidery attitude and said he was the blot that advertises somebody's Blue Black Writing Fluid.

It was Phyllis's turn again, and she was trying to look like the Sphinx that advertises What's-his-name's Personally Conducted Tours up the Nile when the sharp ting of the signal announced the up train. The children rushed out to see it pass. On its engine were the particular driver and fireman who were numbered among the children's dearest friends. Courtesies passed between them. Jim asked after the toy engine, and Bobbie pressed on his acceptance a moist, greasy package of toffee that she had made herself.

Charmed by this attention, the engine-driver consented to consider her request that some day he would take Peter for a ride on the engine.

"Stand back, Mates," cried the engine-driver, suddenly, "and horf she goes."

And sure enough, off the train went. The children watched the tail-lights of the train till it disappeared round the curve of the line, and then turned to go back to the dusty freedom of the General Waiting Room and the joys of the advertisement game.

They expected to see just one or two people, the end of the procession of passengers who had given up their tickets and gone away. Instead, the platform round the door of the station had a dark blot round it, and the dark blot was a crowd of people.

"Oh!" cried Peter, with a thrill of joyous excitement, "something's happened! Come on!"

They ran down the platform. When they got to the crowd, they could, of course, see nothing but the damp backs and elbows of the people on the crowd's outside. Everybody was talking at once. It was evident that something had happened.

"It's my belief he's nothing worse than a natural," said a farmerish-looking person. Peter saw his red, clean-shaven face as he spoke.

"If you ask me, I should say it was a Police Court case," said a young man with a black bag.

"Not it; the Infirmary more like—"

Then the voice of the Station Master was heard, firm and official:

"Now then—move along there. I'll attend to this, if *you* please."

But the crowd did not move. And then came a voice that thrilled the children through and through. For it spoke in a foreign language. And what is more, it was a language that they had never heard. They had heard French spoken and German. Aunt Emma knew German, and tried to sing a song about *bedeuten* and *Zeiten* and *bin* and *Sinn*. Nor was it Latin. Peter had been in Latin for four terms.

It was some comfort, anyhow, to find that none of the crowd understood the foreign language any better than the children did.

"What's that he's saying?" asked the farmer, heavily.

"Sounds like French to me," said the Station Master, who had once been in Boulogne for the day.

"It isn't French!" cried Peter.

"What is it, then?" asked more than one voice. The crowd fell back a little to see who had spoken, and Peter pressed forward, so that when the crowd closed up again, he was in the front rank.

"I don't know what it is," said Peter, "but it isn't French. I know that." Then he saw what it was the crowd had for its centre. It was a man—the man, Peter did not doubt, who had spoken in that strange tongue. A man with long hair and wild eyes, with shabby clothes of a cut Peter had not seen before—a man whose hand and lips trembled, and who spoke again as his eyes fell on Peter.

"No, it's not French," said Peter.

"Try him with French if you know so much about it," said the farmer-man.

"*Parlay voo Frongsay*?" began Peter, boldly, and the next moment the crowd recoiled again, for the man with the wild eyes had left leaning against the wall, and had sprung forward and caught Peter's hands, and began to pour forth a flood of words which, though he could not understand a word of them, Peter knew the sound of.

"There!" said he, and turned, his hands still clasped in the hands of the strange shabby figure, to throw a glance of triumph at the crowd; "there; *that's* French."

"What does he say?"

"I don't know." Peter was obliged to own it.

"Here," said the Station Master again; "you move on if you please. *I'll* deal with this case."

A few of the more timid or less inquisitive travellers moved slowly and reluctantly away. And Phyllis and Bobbie got near to Peter. All three had been *taught* French at school. How deeply they now wished that they had *learned* it! Peter shook his head at the stranger, but he also shook his hands as warmly and looked at him as kindly as he could. A person in the crowd, after some hesitation, said suddenly, "No comprenny!" and then, blushing deeply, backed out of the press and went away.

'"Take him into your room," whispered Bobbie to the Station Master. "Mother can talk French. She'll be here by the next train from Maidbridge."

The Station Master took the arm of the stranger, suddenly but not unkindly. But the man wrenched his arm away, and cowered back coughing and trembling and trying to push the Station Master away.

"Oh, don't" said Bobbie; "don't you see how frightened he is? He thinks you're going to shut him up. I know he does—look at his eyes!"

"They're like a fox's eyes when the beast's in a trap," said the farmer.

"Oh, let me try!" Bobbie went on; "I do really know one or two French words if I could only think of them."

Sometimes, in moments of great need, we can do wonderful things—things that in ordinary life we could hardly even dream of doing. Bobbie had never been anywhere near the top of her French class, but she must have learned something without knowing it, for now, looking at those wild, hunted eyes, she actually remembered and, what is more, spoke, some French words. She said:

"*Vous attendre. Ma mère parlez Français. Nous*—what's the French for 'being kind'?"

Nobody knew.

"*Bong* is 'good'," said Phyllis.

"*Nous être bong pour vous.*"

I do not know whether the man understood her words, but he understood the touch of the hand she thrust into his, and the kindness of the other hand that stroked his shabby sleeve.

She pulled him gently towards the inmost sanctuary of the Station Master. The other children followed, and the Station Master shut the door in the face of the crowd which stood a little while in the booking office talking and looking at the fast-closed yellow door, and then by ones and twos went its way, grumbling.

Inside the Station Master's room Bobbie still held the stranger's hand and stroked his sleeve.

"Here's a go," said the Station Master; "no ticket—doesn't even know where he wants to go. I'm not sure now but what I ought to send for the police."

"Oh, *don't*!" all the children pleaded at once. And suddenly Bobbie got between the others and the stranger, for she had seen that he was crying.

By a most unusual piece of good fortune she had a handkerchief in her pocket. By a still more uncommon accident the handkerchief was moderately clean. Standing in front of the stranger, she got the handkerchief and passed it to him so that the others did not see.

"Wait till Mother comes," Phyllis was saying: "she does speak French beautifully. You'd just love to hear her."

"I'm sure he hasn't done anything like you're sent to prison for," said Peter.

"Looks like without visible means to me," said the Station Master. "Well, I don't mind giving him the benefit of the doubt till your Mamma comes. I *should* like to know what nation's got the credit of *him*, that I should."

Then Peter had an idea. He pulled an envelope out of his pocket, and showed that it was half full of foreign stamps. "Look here," he said, "let's show him these—"

Bobbie looked and saw that the stranger had dried his eyes with her handkerchief. So she said: "All right."

They showed him an Italian stamp, and pointed from him to it and back again, and made signs of questions with their eyebrows. He shook his head. Then they showed him a Norwegian stamp— the common blue kind it was—and again he signed No. Then they showed him a Spanish one, and at that he took the envelope from Peter's hand and searched among the stamps with a hand that trembled. The hand that he reached out at last, with a gesture of one answering a question, contained a *Russian* stamp.

"He's Russian," cried Peter, "or else he's like 'the man who was'—in Kipling, you know."

The train from Maidbridge was signalled.

"I'll stay with him till you bring Mother in," said Bobbie.

"You're not afraid, Missie?"

"Oh, no," said Bobbie, looking at the stranger, as she

might have looked at a strange dog of doubtful temper. "You wouldn't hurt me, would you?"

She smiled at him, and he smiled back, a queer crooked smile. And then he laughed again. And the heavy rattling swish of the incoming train swept past, and the Station Master and Peter and Phyllis went out to meet it. Bobbie was still holding the stranger's hand when they came back with Mother.

The Russian rose and bowed very ceremoniously.

Then Mother spoke in French, and he replied, haltingly at first, but presently in longer and longer sentences.

The children, watching his face and Mother's, knew that he was telling her things that made her angry and pitying, and sorry and indignant all at once.

"Well, Mum, what's it all about?" The Station Master could not restrain his curiosity any longer.

"Oh," said Mother, "it's all right. He's a Russian, and he's lost his ticket. And I'm afraid he's very ill. If you don't mind, I'll take him home with me now. He's really quite worn out. I'll run down and tell you all about him tomorrow."

"I hope you won't find you're taking home a frozen viper," said the Station Master, doubtfully.

"Oh, no," Mother said brightly, and she smiled; "I'm quite sure I'm not. Why, he's a great man in his own country, writes books—beautiful books—I've read some of them; but I'll tell you all about it tomorrow."

She spoke again in French to the Russian, and everyone could see the surprise and pleasure and gratitude in his eyes. He got up and politely bowed to the Station Master, and offered his arm most ceremoniously to Mother. She took it, but anybody could have seen that she was helping him along, and not he her.

"You girls run home and light a fire in the sitting-room," Mother said, "and Peter had better go for the Doctor."

But it was Bobbie who went for the Doctor.

"I hate to tell you," she said breathlessly when she came upon him in his shirt sleeves weeding his pansy-bed, "but Mother's got a very shabby Russian, and I'm sure he'll have to belong to your Club. I'm certain he hasn't got any money. We found him at the station."

"Found him! Was he lost, then?" asked the Doctor, reaching for his coat.

"Yes," said Bobbie, unexpectedly, "that's just what he was. He's been telling Mother the sad, sweet story of his life in French; and she said would you be kind enough to come directly if you were at home. He has a dreadful cough, and he's been crying."

The Doctor smiled.

"Oh, don't," said Bobbie; "please don't. You wouldn't if you'd seen him. I never saw a man cry before. You don't know what it's like."

Dr Forrest wished then that he hadn't smiled.

When Bobbie and the Doctor got to Three Chimneys, the Russian was sitting in the arm-chair that had been Father's, stretching his feet to the blaze of a bright wood fire, and sipping the tea Mother had made him.

"The man seems worn out, mind and body," was what the Doctor said; "the cough's bad, but there's nothing that can't be cured. He ought to go straight to bed, though—and let him have a fire at night."

"I'll make one in my room; it's the only one with a fireplace," said Mother. She did, and presently the Doctor helped the stranger to bed.

There was a big black trunk in Mother's room that none of the children had ever seen unlocked. Now, when she had lighted the fire, she unlocked it and took some clothes out—men's clothes—and set them to air by the newly lighted fire. Bobbie, coming in with more wood for the fire, saw the mark on the night-shirt, and looked over to the open trunk. All the things she could see were men's clothes. And the name marked on the shirt was Father's name. Then Father hadn't taken his clothes with him. And that night-shirt was one of Father's new ones. Bobbie remembered its being made, just before Peter's birthday. Why hadn't Father taken his clothes? Bobbie slipped from the room. As she went she heard the key turned in the lock of the trunk. Her heart was beating horribly. *Why* hadn't Father taken his clothes? When Mother came out of the room, Bobbie flung tightly clasping arms round her waist, and whispered:

"Mother—Daddy isn't—isn't *dead,* is he?"

"My darling, no! What makes you think of anything so horrible?"

"I—I don't know," said Bobbie, angry with herself, but still clinging to that resolution of hers, not to see anything that Mother didn't mean her to see.

Mother gave her a hurried hug. "Daddy was quite, *quite* well when I heard from him last," she said, "and he'll come back to us some day. Don't fancy such horrible things, darling!"

Later on, when the Russian stranger had been made comfortable for the night, Mother came into the girls' room. She was to sleep there in Phyllis's bed, and Phyllis was to have a mattress on the floor, a most amusing adventure for Phyllis. Directly Mother came in, two white figures started up, and two eager voices called:

"Now, Mother, tell us all about the Russian gentleman."

A white shape hopped into the room. It was Peter, dragging his quilt behind him like the tail of a white peacock.

"We have been patient," he said, "and I had to bite my tongue not to go to sleep, and I just nearly went to sleep and I bit too hard, and it hurts ever so. *Do* tell us. Make a nice long story of it."

"I can't make a long story of it tonight," said Mother; "I'm very tired."

Bobbie knew by her voice that Mother had been crying, but the others didn't know.

"Well, make it as long as you can," said Phil, and Bobbie got her arms round Mother's waist and snuggled close to her.

"Well, it's a story long enough to make a whole book of. He's a writer; he's written wonderful books. In Russia at the time of the Tsar one dared not say anything about the rich people doing wrong, or about the things that ought to be done to make poor people better and happier. If one did one was sent to prison."

"But they *can't,*" said Peter; "people only go to prison when they've done wrong."

"Or when Judges *think* they've done wrong," said Mother. "Yes, that's so in England. But in Russia it was different. And he wrote a beautiful book about poor people and how to help them. I've read it. There's nothing in it but goodness and kindness. And they sent him to prison for it. He was three years in a horrible dungeon, with hardly any light, and all damp and dreadful. In prison all alone for three years."

Mother's voice trembled a little and stopped suddenly.

"But Mother," said Peter, "that can't be true *now.* It sounds like something out of a history book—the Inquisition, or something."

"It *was* true," said Mother; "it's all horribly true. Well then they took him out and sent him to Siberia, a convict chained to other convicts—wicked men who'd done all sorts of crimes—a long chain of them, and they walked, and walked, and walked, for days and weeks, till he thought they'd never stop walking. And overseers went behind them with whips—yes, whips—to beat them if they got tired. And some of them went lame, and some fell down, and when they couldn't get up and go on, they beat them, and then left them to die. Oh, it's all too terrible! And at last he got to the mines, and he was condemned to stay there for life—for life, just for writing a good, noble, splendid book."

"How did he get away?"

"When the war came, some of the Russian prisoners were allowed to volunteer as soldiers. And he volunteered. But he deserted at the first chance he got and—"

"But that's very cowardly, isn't it,"—said Peter—"to desert? Especially when it's war."

"Do you think he owed anything to a country that had done *that* to him? If he did, he owed more to his wife and children. He didn't know what had become of them."

"Oh," cried Bobbie, "he had *them* to think about and be miserable about *too,* then, all the time he was in prison?"

"Yes, he had them to think about and be miserable about all the time he was in prison. For anything he knew they might have been sent to prison, too. They did those things in Russia. But while he was in the mines some friends managed to get a message to him that his wife and children had escaped and come to England. So when he deserted he came here to look for them."

"Had he got their address?" said practical Peter.

"No, just England. He was going to London, and he thought he had to change at our station, and then he found he'd lost his ticket and his purse."

"Oh, *do* you think he'll find them?—I mean his wife and children, not the ticket and things."

"I hope so. Oh, I hope and pray that he'll find his wife and children again."

Even Phyllis now perceived that Mother's voice was very unsteady.

"Why, Mother," she said, "how very sorry you seem to be for him!"

Mother didn't answer for a minute. Then she just said, "Yes," and then she seemed to be thinking. The children were quiet.

Presently she said, "Dears, when you say your prayers, I think you might ask God to show His pity upon all prisoners and captives."

"To show His pity," Bobbie repeated slowly, "upon all prisoners and captives. Is that right, Mother?"

"Yes," said Mother, "upon all prisoners and captives. All prisoners and captives."

CHAPTER 6

SAVIOURS OF THE TRAIN

The Russian gentleman was better the next day, and the day after that better still, and on the third day he was well enough to come into the garden. A basket chair was put for him and he sat there, dressed in clothes of Father's which were too big for him. But when Mother had hemmed up the ends of the sleeves and the trousers, the clothes did well enough. His was a kind face now that it was no longer tired and frightened, and he smiled at the children whenever he saw them. They wished very much that he could speak English. Mother wrote several letters to people she thought might know whereabouts in England a Russian gentleman's wife and family might possibly be; not to the people she used to know before she came to live at Three Chimneys—she never wrote to any of them—but strange people—Members of Parliament and Editors of papers, and Secretaries of Societies.

And she did not do much of her story-writing, only corrected proofs as she sat in the sun near the Russian, and talked to him every now and then.

The children wanted very much to show how kindly they felt to this man who had been sent to prison and to Siberia just for writing a beautiful book about poor people. They could smile at him, of course; they could and they did. But if you smile too constantly, the smile is apt to get flexed like the smile of the hyena. And then it no longer looks friendly, but simply silly. So they tried other ways, and brought him flowers till the place where he sat was surrounded by little fading bunches of clover and roses and Canterbury bells.

And then Phyllis had an idea. She beckoned mysteriously to the others and drew them into the back yard, and there, in a concealed spot, between the pump and the water-butt, she said:

"You remember Perks promising me the very first strawberries out of his own garden?" Perks, you will recollect, was the Porter. "Well, I should think they're ripe now. Let's go down and see."

Mother had been down as she had promised to tell the Station Master the story of the Russian Prisoner. But even the charms of the railway had been unable to tear the children away from the neighbourhood of the interesting stranger. So they had not been to the station for three days.

They went now.

And, to their surprise and distress, were very coldly received by Perks.

" 'Ighly honoured, I'm sure," he said when they peeped in at the door of the Porter's Room. And he went on reading his newspaper.

There was an uncomfortable silence.

"Oh, dear," said Bobbie, with a sigh, "I do believe you're *cross*."

"What, me? Not me!" said Perks loftily; "it ain't nothing to me."

"*What* ain't nothing to you?" said Peter, too anxious and alarmed to change the form of words.

"Nothing ain't nothing. What 'appens either 'ere or elsewhere," said Perks; "if you likes to 'ave your secrets, 'ave 'em and welcome. That's what I say."

The secret-chamber of each heart was rapidly examined during the pause that followed. Three heads were shaken.

"We haven't got any secrets from *you*," said Bobbie at last.

"Maybe you 'ave, and maybe you 'aven't," said Perks; "it ain't nothing to me. And I wish you all a very good afternoon." He held up the paper between him and them and went on reading.

"Oh, *don't*!' said Phyllis, in despair; "this is truly dreadful! Whatever it is, do tell us."

"We didn't mean to do it whatever it was."

No answer. The paper was refolded and Perks began on another column.

"Look here," said Peter, suddenly, "it's not fair. Even people who do crimes aren't punished without being told what it's for—as once they were in Russia."

"I don't know nothing about Russia."

"Oh, yes, you do, when Mother came down on purpose to tell you and Mr Gills all about *our* Russian."

"Can't you fancy it?" said Perks, indignantly; "don't you see 'im a-asking of me to step into 'is room and take a chair and listen to what 'er Ladyship 'as to say?"

"Do you mean to say you've not heard?"

"Not so much as a breath. I did go as far as to put a question. And he shuts me up like a rat-trap. 'Affairs of State, Perks,' says he. But I did think one o' you would 'a' nipped down to tell me—you're here sharp enough when you want to get anything out of old Perks"—Phyllis flushed purple at the thought of the strawberries—"information about locomotives or signals or the likes," said Perks.

"We didn't know you didn't know."

"We thought Mother had told you."

"We wanted to tell you only we thought it would be stale news."

The three spoke all at once.

Perks said it was all very well, and still held up the paper. Then Phyllis suddenly snatched it away, and threw her arms round his neck

"Oh, let's kiss and be friends," she said; "we'll say we're sorry first, if you like, but we really didn't know that you didn't know."

"We are so sorry," said the others.

And Perks at last consented to accept their apologies.

Then they got him to come out and sit in the sun on the green Railway bank, where the grass was quite hot to touch, and there, sometimes speaking one at a time, and sometimes all together, they told the Porter the story of the Russian Prisoner.

"Well, I must say," said Perks; but he did not say it—whatever it was.

"Yes, it is pretty awful, isn't it?" said Peter, "and I don't wonder you were curious about who the Russian was."

"I wasn't curious, not so much as interested," said the Porter.

"Well, I do think Mr Gills might have told you about it. It was horrid of him."

"I don't keep no down on 'im for that, Missie," said the Porter; "cos why? I see 'is reasons. 'E wouldn't want to give away 'is own side with a tale like that 'ere. It ain't human nature. A man's got to stand up for his own side whatever they does. That's what it means by Party Politics. I should 'a' done the same myself if that long-'aired chap 'ad 'a' been a Jap."

"But the Japs didn't do cruel, wicked things like that," said Bobbie.

"P'r'aps not," said Perks, cautiously; "still you can't be sure with foreigners. My own belief is they're all tarred with the same brush."

"Then why were you on the side of the Japs?" Peter asked.

"Well, you see, you must take one side or the other. Same as with Liberals and Conservatives. The great thing is to take your side and then stick to it, whatever happens."

A signal sounded.

"There's the 3.14 up," said Perks. "You lie low till she's through, and then we'll go up along to my place, and see if there's any of them strawberries ripe what I told you about."

"If there are any ripe, and you *do* give them to me," said Phyllis, "you won't mind if I give them to the poor Russian, will you?"

Perks narrowed his eyes and then raised his eyebrows.

"So it was them strawberries you come down for this afternoon, eh?" said he.

This was an awkward moment for Phyllis. To say "yes" would seem rude and greedy, and unkind to Perks. But she knew if she said "no", she would not be pleased with herself afterwards. So—

"Yes," she said, "it was."

"Well done!" said the Porter; "speak the truth and shame the—"

"But we'd have come down the very next day if we'd known you hadn't heard the story," Phyllis added hastily.

"I believe you, Missie," said Perks, and sprang across the line six feet in front of the advancing train.

The girls hated to see him do this, but Peter liked it. It was so exciting.

The Russian gentleman was so delighted with the strawberries that the three racked their brains to find some other surprise for him. But all the racking did not bring out any idea more novel than wild cherries. And this idea occurred to them next morning. They had seen the blossom on the trees in the spring, and they knew where to look for wild cherries now that cherry time was here. The trees grew all up and along the rocky face of the cliff out of which the mouth of the tunnel opened. There were all sorts of trees there, birches and beeches and baby oaks and hazels, and among them the cherry blossom had shone like snow and silver.

The mouth of the tunnel was some way from Three Chimneys, so Mother let them take their lunch with them in a basket. And the basket would do to bring the cherries back in if they found any. She also lent them her silver watch so that they should not be late for tea. Peter's Waterbury had taken it into its head not to go since the day when Peter dropped it into the water-butt. And they started. When they got to the top of the cutting, they leaned over the fence and looked down to where the railway lines lay at the bottom of what, as Phyllis said, was exactly like a mountain gorge.

"If it wasn't for the railway at the bottom, it would be as though the foot of man had never been there, wouldn't it?"

The sides of the cutting were of grey stone, very roughly hewn. Indeed, the top part of the cutting had been a little natural glen that had been cut deeper to bring it down to the level of the tunnel's mouth. Among the rocks, grass and flowers grew, and seeds dropped by birds in the crannies of the stone had taken root and grown into bushes and trees that overhung the cutting. Near the tunnel was a flight of steps leading down to the line—just wooden bars roughly fixed into the earth—a very steep and narrow way, more like a ladder than a stair.

"We'd better get down," said Peter; "I'm sure the cherries would be quite easy to get at from the side of the steps. You remember it was there we picked the cherry blossoms that we put on the rabbit's grave."

So they went along the fence towards the little swing gate that is at the top of these steps. And they were almost at the gate when Bobbie said:

"Hush. Stop! What's that?"

'That' was a very odd noise indeed—a soft noise, but quite

plainly to be heard through the sound of the wind in the branches, and the hum and whir of the telegraph wires. It was a sort of rustling, whispering sound. As they listened it stopped and then it began again.

And this time it did not stop, but it grew louder and more rustling and rumbling.

"Look"—cried Peter, suddenly—"the tree over there!"

The tree he pointed at was one of those that have rough grey leaves and white flowers. The berries, when they come, are bright scarlet, but if you pick them, they disappoint you by turning black before you get them home. And, as Peter pointed, the tree was moving—not just the way trees ought to move when the wind blows through them, but all in one piece, as though it were a live creature and were walking down the side of the cutting.

"It's moving!" cried Bobbie. "Oh, look! and so are the others. It's like the woods in *Macbeth*"

"It's magic," said Phyllis, breathlessly. "I always knew the railway was enchanted."

It really did seem a little like magic. For all the trees for about twenty yards of the opposite bank seemed to be slowly walking down towards the railway line, the tree with the grey leaves bringing up the rear like some old shepherd driving a flock of green sheep.

"What is it? Oh, what is it?" said Phyllis; "it's much too magic for me. I don't like it. Let's go home."

But Bobbie and Peter clung fast to the rail and watched breathlessly. And Phyllis made no movement towards going home by herself.

The trees moved on and on. Some stones and loose earth fell down and rattled on the railway metals far below.

"It's *all* coming down," Peter tried to say, but he found there was hardly any voice to say it with. And, indeed, just as he spoke, the great rock, on the top of which the walking trees were, leaned slowly forward. The trees, ceasing to walk, stood still and shivered. Leaning with the rock, they seemed to hesitate a moment, and then rock and trees and grass and bushes, with a rushing sound, slipped right away from the face of the cutting and fell on the line with a blundering crash that could have been heard half a mile off. A cloud of dust rose up.

"Oh," said Peter, in awestruck tones, "isn't it exactly like when coals come in?—if there wasn't any roof to the cellar and you could see down."

"Look what a great mound it's made!" said Bobbie.

"Yes, it's right across the down line," said Phyllis.

"That'll take some sweeping up," said Bobbie.

"Yes," said Peter slowly. He was still leaning on the fence.

"Yes," he said again, still more slowly.

Then he stood upright.

"The 11.29 down hasn't gone by yet. We must let them know at the station, or there'll be a most frightful accident."

"Let's run," said Bobbie, and began.

But Peter cried, "Come back!" and looked at Mother's watch. He was very prompt and businesslike, and his face looked whiter than they had ever seen it.

"No time," he said; "it's ten miles away, and it's past eleven."

"Couldn't we," suggested Phyllis, breathlessly, "couldn't we climb up a telegraph post and do something to the wires?"

"We don't know how," said Peter.

"They do it in war," said Phyllis; "I know I've heard of it."

"They only *cut* them, silly," said Peter, "and that doesn't do any good. And we couldn't cut them even if we got up, and we couldn't get up. If we had anything red, we could go down on the line and wave it."

"But the train wouldn't see us till it got round the corner, and then it could see the mound just as well as us," said Phyllis; "better, because it's much bigger than us."

"If we only had something red," Peter repeated, "we could go round the corner and wave to the train."

"We might wave, anyway."

"They'd only think it was just *us*, as usual. We've waved so often before. Anyway, let's get down."

They got down the steep stairs. Bobbie was pale and

shivering. Peter's face looked thinner than usual. Phyllis was red-faced and damp with anxiety.

"Oh, how hot I am!" she said; "and I thought it was going to be cold; I wish we hadn't put on our—" she stopped short, and then ended in quite a different tone—"our flannel petticoats."

Bobbie turned at the bottom of the stairs.

"Oh, yes," she cried, "*they're* red! Let's take them off."

They did, and with the petticoats rolled up under their arms, ran along the railway, skirting the newly fallen mound of stones and rock and earth, and bent, crushed, twisted trees. They ran at their best pace. Peter led, but the girls were not far behind. They reached the corner that hid the mound from the straight line of railway that ran half a mile without curve or corner.

"Now," said Peter, taking hold of the largest flannel petticoat.

"You're not"—Phyllis faltered—"you're not going to *tear* them?"

"Shut up," said Peter, with brief sternness.

"Oh, yes," said Bobbie, "tear them into little bits if you like. Don't you see, Phil, if we can't stop the train, there'll be a real live accident, with people *killed*. Oh, horrible! Here, Peter, you'll never tear it through the band!"

She took the red flannel petticoat from him and tore it off an inch from the band. Then she tore the other in the same way.

"There!" said Peter, tearing in his turn. He divided each petticoat into three pieces. "Now, we've got six flags." He looked at the watch again. "And we've got seven minutes. We must have flag-staffs."

The knives given to boys are, for some odd reason, seldom of the kind of steel that keeps sharp. The young saplings had to be broken off. Two came up by the roots. The leaves were stripped from them.

"We must cut holes in the flags, and run the sticks through the holes," said Peter. And the holes were cut. The knife was sharp enough to cut flannel with. Two of the flags were set up in heaps of loose stones beneath the sleepers of the down line. Then Phyllis and Roberta took each a flag, and stood ready to wave it as soon as the train came in sight.

"I shall have the other two myself," said Peter, "because it was my idea to wave something red."

"They're our petticoats, though," Phyllis was beginning, but Bobbie interrupted—

"Oh, what does it matter who waves what, if we can only save the train?"

Perhaps Peter had not rightly calculated the number of minutes it would take the 11.29 to get from the station to the place where they were, or perhaps the train was late. Anyway, it seemed a very long time that they waited.

Phyllis grew impatient. "I expect the watch is wrong, and the train's gone by," said she.

Peter relaxed the heroic attitude he had chosen to show off his two flags. And Bobbie began to feel sick with suspense.

It seemed to her that they had been standing there for hours and hours, holding those silly little red flannel flags that no one would ever notice. The train wouldn't care. It would go rushing by them and tear round the corner and go crashing into that awful mound. And everyone would be killed. Her hands grew very cold and trembled so that she could hardly hold the flag. And then came the distant rumble and hum of the metals, and a puff of white steam showed far away along the stretch of line.

"Stand firm," said Peter, "and wave like mad! When it gets to that big furze bush step back, but go on waving! Don't stand *on* the line, Bobbie!"

The train came rattling along very, very fast.

"They don't see us! They won't see us! It's all no good!" cried Bobbie.

The two little flags on the line swayed as the nearing train shook and loosened the heaps of loose stones that held them up. One of them slowly leaned over and fell on the line. Bobbie jumped forward and caught it up, and waved it; her hands did not tremble now.

It seemed that the train came on as fast as ever. It was very near now.

"Keep off the line, you silly cuckoo!" said Peter, fiercely.

"It's no good," Bobbie said again.

"Stand back!" cried Peter, suddenly, and he dragged Phyllis back by the arm.

But Bobbie cried, "Not yet, not yet!" and waved her two flags right over the line. The front of the engine looked black and enormous. Its voice was loud and harsh.

"Oh, stop, stop, stop!" cried Bobbie. No one heard her. At least Peter and Phyllis didn't, for the oncoming rush of the train covered the sound of her voice with a mountain of sound. But afterwards she used to wonder whether the engine itself had not heard her. It seemed almost as though it had—for it slackened swiftly, slackened and stopped, not twenty yards from the place where Bobbie's two flags waved over the line. She saw the great black engine stop dead, but somehow she could not stop waving the flags. And when the driver and the fireman had got off the engine and Peter and Phyllis had gone to meet them and pour out their excited tale of the awful mound just round the corner, Bobbie still waved the flags but more and more feebly and jerkily.

When the others turned towards her she was lying across the line with her hands flung forward and still gripping the sticks of the little red flannel flags.

The engine-driver picked her up, carried her to the train, and laid her on the cushions of a first-class carriage.

"Gone right off in a faint," he said, "poor little woman. And no wonder. I'll just 'ave a look at this 'ere mound of yours, and then we'll run you back to the station and get her seen to."

It was horrible to see Bobbie lying so white and quiet, with her lips blue, and parted.

"I believe that's what people look like when they're dead," whispered Phyllis.

"Don't" said Peter, sharply.

They sat by Bobbie on the blue cushions and the train ran back. Before it reached their station Bobbie sighed and opened her eyes, and rolled herself over and began to cry. This cheered the others wonderfully. They had seen her cry before, but they had never seen her faint, nor anyone else, for the matter of that. They had not known what to do when she was fainting, but now she was only crying they could thump her on the back and tell her not to, just as they always did. And presently, when she stopped crying, they were able to laugh at her for being such a coward as to faint.

When the station was reached, the three were the heroes of an agitated meeting on the platform.

The praises they got for their "prompt action", their "common sense", their "ingenuity", were enough to have turned anybody's head. Phyllis enjoyed herself thoroughly. She had never been a real heroine before, and the feeling was delicious. Peter's ears got very red. Yet he, too, enjoyed himself. Only Bobbie wished they all wouldn't. She wanted to get away.

"You'll hear from the Company about this, I expect," said the Station Master.

Bobbie wished she might never hear of it again. She pulled at Peter's jacket.

"Oh, come away, come away! I want to go home," she said.

So they went. And as they went Station Master and Porter and guards and driver and fireman and passengers sent up a cheer.

"Oh, listen," cried Phyllis; "that's for *us*!"

"Yes," said Peter. "I say, I am glad I thought about something red and waving it."

"How lucky we *did* put on our red flannel petticoats!" said Phyllis.

Bobbie said nothing. She was thinking of the horrible mound, and the trustful train rushing towards it.

"And it was *us* that saved them," said Peter.

"How dreadful if they had all been killed!" said Phyllis; "wouldn't it, Bobbie?"

"We never got any cherries, after all," said Bobbie.

The others thought her rather heartless.

CHAPTER 7

FOR VALOUR

I hope you don't mind my telling you a good deal about Roberta. The fact is I am growing very fond of her. The more I observe her the more I love her. And I notice all sorts of things about her that I like.

For instance, she was quite oddly anxious to make other people happy. And she could keep a secret, a tolerably rare accomplishment. Also she had the power of silent sympathy. That sounds rather dull, I know, but it's not so dull as it sounds. It just means that a person is able to know that you are unhappy, and to love you extra on that account, without bothering you by telling you all the time how sorry she is for you. That was what Bobbie was like. She knew that Mother was unhappy—and that Mother had not told her the reason. So she just loved Mother more and never said a single word that could let Mother know how earnestly her little girl wondered what Mother was unhappy about. This needs practice. It is not so easy as you might think.

Whatever happened—and all sorts of nice, pleasant ordinary things happened—such as picnics, games, and buns for tea, Bobbie always had these thoughts at the back of her mind. "Mother's unhappy. Why? I don't know. She doesn't want me to know. I won't try to find out. But she is unhappy. Why? I don't know. She doesn't—" and so on, repeating and repeating like a tune that you don't know the stopping part of.

The Russian gentleman still took up a good deal of everybody's thoughts. All the Editors and Secretaries of Societies and Members of Parliament had answered Mother's letters as politely as they knew how; but none of them could tell where the wife and children of Mr Szczepansky would be likely to be. (Did I tell you that the Russian's very Russian name was that?)

Bobbie had another quality which you will hear differently described by different people. Some of them call it interfering in other people's business—and some call it "helping lame dogs over stiles", and some call it "loving-kindness". It just means trying to help people.

She racked her brains to think of some way of helping the Russian gentleman to find his wife and children. He had learned a few words of English now. He could say "Good morning" and "Good night", and "Please", and "Thank you", and "Pretty", when the children brought him flowers, and "Ver' good", when they asked him how he had slept.

The way he smiled when he "said his English", was, Bobbie felt, "just too sweet for anything". She used to think of his face because she fancied it would help her to some way of helping him. But it did not. Yet his being there cheered her because she saw that it made Mother happier.

"She likes to have someone to be good to, even beside us," said Bobbie. "And I know she hated to let him have Father's clothes. But I suppose it 'hurt nice', or she wouldn't have."

For many and many a night after the day when she and Peter and Phyllis had saved the train from wreck by waving their little red flannel flags, Bobbie used to wake screaming and shivering, seeing again that horrible mound, and the poor, dear trustful engine rushing on towards it just thinking that it was doing its swift duty, and that everything was clear and safe. And then a warm thrill of pleasure used to run through her at the remembrance of how she and Peter and Phyllis and the red flannel petticoats had really saved everybody.

One morning a letter came. It was addressed to Peter and Bobbie and Phyllis. They opened it with enthusiastic curiosity, for they did not often get letters.

The letter said:

DEAR SIR, AND LADIES,—It is proposed to make a small presentation to you, in commemoration of your prompt and courageous action in warning the train on the—inst., and thus averting what must, humanly speaking, have been a terrible accident. The presentation will take place at the— Station at three o'clock on the 30 inst., if this time and place will be convenient to you.

Yours faithfully,
JABEZ INGLEWOOD
Secretary, Great Northern and Southern Railway Co.

There never had been a prouder moment in the lives of the three children. They rushed to Mother with the letter, and she also felt proud and said so, and this made the children happier than ever.

"But if the presentation is money, you must say, 'Thank you, but we'd rather not take it,' " said Mother. "I'll wash your Indian muslins at once," she added. "You must look tidy on an occasion like this."

"Phil and I can wash them," said Bobbie, "if you'll iron them, Mother."

Washing is rather fun. I wonder whether you've ever done it? This particular washing took place in the back kitchen, which had a stone floor and a very big stone sink under its window.

"Let's put the bath on the sink," said Phyllis; "then we can pretend we're out-of-doors washerwomen like Mother saw in France."

"But they were washing in the cold river," said Peter, his hands in his pockets, "not in hot water."

"This is a *hot* river, then," said Phyllis; "lend a hand with the bath, there's a dear."

"I should like to see a deer lending a hand," said Peter, but he lent his.

"Now to rub and scrub and scrub and rub," said Phyllis, hopping joyously about as Bobbie carefully carried the heavy kettle from the kitchen fire.

"Oh, no!" said Bobbie, greatly shocked; "you don't rub muslin. You put the boiled soap in the hot water and make it all frothy-lathery—and then you shake the muslin and squeeze it, ever so gently, and all the dirt comes out. It's only clumsy things like tablecloths and sheets that have to be rubbed."

The lilac and the Gloire de Dijon roses outside the window swayed in the soft breeze.

"It's a nice drying day—that's one thing," said Bobbie, feeling very grown up. "Oh, I do wonder what wonderful feelings we shall have when we *wear* the Indian muslin dresses!"

"Yes, so do I," said Phyllis, shaking and squeezing the muslin in quite a professional manner.

"*Now* we squeeze out the soapy water. No—we mustn't twist them—and then rinse them. I'll hold them while you and Peter empty the bath and get clean water."

"A presentation! That means presents," said Peter, as his sisters, having duly washed the pegs and wiped the line, hung up the dresses to dry. "Whatever will it be?"

"It might be anything," said Phyllis; "what I've always wanted is a baby elephant—but I suppose they wouldn't know that."

"Suppose it was gold models of steam-engines?" said Bobbie.

"Or a big model of the scene of the prevented accident," suggested Peter, "with a little model train, and dolls dressed like us and the engine-driver and fireman and passengers."

"Do you *like*," said Bobbie, doubtfully, drying her hands on the rough towel that hung on a roller at the back of the scullery door—"do you *like* us being rewarded for saving a train?"

"Yes, I do," said Peter, downrightly; "and don't you try to come it over us that you don't like it, too. Because I know you do."

"Yes," said Bobbie, doubtfully, "I know I do. But oughtn't we to be satisfied with just having done it, and not ask for anything more?"

"Who did ask for anything more, silly?" said her brother. "Victoria Cross soldiers don't *ask* for it; but they're glad enough to get it all the same. Perhaps it'll be medals. Then, when I'm very old indeed, I shall show them to my grand-children and say, 'We only did our duty,' and they'll be awfully proud of me."

"You have to be married," warned Phyllis, "or you don't have any grandchildren."

"I suppose I shall *have* to be married some day," said Peter, "but it will be an awful bother having her round all the time. I'd like to marry a lady who had trances, and only woke up once or twice a year."

"Just to say you were the light of her life and then go to sleep again. Yes. That wouldn't be bad," said Bobbie.

"When *I* get married," said Phyllis, "I shall want him to want me to be awake all the time, so that I can hear him say how nice I am."

"I think it would be nice," said Bobbie, "to marry someone very poor, and then you'd do all the work and he'd love you most frightfully, and see the blue wood smoke curling up among the trees from the domestic hearth as he came home from work every night. I say—we've got to answer that letter and say that the time and place *will* be convenient to us. There's the soap, Peter. We're both as clean as clean. That pink book of writing paper you had on your birthday, Phil."

It took some time to arrange what should be said. Mother had gone back to her writing, and several sheets of pink paper with scalloped gilt edges and green four-leaved shamrocks in the corner were spoiled before the three had decided what to say. Then each made a copy and signed it with its own name.

The threefold letter ran:

DEAR MR JABEZ INGLEWOOD,—Thank you very much. We did not want to be rewarded but only to save the train, but we are glad you think so and thank you very much. The time and place you say will be quite convenient to us. Thank you very much.

Your affecate little friend,

Then came the name, and after it:

P. S. Thank you very much.

"Washing is much easier than ironing," said Bobbie, taking the clean dresses off the line. "I do love to see things come clean. Oh—I don't know how we shall wait till it's time to know what presentation they're going to present!"

When at last—it seemed a very long time after—it was *the* day, the three children went down to the station at the proper time. And everything that happened was so odd that it seemed like a dream. The Station Master came out to meet them—in his best clothes, as Peter noticed at once—and led them into the waiting room where once they had played the advertisement game. It looked quite different now. A carpet had been put down—and there were pots of roses on the mantelpiece and on the window ledges, green branches stuck up, like holly and laurel at Christmas, over the framed advertisement of Cook's Tours and the Beauties of Devon and the Paris – Lyons Railway. There were quite a number of people there besides the Porter—two or three ladies in smart dresses, and quite a crowd of gentlemen in high hats and frock coats—besides everybody who belonged to the station. They recognized several people who had been in the train on the red-flannel-petticoat day. Best of all, their own old gentleman was there, and his coat and hat and collar seemed more than ever different from anyone else's. He shook hands with them and then everybody sat down on chairs, and a gentleman in spectacles—they found afterwards that he was the District Superintendent—began quite a long speech—very clever indeed. I am not going to write the speech down. First, because you would think it dull; and secondly, because it made all the children blush so, and get so hot about the ears that I am quite anxious to get away from this part of the subject; and thirdly, because the gentleman took so many words to say what he had to say that I really haven't time to write them down. He said all sorts of nice things about the children's bravery and presence of mind, and when he had done he sat down, and everyone who was there clapped and said, "Hear, hear."

And then the old gentleman got up and said things, too. It was very like a prize-giving. And then he called the children one by one, by their names, and gave each of them a beautiful gold watch and chain. And inside the watches were engraved after the name of the watch's new owner:

"From the Directors of the Northern and Southern Railway in grateful recognition of the courageous and prompt action which averted an accident on—1905."

The watches were the most beautiful you can possibly imagine, and each one had a blue leather case to live in when it was at home.

"You must make a speech now and thank everyone for their kindness," whispered the Station Master in Peter's ear, and pushed him forward. "Begin 'Ladies and Gentlemen'," he added.

Each of the children had already said "Thank you," quite properly.

"Oh, dear," said Peter, but he did not resist the push.

"Ladies and gentlemen," he said in a rather husky voice. Then there was a pause, and he heard his heart beating in his throat. "Ladies and Gentlemen," he went on with a rush, "it's most awfully good of you, and we shall treasure the watches all our lives—but really we don't deserve it because what we did wasn't anything, really. At least, I mean it was awfully exciting, and what I mean to say—thank you all very, very much."

The people clapped Peter more than they had done the District Superintendent, and then everybody shook hands with them, and as soon as politeness would let them, they got away, and tore up the hill to Three Chimneys with their watches in their hands.

It was a wonderful day—the kind of day that very seldom happens to anybody and to most of us not at all.

"I did want to talk to the old gentleman about something else," said Bobbie, "but it was so public—like being in church."

"What did you want to say?" asked Phyllis.

"I'll tell you when I've thought about it more," said Bobbie.

So when she had thought a little more she wrote a letter.

My dearest old gentleman, [it said] I want most awfully to ask you something. If you could get out of the train and go by the next, it would do. I do not want you to give me anything. Mother says we ought not to. And besides, we do not want any *things*. Only to talk to you about a Prisoner and Captive. Your loving little friend,

BOBBIE

She got the Station Master to give the letter to the old gentleman, and next day she asked Peter and Phyllis to come down to the station with her at the time when the train that brought the old gentleman from town would be passing through.

She explained her idea to them—and they approved thoroughly.

They had all washed their hands and faces, and brushed their hair, and were looking as tidy as they knew how. But Phyllis, always unlucky, had upset a jug of lemonade down the front of her dress. There was no time to change—and the wind happening to blow from the coal yard, her frock was soon powdered with grey, which stuck to the sticky lemonade stains and made her look, as Peter said, "like any little gutter child".

It was decided that she should keep behind the others as much as possible.

"Perhaps the old gentleman won't notice," said Bobbie. "The aged are often weak in the eyes."

There was no sign of weakness, however, in the eyes, or in any other part of the old gentleman, as he stepped from the train and looked up and down the platform.

The three children, now that it came to the point, suddenly felt that rush of deep shyness which makes your ears red and hot, your hands warm and wet, and the tip of your nose pink and shiny.

"Oh," said Phyllis, "my heart's thumping like a steam-engine—right under my sash, too."

"Nonsense," said Peter, "people's hearts aren't under their sashes."

"I don't care—mine is," said Phyllis.

"If you're going to talk like a poetry-book," said Peter, "my heart's in my mouth."

"My heart's in my boots—if you come to that," said Roberta; "but do come on—he'll think we're idiots."

"He won't be far wrong," said Peter, gloomily. And they went forward to meet the old gentleman.

"Hullo," he said, shaking hands with them all in turn. "This is a very great pleasure."

"It *was* good of you to get out," Bobbie said, perspiring and polite.

He took her arm and drew her into the waiting room where she and the others had played the advertisement game the day they found the Russian. Phyllis and Peter followed. "Well?" said the old gentleman, giving Bobbie's arm a kind little shake before he let it go. "Well? What is it?"

"Oh, please!" said Bobbie.

"Yes?" said the old gentleman.

"What I mean to say—" said Bobbie.

"Yes?" said the old gentleman.

"It's all very nice and kind," said she.

"But?" he said.

"I wish I might say something," she said.

"Say it," said he.

"Well, then," said Bobbie—and out came the story of the Russian who had written the beautiful book about poor people, and had been sent to prison and to Siberia for just that.

"And what we want more than anything in the world is to find his wife and children for him," said Bobbie, "but we don't know how. But you must be most horribly clever, or you wouldn't be a Director of the Railway. And if *you* knew how—and would? We'd rather have that than anything else in the world. We'd go without the watches, even, if you could sell them and find his wife with the money."

And the others said so, too, though not with so much enthusiasm.

"Hum," said the old gentleman, pulling down the white

waist-coat that had the big gilt buttons on it, "what did you say the name was—Fryingpansky?"

"No, no," said Bobbie earnestly. "I'll write it down for you. It doesn't really look at all like that except when you say it. Have you a bit of pencil and the back of an envelope?" she asked.

The old gentleman got out a gold pencil-case and a beautiful, sweet-smelling green Russian leather notebook and opened it at a new page.

"Here," he said, "write here."

She wrote down, "Szczepansky," and said:

"That's how you write it. You *call* it Shepansky."

The old gentleman took out a pair of gold-rimmed spectacles and fitted them on his nose. When he had read the name, he looked quite different.

"*That* man? Bless my soul!" he said. "Why, I've read his book! It's translated into every European language. A fine book—a noble book. And so your mother took him in—like the good Samaritan. Well, well. I'll tell you what, youngsters—your mother must be a very good woman."

"Of course she is," said Phyllis, in astonishment.

"And you're a very good man," said Bobbie, very shy, but firmly resolved to be polite.

"You flatter me," said the old gentleman, taking off his hat with a flourish. "And now am I to tell you what I think of you?"

"Oh, please don't," said Bobbie, hastily.

"Why?" asked the old gentleman.

"I don't exactly know," said Bobbie. "Only—if it's horrid, I don't want you to; and if it's nice, I'd rather you didn't."

The old gentleman laughed.

"Well, then," he said, "I'll only just say that I'm very glad you came to me about this—very glad, indeed. And I shouldn't be surprised if I found out something very soon. I know a great many Russians in London, and every Russian knows *his* name. Now tell me all about yourselves."

He turned to the others, but there was only one other, and that was Peter. Phyllis had disappeared.

"Tell me all about yourself," said the old gentleman again. And, quite naturally, Peter was stricken dumb.

"All right, we'll have an examination," said the old gentleman; "you two sit on the table, and I'll sit on the bench and ask questions."

He did, and out came their names and ages—their Father's name and business—how long they had lived at Three Chimneys and a great deal more.

The questions were beginning to turn on a herring and a half for three-halfpence, and a pound of lead and a pound of feathers, when the door of the waiting room was kicked open by a boot; as the boot entered everyone could see that its lace was coming undone—and in came Phyllis, very slowly and carefully.

In one hand she carried a large tin can, and in the other a thick slice of bread and butter.

"Afternoon tea," she announced proudly, and held the can and the bread and butter out to the old gentleman, who took them and said:

"Bless my soul!"

"Yes," said Phyllis.

"It's very thoughtful of you," said the old gentleman, "very."

"But you might have got a cup," said Bobbie, "and a plate."

"Perks always drinks out of the can," said Phyllis, flushing red. "I think it was very nice of him to give it me at all—let alone cups and plates," she added.

"So do I," said the old gentleman, and he drank some of the tea and tasted the bread and butter.

And then it was time for the next train, and he got into it with many good-byes and kind last words.

"Well," said Peter, when they were left on the platform, and the tail-lights of the train disappeared round the corner, "it's my belief that we've lighted a candle today—like Latimer, you know, when he was being burned—and there'll be fireworks for our Russian before long."

And so there were.

It wasn't ten days after the interview in the waiting room

that the three children were sitting on top of the biggest rock in the field below their house watching the 5.15 steam away from the station along the bottom of the valley. They saw, too, the few people who had got out at the station struggling up the road towards the village, and they saw one person leave the road and open the gate that led across the fields to Three Chimneys and to nowhere else.

"Who on earth?" said Peter, scrambling down.

"Let's go and see," said Phyllis.

So they did. And when they got near enough to see who the person was, they saw it was their old gentleman himself, his brass buttons winking in the afternoon sunshine, and his white waistcoat looking whiter than ever against the green of the field.

"Hullo!" shouted the children, waving their hands.

"Hullo!" shouted the old gentleman, waving his hat.

Then the three started to run—and when they got to him they hardly had breath left to say:

"How do you do?"

"Good news," said he. "I've found your Russian friend's wife and child—and I couldn't resist the temptation of giving myself the pleasure of telling him."

But as he looked at Bobbie's face he felt that he *could* resist the temptation.

"Here," he said to her, "you run on and tell him. The other two will show me the way."

Bobbie ran. But when she had breathlessly panted out the news to the Russian and Mother sitting in the quiet garden—when Mother's face had lighted up so beautifully, and she had said half a dozen quick French words to the Exile—Bobbie wished that she had *not* carried the news. For the Russian sprang up with a cry that made Bobbie's heart leap and then tremble—a cry of love and longing such as she had never heard. Then he took Mother's hand and kissed it gently and reverently—and then he sank down in his chair and covered his face with his hands and sobbed. Bobbie crept away. She did not want to see the others just then.

But she was as gay as anybody when the endless French

talking was over, when Peter had torn down to the village for buns and cakes, and the girls had got tea ready and taken it out into the garden.

The old gentleman was most merry and delightful. He seemed to be able to talk in French and English almost at the same moment, and Mother did nearly as well. It was a delightful time. Mother seemed as if she could not make enough fuss about the old gentleman, and she said yes at once when he asked if he might present some "goodies" to his little friends.

The word was new to the children—but they guessed that it meant sweets, for the three large pink and green boxes, tied with green ribbon, which he took out of his bag, held unheard-of layers of beautiful chocolates.

The Russian's few belongings were packed, and they all saw him off at the station.

Then Mother turned to the old gentleman and said:

"I don't know how to thank you for *everything*. It has been a real pleasure to me to see you. But we live very quietly. I am so sorry that I can't ask you to come and see us again."

The children thought this very hard. When they *had* made a friend—and such a friend—they would dearly have liked him to come and see them again.

What the old gentleman thought they couldn't tell. He only said:

"I consider myself very fortunate, Madam, to have been received once at your house."

"Ah," said Mother, "I know I must seem very surly and ungrateful—but—"

"You could never seem anything but a most charming and gracious lady," said the old gentleman, with another of his bows.

And as they turned to go up the hill, Bobbie saw her Mother's face.

"How tired you look, Mammy," she said; "lean on me."

"It's my place to give Mother my arm," said Peter. "I'm the head man of the family when Father's away."

Mother took the arm of each.

"How awfully nice," said Phyllis, skipping joyfully, "to think of the dear Russian embracing his long-lost wife. The baby must have grown a lot since he saw her."

"Yes," said Mother.

"I wonder whether Father will think *I've* grown," Phyllis went on, skipping still more gaily. "I have grown already, haven't I, Mother?"

"Yes," said Mother, "oh, yes," and Bobbie and Peter felt her hands tighten on their arms.

"Poor old Mammy, you *are* tired," said Peter.

Bobbie said, "Come on, Phil; I'll race you to the gate."

And she started the race, though she hated doing it. *You* know why Bobbie did that. Mother only thought that Bobbie was tired of walking slowly. Even Mothers, who love you better than anyone else ever will, don't always understand.

Chapter 8

THE AMATEUR FIREMAN

"That's a likely little brooch you've got on, Miss," said Perks the Porter; "I don't know as ever I see a thing more like a buttercup without it *was* a buttercup."

"Yes," said Bobbie, glad and flushed by this approval. "I always thought it was more like a buttercup almost than even a real one— and I *never* thought it would come to be mine, my very own—and then Mother gave it to me for my birthday."

"Oh, have you had a birthday?" said Perks; and he seemed quite surprised, as though a birthday were a thing only granted to a favoured few.

"Yes," said Bobbie; "when's your birthday, Mr Perks?"

The children were taking tea with Mr Perks in the Porter's room among the lamps and the railway almanacs. They had brought their own cups and some jam turnovers. Mr Perks made tea in a beer can, as usual, and everyone felt very happy and confidential.

"My birthday?" said Perks, tipping some more dark brown tea out of the can into Peter's cup. "I give up keeping of my birthday afore you was born."

"But you must have been born *sometime*, you know," said Phyllis, thoughtfully, "even if it was twenty years ago—or thirty or sixty or seventy."

"Not so long as that, Missie," Perks grinned as he answered. "If you really want to know, it was thirty-two years ago, come the fifteenth of this month."

"Then why don't you keep it?" asked Phyllis.

"I've got something else to keep besides birthdays," said Perks briefly.

"Oh! What?" asked Phyllis, eagerly. "Not secrets?"

"No," said Perks, "the kids and the Missus."

It was this talk that set the children thinking, and, presently, talking. Perks was, on the whole, the dearest friend they had made. Not so grand as the Station Master, but more approachable—less powerful than the old gentleman, but more confidential.

"It seems horrid that nobody keeps his birthday," said Bobbie. "Couldn't *we* do something?"

"Let's go up to the Canal bridge and talk it over," said Peter. "I got a new gut line from the postman this morning. He gave it me for a bunch of roses that I gave him for his sweetheart. She's ill."

"Then I do think you might have given her the roses for nothing," said Bobbie, indignantly.

"Nyang, nyang!" said Peter, disagreeably, and put his hands in his pockets.

"He did, of course," said Phyllis, in haste; "directly we heard she was ill we got the roses ready and waited by the gate. It was when you were making the brekker-toast. And when he'd said 'Thank you' for the roses so many times—much more than he need have—he pulled out the line and gave it to Peter. It wasn't exchange. It was the grateful heart."

"Oh, I *beg* your pardon, Peter," said Bobbie, "I *am* so sorry."

"Don't mention it," said Peter, grandly, "I knew you would be."

So then they all went up to the Canal bridge. The idea was to fish from the bridge, but the line was not quite long enough.

"Never mind," said Bobbie. "Let's just stay here and look at things. Everything's so beautiful."

It was. The sun was setting in red splendour over the grey and purple hills, and the canal lay smooth and shiny in the shadow—no ripple broke its surface. It was like a grey satin ribbon between the dusky green silk of the meadows that were on each side of its banks.

"It's all right," said Peter, "but somehow I can always see how pretty things are much better when I've something to do. Let's get down on to the towpath and fish from there."

Phyllis and Bobbie remembered how the boys on the canal-boats had thrown coal at them, and they said so.

"Oh, nonsense," said Peter. "There aren't any boys here now. If there were, I'd fight them."

Peter's sisters were kind enough not to remind him how he had *not* fought the boys when coal had last been thrown. Instead they said, "All right, then," and cautiously climbed down the steep bank to the towing-path. The line was carefully baited, and for half an hour they fished patiently and in vain. Not a single nibble came to nourish hope in their hearts.

All eyes were intent on the sluggish waters that earnestly pretended they had never harboured a single minnow when a loud, rough shout made them start.

"Hi!" said the shout, in most disagreeable tones, "get out of that, can't you?"

An old white horse coming along the towing-path was within half a dozen yards of them. They sprang to their feet and hastily climbed up the bank.

"We'll slip down again when they've gone by," said Bobbie.

But, alas, the barge, after the manner of barges, stopped under the bridge.

"She's going to anchor," said Peter; "just our luck!"

The barge did not anchor, because an anchor is not part of a canal-boat's furniture, but she was moored with ropes fore and aft—and the ropes were made fast to the palings and to crowbars driven into the ground.

"What you staring at?" growled the Bargee, crossly.

"We weren't staring," said Bobbie; "we wouldn't be so rude."

"Rude be blessed," said the man; "get along with you!"

"Get along yourself," said Peter. He remembered what he had said about fighting boys, and, besides, he felt safe halfway up the bank. "We've as much right here as anyone else."

"Oh, *'ave* you, indeed!" said the man. "We'll soon see about that." And he came across his deck and began to climb down the side of his barge.

"Oh, come away, Peter, come away!" said Bobbie and Phyllis, in agonized unison.

"Not me," said Peter, "but *you'd* better."

The girls climbed to the top of the bank and stood ready to bolt for home as soon as they saw their brother out of danger. The way home lay all downhill. They knew that they all ran well. The Bargee did not look as if *he* did. He was red-faced, heavy, and beefy.

But as soon as his foot was on the towing-path the children saw that they had misjudged him.

He made one spring up the bank and caught Peter by the leg, dragged him down—set him on his feet with a shake—took him by the ear—and said sternly:

"Now, then, what do you mean by it? Don't you know these 'ere waters is preserved? You ain't no right catching fish 'ere—not to say nothing of your precious cheek."

Peter was always proud afterwards when he remembered that, with the Bargee's furious fingers tightening on his ear, the Bargee's crimson countenance close to his own, the Bargee's hot breath on his neck, he had the courage to speak the truth.

"I *wasn't* catching fish," said Peter.

"That's not *your* fault, I'll be bound," said the man, giving Peter's ear a twist—not a hard one—but still a twist.

Peter could not say that it was. Bobbie and Phyllis had been holding on to the railings above and skipping with anxiety. Now suddenly Bobbie slipped through the railings and rushed down the bank towards Peter, so impetuously that Phyllis, following more temperately, felt certain that her sister's descent would end in the waters of the canal. And so it would have done if the Bargee hadn't let go of Peter's ear—and caught her in his jerseyed arm.

"Who are you a-shoving of?" he said, setting her on her feet.

"Oh," said Bobbie, breathless, "I'm not shoving anybody. At least, not on purpose. Please don't be cross with Peter. Of course, it's your canal; we're sorry and we won't fish any more. But we didn't know it was yours."

"Go along with you," said the Bargee.

"Yes, we will; indeed we will," said Bobbie, earnestly; "but we do beg your pardon—and really we haven't caught a single fish. I'd tell you directly if we had, honour bright I would."

She held out her hands and Phyllis turned out her little empty pocket to show that really they hadn't any fish concealed about them.

"Well," said the Bargee, more gently, "cut along, then, and don't you do it again, that's all."

The children hurried up the bank.

"Chuck us a coat, M'ria," shouted the man. And a red-haired woman in a green plaid shawl came out from the cabin door with a baby in her arms and threw a coat to him. He put it on, climbed the bank, and slouched along across the bridge towards the village.

"You'll find me up at the 'Rose and Crown' when you've got the kid to sleep," he called to her from the bridge.

When he was out of sight the children slowly returned. Peter insisted on this.

"The canal may belong to him," he said, "though I don't believe it does. But the bridge is everybody's. Doctor

Forrest told me it's public property. I'm not going to be bounced off the bridge by him or anyone else, so I tell you."

Peter's ear was still sore and so were his feelings.

The girls followed him as gallant soldiers might follow the leader of a forlorn hope.

"I do wish you wouldn't," was all they said.

"Go home if you're afraid," said Peter; "leave me alone. *I'm* not afraid."

The sound of the man's footsteps died away along the quiet road. The peace of the evening was not broken by the notes of the sedge-warblers or by the voice of the woman in the barge, singing her baby to sleep. It was a sad song she sang. Something about Bill Bailey and how she wanted him to come home.

The children stood leaning their arms on the parapet of the bridge; they were glad to be quiet for a few minutes because all three hearts were beating much more quickly.

"I'm not going to be driven away by any old bargeman, I'm not," said Peter, thickly.

"Of course not," Phyllis said soothingly; "you didn't give in to him! So now we might go home, don't you think?"

Nothing more was said till the woman got off the barge, climbed the bank, and came across the bridge.

She hesitated, looking at the three backs of the children, then she said, "Ahem."

Peter stayed as he was, but the girls looked round.

"You mustn't take no notice of my Bill," said the woman; " 'is bark's worse'n 'is bite. Some of the kids down Farley way is fair terrors. It was them put 'is back up calling out about who ate the puppy pie under Marlow bridge."

"Who *did*?" asked Phyllis.

"*I* dunno," said the woman. "Nobody don't know! But somehow, and I don't know the why nor the wherefore of it, them words is p'ison to a barge-master. Don't you take no notice. 'E won't be back for two hours good. You might catch a power o' fish afore that. The light's good an' all," she added.

"Thank you," said Bobbie. "You're very kind. Where's your baby?"

"Asleep in the cabin," said the woman. " 'E's all right. Never wakes afore twelve. Reg'lar as a church clock, 'e is."

"I'm sorry," said Bobbie; "I would have liked to see him, close to."

"And a finer you never did see, Miss, though I says it." The woman's face brightened as she spoke.

"Aren't you afraid to leave it?" said Peter.

"Lor' love you, no," said the woman; "who'd hurt a little thing like 'im? Besides, Spot's there. So long!"

The woman went away.

"Shall we go home?" said Phyllis.

"You can. I'm going to fish," said Peter briefly.

"I thought we came up here to talk about Perk's birthday," said Phyllis.

"Perk's birthday'll keep."

So they got down on the towing-path again and Peter fished. He did not catch anything.

It was almost quite dark, the girls were getting tired, and as Bobbie said, it was past bedtime, when suddenly Phyllis cried, "What's that?"

And she pointed to the canal boat. Smoke was coming from the chimney of the cabin, had indeed been curling softly into the soft evening air all the time—but now other wreaths of smoke were rising, and these were from the cabin door.

"It's on fire—that's all," said Peter, calmly. "Serve him right."

"Oh—how *can* you?" cried Phyllis. "Think of the poor dear dog."

"The *Baby*!" screamed Bobbie.

In an instant all three made for the barge.

Her mooring ropes were slack, and the little breeze, hardly strong enough to be felt, had yet been strong enough to drift her stern against the bank. Bobbie was first—then came Peter, and it was Peter who slipped and fell. He went into the canal up to his neck, and his feet could not feel the bottom, but his arm was on the edge of the barge. Phyllis caught at his hair. It hurt, but it helped him to get out. Next minute he had leaped on to the barge, Phyllis following.

"Not you!" he shouted to Bobbie; "*me*, because I'm wet."

He caught up with Bobbie at the cabin door, and flung her aside very roughly indeed; if they had been playing, such roughness would have made Bobbie weep with tears of rage and pain. Now, though he flung her on to the edge of the hold, so that her knee and her elbow were grazed and bruised, she only cried:

"No—not you—*me*," and struggled up again. But not quickly enough.

Peter had already gone down two of the cabin steps into the cloud of thick smoke. He stopped, remembered all he had ever heard of fires, pulled his soaked handkerchief out of his breast pocket and tied it over his mouth. As he pulled it out he said:

"It's all right, hardly any fire at all."

And this, though he thought it was a lie, was rather good of Peter. It was meant to keep Bobbie from rushing after him into danger. Of course it didn't.

The cabin glowed red. A paraffin lamp was burning calmly in an orange mist.

"Hi," said Peter, lifting the handkerchief from his mouth for a moment. "Hi, Baby—where are you?" He choked.

"Oh, let *me* go," cried Bobbie, close behind him. Peter pushed her back more roughly than before and went on.

Now what would have happened if the baby hadn't cried I don't know—but just at that moment it *did* cry. Peter felt his way through the dark smoke, found something small and soft and warm and alive, picked it up and backed out, nearly tumbling over Bobbie, who was close behind. A dog snapped at his leg—tried to bark, choked.

"I've got the kid," said Peter, tearing off the handkerchief and staggering on to the deck.

Bobbie caught at the place where the bark came from, and her hands met on the fat back of a smooth-haired dog. It turned and fastened its teeth on her hand, but very gently, as much as to say:

"I'm bound to bark and bite if strangers come into my master's cabin, but I know you mean well, so I won't *really* bite."

Bobbie dropped the dog.

"All right, old man. Good dog," said she. "Here—give me the baby, Peter; you're so wet you'll give it cold."

Peter was only too glad to hand over the strange little bundle that squirmed and whimpered in his arms.

"Now," said Bobbie, quickly, "you run straight to the 'Rose and Crown' and tell them. Phil and I will stay here with the precious. Hush, then, a dear, a duck, a darling! Go *now*, Peter! Run!"

"I can't run in these things," said Peter, firmly, "they're as heavy as lead. I'll walk."

"Then *I'll* run," said Bobbie. "Get on the bank, Phil, and I'll hand you the dear."

The baby was carefully handed. Phyllis sat down on the bank and tried to hush the baby. Peter wrung the water from his sleeves and knickerbocker legs as well as he could, and it was Bobbie who ran like the wind across the bridge and up the long white quiet twilight road towards the "Rose and Crown".

There is a nice old-fashioned room at the "Rose and Crown" where Bargees and their wives sit of an evening drinking their supper beer, and toasting their supper cheese at a glowing basketful of coals that sticks out into the room under a great hooded chimney and is warmer and prettier and more comforting than any other fireplace *I* ever saw.

There was a pleasant party of barge people round the fire. You might not have thought it pleasant, but they did; for they were all friends or acquaintances, and they liked the same sort of things, and talked the same sort of talk. This is the real secret of pleasant society. The Bargee Bill, whom the children had found so disagreeable, was considered excellent company by his mates. He was telling a tale of his own wrongs—always a thrilling subject. It was his barge he was speaking about.

"And 'e sent down word 'paint her inside hout,' not namin' no colour, d'ye see? So I gets a lotter green paint and I paints her stem to stern, and I tell yer she looked Al. Then 'e comes along and 'e says. 'Wot yer paint 'er all one colour for?' 'e says. And I says, says I, 'Cause I thought she'd look fust-rate,' says I, 'and I think so still' An' he says, '*Dew* yer? Then ye can just pay for the bloomin' paint yerself,' says he. An' I 'ad to, too." A murmur of sympathy ran round the room. Breaking noisily in on it came Bobbie. She burst open the swing door—crying breathlessly:

"Bill! I want Bill the Bargeman."

There was a stupefied silence. Pots of beer were held in mid-air, paralysed on their way to thirsty mouths.

"Oh," said Bobbie, seeing the bargewoman and making for her. "Your barge cabin's on fire. Go quickly."

The woman started to her feet, and put a big red hand to her waist on the left side, where your heart seems to be when you are frightened or miserable.

"Reginald Horace!" she cried in a terrible voice; "my Reginald Horace!"

"All right," said Bobbie, "if you mean the baby; got him out safe. Dog, too." She had no breath for more, except, "Go on—it's all alight."

Then she sank on the ale-house bench and tried to get that breath of relief after running which people call the "second wind". But she felt as though she would never breathe again.

Bill the Bargee rose slowly and heavily. But his wife was a hundred yards up the road before he had quite understood what was the matter.

Phyllis, shivering by the canal side, had hardly heard the quick approaching feet before the woman had flung herself on the railing, rolled down the bank, and snatched the baby from her.

"Don't," said Phyllis, reproachfully; "I'd just got him to sleep."

*

Bill came up later talking in a language with which the children were wholly unfamiliar. He leaped on to the barge and dipped up pails of water. Peter helped him and they put out the fire. Phyllis, the bargewoman, and the baby—and presently Bobbie, too—cuddled together in a heap on the bank.

"Lord help me, if it was me left anything as could catch alight," said the woman again and again.

But it wasn't she. It was Bill the Bargeman, who had knocked his pipe out and the red ash had fallen on the hearth-rug and smouldered there and at last broken into flame. Though a stern man he was just. He did not blame his wife for what was his own fault, as many bargemen, and other men, too, would have done.

*

Mother was half wild with anxiety when at last the three children turned up at Three Chimneys, all very wet by now, for Peter seemed to have come off on the others. But when she had disentangled the truth of what had happened from their mixed and incoherent narrative, she owned that they had done quite right, and could not possibly have done otherwise. Nor did she put any obstacles in the way of their accepting the cordial invitation with which the bargeman had parted from them.

"Ye be here at seven tomorrow," he had said, "and I'll take you the entire trip to Farley and back, so I will, and not a penny to pay. Nineteen locks!"

They did not know what locks were; but they were at the bridge at seven, with bread and cheese and half a soda cake, and quite a quarter of a leg of mutton in a basket.

It was a glorious day. The old white horse strained at the ropes, the barge glided smoothly and steadily through the still water. The sky was blue overhead. Mr Bill was as nice as anyone could possibly be. No one would have thought that he could be the same man who had held Peter by the ear. As for Mrs Bill, she had always been nice, as Bobbie said, and so had the baby, and even Spot, who might have bitten them quite badly if he had liked.

"It was simply ripping, Mother," said Peter, when they reached home very happy, very tired, and very dirty, "right over that glorious aqueduct. And locks—you don't know what they're like. You sink into the ground and then, when you feel you're never going to stop going down, two great black gates open slowly, slowly—you go out, and there you are on the canal just like you were before."

"I know," said Mother, "there are locks on the Thames. Father and I used to go on the river at Marlow before we were married."

"And the dear, darling, ducky baby," said Bobbie; "it let me nurse it for ages and ages—and it *was* so good. Mother, I wish we had a baby to play with."

"And everybody was so nice to us," said Phyllis, "everybody we met. And they say we may fish whenever we like. And Bill is going to show us the way next time he's in these parts. He says we don't know really."

"He said *you* didn't know," said Peter; "but Mother, he said he'd tell all the bargees up and down the canal that we were the real, right sort, and they were to treat us like good pals, as were we."

"So then I said," Phyllis interrupted, "we'd always each wear a red ribbon when we went fishing by the canal, so they'd know it was *Us*, and we were the real, right sort, and be nice to us!"

"So you've made another lot of friends," said Mother; "first the railway and then the canal!"

"Oh, yes," said Bobbie; "I think everyone in the world is friends if you can only get them to see you don't want to be *un*-friends."

"Perhaps you're right," said Mother; and she sighed. "Come, Chicks. It's bedtime."

"Yes," said Phyllis. "Oh, dear—and we went up there to talk about what we'd do for Perks's birthday. And we haven't talked a single thing about it!"

"No more we have," said Bobbie; "but Peter's saved Reginald Horace's life. I think that's about good enough for one evening."

"Bobbie would have saved him if I hadn't knocked her down; twice I did," said Peter, loyally.

"So would I," said Phyllis, "if I'd known what to do."

"Yes," said Mother, "you've saved a little child's life. I do think that's enough for one evening. Oh, my darlings, thank God *you're* all safe!"

CHAPTER 9

THE PRIDE OF PERKS

It was breakfast-time. Mother's face was very bright as she poured the milk and ladled out the porridge.

"I've sold another story, Chickies," she said; "the one about the King of the Mussels, so there'll be buns for tea. You can go and get them as soon as they're baked. About eleven, isn't it?"

Peter, Phyllis, and Bobbie exchanged glances with each other, six glances in all. Then Bobbie said:

"Mother would you mind if we didn't have the buns for tea tonight, but on the fifteenth? That's next Thursday."

"I don't mind when you have them, dear," said Mother, "but why?"

"Because it's Perks's birthday," said Bobbie; he's thirty-two, and he says he doesn't keep his birthday any more, because he's got other things to keep—not rabbits or secrets—but the kids and the missus."

"You mean his wife and children," said Mother.

"Yes," said Phyllis; "it's the same thing, isn't it?"

"And we thought we'd make a nice birthday for him. He's been so awfully jolly decent to us, you know, Mother," said Peter, "and we agreed that next bun-day we'd ask you if we could."

"But supposing there hadn't been a bun-day before the fifteenth?" said Mother.

"Oh, then, we meant to ask you to let us anti—antipate it, and go without when the bun-day came."

"Anticipate," said Mother. "I see. Certainly. It would be nice to put his name on the buns with pink sugar, wouldn't it?"

"Perks," said Peter, "it's not a pretty name."

"His other name's Albert," said Phyllis; "I asked him once."

"We might put A. P.," said Mother; "I'll show you how when the time comes."

This was all very well as far as it went. But even fourteen half-penny buns with A. P. on them in pink sugar do not of themselves make a very grand celebration.

"There are always flowers, of course," said Bobbie, later, when a really earnest council was being held on the subject in the hay-loft where the broken chaff-cutting machine was, and the row of holes to drop hay through in to the hay-racks over the mangers of the stables below.

"He's got lots of flowers of his own," said Peter.

"But it's always nice to have them given you," said Bobbie, "however many you've got of your own. We can use flowers for trimmings to the birthday. But there must be something to trim besides buns."

"Let's all be quiet and think," said Phyllis; "no one's to speak until it's thought of something."

So they were all quiet and so very still that a brown rat thought that there was no one in the loft and came out very boldly. When Bobbie sneezed, the rat was quite shocked and hurried away, for he saw that a hay-loft where such things could happen was no place for a respectable middle-aged rat that liked a quiet life.

"Hooray!" cried Peter, suddenly, "I've got it." He jumped up and kicked at the loose hay.

"What?" said the others, eagerly.

"Why, Perks is so nice to everybody. There must be lots of people in the village who'd like to help to make him a birthday. Let's go round and ask everybody."

"Mother said we weren't to ask people for things," said Bobbie doubtfully.

"For ourselves, she meant, silly, not for other people. I'll ask the old gentleman too. You see if I don't," said Peter.

"Let's ask Mother first," said Bobbie.

"Oh, what's the use of bothering Mother about every little thing?" said Peter, "especially when she's busy. Come on. Let's go down to the village now and begin."

So they went. The old lady at the Post-office said she

didn't see why Perks should have a birthday any more than anyone else.

"No," said Bobbie. "I should like everyone to have one. Only we know when his is."

"Mine's tomorrow," said the old lady, "and much notice anyone will take of it. Go along with you."

So they went.

And some people were kind, and some were crusty. And some would give and some would not. It is rather difficult work asking for things, even for other people, as you have no doubt found if you have ever tried it.

When the children got home and counted up what had been given and what had been promised, they felt that for the first day it was not so bad. Peter wrote down the lists of the things in the little pocket-book where he kept the numbers of his engines. These were the lists:

Given.

A tobacco pipe from the sweet shop.

Half a pound of tea from the grocer's.

A woollen scarf slightly faded from the draper's, which was the other side of the grocer's.

A stuffed squirrel from the Doctor.

Promised.

A piece of meat from the butcher.

Six fresh eggs from the woman who lived in the old turnpike cottage.

A piece of honeycomb and six bootlaces from the cobbler, and an iron shovel from the blacksmith's.

Very early next morning Bobbie got up and woke Phyllis. This had been agreed on between them. They had not told Peter because they thought he would think it silly. But they told him afterwards, when it had turned out all right.

They cut a big bunch of roses, and put it in a basket with the needle-book that Phyllis had made for Bobbie on her birthday, and a very pretty blue necktie of Phyllis's. Then they wrote on a paper: "For Mrs Ransome, with our best love, because it is her birthday," and they put the paper in the basket, and they took it to the Post-office, and went in and put it on the counter and ran away before the old woman at the Post-office had time to get into her shop.

When they got home Peter had grown confidential over helping Mother to get the breakfast and had told her their plans.

"There's no harm in it," said Mother, "but it depends *how* you do it. I only hope he won't be offended and think it's *charity*. Poor people are very proud, you know."

"It isn't because he's poor," said Phyllis; "it's because we're fond of him."

"I'll find some things that Phyllis has outgrown," said Mother, "if you're quite sure you can give them to him without his being offended. I should like to do some little thing for him because he's been so kind to you. I can't do much because we're poor ourselves. What are you writing, Bobbie?"

"Nothing particular," said Bobbie, who had suddenly begun to scribble. "I'm sure he'd like the things, Mother."

The morning of the fifteenth was spent very happily in getting the buns and watching Mother make A. P. on them with pink sugar. You know how it's done, of course? You beat up whites of eggs and mix powdered sugar with them, and put in a few drops of cochineal. And then you make a cone of clean white paper with a little hole at the pointed end, and put the pink egg-sugar in at the big end. It runs slowly out at the pointed end, and you write the letters with it just as though it were a great fat pen full of pink sugar-ink.

The buns looked beautiful with A. P. on every one, and, when they were put in a cool oven to set the sugar, the children went up to the village to collect the honey and the shovel and the other promised things.

The old lady at the Post-office was standing on her doorstep. The children said "Good morning," politely, as they passed.

"Here, stop a bit," she said.

So they stopped.

"Those roses," said she.

"Did you like them" said Phyllis; "they were as fresh as

fresh. *I* made the needle-book, but it was Bobbie's present." She skipped joyously as she spoke.

"Here's your basket," said the Post-office woman. She went in and brought out the basket. It was full of fat, red gooseberries.

"I dare say Perks's children would like them," said she.

"You *are* an old dear," said Phyllis, throwing her arms around the old lady's fat waist. "Perks *will* be pleased."

"He won't be half so pleased as I was with your needle-book and the tie and the pretty flowers and all," said the old lady, patting Phyllis's shoulder. "You're good little souls, that you are. Look here. I've got a pram round the back in the wood-lodge. It was got for my Emmie's first, that didn't live but six months, and she never had but that one. I'd like Mrs Perks to have it. It 'ud be a help to her with that great boy of hers. Will you take it along?"

"*Oh*!" said all the children together.

When Mrs Ransome had got out the perambulator and taken off the careful papers that covered it, and dusted it all over, she said:

"Well, there it is. I don't know but what I'd have given it to her before if I'd thought of it. Only I didn't quite know if she'd accept it from me. You tell her it was my Emmie's little one's pram—"

"Oh, *isn't* it nice to think there is going to be a real live baby in it again!"

"Yes," said Mrs Ransome, sighing and then laughing; "here, I'll give you some peppermint cushions for the little ones, and then you must run along before I give you the roof off my head and the clothes off my back."

All the things that had been collected for Perks were packed into the perambulator, and at half past three Peter and Bobbie and Phyllis wheeled it down to the little yellow house where the Perkses lived.

The house was very tidy. On the window ledge was a jug of wild flowers, big daisies, and red sorrel, and feathery, flowery grasses.

There was a sound of splashing from the wash-house, and a partly washed boy put his head round the door.

"Mother's a-changing of herself," he said.

"Down in a minute," a voice sounded down the narrow, freshly scrubbed stairs.

The children waited. Next moment the stairs creaked and Mrs Perks came down, buttoning her bodice. Her hair was brushed very smooth and tight, and her face shone with soap and water.

"I'm a bit late changing, Miss," she said to Bobbie, "owing to me having had a extra clean-up today, along o' Perks happening to name its being his birthday. I don't know what put it into his head to think of such a thing. We keeps the children's birthdays, of course; but him and me—we're too old for such like, as a general rule."

"We knew it was his birthday," said Peter, "and we've got some presents for him outside in the perambulator."

As the presents were being unpacked, Mrs Perks gasped. When they were all unpacked, she surprised and horrified the children by sitting suddenly down on a wooden chair and bursting into tears.

"Oh, don't!" said everybody; "oh, please don't!" And Peter added, perhaps a little impatiently: "What on earth is the matter? You don't mean to say you don't like it?"

Mrs Perks only sobbed. The Perks children, now as shiny-faced as anyone could wish, stood at the wash-house door, and scowled at the intruders. There was a silence, an awkward silence.

"*Don't* you like it?" said Peter, again, while his sisters patted Mrs Perks on the back.

She stopped crying as suddenly as she had begun.

"There, there, don't you mind me. *I'm* all right!" she said. "Like it? Why, it's a birthday such as Perks never 'ad, not even when 'e was a boy and stayed with his uncle, who was a corn-chandler on his own account. He failed afterwards. Like it? Oh—" and then she went on and said all sorts of things that I won't write down, because I am sure that Peter and Bobbie and Phyllis would not like me to. Their ears got hotter and hotter, and their faces redder and redder, at the kind things Mrs Perks said. They felt they had done nothing to deserve all this praise.

At last Peter said: "Look here, we're glad you're pleased. But if you go on saying things like that, we must go home. And we did want to stay and see if Mr Perks is pleased, too. But we can't stand this."

"I won't say another single word," said Mrs Perks, with a beaming face, "but that needn't stop me thinking, need it? For if ever—"

"Can we have a plate for the buns?" Bobbie asked abruptly. And then Mrs Perks hastily laid the table for tea, and the buns and the honey and the gooseberries were displayed on plates, and the roses were put in two glass jam jars, and the tea-table looked, as Mrs Perks said, "fit for a Prince".

"To think!" she said, "me getting the place tidy early, and the little 'uns getting the wild flowers and all—when never did I think there'd be anything more for him except the ounce of his pet particular that I got o' Saturday and been saving up for 'im ever since. Bless us! 'e *is* early!"

Perks had indeed unlatched the latch of the little front gate.

"Oh," whispered Bobbie, "let's hide in the back kitchen, and *you* tell him about it. But give him the tobacco first, because you got it for him. And when you've told him, we'll all come in and shout, 'Many happy returns!' "

It was a very nice plan, but it did not quite come off. To begin with, there was only just time for Peter and Bobbie and Phyllis to rush into the wash-house, pushing the young and open-mouthed Perks children in front of them. There was not time to shut the door, so that, without at all meaning it, they had to listen to what went on in the kitchen. The wash-house was a tight fit for the Perks children and the Three Chimneys children, as well as all the wash-house's proper furniture, including the mangle and the copper.

"Hullo, old woman!" they heard Mr Perks's voice say; "here's a pretty set-out!"

"It's your birthday tea, Bert," said Mrs Perks, "and here's a ounce of your extry particular. I got it o' Saturday along o' your happening to remember it was your birthday today."

"Good old girl!" said Mr Perks, and there was a sound of a kiss.

"But what's that pram doing here? And what's all these bundles? And where did you get the sweetstuff, and—"

The children did not hear what Mrs Perks replied, because just then Bobbie gave a start, put her hand in her pocket, and all her body grew stiff with horror.

"Oh!" she whispered to the others, "whatever shall we do? I forgot to put the labels on any of the things! He won't know what's from who. He'll think it's all *us,* and that we're trying to be grand or charitable or something horrid."

"Hush!" said Peter.

And then they heard the voice of Mr Perks, loud and rather angry.

"I don't care," he said; "I won't stand it, and so I tell you straight."

"But," said Mrs Perks, "it's them children you make such a fuss about—the children from the Three Chimneys."

"I don't care," said Perks, firmly, "not if it was a angel from Heaven. We've got on all right all these years and no favours asked. I'm not going to begin these sort of charity goings-on at my time of life, so don't you think it, Nell."

"Oh, hush!" said poor Mrs Perks; "Bert, shut your silly tongue, for goodness' sake. The all three of 'em's in the wash-house a-listening to every word you speaks."

"Then I'll give them something to listen to," said the angry Perks; "I've spoke my mind to them afore now, and I'll do it again," he added, and he took two strides to the wash-house door, and flung it wide open—as wide, that is, as it would go, with the tightly packed children behind it.

"Come out," said Perks, "come out and tell me what you mean by it. 'Ave I ever complained to you of being short as you comes this charity lay over me?"

"*Oh!*" said Phyllis, "I thought you'd be so pleased; I'll never try to be kind to anyone else as long as I live. No, I won't, not never."

She burst into tears.

"We didn't mean any harm," said Peter.

"It ain't what you means so much as what you does," said Perks.

"Oh, *don't*" cried Bobbie, trying hard to be braver than Phyllis, and to find more words than Peter had done for explaining it. "We thought you'd love it. We always have things on our birthdays."

"Oh, yes," said Perks, "your own relations; that's different."

"Oh, no," Bobbie answered. "*Not* our own relations. All the servants always gave us things at home, and us to them when it was their birthdays. And when it was mine, and Mother gave me the brooch like a buttercup, Mrs Viney gave me two lovely glass pots, and nobody thought she was coming the charity lay over us."

"If it had been glass pots here," said Perks, "I wouldn't ha' said so much. It's there being all this heap and heaps of things I can't stand. No—nor won't neither."

"But they're not all from us—" said Peter, "only we forgot to put the labels on. They're from all sorts of people in the village."

"Who put 'em up to it, I'd like to know?" asked Perks.

"Why, we did," said Phyllis.

Perks sat down heavily in the elbow-chair and looked at them with what Bobbie afterwards described as withering glances of gloomy despair.

"So you've been round telling the neighbours we can't make both ends meet? Well, now you've disgraced us as deep as you can in the neighbourhood, you can just take the whole bag of tricks back where it came from. Very much obliged, I'm sure. I don't doubt but what you meant it kind, but I'd rather not be acquainted with you any longer if it's all the same to you." He deliberately turned the chair round so that his back was turned to the children. The legs of the chair grated on the brick floor, and that was the only sound that broke the silence.

Then suddenly Bobbie spoke.

"Look here," she said, "this is most awful."

"That's what I says," said Perks, not turning round.

"Look here," said Bobbie, desperately, "we'll go if you

like—and you needn't be friends with us any more if you don't want, but—"

"*We* shall always be friends with *you*, however nasty you are to us," sniffed Phyllis, wildly.

"Be quiet," said Peter, in a fierce aside.

"But before we go," Bobbie went on desperately, "do let us show you the labels we wrote to put on the things."

"I don't want to see no labels," said Perks, "except proper luggage ones in my own walk of life. Do you think I've kept respectable and outer debt on what I gets, and her having to take in washing, to be give away for a laughing-stock to all the neighbours?"

"Laughing?" said Peter; "you don't know."

"You're a very hasty gentleman," whined Phyllis; "you know you were wrong once before, about us not telling you the secrets about the Russian. Do let Bobbie tell you about the labels!"

"Well. Go ahead!" said Perks, grudgingly.

"Well, then," said, Bobbie, fumbling miserably, yet not without hope, in her tightly-stuffed pocket, "we wrote down all the things everybody said when they gave us the things, with the people's names, because Mother said we ought to be careful—because—but I wrote down what she said—and you'll see."

But Bobbie could not read the labels just at once. She had to swallow once or twice before she could begin.

Mrs Perks had been crying steadily ever since her husband had opened the wash-house door. Now she caught her breath, choked, and said:

"Don't you upset yourself, Missy. *I* know you meant it kind if he doesn't."

"May I read the labels?" said Bobbie, crying on to the slips as she tried to sort them. "Mother's first. It says:

"'Little Clothes for Mrs Perks's children'. Mother said, 'I'll find some of Phyllis's things that she's grown out of if you're quite sure Mr Perks wouldn't be offended and think it's meant for charity. I'd like to do some little thing for him, because he's so kind to you. I can't do much because we're poor ourselves.' "

Bobbie paused.

"That's all right," said Perks, "your Ma's a born lady. We'll keep the little frocks, and what-not, Nell."

"Then there's the perambulator and the gooseberries, and the sweets," said Bobbie, "they're from Mrs Ransome. She said: 'I dare say Mr Perks's children would like the sweets. And the perambulator was got for my Emmie's first—it didn't live but six months, and she's never had but that one. I'd like Mrs Perks to have it. It would be a help with her fine boy. I'd have given it before if I'd been sure she'd accept of it from me.' She told me to tell you," Bobbie added, "that it was her Emmie's little one's pram."

"I can't send the pram back, Bert," said Mrs Perks, firmly, "and I won't. So don't you ask me—"

"I'm not a-asking anything," said Perks, gruffly.

"Then the shovel," said Bobbie. "Mr James made it for you himself. And he said—where is it? Oh, yes here! He said, 'You tell Mr Perks it's a pleasure to make a little trifle for a man as is so much respected,' and then he said he wished he could shoe your children and his own children, like they do the horses, because, well, he knew what shoe leather was."

"James is a good enough chap," said Perks.

"Then the honey," said Bobbie, in haste, "and the bootlaces. *He* said he respected a man that paid his way—and the butcher said the same. And the old turnpike woman said many was the time you'd lent her a hand with her garden when you were a lad—and things like that came home to roost—I don't know what she meant. And everybody who gave anything said they liked you, and it was a very good idea of ours; and nobody said anything about charity or anything horrid like that. And the old gentleman gave Peter a gold pound for you, and said you were a man who knew your work. And I thought you'd *love* to know how fond people are of you, and I never was so unhappy in my life. Good-bye. I hope you'll forgive us some day—"

She could say no more, and she turned to go.

"Stop," said Perks, still with his back to them; "I take

back every word I've said contrary to what you'd wish. Nell, set on the kettle."

"We'll take the things away if you're unhappy about them," said Peter; "but I think everybody'll be most awfully disappointed as well as us."

"I'm not unhappy about them," said Perks; "I don't know," he added, suddenly wheeling the chair round and showing a very odd-looking screwed-up face, "I don't know as ever I was better pleased. Not so much with the presents—though they're an A1 collection—but the kind respect of our neighbours. That's worth having, eh, Nell?"

"I think it's all worth having," said Mrs Perks, "and you've made a most ridiculous fuss about nothing, Bert, if you ask me."

"No, I ain't," said Perks, firmly; "if a man didn't respect hisself, no one wouldn't do it for him."

"But everyone respects you," said Bobbie; "they all said so."

"I knew you'd like it when you really understood," said Phyllis, brightly.

"Humph! You'll stay to tea?" said Mr Perks.

Later on Peter proposed Mr Perks's health. And Mr Perks proposed a toast, also honoured in tea, and the toast was, "May the garland of friendship be ever green," which was much more poetical than anyone had expected from him.

*

"Jolly good little kids, those," said Mr Perks to his wife as they went to bed.

"Oh, they're all right, bless their hearts," said his wife; "it's you that's the aggravatingest old thing that ever was. I was ashamed of you—I tell you—"

"You didn't need to be, old gal. I climbed down handsome soon as I understood it wasn't charity. But charity's what I never did abide, and won't neither."

*

All sorts of people were made happy by that birthday party. Mr Perks and Mrs Perks and the little Perkses by all the nice things and by the kind thoughts of their neighbours; the Three Chimneys children by the success, undoubted though unexpectedly delayed, of their plan; and Mrs Ransome every time she saw the fat Perks baby in the perambulator. Mrs Perks made quite a round of visits to thank people for their kind birthday presents, and after each visit felt that she had a better friend than she had thought.

"Yes," said Perks reflectively, "it's not so much what you does as what you means; that's what I say. Now if it had been charity."

"Oh, drat charity," said Mrs Perks; "nobody won't offer you charity, Bert, however much you was to want it, I lay. That was just friendliness, that was."

When the clergyman called on Mrs Perks, she told him all about it. "It *was* friendliness, wasn't it, Sir?" said she.

"I think," said the clergyman, "it was what is sometimes called loving-kindness."

So you see it was all right in the end. But if one does that sort of thing, one has to be careful to do it in the right way. For, as Mr Perks said, when he had time to think it over, it's not so much what you do, as what you mean.

CHAPTER 10

THE TERRIBLE SECRET

When they first went to live at Three Chimneys, the children had talked a great deal about their Father, and had asked a great many questions about him, and what he was doing and where he was and when he would come home. Mother always answered their questions as well as she could. But as the time went on they grew to speak less of him. Bobbie had felt almost from the first that for some strange miserable reason these questions hurt Mother and made her sad. And little by little the others came to have this feeling, too, though they could not have put it into words.

One day, when Mother was working so hard that she could not leave off even for ten minutes, Bobbie carried up her tea to the big bare room that they called Mother's workshop. It had hardly any furniture. Just a table and chair and a rug. But always big pots of flowers on the windowsills and on the mantelpiece. The children saw to that. And from the three long uncurtained windows the beautiful stretch of meadow and moorland, the far violet of the hills, and the unchanging changefulness of cloud and sky.

"Here's your tea, Mother-love," said Bobbie; "do drink it while it's hot."

Mother laid down her pen among the pages that were scattered all over the table, pages covered with her writing, which was almost as plain as print, and much prettier. She ran her hands into her hair, as if she were going to pull it out by handfuls.

"Poor dear head," said Bobbie, "does it ache?"

"No—yes—not much," said Mother. "Bobbie, do you think Peter and Phil are *forgetting* Father?"

"*No,*" said Bobbie, indignantly. "Why?"

"You none of you ever speak of him now."

Bobbie stood first on one leg and then on the other.

"We often talk about him when we're by ourselves," she said.

"But not to me," said Mother. "Why?"

Bobbie did not find it easy to say why.

"I—you—" she said and stopped. She went over to the window and looked out.

"Bobbie, come here," said her Mother, and Bobbie came.

"Now," said Mother, putting her arm round Bobbie and laying her ruffled head against Bobbie's shoulder, "try to tell me, dear."

Bobbie fidgeted.

"Tell Mother."

"Well, then," said Bobbie, "I thought you were so unhappy about Daddy not being here, it made you worse when I talked about him. So I stopped doing it."

"And the others?"

"I don't know about the others," said Bobbie. "I never said anything about *that* to them. But I expect they felt the same about it as me."

"Bobbie dear," said Mother, still leaning her head against her, "I'll tell you. Besides parting from Father, he and I have had a great sorrow—oh, terrible—worse than anything you can think of, and at first it did hurt to hear you all talking of him as if everything were just the same. But it would be much more terrible if you were to forget him. That would be worse than anything."

"The trouble," said Bobbie, in a very little voice—"I promised I would never ask you any questions, and I never have, have I? But—the trouble—it won't last always?"

"No," said Mother, "the worst will be over when Father comes home to us."

"I wish I could comfort you," said Bobbie.

"Oh, my dear, do you suppose you don't? What should I do without you—you and the others? Do you think I haven't noticed how good you've all been, not quarrelling nearly as much as you used to—and all the little kind things you do for me—the flowers, and cleaning my shoes, and tearing up to make my bed before I get time to do it myself?"

Bobbie *had* sometimes wondered whether Mother noticed these things.

"That's nothing," she said, "to what—"

"I *must* get on with my work," said Mother, giving Bobbie one last squeeze. "Don't say anything to the others."

That evening in the hour before bedtime instead of reading to the children Mother told them stories of the games she and Father used to have when they were children and lived near each other in the country—tales of the adventures of Father with Mother's brothers when they were all boys together. Very funny stories they were, and the children laughed as they listened.

"Uncle Edward died before he was grown up, didn't he?" said Phyllis, as Mother lighted the bedroom candles.

"Yes, dear," said Mother, "you would have loved him. He was such a brave boy, and so adventurous. Always in mischief, and yet friends with everybody in spite of it. And your Uncle Reggie's in Ceylon—yes, and Father's away, too. But I think they'd all like to think we'd enjoyed talking about the things they used to do. Don't you think so?"

"Not Uncle Edward," said Phyllis, in a shocked tone; "he's in Heaven."

"You don't suppose he's forgotten us and all the old times, because God has taken him, any more than I forget him. Oh, no, he remembers. He's only away for a little time. We shall see him some day."

"And Uncle Reggie—and Father, too?" said Peter.

"Yes," said Mother. "Uncle Reggie and Father, too. Good night, my darlings."

"Good night," said everyone. Bobbie hugged her mother more closely even than usual, and whispered in her ear. "Oh, I do love you so, Mummy—I do—I do—"

When Bobbie came to think it all over, she tried not to wonder what the great trouble was. But she could not always help it. Father was not dead—like poor Uncle Edward—Mother had said so. And he was not ill, or Mother would have been with him. Being poor wasn't the trouble. Bobbie knew it was something nearer the heart than money could be.

"I mustn't try to think what it is," she told herself; "no, I mustn't. I *am* glad Mother noticed about us not quarrelling so much. We'll keep that up."

And alas, that very afternoon she and Peter had what Peter called a first-class shindy.

They had not been a week at Three Chimneys before they had asked Mother to let them have a piece of garden each for their very own, and she had agreed, and the south border under the peach trees had been divided into three pieces and they were allowed to plant whatever they liked there.

Phyllis had planted mignonette and nasturtium and Virginia stock in hers. The seeds came up, and though they looked just like weeds, Phyllis believed that they would bear flowers some day. The Virginia stock justified her faith quite soon, and her garden was gay with a band of bright little flowers, pink and white and red and mauve.

"I can't weed for fear I pull up the wrong things," she used to say comfortably; "it saves such a lot of work."

Peter sowed vegetable seeds in his—carrots and onions and turnips. The seed was given to him by the farmer who lived in the nice black-and-white, wood-and-plaster house just beyond the bridge. He kept turkeys and guinea fowls, and was a most amiable man. But Peter's vegetables never had much of a chance, because he liked to use the earth of his garden for digging canals, and making forts and earthworks for his toy soldiers, and the seeds of vegetables rarely come to much in a soil that is constantly disturbed for the purposes of war and irrigation.

Bobbie planted rose-bushes in her garden, but all the little new leaves of the rose-bushes shrivelled and withered, perhaps because she moved them from the other part of the garden in May, which is not at all the right time of the year for moving roses. But she would not own that they were dead, and hoped on against hope, until the day when Perks came up to see the garden, and told her quite plainly that all her roses were as dead as door nails.

"Only good for bonfires, Miss," he said. "You just dig 'em up and burn 'em, and I'll give you some nice fresh roots outer my garden: pansies and stocks, and sweet willies, and forget-me-nots. I'll bring 'em along tomorrow if you get the ground ready."

So next day she set to work, and that happened to be the day when Mother had praised her and the others about not quarrelling. She moved the rose-bushes and carried them to the other end of the garden, where the rubbish heap was that they meant to make a bonfire of when Guy Fawkes' Day came.

Meanwhile Peter had decided to flatten out all his forts and earthworks, with a view to making a model of the railway-tunnel, cutting, embankment, canal, aqueduct, bridges and all.

So when Bobbie came back from her last thorny journey with the dead rose-bushes, he had got the rake and was using it busily.

"*I* was using the rake," said Bobbie.

"Well, I'm using it now," said Peter.

"But I had it first," said Bobbie.

"Then it's my turn now," said Peter. And that was how the quarrel began.

"You're always being disagreeable about nothing," said Peter, after some heated argument.

"I had the rake first," said Bobbie, flushed and defiant, holding on to its handle.

"Didn't I tell you this morning I meant to have it? Didn't I, Phil?"

Phyllis said she didn't want to be mixed up in their rows. And instantly, of course, she was.

"If you remember, you ought to say."

"Of course, she doesn't remember—but she might say so."

"I wish I'd had a brother instead of two whiny little kiddy sisters," said Peter. This was always recognized as indicating the high-water mark of Peter's rage.

Bobbie made the reply she always made to it.

"I can't think why little boys were ever invented," and just as she said it she looked up, and saw the three long windows of Mother's workshop flashing in the red rays of the sun. The sight brought back those words of praise:

"You don't quarrel like you used to do."

"*Oh*" cried Bobbie, just as if she had been hit, or had caught her finger in a door, or had felt the hideous sharp beginning of toothache.

"What's the matter?" said Phyllis.

Bobbie wanted to say: "Don't let's quarrel. Mother hates it so," but though she tried hard, she couldn't. Peter was looking too disagreeable and insulting.

"Take the horrid rake, then," was the best she could manage. And she suddenly let go her hold on the handle. Peter had been holding on to it too, firmly and pullingly, and now that the pull the other way was suddenly stopped, he staggered and fell over backwards, the teeth of the rake between his feet.

"Serve you right," said Bobbie, before she could stop herself.

Peter lay still for half a moment—long enough to frighten Bobbie a little. Then he frightened her a little more, for he sat up—screamed once—turned rather pale, and then lay back and began to shriek, faintly but steadily. It sounded exactly like a pig being killed a quarter of a mile off.

Mother put her head out of the window, and it wasn't half a minute after that she was in the garden kneeling by the side of Peter, who never for an instant ceased to squeal.

"What happened, Bobbie?" Mother asked.

"It was the rake," said Phyllis. "Peter was pulling at it, so was Bobbie, and she let go and he went over."

"Stop that noise, Peter," said Mother. "Come. Stop at once."

Peter used up what breath he had left in a last squeal and stopped.

"Now," said Mother, "are you hurt?"

"If he was really hurt, he wouldn't make such a fuss," said Bobbie, still trembling with fury; "he's not a coward!"

"I think my foot's broken off, that's all," said Peter huffily, and sat up. Then he turned quite white. Mother put her arm round him.

"He *is* hurt," she said; "he's fainted. Here, Bobbie, sit down and take his head on your lap."

Then Mother undid Peter's boots. As she took the right one off, something dripped from his foot on to the ground. It was red blood. And when the stocking came off there were three red wounds in Peter's foot and ankle, where the teeth of the rake had bitten him, and his foot was covered with red smears.

"Run for water—a basinful," said Mother, and Phyllis ran. She upset most of the water out of the basin in her haste, and had to fetch more in a jug.

Peter did not open his eyes again till Mother had tied her handkerchief round his foot, and she and Bobbie had carried him in and laid him on the brown wooden settle in the dining-room. By this time Phyllis was halfway to the Doctor's.

Mother sat by Peter and bathed his foot and talked to him, and Bobbie went out and got tea ready, and put on the kettle.

"It's all I can do," she told herself. "Oh, suppose Peter should die, or be a helpless cripple for life, or have to walk with crutches, or wear a boot with a sole like a log of wood!"

She stood by the back door reflecting on these gloomy possibilities, her eyes focused on the water-butt.

"I wish I'd never been born," she said, and she said it out loud.

"Why, lawk a mercy, what's that for?" asked a voice, and Perks stood before her with a wooden trug basket full of green-leaved things and soft, loose earth.

"Oh, it's you," she said. "Peter's hurt his foot with a rake—three great gaping wounds, like soldiers get. And it was partly my fault."

"That it wasn't I'll go bail," said Perks. "Doctor seen him?"

"Phyllis has gone for the Doctor."

"He'll be all right; you see if he isn't," said Perks. "Why, my father's second cousin had a hay-fork run into him, right into his inside, and he was right as ever in a few weeks, all except his being a bit weak in the head afterwards, and they did say that it was along of his getting a touch of the sun in the hay-field, and not the fork at all. I remember him well. A kind-'earted chap, but soft, as you might say."

Bobbie tried to let herself be cheered by this heartening reminiscence.

"Well," said Perks, "you won't want to be bothered with gardening just this minute, I daresay. You show me where your garden is, and I'll pop the bits of stuff in for you. And I'll hang about, if I may make so free, to see the Doctor as he comes out and hear what he says. You cheer up, Missie. I lay a pound he ain't hurt, not to speak of."

But he was. The Doctor came and looked at the foot and

bandaged it beautifully, and said that Peter must not put it to the ground for at least a week.

"He won't be lame, or have to wear crutches or a lump on his foot, will he?" whispered Bobbie, breathlessly, at the door.

"My aunt! No!" said Dr. Forrest; "he'll be as nimble as ever on his pins in a fortnight. Don't you worry, little Mother Goose."

It was when Mother had gone to the gate with the Doctor to take his last instructions and Phyllis was filling the kettle for tea, that Peter and Bobbie found themselves alone.

"He says you won't be lame or anything," said Bobbie.

"Oh, course I shan't, silly," said Peter, very much relieved all the same.

"Oh, Peter, I *am* so sorry," said Bobbie, after a pause.

"That's all right," said Peter, gruffly.

"It was *all* my fault," said Bobbie.

"Rot," said Peter.

"If we hadn't quarrelled, it wouldn't have happened. I knew it was wrong to quarrel. I wanted to say so, but somehow I couldn't."

"Don't drivel," said Peter. "I shouldn't have stopped if you *had* said it. Not likely. And besides, us rowing hadn't anything to do with it. I might have caught my foot in the hoe, or taken off my fingers in the chaff-cutting machine or blown my nose off with fireworks. It would have been hurt just the same whether we'd been rowing or not."

"But I knew it was wrong to quarrel," said Bobbie, in tears, "and now you're hurt and—"

"Now look here," said Peter, firmly, "you just dry up. If you're not careful you'll turn into a beastly little Sunday-school prig, so I tell you."

"I don't mean to be a prig. But it's so hard not to be when you're really trying to be good."

(The Gentle Reader may perhaps have suffered from this difficulty.)

"Not it," said Peter; "it's a jolly good thing it wasn't you was hurt. I'm glad it was *me*. There! If it had been you, you'd have been lying on the sofa looking like a suffering angel and being the light of the anxious household and all that. And I couldn't have stood it."

"No, I shouldn't," said Bobbie.

"Yes, you would," said Peter.

"I tell you I shouldn't."

"I tell you you would."

"Oh, children," said Mother's voice at the door. "Quarrelling again? Already?"

"We aren't quarrelling—not really," said Peter. "I wish you wouldn't think it's rows every time we don't agree!" When Mother had gone out again, Bobbie broke out:

"Peter, I *am* sorry you're hurt. But you *are* a beast to say I'm a prig."

"Well," said Peter unexpectedly, "perhaps I am. You did say I wasn't a coward, even when you were in such a wax. The only thing is—don't you be a prig, that's all. You keep your eyes open and if you feel priggishness coming on just stop in time. See?"

"Yes," said Bobbie, "I see."

"Then let's call it Pax," said Peter magnanimously: "bury the hatchet in the fathoms of the past. Shake hands on it. I say, Bobbie, old chap, I am tired."

He was tired for many days after that, and the settle seemed hard and uncomfortable in spite of all the pillows and bolsters and soft folded rugs. It was terrible not to be able to go out. They moved the settle to the window, and from there Peter could see the smoke of the trains winding along the valley. But he could not see the trains.

At first Bobbie found it quite hard to be as nice to him as she wanted to be, for fear he should think her priggish. But that soon wore off, and both she and Phyllis were, as he observed, jolly good sorts. Mother sat with him when the sisters were out. And the words, "he's not a coward," made Peter determined not to make any fuss about the pain in his foot, though it was rather bad, especially at night.

Praise helps people very much sometimes.

There were visitors, too. Mrs Perks came up to ask how he was, and so did the Station Master, and several of the village people. But the time went slowly, slowly.

"I do wish there was something to read," said Peter, "I've read all our books about fifty times over."

"I'll go to the Doctor's," said Phyllis; "he's sure to have some."

"Only about how to be ill, and about people's nasty insides, I expect," said Peter.

"Perks has a whole heap of Magazines that came out of trains when people are tired of them," said Bobbie. "I'll run down and ask him."

So the girls went their two ways.

Bobbie found Perks busy cleaning lamps.

"And how's the young gent?" said he.

"Better, thanks," said Bobbie, "but he's most frightfully bored. I came to ask if you'd got any Magazines you could lend him."

"There, now," said Perks, regretfully, rubbing his ear with a black and oily lump of cotton waste, "why didn't I think of that, now? I was trying to think of something as 'ud amuse him only this morning, and I couldn't think of anything better than a guinea-pig. And a young chap I know's going to fetch that over for him this teatime."

"How lovely! A real live guinea-pig! He will be pleased. But he'd like the Magazines as well."

"That's just it," said Perks. "I've just sent the pick of 'em to Snigson's boy—him what's just getting over the pneumonia. But I've lots of illustrated papers left."

He turned to the pile of papers in the corner and took up a heap six inches thick.

"There!" he said. "I'll just slip a bit of string and a bit of paper round 'em."

He pulled an old newspaper from the pile and spread it on the table, and made a neat parcel of it.

"There," said he, "there's lots of pictures, and if he likes to mess 'em about with his paint-box or coloured chalks or what not, why let him. *I* don't want 'em."

"You're a dear," said Bobbie, took the parcel, and started. The papers were heavy, and when she had to wait at the level-crossing while a train went by, she rested the parcel on the top of the gate. And idly she looked at the printing on the paper that the parcel was wrapped in.

Suddenly she clutched the parcel tighter and bent her head over it. It seemed like some horrible dream. She read on—the bottom of the column was torn off—she could read no farther.

She never remembered how she got home. But she went on tip-toe to her room and locked the door. Then she undid the parcel and read that printed column again, sitting on the edge of her bed, her hands and feet icy cold and her face burning. When she had read all there was, she drew a long, uneven breath.

"So now I know," she said.

What she had read was headed, "End of the Trial. Verdict. Sentence".

The name of the man who had been tried was the name of her Father. The verdict was "Guilty". And the sentence was "Five years' Penal Servitude".

"Oh, Daddy," she whispered, crushing the paper hard, "it's not true—I don't believe it. You never did it! Never, never, never!"

There was a hammering at the door.

"What is it?" said Bobbie.

"It's me," said the voice of Phyllis; "tea's ready, and a boy's brought Peter a guinea-pig. Come along down."

And Bobbie had to.

Chapter 11

THE HOUND IN THE RED JERSEY

Bobbie knew the secret now. A sheet of old newspaper wrapped round a parcel—just a little chance like that—had given the secret to her. And she had to go down to tea and pretend that there was nothing the matter. The pretence was bravely made, but it wasn't very successful.

For when she came in, everybody looked up from tea and saw her pink-lidded eyes and her pale face with red tear-blotches on it.

"My darling," cried Mother, jumping up from the tea-tray, "whatever *is* the matter?"

"My head aches, rather," said Bobbie. And indeed it did.

"Has anything gone wrong?" Mother asked.

"I'm all right, really," said Bobbie, and she telegraphed her Mother from her swollen eyes this brief, imploring message—"*Not* before the others!"

Tea was not a cheerful meal. Peter was so distressed by the obvious fact that something horrid had happened to Bobbie that he limited his speech to repeating, "More bread and butter, please," at startlingly short intervals. Phyllis stroked her sister's hand under the table to express sympathy, and knocked her cup over as she did it. Fetching a cloth and wiping up the spilt milk helped Bobbie a little. But she thought that tea would never end. Yet at last it did end, as all things do at last, and when Mother took out the tray, Bobbie followed her.

"She's gone to own up," said Phyllis to Peter; "I wonder what she's done."

"Broken something, I suppose," said Peter, "but she needn't be so silly over it. Mother never rows for accidents. Listen! Yes, they're going upstairs. She's taking Mother up to show her—the waterjug with storks on it, I expect it is."

Bobbie, in the kitchen, had caught hold of Mother's hand as she set down the tea-things.

"What is it?" Mother asked.

But Bobbie only said, "Come upstairs, come up where nobody can hear us."

When she had got Mother alone in her room she locked the door and then stood quite still, and quite without words.

All through tea she had been thinking of what to say; she had decided that "I know all", or "All is known to me", or

"The terrible secret is a secret no longer", would be the proper thing. But now that she and her Mother and that awful sheet of newspaper were alone in the room together, she found that she could say nothing.

Suddenly she went to Mother and put her arms round her and began to cry again. And still she could find no words, only "Oh, Mammy, oh, Mammy, oh, Mammy!" over and over again.

Mother held her close and waited.

Suddenly Bobbie broke away from her and went to her bed. From under her mattress she pulled out the paper she had hidden there, and held it out, pointing to her Father's name with a finger that shook.

"Oh, Bobbie," Mother cried, when one little quick look had shown her what it was, "you don't *believe* it? You don't believe Daddy did it?"

"*No,*" Bobbie almost shouted. She had stopped crying.

"That's all right," said Mother. "It's not true. And they've shut him up in prison, but he's done nothing wrong. He's good and noble and honourable, and he belongs to us. We have to think of that, and be proud of him and wait."

Again Bobbie clung to her Mother, and again only one word came to her, but now that word was "Daddy," and "Oh, Daddy, oh, Daddy, oh, Daddy!" again and again.

"Why didn't you tell me, Mammy?" she asked presently.

"Are you going to tell the others?" Mother asked.

"No."

"Why?"

"Because—"

"Exactly," said Mother; "so you understand why I didn't tell you. We two must help each other to be brave."

"Yes," said Bobbie. "Mother, will it make you more unhappy if you tell me all about it? I want to understand."

So then, sitting cuddled up close to her Mother, Bobbie heard "all about it". She heard how those men, who had asked to see Father on that remembered last night when the Engine was being mended, had come to arrest him, charging him with selling State secrets to the Russians—with being, in fact, a spy and a traitor. She heard about the trial, and about the evidence—letters, found in Father's desk at the office, letters that convinced the jury that Father was guilty.

"Oh, how could they look at him and believe it!" cried Bobbie; "and how could *anyone* do such a thing!"

"*Someone* did it," said Mother, "and all the evidence was against Father. Those letters—"

"Yes. How did the letters get into his desk?"

"Someone put them there. And the person who put them there was the person who was really guilty."

"*He* must be feeling pretty awful all this time," said Bobbie, thoughtfully.

"I don't believe he had any feelings," Mother said hotly; "he couldn't have done a thing like that if he had."

"Perhaps he just shoved the letters into the desk to hide them when he thought he was going to be found out. Why don't you tell the lawyers, or someone, that it must have been that person? There wasn't anyone that would have hurt Father on purpose, was there?"

"I don't know—I don't know. The man under him who got Daddy's place when he—when the awful thing happened—he was always jealous of your Father because Daddy was so clever and everyone thought such a lot of him. And Daddy never quite trusted that man."

"Couldn't we explain all that to someone?"

"Nobody will listen," said Mother, very bitterly, "nobody at all. Do you suppose I've not tried everything? No, my dearest, there's nothing to be done. All we can do, you and I and Daddy, is to be brave, and patient, and"—she spoke very softly—"to pray, Bobbie, dear."

"Mother, you've got very thin," said Bobbie, abruptly.

"A little perhaps."

"And oh," said Bobbie, "I do think you're the bravest person in the world as well as the nicest!"

"We won't talk of all this any more, will we, dear?" said Mother; "we must bear it and be brave. And darling, try not to think of it. It's much easier for me if you can be a little bit happy and enjoy things. Wash your poor little round face, and let's go out into the garden for a bit."

The other two were very gentle and kind to Bobbie. And they did not ask her what was the matter. This was Peter's idea, and he had drilled Phyllis, who would have asked a hundred questions if she had been left to herself.

A week later Bobbie managed to get away alone. And once more she wrote a letter. And once more it was to the old gentleman.

MY DEAR FRIEND, [she said] you see what is in this paper. It is not true. Father never did it. Mother says someone put the papers in Father's desk, and she says the man under him that got Father's place afterwards was jealous of Father, and Father suspected him a long time. But nobody listens to a word she says, but you are so good and clever, and you found out about the Russian gentleman's wife directly. Can't you find out who did the treason because he wasn't Father upon my honour; he is an Englishman and uncapable to do such things, and then they would let Father out of prison. It is dreadful, and Mother is getting so thin. She told us once to pray for all prisoners and captives. I see now. Oh, do help me—there is only just Mother and me know, and we can't do anything. Peter and Phil don't know. I'll pray for you twice every day as long as I live if you'll only try—just try to find out. Think if it was *your* Daddy, what you would feel. Oh, do, *do*, help me. With love

I remain Your affectionately little friend
ROBERTA

P.S. Mother would send her kind regards if she knew I am writing—but it is no use telling her I am, in case you can't do anything. But I know you will. Bobbie, with best love.

She cut the account of her Father's trial out of the newspaper with Mother's big cutting-out scissors, and put it in the envelope with her letter.

Then she took it down to the station, going out the back way and round by the road, so that the others should not see her and offer to come with her, and she gave the letter to the Station Master to give to the old gentleman next morning.

"Where *have* you been?" shouted Peter, from the top of the yard wall where he and Phyllis were.

"To the station, of course," said Bobbie; "give us a hand, Pete."

She set her foot on the lock of the yard door. Peter reached down a hand.

"What on earth?" she asked as she reached the wall top—for Phyllis and Peter were very muddy. A lump of wet clay lay between them on the wall, they had each a slip of slate in a very dirty hand, and behind Peter, out of the reach of accidents, were several strange rounded objects rather like very fat sausages, hollow, but closed up at one end.

"It's nests," said Peter, "swallows' nests. We're going to dry them in the oven and hang them up with string under the eaves of the coach-house."

"Yes," said Phyllis; "and then we're going to save up all the wool and hair we can get, and in the spring we'll line them, and then how pleased the swallows will be!"

"I've often thought people don't do nearly enough for dumb animals," said Peter with an air of virtue. "I do think people might have thought of making nests for poor little swallows before this."

"Oh," said Bobbie, vaguely, "if everybody thought of everything, there'd be nothing left for anybody else to think about."

"Look at the nests—aren't they pretty?" said Phyllis, reaching across Peter to grasp a nest.

"Look out, Phil, you goat," said her brother. But it was too late; her strong little fingers had crushed the nest.

"There now," said Peter.

"Never mind," said Bobbie.

"It *is* one of my own," said Phyllis, "so you needn't jaw, Pete. Yes, we've put our initial names on the ones we've done, so that the swallows will know who they've got to be so grateful to and fond of."

"Swallows can't read, silly," said Peter.

"Silly yourself," retorted Phyllis; "how do you know?"

"Who thought of making the nests, anyhow?" shouted Peter.

"I did," screamed Phyllis.

"Nya," rejoined Peter, "you only thought of making hay ones and sticking them in the ivy for the sparrows, and they'd have been sopping *long* before egg-laying time. It was me said clay and swallows."

"I don't care what you said."

"Look," said Bobbie, "I've made the nest all right again. Give me the bit of stick to mark your initial name on it. But how can you? Your letter and Peter's are the same. P. for Peter, P. for Phyllis."

"I put F. for Phyllis," said the child of that name. "That's how it sounds. The swallows wouldn't spell Phyllis with a P., I'm certain sure."

"They can't spell at all," Peter was still insisting.

"Then why do you see them always on Christmas cards and Valentines with letters round their necks? How would they know where to go if they couldn't read?"

"That's only in pictures. You never saw one really with letters round its neck."

"Well, I have a pigeon, then; at least Daddy told me they did. Only it was under their wings and not round their necks, but it comes to the same thing, and—"

"I say," interrupted Bobbie, "there's to be a paper-chase tomorrow."

"Who?" Peter asked.

"Grammar School. Perks thinks the hare will go along by the line at first. We might go along the cutting. You can see a long way from there."

The paper-chase was found to be a more amusing subject of conversation than the reading powers of swallows. Bobbie had hoped it might be. And next morning Mother let them take their lunch and go out for the day to see the paper-chase.

"If we go to the cutting," said Peter, "we shall see the workmen, even if we miss the paper-chase."

Of course it had taken some time to get the line clear

from the rocks and earth and trees that had fallen on it when the great land-slip happened. That was the occasion, you will remember, when the three children saved the train from being wrecked by waving six little red-flannel-petticoat flags. It is always interesting to watch people working, especially when they work with such interesting things as spades and picks and shovels and planks and barrows, when they have cindery red fires in iron pots with round holes in them, and red lamps hanging near the works at night. Of course the children were never out at nights; but once, at dusk, when Peter had got out of his bedroom skylight on to the roof, he had seen the red lamp shining far away at the edge of the cutting. The children had often been down to watch the work, and this day the interest of picks and spades, and barrows wheeled along planks, completely put the paper-chase out of their heads, so that they quite jumped when a voice just behind them panted, "Let me pass, please." It was the hare—a big-boned, loose-limbed boy, with dark hair lying flat on a very damp forehead. The bag of torn paper under his arm was fastened across one shoulder by a strap. The children stood back. The hare ran along the line, and the workmen leaned on their picks to watch him. He ran on steadily and disappeared into the mouth of the tunnel.

"That's against the by-laws," said the foreman.

"Why worry?" said the oldest workman; "live and let live's what I always say. Ain't you never been young yourself, Mr Bates?"

"I ought to report him," said the foreman.

"Why spoil sport's what I always say."

"Passengers are forbidden to cross the line on any pretence," murmured the foreman, doubtfully.

"He ain't no passenger," said one of the workmen.

"Nor 'e ain't crossed the line, not where we could see 'im do it," said another.

"Nor yet 'e ain't made no pretences," said a third.

"And," said the oldest workman, "'e's outer sight now. What the eye don't see the 'art needn't take no notice of's what I always say."

And now, following the track of the hare by the little white blots of scattered paper, came the hounds. There were thirty of them, and they all came down the steep, ladder-like steps by ones and twos and threes and sixes and sevens. Bobbie and Phyllis and Peter counted them as they passed. The foremost ones hesitated a moment at the foot of the ladder, then their eyes caught the gleam of scattered whiteness along the line and they turned towards the tunnel, and, by ones and twos and threes and sixes and sevens, disappeared in the dark mouth of it. The last one, in a red jersey, seemed to be extinguished by the darkness like a candle that is blown out.

"They don't know what they're in for," said the foreman; "it isn't so easy running in the dark. The tunnel takes two or three turns."

"They'll take a long time to get through, you think?" Peter asked.

"An hour or more, I shouldn't wonder."

"Then let's cut across the top and see them come out at the other end," said Peter; "we shall get there long before they do." The counsel seemed good, and they went.

They climbed the steep steps from which they had picked the wild cherry blossom for the grave of the little wild rabbit, and reaching the top of the cutting, set their faces towards the hill through which the tunnel was cut. It was stiff work.

"It's like Alps," said Bobbie, breathlessly.

"Or Andes," said Peter.

"It's like Himmy what's its names?" gasped Phyllis. "Mount Everlasting. Do let's stop."

"Stick to it," panted Peter; "you'll get your second wind in a minute."

Phyllis consented to stick to it—and on they went, running when the turf was smooth and the slope easy, climbing over stones, helping themselves up rocks by the branches of trees, creeping through narrow openings between tree trunks and rocks, and so on and on, up and up, till at last they stood on the very top of the hill where they had so often wished to be.

"Halt!" cried Peter, and threw himself flat, on the grass. For the very top of the hill was a smooth, turfed table-land, dotted with mossy rocks and little mountain-ash trees.

The girls also threw themselves down flat.

"Plenty of time," Peter panted; "the rest's all downhill."

When they were rested enough to sit up and look round them, Bobbie cried:

"Oh, look!"

"What at?" said Phyllis.

"The view," said Bobbie.

"I hate views," said Phyllis, "don't you, Peter?"

"Let's get on," said Peter.

"But this isn't like a view they take you to in carriages when you're at the seaside, all sea and sand and bare hills. It's like the 'coloured counties' in one of Mother's poetry books."

"It's not so dusty," said Peter: "look at the aqueduct straddling slap across the valley like a giant centipede, and then the town's church spires sticking up out of the trees like pens out of an ink-stand. *I* think it's more like

> *"There could we see the banners*
> *Of twelve fair cities shine."*

"I love it," said Bobbie; "it's worth the climb."

"The paper-chase is worth the climb," said Phyllis, "if we don't lose it. Let's get on. It's all downhill now."

"*I* said that ten minutes ago," said Peter.

"Well, *I've* said it now," said Phyllis; "come on."

"Loads of time," said Peter. And there was. For when they had got down to a level with the top of the tunnel's mouth—they were a couple of hundred yards out of their reckoning and had to creep along the face of the hill—there was no sign of the hare or the hounds.

"They've gone long ago, of course," said Phyllis, as they leaned on the brick parapet above the tunnel.

"I don't think so," said Bobbie, "but even if they had, it's ripping here, and we shall see the trains come out of the tunnel like dragons out of lairs. We've never seen that from the top side before."

"No more we have," said Phyllis, partially appeased.

It was really a most exciting place to be in. The top of the tunnel seemed ever so much farther from the line than they had expected, and it was like being on a bridge, but a bridge overgrown with bushes and creepers and grass and wild flowers.

"I *know* the paper-chase has gone long ago," said Phyllis every two minutes, and she hardly knew whether she was pleased or disappointed when Peter, leaning over the parapet, suddenly cried:

"Look out. Here he comes!"

They all leaned over the sun-warmed brick wall in time to see the hare, going very slowly, come out from the shadow of the tunnel.

"There now," said Peter, "what did I tell you? Now for the hounds!"

Very soon came the hounds—by ones and twos and threes and sixes and sevens—and they also were going slowly and seemed very tired. Two or three who lagged far behind came out long after the others.

"There," said Bobbie, "that's all—now what shall we do?"

"Go along into the tulgy wood over there and have lunch," said Phyllis; "we can see them for miles from up there."

"Not yet," said Peter. "That's not the last. There's the one in the red jersey to come yet. Let's see the last of them come out."

But though they waited and waited and waited, the boy in the red jersey did not appear.

"Oh, let's have lunch," said Phyllis; "I've got a pain in my front with being so hungry. You must have missed seeing the red-jerseyed one when he came out with the others—"

But Bobbie and Peter agreed that he had not come out with the others.

"Let's go down to the tunnel mouth," said Peter: "then perhaps we shall see him coming along from the inside. I expect he felt spun-chuck, and rested in one of the manholes. You stay up here and watch, Bob, and when I signal from below, you come down. We might miss seeing him on the way down, with all these trees."

So the others climbed down and Bobbie waited till they signalled to her from the line below. And then she, too, scrambled down the roundabout slippery path among roots and moss till she stepped out between two dogwood trees and joined the others on the line. And still there was no sign of the hound with the red jersey.

"Oh, do, do let's have something to eat," wailed Phyllis. "I shall die if you don't and then you'll be sorry."

"Give her the sandwiches, for goodness' sake, and stop her silly mouth," said Peter, not quite unkindly. "Look here," he added, turning to Bobbie, "perhaps we'd better have one each, too. We may need all our strength. Not more than one, though. There's no time."

"What for?" asked Bobbie, her mouth already full, for she was just as hungry as Phyllis.

"Don't you see," replied Peter, impressively, "that red-jerseyed hound has had an accident—that's what it is. Perhaps even as we speak he's lying with his head on the metals, an unresisting prey to any passing express—"

"Oh, don't try to talk like a book," cried Bobbie, bolting what was left of her sandwich; "come on, Phil, keep close behind me. If a train comes, stand flat against the tunnel wall and hold your petticoats close to you."

"Give me one more sandwich," pleaded Phyllis, "and I will." "I'm going first," said Peter; "it was my idea," and he went.

Of course you know what going into a tunnel is like? The engine gives a scream and then suddenly the noise of the running, rattling train changes and grows different and much louder. Grown-up people pull up the windows and hold them by the strap. The railway carriage suddenly grows like night—with lamps, of course, unless you are in a slow local train, in which case lamps are not always provided. Then by and by the darkness outside the carriage window is touched by puffs of cloudy whiteness, then you see a blue light on the walls of the tunnel, then the sound of the moving train changes once more, and you are out in the good open air again, and grown-ups let the straps go. The windows, all dim with the yellow breath of the tunnel, rattle down into their places, and you see once more the dip and catch of the telegraph wires beside the line, and the straight-cut hawthorn hedges with the tiny baby trees growing up out of them every thirty yards.

All this, of course, is what a tunnel means when you are in a train. But everything is quite different when you walk into a tunnel on your own feet, and tread on shifting, sliding stones and gravel on a path that curves downwards from the shining metals to the wall. Then you see slimy, oozy trickles of water running down the inside of the tunnel, and you notice that the bricks are not red or brown, as they are at the tunnel's mouth, but dull, sticky, sickly green. Your voice, when you speak, is quite changed from what it was out in the sunshine, and it is a long time before the tunnel is quite dark.

It was not yet quite dark in the tunnel when Phyllis caught at Bobbie's skirt, ripping out half a yard of gathers, but no one noticed this at the time.

"I want to go back," she said, "I don't like it. It'll be pitch dark in a minute. I *won't* go on in the dark. I don't care what you say, I *won't*."

"Don't be a silly cuckoo," said Peter; "I've got a candle end and matches, and what's that?"

'That' was a low, humming sound on the railway line, a trembling of the wires beside it, a buzzing humming sound that grew louder and louder as they listened.

"It's a train," said Bobbie.

"Which line?"

"Let me go back," cried Phyllis, struggling to get away from the hand by which Bobbie held her.

"Don't be a coward," said Bobbie; "it's quite safe. Stand back."

"Come on," shouted Peter, who was a few yards ahead. "Quick! Manhole!"

The roar of the advancing train was now louder than the noise you hear when your head is under water in the bath and both taps are running, and you are kicking with your heels against the bath's tin sides. But Peter had shouted for all he was worth, and Bobbie heard him. She dragged Phyllis along to the manhole. Phyllis, of course, stumbled over the wires and grazed both her legs. But they dragged her in, and all three stood in the dark, damp, arch recess while the train roared louder and louder. It seemed as if it would deafen them. And, in the distance, they could see its eyes of fire growing bigger and brighter every instant.

"It *is* a dragon—I always knew it was—it takes its own shape in here, in the dark," shouted Phyllis. But nobody heard her. You see the train was shouting, too, and its voice was bigger than hers.

And now, with a rush and a roar and a rattle and a long dazzling flash of lighted carriage windows, a smell of smoke, and blast of hot air, the train hurtled by, clanging and jangling and echoing in the vaulted roof of the tunnel. Phyllis and Bobbie clung to each other. Even Peter caught hold of Bobbie's arm, "in case she should be frightened," as he explained afterwards.

And now, slowly and gradually, the tail-lights grew smaller and smaller, and so did the noise, till with one last *whiz* the train got itself out of the tunnel, and silence settled again on its damp walls and dripping roof

"Oh!" said the children, all together in a whisper.

Peter was lighting the candle end with a hand that trembled.

"Come on," he said; but he had to clear his throat before he could speak in his natural voice.

"Oh," said Phyllis, "if the red-jerseyed one was in the way of the train!"

"We've got to go and see," said Peter.

"Couldn't we go and send someone from the station?" said Phyllis.

"Would you rather wait here for us?" asked Bobbie, severely, and of course, that settled the question.

So the three went on into the deeper darkness of the tunnel. Peter led, holding his candle end high to light the way. The grease ran down his fingers, and some of it right up his sleeve. He found a long streak from wrist to elbow when he went to bed that night.

It was not more than a hundred and fifty yards from the spot where they had stood while the train went by that Peter stood still, shouted "Hullo" and then went on much quicker than before. When the others caught him up, he stopped. And he stopped within a yard of what they had come into the tunnel to look for. Phyllis saw a gleam of red, and shut her eyes tight. There, by the curved, pebbly down line, was the red-jerseyed hound. His back was against the wall, his arms hung limply by his sides, and his eyes were shut.

"Was the red, blood? Is he all killed?" asked Phyllis, screwing her eyelids more tightly together.

"Killed? Nonsense!" said Peter. "There's nothing red about him except his jersey. He's only fainted. What on earth are we to do?"

"Can we move him?" asked Bobbie.

"I don't know; he's a big chap."

"Suppose we bathe his forehead with water. No, I know we haven't any, but milk's just as well. There's a whole bottle."

"Yes," said Peter, "and they rub people's hands, I believe."

"They burn feathers, I know," said Phyllis.

"What's the use of saying that when we haven't any feathers!"

"As it happens," said Phyllis, in a tone of exasperated triumph, "I've got a shuttlecock in my pocket. So there!"

And now Peter rubbed the hands of the red-jerseyed one. Bobbie burned the feathers of the shuttlecock one by one under his nose, Phyllis splashed warmish milk on his forehead, and all three kept on saying as fast and as earnestly as they could:

"Oh, look up, speak to me! For my sake, speak!"

CHAPTER 12

WHAT BOBBIE BROUGHT HOME

"Oh, look up! Speak to me! For *my* sake, speak!" The children said the words over and over again to the unconscious hound in a red jersey, who sat with closed eyes and pale face against the side of the tunnel.

"Wet his ears with milk," said Bobbie. "I know they do it to people that faint—with eau-de-Cologne. But I expect milk's just as good."

So they wetted his ears, and some of the milk ran down his neck under the red jersey. It was very dark in the tunnel. The candle end Peter had carried, and which now burned on a flat stone, gave hardly any light at all.

"Oh, *do* look up," said Phyllis. "For *my* sake! I believe he's dead."

"For *my* sake," repeated Bobbie. "No, he isn't."

"For *any* sake," said Peter; "come out of it." And he shook the sufferer by the arm.

And then the boy in the red jersey sighed, and opened his eyes, and shut them again and said in a very small voice, "Chuck it."

"Oh, he's *not* dead," said Phyllis. "I *knew* he wasn't," and she began to cry.

"What's up? I'm all right," said the boy.

"Drink this," said Peter, firmly, thrusting the nose of the milk bottle into the boy's mouth. The boy struggled, and some of the milk was upset before he could get his mouth free to say:

"What is it?"

"It's milk," said Peter. "Fear not, you are in the hands of friends. Phil, you stop bleating this minute."

"Do drink it," said Bobbie gently; "it'll do you good."

So he drank. And the three stood by without speaking to him.

"Let him be a minute," Peter whispered; "he'll be all right as soon as the milk begins to run like fire through his veins."

He was.

"I'm better now," he announced. "I remember all about it." He tried to move, but the movement ended in a groan. "Bother! I believe I've broken my leg," he said.

"Did you tumble down?" asked Phyllis, sniffing.

"Of course not—I'm not a kiddie," said the boy, indignantly; "it was one of those beastly wires tripped me up, and when I tried to get up again I couldn't stand, so I sat down. Gee whillikins! It does hurt though. How did *you* get here?"

"We saw you all go into the tunnel and then we went across the hill to see you all come out. And the others did—all but you, and you didn't. So we are a rescue party," said Peter, with pride.

"You've got some pluck, I will say," remarked the boy.

"Oh, that's nothing," said Peter with modesty. "Do you think you could walk if we helped you?"

"I could try," said the boy.

He did try. But he could only stand on one foot; the other dragged in a very nasty way.

"Here, let me sit down. I feel like dying," said the boy. "Let go of me—let go, quick—" He lay down and closed his eyes. The others looked at each other by the dim light of the little candle.

"What on earth!" said Peter.

"Look here," said Bobbie quickly, "you must go and get help. Go to the nearest house."

"Yes, that's the only thing," said Peter. "Come on."

"If you take his feet and Phil and I take his head, we could carry him to the manhole."

They did it. It was perhaps as well for the sufferer that he had fainted again.

"Now," said Bobbie, "I'll stay with him. You take the longest bit of candle, and, oh—be quick, for this bit won't burn long."

"I don't think Mother would like me leaving you," said Peter, doubtfully. "Let me stay, and you and Phil go."

"No, no," said Bobbie, "you and Phil go—and lend me your knife. I'll try to get his boot off before he wakes up again."

"I hope it's all right what we're doing," said Peter.

"Of course it's right," said Bobbie, impatiently. "What else *would* you do? Leave him here all alone because it's dark? Nonsense. Hurry up, that's all."

So they hurried up.

Bobbie watched their dark figures and the little light of the little candle with an odd feeling of having come to the end of everything. She knew now, she thought, what nuns who were bricked up alive in convent walls felt like. Suddenly she gave herself a little shake.

"Don't be a silly little girl," she said. She was always very angry when anyone else called her a little girl, even if the adjective that went first was not "silly" but "nice" or "good" or "clever". And it was only when she was very angry with herself that she allowed Roberta to use that expression to Bobbie.

She fixed the little candle end on a broken brick near the red-jerseyed boy's foot. Then she opened Peter's knife. It was always hard to manage—a halfpenny was generally needed to get it open at all. This time Bobbie somehow got it open with her thumbnail. She broke the nail, and it hurt horribly. Then she cut the boy's bootlace, and got the boot off. She tried to pull off his stocking, but his leg was dreadfully swollen, and it did not seem to be the proper shape. So she cut the stocking down, very slowly and carefully. It was a brown knitted stocking, and she wondered who had knitted it, and whether it was the boy's mother, and whether she was feeling anxious about him, and how she would feel when he was brought home with his leg broken. When Bobbie got the stocking off and saw the poor leg, she felt as though the tunnel was growing darker, and the ground felt unsteady, and nothing seemed quite real.

"*Silly* little girl!" said Roberta to Bobbie, and felt better.

"The poor leg," she told herself; "it ought to have a cushion—ah!"

She remembered the day when she and Phyllis had torn up their red flannel petticoats to make danger signals to stop the train and prevent an accident. Her flannel petticoat today was white, but it would be quite as soft as a red one. She took it off.

"Oh, what useful things flannel petticoats are!" she said; "the man who invented them ought to have a statue directed to him." And she said it aloud, because it seemed that any voice, even her own, would be comfort in that darkness.

"*What* ought to be directed? Who to?" asked the boy, suddenly and very feebly.

"Oh," said Bobbie, "now you're better! Hold your teeth and don't let it hurt too much. Now!"

She had folded the petticoat, and lifting his leg laid it on the cushion of folded flannel.

"Don't faint again, *please* don't," said Bobbie, as he groaned. She hastily wetted her handkerchief with milk and spread it over the poor leg.

"Oh, that hurts," cried the boy, shrinking. "Oh—no, it doesn't— it's nice, really."

"What's your name?" said Bobbie.

"Jim."

"Mine's Bobbie."

"But you're a girl, ain't you?"

"Yes, my long name's Roberta."

"I say—Bobbie."

"Yes?"

"Wasn't there some more of you just now?"

"Yes, Peter and Phil—that's my brother and sister. They've gone to get someone to carry you out."

"What rum names. All boys."

"Yes—I wish I was a boy, don't you?"

"I think you're all right as you are."

"I didn't mean that—I meant don't you wish *you* were a boy, but of course you are without wishing."

"You're just as brave as a boy. Why didn't you go with the others?"

"Somebody had to stay with you," said Bobbie.

"Tell you what, Bobbie," said Jim, "you're a brick. Shake." He reached out a red-jerseyed arm and Bobbie squeezed his hand.

"I won't shake it," she explained, "because it would shake *you*, and that would shake your poor leg, and that would hurt. Have you got a hanky?"

"I don't expect I have." He felt in his pocket. "Yes, I have. What for?"

She took it and wetted it with milk and put it on his forehead.

"That's jolly," he said; "what is it?"

"Milk," said Bobbie. "We haven't any water—"

"You're a jolly good little nurse," said Jim.

"I do it for Mother sometimes," said Bobbie—"not milk, of course, but scent, or vinegar and water. I say, I must put the candle out now, because there mayn't be enough of the other one to get you out by."

"By George," said he, "you think of everything."

Bobbie blew. Out went the candle. You have no idea how black-velvety the darkness was.

"I say, Bobbie," said a voice through the blackness, "aren't you afraid of the dark?"

"Not—not—very, that is—"

"Let's hold hands," said the boy, and it was really rather good of him, because he was like most boys of his age and hated all material tokens of affection, such as kissing, and holding of hands. He called all such things "pawing", and detested them.

The darkness was more bearable to Bobbie now that her hand was held in the large rough hand of the red-jerseyed sufferer; and he, holding her little smooth hot paw, was surprised to find that he did not mind it so much as he expected. She tried to talk, to amuse him, and "take his mind off" his sufferings, but it is very difficult to go on talking in the dark, and presently they found themselves in a silence, only broken now and then by a—

"You all right, Bobbie?"

Or an—

"I'm afraid it's hurting you most awfully, Jim. I *am* so sorry."

And it was very cold.

*

Peter and Phyllis tramped down the long way of the tunnel towards daylight, the candle-grease dripping over Peter's fingers. There were no accidents unless you count Phyllis's catching her frock on a wire, and tearing a long, jagged slit in it, and tripping over her bootlace when it came undone, or going down on her hands and knees, all four of which were grazed.

"There's no end to this tunnel," said Phyllis—and indeed it did seem very, very long.

"Stick to it," said Peter; "everything has an end, and you get to it if you only keep on."

Which is quite true, if you come to think of it, and a useful thing to remember in seasons of trouble—such as measles, arithmetic, impositions, and those times when you are in disgrace, and feel as though no one would ever love you again, and you could never—never again—love anybody.

"Hurray," said Peter, suddenly, "there's the end of the tunnel— looks just like a pin-hole in a bit of black paper, doesn't it?"

The pin-hole got larger—blue lights lay along the sides of the tunnel. The children could see the gravel way that lay in front of them; the air grew warmer and sweeter. Another twenty steps and they were out in the good glad sunshine with the green trees on both sides.

Phyllis drew a long breath.

"I'll never go into a tunnel again, as long as ever I live," said she, "not if there are twenty hundred thousand million hounds inside with red jerseys and their legs broken."

"Don't be a silly cuckoo," said Peter, as usual. "You'd *have* to."

"I think it was very brave and good of me," said Phyllis.

"Not it," said Peter; "you didn't go because you were brave, but because Bobbie and I aren't skunks. Now where's the nearest house, I wonder? You can't see anything here for the trees."

"There's a roof over there," said Phyllis, pointing down the line.

"That's the signal-box," said Peter, "and you know

you're not allowed to speak to signalmen on duty. It's wrong."

"I'm not near so afraid of doing wrong as I was of going into that tunnel," said Phyllis. "Come on," and she started to run along the line. So Peter ran, too.

It was very hot in the sunshine, and both children were hot and breathless by the time they stopped, and bending their heads back to look up at the open windows of the signal-box, shouted "Hi!" as loud as their breathless state allowed. But no one answered. The signal-box stood quiet as an empty nursery, and the handrail of its steps was hot to the hands of the children as they climbed softly up. They peeped in at the open door. The signalman was sitting on a chair tilted back against the wall. His head leaned sideways, and his mouth was open. He was fast asleep.

"My hat!" cried Peter; "wake up!" And he cried it in a terrible voice, for he knew that if a signalman sleeps on duty, he risks losing his situation, let alone all the other dreadful risks to trains which expect him to tell them when it is safe for them to go their ways.

The signalman never moved. Then Peter sprang to him and shook him. And slowly, yawning and stretching, the man awoke. But the moment he *was* awake he leapt to his feet, put his hands to his head "like a mad maniac", as Phyllis said afterwards, and shouted:

"Oh, my heavens—what's o'clock?"

"Twelve thirteen," said Peter, and indeed it was by the white-faced, round-faced clock on the wall of the signal-box.

The man looked at the clock, sprang to the levers, and wrenched them this way and that. An electric bell tingled—the wires and cranks creaked, and the man threw himself into a chair. He was very pale, and the sweat stood on his forehead "like large dewdrops on a white cabbage," as Phyllis remarked later. He was trembling, too; the children could see his big hairy hands shake from side to side, "with quite extra-sized trembles," to use the subsequent words of Peter. He drew long breaths. Then suddenly he cried, "Thank God, thank God you come in when you did—oh, thank God!" and his shoulders began to heave and his face grew red again, and he hid it in those large hairy hands of his.

"Oh, don't cry—don't," said Phyllis, "it's all right now," and she patted him on one big, broad shoulder, while Peter conscientiously thumped the other.

But the signalman seemed quite broken down, and the children had to pat him and thump him for quite a long time before he found his handkerchief—a red one with mauve and white horse-shoes on it—and mopped his face and spoke. During this patting and thumping interval a train thundered by.

"I'm downright shamed, that I am," were the words of the big signalman when he had stopped crying; "snivelling like a kid." Then suddenly he seemed to get cross. "And what was you doing up here, anyway?" he said; "you know it ain't allowed."

"Yes," said Phyllis, "we knew it was wrong—but I wasn't afraid of doing wrong, and it so turned out right. You aren't sorry we came?"

"Lor' love you—if you hadn't 'a' come—" he stopped and then went on. "It's a disgrace, so it is, sleeping on duty. If it was to come to be known—even as it is, when no harm's come of it."

"It won't come to be known," said Peter; "we aren't sneaks. All the same, you oughtn't to sleep on duty—it's dangerous."

"Tell me something I don't know," said the man, "but I can't help it. I know'd well enough just how it 'ud be. But I couldn't get off. They couldn't get no one to take on my duty. I tell you, I ain't had ten minutes' sleep this last five days. My little chap's ill—pewmonia, the Doctor says—and there's no one but me and 'is little sister to do for him. That's where it is. The gell must 'ave her sleep. Dangerous? Yes, I believe you. Now go and split on me if you like."

"Of course we won't," said Peter, indignantly, but Phyllis ignored the whole of the signalman's speech, except the first six words.

"You asked us," she said, "to tell you something you

don't know. Well, I will. There's a boy in the tunnel over there with a red jersey and his leg broken."

"What did he want to go into the blooming tunnel for, then?" said the man.

"Don't be so cross," said Phyllis, kindly. "*We* haven't done anything wrong except coming and waking you up and that was right, as it happens."

Then Peter told how the boy came to be in the tunnel.

"Well," said the man, "I don't see as I can do anything. I can't leave the box."

"You might tell us where to go after someone who isn't in a box, though," said Phyllis.

"There's Brigden's farm over yonder—where you see the smoke a-coming up through the trees," said the man, more and more grumpy, as Phyllis noticed.

"Well, good-bye then," said Peter.

But the man said, "Wait a minute." He put his hand in his pocket and brought out some money—a lot of pennies and one or two shillings and sixpence and half a crown. He picked out two shillings and held them out.

"Here," he said. "I'll give you this to hold your tongues about what's taken place today."

There was a short, unpleasant pause. Then:

"You *are* a nasty man, though, aren't you?" said Phyllis.

Peter took a step forward and knocked the man's hand up, so that the shillings leapt out of it and rolled on the floor.

"If anything *could* make me sneak, *that* would!" he said. "Come, Phil," and marched out of the signal-box with flaming cheeks.

Phyllis hesitated. Then she took the hand, still held out stupidly, that the shillings had been in.

"I forgive you," she said, "even if Peter doesn't. You're not in your proper senses, or you'd never have done that. I know want of sleep sends people mad. Mother told me. I hope your little boy will soon be better, and—"

"Come on, Phil," cried Peter, eagerly.

"I'll give you my sacred honour-word we'll never tell anyone. Kiss and be friends," said Phyllis, feeling how noble it was of her to try to make up a quarrel in which she was not to blame.

The signalman stooped and kissed her.

"I do believe I'm a bit off my head, Missie," he said. "Now run along home to Mother. I didn't mean to put you about—there."

So Phil left the hot signal-box and followed Peter across the fields to the farm.

When the farm men, led by Peter and Phyllis and carrying a hurdle covered with horse-cloths, reached the manhole in the tunnel, Bobbie was fast asleep and so was Jim. Worn out with the pain, the Doctor said afterwards.

"Where does he live?" the bailiff from the farm asked, when Jim had been lifted on to a hurdle.

"In Northumberland," answered Bobbie.

"I'm at school at Maidbridge," said Jim. "I suppose I've got to get back there, somehow."

"Seems to me the Doctor ought to have a look in first," said the bailiff.

"Oh, bring him up to our house," said Bobbie. "It's only a little way by the road. I'm sure Mother would say we ought to."

"Will your Ma like you bringing home strangers with broken legs?"

"She took the poor Russian home herself," said Bobbie. "I know she'd say we ought."

"All right," said the bailiff, "you ought to know what your Ma 'ud like. I wouldn't take it upon me to fetch him up to our place without I asked the Missus first, and they call me the Master, too."

"Are you sure your Mother won't mind?" whispered Jim.

"Certainly," said Bobbie.

"Then we're to take him up to Three Chimneys?" said the bailiff.

"Of course," said Peter.

"Then my lad shall nip up to the Doctor's on his bike,

and tell him to come down there. Now, lads, lift him quiet and steady. One, two, three!"

*

Thus it happened that Mother, writing away for dear life at a story about a Duchess, a designing villain, a secret passage, and a missing will, dropped her pen as her work-room door burst open, and turned to see Bobbie hatless and red with running.

"Oh, Mother," she cried, "do come down. We found a hound in a red jersey in the tunnel, and he's broken his leg and they're bringing him home."

"They ought to take him to the vet," said Mother, with a worried frown; "I really *can't* have a lame dog here."

"He's not a dog, really—he's a boy," said Bobbie, between laughing and choking.

"Then he ought to be taken home to his mother."

"His mother's dead," said Bobbie, "and his father's in Northumberland. Oh, Mother, you will be nice to him? I told him I was sure you'd want us to bring him home. You always want to help everybody."

Mother smiled, but she sighed, too. It is nice that your children should believe you willing to open house and heart to any and every one who needs help. But it is rather embarrassing sometimes, too, when they act on their belief.

"Oh, well," said Mother, "we must make the best of it."

When Jim was carried in, dreadfully white and with set lips whose red had faded to a horrid bluey violet colour, Mother said:

"I am glad you brought him here. Now, Jim, let's get you comfortable in bed before the Doctor comes!"

And Jim, looking at her kind eyes, felt a little, warm, comforting flush of new courage.

"It'll hurt rather, won't it?" he said. "I don't mean to be a coward. You won't think I'm a coward if I faint again, will you? I really and truly don't do it on purpose. And I do hate to give you all this trouble."

"Don't you worry," said Mother; "it's you that have the trouble, you poor dear—not us."

And she kissed him just as if he had been Peter. "We love to have you here—don't we, Bobbie?"

"Yes," said Bobbie—and she saw by her Mother's face how right she had been to bring home the wounded hound in the red jersey.

CHAPTER 13

THE HOUND'S GRANDFATHER

Mother did not get back to her writing all that day, for the red-jerseyed hound whom the children had brought to Three Chimneys had to be put to bed. And then the Doctor came, and hurt him most horribly. Mother was with him all through it, and that made it a little better than it would have been, but "bad was the best," as Mrs Viney said.

The children sat in the parlour downstairs and heard the sound of the Doctor's boots going backwards and forwards over the bedroom floor. And once or twice there was a groan.

"It's horrible," said Bobbie. "Oh, I wish Dr Forrest would make haste. Oh, poor Jim!"

"It *is* horrible," said Peter, "but it's very exciting. I wish Doctors weren't so stuck-up about who they'll have in the room when they're doing things. I should most awfully like to see a leg set. I believe the bones crunch like anything."

"Don't!" said the two girls at once.

"Rubbish!" said Peter. "How are you going to be Red Cross Nurses, like you were talking of coming home, if you can't even stand hearing me say about bones crunching? You'd have to *hear* them crunch on the field of battle—

and be steeped in gore up to the elbows as like as not, and—"

"Stop it!" cried Bobbie, with a white face; "you don't know how funny you're making me feel."

"Me, too," said Phyllis, whose face was pink.

"Cowards!" said Peter.

"I'm not," said Bobbie. "I helped Mother with your rake-wounded foot, and so did Phil—you know we did."

"Well, then!" said Peter. "Now look here. It would be a jolly good thing for you if I were to talk to you every day for half an hour about broken bones and people's insides, so as to get you used to it."

A chair was moved above.

"Listen," said Peter, "that's the bone crunching."

"I do wish you wouldn't," said Phyllis. "Bobbie doesn't like it."

"I'll tell you what they do," said Peter. I can't think what made him so horrid. Perhaps it was because he had been so very nice and kind all the earlier part of the day, and now he had to have a change. This is called reaction. One notices it now and then in oneself. Sometimes when one has been extra good for a longer time than usual, one is suddenly attacked by a violent fit of not being good at all. "I'll tell you what they do," said Peter; "they strap the broken man down so that he can't resist or interfere with their doctorish designs, and then someone holds his head, and someone holds his leg—the broken one, and pulls it till the bones fit in—with a crunch, mind you! Then they strap it up and—let's play at bone-setting!"

"Oh, no!" said Phyllis.

But Bobbie said suddenly: "All right—*let's*! I'll be the doctor, and Phil can be the nurse. You can be the broken boner; we can get at your legs more easily, because you don't wear petticoats."

"I'll get the splints and bandages," said Peter; "you get the couch of suffering ready."

The ropes that had tied up the boxes that had come from home were all in a wooden packing-case in the cellar. When

Peter brought in a trailing tangle of them, and two boards for splints, Phyllis was excitedly giggling.

"Now, then," he said, and lay down on the settle, groaning most grievously.

"Not so loud!" said Bobbie, beginning to wind the rope round him and the settle. "You pull, Phil."

"Not so tight," moaned Peter. "You'll break my other leg."

Bobbie worked on in silence, winding more and more rope round him.

"That's enough," said Peter. "I can't move at all. Oh, my poor leg!" He groaned again.

"*Sure* you can't move?" asked Bobbie, in a rather strange tone.

"Quite sure," replied Peter. "Shall we play it's bleeding freely or not?" he asked cheerfully.

"*You* can play what you like," said Bobbie, sternly, folding her arms and looking down at him where he lay all wound round and round with cord. "Phil and I are going away. And we shan't untie you till you promise never, never to talk to us about blood and wounds unless we say you may. Come, Phil!"

"You beast!" said Peter, writhing. "I'll never promise, never. I'll yell, and Mother will come."

"Do," said Bobbie, "and tell her why we tied you up! Come on, Phil. No, I'm not a beast, Peter. But you wouldn't stop when we asked you and—"

"Yah," said Peter, "it wasn't even your own idea. You got it out of Stalky!"

Bobbie and Phil, retiring in silent dignity, were met at the door by the Doctor. He came in rubbing his hands and looking pleased with himself.

"Well," he said, "*that* job's done. It's a nice clean fracture, and it'll go on all right, I've no doubt. Plucky young chap, too—hullo! What's all this?"

His eye had fallen on Peter who lay mousey-still in his bonds on the settle.

"Playing at prisoners, eh?" he said; but his eyebrows had gone up a little. Somehow he had not thought that Bobbie would be playing while in the room above someone was having a broken bone set.

"Oh, no!" said Bobbie, "not at *prisoners.* We were playing at setting bones. Peter's the broken boner, and I was the doctor."

"I was the nurse," put in Phyllis cheerfully.

The Doctor frowned.

"Then I must say," he said, and he said it rather sternly, "that it's a very heartless game. Haven't you enough imagination even to faintly picture what's been going on upstairs? That poor chap, with drops of sweat on his forehead, and biting his lips so as not to cry out, and every touch on his leg agony and—"

"*You* ought to be tied up," said Phyllis; "you're as bad as—"

"Hush," said Bobbie; "I'm sorry, but we weren't heartless, really."

"I was, I suppose," said Peter, crossly. "All right, Bobbie, don't you go on being noble and screening me, because I jolly well won't have it. It was only that I kept on talking about blood and wounds. I wanted to train them for Red Cross Nurses. And I wouldn't stop when they asked me."

"Well?" said Dr Forrest, sitting down.

"Well—then I said, 'Let's play at setting bones.' It was all rot. I knew Bobbie wouldn't. I only said it to tease her. And then when she said 'yes', of course I had to go through with it. And they tied me up. They got it out of Stalky. And I think it's a beastly shame."

He managed to writhe over and hide his face against the wooden back of the settle.

"I didn't think that anyone would know but us," said Bobbie, indignantly answering Peter's unspoken reproach. "I never thought of your coming in. And hearing about blood and wounds does really make me feel most awfully funny. It was only a joke our tying him up. Let me untie you, Peter."

"I don't care if you never untie me," said Peter; "and if that's your idea of a joke—"

"If I were you," said the Doctor, though really he did not

quite know what to say, "I should be untied before your Mother comes down. You don't want to worry her just now, do you?"

"I don't promise anything about not saying about wounds, mind," said Peter, in very surly tones, as Bobbie and Phyllis began to untie the knots.

"I'm very sorry, Pete," Bobbie whispered, leaning close to him as she fumbled with the big knot under the settle; "but if you only knew how sick you made me feel."

"You've made *me* feel pretty sick, I can tell you," Peter rejoined. Then he shook off the loose cords, and stood up.

"I looked in," said Dr Forrest, "to see if one of you would come along to the surgery. There are some things that your Mother will want at once, and I've given my man a day off to go and see the circus; will you come, Peter?"

Peter went without a word or a look to his sisters.

The two walked in silence up to the gate that led from the Three Chimneys field to the road. Then Peter said:

"Let me carry your bag. I say, it is heavy—what's in it?"

"Oh, knives and lancets and different instruments for hurting people. And the ether bottle. I had to give him ether, you know—the agony was so intense."

Peter was silent.

"Tell me all about how you found that chap," said Dr Forrest.

Peter told. And then Dr Forrest told him stories of brave rescues; he was a most interesting man to talk to, as Peter had often remarked.

Then in the surgery Peter had a better chance than he had ever had of examining the Doctor's balance, and his microscope, and his scales and measuring glasses. When all the things were ready that Peter was to take back, the Doctor said suddenly:

"You'll excuse my shoving my oar in, won't you? But I should like to say something to you."

"Now for a rowing," thought Peter, who had been wondering how it was that he had escaped one.

"Something scientific," added the Doctor.

"Yes," said Peter, fiddling with the fossil ammonite that the Doctor used for a paper-weight.

"Well," said the Doctor, "you know men have to do the work of the world and not be afraid of anything—so they have to be hardy and brave. But women have to take care of their babies and cuddle them and nurse them and be very patient and gentle."

"Yes," said Peter, wondering what was coming next.

"Well then, you see. Boys and girls are only little men and women. And *we* are much harder and hardier than they are"—(Peter liked the "we". Perhaps the Doctor had known he would.)—"and much stronger, and things that hurt *them* don't hurt us. You know you mustn't hit a girl—"

"I should think not, indeed," muttered Peter, indignantly.

"Not even if she's your own sister. That's because girls are so much softer and weaker than we are; they have to be, you know," he added, "because if they weren't, it wouldn't be nice for the babies. And that's why all the animals are so good to the mother animals. They never fight them, you know."

"I know," said Peter, interested; "two buck rabbits will fight all day if you let them, but they won't hurt a doe."

"No; and quite wild beasts—lions and elephants—they're immensely gentle with the female beasts. And we've got to be, too."

"I see," said Peter.

"And their hearts are soft, too," the Doctor went on, "and things that we shouldn't think anything of hurt them dreadfully. So that a man has to be very careful, not only of his fists, but of his words. They're awfully brave, you know," he went on. "Think of Bobbie waiting alone in the tunnel with that poor chap. It's an odd thing—the softer and more easily hurt a woman is the better she can screw herself up to do what *has* to be done. I've seen some brave women—your Mother's one," he ended abruptly.

"Yes," said Peter.

"Well, that's all; excuse my mentioning it. But nobody

knows everything without being told. And you see what I mean, don't you?"

"Yes," said Peter. "I'm sorry. There!"

"Of course you are! People always are—directly they understand. Everyone ought to be taught these scientific facts. So long!"

They shook hands heartily. When Peter came home, his sisters looked at him doubtfully.

"It's Pax," said Peter, dumping down the basket on the table. "Dr Forrest has been talking scientific to me. No, it's no use my telling you what he said; you wouldn't understand. But it all comes to you girls being poor, soft, weak, frightened things like rabbits, so us men have just got to put up with them. He said you were female beasts. Shall I take this up to Mother, or will you?"

"I know what *boys* are," said Phyllis, with flaming cheeks; "they're just the nastiest, rudest—"

"They're very brave," said Bobbie, "sometimes."

"Ah, you mean the chap upstairs? I see. Go ahead, Phil—I shall put up with you whatever you say because you're a poor, weak, frightened, soft—"

"Not if I pull your hair you won't," said Phyllis, springing at him.

"He said 'Pax'," said Bobbie, pulling her away. "Don't you see," she whispered as Peter picked up the basket and stalked out with it, "he's sorry, really, only he won't say so? Let's say we're sorry."

"It's so goody-goody," said Phyllis, doubtfully; "he said we were female beasts, and soft and frightened—"

"Then let's show him we're not frightened of him thinking us goody-goody," said Bobby; "and we're not any more beasts than he is."

And when Peter came back, still with his chin in the air, Bobbie said:

"We're sorry we tied you up, Pete."

"I thought you would be," said Peter, very stiff and superior.

This was hard to bear. But—

"Well, so we are," said Bobbie. "Now let honour be satisfied on both sides."

"I did call it Pax," said Peter, in an injured tone.

"Then let it *be* Pax," said Bobbie. "Come on, Phil, let's get the tea. Peter, you might lay the cloth."

"I say," said Phyllis, when peace was really restored, which was not till they were washing up the cups after tea, "Dr Forrest didn't really say we were female beasts, did he?"

"Yes," said Peter, firmly, "but I think he meant we men were wild beasts, too."

"How funny of him!" said Phyllis, breaking a cup.

*

"May I come in, Mother?" Peter was at the door of Mother's writing-room, where Mother sat at her table with two candles in front of her. Their flames looked orange and violet against the clear grey blue of the sky where already a few stars were twinkling.

"Yes, dear," said Mother, absently, "anything wrong?" She wrote a few more words and then laid down her pen and began to fold up what she had written. "I was just writing to Jim's grandfather. He lives near here, you know."

"Yes, you said so at tea. That's what I want to say. Must you write to him, Mother? Couldn't we keep Jim, and not say anything to his people till he's well? It would be such a surprise for them."

"Well, yes," said Mother, laughing. "I think it would."

"You see," Peter went on, "of course the girls are all right and all that—I'm not saying anything against *them*. But I should like it if I had another chap to talk to sometimes."

"Yes," said Mother, "I know it's dull for you, dear. But I can't help it. Next year perhaps I can send you to school—you'd like that, wouldn't you?"

"I do miss the other chaps, rather," Peter confessed; "but if Jim could stay after his leg was well, we could have awful larks."

"I've no doubt of it," said Mother. "Well—perhaps he could, but you know, dear, we're not rich. I can't afford to get him everything he'll want. And he must have a nurse."

"Can't you nurse him, Mother? You do nurse people so beautifully."

"That's a pretty compliment, Pete—but I can't do nursing and my writing as well. That's the worst of it."

"Then you *must* send the letter to his grandfather?"

"Of course—and to his schoolmaster, too. We telegraphed to them both, but I must write as well. They'll be most dreadfully anxious."

"I say, Mother, why can't his grandfather pay for a nurse?" Peter suggested. "That would be ripping. I expect the old boy's rolling in money. Grandfathers in books always are."

"Well, this one isn't in a book," said Mother, "so we mustn't expect him to roll much."

"I say," said Peter, musingly, "wouldn't it be jolly if we all *were* in a book and you were writing it? Then you could make all sorts of jolly things happen, and make Jim's legs get well at once and be all right tomorrow, and Father come home soon and—"

"Do you miss your Father very much?" Mother asked, rather coldly, Peter thought.

"Awfully," said Peter, briefly.

Mother was enveloping and addressing the second letter.

"You see," Peter went on slowly, "you see, it's not only him *being* Father, but now he's away there's no other man in the house but me—that's why I want Jim to stay so frightfully much. Wouldn't you like to be writing that book with us all in it, Mother, and make Daddy come home soon?"

Peter's mother put her arm round him suddenly, and hugged him in silence for a minute. Then she said:

"Don't you think it's rather nice to think that we're in a book that God's writing? If I were writing a book, I might make mistakes. But God knows how to make the story end just right—in the way that's best for us."

"Do you really believe that, Mother?" Peter asked quietly.

"Yes," she said, "I do believe it—almost always—except when I'm so sad that I can't believe anything. But even when I can't believe it, I know it's true—and I try to believe it. You don't know how I try, Peter. Now take the letters to the post and don't let's be sad any more. Courage, courage! That's the finest of all the virtues! I dare say Jim will be here for two or three weeks yet."

For what was left of the evening Peter was so angelic that Bobbie feared he was going to be ill. She was quite relieved in the morning to find him plaiting Phyllis's hair on to the back of her chair in quite his old manner.

It was soon after breakfast that a knock came at the door. The children were hard at work cleaning the brass candlesticks in honour of Jim's visit.

"That'll be the Doctor," said Mother. "I'll go. Shut the kitchen door—you're not fit to be seen."

But it wasn't the Doctor. They knew that by the voice and by the sound of the boots that went upstairs. They did not recognize the sound of the boots, but everyone was certain that they had heard the voice before.

There was a longish interval. The boots and the voice did not come down again.

"Who can it possibly be?" they kept on asking themselves and each other.

"Perhaps," said Peter at last, "Dr Forrest has been attacked by highwaymen and left for dead, and this is the man he's telegraphed for to take his place. Mrs Viney said he had a local tenant to do his work when he went for a holiday, didn't you, Mrs Viney?"

"I did so, my dear," said Mrs Viney from the back kitchen.

"He's fallen down in a fit, more likely," said Phyllis, "all human aid despaired of. And this is his man come to break the news to Mother."

"Nonsense!" said Peter, briskly. "Mother wouldn't have taken the man up into Jim's bedroom. Why should she? Listen—the door's opening. Now they'll come down. I'll open the door a crack."

He did.

"It's not listening," he replied indignantly to Bobbie's scandalized remarks; "nobody in their senses would talk secrets on the stairs. And Mother can't have secrets to talk with Dr Forrest's stable-man—and you said it was him."

"Bobbie," called Mother's voice.

They opened the kitchen door, and Mother leaned over the stair railing.

"Jim's grandfather has come," she said; "wash your hands and faces and then you can see him. He wants to see you!" The bedroom door shut again.

"There now!" said Peter; "fancy us not even thinking of that! Let's have some hot water, Mrs Viney. I'm as black as your hat."

The three were indeed dirty, for the stuff you clean brass candlesticks with is very far from cleaning to the cleaner.

They were still busy with soap and flannel when they heard the boots and the voice come down the stairs and go into the dining-room. And when they were clean, though still damp—because it takes such a long time to dry your hands properly, and they were very impatient to see the grandfather—they filed into the dining-room.

Mother was sitting in the window-seat, and in the leather-covered arm-chair that Father always used to sit in at the other house sat—

THEIR OWN OLD GENTLEMAN!

"Well, I never did," said Peter, even before he said, "How do you do?" He was, as he explained afterwards, too surprised even to remember that there was such a thing as politeness—much less to practise it.

"It's our own old gentleman!" said Phyllis.

"Oh, it's you!" said Bobbie. And then they remembered themselves and their manners and said, "How do you do?" very nicely.

"This is Jim's grandfather, Mr— " said Mother, naming the old gentleman's name.

"How splendid!" said Peter; "that's just exactly like a book, isn't it, Mother?"

"It is, rather," said Mother, smiling; things do happen in real life that are rather like books, sometimes."

"I am so awfully glad it *is* you," said Phyllis; "when you think of the lots of old gentlemen there are in the world—it might have been almost anyone."

"I say, though," said Peter, "you're not going to take Jim away, though, are you?"

"Not at present," said the old gentleman. "Your Mother has most kindly consented to let him stay here. I thought of sending a nurse, but your Mother is good enough to say that she will nurse him herself."

"But what about her writing?" said Peter, before anyone could stop him. "There won't be anything for him to eat if Mother doesn't write."

"That's all right," said Mother hastily.

The old gentleman looked very kindly at Mother.

"I see," he said, "you trust your children, and confide in them."

"Of course," said Mother.

"Then I may tell them our little arrangement," he said. "Your Mother, my dears, has consented to give up writing for a little while and to become a Matron of my Hospital."

"Oh!" said Phyllis, blankly; "and shall we have to go away from Three Chimneys and the Railway and everything?"

"No, no, darling," said Mother, hurriedly.

"The Hospital is called Three Chimneys Hospital," said the old gentleman, "and my unlucky Jim's the only patient, and I hope he'll continue to be so. Your Mother will be Matron, and there'll be a hospital staff of a housemaid and a cook—till Jim's well."

"And then will Mother go on writing again?" asked Peter.

"We shall see," said the old gentleman, with a swift, slight glance at Bobbie; "perhaps something nice may happen and she won't have to."

"I love my writing," said Mother, very quickly.

"I know," said the old gentleman; "don't be afraid that I'm going to try to interfere. But one never knows. Very wonderful and beautiful things do happen, don't they? And we live most of our lives in the hope of them. I may come again to see the boy?"

"Surely," said Mother, "and I don't know how to thank you for making it possible for me to nurse him. Dear boy!"

"He kept calling Mother, Mother, in the night," said Phyllis. "I woke up twice and heard him."

"He didn't mean me," said Mother, in a low voice to the old gentleman; "that's why I wanted so much to keep him."

The old gentleman rose.

"I'm so glad," said Peter, "that you're going to keep him, Mother."

"Take care of your Mother, my dears," said the old gentleman. "She's a woman in a million."

"Yes, isn't she?" whispered Bobbie.

"God bless her," said the old gentleman, taking both Mother's hands, "God bless her! Ay, and she shall be blessed. Dear me, where's my hat? Will Bobbie come with me to the gate?"

At the gate he stopped and said:

"You're a good child, my dear—I got your letter. But it wasn't needed. When I read about your Father's case in the papers at the time, I had my doubts. And ever since I've known who you were, I've been trying to find out things. I haven't done very much yet. But I have hopes, my dear—I have hopes."

"Oh!" said Bobbie, choking a little.

"Yes—I may say great hopes. But keep your secret a little longer. Wouldn't do to upset your Mother with a false hope, would it?"

"Oh, but it isn't false!" said Bobbie; "I *know* you can do it. I knew you could when I wrote. It isn't a false hope, is it?"

"No," he said, "I don't think it's a false hope, or I wouldn't have told you. And I think you deserve to be told that there *is* a hope."

"And you don't think Father did it, do you? Oh, say you don't think he did."

"My dear," he said, "I'm perfectly *certain* he didn't."

If it was a false hope, it was none the less a very radiant one that lay warm at Bobbie's heart, and through the days that followed lighted her little face as a Japanese lantern is lighted by the candle within.

Chapter 14

THE END

Life at Three Chimneys was never quite the same again after the old gentleman came to see his grandson. Although they now knew his name, the children never spoke of him by it—at any rate, when they were by themselves. To them he was always the old gentleman, and I think he had better be the old gentleman to us, too. It wouldn't make him seem any more real to you, would it, if I were to tell you that his name was Snooks or Jenkins (which it wasn't)?—and, after all, I must be allowed to keep one secret. It's the only one; I have told you everything else, except what I am going to tell you in this chapter, which is the last. At least, of course, I haven't told you *everything*. If I were to do that, the book would never come to an end, and that would be a pity, wouldn't it?

Well, as I was saying, life at Three Chimneys was never quite the same again. The cook and the housemaid were very nice (I don't mind telling you their names—they were Clara and Ethelwyn), but they told Mother they did not seem to want Mrs Viney, and that she was an old muddler. So Mrs Viney came only two days a week to do washing and ironing. Then Clara and Ethelwyn said they could do the work all right if they weren't interfered with, and that meant that the children no longer got the tea and cleared it away and washed up the tea-things and dusted the rooms.

This would have left quite a blank in their lives, although they had often pretended to themselves and to each other that they hated housework But now that Mother had no writing and no housework to do, she had time for lessons. And lessons the children had to do. However nice the person who is teaching you may be, lessons are lessons all the world over, and at their best are worse fun than peeling potatoes or lighting a fire.

On the other hand, if Mother now had time for lessons, she also had time for play, and to make up little rhymes for the children as she used to do. She had not had much time for rhymes since she came to Three Chimneys.

There was one very odd thing about these lessons. Whatever the children were doing, they always wanted to be doing something else. When Peter was doing his Latin, he thought it would be nice to be learning History like Bobbie. Bobbie would have preferred Arithmetic, which was what Phyllis happened to be doing, and Phyllis of course thought Latin much the most interesting kind of lesson. And so on.

So, one day, when they sat down to lessons, each of them found a little rhyme at its place. I put the rhymes in to show you that their Mother really did understand a little how children feel about things, and also the kind of words they use, which is the case with very few grown-up people. I suppose most grown-ups have very bad memories, and have forgotten how they felt when they were little. Of course, the verses are supposed to be spoken by the children.

PETER

I once thought Caesar easy pap—
How very soft I must have been!
When they start Caesar with a chap
He little knows what that will mean.
Oh, verbs are silly stupid things.
I'd rather learn the dates of kings!

BOBBIE

The worst of all my lesson things
Is learning who succeeded who
In all the rows of queens and kings,
With dates to everything they do;
With dates enough to make you sick;—
I wish it was Arithmetic!

PHYLLIS

Such pounds and pounds of apples fill
My slate—what is the price you'd spend!
You scratch the figures out until
You cry upon the dividend
I'd break the slate and scream for joy
If I did Latin like a boy!

This kind of thing, of course, made lessons much jollier. It is something to know that the person who is teaching you sees that it is not all plain sailing for you, and does not think that it is just your stupidness that makes you not know your lessons till you've learned them!

Then as Jim's leg got better it was very pleasant to go up and sit with him and hear tales about his school life and the other boys. There was one boy, named Parr, of whom Jim seemed to have formed the lowest possible opinion, and another boy named Wigsby Minor, for whose views Jim had a great respect. Also there were three brothers named Paley, and the youngest was called Paley Terts, and was much given to fighting.

Peter drank in all this with deep joy, and Mother seemed to have listened with some interest, for one day she gave Jim a sheet of paper on which she had written a rhyme about Parr, bringing in Paley and Wigsby by name in a most wonderful way, as well as all the reasons Jim had for not liking Parr, and Wigsby's wise opinion on the matter. Jim was immensely pleased. He had never had a rhyme written expressly for him before. He read it till he knew it by heart and then he sent it to Wigsby, who liked it almost as much as Jim did. Perhaps you may like it, too.

THE NEW BOY

His name is Parr; he says that he
Is given bread and milk for tea.
He says his father killed a bear.
He says his mother cuts his hair.

He wears goloshes when it's wet.
I've heard his people call him "Pet"!
He has no proper sense of shame;
He told the chaps his Christian name.

He cannot wicket-keep at all
He's frightened of a cricket ball.
He reads indoors for hours and hours,
He knows the names of beastly flowers.

He says his French just like Mossoo—
A beastly stuck-up thing to do—
He won't keep cave, *shirks his turn*
And says he came to school to learn!

He won't play football, says it hurts;
He wouldn't fight with Paley Terts;
He couldn't whistle if he tried,
And when we laughed at him he cried!

Now, Wigsby Minor says that Parr
Is only like all new boys are.
I know when I *first came to school*
I wasn't such a jolly fool!

Jim could never understand how Mother could have been clever enough to do it. To the others it seemed nice, but natural. You see they had always been used to having a mother who could write verses just like the way people talk, even to the shocking expression at the end of the rhyme, which was Jim's very own.

Jim taught Peter to play chess and draughts and dominoes, and altogether it was a nice quiet time.

Only Jim's leg got better and better, and a general feeling began to spring up among Bobbie, Peter, and Phyllis that something ought to be done to amuse him; not just games, but something really handsome. But it was extraordinarily difficult to think of anything.

'It's no good," said Peter, when all of them had thought

and thought till their heads felt quite heavy and swollen; "if we can't think of anything to amuse him, we just can't, and there's an end to it. Perhaps something will just happen of its own accord that he'll like."

"Things *do* happen by themselves sometimes, without your making them," said Phyllis, rather as though, usually, everything that happened in the world was her doing.

"I wish something would happen," said Bobbie, dreamily, "something wonderful."

And something wonderful did happen exactly four days after she had said this. I wish I could say it was three days after, because in fairy tales it is always three days after that things happen. But this is not a fairy story, and besides, it really was four and not three, and I am nothing if not strictly truthful.

They seemed to be hardly Railway children at all in those days, and as the days went on each had an uneasy feeling about this which Phyllis expressed one day.

"I wonder if the Railway misses us," she said, plaintively. "We never go to see it now."

"It seems ungrateful," said Bobbie; "we loved it so when we hadn't anyone to play with."

"Perks is always coming up to ask after Jim," said Peter, "and the signalman's little boy is better. He told me so."

"I didn't mean the people," explained Phyllis; "I meant the dear Railway itself."

"The thing I don't like," said Bobbie, on this fourth day, which was a Tuesday, "is our having stopped waving to the 9.15 and sending our love to Father by it."

"Let's begin again," said Phyllis. And they did.

Somehow the change of everything that was made by having servants in the house and Mother not doing any writing, made the time seem extremely long since that strange morning at the beginning of things, when they had got up so early and burnt the bottom out of the kettle and had apple pie for breakfast and first seen the Railway.

It was September now, and the turf on the slope to the Railway was dry and crisp. Little long grass spikes stood up like bits of gold wire, frail blue harebells trembled on their tough, slender stalks. Gipsy roses opened wide and flat their lilac-coloured discs, and the golden stars of St John's Wort shone at the edges of the pool that lay half-way to the Railway. Bobbie gathered a generous handful of the flowers and thought how pretty they would look lying on the green-and-pink blanket of silk waste that now covered Jim's poor broken leg.

"Hurry up," said Peter, "or we shall miss the 9.15!"

"I can't hurry more than I am doing," said Phyllis. "Oh, bother it! My bootlace has come undone *again*!"

"When you're married," said Peter, "your bootlace will come undone going up the church aisle, and your man that you're going to get married to will tumble over it and smash his nose in on the ornamented pavement; and then you'll say you won't marry him, and you'll have to be an old maid."

"I shan't," said Phyllis. "I'd much rather marry a man with his nose smashed in than not marry anybody."

"It would be horrid to marry a man with a smashed nose all the same," went on Bobbie. "He wouldn't be able to smell the flowers at the wedding. Wouldn't that be awful!"

"Bother the flowers at the wedding!" cried Peter. "Look! the signal's down. We must run!"

They ran. And once more they waved their handkerchiefs, without at all minding whether the handkerchiefs were clean or not, to the 9.15.

"Take our love to Father!" cried Bobbie. And the others, too, shouted:

"Take our love to Father!"

The old gentleman waved from his first-class carriage window. Quite violently he waved. And there was nothing odd in that, for he always had waved. But what was really remarkable was that from every window handkerchiefs fluttered, newspapers signalled, hands waved wildly. The train swept by with a rustle and roar, the little pebbles jumped and danced under it as it passed, and the children were left looking at each other.

"Well!" said Peter.

"*Well!*" said Bobbie.

"WELL!" said Phyllis.

"Whatever on earth does that mean?" asked Peter, but he did not expect any answer.

"I *don't* know," said Bobbie. "Perhaps the old gentleman told the people at his station to look out for us and wave. He knew we should like it!"

Now, curiously enough, this was just what had happened. The old gentleman, who was very well known and respected at this particular station, had got there early this morning, and he had waited at the door where the young man stands holding the interesting machine that clips the tickets, and he had said something to every single passenger who passed through that door. And after nodding to what the old gentleman had said—and the nods expressed every shade of surprise, interest, doubt, cheerful pleasure, and grumpy agreement—each passenger had gone on to the platform and read one certain part of his newspaper. And when the passengers got into the train, they had told the other passengers who were already there what the old gentleman had said, and then the other passengers had also looked at their newspapers and seemed very astonished and, mostly, pleased. Then, when the train passed the fence where the three children were, newspapers and hands and handkerchiefs were waved madly, till all that side of the train was fluttery with white, like pictures of the King's Coronation in the biograph at Maskelyne and Cook's. To the children it almost seemed as though the train itself was alive, and was at last responding to the love that they had given it so freely and so long.

"It is most extraordinarily rum!" said Peter.

"Most stronery!" echoed Phyllis.

But Bobbie said, "Don't you think the old gentleman's waves seemed more significating than usual?"

"No," said the others.

"I do," said Bobbie. "I thought he was trying to explain something to us with his newspaper."

"Explain what?" asked Peter, not unnaturally.

"*I* don't know," Bobbie answered, "but I do feel most

awfully funny. I feel just exactly as if something was going to happen."

"What is going to happen," said Peter, "is that Phyllis's stocking is going to come down."

This was but too true. The suspender had given way in the agitation of the waves to the 9.15. Bobbie's handkerchief served as first aid to the injured, and they all went home.

Lessons were more than usually difficult to Bobbie that day. Indeed, she disgraced herself so deeply over a quite simple sum about the division of 48 pounds of meat and 36 pounds of bread among 144 hungry children that Mother looked at her anxiously.

"Don't you feel quite well, dear?" she asked.

"I don't know," was Bobbie's unexpected answer. "I don't know how I feel. It isn't that I'm lazy. Mother, will you let me off lessons today? I feel as if I wanted to be quite alone by myself."

"Yes, of course I'll let you off," said Mother: "but—"

Bobbie dropped her slate. It cracked just across the little green mark that is so useful for drawing patterns round, and it was never the same slate again. Without waiting to pick it up she bolted. Mother caught her in the hall feeling blindly among the water-proofs and umbrellas for her garden hat.

"What is it, my sweetheart?" said Mother. "You don't feel ill, do you?"

"I *don't* know," Bobbie answered, a little breathlessly, "but I want to be by myself and see if my head really is all silly and my inside all squirmy-twisty."

"Hadn't you better lie down?" Mother said, stroking her hair back from her forehead.

"I'd be more alive in the garden, I think," said Bobbie.

But she could not stay in the garden. The hollyhocks and the asters and the late roses all seemed to be waiting for something to happen. It was one of those still, shiny autumn days, when everything does seem to be waiting.

Bobbie could not wait.

"I'll go down to the station," she said, "and talk to Perks and ask about the signalman's little boy."

So she went down. On the way she passed the old lady from the Post-office, who gave her a kiss and a hug, but rather to Bobbie's surprise, no words except:

"God bless you, love—" and, after a pause, "run along—do."

The draper's boy, who had sometimes been a little less than civil and a little more than contemptuous, now touched his cap, and uttered the remarkable words:

"Morning, Miss. I'm sure—"

The blacksmith, coming along with an open newspaper in his hand, was even more strange in his manner. He grinned broadly, though, as a rule, he was a man not given to smiles, and waved the newspaper long before he came up to her. And as he passed her, he said, in answer to her "Good morning":

"Good morning to you, Missie, and many of them! I wish you joy, that I do!"

"Oh!" said Bobbie to herself, and her heart quickened its beats, "something *is* going to happen! I know it is—everyone is so odd, like people are in dreams."

The Station Master wrung her hand warmly. In fact he worked it up and down like a pump-handle. But he gave her no reason for this unusually enthusiastic greeting. He only said:

"The 11.54's a bit late, Miss—the extra luggage this holiday time," and went away very quickly into that inner Temple of his into which even Bobbie dared not follow him.

Perks was not to be seen, and Bobbie shared the solitude of the platform with the Station Cat. This tortoiseshell lady, usually of a retiring disposition, came today to rub herself against the brown stockings of Bobbie with arched back, waving tail, and reverberating purrs.

"Dear me!" said Bobbie, stooping to stroke her, "how very kind everybody is today—even you, pussy!"

Perks did not appear until the 11.54 was signalled, and then he, like everybody else that morning, had a newspaper in his hand.

"Hullo!" he said, " 'ere you are. Well, if *this* is the train, it'll be smart work! Well, God bless you, my dear! I see it in the paper, and I don't think I was ever so glad of anything in all my born days!" He looked at Bobbie a moment, then said, "One I must have, Miss, and no offence, I know, on a day like this 'ere!" and with that he kissed her, first on one cheek and then on the other.

"You ain't offended, are you?" he asked anxiously. "I ain't took too great a liberty? On a day like this, you know—"

"No, no," said Bobbie, "of course it's not a liberty, dear Mr Perks; we love you quite as much as if you were an uncle of ours—but—on a day like *what*?"

"Like this 'ere!" said Perks. "Don't I tell you I see it in the paper?"

"Saw *what* in the paper?" asked Bobbie, but already the 11.54 was steaming into the station and the Station Master was looking at all the places where Perks was not and ought to have been.

Bobbie was left standing alone, the Station Cat watching her from under the bench with friendly golden eyes.

Of course you know already exactly what was going to happen. Bobbie was not so clever. She had the vague, confused, expectant feeling that comes to one's heart in dreams. What her heart expected I can't tell—perhaps the very thing that you and I know was going to happen—but her mind expected nothing; it was almost blank, and felt nothing but tiredness and stupidness and an empty feeling like your body has when you have been for a long walk and it is very far indeed past your proper dinner-time.

Only three people got out of the 11.54. The first was a country-woman with two baskety boxes full of live chickens who stuck their russet heads out anxiously through the wicker bars; the second was Miss Peckitt, the grocer's wife's cousin, with a tin box and three brown-paper parcels; and the third—

"Oh! my Daddy, my Daddy!" That scream went like a knife into the heart of everyone in the train, and people put their heads out of the windows to see a tall pale man with lips set in a thin close line, and a little girl clinging to him with arms and legs, while his arms went tightly round her.

*

"I knew something wonderful was going to happen," said Bobbie, as they went up the road, "but I didn't think it was going to be this. Oh, my Daddy, my Daddy!"

"Then didn't Mother get my letter?" Father asked.

"There weren't any letters this morning. Oh! Daddy! it *is* really you, isn't it?"

The clasp of a hand she had forgotten assured her that it was.

"You must go in by yourself, Bobbie, and tell Mother quite quietly that it's all right. They've caught the man who did it. Everyone knows now that it wasn't your Daddy."

"*I* always knew it wasn't," said Bobbie. "Me and Mother and our old gentleman."

"Yes," he said, "it's all his doing. Mother wrote and told me you had found out. And she told me what you'd been to her. My own little girl!" They stopped a minute then.

And now I see them crossing the field. Bobbie goes into the house, trying to keep her eyes from speaking before her lips have found the right words to "tell Mother quite quietly" that the sorrow and the struggle and the parting are over and done, and that Father has come home.

I see Father walking in the garden, waiting—waiting. He is looking at the flowers, and each flower is a miracle to eyes that all these months of Spring and Summer have seen only flag-stones and gravel and a little grudging grass. But his eyes keep turning towards the house. And presently he leaves the garden and goes to stand outside the nearest door. It is the back door, and across the yard the swallows are circling. They are getting ready to fly away from cold winds and keen frost to the land where it is always summer. They are the same swallows that the children built the little clay nests for.

Now the door opens. Bobbie's voice calls:

"Come in, Daddy; come in!"

He goes in and the door is shut. I think we will not open the door to follow him. I think that just now we are not wanted there. I think it will be best for us to go quickly and quietly away. At the end of the field, among the thin gold spikes of grass and the hare-bells and Gipsy roses and St John's Wort, we may just take one last look, over our shoulders, at the white house where neither we nor anyone else is wanted now.